PENGUIN CLASSICS

IVANHOE

WALTER SCOTT was born in Edinburgh in 1771, educated at the High School and University there and admitted to the Scottish Bar in 1792. From 1799 until his death he was Sheriff of Selkirkshire, and from 1806 to 1830 he held a well-paid office as a principal clerk to the Court of Session in Edinburgh, the supreme Scottish civil court. From 1805, too, Scott was secretly an investor in, and increasingly controller of, the printing and publishing businesses of his associates, the Ballantyne brothers.

Despite crippling polio in infancy, conflict with his Calvinist lawyer father in adolescence, rejection by the woman he loved in his twenties and financial ruin in his fifties, Scott displayed an amazingly productive energy and his personal warmth was attested by almost everybody who met him. His first literary efforts, in the late 1790s, were translations of romantic and historical German poems and plays. In 1805 Scott's first considerable original work, *The Lay of the Last Minstrel*, began a series of narrative poems that popularized key incidents and settings of early Scottish history, and brought him fame and fortune.

In 1813 Scott, having declined the poet laureateship and recommended Southey instead, moved towards fiction and devised a new form that was to dominate the early-nineteenth-century novel. *Waverley* (1814) and its successors draw on the social and cultural contrasts and the religious and political conflicts of recent Scottish history to illustrate the nature and cost of political and cultural change and the relationship between the historical process and the individual. *Waverley* was published anonymously and, although many people guessed, Scott did not acknowledge authorship of the Waverley Novels until 1827. Many of the novels from *Ivanhoe* (1819) on extended their range to the England and Europe of the Middle Ages and Renaissance. Across the English-speaking world, and by means of innumerable translations throughout Europe, the Waverley Novels changed forever the way people constructed their personal and national identities.

Scott was created a baronet in 1820. During the financial crisis of 1825–6 Scott, his printer Ballantyne, and his publishers Constable and their London partner became insolvent. Scott chose not to be declared bankrupt, determining instead to work to generate funds to pay his creditors. Despite his failing health he continued to write new novels, to revise and annotate the earlier ones for a new edition, and to write a nine-volume *Life of Napoleon* and a history of Scotland under the title *Tales of a Grandfather*. His private thoughts during and after his financial crash are set down in a revealing and moving *Journal*. Scott died in September 1832; his creditors were finally paid in full in 1833 from the proceeds of his writing.

GRAHAM TULLOCH is Professor of English at Flinders University, Adelaide. He was educated at the universities of Adelaide and Leicester and is the author of *The Language of Walter Scott* (1980) and other works on Scottish literature and language. He has also edited Marcus Clarke's *His Natural Life* and Catherine Martin's *An Australian Girl*.

DAVID HEWITT, born in 1942, was brought up in the Borders, and studied English at the University of Edinburgh. Since 1994 he has been Professor in Scottish Literature at the University of Aberdeen. He has published widely on Scottish and Romantic literature, and is editor-in-chief of the Edinburgh Edition of the Waverley Novels. He is editor of Scott's *The Antiquary* for Penguin Classics.

CLAIRE LAMONT is a graduate of the universities of Edinburgh and Oxford and is currently a Senior Lecturer in English at the University of Newcastle. She specializes in late-eighteenth and early-nineteenth-century English and Scottish literature. She has published editions of Scott's *Waverley* (1981) and *The Heart of Midlothian* (1982), and is editing *Chronicles of the Canongate* for the Edinburgh Edition of the Waverley Novels. She is Advisory Editor for the Waverley Novels in Penguin and the Textual Advisor for the new Penguin edition of the novels of Jane Austen.

WALTER SCOTT

IVANHOE

Edited with an introduction by
GRAHAM TULLOCH

PENGUIN BOOKS

PENGUIN BOOKS

Published by the Penguin Group
Penguin Books Ltd, 80 Strand, London WC2R 0RL, England
Penguin Putnam Inc., 375 Hudson Street, New York, New York 10014, USA
Penguin Books Australia Ltd, 250 Camberwell Road, Camberwell, Victoria 3124, Australia
Penguin Books Canada Ltd, 10 Alcorn Avenue, Toronto, Ontario, Canada M4V 3B2
Penguin Books India (P) Ltd, 11 Community Centre, Panchsheel Park, New Delhi – 110 017, India
Penguin Books (NZ) Ltd, Cnr Rosedale and Airborne Roads, Albany, Auckland, New Zealand
Penguin Books (South Africa) (Pty) Ltd, 24 Sturdee Avenue, Rosebank 2196, South Africa

Penguin Books Ltd, Registered Offices: 80 Strand, London WC2R 0RL, England

www.penguin.com

First published 1814
Published in the Edinburgh Edition of the Waverley Novels by the Edinburgh University Press 1998
Published with revised critical apparatus in Penguin Classics 2000
6

Typeset in Linotype Ehrhardt
Printed in England by Clays Ltd, St Ives plc

CONTENTS

ACKNOWLEDGEMENTS

The editors of a critical edition incur many debts, but the indebtedness of the editors of the Edinburgh Edition of the Waverley Novels and of its paperback progeny in the Penguin Scott is particularly heavy. The universities which employ the editors (in this case Flinders University, South Australia) have, in practice, provided the most substantial assistance, but in addition the Universities of Edinburgh and of Aberdeen have been particularly generous with their grants towards the costs of editorial preparation, and it has been the support of the Humanities Research Board of the British Academy that has allowed the Edition to employ a research fellow.

The Edinburgh Edition of the Waverley Novels has been most fortunate in having as its principal financial sponsor the Bank of Scotland, which has continued its long and fruitful involvement with the affairs of Walter Scott. In addition the P.F. Charitable Trust and the Robertson Trust have given generous grants, and the Carnegie Trust for the Universities of Scotland has been most helpful.

The manuscript of *Ivanhoe* is owned by the Pierpont Morgan Library in New York, and most of the relevant letters and papers relating to the publication of the novel are in the National Library of Scotland in Edinburgh. Without the preparedness of these libraries to make manuscripts readily accessible, and to provide support beyond the ordinary, this edition would not have been feasible.

The editors have had, perforce, to seek specialist advice on many matters, and they are most grateful to their consultants Dr John Cairns, Professor Thomas Craik, Dr Caroline Jackson-Houlston, Professor David Nordloh, Roy Pinkerton, and Professor David Stevenson. They owe much to their research fellows, Mairi Robinson, Dr Alison Lumsden, and Gerard Carruthers. They have asked many colleagues far and wide for information. They have continuously sought advice from the members of the Scott Advisory Board, and are particularly grateful for the support of Sir Kenneth Alexander, Professor David Daiches, Dr Douglas Mack, Professor Jane Millgate, and Dr Archie Turnbull.

The editor of *Ivanhoe* would particularly like to express his gratitude to his principal research assistant, Anne Chittleborough, and also to thank Judy King, Sue Tulloch and the staff of Flinders University Library and of the Baillieu Library at the University of Melbourne.

To all of these the editors express their thanks, and acknowledge that the production of the Edinburgh Edition of the Waverley Novels and the Penguin Scott has involved a collective effort to which all those mentioned by name, and very many others, have contributed generously and with enthusiasm.

David Hewitt
Editor-in-chief

Claire Lamont
Advisory editor, the Penguin Scott

J. H. Alexander,
P. D. Garside,
G. A. M. Wood
General editors

THE WAVERLEY NOVELS IN PENGUIN

The novels of Walter Scott published in Penguin are based on the volumes of the Edinburgh Edition of the Waverley Novels (EEWN). This series, which started publication in 1993 and which when complete will run to thirty volumes, is published in hardback by Edinburgh University Press. The Penguin edition of *Ivanhoe* reproduces the text of the novel, Historical Note, Explanatory Notes and Glossary unaltered from the EEWN volume. It does not reproduce the substantial amount of textual information in the Edinburgh Edition but instead provides, in the following paragraphs, a summary of general issues common to all Scott's novels and, in the Note on the Text, a succinct statement of the textual history of *Ivanhoe*. A new critical introduction has been written specifically for the paperback, as well as a Chronology of Scott's life and a list of recommended Further Reading.

The most important aspect of the EEWN is that the text of the novels is based on the first editions, corrected so as to present what may be termed an 'ideal first edition'. Normally Scott's novels gestated over a long period: for instance, the historical works on which he drew for *The Tale of Old Mortality* (1816) had all been read by 1800. By contrast the process of committing a novel to paper, and of converting the manuscript into print, was in most cases extremely rapid. Scott wrote on only one side of his paper, and he used the blank back of the preceding leaf for additions and corrections, made both as he wrote and as he read over what he had written the previous day. Scott's novels were published anonymously – hence the title 'the Waverley Novels', named after the first of them – which meant that only a few people could be allowed to see his handwritten manuscript. Before delivery to the printing-house, therefore, the manuscript was copied and it was the copy that went to the compositor. The person who oversaw the printing of Scott's novels was his friend and business partner James Ballantyne, with whom he jointly owned the printing firm of James Ballantyne & Co. from 1805 (except for the period 1816–22 when Scott was sole partner) until they both became insolvent in 1826.

The compositors in the printing-house set the novels as copy arrived, and while doing so they inserted the great majority of the punctuation marks, normalised and regularised the spelling without standardising it, and corrected many small errors. It was in the printing-house that the presentation of the texts of the novels was changed from the conventions appropriate to manuscript to those of a printed novel of the early nineteenth century. Proofs were corrected in-house, and then a new set of proofs was given to Ballantyne who annotated them prior to sending them to the author. Scott did not read his proofs against his manuscript or against the printer's copy; he read for sense and, making full use of the prerogatives of ownership, he took the opportunity of revising, amplifying, and even introducing new ideas. Thus for Scott reading proofs was a creative rather than just a corrective engagement with his texts. The proofs went back to Ballantyne who oversaw the copying of Scott's new material on to a clean set of proofs and its incorporation into the printed text. Only occasionally did Scott see revised proofs. Two points in particular might be noted about the above procedures. First, Scott delivered his manuscript in batches as he wrote it, and the result was that the first part of a novel was set in type, and proofs corrected, before the end was written. And secondly, in the business of turning a rapidly written text from manuscript to print Scott was indebted to a series of people, copyist, printer, proof-reader, whom Scott editors have come to refer to as 'the intermediaries'.

The business of producing a Waverley novel was so pressurised that mistakes were inevitable. The manuscript was sometimes misread or misunderstood (Scott's handwriting is neat but his letters poorly differentiated); punctuation was often inserted in a mechanical way and the implication of Scott's light manuscript punctuation lost; period words were sometimes not recognised and more obvious, modern terms were substituted for them. The EEWN has examined every aspect of the first-edition texts in the light of the manuscript and the full textual history of the novel. This has enabled the editors to correct the text where Scott's intentions were clearly not fulfilled in the first edition. The EEWN corrects errors, but it does so conservatively bearing in mind that the production of the printed text was a collective effort to which Scott had given his sanction.

Most of the Waverley Novels went through many editions in Scott's lifetime; Scott was not normally involved in the later editions although very occasionally he did see proofs. But in 1827, after his insolvency the previous year, it was decided to issue the first full collected edition of the Waverley Novels, and much of Scott's time in the last years of his life was committed to writing introductions and notes, and to reviewing his text for what he called his 'Magnum Opus' ('Great Work'), or Magnum for short. Scott had acknowledged his authorship of the novels in 1827, and this enabled him to describe the origins of his novels in the introductions to the Magnum edition in a way which was impossible to an author seeking anonymity. The Magnum has formed the basis of every edition of the Waverley Novels published from Scott's death in 1832 until the EEWN chose the first editions as its base-text. In the EEWN the additions made for the Magnum will be published in two volumes at the end of the series. In the volumes published in Penguin passages from the Magnum Introduction relating to the genesis of the novel are included in the new original material produced for the paperback edition.

This edition of Scott in Penguin offers the reader a text which is not only closer to what the author actually wrote and intended but is also new in that it uses for the first time material recovered from manuscripts and proof-sheets, revealing to fuller view the flair and precision of Scott's writing. In addition it supplies the editorial assistance necessary for a modern reader to interpret and enjoy the novel.

David Hewitt
Editor-in-chief
The Edinburgh Edition of the Waverley Novels

INTRODUCTION

The year 1819 was one of discontent in Britain. With the Napoleonic wars finally over and peace re-established in Europe, problems at home became prominent. On 16 August 1819 a large crowd at St Peter's Fields in Manchester demonstrated in favour of the reform of parliament. When the authorities responded by sending in troops, eleven of the demonstrators were killed. In ironic reference and contrast to Wellington's victory over Napoleon four years before at Waterloo, the massacre was nicknamed Peterloo. This was the year in which Shelley wrote of 'An old, mad, blind, despised, and dying king', of 'Princes, the dregs of their dull race', of 'Rulers who . . . leech-like to their fainting country cling', and of 'A people starved and stabbed in the untilled field'[1] and this was the year in which Scott wrote *Ivanhoe*.

For his new novel Scott moved far away from the setting of his own turbulent time. He went back five centuries earlier than any of his previous novels, to the late twelfth century, and to England rather than the Scottish setting of all his previous novels. Yet writing about the past can be a way of writing about the present and Scott in his mind connected his writing *Ivanhoe* with his concerns about contemporary events. Unlike Shelley, who hoped that the tumult of 1819 would lead on to a revolution, Scott was deeply disturbed by the radical agitation taking place and published a long letter supporting the authorities' actions at Peterloo in the *Edinburgh Weekly Journal* of 8 September 1819, signing it 'L. T.', the initials of the supposed author of *Ivanhoe*, Laurence Templeton, whose name appears at the end of the Dedicatory Epistle which opens the novel. It has further been suggested that another connection with contemporary events may lie hidden in the Dedicatory Epistle. It is dated 17 November 1817, a date of no obvious relevance to either the publication of *Ivanhoe* in December 1819 or its composition between June and November of the same year. In a recent article Gary Dyer has drawn attention to a murder case of 1817 in which the accused, Abraham Thornton, whose acquittal (despite strong evidence of his guilt) was subject to appeal, avoided answering the appeal in court by claiming the right of trial by combat. Since the climax of *Ivanhoe* is a trial by combat, it may be significant that the date on which Thornton claimed his right of combat was this very same 17 November 1817.[2] We cannot know whether this is merely a striking coincidence or a deliberate hint of a link but what is certain is that the case attracted enormous publicity and that Scott knew about it and mentioned it elsewhere. This contrast between a remote setting and contemporary relevance is one of the many oppositions that characterize the novel.

The first recorded reaction to *Ivanhoe* is that of Robert Cadell of Archibald Constable and Co., the novel's original publishers. Having travelled south to London with a copy of Volume I to seek a London agent for the novel's distribution, Cadell writes back to his partner in Edinburgh that he has read the book *en route* 'so anxiously that I did not take almost any exercise at the stages'. It is, he asserts, 'a most extraordinary book'.[3] The comments have the ring of more than merely commercial enthusiasm, hard-headed as Cadell was. Many later readers shared his enthusiasm but increasingly associated it with a view of the novel as a great romantic tale, a wonderful story for boys, but full of historical inaccuracies and improbabilities and lacking real substance of ideas. Andrew Lang summed up some of these attitudes in 1893 in his introduction to the Border Edition of the novel: 'Many a trumpet of romance has shrilled since Ivanhoe's in the lists of fancy, many a spear has been shivered, many a sword-stroke and axe-stroke dealt. But in "Ivanhoe" all these came first and freshest, and, while youth dwells in day-dreams that manhood does not forget, this gay and glorious pageant will hold its own, eminent among the greatest works of the great Magician.'[4] It further became customary to consider it as inferior to his Scottish novels: for John Buchan in 1932, 'In *Ivanhoe* Scott opened a new lode in the mine of his fancy, a vein of poorer but most marketable ore,'[5] and for David Daiches, in a seminal article of 1951, 'The novels on which Scott's reputation as a novelist must stand or fall are his "Scotch novels" – those that deal with Scottish history and manners – and not even all of those.'[6] One of the first challenges to the prevailing opinion that *Ivanhoe* is a romantic tale for boys without serious substance comes from Joseph E. Duncan in 1955, claiming that 'the basic point of view in *Ivanhoe* is neither juvenile nor romantic, but thoughtful, mature, and in a sense anti-romantic'.[7] While, for some time after this, critical attention continued to focus on the Scottish novels, thus avoiding a serious consideration of *Ivanhoe*, more recent writers of books and articles have been much more willing to recognize the seriousness and complexities of its concerns and, like Judith Wilt in her *Secret Leaves* of 1985, to argue for its centrality to Scott's work. At the same time, a continuing view of *Ivanhoe* as a romance without the moral complexity of Scott's earlier work appears in a more sophisticated form in Bruce Beiderwell's *Power and Punishment in Scott's Novels* of 1992.

These differing opinions of the novel can partly be explained in terms of changes in Scott's general reputation and the reputation of historical novels. But it would be wrong to see them as arising purely from external forces. In fact the text offers internal support for conflicting opinions since it is built on a series of interlinked oppositions or conflicts which allow for a good deal of ambivalence within the text. Some of the conflicts are immediately obvious: Saxon versus Norman, Christian versus Jew, men versus women. Others reveal themselves with further reflection: medieval versus modern, history versus romance, reality versus fantasy, disguise versus revelation, disinheritance versus the return of the true heir, deracination versus settlement. Examining some of these multiple conflicts provides a useful entry into a complex text.

One way of taking up these conflicts is to begin at the beginning – with the opening point that Scott himself devised, the Dedicatory Epistle, already referred to, which precedes the first chapter. The publication of *Ivanhoe* represented a major turning point in Scott's career and it was natural for him to stop and reflect on the significance of this change for his work. However, any public reflection had to be oblique; the novel was to be published anonymously like all his previous novels. Hence the appearance of a new figure presenting himself as the supposed author of *Ivanhoe*, Laurence Templeton. In the Dedicatory Epistle Templeton dedicates his work to his antiquarian friend Dr Dryasdust of York. The name Dryasdust warns us at once that the Epistle is a piece of play on the author's part, but this should not prevent us from taking it seriously.

From its first paragraph the Dedicatory Epistle deals with one of the major conflicts we have identified, that between romance and history. As we shall see, this conflict also encompasses some of the other major conflicts. *Ivanhoe* now comes to us as one of the Waverley Novels and no one is likely to question its status as a novel. But the Dedicatory Epistle begins by making a surprising claim, that *Ivanhoe* is 'a work designed to illustrate the domestic antiquities of England, and particularly of our Saxon forefathers'. In other words it is a historical work, and more specifically a work of social history like the writings of Robert Henry, Sharon Turner and Joseph Strutt referred to later in the Epistle.[8] Almost immediately, it is true, Templeton remarks that 'the more grave antiquary will perhaps class [it] with the idle novels and romances of the day'. (5) Within a few lines the reader is thus presented with two apparently contradictory classifications. It is tempting to simply dismiss the claim to status as history as part of the joke of the Epistle, since to modern perceptions *Ivanhoe* is quite obviously a novel even if it is not 'idle' and even if 'romance', the other term on offer, may not immediately strike us as appropriate. But the claim that this is history should not be dismissed; after all, the rest of the Epistle takes it seriously and examines the issues with a thoroughness that cannot be set aside as mere fun.

Yet at the same time the title page of the novel bears a subtitle, *Ivanhoe: A Romance*. The two terms 'history' and 'romance' seem incompatible but these apparently contradictory classifications are more helpful than they at first seem. Scott in his 'Essay on Romance' comments on how early romances are often also histories: 'romantic histories, or historical romances'.[9] The 'historical romance' is nowadays a recognized genre and it is tempting to simply say that *Ivanhoe* belongs to that mixed genre and go no further. But the Epistle never calls the novel a historical romance and it proves to be more illuminating not to examine it at first as an example of a single blended genre but as both a history and a romance, or more particularly as a history moving towards romance and a romance moving towards history.

To say that it is a history is not to suggest that it is either a medieval chronicle or a modern work of economic, social or political history. Nor is it to take seriously the claim in the Dedicatory Epistle that the novel is based on an 'Anglo-Norman' manuscript 'which Sir Arthur Wardour preserves with such jealous care in the third drawer of his oaken cabinet'. (12) Even if the supposed owner of the manuscript were not easily recognized as a fictional character in Scott's *The Antiquary*, readers have long since learnt to be sceptical about such claims. Yet if not a history in these senses, *Ivanhoe* can legitimately claim to be 'a work designed to illustrate the domestic antiquities of England, and particularly of our Saxon forefathers'. It is full of minute details of medieval life which Scott culled from the best authorities available to him: a mass of information about food, clothing, physical appearance, buildings, social classes, money, religious beliefs and superstitions. Moreover these details are not merely background decoration but often assume a central position in the story or the characterisation so that they achieve considerable prominence. The tournament at Ashby-de-la-Zouche provides much historical (if anachronistic) detail but it is also used to illustrate social tensions in English society and attitudes towards love and the relationship of the sexes and is tied to the powerful literary themes of disguise and disinheritance. Scott also understood how the physical shape and attitudinal shape of the past are interrelated. A footnote on the barriers which he describes as a feature of 'Every Gothic castle and city' leads straight into his recognition that fights around barriers became an accepted location of admired feats of arms (246n): what is admired in an age is what that age makes physically possible. He then proceeds to make such a fight a central scene of the novel and builds around it a discussion of the value of chivalry.

Some broader elements of social history are also observed. There have always been readers who would have preferred Ivanhoe to have married the Jewess Rebecca rather than his childhood sweetheart, the Saxon Rowena. There are literary reasons why this did not happen which will be considered later but there are also historical reasons expressed succinctly by Scott in the Introduction to the Magnum edition: 'the prejudices of the age rendered such a union almost impossible'.[10] Scott preserves an essential if unpalatable historical truth in refusing to marry the Christian Ivanhoe to the Jewish Rebecca.

The novel also contains accurate details of political history: Prince John was plotting with the French king against Richard's interests in his absence and there was a rebellion by some of John's supporters against Richard on his return. But it is here that the novel most drastically departs from history. The central historical fact of the novel, Richard's return to England from captivity in Germany, is presented in almost entirely fictional form. In the novel Richard returns disguised and unknown and wanders around the country playing the role of a knight errant until his supporters have gathered and he is ready to reveal himself. In reality he arrived openly at Sandwich and proceeded in full public view to London before going on to Bury St Edmunds, Nottingham and a short visit to Sherwood Forest.

Richard's wanderings in disguise in *Ivanhoe* move away from history to romance, where the figure of a disguised knight wandering the country and undertaking various deeds of chivalry is a familiar one. Moreover a specific romance, known to Scott as *Richard Coeur de Lion*, tells of Richard appearing at a tournament in disguise, wearing black armour, defeating various knights and disappearing into the forest just as he does at the tournament in *Ivanhoe*.[11] Another incident during Richard's period of disguise, when he is entertained by a jolly hermit, is based on a fragmentary medieval comic romance, 'The Kyng and the Hermite', as Scott revealed in the Magnum edition Introduction.[12] The king in this story is an unidentified Edward who enjoys a night of revelry with the hermit but Scott transfers the story to Richard – with far-reaching consequences. The original romance mentions no linguistic barrier between king and hermit and they must be assumed to converse in English; when the story is transferred to Richard he, too, is presented as freely speaking English and the effect is further heightened by presenting his brother as 'affecting not to understand the Saxon language, in which, however, he was well-skilled'. (91) Yet it is very doubtful that the historical Richard could actually speak English. This non-historical presentation of Richard as an English speaker is all the more significant when we notice that the linguistic divide between Saxons and Normans is a prominent topic in the first half of the novel and an important part of Scott's attempt to present the historical realities of twelfth century England. However with a historical figure who is known to have had little interest in English or England (Richard spent only a few months of his reign there) Scott chooses to go against history. Evidently an English-speaking Richard offers valuable literary opportunities. Certainly by portraying Richard as an English-speaker Scott can show him drinking with Friar Tuck, feasting with Robin Hood and organising an attack by Saxons on a Norman castle. In a year of social turmoil like 1819 the political symbolism of an English king and his subjects united in harmony cannot be ignored. By departing from history in the direction of romance Scott has been able to make a plea for the social harmony he feared was disappearing in radical revolt. The Richard of romance is in this respect more helpful to him than the Richard of history.

Paradoxically the status of the text as history is often reinforced by claims within the text itself that it is no more than a novel: when the narrator describes De Bracy's attempt to force Rowena to marry him, he appeals to history (specifically Henry) to 'offer some better proof than the incidents of an idle tale, to vindicate the melancholy representation of manners which has just been laid before the reader'. (192) On the surface this disclaims any authority for the novel as history – it is merely an idle tale. In reality the novel's validity as history is actually reinforced by the fact that it is possible to cite historians as evidence of the accuracy of its picture of the manners of the times.

The biggest qualification of the novel's claims to status as history lies in the presence of some anachronisms, as Templeton acknowledges in the Dedicatory Epistle, disarming criticism by admitting that 'it is extremely probable that I may have confused the manners of two or three centuries'. (12) To take just a couple of examples, Scott does his best to present an accurate picture of Anglo-Saxon life but it can be queried whether such a lifestyle survived unchanged in the late twelfth century and, while he drew on authentic sources such as Chaucer and Froissart for description of the tournament, he necessarily as a result gives us a carefully staged and organized late medieval event very different to the free and easy style of tournaments in Richard I's reign. However, as the Dedicatory Epistle points out, complete accuracy is impossible:

> the same motive which prevents my writing the dialogue of the piece in Anglo-Saxon or in Norman-French, and which prohibits my sending forth to the public this essay printed with the types of Caxton or Wynken de Worde, prevents my attempting to confine myself within the limits of the period in which my story is laid. (9)

Templeton's argument is that excessive concentration on the difference of the past from the present will arouse the readers' resistance to 'the repulsive dryness of mere antiquity' but that this can be avoided by concentrating on 'that extensive neutral ground, the proportion, that is, of manners and sentiments which are common to us and to our ancestors'. (9) In theory this might be seen as weakening the historicity of the text but in practice it is used to help the reader respond to the past so that more, rather than less, historical material can be introduced. Thus, when describing the preparations for witch-burning towards the end of the novel, the narrator is able to present this obsolete practice by reference to the 'extensive neutral ground' of continuing human traits:

> the evident desire to look on blood and death, is not peculiar to these dark ages; though in the gladiatorial exercises of single combat and general tourney, they were habituated to the bloody spectacle of brave men falling by each other's hands. Even in our own days, when morals are better understood, an execution, a bruising match between two professors, a riot, or a meeting of radical reformers, collects at considerable hazard to themselves immense crowds of spectators, otherwise little interested, excepting to see how matters are to be conducted. (382)

Scott's antipathy to meetings of radical reformers is evident in his placing them alongside boxing matches and executions but this passage serves a more important purpose by simultaneously drawing past and present apart by their difference and bringing them together by their similarity. At this stage, at least, the conflict between past and present is thus both resolved and unresolved.

At other times the reader's attention is drawn rather more to differences from the past than to similarities. One such difference is medieval superstition compared to modern rationalism: when Malvoisin's henchmen present ridiculous evidence that Rebecca is a witch, the narrator comments that 'The circumstances of their evidence would have been, in modern days, divided into two classes – those which were immaterial, and those which were actually and physically impossible. But both were, in those ignorant and superstitious days, eagerly credited as proofs of guilt.' (327) Rebecca, with her usual clear-sightedness and an understanding born of years of experience of racial prejudice, repeats the same argument as the narrator: 'to plead that many things which these men . . . have spoken against me are impossible, would avail me but little, since you believe in their possibility; and still less would it advantage me to explain, that the peculiarities of my dress, language, and manners, are those of my people'. (328) Similarly Bois-Guilbert, from his atheist viewpoint, is able to ask: 'Will future ages believe that such stupid bigotry ever existed?' (315) By emphasising the differences from modern viewpoints the text is once again able to demonstrate its validity as history.

History, as we know, is not just facts but also interpretation. By locating *Ivanhoe* close to the Norman Conquest Scott is placing it beside one of the central facts of English history but he is also placing it near one of the great loci of historical interpretation. Wamba responds to an offer to serve a Norman lord by quoting an alleged 'proverb':

Norman saw on English oak,
On English neck a Norman yoke;
Norman spoon in English dish,
And England ruled as Normans wish;
Blithe world in England ne'er will be more
Till England's rid of all the four. (225)

Although for a modern reader the Norman yoke has no greater resonance than the Norman saw and the Norman spoon, it would have had special meaning for many of Scott's original readers. A long-standing interpretation of English history saw the Norman Conquest as the point in time when what Scott calls 'the milder and more free spirit of the Saxon constitution' (16) was replaced by the 'Norman yoke' of feudalism. According to their various political persuasions, various writers saw this yoke as having been subsequently lifted at some significant point or other in English history, resulting in the restoration of the lost Anglo-Saxon liberties.[13] Such an interpretation of history sets Saxon against Norman and assumes the ultimate triumph of one over the other. Scott, however, influenced by Sharon Turner's views, as Clare A. Simmons has shown,[14] did not present the outcome of history as a triumph of Saxon over Norman but rather as a blending of the two races into a new race, the English, who preserve the best characteristics of both. By entering the controversial area of historical interpretation Scott added another important level of 'history' to the text.

If the discussion has so far been able to avoid directly addressing the question 'what is a history?' by accepting a view of history as defined by the works of historians of Scott's time like Henry, Strutt and Turner, to whom he refers, it is not possible to discuss *Ivanhoe* as a romance without addressing the question 'what is a romance?' since it is by no means clear what kinds of romance Scott is referring to in his subtitle. Scott begins his own 'Essay on Romance' by quoting Johnson's definition of a romance as 'a military fable of the middle ages; a tale of wild adventures in love and chivalry', but finds it 'not sufficiently comprehensive' and instead he offers his own definition of a romance as 'a fictitious narrative in prose or verse; the interest of which turns upon marvellous and uncommon incidents'. (129) One's first reaction might be to say that Johnson's definition fits *Ivanhoe* better than Scott's since it explicitly mentions things that are clearly in the novel: military matters, love and chivalry. But this is to ignore the difficulty raised by the vagueness of Johnson's 'wild adventures' which Scott considered to be 'almost the only absolutely essential ingredient in Johnson's definition' and which are represented in his own definition as 'marvellous and uncommon incidents'. If we take the term 'marvellous' to mean 'supernatural', as it often did in discussions of literature, then *Ivanhoe* does not qualify: unlike with many medieval romances, nothing in the novel needs to be explained in supernatural terms. However, if we take 'marvellous' to mean simply 'surprising', then there are certainly many wild, surprising and uncommon events in the novel: the love of a Templar for a Jewess, a trial by combat, a band of honest outlaws, the siege and burning of a castle, to name a few. At the same time other wild and uncommon events are entertained as real possibilities in the novel but remain only as potential without actually taking place. The lurking possibility of rape for Rebecca and Rowena, of being roasted and basted for Isaac, of being burned alive for Rebecca, of being scalped and hung from the battlements for Wamba: all of these are very real threats but never happen. A dramatic illustration of this is the three scenes in which Rowena, Rebecca and Isaac are threatened in Torquilstone: all end with the same horn blast at the gates. It is here that the links of the novel with another kind of romance become obvious. Scott's definition, broader than Johnson's, encompasses such later works as the Gothic romances of the eighteenth century. Medieval romance can involve real violence and a particularly pertinent example is to be found in the romance *Richard Coeur de Lion*. Here Richard is depicted as a cannibal happily dining on the heads of Saracens. The story is too ridiculous to find a place in a work that claims to be a serious history and it is incompatible with Scott's portrayal of Richard but the novel also avoids more plausible and historically accurate violence; instead, by relegating similar violence and cruelty to the status of real but unfulfilled threats, Scott shows himself in this respect much closer to eighteenth century Gothic romance than to medieval romance. Nevertheless other aspects of the novel show the influence of medieval romance. Some of Scott's specific borrowings have already been mentioned and Jerome Mitchell in his *Scott, Chaucer and Medieval Romance* has illustrated just how many events in *Ivanhoe* have parallels in medieval romances including such motifs as the hero being disguised as a palmer, like Ivanhoe at the beginning of the novel. For this Mitchell offers no less than five parallels, two of which deal with the return of a Crusader and three with his visit in disguise to his lady.[15]

But if there are strong elements of romance in the novel, it still remains within the conventions of a realistic novel. Events and characters are realistic. Richard, the subject of an extravagant medieval romance, is developed as a realistic character, a complex mixture of pride, rashness and arbitrariness with generosity and good humour. This is not romance: it is history in so far as Scott's picture conforms with that of historians of his time. Paradoxically, though, part of the realism of character proceeds from romance of events. As has already been noted, the historical Richard did not wander around England in disguise playing the knight errant. Scott creates this from romance sources but uses it to portray what he sees as a central facet of Richard's historical character. At one point Ivanhoe reproaches Richard with playing the knight errant, endangering his own life and not caring for this kingdom. (363) His words very closely reflect those of Richard's historical followers in Palestine when Richard indulged in similar exploits and function to reinforce what was currently seen as a historically accurate view of Richard's character but are transferred to non-historical English exploits.

One way of describing this would be to say that we have romance of event and historical realism of character. In fact, history and romance are even more deeply interconnected than that. We have already seen how events taken from romance have been kept within the bounds of historical realism but we can also show how historically realistic characters have within them deeply entrenched elements of romance. For this the crucial connecting point is chivalry. When we read Scott's essays on both romance and chivalry, it becomes clear that the two are intimately linked in his mind. It is not just that chivalry is the primary subject of medieval romance, it is also that Scott's conceptions of romance and chivalry are deeply akin. Chivalry can be seen as romance lived in real life, a view evident in these comments from the 'Essay on Chivalry' on 'the strain of sentiment . . . which Chivalry inspired' in Spain:

> The warriors whom she sent to the New World sought and found marvels which resembled those of romance; they achieved deeds of valour against such odds of numbers as are only recorded in the annals of knight-errantry.[16]

Romance, however extravagant in its claims, forms the model for chivalry. At the same time chivalry in its often extreme manifestations forms the subject-matter of romance, to the extent that Scott in the same essay has

> no hesitation in quoting the romances of Chivalry as good evidence of the laws and customs of knighthood. The authors, like the painters of the period, invented nothing, but copying the manners of the age in which they lived, transferred them, without doubt or scruple, to the period and personages of whom they treated. (8n)

Chivalry imitates romance and romance imitates chivalry: fiction and reality become one. The embodiment of this within the novel is Richard: as Scott says, 'In the lion-hearted King, the brilliant, but useless character, of a knight of romance, was in great measure realized' (365). A character of romance is realized as history. As a result Scott is able to deal simultaneously with history and romance; in the subject matter of chivalry the two genres of history and romance converge.

One manifestation of this convergence is the critique of chivalry which the novel offers. Chivalry is presented as a historical reality but with strong emphasis on the fantastic and extravagant qualities which connect it with romance. The narrator writes of 'the most frantic excess of chivalrous zeal' (323) and 'the wild spirit of chivalry' which impels Richard to look for dangers 'which it was unpardonable in him to have sought out' (364) and the 'excited imagination' which values glory more than political wisdom and impels Richard towards 'feats of chivalry' which are of no solid benefit to his country. (365) Characters also join in this chorus of criticism with Cedric the Saxon predictably objecting to the 'fantastic fashions of Norman chivalry' (52) and Rebecca reflecting on the 'fantastic chivalry of the Nazarenes'. (250)

Rebecca's comments come as part of a debate with Ivanhoe about chivalry. For Ivanhoe chivalry is the pursuit of glory:

> 'we live not – we wish to live no longer than while we are victorious and renowned – Such, maiden, are the laws of chivalry to which we are sworn, and to which we offer all that we hold dear.' (249)

It is only after Rebecca questions the value of this glory that Ivanhoe replies in slightly more altruistic terms:

> 'Chivalry! – why, maiden, it is the nurse of pure and high affection – the stay of the oppressed, the redresser of grievances, the curb of the power of the tyrant – nobility were but an empty name without her, and liberty finds the best protector in her lance and sword.' (249)

By asserting the noblest aspirations of chivalry, the protection of the weak, Ivanhoe deflects Rebecca's criticism but does not really answer it. Soon after he falls asleep and the debate remains unresolved although the final word rests for the moment with Rebecca's censure of 'the fantastic chivalry of the Nazarenes'. Given that Rebecca is the most thoroughly admirable and clear-sighted character in the book we might be inclined to take her judgement as final but, as Ivanhoe sleeps, she expresses her growing love for him and then berates herself for forgetting her father. She thus effectively moves aside from the debate about chivalry and leaves it without resolution.

Other parts of the novel suggest a kinder judgement of chivalry. De Bracy hardly plays a chivalric part in kidnapping Rowena in an effort to force her to marry him. Yet he refrains from betraying Rowena's injured lover to his enemy because 'The ideas of chivalrous honour, which, amidst his wildness and levity, never utterly abandoned [him], prohibited him from doing the knight any injury in his defenceless condition'. (240) Just as the novel as a whole is both a history and a romance, so Scott's modern romance of chivalry offers us both the romantic ideal which Scott saw as its romance and the excess that he saw as its historical reality or, as he said elsewhere of the 'knights and ladies' of the Middle Ages, 'their purity is that of romance, their profligacy that of reality'.[17] In chivalry history and romance are one: the conflict between the two is dissolved.

The contrast between disguise and revelation provides another of the major conflicts in the novel. Disguise is everywhere and one of the most persistently disguised is the hero. Ivanhoe first appears disguised as a palmer; he then takes part in the tournament under the name of El Desdichado; next he uses his hood to cover his face after the first day of the tournament; finally he conceals his face on entering Coningsburgh Castle. Gurth, as Ivanhoe's squire, 'seemed to affect the incognito as much as his master' (93). De Bracy and Bois-Guilbert dress themselves as Saxon outlaws, Wamba disguises himself as a monk and then hands this disguise over to Cedric and Richard appears as the Black Knight at the tournament and as the Knight of the Fetterlock at the siege of Torquilstone. Finally Ulrica disguises her true identity under the name Urfried.

Disguise is a romance motif and *Ivanhoe* is a romance, but it is the special association of disguise with chivalry that lends it particular prominence in the novel. On Ivanhoe's refusal to uncover his face to receive his prize from Prince John the narrator's comments that 'amidst the capricious vows by which knights were accustomed to bind themselves in those days of chivalry, there was none more common than those by which they engaged to remain incognito for a certain space'. (85–6) Even the incidental trappings of chivalry include disguise with squires at the tournament 'quaintly disguised as a savage or sylvan man, or in some other fantastic dress'. (67) It is particularly in the quintessential chivalric role of the knight errant that disguise is favoured, as Bois-Guilbert makes clear in his plan to save Rebecca by appearing as her champion 'disguised indeed in the fashion of a roving knight, who seeks adventures to prove his shield and spear'. (341) It is no surprise, then, to find Richard, the embodiment of the knight errant, adopting a disguise.

Disguise is balanced by revelation and the throwing off of disguise provides some of the most dramatic scenes of the novel. Ivanhoe uncovers himself twice in the presence of his father, at the tournament and at Coningsburgh. Richard's revelation of himself as king leads to the scene of symbolic social harmony with which Scott balanced the social disharmony of his own time. Ulrica finally redeems herself when she reveals her name and ancestry to the full view of all 'on a turret, in the guise [not *dis*guise] of one of the ancient Furies, yelling forth a war-song, such as was of yore chaunted on the field of battle by the scalds of the yet heathen Saxons' (269). Her invocation of Zernebock and Valhalla, anachronistic and inaccurate as it may be in historical terms, expresses the deepest roots of her identity, a rejection of her shameful relationship with the Norman Front-de-Boeuf.

In this world one character stands out as never adopting disguise: Rebecca. She does appear veiled, but this is out of modesty not an intention to hide her identity. It is only the prejudice or imagination of others that disguises her true identity: when she unexpectedly appears dressed in white Gurth is worried and affected by 'all the characteristic terrors of a Saxon respecting fawns, forest-fiends [and] white women' (100) while Ivanhoe's 'fancy' (235) interferes with his ability to recognize her for what she is when she tends to his wounds. Rebecca refuses to make use of these deceptions. As soon as Ivanhoe addresses her as 'Noble damsel', placing her by those words in the same rank and class as himself, she reveals that 'your hand-maiden is a poor Jewess' (235) despite the prejudices this will excite.

If Rebecca is associated with revelation in this sense she is also associated with revelation in another sense of the word, the revealed truth of religion. Of all the characters in the novel, she is the one most deeply and consciously committed to the beliefs shared by Christians and Jews. While others may refer to aspects of Christianity, the Prior to his Vulgate Bible and the Grand Master to scriptural quotations from the Templar Rule, she alone appeals to the fundamental beliefs of Christians and Jews, as when she calls on Rowena 'in the great name of the God whom they both worshipped, and by that revelation of the Law in which they both believed'.(160) Rebecca's acceptance of divine revelation gives her access to a level of understanding and clear-sightedness shared by no other character. She is able therefore to see Bois-Guilbert's plans to save her for the 'dream' (343) it is; by contrast

Bois-Guilbert sees the very real preparations for her burning as 'hideous fantasies' and 'something unreal' and her equally real hopes of Heaven (the expression of her faith in the revelation of religion) as 'dreams . . . idle visions' (388).

Ivanhoe's disguise at the tournament is that of El Desdichado, the Disinherited Knight, because his father has disinherited him. Apart from indicating the ability of disguise to symbolically express the truth, this links disguise to the closely related theme of disinheritance. Like disguise, disinheritance involves the false displacing the true; the true heir is displaced by the false claimant. At its most literal and obvious level this applies to individuals like Ivanhoe himself, to the Anglo-Saxon claimants of the throne, displaced by Richard and, ironically, also to Richard himself, the true king whom his brother has temporarily displaced, but it applies equally to the Jews robbed of their promised land and the Saxons who live on in England seeing their inherited homeland owned by the Normans. The idea of disinheritance is one of special significance for Scott because it is central to the Jacobite theme which he had already dealt with in his first novel *Waverley* and subsequently in *Rob Roy*: the Jacobites claimed to be the true heirs displaced by the Hanoverian kings and Scott felt a strong emotional pull towards the validity of their claim. Using the fictional Athelstane and the historical Richard as surrogate Jacobite claimants, Scott is able to explore different aspects and outcomes of the Jacobite theme including one ending in which the true king is restored. Yet this text, while constantly creating cases of disinheritance, eschews a disinheritance narrative traditionally associated with one of its main characters; over time Robin Hood had come to be identified, in accounts well known to Scott, as a disinherited nobleman but in *Ivanhoe* he appears merely as a yeoman.

By a further symbolic linkage the device that Ivanhoe uses to symbolize his disinherited state is a deracinated oak. Deracination is another aspect of disinheritance and the novel is appropriately full of wandering and deracinated people: Gurth remarks that he is surrounded by 'errant knights and errant squires, errant monks and errant minstrels, errant jugglers and errant jesters' (102), the word 'wandering' is applied to pilgrims (20), the Jews (97, 230), a minstrel (138), a bard (249), 'errant knights . . . whose trade is wandering' (275) and 'wandering palmers, hedge-priests, Saxon minstrels, and Welch bards' (369) and the word 'roving' is used to describe knights (341) and the lifestyle of outlaws (159). This is a radically unsettled society in contrast to the settlement and order that the return of the true heir is supposed to bring. For some of these wanderers the wandering, deracinated lifestyle is desirable, for others it is a cause of lament but the novel offers little prospect of the recovery of inheritance and the end of wandering until near its conclusion and then it is only partial.

According to Scott the very first seed of *Ivanhoe* in his mind was an opposition, between Saxon and Norman, which he had seen represented on the stage in John Logan's play *Runnamede*,[18] but by the end of the novel this opposition has been resolved. The marriage of Ivanhoe and Rowena is explicitly presented as a symbol of the reconciliation of the two races:

> these distinguished nuptials were celebrated by the attendance of the high-born Normans, as well as Saxons, joined with the universal jubilee of the lower orders, that marked the marriage of two individuals as a type of the future peace and harmony betwixt two races, which, since that period, have been so completely mingled, that the distinction has become utterly invisible. (398)

Not only are Saxon and Norman reconciled but also the distinction between medieval and modern viewpoints is overturned by making the past a symbol of the present.

The symbolic effect of the marriage of Ivanhoe and Rowena extends to many of the novel's other conflicts. Marriage is a traditional ending for romance but by linking this marriage with the historical evolution of the English race the text continues that drawing together of history and romance that has been operating since the first chapter. By its very nature marriage also bridges the conflict between men and women. Ivanhoe's acceptance by his father and Richard's presence as the acknowledged king of England at the wedding resolves the conflict between disinheritance and the acceptance of the true heir. Even the conflict within chivalry between idealism and excess is to some extent reconciled in the figure of Ivanhoe, a true knight errant in his defence of Rebecca but willing nevertheless to settle down with Rowena. Finally marriage, as a public expression of private feelings, pushes aside the disjunction between outward and inward which expresses itself in disguise. Thus the last chapter of the book presents us with a picture of harmony and reconciliation involving the resolution of the conflicts on which so much of the story had been based.

It is a satisfying conclusion – but it is not the only conclusion to the novel. Alongside the wedding of Ivanhoe and Rowena, the final chapter offers us another conclusion, not of reconciliation and harmony but of exclusion. After the wedding Rebecca comes to Rowena and announces that she must leave England and find security at the court of the Muslim Mohammed Boabdil in Granada. The historical details are anachronistic but for the reader this does not lessen in any way the profound impact of Rebecca's exile. Here is the novel's most admirable character unable to find a place in the new world that the wedding has symbolized.

There are others who are excluded from the harmonious ending. The Templars, an international order that defies the national authority, have no place in the developing nation state. Prince John retreats to France. The Malvoisins, unfortunate in their name, have no place in the quiet neighbourhood which will displace Norman violence. But no one is so prominently excluded as the Jews. In many ways this is puzzling. The text begins with Shylock's powerful plea for recognition of the shared humanity of Christians and Jews, 'Hath not a Jew eyes? Hath not a Jew hands, organs, dimensions, senses, affections, passions? Fed with the same food, hurt with the same weapons, subject to the same diseases, healed by the same means, warmed and cooled by the same winter and summer, as a Christian is?' Alluded to in the Dedicatory Epistle, (10) it is quoted in full as the motto to Chapter 5. (46) As the novel progresses we are continually invited to recognize this shared humanity by historical explanations of cases of Jewish avarice and obsequiousness as the natural consequence of their oppression by Christians rather than as derived from inherent racial characteristics. In Isaac Scott presents the traditional comic avarice of the stereotypical Jew but overwhelms and obliterates it with the depth of Isaac's love for his daughter. In Rebecca he portrays everything that is beautiful and noble. And yet there is no place for them. Why?

Some reasons apply specifically to Rebecca. Amongst these Scott's sense of literary appropriateness no doubt played a part: as one of the novel's most vibrant and interesting characters, Rebecca needs an ending of equal weight but different to that accorded to Rowena. Scott explicitly rules out the traditional literary ending to such tales, the conversion of the young Jewess, but exile provides him with an ending of appropriate significance. Traditionally readers and critics have concentrated on her as the other woman, the woman that Ivanhoe cannot marry because he must marry Rowena, and the narrator himself lends support to this by speculating whether 'the recollection of Rebecca's beauty and magnanimity did not recur to his mind more frequently than the fair descendant of Alfred might altogether have approved' (401) but Rebecca is not just the other woman she is the Other in a much broader sense. She has continually been presented throughout the novel as an exotic figure, often, with her Eastern dress, as the oriental other. Although she asserts her Englishness, she is perceived as, to use Ulrica's term, 'outlandish' (194) and as belonging elsewhere. Also, though unharmed at the end, she has not lost her role as the symbol of all that women can suffer from men. This role can no longer apply to Rowena who, by her marriage to Ivanhoe, avoids the threat of rape or, at best, forced marriage to De Bracy; but Rebecca, the woman who has been most seriously threatened by the power of men and faced with the possibility not just of rape but of being burnt to death, remains. She is not all women but she symbolizes all women's potential to be the victims of men's violence and oppression. Finally as the non-disguiser, the character who is most completely identified with revealed truth she does not belong in the necessarily compromised real world that the other characters inhabit.

Other reasons apply more generally to the Jews. Firstly, Scott's sense of history undoubtedly played a part: he knew that the Jews were not long after expelled from England. Secondly, as the representative Jews of the novel, Rebecca and her father are threatened with more horrific violence than any other characters of the novel: for Isaac with being basted and roasted alive, for Rebecca with being burnt at the stake. In both cases a champion intervenes to save them but their potentiality as victims of monstrous violence remains. Those who planned this violence are dead or in exile; ironically the only figures who remain and can symbolize that dark potential in human beings are their intended victims. Though in exile, Rebecca and Isaac are still there, reminding us of the cruelty of which they were so nearly victims, of that dark side to humanity that cannot be accommodated within the happy romance conclusion. Thirdly, the Jews, like the Templars, are a nation without a state, dispersed and wandering as the novel so often calls them, and have no place in the new English state. Finally, and perhaps most importantly, Rebecca and Isaac represent that residue which always remains excluded in some way or other at a time of racial integration. Why was Scott so taken with Logan's image of opposed Saxons and Normans which he tells us was the seed of the novel? Surely it cannot have been unconnected with his recognition of racial divisions in his own country, between Highlanders and Lowlanders. At one level he accepted the necessity for Highland integration with the Lowlands, but he was aware that many Highlanders had been forced into exile to achieve this. His novels do not deal with this exile directly but he does deal with those who are left behind unable to accept the new integrated world; one of the most poignant portraits in his later writing is that of Elspat in 'The Highland Widow' who cannot accept the integration of the Highlands into the new Britain. The Jews, as people who are to have for a long time no part in the new racially integrated England, are a potent symbol of that residue which is always left over when integration takes place.

Ivanhoe is thus a novel which begins and, partly, ends in division. The division with which it began is resolved, as are various other conflicts set up within the novel but at the end there remains a division between those who can take part in that resolution and those whose place remains unresolved, other and apart. If one ending of the novel, the vision of the blending of races and harmony between social classes, can be seen as a counterbalance to the traumatic events of 1819 and, as Dyer has suggested, the worrying implications of the 1817 appeal to trial by combat, the other ending, exile and exclusion, cannot be seen as offering any such visions of hope. Traditionally readers have been more affected by one ending or the other. But the text offers us both equally. The best response may be one that encompasses both endings. Perhaps it is here that Scott's Scottish background becomes most relevant. It is ironic that one of the great defining myths of Englishness, for that is what *Ivanhoe* became, was written by a Scotsman. Perhaps the dual ending of the novel reflects the essential ambivalence of Scott's position as a Scot, both an outsider and an insider of English culture. The dual sense of integration and exclusion is central to the Scottish experience. This is not to suggest that *Ivanhoe* is really a novel about Scotland rather than England. Rather it is to propose that literary understanding of the end of the novel should be built on a recognition that it offers both integration and exclusion, both settlement and deracination, both peace and the continuing potential for violence and that it is the combination of these opposites that constitutes the final statement of the novel.

NOTES

1 Percy Bysshe Shelley, 'Sonnet: England in 1819', in *The Complete Poetical Works of Percy Bysshe Shelley*, ed. Thomas Hutchinson (London, 1904), lines 1–7.

2 Gary R. Dyer, '*Ivanhoe*, Chivalry, and the Murder of Mary Ashford', *Criticism*, 39 (1997), 383–408.

3 National Library of Scotland, MS 323, ff. 6v-7r.

4 Andrew Lang, Editor's Introduction to *Ivanhoe*, in *Waverley Novels*, Border Edition, 48 vols (London, 1892–4), 17.xix.

5 John Buchan, *Sir Walter Scott* (London, 1932), 198.

6 David Daiches, 'Scott's Achievement as a Novelist', *Nineteenth Century Fiction*, 6 (1951), 81–95, 153–73, at 84; reprinted in *Literary Essays*, (Edinburgh, 1966), 88–121 and in *Scott's Mind and Art*, ed. A. Norman Jeffares (Edinburgh, 1969), 21–52.

7 'The Anti-Romantic in "Ivanhoe"', *Nineteenth-Century Fiction*, 9 (1955), 293–300, at 293–4.

8 Robert Henry, *The History of Great Britain, from the First Invasion of it by the Romans* (1771–93); Sharon Turner, *The History of the Anglo-Saxons* (1799–1805); Joseph Strutt, *A Complete View of the Dress and Habits of the People of England*, (1796–9) and *Sports and Pastimes of the People of England* (1801).

9 'Essay on Romance', in *The Prose Works of Sir Walter Scott, Bart.*, 28 vols (Edinburgh, 1834–6), 6.134.

10 Walter Scott, *Waverley Novels*, in 48 vols (Edinburgh, 1829–33), 16.xxi. (Hereafter 'Magnum').
11 George Ellis, *Specimens of Early English Romances,* 3 vols (London, 1805), 3.186–7.
12 Magnum, 16.xii-xviii.
13 For a full account of the development of this notion see Christopher Hill, 'The Norman Yoke' in *Puritanism and Revolution* (London, 1958), 50–122.
14 Clare A. Simmons, *Reversing the Conquest: History and Myth in Nineteenth-Century British Literature* (New Brunswick, 1990), 79.
15 Jerome Mitchell, *Scott, Chaucer and Medieval Romance: A Study of Sir Walter Scott's Indebtedness to the Literature of the Middle Ages* (Lexington, 1987), 127–9
16 'Essay on Chivalry', in *The Prose Works of Sir Walter Scott, Bart*., 28 vols (Edinburgh, 1834–6), 6.19.
17 'Essay on Chivalry', 41.
18 Magnum, 16.vii-viii.

CHRONOLOGY OF WALTER SCOTT

1771 *15 August*. Born in College Wynd, Edinburgh. His father, Walter (1729–99), son of a sheep-farmer at Sandyknowe, near Smailholm Tower, Roxburghshire, was a lawyer. His mother, Anne Rutherford (1732–1819), was daughter of Dr John Rutherford, Professor of Medicine in the University of Edinburgh. His parents married in April 1758; Walter was their ninth child. The siblings who survived were Robert (1767–87), John (1769–1816), Anne (1772–1801), Thomas (1774–1823), and Daniel (?1776–1806).

1772–73 *Winter*. Contracted what is now termed poliomyelitis, and became permanently lame in his right leg. His grandfather Rutherford advised that he be sent to Sandyknowe to benefit from country air, and, apart from a period of 'about a year' in 1775 spent in Bath, a spell in 1776 with his family in their new home on the west side of George Square, Edinburgh, and a time in 1777 at Prestonpans, near Edinburgh, he lived there until 1778. From his grandmother and his aunt Janet he heard many ballads and stories of the Border past, and these narratives were crucial to his intellectual and imaginative development.

1779–83 Attended the High School of Edinburgh; he was particularly influenced by the Rector, Dr Alexander Adam, and his teaching of literature in Latin. After the High School, he spent 'half a year' with his aunt Janet in Kelso, where he attended the grammar school, and read for the first time Thomas Percy's *Reliques of Ancient English Poetry*.

1783–86 Attended classes in Edinburgh University, including Humanity (Latin), Greek, Logic and Metaphysics, and Moral Philosophy.

1786 Studies terminated by serious illness; convalescence in Kelso. Apprenticed as a lawyer to his father.

1787 Met Robert Burns at the house of the historian and philosopher, Adam Ferguson.

1789 Decided to prepare for the Bar.

1789–92 Attended classes at Edinburgh University, including History, Moral Philosophy, Scots Law, and Civil Law.

1792 *11 July*. Admitted to the Faculty of Advocates.

Autumn. First visit to Liddesdale, in the extreme south of Scotland, with Robert Shortreed, in search of ballads and ballad-singers. Seven such 'raids' followed over seven years. Shortreed later commented: 'He was makin' himsell a' the time'. His tours took him into many parts of Scotland and the north of England: e.g. in 1793 to Perthshire and the Trossachs; in 1796 to the north-east of Scotland; and in 1797 to Cumberland and the Lake District.

1794 In April involved in a brawl with some political radicals and bound to keep the peace. In September attended the trials of the radicals Watt and Downie, and in November Watt's execution.

*c.*1794–96 In love with Williamina Belsches, culminating in April 1796 with an invitation to her home, Fettercairn House, Kincardineshire.

1796 Anonymous publication of *The Chase and William and Helen*, Scott's translations of two of Bürger's poems.

October. Announcement of the engagement of Williamina Belsches to William Forbes.

1797 Volunteered for the new volunteer cavalry regiment, the Royal Edinburgh Light Dragoons, and appointed quartermaster.

September. Met Charlotte Carpenter (1770–1826), at Gilsland, Cumberland, and within three weeks proposed marriage. Charlotte's parents were Jean François Charpentier and Margaret Charlotte Volère (d. 1788), of Lyons. Sometime after the break-up of the marriage around 1780, her mother brought Charlotte and her brother Charles (1772–1818) to England; Charlotte and Charles later became the wards of the 2nd Marquess of Downshire, and changed their name to Carpenter.

24 December. Married Charlotte in Carlisle, and set up house at 50 George Street, Edinburgh.

1798 Met Matthew Gregory ('Monk') Lewis, and agreed to contribute to *Tales of Wonder* (published 1801).

Rented cottage in Lasswade near Edinburgh for the summer, and made many political and literary contacts, including Lady Louisa Stuart, who proved to be one of the most acute and trusted of his friends and critics.

Moved to 19 Castle Street, Edinburgh.

October. Birth and death of first son.

1799 Publication of *Goetz of Berlichingen*, Scott's translation of Goethe's tragedy.

April. Death of Scott's father.
Met John Leyden and the publisher Archibald Constable, and had his first discussion with the printer James Ballantyne about undertaking book-printing: Ballantyne brought out Scott's anthology *An Apology for Tales of Terror* in 1800.
October. Birth of daughter, Charlotte Sophia Scott.
December. Appointed Sheriff-Depute of Selkirkshire.

1801 *October*. Birth of son, Walter Scott.
Moved to 39 Castle Street, Edinburgh.

1802 Publication of *Minstrelsy of the Scottish Border*, Vols 1 and 2. The *Minstrelsy* was the first publication in a lifetime of scholarly editing, and it shows both the strengths and weaknesses of Scott as editor. He found new texts (of the 72 ballads he published, 38 had not appeared in print before), and his literary, historical, and anthropological essays and notes are always illuminating; but, following the editorial practice of the time, he had no settled methods or principles for choosing or establishing a text.
Met James Hogg.

1803 *February*. Birth of daughter, Anne Scott.
Second edition of *Minstrelsy of the Scottish Border*, Vols 1 and 2, and first edition of Vol. 3.
Began to contribute reviews to the *Edinburgh Review*. Scott was an acute reviewer, in the expansive manner characteristic of heavyweight reviews in the early nineteenth century, and was particularly perceptive about such contemporaries as Jane Austen, Byron, and Mary Shelley.
September. Visit from William and Dorothy Wordsworth.

1804 Took the lease of Ashestiel near Selkirk as his country house in place of the cottage in Lasswade.
Publication of Scott's edition of the medieval metrical romance, *Sir Tristrem*.

1805 Publication of *The Lay of the Last Minstrel*, the first of a series of verse romances which established his fame as a poet.
Entered into partnership with James Ballantyne in the printing business of James Ballantyne & Co. Until the financial crash in 1826, the partnership was not just a financial arrangement, but a unique collaboration: Ballantyne managed the business, but also acted as Scott's editor; Scott seems to have been responsible for much of the financial planning, and it was a standard part of his

contracts with publishers that his works should be printed by James Ballantyne & Co.

December. Birth of son, Charles Scott.

1806 Hurried to London to secure his appointment as one of the Principal Clerks to the Court of Session, a position which had been under negotiation for much of the previous year but which was imperilled by the advent of a new government after the death of William Pitt on 23 January. The appointment was announced on 8 March. Scott took the place of an elderly Clerk, but, as there was no retirement and pension scheme, allowed his predecessor to keep the salary of £800 per annum for life. While in London Scott was 'taken up' by high society.

1807 Brother Tom bankrupt. It also emerged that Tom, a lawyer who had inherited his father's practice, and who had been retained as agent for the Duddingston estate of the Marquess of Abercorn, had misappropriated some of his client's money. Scott felt financially and morally endangered by his brother's breach of trust, and extended efforts were required over several years to protect his own financial credit and provide for his brother and his family.

1808 Publication of poem *Marmion* (the rights of which the publisher Archibald Constable had bought for £1050 in 1807).

Appointed secretary to the Parliamentary Commission to Inquire into the Administration of Justice in Scotland. The Commission ended its work in 1810.

Publication of *The Works of John Dryden . . . with Notes . . . and a Life of the Author*, 18 vols.

Cancelled his subscription to the *Edinburgh Review* because of its 'defeatist' view of the war in Spain, and began (with others) planning the *Quarterly Review* and the *Edinburgh Annual Register*, both launched in 1810. The political disagreement developed into a quarrel with Archibald Constable & Co., and Scott and the Ballantyne brothers, James and John, set up and became the partners in a rival publishing business, John Ballantyne & Co. Scott entrusted his own works to the new business and whenever possible directed other writers and new ventures to it, but Constable withdrew printing work from James Ballantyne & Co., and the printing firm stopped making significant profits.

1809 Publication of *A Collection of Scarce and Valuable Tracts*

(Somers' Tracts), Vols 1–3; completed in 13 vols 1812.

1810 Publication of *The Lady of the Lake*, his most commercially successful poem.

1811 Scott's predecessor as Clerk of Session agreed to apply for a pension, and from 1812 Scott was paid a salary of £1300 per annum.

Publication of poem *The Vision of Don Roderick*.

Purchase of Cartley Hole, the nucleus of the Abbotsford Estate, between Galashiels and Melrose.

1812 Byron began correspondence with Scott.

Removal from Ashestiel to Abbotsford, and plans for rebuilding the small farmhouse there.

1813 Publication of poems *Rokeby* and *The Bridal of Triermain*.

First financial crisis. It became apparent in 1812 that the publishing firm of John Ballantyne & Co. was making losses on every publication except Scott's poetry, and that the *Edinburgh Annual Register* was losing £1000 per issue. The firm was undercapitalised, and depended overmuch on bank credit. The national financial crisis of 1812–14 led to reduced orders for books from retailers, late payments, and to the bankruptcy of many companies whose debts to John Ballantyne & Co. were either not paid or paid in part. John Ballantyne & Co. found itself unable to pay its own bills and repay the banks on time, and *Rokeby*, greatly profitable though it was, failed to generate enough ready money to meet obligations. Protracted negotiations with Constable over much of 1813 led to the purchase of Ballantyne stock, on the condition that John Ballantyne & Co. ceased to be an active publisher, to the sale of a share in *Rokeby*, and later to the advance sale to Constable of rights for the publication of the long poem *The Lord of the Isles*. Scott had to ask the Duke of Buccleuch to guarantee a bank loan of £4000, and many friends gave small loans. All the personal loans were repaid in 1814, and the publishing business was eventually wound up profitably in 1817, largely through Scott's efforts. As part of the reconciliation Constable commissioned essays on Chivalry and the Drama for the Supplement to the *Encyclopaedia Britannica* (published 1818 and 1819 respectively).

Offered and declined the Poet Laureateship.

1814 Publication of his first novel, *Waverley*. The novel was probably begun in 1808 (the date '1st November, 1805' in the first chapter is part of the fiction), continued in 1810, and completed 1813–14; it was first advertised in 1810, and again in January 1814. The early parts (up to the beginning of Chapter 5, and Chapters 5–7) were probably written in parallel with Scott's autobiography (first published at the beginning of Lockhart's *Life of Scott* in 1837).

Publication of *The Works of Jonathan Swift . . . with Notes and a Life of the Author*, 19 vols.

Toured the northern and western isles of Scotland with the Lighthouse Commissioners. His diary of the voyage is published in Lockhart's *Life of Scott* (1837).

1815 Publication of poem *The Lord of the Isles*, and *Guy Mannering*, his second novel.

First visit to the Continent, including Waterloo and Paris, where he was lionised.

1816 Publication of *Paul's Letters to his Kinsfolk, The Antiquary*, and *Tales of my Landlord* (*The Black Dwarf* and *The Tale of Old Mortality*).

1817 Publication of *Harold the Dauntless* (Scott's last long poem), and *Rob Roy* (1818 on title page).

1817–19 First phase of the building of Abbotsford.

1818 Publication of *Tales of my Landlord*, second series (*The Heart of Mid-Lothian*).

Offered and accepted a baronetcy (announced March 1820).

1819 Seriously ill, probably from gall-stones. From 1817 Scott had been suffering stomach cramps, but in the spring and early summer of 1819 he was thought to be dying. Nonetheless he continued to work, dictating to an amanuensis when he was too ill to write. He completed *The Bride of Lammermoor* in April (the greater part of the manuscript is in his own hand) but the latter part of the novel and most of *A Legend of the Wars of Montrose* must have been dictated. The two tales constitute *Tales of my Landlord*, third series, and were published in June 1819.

Purchase by Constable of the copyrights of the 'Scotch novels' and publication of the first collection of Scott's fiction as *Novels and Tales of the Author of Waverley*, 16 vols. All the novels eventually appeared in collected editions in three formats: 8vo, 12mo and 18mo. Publication of three articles in the *Edinburgh Weekly Journal*, later issued as a pamphlet entitled *The Visionary*, which was in

essence political propaganda for the constitutional status quo in the period after Peterloo, when there was a real possibility of a radical rising in the west of Scotland.
December. Death of Scott's mother.
Publication of *Ivanhoe* (1820 on title-page).

1820 Publication of *The Monastery*, and *The Abbot*.
Marriage of daughter Sophia to John Gibson Lockhart.
Elected president of the Royal Society of Edinburgh.

1821 Publication of *Kenilworth*, and *The Pirate* (1822 on title-page).

1821–24 Publication of *Ballantyne's Novelist's Library*, for which Scott wrote the lives of the novelists.

1822 Publication of *The Fortunes of Nigel*, and *Peveril of the Peak* (1823 on title-page).
Visit of King George IV to Edinburgh.

1822–25 Demolition of the original house and second phase of the building of Abbotsford.

1823 Bannatyne Club founded and Scott made first president.
Publication of *Quentin Durward*, and *St Ronan's Well* (1824 on title-page).

1824 Publication of *Redgauntlet*.

1825 Marriage of son Walter to Jane Jobson.
Publication of *Tales of the Crusaders* (*The Betrothed* and *The Talisman*).
Began his Journal.

1826 *January*. Scott insolvent. There was a severe economic recession in the winter of 1825–26 and many companies and individuals became bankrupt. Scott's principal publishers, Archibald Constable & Co., and the printers James Ballantyne & Co. in which he was co-partner, had always been undercapitalised, and relied on bank borrowings for working capital. In paying for goods and services, including such things as paper, printing, and publication rights, all parties used promissory bills, a system in which the drawer promised to pay stated sums on stated dates, and which the acceptor 'discounted' at the banks, i.e. got the money in advance of the date less the amount the banks charged in interest for what was in fact a loan. Both Constable's and Ballantyne's hoped that the money coming in from the sale of books when they were published would be sufficient to pay off the money due to the banks, but in practice both firms too often borrowed more money to pay off debts when they were due, and acted as guarantors for each other's loans. In December 1825 it was realised that they were unable to get further credit from the banks; and in January the bankruptcy of the London publishers of Scott's works, Hurst, Robinson & Co., precipitated the collapse of Constable's, then Ballantyne's, and the ruin of all the partners. Scott, the only one of those involved with a capacity to generate a large income, signed a trust deed undertaking to repay his own private debts (£35,000), all the debts of the printing business for which he and James Ballantyne were jointly liable (£41,000), the debts of Archibald Constable & Co. for which he was legally liable (£40,000), and a mortgage on Abbotsford (£10,000), amounting in all to over £126,000. Such were the profits from works like *Woodstock*, *The Life of Napoleon Buonaparte*, and above all the Magnum Opus, the collected edition of the Waverley Novels with introductions and notes specially written by Scott, and issued in monthly parts from 1829–33, that by Scott's death in 1832 more than £53,000 had been repaid, and the remaining debts were paid in 1833.

Publication of three letters in the *Edinburgh Weekly Journal*, later issued as *The Letters of Malachi Malagrowther*, in which Scott attacked a government proposal to restrict the rights of the Scottish banks to issue their own banknotes; Scott was so effective that the government withdrew its proposal.

Sale of 39 Castle Street, Edinburgh, on behalf of creditors.

15 May. Death of wife, Charlotte Scott.

Publication of *Woodstock*.

Autumn. Visit to Paris.

1827 Public acknowledgement of the authorship of the Waverley Novels.

Publication of *The Life of Napoleon Buonaparte*, 9 vols, *Chronicles of the Canongate* (Chrystal Croftangry's Narrative, 'The Highland Widow', 'The Two Drovers' and 'The Surgeon's Daughter'), and *Tales of a Grandfather* (Scotland to 1603).

1828 Publication of *Chronicles of the Canongate*, second series (*The Fair Maid of Perth*), and *Tales of a Grandfather*, second series (Scotland 1603–1707).

1829 Publication of *Anne of Geierstein*, *History of Scotland*, Vol. 1, and *Tales of a Grandfather*, third series (Scotland 1707–45). The first volume of the Magnum Opus, completed in 48 vols in 1833, appeared on 1 June.

1830 *February*. First stroke.
November. Retired as Clerk to the Court of Session with pension of £864 per annum. Second stroke.
Publication of *Letters on Demonology and Witchcraft, Tales of a Grandfather* (France), and *History of Scotland*, Vol. 2.

1831 *April*. Third stroke.
Publication of *Tales of my Landlord*, fourth series (*Count Robert of Paris* and *Castle Dangerous*).
October. Departure on HMS *Barham* to the Mediterranean, Malta and Naples.

1832 Overland journey home, via Rome, Florence, Venice, Verona, the Brenner Pass, Augsburg, Mainz, and down the Rhine, but had his fourth stroke at Nijmegen. Travelling by sea to London and then Edinburgh, he reached Abbotsford on 11 July.
21 September. Death at Abbotsford.

FURTHER READING

THE WORKS OF SCOTT

The Journal of Sir Walter Scott, ed. W. E. K. Anderson (Oxford, 1972).
The Letters of Sir Walter Scott, ed. H. J. C. Grierson and others, 12 vols (London, 1932–37). The index to this edition is by James C. Corson, *Notes and Index to Sir Herbert Grierson's Edition of the Letters of Sir Walter Scott* (Oxford, 1979).
'Memoirs', in *Scott on Himself: A Selection of the Autobiographical Writings of Sir Walter Scott*, ed. David Hewitt (Edinburgh, 1981).
The Poetical Works of Sir Walter Scott, ed. J. Logie Robertson (Oxford, 1904; frequently reprinted).
The Poetical Works of Sir Walter Scott, Bart., [ed. J. G. Lockhart], 12 vols (Edinburgh, 1833–34).
The Prose Works of Sir Walter Scott, Bart., 28 vols (Edinburgh, 1834–36).
Waverley Novels, 48 vols (Edinburgh, 1829–33), known as the 'Magnum Opus'.

The Waverley Novels were among the most frequently reprinted works of the nineteenth century, and all editions after Scott's death were based upon the edition of 1829–33. Of these, the best are the Centenary Edition, 25 vols (London, 1871), the Dryburgh Edition, 25 vols (London, 1892–94), and the Border Edition, ed. Andrew Lang, 48 vols (London, 1892–94). The first critical edition is the Edinburgh Edition of the Waverley Novels (1993–) on which the volumes of the new Penguin Scott are based.

The complete listing of the works of Scott is in:

William B. Todd and Ann Bowden, *Sir Walter Scott: A Bibliographical History 1796–1832* (New Castle, DE, 1998).

There are two simpler, non-comprehensive listings:

J. G. Lockhart, 'Chronological List of the Publications of Sir Walter Scott', in *Memoirs of the Life of Sir Walter Scott, Bart.*, 7 vols (Edinburgh, 1837; many times republished), 7.433–39.
James C. Corson, 'Sir Walter Scott', in *The New Cambridge Bibliography of English Literature*, ed. George Watson, 5 vols (Cambridge, 1969–77), 3.670–79.

BIOGRAPHY

There are very many biographies of Scott. The most important is still by J. G. Lockhart for although it is unreliable in much of its detail it is the work of a writer and an intimate. The most comprehensive of the modern works is by Edgar Johnson; it is generally reliable. John Buchan's one-volume life is the most sympathetic of all the studies of Scott, while John Sutherland takes a harsher view of the way in which Scott used those in his circle for his own advantage.

James Hogg, *Anecdotes of Scott*, ed. Jill Rubinstein (Edinburgh, 1999).

J. G. Lockhart, *Memoirs of the Life of Sir Walter Scott, Bart.*, 7 vols (Edinburgh, 1837–38; many times republished).

John Buchan, *Sir Walter Scott* (London, 1932).

Sir Herbert Grierson, *Sir Walter Scott, Bart.: A New Life supplementary to, and corrective of, Lockhart's Biography* (London, 1938).

Arthur Melville Clark, *Sir Walter Scott: The Formative Years* (Edinburgh, 1969).

Edgar Johnson, *Sir Walter Scott: The Great Unknown*, 2 vols (London, 1970).

John Sutherland, *The Life of Walter Scott* (Oxford, 1995).

CRITICISM

Complete listings of critical works on Scott are to be found in:

James C. Corson, *A Bibliography of Sir Walter Scott: A Classified and Annotated List of Books and Articles relating to his Life and Works 1797–1940* (Edinburgh, 1943).

Jill Rubenstein, *Sir Walter Scott: A Reference Guide* (Boston, MA, 1978) [covers the period 1932–77].

Jill Rubenstein, *Sir Walter Scott: An Annotated Bibliography of Scholarship and Criticism 1975–1990* (Aberdeen, 1994).

THE FOLLOWING ARE USEFUL FOR THE STUDY OF *IVANHOE*:

Joseph Duncan, 'The Anti-Romantic in *Ivanhoe*', *Nineteenth Century Fiction*, 9 (1955), 293–300.

Edgar Rosenberg, *From Shylock to Svengali: Jewish Stereotypes in English Fiction* (Stanford, 1960), Chapter 4.

William E. Simeone, 'The Robin Hood of *Ivanhoe*', *Journal of American Folklore*, 74 (1961), 230–34.

Alexander Welsh, *The Hero of the Waverley Novels* (Princeton, 1963).

Francis Russell Hart, *Scott's Novels: The Plotting of Historical Survival* (Charlottesville, 1966).

Alice Chandler, *A Dream of Order: The Medieval Ideal in Nineteenth-Century English Literature* (Lincoln, Nebr., 1970).

Livia G. Bitton, 'The Jewess as Fictional Sex Symbol', *Bucknell Review*, 21 (1973), 63–86.

Alice Chandler, 'Chivalry and Romance: Scott's Medieval Novels', *Studies in Romanticism*, 14 (1975), 185–200.

U. C. Knoepflmacher, 'The Counterworld of Victorian Fiction and *The Woman in White*', in *The Worlds of Victorian Fiction*, ed. Jerome H. Buckley (Cambridge, Mass., 1975), 351–57.

Francis Russell Hart, 'Scott's Endings: The Fiction of Authority', *Nineteenth Century Fiction*, 33 (1978), 48–68.

David Brown, *Walter Scott and the Historical Imagination* (London, 1979).

Kenneth M. Sroka, 'The Function of Form: *Ivanhoe* as Romance', *Studies in English Literature 1500–1900*, 19 (1979), 645–60.

Mary Lascelles, *The Story-Teller Retrieves the Past* (Oxford, 1980).

Graham Tulloch, *The Language of Walter Scott: A Study of his Scottish and Period Language*, The Language Library (London, 1980).

Anne Aresty Naman, *The Jew in the Victorian Novel* (New York, 1980).

Graham McMaster, *Scott and Society* (Cambridge, 1981).

Linda Gertner Zatlin, *The Nineteenth Century Anglo-Jewish Novel* (Boston, Mass., 1981), Chapter 1.

John Henry Raleigh, '*Ulysses* and Scott's *Ivanhoe*', *Studies in Romanticism*, 22 (1983), 569–86.

Marinella Salari, '*Ivanhoe*'s Middle Ages', in *Medieval and Pseudo-Medieval Literature*, ed. Piero Boitani and Anna Torti, Tübinger Beiträge zur Anglistik, 6 (Tübingen, 1984), 149–60.

Daniel Cottom, *The Civilized Imagination: A Study of Ann Radcliffe, Jane Austen and Sir Walter Scott* (Cambridge, 1985).

Judith Wilt, *Secret Leaves: The Novels of Walter Scott* (Chicago, 1985).

Alfred David, 'An Iconography of Noses: Directions in the History of a Physical Stereotype', in *Mapping the Cosmos*, ed. Jane Chance and R. O. Wells, Jr (Houston, 1985), 76–97.

Jerome Mitchell, *Scott, Chaucer, and Medieval Romance* (Lexington, 1987).

Chris R. Vanden Bossche, 'Culture and Economy in *Ivanhoe*', *Nineteenth Century Literature*, 42 (1987), 46–72.

Alide Cagidemetrio, 'A Plea for Fictional Histories and Old-Time "Jewesses"', in *The Invention of Ethnicity*, ed. Werner Sollors (New York, 1989), 14–43.

Gary Kelly, 'Social Conflict, Nation and Empire: From Gothicism to Romantic Orientalism', *Ariel*, 20 (1989), 3–18.

Clare A. Simmons, *Reversing the Conquest: History and Myth in Nineteenth Century British Literature* (New Brunswick, 1990).

Ina Ferris, *The Achievement of Literary Authority: Gender, History, and the Waverley Novels* (Ithaca, N.Y., 1991).

Ian Duncan, *Modern Romance and Transformations of the Novel: The Gothic, Scott, Dickens* (Cambridge, 1992).

Bruce Beiderwell, *Power and Punishment in Scott's Novels* (Athens, Ga., 1992).

Michael Ragussis, 'Writing Nationalist History: England, the Conversion of the Jews, and *Ivanhoe*', *ELH*, 60 (1993), 181–215.

James Diedrick, 'Dialogical History in *Ivanhoe*', in *Scott in Carnival: Selected Papers of the Fourth International Scott Conference, Edinburgh 1991*, ed. J. H. Alexander and David Hewitt (Aberdeen, 1993), 280–93.

Sylvia Mergenthal, 'The Shadow of Shylock: Scott's *Ivanhoe* and Edgeworth's *Harrington*', in *Scott in Carnival: Selected Papers of the Fourth International Scott Conference, Edinburgh 1991*, ed. J. H. Alexander and David Hewitt (Aberdeen, 1993), 320–31.

Graham Tulloch, '*Ivanhoe* and Bibles', in *Scott in Carnival: Selected Papers of the Fourth International Scott Conference, Edinburgh 1991*, ed. J. H. Alexander and David Hewitt (Aberdeen, 1993), 309–19.

Tara Ghosal Wallace, 'Competing Discourses in *Ivanhoe*', in *Scott in Carnival: Selected Papers of the Fourth Internationl Scott Conference, Edinburgh 1991*, ed. J. H. Alexander and David Hewitt (Aberdeen, 1993), 294–308.

Fiona Robertson, *Legitimate Histories: Scott, Gothic and the Authority of Fiction* (Oxford, 1994).

Paul J. deGategno, *Ivanhoe: The Mask of Chivalry*, Twayne's Masterwork Studies, 125 (New York, 1994).

Jane Millgate, 'Making it New: Scott, Constable, Ballantyne and the Publication of *Ivanhoe*', *Studies in English Literature 1500–1900*, 34 (1994), 795–811.

Ian Duncan, Introduction to Walter Scott, *Ivanhoe*, The World's Classics (Oxford, 1996), vii–xxvi.

Gary R. Dyer, '*Ivanhoe*, Chivalry, and the Murder of Mary Ashford', *Criticism*, 39 (1997), 383–408.

A NOTE ON THE TEXT

Ivanhoe was in Scott's mind from at least 8 June 1819 when his agent John Ballantyne began negotiations for its publication with the Edinburgh publisher, Archibald Constable and Co. At this time he was still suffering the last stage of a long illness caused by gall-stones but, in the course of his writing *Ivanhoe*, his health improved considerably. Because of his illness he had to dictate the first part of the novel but nevertheless proceeded quickly with it in July and early August. The original intention was to bring the novel out in September but delays in the printing house led him to put the novel aside, perhaps on more than one occasion, to begin work on his next novel *The Monastery* and it was not until 10 November that *Ivanhoe* was finally finished. At first it was planned to print 6000 copies for the first edition but, after seven gatherings (the section to 45.41 in this edition) had been printed, Constable's decided to increase this to 8000. *Ivanhoe* was finally published in Edinburgh in mid-December in the three volume format normal at the time; copies were not available in London until after Christmas because the ship carrying copies there was delayed by a storm. A second edition followed shortly after and a third edition in 1821. *Ivanhoe* was included in the collection *Historical Romances* published in three formats between 1822 and 1824 and in the complete collection of Scott's novels known as the Magnum (1829–32).

The present edition, as is the normal practice of the Edinburgh Edition of the Waverley Novels from which the Penguin Scott derives, is based on the first edition but has been corrected by reference to the manuscript and proofs and to all editions published in Scott's lifetime. The manuscript of *Ivanhoe* is in the Pierpont Morgan Library in New York (MS MA 440). It begins with the words 'Let the old tree wither' at a point corresponding to 212.31 in this edition; this is presumably the point at which Scott resumed writing the manuscript himself after dictating the earlier part of the novel. The proofs cover a large part of Volume I (9.20–82.38 in this edition) and a short section of Volume II (145.8–151.27).

Although the original process of converting the manuscript into text was very carefully and generally accurately carried out and Scott himself checked proofs and made corrections at that stage, there are a number of cases where the first edition clearly represents a misreading of the manuscript. Scott's style has been criticized as slack but the fault sometimes lies with the intermediaries who converted his manuscript into printed text. For instance, after saving Richard from one ambush Robin Hood sends out a group to search the road ahead; in the manuscript he tells Richard that they will alert him to 'any second ambuscade' (367.34) but in the first edition the adjective is changed to 'secret' introducing a redundancy of expression not intended by Scott. One of the features of *Ivanhoe* is its use of archaic language but the intermediaries do not always understand it. The transcriber evidently did not know 'patch', an old word for a jester applied by De Bracy to Wamba. Furthermore it looks like 'putch' in Scott's handwriting. In the first edition it becomes the less explicit and less appropriate 'wretch' (224.34). Archaic spellings are also removed in the first edition but have been restored in this edition, which reads 'avised', 'nigromancy', 'popingay', and 'debitors' (279.40, 303.34, 307.42, 355.16) rather than following the first edition's 'advised', 'necromancy', 'popinjay' and 'debtors'. Scott's punctuation in the manuscript is not completely consistent and the first edition intermediaries have often had to make changes to it. For the most part these carry through what Scott would have himself expected but there are certainly cases where Scott's own punctuation is ignored to the detriment of the text. For instance, when Friar Tuck tells Isaac 'thou didst promise to give all thy substance to our holy order', Isaac in the manuscript replies 'So help me the Promise . . . as no such sounds ever crossed my lips'. The Promise referred to here is the promise of the Lord to Abraham, whereas the first edition's substitution of a lower-case *p* (280.38) causes confusion with the promise Isaac allegedly gave to Friar Tuck. Occasionally the first edition corrects Scott's grammar, not always appropriately; for example his use of 'which' applied to a person (335.18) fittingly imitates the language of the Authorized Version and should not have yielded to the first edition's 'who'. The present edition makes a large number of emendations of the text on the authority of the manuscript. Amongst these, over 600 words here follow the manuscript where other words were substituted for them in the first edition, something over 270 words (singly or in short phrases) and five longer passages (including two footnotes) omitted from the first edition have been restored from the manuscript and the manuscript spelling has been preferred to the first edition's in about thirty cases. All of these emendations, along with others based on the proofs and printed editions, are listed in the *Ivanhoe* volume of the Edinburgh Edition of the Waverley Novels.[1] About thirty relatively minor emendations are based on the proofs.

1 *Ivanhoe*, ed. Graham Tulloch, EEWN 8 (Edinburgh; Edinburgh University Press, 1998).

A few corrections of obvious errors have been adopted from the second setting of the first part of Volume I (required to make up a full 8000 copies of the first edition) as well as one more substantial change on the grounds that this resetting is part of the original creative process of the novel. However, since later editions are not part of this process, they are used sparingly as a basis for emendations and only where there is a clear indication of a mistake in the first edition. Successive editions corrected various mistakes but not all of these corrections ended up in the Magnum which is based on the octavo edition of *Historical Romances*, itself based for *Ivanhoe* on the third edition which in its turn was based on a copy of the first edition with the original setting of the first seven gatherings. Some corrections in the second edition and the 18mo *Historical Romances* (which was derived from the third edition independently of the octavo edition) were consequently lost in subsequent editions and have been restored here. On the other hand, editions after the first edition, as well as perpetuating mistakes in transcribing the manuscript, introduced new errors which were carried on from edition to edition and not discovered by Scott when he corrected a copy of the octavo *Historical Romances* in preparing for the Magnum edition. The current edition thus reflects the period of Scott's original and most intense involvement with the novel and attempts as far as possible to reproduce the text that Scott would have hoped to emerge as he first dictated and then wrote the manuscript and later corrected the proofs of the first edition. In the process *Ivanhoe* emerges as a tauter and more carefully composed text than it has appeared in all the multitude of editions based on the Magnum.

IVANHOE;

A ROMANCE.

BY "THE AUTHOR OF WAVERLEY," &c.

Now fitted the halter, now traversed the cart,
And often took leave,—but seem'd loth to depart!

PRIOR.

IN THREE VOLUMES.

VOL. I.

EDINBURGH:

PRINTED FOR ARCHIBALD CONSTABLE AND CO. EDINBURGH;
AND HURST, ROBINSON, AND CO. 90, CHEAPSIDE, LONDON.

1820.

ADVERTISEMENT.

It was the Author's intention, that this Work should have been concluded, as it commenced, in the fictitious character. But a circumstance, to which more importance has been attached than it deserved, induced his respectable publishers to request, that some guarantee should appear upon the Title-page, in order to satisfy the Public that these Volumes were written by

THE AUTHOR OF WAVERLEY.

DEDICATORY EPISTLE

TO

THE REV. DR DRYASDUST, F. A. S.

Residing in the Castle-Gate, York.

MUCH ESTEEMED AND DEAR SIR,

IT IS SCARCE necessary to mention the various and concurring reasons which induce me to place your name at the head of the following work. Yet the chief of these reasons may perhaps be refuted by the imperfections of the performance. Could I have hoped to render it worthy of your patronage, the public would at once have seen the propriety of inscribing a work designed to illustrate the domestic antiquities of England, and particularly of our Saxon forefathers, to the learned author of the Essays upon the Horn of King Ulphus, and on the Lands bestowed by him upon the patrimony of St Peter. I am conscious, however, that the slight, unsatisfactory, and trivial manner in which the result of my antiquarian researches has been recorded in the following pages, takes the work from under that class which bears the proud motto *Detur digniori*. On the contrary, I fear I shall incur the censure of presumption in placing the venerable name of Dr Jonas Dryasdust at the head of a publication, which the more grave antiquary will perhaps class with the idle novels and romances of the day. I am anxious to vindicate myself from such a charge; for although I might trust to your friendship for an apology in your own eyes, yet I would not willingly stand convicted in those of the public of so grave a crime, as my fears lead me to anticipate my being charged with.

I must therefore remind you, that when we first talked over together that class of productions, in one of which the private and family affairs of your learned northern friend, Mr Oldbuck of Monkbarns, were so unjustifiably exposed to the public, some discussion occurred between us concerning the cause of the popularity which works, which, whatever other merit they possess, must be admitted to be hastily written, and in violation of every rule assigned to the epopeia, have attained in this idle age. It seemed then to be your opinion, that the charm lay entirely in the art with which the unknown author had availed himself, like a second M'Pherson, of the stores of antiquity which lay scattered around him, supplying his own indolence or poverty of invention, by the incidents which had actually taken place in his country at no distant period, introducing real characters, and scarcely suppressing real names. It was not above sixty or seventy years, you observed, that the whole north of Scotland was under a state of government nearly as simple and as patriarchal as those of our good allies the Mohawks and Iroquois. Admitting that the author cannot himself be supposed to have witnessed these times, he must have lived, you observed, among persons who had acted and suffered in them; and even within these thirty years, such an infinite change has taken place in the manners of Scotland, that men look back upon their fathers' habits of society, as we do on those of the reign of Queen Anne. Having thus materials of every kind lying strewed around him, there was little, you observed, to embarrass the author, but the facility of choice. It was no wonder, therefore, that, having begun to work a mine so plentiful, he should have derived from his works fully more credit and profit than the facility of his labours merited.

Admitting (as I could not deny) the general truth of these conclusions, I cannot but think it strange that no attempt has been made to obtain an interest for the traditions and manners of Old England, similar to that which has been excited in behalf of those of our poorer and less celebrated neighbours. The Kendal green, though its date is more ancient, ought surely to be as dear to our feelings as the variegated tartans of the north. The name of Robin Hood, if duly conjured with, should raise a spirit as soon as that of Rob Roy; and the patriots of England deserve no less their renown in our modern circles, than the Bruces and Wallaces of Caledonia. If the scenery of the south be less romantic and sublime than that of the northern mountains, it must be allowed to possess in the same proportion superior softness and beauty; and upon the whole, we feel ourselves entitled to exclaim with the patriotic Syrian—"Are not Pharphar and Abana, rivers of Damascus, better than all the rivers of Israel!"

Your objections to such an attempt, my dear doctor, were, you may remember, two-fold. You insisted upon the advantages which the Scotsman possessed from the very recent existence of that state of society in which his scene was to be laid. Many men alive, you remarked, well remembered persons who had not only seen the celebrated Roy M'Gregor, but had feasted, and even fought with him. All those minute circumstances belonging to private life and domestic character, all that gives verisimilitude to a narrative and individuality to the persons introduced, is still known and remembered in Scotland; whereas in England, civilization has been so long complete, that our ideas of our ancestors are only to be gleaned from musty records and chronicles, the authors of which seem perversely to have conspired to suppress in their narratives all interesting details, in order to find room for flowers of monkish eloquence, or trite reflections upon morals. To match an English and a Scottish author in the rival task of embodying and reviving the traditions of their respective countries, would be, you alleged, in the highest degree unequal and unjust. The Scottish magician, you said, was like Lucan's witch, at liberty to walk over the recent field of battle, and to select for the subject of resuscitation by his sorceries, a body whose limbs had recently quivered with existence, and whose throat had but just uttered the last note of agony. Such a subject even the powerful Erictho was compelled to select, as alone capable of being reanimated even by *her* potent magic—

> ——gelidas leto scrutata medullas,
> Pulmonis rigidi stantes sine vulnere fibras
> Invenit, et vocem defuncto in corpore quærit.

The English author, on the other hand, without supposing him less of a conjuror than the Northern Warlock, can, you observed, only have the liberty of selecting his subject amidst the dust of antiquity, where nothing was to be found but dry, sapless, mouldering and disjointed bones, such as those which filled the valley of Jehoshaphat. You expressed, besides, your apprehension, that the unpatriotic prejudices of my countrymen would not allow fair play to such a work as that of which I endeavoured to demonstrate the probable success. And this, you said, was not entirely owing to the more general prejudice in favour of that which is foreign, but rested partly upon improbabilities, arising out of the circumstances in which the English reader is placed. If you describe to him a set of wild manners, and a state of primitive society existing in the Highlands of Scotland, he was much disposed to acquiesce in the truth of what was asserted. And reason good. If he was of the ordinary class of readers, he had either never seen those remote districts at all, or he had wandered through those desolate regions in the course of a summer-tour, eating bad dinners, sleeping on truckle beds, stalking from desolation to desolation, and fully prepared to believe the strangest things that could be told him of a people wild and extravagant enough to be attached to scenery so extraordinary. But the same worthy person, when placed in his own snug parlour, and surrounded by all the comforts of an Englishman's fire-side, is not half so much disposed to believe that his own ancestors led a very different life from himself; that the shattered tower, which now forms a vista from his window, once held a baron who would have hung him up at his own door without any form of trial; that the hinds, by whom his little pet-farm is managed, would have, a few centuries ago, been his slaves; and that the complete influence of feudal tyranny once extended over the neighbouring village, where the attorney is now a man of more importance than the lord of the manor.

While I own the force of these objections, I must confess, at the same time, that they do not appear to me to be altogether insurmountable. The scantiness of materials is indeed a formidable difficulty; but no one knows better than Dr Dryasdust, that to those deeply read in antiquity, hints concerning the private life of our ancestors lie scattered through our various historians, bearing, indeed, a slender proportion to the other matters of which they treat, but still, when collected together, sufficient to throw considerable light upon the *vie privée* of our forefathers; indeed, I am convinced that however I myself might fail in the ensuing attempt, yet, with more labour in collecting, or more skill in using, the materials within their reach, illustrated as they have been by the labours of Dr Henry, of the late Mr Strutt, and, above all, of Mr Sharon Turner, an abler hand would have been successful; and therefore I protest, beforehand, against any argument which may be founded in the failure of the present experiment.

On the other hand, I have already said, that if any thing like a true picture of old English manners could be drawn, I would trust to the good nature and good sense of my countrymen for insuring its favourable reception.

Having thus replied to the best of my power to the first class of your objections, or at least having shewn my resolution to overleap the barriers which your prudence has raised, I will be brief in noticing that which is more peculiar to myself. It seemed to be your opinion, that the very office of an antiquary, employed in grave, and, as the vulgar will sometimes allege, in minute and trivial research, must be considered as incapacitating him from successfully compounding a tale of this sort. But permit me to say, my dear doctor, that this objection is rather formal than substantial. It is true, that such slighter compositions might not suit the severer genius of our friend Mr Oldbuck. Yet Horace Walpole wrote a goblin tale which has thrilled many a bosom; and George Ellis could transfer all the playful fascination of a humour, as delightful as it was uncommon, into his Abridgement of the Ancient Metrical Romances.

So that, however I may have occasion to rue my present audacity, I have at least the most respectable precedents in my favour.

Still the severer antiquary may think that, by thus intermingling fiction with truth, I am polluting the well of history with modern inventions, and impressing upon the rising generation false ideas of the age which I describe. I cannot but in some sense admit the force of this reasoning, which I yet hope to traverse by the following considerations.

It is true, that I neither can, nor do pretend, to the observation of complete accuracy, even in matters of outward costume, much less in the more important points of language and manners. But the same motive which prevents my writing the dialogue of the piece in Anglo-Saxon or in Norman-French, and which prohibits my sending forth to the public this essay printed with the types of Caxton or Wynken de Worde, prevents my attempting to confine myself within the limits of the period in which my story is laid. It is necessary, for exciting interest of any kind, that the subject assumed should be, as it were, translated into the manners as well as the language of the age we live in. No fascination has ever been attached to oriental literature, equal to that produced by Mr Galland's first translation of the Arabian Tales; in which, retaining on the one hand the splendour of eastern costume, and on the other the wildness of eastern fiction, he mixed these with just so much ordinary feeling and expression, as rendered them interesting and intelligible, while he abridged the long-winded narratives, curtailed the monotonous reflections, and rejected the endless repetitions of the Arabian original. The tales, therefore, though less purely oriental than in their first concoction, were eminently better fitted for the European market, and obtained an unrivalled degree of public favour, which they certainly would never have gained had not the manners and style been in some degree familiarized to the feelings and habits of the western reader.

In point of justice, therefore, to the multitudes who will, I trust, devour this book with avidity, I have so far explained our ancient manners in modern language, and so far detailed the characters and sentiments of my persons, that the modern reader will not find himself, I should hope, much trammelled by the repulsive dryness of mere antiquity. In this, I respectfully contend, I have in no respect exceeded the fair license due to the author of a fictitious composition. The late ingenious Mr Strutt, in his romance of Queen-Hoo-Hall, acted upon another principle, and in distinguishing between what was ancient and modern, forgot, as it appears to me, that extensive neutral ground, the proportion, that is, of manners and sentiments which are common to us and to our ancestors, which have been handed down unaltered from them to us, or which, arising out of the principles of our common nature, must have existed alike in either state of society. In this manner, a man of talent, and of great antiquarian erudition, limited the popularity of his work, by excluding from it every thing which was not sufficiently obsolete to be altogether forgotten and unintelligible.

The licence which I would here vindicate, is so necessary to the execution of my plan, that I will crave your patience while I illustrate my argument a little farther.

He who first opens Chaucer, or any other ancient poet, is so much struck with the obsolete spelling, multiplied consonants, and antiquated appearance of the language, that he is apt to lay the work down in despair, as encrusted too deep with the rust of antiquity, to permit his judging of its merits or tasting its beauties. But if some intelligent friend points out to him, that the difficulties by which he is startled are more in appearance than reality, if, by reading aloud to him, or by reducing the ordinary words to the modern orthography, he satisfies his proselyte that only about one-tenth part of the words employed are in fact obsolete, the novice may be easily persuaded to approach the "well of English undefiled," with the certainty that a slender degree of patience will enable him to enjoy both the humour and the pathos with which old Geoffrey delighted the age of Cressy and of Poictiers.

To pursue this a little farther, if our neophyte, strong in the new-born love of antiquity, were to undertake to imitate what he had learnt to admire, it must be allowed he would act very injudiciously, if he were to select from the Glossary the obsolete words which it contains, and employ those exclusively of all others. This was the error of the unfortunate Chatterton. In order to give his language the appearance of antiquity, he rejected every word that was modern, and produced a dialect entirely different from any that had ever been spoken in Great Britain. He who would imitate the ancient language with success, will attend rather to its grammatical character, turn of expression, and mode of arrangement, than labour to collect extraordinary and antiquated terms, which, as I have already averred, do not in ancient authors approach the number of words still in use, though perhaps somewhat altered in sense and spelling, in the proportion of one to ten.

What I have applied to language, is still more justly applicable to sentiments and manners. The passions, the sources from which these must spring in all their modifications, are generally the same in all ranks and conditions, all countries and ages; and it follows, as a matter of course, that the opinions, habits of thinking, and actions, however influenced by the peculiar state of society, must still, upon the whole, bear a strong resemblance to each other. Our ancestors were not more distinct from us, surely, than Jews are from Christians; they had "eyes, hands, organs, dimensions, senses, affections, passions;" were "fed with the same food, hurt with the same weapons, subject to the same diseases, warmed and cooled by the same winter and summer" as ourselves. The tenor, therefore, of their affections and feelings, must have borne the same general proportion to our own.

It follows, therefore, that of the materials which he has to use in a romance, or fictitious composition, such as I have ventured to attempt, the author will find that a great proportion, both of language and manners, are as proper to the present time as to those in which he has laid his time of action. The freedom of choice which this allows him, is therefore much greater, and the difficulty of his task much more diminished, than at first appears. To take an illustration from a sister art, the antiquarian details may be said to represent the peculiar features of a landscape under delineation of the pencil. His feudal tower must arise in due majesty; the figures which he introduces must have the costume and character of their age; the piece must represent the peculiar features of the scene which he has chosen for his subject, with all its appropriate elevation of rock, or precipitate descent of cataract. His general colouring, too, must be copied from Nature: The sky must be clouded or serene, according to the climate, and the general tints must be those which prevail in a natural landscape. So far the painter is bound down by the rules of his art, to a precise imitation of the features of Nature; but it is not required that he should descend to copy all her more minute features, or represent with absolute exactness the very herbs, flowers, and trees, with which the spot is decorated. These, as well as all the more minute points of light and shadow, are attributes proper to scenery in general, natural to each situation, and subject to the artist's disposal, as his taste or pleasure may dictate.

It is true, that this licence is confined in either case within legitimate bounds. The painter must introduce no ornament inconsistent with the climate or country of his landscape; he must not plant cypress trees upon Inch-Merrin, or Scottish firs among the ruins of Persepolis; and the author lies under a corresponding restraint. However far he may venture in a more full detail of passions and feelings, than is to be found in the ancient compositions which he imitates, he must introduce nothing inconsistent with the manners of the age; his knights, squires, grooms, and yeomen, may be more fully drawn than in the hard, dry delineations of an ancient illuminated manuscript, but the character and costume of the age must remain inviolate; they must be the same figures, drawn by a better pencil, or, to speak more modestly, executed in an age when the principles of art were better understood. His language must not be exclusively obsolete and unintelligible; but he should admit, if possible, no word or turn of phraseology betraying an origin directly modern. It is one thing to make use of the language and sentiments which are common to ourselves and our forefathers, and it is another to invest them with the sentiments and dialect exclusively proper to their descendants.

This, my dear friend, I have found the most difficult part of my task; and, to speak frankly, I hardly expect to satisfy your less partial judgment, and more extensive knowledge of such subjects, since I have hardly been able to please my own.

I am conscious that I shall be found still more faulty in the tone of keeping and costume, by those who may be disposed rigidly to examine my Tale, with reference to the manners of the exact period in which my actors flourished: It may be, that I have introduced little which can positively be termed modern; but, on the other hand, it is extremely probable that I may have confused the manners of two or three centuries, and introduced, during the reign of Richard the First, circumstances appropriated to a period either considerably earlier, or a good deal later than that era. It is my comfort, that errors of this kind will escape the general class of readers, and that I may share in the ill-deserved applause of those architects, who, in their modern Gothic, do not hesitate to introduce, without rule or method, ornaments proper to different styles and to different periods of the art. Those whose extensive researches have given them the means of judging my backslidings with more severity, will probably be lenient in proportion to their knowledge of the difficulty of my task. My honest and neglected friend Ingulphus, has furnished me with many a valuable hint, but the light afforded by the Monk of Croydon, and Geoffrey de Vinsauff, is dimmed by such a conglomeration of uninteresting and unintelligible matter, that we gladly fly for relief to the delightful pages of the gallant Froissart, although he flourished at a period so much more remote from the date of my history. If, therefore, my dear friend, you have generosity enough to pardon the presumptuous attempt, to frame for myself a minstrel coronet, partly out of the pearls of pure antiquity, and partly from the Bristol stones and paste, with which I have endeavoured to imitate them, I am convinced your opinion of the difficulty of the task will reconcile you to the imperfect manner of its execution.

Of my materials I have but little to say: They may be chiefly found in the singular Anglo-Norman MS., which Sir Arthur Wardour preserves with such jealous care in the third drawer of his oaken cabinet, scarcely allowing any one to touch it, and being himself not able to read one syllable of its contents. I should never have got his consent, on my visit to Scotland, to read in these precious pages for so many hours, had I not promised to designate it by some emphatic mode of printing, as **The Wardour Manuscript**; giving it, thereby, an individuality as important as the Bannatyne MS., the Auchinleck MS., and any other monument of the patience of a Gothic scrivener. I have sent, for your private consideration, a list of the contents of this curious piece, which I shall perhaps subjoin, with your approbation, to the third volume of my Tale, in case the printer's devil should become impatient for copy, when the whole of my narrative has been imposed.

Adieu, my dear friend; I have said enough to explain, if not to vindicate, the attempt which I have made, and which, in spite of your doubts, and my own incapacity, I am still willing to believe has not been altogether made in vain.

I hope you are now well recovered from your spring fit of the gout, and shall be happy if the advice of your learned physician should recommend a tour to these parts: Several curiosities have been lately dug up near the Wall, as well as at the ancient station of Habitancum. Talking of the latter, I suppose you have long since heard the news, that a sulky churlish boor has destroyed the ancient statue, or rather bas-relief, popularly called Robin of Redesdale. It seems Robin's fame attracted more visitants than was consistent with the growth of the heather, upon a moor worth a shilling an acre. Reverend as you write yourself, be revengeful for once, and pray with me that he may be visited with such a fit of the stone, as if he had all the fragments of poor Robin in that region of his viscera where the disease holds its seat. Tell this not in Gath, lest the Scots rejoice that they have at length found a parallel instance among their neighbours, to that barbarous deed which demolished Arthur's oven. But there is no end to lamentation, when we betake ourselves to such subjects. My respectful compliments attend Miss Dryasdust; I endeavoured to match the spectacles agreeable to her commission, during my late journey to London, and hope she has received them safe, and found them satisfactory. I send this by the blind carrier, so that probably it may be sometime upon its journey.* The last news which I hear from Edinburgh is, that the gentleman who fills the situation of Secretary to the Antiquarian Society, is the best amateur draftsman in that kingdom, and that much is expected from his skill and zeal in delineating those specimens of national antiquity, which are either mouldering under the slow touch of time, or swept away by modern taste, with the same besom of destruction which John Knox used at

*This anticipation proved but too true; as my learned correspondent did not receive my letter until a twelvemonth after it was written. I mention this circumstance, that a gentleman attached to the cause of learning, who now holds the principal controul of the post-office, may consider whether by some mitigation of the present enormous rates, some favour might not be shewn to the correspondents of the principal Literary and Antiquarian Societies. I understand, indeed, that this experiment was once tried, but that the mail-coach having broke down under the weight of packages addressed to members of the Antiquarian Society, it was relinquished as a hazardous experiment. Surely, however, it would be possible to build these vehicles in a form more substantial, heavier in the perch and broader in the wheels, so as to support the weight of antiquarian learning; when, if they should be found to travel more slowly, they would be not the less agreeable to quiet travellers like myself.

the Reformation. Once more adieu; *vale tandem, non immemor mei.* Believe me to be,

Reverend, and very dear Sir,
Your most faithful humble Servant,
LAURENCE TEMPLETON.

Toppingwold, near Egremont,
Cumberland, Nov. 17, 1817.

IVANHOE

VOLUME I

Chapter One

Thus commun'd these; while to their lowly dome,
The full-fed swine returned with evening home;
Compelled, reluctant, to the several sties,
With din obstreperous, and ungrateful cries.
POPE'S *Odyssey.*

IN THAT pleasant district of merry England which is watered by the river Don, there extended in ancient times a large forest, covering the greater part of the beautiful hills and vallies which lie between Sheffield and the pleasant town of Doncaster. The remains of this extensive wood are still to be seen at the noble seats of Wentworth, of Warncliffe Park, and around Rotherham. Here haunted of yore the fabulous Dragon of Wantley; here were fought many of the most desperate battles during the civil wars of the Roses; and here also flourished in ancient times those bands of gallant outlaws, whose deeds have been rendered so popular in English song.

Such being our chief scene, the date of our story refers to a period towards the end of the reign of Richard I., when his return from his long captivity had become an event rather wished than hoped for by his despairing subjects, who were in the meantime subjected to every species of subordinate oppression. The nobles, whose power had become exorbitant during the reign of Stephen, and whom the prudence of Henry the Second had scarce reduced into some degree of subjection to the crown, had now resumed their ancient licence in its utmost extent; despising the feeble interference of the English Council of State, fortifying their castles, increasing the number of their dependants, reducing all around them to a state of vassalage, and striving by every means in their power, to place themselves each at the head of such forces as might enable him to make a figure in the national convulsions which appeared to be impending.

The situation of the inferior gentry, or Franklins, as they were called, who, by the law and spirit of the English constitution, were entitled to hold themselves independent of feudal tyranny, became now unusually precarious. If, as was most generally the case, they placed themselves under the protection of any of the petty kings in their vicinity, accepted of feudal offices in his household, or bound themselves, by mutual treaties of alliance and protection, to support him in his enterprizes, they might indeed purchase temporary repose; but it must be with the sacrifice of that independence which was so dear to every English bosom, and at the certain hazard of being involved as a party in whatever rash expedition the ambition of their protector might lead him to undertake. On the other hand, such and so multiplied were the means of vexation and oppression possessed by the great Barons, that they never wanted the pretext, and seldom the will, to harass and pursue, even to the very edge of destruction, any of their less powerful neighbours, who attempted to separate themselves from their authority, and to trust for their protection, during the dangers of the times, to their own inoffensive conduct, and to the laws of the land.

A circumstance which greatly tended to enhance the tyranny of the nobility, and the sufferings of the inferior classes, arose from the consequences of the conquest by Duke William of Normandy. Four generations had not sufficed to blend the hostile blood of the Normans and Anglo-Saxons, or to unite, by a common language and mutual interests, two hostile races, one of which still felt the elation of triumph, while the other groaned under all the consequences of defeat. The power had been completely placed in the hands of the Norman nobility, by the event of the battle of Hastings, and it had been used, as our histories assure us, with no moderate hand. The whole race of Saxon princes and nobles had been extirpated or disinherited, with few or no exceptions; nor were the numbers great who possessed land in the country of their fathers, even as proprietors of the second, or of yet inferior classes. The royal policy had long been to weaken, by every means, legal or illegal, the strength of a part of the population which was justly considered as nourishing the most inveterate antipathy to their victors. All the monarchs of the Norman race had shewn the most marked predilection for their Norman subjects; the laws of the chase, and many others, equally unknown to the milder and more free spirit of the Saxon constitution, had been fixed upon the necks of the subjugated inhabitants, to add weight, as it were, to the feudal chains with which they were loaded. At court, and in the castles of the great nobles, where the pomp and state of a court was emulated, Norman French was the only language employed; in courts of law, the pleadings and judgments were delivered in the same tongue. In short, French was the language of honour, of chivalry, and even of justice, while the far more manly and expressive Anglo-Saxon was abandoned to the use of rustics and hinds, who knew no other. Still, however, the necessary intercourse between the lords of the soil, and those inferior beings by whom that soil was cultivated, occasioned the gradual formation of a dialect, compounded betwixt the French and the Anglo-Saxon, in which they could render themselves mutually intelligible to each other; and from this necessity arose by degrees the structure of our present English language, in which the speech of the victors and the vanquished have been so happily blended together; and which has since been so richly improved by importations from the classical languages, and from those spoken by the southern nations of Europe.

This state of things I have thought it necessary to premise for the information of the general reader, who might be apt to forget, that, although no great historical events, such as war or insurrection, mark the existence of the Anglo-Saxons as a separate people subsequent to the reign of William the Second; yet the great national distinctions betwixt them and their conquerors, the recollection of what they had formerly been, and to what they were now reduced, continued, down to the reign of Edward the Third, to keep open the wounds which the Conquest had inflicted, and to maintain a line of separation betwixt the descendants of the victor Normans and the vanquished Saxons.

The sun was setting upon one of the rich grassy glades of that forest, which we have mentioned in the beginning of the chapter. Hundreds of broad short-stemmed oaks, which had witnessed perhaps the stately march of the Roman soldiery, flung their broad gnarled arms over a thick carpet of the most delicious green sward; in some places they were intermingled with beeches, hollies, and copsewood of various descriptions, so closely as totally to intercept the level beams of the sinking sun; in others they receded from each other, forming those long sweeping vistas, in the intricacy of which the eye delights to lose itself, while imagination considers them as the paths to yet wilder scenes of sylvan solitude. Here the red rays of the sun shot a broken and discoloured light, that partially hung upon the scattered boughs and mossy trunks of the trees, and there they illuminated in brilliant patches the portions of turf to which they made their way. A considerable open space, in the midst of this glade, seemed formerly to have been dedicated to the rites of Druidical superstition; for, on the summit of a hillock, so regular as to seem artificial, there still remained part of a circle of rough unhewn stones, of large dimensions. Seven stood upright; the rest had been dislodged from their places, probably by the zeal of some convert to Christianity, and lay, some prostrate near their former site, and others on the side of the hill. One large stone only had found its way to the bottom, and in stopping the course of a small brook, which glided smoothly round the foot of the eminence, gave, by its opposition, a feeble voice of murmur to the placid and elsewhere silent streamlet.

The human figures which completed this landscape, were in number two, partaking, in their dress and appearance, of that wild and rustic character which belonged to the woodlands of the West-Riding of Yorkshire at this early period. The eldest of these men had a stern, savage, and wild aspect. His garment was of the simplest form imaginable, being a close jacket with sleeves, composed of the tanned skin of some animal, on which the hair had been originally left, but which had been worn off in so many places, that it would have been difficult to distinguish from the patches that remained, to what creature the fur had belonged. This primeval vestment reached from the throat to the knees, and served at once all the usual purposes of body-clothing; there was no wider opening at the collar, than was necessary to admit the passage of the head, from which it may be inferred, that it was put on by slipping it over the head and shoulders, in the manner of a modern shirt, or ancient hauberk. Sandals, bound with thongs made of boars' hide, protected the feet, and a sort of roll of thin leather was twined artificially round the legs, and, ascending above the calf, left the knees bare, like those of a Scottish Highlander. To make the jacket sit yet more close to the body, it was gathered at the middle by a broad leathern belt, secured by a brass buckle; to one side of which was attached a sort of scrip, and to the other a ram's horn, accoutred with a mouth-piece, for the purpose of blowing. In the same belt was stuck one of those long, broad, sharp-pointed, and two-edged knives, with a buck's-horn handle, which were fabricated in the neighbourhood, and bore even at this early period the name of a Sheffield whittle. The man had no covering upon his head, which was only defended by his own thick hair, matted and twisted together, and scorched by the influence of the sun into a rusty dark red colour, forming a contrast with the overgrown beard upon his cheeks, which was rather of a yellow or amber hue. One part of his dress only remains, but it is too remarkable to be suppressed; it was a brass ring, resembling a dog's collar, but without any opening, and soldered fast round his neck, so loose as to form no impediment to his breathing, yet so tight as to be incapable of being removed, excepting by the use of the file. On this singular gorget was engraved in Saxon characters, an inscription of the following purport:—"Gurth, the son of Beowolf, is the born thrall of Cedric of Rotherwood."

Beside this swine-herd, for such was Gurth's occupation, was seated, upon one of the fallen Druidical monuments, a person who looked ten years younger in appearance, and whose dress, though resembling his companion's in form, was of better materials, and of a more fantastic appearance. His jacket had been stained of a bright purple hue, upon which there had been some attempt to paint grotesque ornaments in different colours. To the jacket he added a short cloak, which scarcely reached half-way down his thigh; it was of crimson cloth, though a good deal soiled, lined with bright yellow; and as he could transfer it from one shoulder to the other, or at his pleasure draw it all around him, its width, contrasted with its want of longitude, formed a fantastic piece of drapery. He had thin silver bracelets upon his arms, and on his neck a collar of the same metal, bearing the inscription, "Wamba, the son of Witless, is the thrall of Cedric of Rotherwood." This personage had the same sort of sandals with his companion, but instead of the roll of leather thong, his legs were cased in a sort of gaiters, of which one was red and the other yellow. He was provided also with a cap, having around it more than one bell, about the size of those attached to hawks, which jingled as he turned his head to one side or other, and as he seldom remained a minute in the same posture, the sound might be considered as incessant. Around the edge of this cap was a stiff bandeau of leather, cut at the top into open work, resembling a coronet, while a prolonged bag arose from within it, and fell down on one shoulder like an old-fashioned night-cap, or a jelly-bag, or the head-gear of a modern hussar. It was to this part of the cap that the bells were attached; which circumstance, as well as the shape of his head-dress, and his own half-crazed, half-cunning expression of countenance, sufficiently pointed him out as belonging to the race of domestic clowns or jesters, maintained in the houses of the wealthy, to help away the tedium of those lingering hours which they were obliged to spend within doors. He bore, like his companion, a scrip, attached to his belt, but had neither horn nor knife, being probably considered as belonging to a class whom it is esteemed dangerous to entrust with edge-tools. In place of these, he was equipped with a sword of lath, resembling that with which Harlequin operates his wonders upon the modern stage.

The outward appearance of these two men formed scarce a stronger contrast than their different look and demeanour. That of the serf, or bondsman, was sad and sullen; his aspect was bent on the ground with an appearance of deep dejection, which might be almost construed into apathy, had not the fire which occasionally sparkled in his red eye manifested that there slumbered under the appearance of sullen despondency a sense of oppression, and a disposition to resistance. The looks of Wamba, on the other hand, indicated, as usual with his class, a sort of vacant curiosity, and fidgetty impatience of any posture of repose, together with the utmost self-satisfaction respecting his own situation, and the appearance which he made. The dialogue which they maintained between them, was carried on in Anglo-Saxon, which, as we said before, was universally spoken by the inferior classes, excepting the Norman soldiers, and the immediate personal dependants of the great feudal nobles. But to give their conversation in the original would convey but little information to the modern reader, for whose benefit we beg to offer the following translation.

"The curse of St Withold upon these infernal porkers," said the swine-herd, after blowing his horn obstreperously, to collect together the scattered herd of swine, which, answering his call with notes equally melodious, made, however, no haste to remove themselves from the luxurious banquet of beech-mast and acorns on which they had fattened, or to forsake the marshy banks of the rivulet, where several of them, half plunged in mud, lay stretched at their ease, altogether regardless of the voice of their keeper. "The curse of St Withold upon them and upon me," said Gurth; "if the two-legged wolf snap not up some of them ere nightfall, I am no true man.—Here, Fangs! Fangs!" he ejaculated at the top of his voice to a rugged wolfish-looking dog, a sort of lurcher, half mastiff, half greyhound, which ran limping about as if with a purpose of seconding his master in collecting the refractory grunters; but which, in fact, from misapprehension of the swine-herd's signals, ignorance of his own duty, or malice prepense, only drove them hither and thither, and increased the evil which he seemed to design to remedy. "A devil draw the teeth of him," said Gurth, "and the mother of mischief confound the ranger of the forest that cuts the fore-claws of our dogs, and makes them unfit for their trade!—Wamba, up and help me an' thou be'st a man; take a turn round the back o' the hill to gain the wind on them; and when thou'st got the weather-gage, thou may'st drive them before thee as gently as so many innocent lambs."

"Truly," said Wamba, without stirring from the spot, "I have consulted my legs upon this matter, and they are altogether of opinion, that to carry my gay garments through these sloughs, would be an act of unfriendship to my sovereign person and royal wardrobe; wherefore, Gurth, I advise thee to call off Fangs, and leave the herd to their destiny, which, whether they meet with bands of travelling soldiers, or of outlaws, or of wandering pilgrims, can be little else than to be converted into Normans before morning, to thy no small ease and comfort."

"The swine turned Normans to my comfort!" quoth Gurth; "expound that to me, Wamba, for my brain is too dull, and my mind too vexed, to read riddles."

"Why, how call you these grunting brutes running about on their four legs?" demanded Wamba.

"Swine, fool, swine," said the herd, "every fool knows that."

"And swine is good Saxon," said the jester; "but how call you the sow when she is flayed, and drawn, and quartered, and hung up by the heels, like a traitor?"

"Pork," answered the swine-herd.

"I am very glad every fool knows that too," said Wamba, "and pork, I think, is good Norman French; and so when the brute lives, and is in the charge of a Saxon slave, she goes by her Saxon name; but becomes a Norman, and is called pork, when she is carried to the Castle-hall to feast among the nobles; what do'st thou think of this, friend Gurth, ha?"

"It is but too true doctrine, friend Wamba, however it got into thy fool's pate."

"Nay, I can tell you more," said Wamba, in the same tone; "there is old Alderman Ox continues to hold his Saxon epithet, while he is under the charge of serfs and bondsmen such as thou, but becomes Beef, a fiery French gallant, when he arrives before the worshipful jaws that are destined to consume him. Mynheer Calve, too, becomes Monsieur de Veau in the like manner; he is Saxon when he requires tendance, and takes a Norman name when he becomes matter of enjoyment."

"By St Dunstan," answered Gurth, "thou speakest but sad truths; little is left to us but the air we breathe, and that appears to have been reserved with much hesitation, clearly for the purpose of enabling us to endure the tasks they lay upon our shoulders. The finest and the fattest is for their board; the loveliest is for their couch; the best and bravest supply their foreign masters with soldiers, and whiten distant lands with their bones, leaving few here who have either will or power to protect the unfortunate Saxon. God's blessing on our master Cedric, he hath done the work of a man in standing in the gap; but Reginald Front-de-Bœuf is coming down to this country in person, and we shall soon see how little Cedric's trouble will avail him.—Here, here," he exclaimed again, raising his voice, "So ho! so ho! well done, Fangs! thou hast them all before thee now, and bring'st them on bravely, lad."

"Gurth," said the jester, "I know thou thinkest me a fool, or thou would'st not be so rash in putting thy head into my mouth. One word to Reginald Front-de-Bœuf, or Philip de Malvoisin, that thou hast spoken treason against the Norman, and thou art but a cast-away swine-herd,—thou would'st waver on one of these trees as a terror to all evil speakers against dignities."

"Dog, thou would'st not betray me," said Gurth, "after having led me on to speak so much at disadvantage?"

"Betray thee!" answered the jester; "no, that were the trick of a wise man; a fool cannot half so well help himself—but soft, whom have we here?" he said, listening to the trampling of several horses which became then audible.

"Never mind whom," answered Gurth, who had now got his herd before him, and, with the aid of Fangs, was driving them down one of the long dim vistas which we have endeavoured to describe.

"Nay, but I must see the riders," answered Wamba; "perhaps they are come from Fairy-land with a message from King Oberon."

"A murrain take thee," rejoined the swine-herd; "wilt thou talk of such things, while a terrible storm of thunder and lightning is raging within a few miles of us? Hark, how the thunder rumbles! and for summer rain, I never saw such broad downright flat drops fall out of the clouds; the oaks too, notwithstanding the calm weather, sob and creak with their great boughs as if announcing a tempest. Thou can'st play the rational if thou wilt; credit me for once, and let us home ere the storm begins to rage, for the night will be fearful."

Wamba seemed to feel the force of this appeal, and accompanied his companion, who began his journey after catching up a long quarter-staff which lay upon the grass beside him. This second Eumæus strode hastily down the forest glade, driving before him, with the assistance of Fangs, the whole herd of his inharmonious charge.

Chapter Two

A Monk there was, a fayre for the maistrie,
An outrider that loved venerie;
A manly man, to be an Abbot able,
Full many a daintie horse had he in stable:
And whan he rode, men might his bridle hear
Gingeling in a whistling wind as clear,
And eke as loud, as doth the chapell bell,
There as this lord was keeper of the cell.

CHAUCER.

NOTWITHSTANDING the occasional exhortation and chiding of his companion, the noise of the horses' feet continuing to approach, Wamba could not be prevented from lingering occasionally on the road upon every pretence which occurred; now catching from the hazel a cluster of half-ripe nuts, and now turning his head to leer after a cottage maiden who crossed their path. The horsemen, therefore, soon overtook them upon the road.

Their numbers amounted to ten men, of whom the two who rode foremost seemed to be persons of considerable importance, and the others their attendants. It was not difficult to ascertain the condition and character of one of these personages. He was obviously an ecclesiastic of high rank; his dress was that of a Cistercian Monk, but composed of materials much finer than those which the rule of that order admitted. His mantle and hood were of the best Flanders cloth, and fell in ample, and not ungraceful folds around a handsome though somewhat corpulent person. His countenance bore as little the marks of self-denial, as his habit indicated contempt of worldly splendour. His features might have been called good, had there not lurked under the pent-house of his eye, that sly epicurean twinkle which indicates the cautious voluptuary. In other respects, his profession and situation had taught him a ready command over his countenance, which he could contract at pleasure into solemnity, although its natural expression was that of good-humoured social indulgence. In defiance of conventual rules, and the edicts of popes and councils, the sleeves of this dignitary were lined and turned up with rich furs, his mantle secured at the throat with a golden clasp, and the whole dress proper to his order as much refined upon and ornamented, as that of a quaker beauty of the present day, who, while she retains the garb and costume of her sect, continues to give to its simplicity, by the choice of materials and the mode of disposing them, a certain air of coquettish attraction, savouring but too much of the vanities of the world.

This worthy churchman rode upon a well-fed ambling mule, whose furniture was highly decorated, and whose bridle, according to the fashion of the day, was ornamented with silver bells. In his seat he had nothing of the awkwardness of the convent, but displayed the easy and habitual grace of a well-trained horseman. Indeed, it seemed that so humble a conveyance as a mule, in however good case, and however well broken to a pleasant and accommodating amble, was only used by the gallant monk for travelling on the road. A lay brother, one of those who followed in the train, had, for his use upon other occasions, one of the most handsome Spanish jennets ever bred in Andalusia, which merchants used at that time to import, with great trouble and risk, for the use of persons of wealth and distinction. The saddle and housings of this superb palfrey were covered by a long foot-cloth, which reached nearly to the ground, and on which were richly embroidered, mitres, crosses, and other ecclesiastical emblems. Another lay brother led a sumpter mule, loaded probably with his superior's baggage; and two monks of his own order, of inferior station, rode together in the rear, laughing and conversing with each other, without taking much notice of the other members of the cavalcade.

The companion of the church dignitary was a man past forty, thin, strong, tall, and muscular; an athletic figure, which long fatigue and constant exercise seemed to have left none of the softer part of the human form, having reduced the whole to brawn, bones, and sinews, which had sustained a thousand toils, and were ready to dare a thousand more. His head was covered with a scarlet cap, faced with fur,—of that kind which the French call *mortier*, from its resemblance to the shape of an inverted mortar. His countenance was therefore fully displayed, and its expression was calculated to impress a degree of awe, if not of fear, upon strangers. High features, naturally strong and powerfully expressive, had been burned almost into Negro blackness by constant exposure to the tropical sun, and might, in their ordinary state, be said to slumber after the storm of passion had passed away; but the projection of the veins of the forehead, the readiness with which the upper lip and its thick black moustaches quivered upon the slightest emotion, plainly intimated that the tempest might be again and easily awakened. His keen, piercing, dark eyes, told in every glance a history of difficulties subdued, and dangers dared, and seemed to challenge opposition to his wishes, for the pleasure of sweeping it from his road by a determined exertion of courage and of will; a deep scar on his brow gave additional sternness to his countenance, and a sinister expression to one of his eyes, which had been slightly injured upon the same occasion, and of which the vision, though perfect, was in a slight and partial degree distorted.

The upper dress of this personage resembled that of his companion in shape, being a long monastic mantle, but the colour being scarlet, shewed that he did not belong to any of the four regular orders of monks. On the right shoulder of the mantle there was cut, in white cloth, a cross of a peculiar form. This upper robe concealed what at first view seemed rather inconsistent with its form, a shirt, namely, of linked mail, with sleeves and gloves of the same, curiously plaited and interwoven, as flexible to the body as those which are now wrought in the stocking loom, and of less obdurate materials. The fore-part of his thighs, where the folds of his mantle permitted them to be seen, were also covered with linked mail; the knees and feet were defended by splints, or thin plates of steel, ingeniously jointed upon each other; and mail hose reaching from the ancle to the knee, effectually protected the legs, and completed the rider's defensive armour. In his girdle he wore a long and double-edged dagger, which was the only offensive weapon about his person.

He rode not a mule, like his companion, but a strong hackney for the road, to save his gallant war-horse, which a squire led behind, fully accoutred for battle, with a chamfrom or plaited head-piece upon his head, having a short spike projecting from the front. On one side of the saddle hung a short battle-axe, richly inlaid with Damascene carving; on the other the rider's plumed head-piece and hood of mail, with a long two-handled sword, used by the chivalry of the period. A second squire held aloft his master's lance, from the extremity of which fluttered a small banderole, or streamer, bearing a cross of the same form with that embroidered upon his cloak. He also carried his small triangular shield, broad enough at the top to protect the breast, and from thence diminishing to a point. It was covered with a scarlet cloth, which prevented the device from being seen.

These two squires were followed by two attendants, whose dark visages, white turbans, and the oriental form of their garments, shewed them to be natives of some distant eastern country. The whole appearance of this warrior and his retinue was wild and outlandish; the dress of his squires was gorgeous, and his eastern attendants wore silver collars round their throats, and bracelets of the same metal upon their swarthy arms and legs, of which the former were naked from the elbow, and the latter from mid-leg to ancle. Silk and embroidery distinguished their dresses, and marked the wealth and importance of their master; forming, at the same time, a striking contrast with the martial simplicity of his own attire. They were armed with crooked sabres, having the hilt and baldrick inlaid with gold, and matched with Turkish daggers of yet more costly workmanship. Each of them bore at his saddle-bow a bundle of darts or javelins, about four feet in length, having sharp steel heads, a weapon much in use among the Saracens, and of which the memory is yet preserved in the martial exercise called *El Jerrid*, still practised in the eastern countries.

The steeds of these attendants were in appearance as foreign as their riders; they were of Saracen origin, and consequently of Arabian descent, and their fine slender limbs, small fetlocks, thin manes and easy springy motion, formed a marked contrast with the large-jointed heavy horses, of which the race was cultivated in Flanders and in Normandy, for mounting the men-at-arms of the period in all the panoply of plate and mail; and which, placed by the side of those eastern coursers, might have passed for a personification of substance and of shadow.

The singular appearance of this cavalcade not only attracted the curiosity of Wamba, but excited even that of his less volatile companion. The monk he instantly knew to be the Prior of Jorvaulx Abbey, well known for many miles around as a lover of the chase, of the banquet, and, if fame did him not wrong, of other worldly pleasures still more inconsistent with his monastic vows.

Yet so loose were the ideas of the times respecting the conduct of the clergy, whether secular or regular, that the Prior Aymer maintained a fair character in the neighbourhood of his abbey. His free and jovial temper, and the readiness with which he granted absolution from all ordinary delinquencies, rendered him a favourite among the nobility and principal gentry, to several of whom he was allied by birth, being of a distinguished Norman family. The ladies, in particular, were not disposed to scan too nicely the morals of a man who was a professed admirer of their sex, and who possessed many means of dispelling the ennui which was too apt to intrude upon the halls and bowers of an ancient feudal castle. The Prior mingled in the sports of the field with more than due eagerness, and was allowed to possess the best trained hawks, and the fleetest greyhounds in the North Riding; circumstances which strongly recommended him to the youthful gentry. With the old, he had another part to play, which, when needful, he could sustain with great decorum. His knowledge of books, however superficial, was sufficient to impress upon their ignorance respect for his supposed learning; and the gravity of his deportment and language, with the high tone which he exerted in setting forth the authority of the church and of the priesthood, impressed them no less with an opinion of his sanctity. Even the common people, the severest critics of the conduct of their betters, had commiseration with the follies of Prior Aymer. He was generous; and charity, as it is well known, covereth a multitude of sins, in another sense than that in which it is said to do so in Scripture. The revenues of the monastery, of which a large part was at his disposal, while they gave him the means of supplying his own very considerable expences, afforded also those largesses which he bestowed among the peasantry, and with which he frequently relieved the distresses of the oppressed. If Prior Aymer rode hard in the chase, remained long at the banquet,—if Prior Aymer was seen, at the early peep of dawn, to enter the postern of the abbey, as he glided home from some rendezvous which had occupied the hours of darkness, men only shrugged up their shoulders, and reconciled themselves to his irregularities, by recollecting that the same were practised by many of his brethren who had no redeeming qualities whatsoever to atone for them. Prior Aymer, therefore, and his character, were well known to our Saxon serfs, who made their rude obeisance, and received his "*benedicite, mes filz,*" in return.

But the singular appearance of his companion and his attendants, arrested their attention and excited their wonder, and they could scarcely attend to the Prior of Jorvaulx' question, when he demanded if they knew of any place of harbourage in the vicinity; so much were they surprised at the half monastic, half military appearance of the swarthy stranger, and at the uncouth dress and arms of his eastern attendants. It is probable, too, that the language in which the benediction was conferred, and the information asked, sounded ungracious, though not probably unintelligible, in the ears of the Saxon peasants.

"I asked you, my children," said the Prior, raising his voice, and using the lingua Franca, or mixed language in which the Norman and Saxon races conversed with each other, "if there be in this neighbourhood any good man, who, for the love of God, and devotion to Mother Church, will give two of her humblest servants, with their train, a night's hospitality and refreshment?"

This he spoke with a tone of conscious importance, which formed a strong contrast to the modest terms which he thought it proper to employ.

"Two of the humblest servants of Mother Church!" repeated Wamba to himself,—but, fool as he was, taking care not to make his observation audible; "I should like to see her seneschals, her chief butlers, and her other principal domestics!"

After this internal commentary on the Prior's speech, he raised his eyes, and replied to the question which had been put.

"If the reverend fathers," he said, "loved good cheer and soft lodging, few miles of riding would carry them to the priory of Brinxworth, where their quality could not but secure them the most honourable reception; or if they preferred spending a penitential evening, they might turn down yonder wild glade, which would bring them to the hermitage of Copmanhurst, where a pious anchoret would make them sharers for the night of the shelter of his roof and the benefit of his prayers."

The Prior shook his head at both proposals.

"Mine honest friend," said he, "if the jangling of thy bells had not dizzied thine understanding, thou might'st know *Clericus clericum non decimat;* that is to say, we churchmen do not exhaust each other's hospitality, but rather require that of the laity, giving them thus an opportunity to serve God in honouring and relieving his appointed servants."

"It is true," replied Wamba, "that I, being but an ass, am, nevertheless, honoured to bear the bells as well as your reverence's mule; notwithstanding, I did conceive that the charity of Mother Church and her servants might be said, with other charity, to begin at home."

"A truce to thine insolence, fellow," said the armed rider, breaking in on his prattle with a high and stern voice, "and tell us, if thou can'st, the road to——How call'd you your Franklin, Prior Aymer?"

"Cedric," answered the Prior; "Cedric the Saxon.—Tell me, good fellow, are we near his dwelling, and can you shew us the road?"

"The road will be uneasy to find," answered Gurth, who broke silence for the first time, "and the family of Cedric retire early to rest."

"Tush, tell not me, fellow," said the military rider; "'tis easy for them to arise and supply the wants of travellers such as we are, who will not stoop to beg the hospitality which we have a right to command."

"I know not," said Gurth, sullenly, "if I should shew the way to my master's house, to those who demand as a right, the shelter which most are fain to ask as a favour."

"Do you dispute with me, slave!" said the soldier; and, setting spurs to his horse, he caused him make a demivolte across the path, raising at the same time the riding rod which he held in his hand, with a purpose of chastising what he considered as the insolence of the peasant.

Gurth darted at him a savage and revengeful scowl, and with a fierce, yet hesitating motion, laid his hand on the haft of his knife; but the interference of Prior Aymer, who pushed his mule betwixt his companion and the swine-herd, prevented the meditated violence.

"Nay, by St Mary, brother Brian, you must not think you are now in Palestine, predominating over heathen Turks and infidel Saracens; we islanders love not blows, save those of holy Church, who chasteneth whom she loveth.—Tell me, good fellow," said he to Wamba, and seconded his speech by a small piece of silver coin, "the way to Cedric the Saxon's; you cannot be ignorant of it, and it is your duty to direct the wanderer even when his character is less sanctified than ours."

"In truth, venerable father," answered the jester, "the Saracen head of your right reverend companion has frightened out of mine the way home—I am not sure I shall get there to-night myself."

"Tush," said the Abbot, "thou can'st tell us if thou wilt. This reverend brother has been all his life engaged in fighting among the Saracens for the recovery of the Holy Sepulchre; he is of the order of Knights Templars, whom you may have heard of; he is half a monk, half a soldier."

"If he is but half a monk," said the jester, "he should not be wholly unreasonable with those whom he meets upon the road, even if they should be in no hurry to answer questions that no way concern them."

"I forgive thy wit," replied the Abbot, "on condition thou wilt shew me the way to Cedric's mansion."

"Well, then," answered Wamba, "your reverences must hold on this path till you come to a sunken-cross, of which scarce a cubit's length remains above ground; then take the path to the left, for there are four which meet at Sunken Cross, and I trust your reverences will obtain shelter before the storm comes on."

The Abbot thanked his sage adviser; and the cavalcade, setting spurs to their horses, rode on as men do who wish to reach their inn before the bursting of a night-storm. As their horses' hoofs died away, Gurth said to his companion, "If they follow thy wise direction, the reverend fathers will hardly reach Rotherwood this night."

"No," said the jester, grinning, "but they may reach Sheffield if they have good luck, and that is as fit a place for them. I am not so bad a woodsman as to shew the dog where the deer lies, if I have no mind he should chase him."

"Thou art right," said Gurth; "it were ill that Aymer saw the lady Rowena; and it were worse, it may be, for Cedric to quarrel, as is most likely, with this military monk. But, like good servants, let us hear and see and say nothing."

We return to the riders, who had soon left the bondsmen far behind them, and who maintained the following conversation in the Norman-French language, usually employed by the superior classes, with the exception of the few who were still inclined to boast their Saxon descent.

"What mean these fellows by their capricious insolence," said the Templar to the Cistercian, "and why did you prevent me from chastising it?"

"Marry, brother Brian," replied the Prior, "touching the one of them, it were hard for me to render a reason for a fool speaking according to his folly; and the other churl is of that savage, fierce, intractable race, some of whom, as I have often told you, are still to be found among the descendants of the conquered Saxons, and whose supreme pleasure it is to testify by all means in their power their aversion to their conquerors."

"I would soon have beat him into courtesy," observed Brian; "I am accustomed to deal with such spirits: Our Turkish captives are as fierce and intractable as Odin himself could have been; yet two months in my household, under the management of my master of the slaves, has made them humble, submissive, serviceable, and observant of your will. Marry, sir, you must beware of the poison and the dagger, for they use either with free will when you give them the slightest opportunity."

"Ay, but," answered Prior Aymer, "every land has its own manners and fashions; and, besides that beating this fellow could procure us no information respecting the road to Cedric's house, it would have been sure to have established a quarrel betwixt you and him had we found our way thither. Remember what I told you, this wealthy Franklin is proud, fierce, jealous, and irritable; a withstander of the nobility, and even of his neighbours, Reginald Front-de-Bœuf, and Philip Malvoisin, who are no babes to strive withall. He stands up so sternly for the privileges of his race, and is so proud of his uninterrupted descent from Hereward, a renowned champion of the Heptarchy, that he is universally called Cedric the Saxon; and makes a boast of his belonging to a people from whom many others endeavour to hide their descent, lest they should encounter a share of the *vae victis*, or severities imposed upon the vanquished."

"Prior Aymer," said the Templar, "you are a man of gallantry, learned in the study of beauty, and as expert as a troubadour in all matters concerning the arrests of love; but I shall expect much beauty in this celebrated Rowena, to counterbalance the self-denial and forbearance which I must exert, if I am to court the favour of such a seditious churl as you have described her father Cedric."

"Cedric is not her father," replied the Prior, "and is but of remote relation; she is descended from higher blood than even he pretends to, and is but distantly connected with him by birth. Her guardian, however, he is, self-constituted as I believe; but his ward is as dear to him as if she were his own child. Of her beauty you shall soon be judge; and if the purity of her complexion, and the majestic, yet soft expression of a mild blue eye, do not chase from your memory the black-tressed girls of Palestine, ay, or the houris of old Mahound's paradise, I am an infidel, and no true son of the church."

"Should your boasted beauty," said the Templar, "be weighed in the balance and found wanting, you know our wager?"

"My gold collar," answered the Prior, "against ten butts of Chian wine;—they are mine as securely as if they were already in the convent vaults, under the key of old Dennis the cellarer."

"And I am myself to be judge," said the Templar, "and am only to be convicted on my own admission, that I have seen no maiden so beautiful since Pentecost was a twelve-month. Ran it not so?—Prior, your collar is in danger, I will wear it over my gorget in the lists at Ashby-de-la-Zouche."

"Win it fairly," said the Prior, "and wear it as ye will; I shall trust your giving true response, on your word as a knight and as a churchman. Yet, brother, take my advice, and file your tongue to a little more courtesy than your habits of predominating over infidel captives and eastern bondsmen have accustomed you. Cedric the Saxon, if offended,—and he is noway slack in taking offence,—is a man who, without respect to your knighthood, my high office, or the sanctity of either, would clear his house of us, and send us to lodge with the larks, though the hour were midnight. And be careful how you look on Rowena, whom he cherishes with the most jealous care; an' he take the least alarm in that quarter we are but lost men. It is said he banished his only son from his family for lifting his eyes in the way of affection towards this beauty, who may be worshipped, it seems, at a distance, but is not to be approached with other thoughts than such as we bring to the shrine of the Blessed Virgin."

"Well, you have said enough," answered the Templar; "I will for a night put on the needful restraint, and deport me as meekly as a maiden; but as for the fear of his expelling us by violence, myself and squires, with Hamet and Abdalla, will warrant you against that disgrace. Doubt not that we shall be strong enough to make good our quarters."

"We must not let it come so far—" answered the Prior; "but here is the clown's sunken cross, and the night is so dark that we can hardly see which of the roads we are to follow. He bid us turn, I think, to the left."

"To the right," said Brian, "to the best of my remembrance."

"The left, certainly, the left; I remember his pointing with his wooden sword."

"Ay, but he held his sword in his left hand, and so pointed across his body with it," said the Templar.

Each maintained his opinion with sufficient obstinacy, as is usual in all such cases; the attendants were appealed to, but they had not been near enough to hear Wamba's directions. At length Brian remarked, what had at first escaped him in the twilight; "Here is some one either asleep, or lying dead at the foot of this cross—Hugo, stir him with the butt-end of the lance."

This was no sooner done than the figure arose, exclaiming in good French, "Whosoever thou art, it is discourteous in you to disturb my thought."

"We did but wish to ask you," said the Prior, "the road to Rotherwood, the abode of Cedric the Saxon."

"I myself am bound thither," replied the stranger; "and if I had a horse, I would be your guide, for the way is somewhat intricate, though perfectly well known to me."

"Thou shalt both have thanks and reward, my friend," said the Prior, "if thou wilt bring us to Cedric's in safety."

And he caused one of his attendants to mount his own led horse, and give that upon which he had hitherto ridden to the stranger, who was to serve for a guide.

Their conductor pursued an opposite road from that which Wamba had recommended for the purpose of misleading them. The path soon led deeper into the woodland, and crossed more than one brook, the approach to which was rendered perilous by the marshes through which it flowed; but the stranger seemed to know, as if by instinct, the soundest ground and the safest points of passage; and by dint of caution and attention, brought the party safely into a wider avenue than any they had yet seen; and, pointing to a large low irregular building at the upper extremity, he said to the Prior, "Yonder is Rotherwood, the dwelling of Cedric the Saxon."

This was a joyful intimation to Aymer, whose nerves were none of the strongest, and who had suffered such agitation and alarm in the course of passing through the dangerous bogs, that he had not yet had the curiosity to ask his guide a single question. Finding himself now at his ease and near shelter, his curiosity began to awake, and he demanded of the guide who and what he was.

"A Palmer, just returned from the Holy Land," was the answer.

"You had better have tarried there to fight for the recovery of the Holy Sepulchre," said the Templar.

"True, Reverend Sir Knight," answered the Palmer, to whom the appearance of the Templar seemed perfectly familiar; "but when those who are under oath to recover the holy city, are found travelling at such a distance from the scene of their duties, can you wonder that a peaceful peasant like me should decline the task which they have abandoned?"

The Templar would have made an angry reply, but was interrupted by the Prior, who again expressed his astonishment that their guide, after such long absence, should be so perfectly acquainted with the passes of the forest.

"I was born a native of these parts," answered their guide, and as he made the reply they stood before the mansion of Cedric;—a low irregular building, containing several court-yards or enclosures, extending over a considerable space of ground, and which, though its size argued the inhabitant to be a person of wealth, differed entirely from the tall, turretted, and castellated buildings in which the Norman nobility resided, and which had become the universal style of architecture throughout England.

Rotherwood was not, however, without defences; no habitation, in that disturbed period, could have been so, without the risk of being plundered and burnt before the next morning. A deep fosse, or ditch, was drawn round the whole building, and filled with water from a neighbouring stream. A double stockade, or pallisade, composed of pointed beams, which the adjacent forest supplied, defended the outer and inner bank of the fosse. There was an entrance from the west through the outer stockade, which communicated by a drawbridge, with a similar opening in the interior defences. Some precautions had been taken to place those entrances under the protection of projecting angles, by which they might be flanked in case of need by archers or slingers.

Before this entrance the Templar wound his horn loudly; for the rain, which had long threatened, began now to descend with great violence.

Chapter Three

Then (sad relief!) from the bleak coast that hears
The German Ocean roar, deep-blooming, strong,
And yellow hair'd, the blue ey'd Saxon came.
THOMSON'S *Liberty.*

IN A HALL, the height of which was greatly disproportioned to its extreme length and width, a long oaken table, formed of planks rough-hewn from the forest, and which had scarcely received any polish, stood ready prepared for the evening meal of Cedric the Saxon. The roof composed of beams and rafters, had nothing to divide the apartment from the sky excepting the planking and thatch; there was a huge fire-place at either end of the hall, but as the chimnies were constructed in a very clumsy manner, at least as much of the smoke found its way into the apartment as escaped by the proper vent. The constant vapour which this occasioned, had polished the rafters and beams of the low-browed hall, by encrusting them with a black varnish of soot. On the sides of the apartment hung implements of war and of the chace, and there were at each corner folding doors, which gave access to other parts of the extensive building.

The other appointments of the mansion partook of the rude simplicity of the Saxon period, which Cedric piqued himself upon maintaining. The floor was composed of earth mixed with lime, trodden into such a hard substance, as is often employed in flooring our modern barns. For about one quarter of the length of the apartment, the floor was raised by a step, and this space, which was called the dais, was occupied only by the principal members of the family and visitors of distinction. For this purpose, a table richly covered with scarlet cloth was placed transversely across the platform, from the middle of which run the longer and lower board, at which the domestics and inferior persons fed, down towards the bottom of the hall. The whole resembled the form of the letter T, or some of those ancient dinner-tables, which, arranged on the same principle, may be still seen in the antique Colleges of Oxford and Cambridge. Massive chairs and settles of carved oak were placed upon the dais, and over these seats and the more elevated table was fastened a canopy of cloth, which served in some degree to protect the dignitaries who occupied that distinguished station from the weather, and from the rain, which in some places found its way through the ill-constructed roof.

The walls of this upper end of the hall, as far as the dais extended, were covered with hangings or curtains, and upon the floor there was a carpet, both of which were adorned with some attempts at tapestry, or embroidery, executed in brilliant or rather with gaudy colouring. Over the lower range of table, the roof, as we have noticed, had no covering; the rough plastered walls were left bare, and the rude earthen floor was uncarpetted; the board was uncovered by a cloth, and rude massive benches supplied the place of chairs.

In the centre of the upper table, were placed two chairs more elevated than the rest, for the master and mistress of the family, who presided over the scene of hospitality, and from doing so derived their Saxon title of honour, which signifies "The Dividers of Bread."

To each of these chairs was added a footstool, curiously carved and inlaid with ivory, which mark of distinction was peculiar to them. One of these seats was at present occupied by Cedric the Saxon, who, though but in rank a thane, or, as the Normans called him, a Franklin, felt, at the delay of his evening meal, an irritable impatience, which might have become an alderman whether of ancient or of modern times.

It appeared, indeed, from the countenance of this proprietor, that he was of a frank, but hasty and choleric temper. He was not above the middle stature, but broad-shouldered, long-armed, and powerfully made, like one accustomed to endure the fatigue of war or of the chase; his face was broad, with large blue eyes, open and frank features, fine teeth, and a well formed head, altogether expressive of that sort of good humour which often lodges with a sudden and hasty temper. Pride and jealousy there was in his eye, for his life had been spent in asserting rights which were constantly liable to invasion; and the prompt, fiery, and resolute disposition of the man, had been kept constantly upon the alert by the circumstances of his situation. His long yellow hair was equally divided upon the top of his head and upon his brow, and combed down on each side to the length of his shoulders; it had but little tendency to grey, although Cedric was approaching to his sixtieth year.

His dress was a tunic of forest green, furred at the throat and cuffs with what was called minever; a kind of fur inferior in quality to ermine, and formed, it is believed, of the skin of the grey squirrel. This doublet hung unbuttoned over a close dress of scarlet which sate tight to his body; he had breeches of the same, but they did not reach lower than the thigh, leaving the knee exposed. His feet had sandals of the same fashion with the peasants, but of finer materials, and secured in the front with golden clasps. He had bracelets of gold upon his arms, and a broad collar of the same precious metal around his neck. About his waste he wore a richly-studded belt, in which was stuck a short straight two-edged sword, with a sharp point, so disposed as to hang almost perpendicularly by his side. Behind his seat was hung a scarlet cloth cloak lined with fur, and a cap of the same materials richly embroidered, which completed the dress of the opulent landholder when he chose to go forth. A short boar spear, with a broad and bright steel head, also reclined against the back of his chair, which served him, when he walked abroad, for the purposes of a staff or of a weapon, as chance might require.

Several domestics, whose dress held various proportions betwixt the richness of their master's, and the coarse and simple attire of Gurth the swineherd, watched the looks and waited the commands of the Saxon dignitary. Two or three servants of a superior order stood behind their master upon the dais; the rest occupied the lower part of the hall. Other attendants there were of a different description; two or three large and shaggy greyhounds, such as were then employed in hunting the stag and wolf; as many slow-hounds of a large bony breed, with thick necks, large heads, and long ears; and one or two of the smaller dogs, now called terriers, which waited with impatience the arrival of the supper; but with the sagacious knowledge of physiognomy peculiar to their race, forbore to intrude upon the moody silence of their master, apprehensive probably of a small white truncheon which lay by Cedric's trencher, for the purpose of repelling the advances of his four-legged dependents. One grisly old wolf-dog alone, with the liberty of an indulged favourite, had planted himself close by the chair of state, and occasionally ventured to solicit notice by putting his large hairy head upon his master's knee, or pushing his nose into his hand. Even he was repelled by the stern command, "Down, Balder, down! I am not in the humour for foolery."

In fact, Cedric, as we have observed, was in no very placid state of mind. The Lady Rowena, who had been absent to attend an evening mass at a distant church, had but just returned, and was changing her garments, which had been wetted by the storm. There were as yet no tidings of Gurth and his charge, which should long since have been driven home from the forest; and such was the insecurity of property, as to render it probable that the delay would be explained by some depredation of the outlaws, with whom the neighbouring forest abounded, or by the violence of some neighbouring baron, whose consciousness of strength made him equally negligent of the laws of property. The matter was of consequence, for great part of the domestic wealth of the Saxon proprietors consisted in numerous herds of swine, especially in forest-land, where these animals easily found their food.

Besides these subjects of anxiety, the Saxon thane was impatient for the presence of his favourite clown Wamba, whose jests, such as they were, served for a sort of seasoning to his evening meal, and to the deep draughts of wine with which he was in the habit of accompanying it. Add to all this, Cedric had not fed since noon, and his usual supper hour was long past, a cause of irritation common to country squires, both in ancient and modern times. His displeasure was expressed in broken sentences, partly muttered to himself, partly addressed to the domestics who stood around; and particularly to his cup-bearer, who offered him from time to time, as a sedative, a silver goblet filled with wine—"Why tarries the Lady Rowena?"

"She is but changing her head gear," replied a female attendant, with as much confidence as the favourite lady's maid usually answers the master of a modern family; "you would not wish her to sit down to the banquet in her wet hood and kirtle? and no lady within the shire can be quicker in arraying herself than my mistress."

This undeniable argument produced a sort of acquiescent umph! on the part of the Saxon, with the addition, "I wish her devotion may choose fair weather for the next visit to St John's Kirk;—but what, in the name of ten devils," continued he, turning to the cup-bearer, and raising his voice as if happy to have found a channel into which he might divert his indignation without fear or controul—"what, in the name of ten devils, keeps Gurth so long a-field? I suppose we shall have an evil account of the herd; he was wont to be a faithful and cautious drudge, and I had destined him for something better; perchance I might even have made him one of my warders."*

Oswald the cup-bearer modestly suggested, "that it was scarce an hour since the tolling of the curfew;" an ill chosen apology, since it turned upon a topic so harsh to Saxon ears.

"The foul fiend," exclaimed Cedric, "take the curfew-bell, and the tyrannical bastard by whom it was devised, and the heartless slave who names it with a Saxon tongue to a Saxon ear! The curfew!" he added, pausing, "ay, the curfew; which compels true men to extinguish their

*The original has *Cnichts*, by which the Saxons seem to have designated a class of military attendants, sometimes free, sometimes bondsmen, but always ranking above an ordinary domestic, whether in the royal household or in those of the aldermen and thanes. But the term cnicht, now spelt knight, having been received into the English language as equivalent to the Norman chevalier, I have avoided using it in its more ancient sense, to prevent confusion. L. T.

lights, that thieves and robbers may work their deeds in darkness! Ay, the curfew;—Reginald Front-de-Bœuf and Philip de Malvoisin know the use of the curfew as well as William the Bastard himself, or e'er a Norman adventurer that fought at Hastings. I shall hear, I guess, that my property has been swept off to save from starving the hungry banditti, whom they cannot support but by theft and robbery. My faithful slave is murdered, and my goods are taken for a prey—and Wamba—where is Wamba? Said not some one he had gone forth with Gurth?"

Oswald replied in the affirmative.

"Ay, why this is better and better; he is carried off too, the Saxon fool, to serve the Norman lord. Fools are we all indeed that serve them, and fitter subjects for their scorn and laughter, than if we were born with but half our wits. But I will be avenged," he added, starting from his chair in impatience at the supposed injury, and catching hold of his boar-spear; "I will go with my complaint to the great council; I have friends, I have followers—man to man will I appeal the Norman to the lists; let him come in his plate and his mail, and all that can render cowardice bold; I have sent such a javelin as this through a stronger fence than three of their war shields!—Haply they think me old; but they shall find, alone and childless as I am, the blood of Hereward is in the veins of Cedric.—Ah, Wilfred, Wilfred!" he exclaimed in a lower tone, "could'st thou have ruled thine unreasonable passion, thy father had not been left in his age like the solitary oak that throws out its shattered and unprotected branches against the full sweep of the tempest!" The reflection seemed to conjure into sadness his irritated feelings. Replacing his javelin, he resumed his seat, bent his looks downward, and appeared to be absorbed in melancholy reflection.

From his musing, Cedric was suddenly awakened by the blast of a horn, which was replied to by the clamorous yells and barking of all the dogs in the hall, and some twenty or thirty which were quartered in other parts of the building. It cost much exercise of the white truncheon, well seconded by the exertions of the domestics, to silence this canine clamour.

"To the gate, knaves!" said the Saxon, hastily, as soon as the tumult was so much appeased that the dependants could hear his voice. "See what tidings that horn tells of—to announce, I ween, some hership and robbery which has been done upon my lands."

Returning in less than three minutes, a warder announced "that the Prior Aymer of Jorvaulx, and the good knight Brian de Bois-Guilbert, commander of the valiant and venerable order of Knights Templars, with a small retinue, requested hospitality and lodging for the night, being on their way to a tournament which was to be held not far from Ashby-de-la-Zouche, on the second day from the present."

"Aymer, the Prior Aymer? Brian de Bois-Guilbert?" muttered Cedric; "Normans both;—but Norman or Saxon, the hospitality of Rotherwood must not be impeached; they are welcome, since they have chosen to halt—more welcome would they have been to have ridden further on their way—But it were unworthy to murmur for a night's lodging and a night's food; in the quality of guests at least, even Normans must suppress their insolence.—Go, Hundebert," he added, to a sort of major-domo who stood behind him with a white wand; "take six of the attendants, and introduce the strangers to the guests' lodging. Look after their horses and mules, and see their train lack nothing. Let them have change of vestments if they require it, and fire, and water to wash, and wine and ale; and bid the cooks add what they hastily can to our evening meal; and let it be put on the board when those strangers are ready to share it. Say to them, Hundebert, that Cedric would himself bid them welcome, but he is under a vow never to step more than three steps from the dais of his own hall to meet any who shares not the blood of Saxon royalty. Begone! see them carefully tended; let them not say in their pride, the Saxon churl has shewn at once his poverty and his avarice."

The major-domo departed with several attendants to execute his master's commands. "The Prior Aymer!" repeated Cedric, looking to Oswald, "the brother, if I mistake not, of Giles de Mauleverer, now lord of Middleham?"

Oswald made a respectful sign of assent. "His brother sits in the seat, and usurps the patrimony, of a better race, the race of Ulfgar of Middleham; but what Norman lord doth not the same? This Prior is, they say, a free and jovial priest, who loves the wine-cup and the bugle-horn better than bell and book: Good; let him come; he shall be welcome. How named ye the Templar?"

"Brian de Bois-Guilbert."

"Bois-Guilbert," said Cedric, still in the musing, self-arguing tone, which the habit of living among dependants had accustomed him to employ, and which resembled a man who talks to himself rather than to those around him—"Bois-Guilbert? that name has been spread wide both for good and evil. They say he is valiant as the bravest of his order; but stained with their usual vices, pride, arrogance, cruelty, and voluptuousness; a hard-hearted man, who knows neither fear of earth nor awe of heaven. So say the few warriors who have returned from Palestine.—Well; it is but for one night; he shall be welcome too.—Oswald, broach the oldest wine-cask; place the best mead, the richest morat, the most sparkling cyder, the most odoriferous pigment, upon the board; fill the largest horns*—Templars and Abbots love good wines and good measure. Elgitha, let thy Lady Rowena know we shall not this night expect her in the hall, unless such be her especial pleasure."

"But it will be her especial pleasure," answered Elgitha, with great readiness, "for she is ever desirous to hear the latest news from Palestine."

Cedric darted at the forward damsel a glance of hasty resentment; but Rowena, and whatever belonged to her, were privileged and secure from his anger. He only replied, "Silence, maiden; thy tongue outruns thy discretion. Say my message to thy mistress, and let her do her pleasure. Here, at least, the descendant of Alfred still reigns a princess." Elgitha left the apartment.

"Palestine!" repeated the Saxon; "Palestine! how many ears are turned to the tales which dissolute crusaders, or hypocritical pilgrims, bring from that fatal land! I too might ask—I too might enquire—I too might listen with a beating heart to fables which the wily strollers devise to cheat us into hospitality—but no—The son who has disobeyed me is no longer mine; nor will I concern myself more for his fate than for that of the most worthless among the millions that ever shaped the cross on their shoulder, rushed into excess and blood-guiltiness, and called it an accomplishment of the will of God."

He knit his brows, and fixed his eyes for an instant on the ground; as he raised them, the folding doors at the bottom of the hall were cast wide, and, preceded by the major-domo with his wand, and four domestics bearing blazing torches, the guests of the evening entered the apartment.

* These were drinks used by the Saxons, as we are informed by Mr Turner: Morat was made of honey flavoured with the juice of mulberries; Pigment was a sweet and rich liquor, composed of wine highly spiced, and sweetened also with honey; the other liquors need no explanation. L. T.

Chapter Four

With sheep and shaggy goats the porkers bled,
And the proud steer was on the marble spread;
With fire prepared, they deal the morsels round,
Wine rosy bright the brimming goblets crown'd.

\- - - -

Disposed apart, Ulysses shares the treat;
A trivet table and ignobler seat,
The Prince assigns——

Odyssey, Book 21.

THE PRIOR AYMER had taken the opportunity afforded him, of changing his riding robe for one of yet more costly materials, over which he wore a cope curiously embroidered. Besides the huge golden signet ring, which marked his ecclesiastical dignity, his fingers, though contrary to the canon, were loaded with precious gems; his sandals were of the finest leather which was imported from Spain; his beard trimmed to as small dimensions as his order would possibly permit, and his shaven crown concealed by a scarlet cap richly embroidered.

The appearance of the Knight Templar was also changed; and, though less studiously bedecked with ornament, his dress was as rich, and his appearance far more commanding, than that of his companion. He had exchanged his shirt of mail for an under tunic of dark purple silk, garnished with furs, over which flowed his long robe of spotless white, in ample folds. The eight-pointed cross of his order was cut on the shoulder of his mantle in black velvet. The high cap no longer invested his brows, which were only shaded by short and thick curled hair of a raven blackness, corresponding to his unusually swart complexion. Nothing could be more majestic than his step and manner, had they not been marked by a predominant air of haughtiness, easily acquired by the exercise of unresisted authority.

These two dignified persons were followed by their respective attendants, and at a more humble distance by their guide, whose figure had nothing more remarkable than it derived from the usual weeds of a pilgrim. A cloak or mantle of coarse black serge, enveloped his whole body. It was in shape something like the cloak of a modern hussar, having similar flaps for covering the arms, and was called a *Sclaveyn* or *Slavonian*. Coarse sandals, bound with thongs, on his bare feet; a broad and shadowy hat, with cockle-shells stitched on its brim, and a long staff shod with iron, to the upper end of which was attached a branch of palm, completed the palmer's attire. He followed modestly the last of the train which entered the hall, and, observing that the lower table scarce afforded room sufficient for the domestics of Cedric and the retinue of his guests, he withdrew to a settle placed beside and almost under one of the large chimnies, and seemed to employ himself in drying his garments, until the retreat of some one should make room at the board, or the hospitality of the steward should supply him with refreshments in the place he had chosen apart.

Cedric rose to receive his guests with an air of dignified hospitality, and, descending from the dais, or elevated part of his hall, made three steps towards them, and then awaited their approach.

"I grieve," he said, "reverend Prior, that my vow binds me to advance no farther upon this floor of my fathers, even to receive such guests as you, and this valiant Knight of the Holy Temple. But my steward has expounded to you the cause of my seeming discourtesy. Let me also pray, that you will excuse my speaking to you in my native language, and that you will reply in the same if your knowledge of it permits; if not, I sufficiently understand Norman to follow your meaning."

"Vows," said the Abbot, "must be unloosed, worthy Franklin, or permit me rather to say, worthy Thane, though the title is antiquated. Vows are the knots which tie us to heaven—they are the cords which bind the sacrifice to the horns of the altar,—and are therefore,—as I said before,—to be unloosed and discharged, unless our holy Mother Church shall pronounce the contrary. And respecting language, I willingly hold communication in that spoken by my respected grandmother, Hilda of Middleham, who died in odour of sanctity, little short, if we may presume to say so, of her glorious name-sake, the blessed Saint Hilda of Whitby, God be gracious to her soul!"

When the Prior had ceased what he meant as a conciliatory harangue, his companion said briefly and emphatically, "I speak ever French, the language of King Richard and his nobles; but I understand English sufficiently to communicate with the natives of the country."

Cedric darted at the speaker one of those hasty and impatient glances, which comparisons between the two rival nations seldom failed to call forth; but recollecting the duties of hospitality, he suppressed further shew of resentment, and, motioning with his hand, caused his guests to assume two seats a little lower than his own, but placed close beside him, and gave a signal that the evening meal should be placed upon the board.

While the attendants hastened to obey Cedric's commands, his eye distinguished Gurth the swine-herd, who, with his companion Wamba, had just entered the hall. "Send these loitering knaves up hither," said the Saxon, impatiently. And when the culprits came before the dais,—"How comes it, villains! that you have loitered abroad so late as this? Hast thou brought home thy charge, sirrah Gurth, or hast thou left them to outlaws and marauders?"

"The herd is safe, so please ye," said Gurth.

"But it does not please me, thou knave," said Cedric, "that I should be made to suppose otherwise for two hours, and sit here devising vengeance against my neighbours for wrongs they have not done me. I tell thee, shackles and the prison-house shall punish the next offence of this kind."

Gurth, knowing his master's irritable temper, attempted no exculpation; but the Jester, who could presume upon Cedric's tolerance, by virtue of his privileges as a fool, replied for them both; "In troth, uncle Cedric, you are neither wise nor reasonable to-night."

"How, sir?" said his master; "you shall to the porter's lodge, and taste of the discipline there, if you give your foolery such license."

"First let your wisdom tell me," said Wamba, "is it just and reasonable to punish one person for the fault of another?"

"Certainly not, fool," answered Cedric.

"Then why should you shackle poor Gurth, uncle, for the fault of his dog Fangs? for I dare be sworn we lost not a minute by the way when we had got our herd together, which Fangs did not manage until we heard the vesper-bell."

"Then hang up Fangs," said Cedric, turning hastily towards the swine-herd, "if the fault is his, and get thee another dog."

"Under favour, uncle," said the Jester, "that were still somewhat on the bow-hand of fair justice; for it was no fault of Fangs that he was lame and could not gather the herd, but the fault of those that struck off two of his fore-claws, an operation for which, if the poor fellow had been consulted, he would scarce have given his voice."

"And who dared to lame an animal which belonged to my bondsman?" said the Saxon, kindling in wrath.

"Marry, that did old Hubert," said Wamba, "Sir Philip de Malvoisin's keeper of the chace. He caught Fangs strolling in the forest, and said, he chased the deer contrary to his master's right, as warden of the walk."

"The foul fiend take Malvoisin," answered the Saxon, "and his keeper both! I will teach them that the wood was disforested in terms of the great Forest Charter. But enough of this. Go to, knave, go to thy place—and thou, Gurth, get thee another dog, and should the keeper dare to touch it, I will mar his archery; the curse of a coward on my head, if I strike not off the fore-finger of his right hand—he shall draw bow-string no more.—I crave your pardon, my worthy guests. I am beset here with neighbours that match your infidels, Sir Knight, in

Holy Land. But your homely fare is before you; feed, and let welcome make amends for hard fare."

The feast, however, which was spread upon the board, needed no apologies from the lord of the mansion. Swine's flesh, dressed in several modes, appeared on the lower part of the board, as also that of fowls, deer, goats, and hares, and various kinds of fish, together with huge loaves and cakes of bread, and sundry confections made of fruits and honey. The smaller sorts of wild-fowl, of which there was abundance, were not served up in platters, but brought in upon small wooden spits or broaches, and offered by the pages and domestics who bore them, to each guest in succession, who cut from them such a portion as he pleased. Beside each person of rank, was placed a goblet of silver; the lower board was accommodated with large drinking horns.

When the repast was about to commence, the major-domo, or steward, suddenly raising his wand, said aloud, "Forbear!—Place for the Lady Rowena." A side door at the upper end of the hall now opened behind the banquet table, and Rowena, followed by four female attendants, entered the apartment. Cedric, though surprised, and perhaps not altogether agreeably so, at his ward appearing in public upon this occasion, hastened to meet her, and to conduct her, with respectful ceremony, to the elevated seat at his own right hand, appropriated to the lady of the mansion. All stood up to receive her; and, replying to their courtesy by a mute gesture of salutation, she moved gracefully forwards to assume her place at the board. Ere she had time to do so, the Templar whispered to the Prior, "I shall wear no collar of gold of yours at the tournament. The Chian wine is your own."

"Said I not so?" answered the Prior; "but check your raptures, the Franklin observes you."

Unheeding this remonstrance, and accustomed only to act upon the immediate impulse of his own wishes, Brian de Bois-Guilbert kept his eyes rivetted on the Saxon beauty, more striking perhaps to his imagination, because differing widely from those of the eastern sultanas.

Formed in the best proportions of her sex, Rowena was tall in stature, yet not so much so as to attract observation on account of superior height. Her complexion was exquisitely fair, but the noble cast of her head and features prevented the insipidity which sometimes attaches to fair beauties. Her clear blue eye, which sate enshrined beneath a graceful eye-brow of brown sufficiently marked to give expression to the forehead, seemed capable to kindle as well as melt, to command as well as to beseech. If mildness were the more natural expression of such a combination of features, it was plain, that in the present instance, the exercise of habitual superiority, and the reception of general homage, had given to the Saxon lady a loftier character, which mingled with and qualified that bestowed by nature. Her profuse hair, of a colour betwixt brown and flaxen, was arranged in a fanciful and graceful manner in numerous ringlets, to form which art had probably aided nature. These locks were braided with gems, and, being worn at full length, intimated the noble birth and free-born condition of the maiden. A golden chain, to which was attached a small reliquary of the same metal, hung round her neck. She wore bracelets on her arms, which were bare. Her dress was an under-gown and kirtle of pale sea-green silk, over which hung a long loose robe, which reached to the ground, having very wide sleeves, which came down, however, very little below the elbow. This robe was crimson, and manufactured out of the very finest wool. A veil of silk, interwoven with gold, was attached to the upper part of it, which could be, at the wearer's pleasure, either drawn over the face and bosom after the Spanish fashion, or disposed as a sort of drapery round the shoulders.

When Rowena perceived the Knight Templar's eyes bent on her with an ardour, that, compared with the dark caverns under which they moved, gave them the effect of lighted charcoal, she drew with dignity the veil around her face, as an intimation that the determined freedom of his glance was disagreeable. Cedric saw the motion and its cause. "Sir Templar," said he, "the cheeks of our Saxon maidens have seen too little of the sun to enable them to bear the fixed glance of a crusader."

"If I have offended," replied Sir Brian, "I crave your pardon,—that is, I crave the Lady Rowena's pardon,—for my humility will carry me no lower."

"The Lady Rowena," said the Prior, "has punished us all, in chastising the boldness of my friend. Let me hope she will be less cruel to the splendid train which are to meet at the tournament."

"Our going thither," said Cedric, "is uncertain. I love not these vanities, which were unknown to my fathers when England was free."

"Let us hope, nevertheless," said the Prior, "our company may determine you to travel thitherward; when the roads are so unsafe, the escort of Sir Brian de Bois-Guilbert is not to be despised."

"Sir Prior," answered the Saxon, "wheresoever I have travelled in this land, I have hitherto found myself, with the assistance of my good sword and faithful followers, in no respect needful of other aid. At present, if we indeed journey to Ashby-de-la-Zouche, we do so with my noble neighbour and countryman Athelstane of Coningsburgh, and with such a train as would set outlaws and feudal enemies alike at defiance.——I drink to you, Sir Prior, in this cup of wine, which I trust your taste will approve, and I thank you for your courtesy. Should you be so rigid in adhering to monastic rule," he added, "as to prefer your acid preparation of milk, I hope you will not strain courtesy to do me reason."

"Nay," said the Priest, laughing, "it is only in our abbey that we confine ourselves to the *lac dulce* or the *lac acidum* either. Conversing with the world, we use the world's fashions, and therefore I answer your pledge in this honest wine, and leave the weaker liquor to my lay-brother."

"And I," said the Templar, filling his goblet, "drink wassail to the fair Rowena; for since her name-sake introduced the word into England, has never been one more worthy of such a tribute. By my faith, I could pardon the unhappy Vortigern, had he half the cause that we now witness for making shipwreck of his honour and his kingdom."

"I will spare your courtesy, Sir Knight," said Rowena with dignity, and without unveiling herself; "or rather I will tax it so far as to require of you the latest news from Palestine, a theme more agreeable to our English ears than the compliments which your French breeding teaches."

"I have little of importance to say, lady," answered Sir Brian de Bois-Guilbert, "excepting the confirmed tidings of a truce with Saladin."

He was interrupted by Wamba, who had taken his appropriated seat upon a chair, the back of which was decorated with two ass's ears, and which was placed about two steps behind that of his master, who, from time to time, supplied him with victuals from his own trencher; a favour, however, which the Jester shared with the favourite dogs, of whom, as we have already noticed, there were several in attendance. Here sat Wamba, with a small table before him, his heels tucked up against the bar of the chair, his cheeks sucked up so as to make his jaws resemble a pair of nut-crackers, and his eyes half shut, yet watching with alertness every opportunity to exercise his licensed foolery.

"These truces with the infidels," he exclaimed, without caring how suddenly he interrupted the stately Templar, "make an old man of me!"

"Go to, knave, how so?" said Cedric, his features prepared to receive favourably the expected jest.

"Because," answered Wamba, "I remember three of them in my day, each of which was to endure for the course of fifty years; so that, by computation, I must be at least a hundred and fifty years old."

"I will warrant you against dying of old age, however," said the Templar, who now recognised his friend of the forest; "I will assure you from all deaths but a violent one, if you give such directions to way-farers, as you did this night to the Prior and me."

"How, sirrah!" said Cedric, "misdirect travellers? We must have you whipt; you are at least as much rogue as fool."

"I pray thee, uncle," answered the Jester, "let my folly, for once, protect my roguery. I did but make a mistake between my right hand and my left, and he might have pardoned a greater who took a fool for his counsellor and guide."

Conversation was here interrupted by the entrance of the porter's page, who announced that there was a stranger at the gate, imploring admittance and hospitality.

"Admit him," said Cedric, "be he who or what he may;—a night like that which roars without, compels even wild animals to herd with tame, and to seek the protection of man, their mortal foe, rather than perish by the elements. Let his wants be ministered to with all care—look to it, Oswald."

And the steward left the banqueting hall to see the commands of his patron obeyed.

Chapter Five

> Hath not a Jew eyes? Hath not a Jew hands, organs, dimensions, senses, affections, passions? Fed with the same food, hurt with the same weapons, subject to the same diseases, healed by the same means, warmed and cooled by the same winter and summer, as a Christian is?
>
> *Merchant of Venice.*

OSWALD, returning, whispered into the ear of his master, "It is a Jew, who calls himself Isaac of York; is it fit I should marshall him into the hall?"

"Let Gurth do thine office, Oswald," said Wamba with his usual effrontery; "the swine-herd will be a fit usher to the Jew."

"St Mary," said the Abbot, crossing himself, "an unbelieving Jew, and admitted into this presence!"

"A dog Jew," echoed the Templar, "to approach a defender of the Holy Sepulchre!"

"By my faith," said Wamba, "it would seem the Templars love the Jews' inheritance better than they do their company."

"Peace, my worthy guests," said Cedric; "my hospitality must not be bounded by your dislikes. If Heaven bore with the whole nation of stiff-necked unbelievers for more years than a layman can number, we may endure the presence of one Jew for a few hours. But I constrain no man to converse or to feed with him.—Let him have a board and morsel apart,—unless," he said smiling, "these turban'd strangers will admit his society."

"Sir Franklin," answered the Templar, "my Saracen slaves are true Moslems, and scorn as much as any Christian to hold intercourse with a Jew."

"Now, in faith," said Wamba, "I cannot see that the worshippers of Mahound and Termagaunt have so greatly the advantage over the people once chosen of Heaven."

"He shall sit with thee, Wamba," said Cedric; "the fool and the knave will be well met."

"The fool," answered Wamba, raising the relics of a gammon of bacon, "will take care to erect a bulwark against the knave."

"Hush," said Cedric, "for here he comes."

Introduced with little ceremony, and advancing with fear and hesitation, and many a bow of deep humility, a tall thin old man, who, however, had lost by the habit of stooping much of his actual height, approached the lower end of the board. His features, keen and regular, with an aquiline nose, and piercing black eyes; his high and wrinkled forehead, and long grey hair and beard, would have been considered as handsome, had they not been the marks of a physiognomy peculiar to a race, which, during these dark ages, was alike detested by the credulous and prejudiced vulgar, and persecuted by the greedy and rapacious nobility, and who, perhaps, owing to that very hatred and persecution, had adopted a national character, in which there was much, to say the least, mean and unamiable.

The Jew's dress, which appeared to have suffered considerably from the storm, was a plain russet cloak of many folds, covering a dark purple tunic. He had large boots, lined with fur, and a belt around his waist, which sustained a small knife, together with a case for writing materials, but no weapon. He wore a high square yellow cap of a peculiar fashion, assigned to his nation to distinguish them from Christians, and which he doffed with great humility at the door of the hall.

The reception of this person in the hall of Cedric the Saxon, was such as might have satisfied the most prejudiced enemy of the tribes of Israel. Cedric himself coldly nodded in answer to the Jew's repeated salutations, and signed to him to take place at the lower end of the table, where, however, no one offered to make room for him. On the contrary, as he passed along the file, casting a timid supplicating glance, and turned towards each of those who occupied the lower end of the board, the Saxon domestics squared their shoulders, and continued to devour their supper with great perseverance, paying not the least attention to the wants of the new guest. The attendants of the Abbot crossed themselves, with looks of pious horror, and the very heathen Saracens, as Isaac drew near them, curled up their whiskers with indignation, and laid their hands on their poniards, as if ready to rid themselves by the most desperate means from the apprehended contamination of his nearer approach.

Probably the same motives which induced Cedric to open his hall to this son of a rejected people, would have made him insist on his attendants receiving Isaac with more courtesy. But the Abbot had, at this moment, engaged him in a most interesting discussion on the breed and character of his favourite hounds, which he would not have interrupted for matters of much greater importance than that of a Jew going to bed supperless. While Isaac thus stood an outcast in the present society, like his people among the nations, looking in vain for welcome or resting place, the Pilgrim who sat by the chimney took compassion upon him, and resigned his seat, saying briefly, "Old man, my garments are dried, my hunger is appeased, thou art both wet and fasting." So saying, he gathered together, and brought to a flame, the decaying brands which lay scattered on the ample hearth; took from the larger board a mess of pottage and seethed kid, placed it upon the small table at which he had himself supped, and without waiting the Jew's thanks, went to the other side of the hall;—whether from unwillingness to hold more close communication with the object of his benevolence, or from a wish to draw near to the upper end of the table, seemed uncertain.

Had there been painters in those days capable to execute such a subject, the Jew, as he bent his withered form, and expanded his chilled and trembling hands over the fire, would have formed no bad emblematical personification of the winter season. Having dispelled the cold, he turned eagerly to the smoking mess which was placed before him, and eat with a haste and an apparent relish, that seemed to betoken long abstinence from food.

Meanwhile the Abbot and Cedric continued their discourse upon hunting; the Lady Rowena seemed engaged in conversation with one of her attendant females; and the haughty Templar, whose eye seemed to wander from the Jew to the Saxon beauty, revolved in his mind thoughts which appeared deeply to interest him.

"I marvel, worthy Cedric," said the Abbot, as their discourse proceeded, "that, great as your predilection is for your own manly language, you do not at least receive the Norman French into your favour, so far as the mystery of wood-craft and hunting is concerned. Surely no tongue is so rich in the various phrases which the field sports demand, or furnishes means to the experienced woodsman so well to express his jovial art."

"Good Father Aymer," said the Saxon, "be it known to you, I care not for those over-sea refinements, without which I can well enough take my pleasure in the woods. I can wind my horn, though I call not the blast either a *recheate* or a *morte*—I can cheer my dogs on the prey, and I can flay and quarter the animal when it is brought down, without using the new-fangled jargon of *curee*, *arbor*, *nombles*, and all the babble of the fabulous Sir Tristrem."

"The French," said the Templar, raising his voice with the presumptuous and authoritative tone which he used upon all occasions, "is not only the natural language of the chase, but that of love and of war, in which ladies should be won and enemies defied."

"Pledge me in a cup of wine, Sir Templar," said Cedric, "and fill another to the Abbot, while I look back some thirty years to tell you another tale. As Cedric the Saxon then was, his plain English tale needed no garnish from French troubadours, when it was told in the ear of beauty; and the field of Northallerton, upon the day of the Holy Standard, could tell whether the Saxon war-cry was not heard as far within the ranks of the Scottish host as the *cri de guerre* of the boldest Norman baron. To the memory of the brave who fought there!—Pledge me, my guests." He drank deep, and went on with increasing warmth. "Ay, that was a day of cleaving of shields, when a hundred banners were bent forwards over the head of the valiant, and blood flowed round like water, and death was held better than flight. A Saxon bard had called it a feast of the swords—a gathering of the eagles to the prey—the clashing of bills upon shield and helmet, the shouting of battle more joyful than the clamour of a bridal. But our bards are no more," said he; "our deeds are lost in those of another race—our language—our very name is hastening to decay, and none mourns for it save one solitary old man—Cup-bearer! knave, fill the goblets—To the strong in arms, Sir Templar, be their race or language what it will, who now bear them best in Palestine among the champions of the Cross."

"It becomes not one wearing this badge to answer," said Sir Brian de Bois-Guilbert; "yet to whom, besides the sworn champions of the Holy Sepulchre, can the palm be assigned among the champions of the Cross?"

"To the Knights Hospitallers," said the Abbot; "I have a brother of their order."

"I impeach not their fame," said the Templar; "nevertheless"——

"I think, friend Cedric," said Wamba, interfering, "that had Richard of the Lion's Heart been wise enough to have taken a fool's advice, he might have staid at home with his merry Englishmen, and left the recovery of Jerusalem to those same Knights who had most to do with the loss of it."

"Were there then none in the English army," said the Lady Rowena, "whose names are worthy to be mentioned with the Knights of the Temple, and of St John?"

"Forgive me, lady," replied De Bois-Guilbert; "the English monarch did, indeed, bring to Palestine a host of gallant warriors, second only to those whose breasts have been the unceasing bulwark of that blessed land."

"Second to NONE," said the Pilgrim, who had stood near enough to hear, and had listened to this conversation with marked impatience. All turned toward the spot from whence this unexpected asseveration was heard. "I say," repeated the Pilgrim in a firm and strong voice, "that the English chivalry were second to NONE who ever drew sword in defence of the Holy Land. I say besides, for I saw it, that King Richard himself, and five of his knights, held a tournament after the taking of St John-de-Acre, as challengers against all comers. I say that, on that day, each knight ran three courses, and cast to the ground three antagonists. I add, that seven of these assailants were Knights of the Temple—and Sir Brian de Bois-Guilbert well knows the truth of what I tell you."

It is impossible for language to describe the bitter scowl of rage which rendered yet darker the swarthy countenance of the Templar. In the extremity of his resentment and confusion, his quivering fingers griped towards the handle of his sword, and perhaps only withdrew from the consciousness that no act of violence could be safely executed in that place and presence. Cedric, whose feelings were all of a right onward and simple kind, and were seldom occupied by more than one object at once, omitted, in the joyous glee with which he heard of the glory of his countrymen, to remark the angry confusion of his guest; "I would give thee this golden bracelet, Pilgrim, could'st thou tell me the names of those knights who upheld so gallantly the renown of merry England."

"That will I do blythely," replied the Pilgrim, "and that without guerdon; my oath, for a time, prohibits me touching gold."

"I will wear the bracelet for you, if you will, friend Palmer," said Wamba.

"The first in honour as in arms, in renown as in place," said the Pilgrim, "was the brave Richard, King of England."

"I forgive him," said Cedric; "I forgive him his descent from the tyrant Duke William."

"The Earl of Leicester was the second," continued the Pilgrim;

"Sir Thomas Multon of Gilsland was the third."

"Of Saxon descent, he at least," said Cedric, with exultation.

"Sir Foulk Doilly the fourth," said the Pilgrim.

"Saxon also, at least by the mother's side," continued Cedric, who listened with the utmost eagerness, and forgot, in part at least, his hatred to the Normans, in the common triumph of the King of England and his islanders. "And who was the fifth?" he demanded.

"The fifth was Sir Edwin Turneham."

"Genuine Saxon, by the soul of Hengist!" shouted Cedric—"And the sixth?" he continued with eagerness—"how name you the sixth?"

"The sixth," said the Palmer, after a pause, in which he seemed to recollect himself, "was a young knight of lesser renown and lower rank, assumed into that honourable company less to aid their enterprize than to make up their numbers—his name dwells not in my memory."

"Sir Palmer," said Sir Brian de Bois-Guilbert scornfully, "this assumed forgetfulness, after so much has been remembered, comes too late to serve your purpose. I will myself tell the name of the knight before whose lance fortune and my horse's fault occasioned my falling—it was the Knight of Ivanhoe; nor was there one of the six that, for his years, had more renown in arms.—Yet this will I say, and loudly—that were he in England, and durst repeat, in this week's tournament, the challenge of St John de Acre, I, mounted and armed as I now am, would give him every advantage of weapons, and abide the result."

"Your challenge would be soon answered," replied the Palmer, "were your antagonist near you. As the matter is, disturb not the peaceful hall with vaunts of the issue of a conflict, which you well know cannot take place. If Ivanhoe ever returns from Palestine, I will be his surety that he meets you."

"A goodly security," said the Knight Templar; "and what do you proffer as a pledge?"

"This reliquary," said the Palmer, taking a small ivory box from his bosom, and crossing himself, "containing a portion of the true cross, brought from the monastery of Mount Carmel."

The Prior of Jorvaulx crossed himself and repeated a pater noster, in which all devoutly joined, excepting the Jew, the Mahomedans, and the Templar, the latter of whom, without vailing his bonnet or testifying any reverence for the alleged sanctity of the relique, took from his neck a gold chain, which he flung on the board, saying—"Let Prior Aymer hold my pledge and that of this nameless vagrant, in token that when the Knight of Ivanhoe comes within the four seas of Britain, he underlies the challenge of Brian de Bois-Guilbert, which, if he answer not, I will proclaim him as a coward on the walls of every Temple Court in Europe."

"It will not need," said the Lady Rowena, breaking silence; "My voice shall be heard, if no other in this hall is raised on behalf of the absent Ivanhoe. I affirm he will meet fairly every honourable challenge. Could my weak warrant add security to the inestimable pledge of this holy pilgrim, I would pledge name and fame that Ivanhoe gives this proud knight the meeting he desires."

A crowd of conflicting emotions seemed to have occupied Cedric, and kept him silent during this discussion. Gratified pride, resentment, embarrassment, chased each other over his broad and open brow, like the shadow of cloud drifting over a harvest-field; whilst his attendants, on whom the name of the sixth knight seemed to produce an effect almost electrical, hung in suspense upon their master's looks. But when Rowena spoke, the sound of her voice seemed to startle him from his silence.

"Lady," said Cedric, "this beseems not; were further pledge necessary, I myself, offended, and justly offended, as I am, would yet gage my honour for the honour of Ivanhoe. But the wager of battle is complete, even according to the fantastic fashions of Norman chivalry —Is it not, Father Aymer?"

"It is," replied the Prior; "and the blessed relique and rich chain will I bestow safely in the treasury of our convent, until the decision of this warlike challenge."

Having thus spoken, he crossed himself again and again, and after many genuflections and muttered prayers, he delivered the reliquary to Brother Ambrose, his attendant monk, while he himself swept up with less ceremony, but perhaps with no less internal satisfaction, the golden chain, and bestowed it in a pouch lined with perfumed leather, which opened under his arm. "And now, Sir Cedric," he said, "my ears are chiming vespers with the strength of your good wine—permit us another pledge to the welfare of the fair Lady Rowena, and indulge us with liberty to pass to our repose."

"By the rood of Bromholme," said the Saxon, "you do but small credit to your fame, Sir Prior; report speaks you a bonny monk, that would hear the mattin chime ere he quitted his bowl; and, old as I am, I feared to have shame in encountering you. But, by my faith, a Saxon boy of twelve, in my time, would not so soon have relinquished his goblet."

The Prior had his own reasons, however, for persevering in the course of temperance which he had adopted. He was not only a professional peace-maker, but from practice a hater of all feuds and brawls. It was not altogether from a love to his neighbour, or to himself, or from a mixture of both. On the present occasion he had an instinctive apprehension of the fiery temper of the Saxon, and saw the danger that the reckless and presumptuous spirit, of which his companion had already given so many proofs, might at length end by producing some disagreeable explosion. He therefore gently insinuated the incapacity of the native of any other country engaging in the genial conflict of the bowl with the hardy and strong-headed Saxons; something he mentioned, but slightly, about his own holy character, and ended by pressing his proposal to depart to repose.

The grace-cup was accordingly served round, and the guests, after making deep obeisance to their landlord and to the Lady Rowena, arose and mingled in the hall, while the heads of the family, by separate doors, retired with their attendants.

"Unbelieving dog," said the Templar to Isaac the Jew, as he passed him in the throng, "dost thou bend thy course to the tournament?"

"I do so purpose," replied Isaac, bowing in all humility, "if it please your reverend valour."

"Ay," said the Knight, "to gnaw the bowels of our nobles with usury, and to gull women and boys with gauds and toys—I warrant thee store of shekels in thy Jewish scrip."

"Not a shekel, not a silver penny, not a halfling—so help me the God of Abraham!" said the Jew, clasping his hands; "I go but to seek the assistance of some brethren of my tribe to aid me to pay the fine which the Exchequer of the Jews* have imposed upon me—Father Jacob be my speed!—I am an impoverished wretch—the very gaberdine I wear is borrowed from Reuben of Tadcaster."

The Templar smiled sourly as he replied, "Beshrew thee for a false-hearted liar!" and passing onward, as if disdaining farther conference, he communed with his Moslem slaves in a language unknown to the by-standers. The poor Israelite seemed so staggered by the address of the military monk, that the Templar had passed on to the extremity of the hall ere he raised his head from the humble posture which he had assumed, so far as to be sensible of his departure. And when he did look around, it was with the astounded air of one at whose feet a thunderbolt has just burst, and who hears still the astounding report ringing in his ears.

The Templar and Prior were shortly after marshalled to their sleeping apartments by the steward and the cup-bearer, each attended by two torch-bearers and two servants carrying refreshments, while servants of inferior condition indicated to their retinue and to the other guests their respective places of repose.

*In those days the Jews were subjected to an Exchequer, specially dedicated to that purpose.—L. T.

Chapter Six

To buy his favour I extend this friendship:
If he will take it, so; if not, adieu;
And, for my love, I pray you wrong me not.
Merchant of Venice.

AS THE PALMER, lighted by a domestic with a torch, past through the intricate combination of apartments of this large and irregular mansion, the cup-bearer coming behind him whispered in his ear, that if he had no objection to a cup of good mead in his apartment, there were many domestics in that family who would gladly hear the news he had brought from the Holy Land, and particularly that which concerned the Knight of Ivanhoe. Wamba presently appeared to urge the same request, observing that a cup after midnight was worth three after curfew. Without disputing a maxim urged by such grave authority, the Palmer thanked them for their courtesy, but observed that he had included in his religious vow, an obligation never to speak in the kitchen on matters which were prohibited in the hall. "That vow," said Wamba to the cup-bearer, "would scarce suit a serving-man."

The cup-bearer shrugged his shoulders in displeasure. "I thought to have lodged him in the solere chamber," said he; "but since he is so unsocial to Christians, e'en let him take the next stall to Isaac the Jew's.—Anwold," said he to the torch-bearer, "carry the Pilgrim to the southern cell.—I give you good night," he added; "Sir Palmer, with small thanks for short courtesy."

"Good night, and our Lady's benison," said the Palmer, with composure, and his guide moved forward.

In a small anti-chamber, into which several doors opened, and which was lighted by a small iron lamp, they met a second interruption from the waiting-maid of Rowena, who, saying in a tone of authority, that her mistress desired to speak with the Pilgrim, took the torch from the hand of Anwold, and, bidding him await her return, made a sign to the Palmer to follow. Apparently he did not think it proper to decline this invitation as he had done the former; for, though his gesture indicated some surprise at the summons, he obeyed it without answer or remonstrance.

A short passage, and an ascent of seven steps, each of which was composed of a solid beam of oak, led him to the apartment of the Lady Rowena, the rude magnificence of which corresponded to the respect which was paid to her by the lord of the mansion. The walls were covered with embroidered hangings, on which different coloured silks, interwoven with gold and silver threads, had been employed with all the art of which the age was capable, to represent the sports of hunting and hawking. The bed was adorned with the same rich tapestry, and surrounded with curtains dyed with purple. The seats had also their stained coverings, and one, which was higher than the rest, was accommodated with a footstool of ivory, curiously carved.

No less than four silver candelabra, holding great waxen torches, served to illuminate this apartment. Yet let not modern beauty envy the magnificence of a Saxon princess. The walls of the apartment were so ill finished and so full of crevices, that the rich hangings shook to the night blast, and, in despite of a sort of screen intended to protect them from the wind, the flame of the torches streamed sideways into the air, like the unfurled pennon of a chieftain. Magnificence there was, with some rude attempt at taste; but of comfort there was little, and, being unknown, it was unmissed.

The Lady Rowena, with three of her attendants standing at her back, and arranging her hair ere she lay down to rest, was seated in the sort of throne already mentioned, and looked as if born to exact general homage. The Pilgrim acknowledged her claim to it by a low genuflection.

"Rise, Palmer," said she, graciously. "The defender of the absent has a right to favourable reception from all who value truth, and honour manhood." She then said to her train, "Retire, excepting only Elgitha; I would speak with this holy Pilgrim."

The maidens, without leaving the apartment, retired to its further extremity, and sat down on a small bench against the wall, where they remained mute as statues, though at such a distance that their whispers could not have interrupted the conversation of their mistress.

"Pilgrim," said the lady, after a moment's pause, during which she seemed uncertain how to address him; "you this night mentioned a name—I mean," she said, with a sort of effort, "the name of Ivanhoe, in the halls where by nature and kindred it should have sounded most acceptably; and yet, such is the perverse course of fate, that of many whose hearts must have throbbed at the sound, I only dare ask you where, and in what condition, you left him of whom you spoke?—We heard, that, having remained in Palestine, on account of his impaired health, after the departure of the English army, he had experienced the persecution of the French faction, to whom the Templars are known to be attached."

"I know little of the Knight of Ivanhoe," answered the Palmer, with a troubled voice. "I would I knew him better, since you, lady, are interested in his fate. He hath, I believe, surmounted the persecution of his enemies in Palestine, and is on the eve of returning to England, where you, lady, must know better than I, what is his chance of happiness."

The Lady Rowena sighed deeply, and asked more particularly when the Knight of Ivanhoe might be expected in his native country, and whether he would not be exposed to great dangers by the road. On the first point, the Palmer professed ignorance; on the second, he said that the voyage might be safely made by the way of Venice and Genoa, and from thence through France to England. "Ivanhoe," he said, "was so well acquainted with the language and manners of the French, that there was no fear of his incurring any hazard during that part of his travels."

"Would to God," said the Lady Rowena, "he were here safely arrived, and able to bear arms in the approaching tourney, in which the chivalry of this land are expected to display their address and valour. Should Athelstane of Coningsburgh obtain the prize, Ivanhoe is like to hear evil tidings when he reaches England. How looked he, stranger, when you last saw him? Had disease laid her hand heavy upon his strength and comeliness?"

"He was darker," said the Palmer, "and thinner, than when he came from Cyprus in the train of Cœur de Lion, and care seemed to sit heavy on his brow; but I approached not his presence, because he is unknown to me."

"He will," said the lady, "I fear, find little in his native land to clear those clouds from his countenance. Thanks, good Pilgrim, for your information concerning the companion of my childhood. Maidens," she said, "draw near—offer the sleeping cup to this holy man, whom I will no longer detain from repose."

One of the maidens presented a silver cup, containing a rich mixture of wine and spice, which Rowena barely put to her lips. It was then offered to the Palmer, who, after a low obeisance, tasted a few drops.

"Accept this alms, friend," continued the lady, offering a piece of gold, "in acknowledgment of thy painful travel, and of the shrines thou hast visited."

The Palmer accepted the boon with another low reverence, and followed Elgitha out of the apartment.

In the anti-room he found his attendant Anwold, who, taking the torch from the hand of the waiting-maid, conducted him with more haste than ceremony to an exterior and ignoble part of the building, where a number of small apartments, or rather cells, served for sleeping places to the lower order of domestics, and to strangers of mean degree.

"In which of these sleeps the Jew?" said the Pilgrim.

"The unbelieving dog," answered Anwold, "kennels in the cell next your holiness. St Dunstan, how it must be scraped and cleansed ere it be again fit for a Christian!"

"And where sleeps Gurth the swineherd?" said he.

"Gurth," replied the bondsman, "sleeps in the cell on your right, as the Jew in that to your left; you serve to keep the child of circumcision separate from the abomination of his tribe. You might have occupied a more honourable place had you accepted of Oswald's invitation."

"It is well as it is," said the Palmer; "the company, even of a Jew, can hardly spread contamination through an oaken partition."

So saying, he entered the cabin allotted to him, and taking the torch from the domestic's hand, thanked him and wished him good night. Having shut the door of his cell, he placed the torch in a candlestick made of wood, and looked around his sleeping apartment, the furniture of which was of the most simple kind. It consisted of a rude wooden stool, and still ruder hutch or bed-frame, stuffed with clean straw, and accommodated with two or three sheep's skins by way of bed-clothes.

The Palmer, having extinguished his torch, threw himself, without taking off any part of his clothes, on this rude couch, and slept, or at least retained his recumbent posture, until the earliest sunbeams found their way through the little grated window, which served at once to admit both air and light to his uncomfortable cell. He then started up, and after repeating his matins, and adjusting his dress, he left it, and entered that of Isaac the Jew, lifting the latch as gently as he could.

The inmate was lying in troubled slumber upon a couch similar to that on which the Palmer himself had passed the night. Such parts of his dress as the Jew had laid aside on the preceding evening, were disposed carefully around his person, as if to prevent the hazard of their being abstracted during his slumbers. There was a trouble on his brow amounting almost to agony. His hands and arms moved convulsively, as if struggling with the night-mare; and besides several ejaculations in Hebrew, the following were distinctly heard in the Norman-English, or mixed language of the country. "For the sake of the God of Abraham, spare an unhappy old man! I am poor, I am pennyless—should your irons wrench my limbs asunder, I could not gratify you!"

The Palmer awaited not the end of the Jew's vision, but stirred him with his pilgrim's staff. The touch probably associated, as is usual, with some of the apprehensions excited by his dream; for the old man started up, his grey hair standing almost erect upon his head, and huddling some part of his garments about him, while he held the detached pieces with the tenacious grasp of a falcon, he fixed upon the

Palmer his keen black eyes, expressive of wild surprise and of bodily apprehension.

"Fear nothing from me, Isaac," said the Palmer, "I come as your friend."

"The God of Israel requite you," said the Jew, greatly relieved; "I dreamed—but Father Abraham be praised, it was but a dream." Then collecting himself, he added in his usual tone, "And what may it be your pleasure to want at so early an hour with the poor Jew?"

"It is to tell you," said the Palmer, "that if you leave not this mansion instantly, and travel not with some haste, your journey may prove a dangerous one."

"Holy Father," said the Jew, "whom could it interest to endanger so poor a wretch as I am?"

"The purpose you can best guess," said the Pilgrim; "but rely on this, that when the Templar crossed the hall yesternight, he spoke to his Musselman slaves in the Saracen language, which I well understand, and charged them this morning to watch the journey of the Jew, to seize upon him when at a convenient distance from the mansion, and to conduct him to the castle of Philip de Malvoisin, or to that of Reginald Front-de-Bœuf."

It is impossible to describe the extremity of terror which seized upon the Jew at this information, and seemed at once to overpower his whole faculties. His arms fell down to his sides, and his head drooped on his breast, his knees bent under his weight, every nerve and muscle of his frame seemed to collapse and lose its energy, and he sunk at the foot of the Palmer, not in the fashion of one who intentionally stoops, kneels, or prostrates himself to excite compassion, but like a man borne down on all sides by the pressure of some invisible force which crushes him to the earth without the power of resistance.

"Holy God of Abraham!" was his first exclamation, folding and elevating his wrinkled hands, but without raising his grey head from the pavement; "Oh! holy Moses! O! blessed Aaron! the dream is not dreamed for nought, and the vision cometh not in vain! I feel their irons already tear my sinews! I feel the rack pass over my body like the saws and harrows and axes of iron over the men of Rabbah and of the cities of the children of Ammon!"

"Stand up, Isaac, and hearken to me," said the Palmer, who viewed the extremity of his distress with a compassion in which contempt was largely mingled; "you have cause for your terror, considering how your brethren have been used, in order to extort from them their hoards, both by princes and nobles; but stand up, I say, and I will point out to you the means of escape. Leave this mansion instantly, while its inmates sleep sound after the last night's revel. I will guide you by the secret paths of the forest, known as well to me as to any forester that ranges it, and I will not leave you till you are under safe conduct of some chief or baron going to the tournament, whose good will you have probably the means of securing."

As the ears of Isaac received the hopes of escape which this speech intimated, he began gradually, and inch by inch as it were, to raise himself up from the ground, until he fairly rested upon his knees, throwing back his long grey hair and beard, and fixing his keen black eyes upon the Palmer's face, with a look expressive at once of hope and fear, not unmingled with suspicion. But when he heard the concluding part of the sentence, his original terror appeared to revive in full force, and he dropt once more on his face, exclaiming, "*I* possess the means of securing good will! alas! there is but one road to the favour of a Christian, and how can the poor Jew find it, whom extortions have already reduced to the misery of Lazarus?" Then, as if suspicion had overpowered his other feelings, he suddenly exclaimed, "For the love of God, young man, betray me not—for the sake of the Great Father who made us all, Jew as well as Gentile, Israelite and Ishmaelite—do me no treason! I have not means to secure the good-will of a Christian beggar, were he rating it at a single penny." As he said these last words, he raised himself and grasped the Palmer's mantle with a look of the most earnest entreaty. The Pilgrim extricated himself, as if there were contamination in the touch.

"Wert thou loaded with all the wealth of thy tribe," he said, "what interest have I to injure thee?—In this dress I am vowed to poverty, nor do I change it for aught save a horse and a coat of mail. Yet think not that I care for thy company, or propose myself advantage by it; remain here if thou wilt—Cedric the Saxon may protect thee."

"Alas!" said the Jew, "he will not let me travel in his train—Saxon or Norman will be equally ashamed of the poor Israelite; and to travel by myself through the domains of Philip de Malvoisin and Reginald Front-de-Bœuf—Good youth, I will go with you!—Let us haste—let us gird up our loins—let us flee!—Here is thy staff, why wilt thou tarry?"

"I tarry not," said the Pilgrim, giving way to the urgency of his companion; "but I must secure the means of leaving this place—follow me."

He led the way to the adjoining cell, which, as the reader is apprised, was occupied by Gurth the swine-herd.—"Arise, Gurth," said the Pilgrim, "undo the postern gate, and let out the Jew and me."

Gurth, whose occupation, though now held so mean, gave him as much consequence in Saxon England as that of Eumæus in Ithaca, was offended at the familiar and commanding tone assumed by the

Palmer. "The Jew leaving Rotherwood," said he, raising himself on his elbow, and looking superciliously at him without quitting his pallet, "and travelling in company with the Palmer to boot"——

"I should as soon have dreamt," said Wamba, who entered the apartment at the instant, "of his stealing away with a gammon of bacon."

"Nevertheless," said Gurth, again laying down his head on the wooden log, which served him for a pillow, "both Jew and Gentile must be content to abide the opening of the great gate—we suffer no visitors to depart by stealth at these unseasonable hours."

"Nevertheless," said the Pilgrim, in a commanding tone, "you will not, I think, refuse me that favour."

So saying, he stooped over the bed of the recumbent swine-herd, and whispered something in his ear in Saxon. Gurth started up as if electrified. The Pilgrim, raising his finger in an attitude as if to express caution, added, "Gurth, beware—thou art wont to be prudent. I say, undo the postern—thou shalt know more anon."

With hasty alacrity Gurth obeyed him, while Wamba and the Jew followed, both wondering at the sudden change in the swine-herd's demeanour.

"My mule, my mule?" said the Jew, as soon as they stood without the postern.

"Fetch him his mule," said the Pilgrim; "and, hearest thou,—let me have another, that I may bear him company till he is beyond these parts—I will return it safely to some of Cedric's train at Ashby. And do thou"—he whispered the rest in Gurth's ear.

"Willingly, most willingly shall it be done," said Gurth, and instantly departed to execute the commission.

"I wish I knew," said Wamba, when his comrade's back was turned, "what you Palmers learn in the Holy Land."

"To say our prayers, fool," answered the Pilgrim, "to repent our sins, and to mortify ourselves with fasting, vigils, and long prayers."

"Something more potent than that," answered the Jester; "for when would repentance or prayer make Gurth do a courtesy, or fasting or vigil persuade him to lend you a mule?—I trow you might as well have told his favourite black boar of thy vigils and penance, and wouldst have gotten as civil an answer."

"Go to," said the Pilgrim, "thou art but a Saxon fool."

"Thou say'st well," said the Jester; "had I been born a Norman, as I think thou art, I would have had luck on my side, and been next door to a wise man."

At this moment Gurth appeared on the opposite side of the moat with the mules. The travellers crossed the ditch upon a draw-bridge of only two planks breadth, the narrowness of which was matched with the straitness of the postern, and with a little wicket in the exterior palisade, which gave access to the forest. No sooner had they reached the mules, than the Jew, with hasty and trembling hands, secured upon the saddle a small bag of blue buckram, which he took from under his cloak, containing, as he muttered, "a change of raiment—only a change of raiment." Then getting upon the animal with more alacrity and haste than could have been anticipated from his years, he lost no time in so disposing the skirts of his gaberdine as to conceal completely from observation the burthen which he had thus exposed *en croupe*.

The Pilgrim mounted with more deliberation, reaching, as he departed, his hand to Gurth, who kissed it with the utmost possible veneration. The swine-herd stood gazing after the travellers until they were lost under the boughs of the forest path, when he was disturbed from his reverie by the voice of Wamba.

"Knowest thou," said the Jester, "my good friend Gurth, that thou art strangely courteous and most unwontedly pious on this summer morning—I would I were a black Prior or a barefoot Palmer, to avail myself of thy unwonted zeal and courtesy—certes, I would make more out of it than a kiss of the hand!"

"Thou art no fool thus far, Wamba," answered Gurth, "though thou arguest from appearances, and the wisest of us can do no more—But it is time for us to look after my charge."

So saying, he turned back to the mansion, attended by the Jester.

Meanwhile the travellers continued to press on their journey with a dispatch which argued the extremity of the Jew's fears, since persons at his age are seldom fond of rapid motion. The Palmer, to whom every path and outlet in the wood appeared to be familiar, led the way through the most devious paths, and more than once excited anew the suspicion of the Israelite, that he intended to betray him into some ambuscade of his enemies.

His doubts might have been indeed pardoned; for, except perhaps the flying fish, there was no race existing on the earth, in the air, or the waters, who were the object of such an unintermitting, general, and relentless persecution as the Jews of this period. Upon the slightest and most unreasonable pretences, as well as upon accusations the most absurd and groundless, their persons and property were exposed to every turn of popular fury; for Norman, Saxon, Dane, and Briton, however adverse these races were to each other, contended which should look with greatest detestation upon a people, whom it was accounted a point of religion to hate, to revile, to despise, to plunder, and to persecute. The kings of the Norman race, and the independent nobles, who followed their example in all acts of tyranny, maintained against this devoted people a persecution of a more regular, calculated, and self-interested kind. It is a well-known story of King John, that he confined a wealthy Jew in one of the royal castles, and daily caused one of his teeth to be torn out, until, when the jaw of the unhappy Israelite was half disfurnished, he consented to pay a large sum, which it was the tyrant's object to extort from him. The little ready money which was in the country was chiefly in possession of this persecuted people, and the nobility hesitated not to follow the example of their sovereign, in wringing it from them by every species of oppression, and even personal torture. Yet the passive courage inspired by the love of gain induced the Jews to dare the various evils to which they were subjected, in consideration of the immense profits which they were enabled to realize in a country naturally so wealthy as England. In spite of every species of discouragement, and even of a special court of taxations, called the Jews' Exchequer, erected for the very purpose of despoiling and distressing them, the Jews increased, multiplied, and accumulated huge sums, which they transferred from one hand to another by means of bills of exchange—an invention for which commerce is said to be indebted to them, and which enabled them to transfer their wealth from land to land, that when threatened with oppression in one country, their treasure might be secured in another.

The obstinacy and avarice of the Jews being thus in a measure placed in opposition to the fanaticism and tyranny of those under whom they lived, seemed as it were to increase in proportion to the persecution with which they were visited; and the immense wealth they usually acquired in commerce, while it frequently placed them in danger, was at other times used to extend their influence and to secure to them a certain degree of protection. On these terms they lived, and their character, influenced accordingly, was watchful, suspicious, and timid—yet obstinate, uncomplying, and skilful in evading the dangers to which they were exposed.

When the travellers had pushed on at a rapid rate through many devious paths, the Palmer at length broke silence.

"That large decayed oak," he said, "marks the boundaries over which Front-de-Bœuf claims authority—we are long since far from those of Malvoisin. There is now no fear of pursuit."

"May the wheels of their chariots be taken off," said the Jew, "like those of the host of Pharaoh, that they may drive heavily!—But leave me not, good Pilgrim—Think but of that fierce and savage Templar, with his Saracen slaves—they will regard neither territory, nor manor, nor lordship."

"Our road," said the Palmer, "should here separate; for it beseems not men of my character and thine to travel together longer than needs must be. Besides, what succour couldst thou have from me, a peaceful Pilgrim, against two armed heathens?"

"O good youth," answered the Jew, "thou canst defend me, and I know thou wouldst. Poor as I am, I will requite it—not with money, for money, so help me my Father Abraham, I have none—but——"

"Money and recompense," said the Palmer interrupting him, "I have already said I require not of thee. Guide thee I can; and it may be, even defend thee; since to protect a Jew against a Saracen, can scarce be accounted unworthy of a Christian. Therefore, Jew, I will see thee safe under some fitting escort. We are now not far from the town of Sheffield, where thou mayest easily find many of thy tribe with whom to take refuge."

"The blessing of Jacob be upon thee, good youth!" said the Jew; "in Sheffield I can harbour with my kinsman Zareth, and find some means of travelling forth with safety."

"Be it so," said the Palmer; "at Sheffield then we part, and half an hour's riding will bring us in sight of that town."

The half hour was spent in perfect silence on both parts; the Pilgrim perhaps disdaining to address the Jew, except in case of absolute necessity, and the Jew not presuming to force a conversation with a person, whose journey to the Holy Sepulchre gave a sort of sanctity to his character. They paused on the top of a gently rising bank, and the Pilgrim pointing to the town of Sheffield, which lay beneath them, repeated the words, "Here then we part."

"Not till you have had the poor Jew's thanks," said Isaac; "for I presume not to ask you to go with me to my kinsman Zareth's, who might aid me with some means of repaying your good offices."

"I have already said," answered the Pilgrim, "that I desire no recompense. If, among the huge list of thy debtors, thou wilt, for my sake, spare the gyves and the dungeon to some unhappy Christian who stands in thy danger, I shall hold this morning's service to thee well bestowed."

"Stay, stay," said the Jew, laying hold of his garment; "something would I do more than this, something for thyself.—God knows the Jew is poor—yes, Isaac is the beggar of his tribe—but forgive me should I guess what thou most lackest at this moment."

"If thou wert to guess truly," said the Palmer, "it is what thou canst not supply, wert thou as wealthy as thou say'st thou art poor."

"As I say?" echoed the Jew; "O! believe it, I say but the truth; I am a plundered, indebted, distressed man. Hard hands have wrung from me my goods, my money, my ships, and all that I possessed—Yet I can tell thee what thou lackest, and it may be, supply it too. Thy wish even now is for a horse and armour."

The Palmer started, and turned suddenly towards the Jew:—"What fiend prompted that guess?" said he hastily.

"No matter," said the Jew, smiling, "though it be a true one—and, as I can guess thy want, so I can supply it."

"But consider," said the Palmer, "my character, my dress, my vow."

"I know you Christians," replied the Jew, "and that the noblest of you will take the staff and sandal in superstitious penance, and walk afoot to visit the graves of dead men."

"Blaspheme not, Jew," said the Pilgrim sternly.

"Forgive me!" said the Jew; "I spoke rashly. But there dropt words from you last night and this morning, that, like sparks from flint, shewed the metal within; and in the bosom of that Palmer's gown, is hidden a knight's chain and spurs of gold. They glanced as you stooped over my bed in the morning."

The Pilgrim could not forbear smiling. "Were thy garments searched by as curious an eye, Isaac," said he, "what discoveries might not be made?"

"No more of that," said the Jew, changing colour; and drawing forth his writing materials in haste, as if to stop the conversation, he began to write upon a piece of paper which he supported on the top of his yellow cap, without dismounting from his mule. When he had finished, he delivered the scroll, which was in the Hebrew character, to the Pilgrim, saying, "In the town of Leicester all men know the rich Jew, Kirjath Jairam of Lombardy; give him this scroll—he hath on sale six Milan harnesses, the worst would suit a crowned head—ten goodly steeds, the worst might mount a king, were he to do battle for his throne. Of these he will give thee thy choice, with every thing else that can furnish thee forth for the tournament: when it is over, thou wilt return them safely—unless thou shouldst have wherewith to pay their value to the owner."

"But, Isaac," said the Pilgrim, smiling, "dost thou know that in these sports, the arms and steed of the knight who is unhorsed are forfeit to his victor? Now I may be unfortunate, and so lose what I cannot replace or repay."

The Jew looked somewhat astounded at this possibility; but collecting his courage, he replied hastily, "No—no—no—It is impossible—I will not think so. The blessing of our Father will be upon thee. Thy lance will be powerful as the rod of Moses."

So saying, he was turning his mule's head away, when the Palmer, in his turn, took hold of his gaberdine. "Nay, but Isaac, thou knowest not all the risk. The steed may be slain, the armour injured—for I will spare neither horse nor man. Besides, those of thy tribe give nothing for nothing; something there must be paid for their use."

The Jew twisted himself in his saddle, like a man in a fit of the cholic; but his better feelings predominated over those which were most familiar to him. "I care not," he said, "I care not—let me go. If there is damage, it will cost you nothing—if there is usage money, Kirgath Jairam will forgive it for the sake of his kinsman Isaac. Fare thee well!—Yet hark thee, good youth," said he, turning about, "thrust thyself not too forward into this vain hurley burley—I speak not for endangering the steed, and coat of armour, but for the sake of thine own life and limbs."

"Gramercy for thy caution," said the Palmer, again smiling; "I will use thy courtesy frankly, and it will go hard with me but I will requite it."

They parted, and took different roads for the town of Sheffield.

Chapter Seven

Knights, with a long retinue of their squires,
In gaudy liveries march and quaint attires;
One laced the helm, another held the lance,
A third the shining buckler did advance.
The courser paw'd the ground with restless feet,
And snorting foam'd and champ'd the golden bit.
The smiths and armourers on palfreys ride,
Files in their hands, and hammers at their side;
And nails for loosen'd spears, and thongs for shields provide.
The yeomen guard the streets in seemly bands;
And clowns come crowding on, with cudgels in their hands.

Palamon and Arcite.

THE CONDITION of the English nation was at this time sufficiently miserable. King Richard was absent a prisoner, and in the power of the perfidious and cruel Duke of Austria. Even the very place of his captivity was uncertain, and his fate but very imperfectly known to the generality of his subjects, who were, in the mean time, a prey to every species of subaltern oppression.

Prince John, in league with Philip of France, Richard's mortal enemy, was using every species of influence with the Duke of Austria, to prolong the captivity of his brother Richard, to whom he stood indebted for so many favours. In the mean time he was strengthening his faction in the kingdom, of which he proposed to dispute the succession, in case of the king's death, with the legitimate heir, Arthur Duke of Brittany, son of Geoffrey Plantagenet, the elder brother of John. This usurpation, it is well known, he afterwards effected.

His own character being light, profligate, and perfidious, John easily attached to his person and faction, not only all who had reason to dread the resentment of Richard for proceedings during his absence, but also the numerous class of "lawless resolutes," whom the crusades had turned back on their country, accomplished in the vices of the east, impoverished in substance, and hardened in character, and who placed their hopes of harvest in civil commotion.

To these causes of public distress and apprehension, fall to be added the multitude of outlaws, who, driven to despair by the oppression of the feudal nobility, and the severe exercise of the forest laws, banded together in large gangs, and keeping possession of the forests and the wastes, set at defiance the justice and magistracy of the country. The nobles themselves, each fortified within his own castle, and playing the petty sovereign over his own domains, were the leaders of bands scarce less lawless and oppressive than those of the avowed depredators. To maintain these retainers, and to support the extravagance and magnificence which their pride induced them to affect, the nobility borrowed sums of money from the Jews at the most usurious interest, which gnawed into their estates like consuming cankers, scarce to be cured unless when circumstances gave them an opportunity of getting free by exercising upon their creditors some act of unprincipled violence.

Under the various burdens imposed by this unhappy state of affairs, the people of England suffered deeply for the present, and had yet more dreadful cause to fear for the future. To augment their misery, a contagious disorder of a dangerous nature spread through the land; and, rendered more virulent by the uncleanness, the indifferent food, and the wretched lodging of the lower classes, swept off many whose fate the survivors were tempted to envy, as exempting them from the evils which were to come.

Yet amid these accumulated distresses, the poor as well as the rich, the vulgar as well as the noble, in the event of a tournament, which was the grand spectacle of that age, felt as much interest as the half-starved citizen of Madrid, who has not a real left to buy provisions for his family, feels in the issue of a bull-feast. Neither duty nor infirmity could keep youth or age from such exhibitions. The Passage of Arms, as it was called, which was to take place at Ashby, in the county of Leicester, as champions of the first renown were to take the field in the presence of Prince John himself, who was expected to grace the lists, had attracted universal attention, and an immense confluence of persons of all ranks hastened upon the appointed morning to the place of combat.

The scene was singularly romantic. On the verge of a wood, which approached to within a mile of the town of Ashby, was an extensive meadow of the finest and most beautiful green turf, surrounded on one side by the forest, and fringed on the other by straggling oak-trees, some of which had grown to an immense size. The ground, as if fashioned on purpose for the martial display which was intended, sloped gradually down on all sides to a level bottom, which was inclosed for the lists with strong palisades, forming a space of a quarter of a mile in length, and about half as broad. The form was square, save that the corners were considerably rounded off, in order to afford more convenience for the spectators. The openings for the entry of the combatants were at the northern and southern extremities of the lists, accessible by strong wooden gates, each wide enough to admit two horsemen riding abreast. At each of these portals were stationed two heralds, attended by six trumpets, as many pursuivants, and a strong body of men-at-arms for maintaining order, and ascertaining the quality of the knights who proposed to engage in this martial game.

On a platform beyond the southern entrance, formed by a natural elevation of the ground, were pitched five magnificent pavilions, adorned with pennons of russet and black, the chosen colour of the five knights challengers. The cords of the tents were of the same colour. Before each pavilion was suspended the shield of the knight by whom it was occupied, and beside it stood his squire, quaintly disguised as a savage or sylvan man, or in some other fantastic dress, according to the taste of his master, and the character which he was pleased to assume during the game. The central pavilion, as the place of honour, had been assigned to Brian de Bois-Guilbert, whose renown, in all games of chivalry, no less than his connection with the knights who had undertaken this Passage of Arms, had occasioned him to be eagerly received into the company of the challengers, and even adopted as a chief. On one side of his tent were pitched those of Reginald Front-de-Bœuf and Philip de Malvoisin, and on the other was the pavilion of Hugh de Grantmesnil, a noble baron in the vicinity, whose ancestor had been Lord High Steward of England in the time of the Conqueror and his son William Rufus. Ralph de Vipont, a Knight of St John of Jerusalem, who had some ancient possessions at a place called Heather, near Ashby-de-la-Zouche, occupied the fifth pavilion. From the entrance into the lists, a gently sloping passage, ten yards in breadth, led up to the platform on which the tents were pitched. It was strongly secured by a palisade on each side, as was the esplanade in front of the pavilions, and the whole was guarded by men-at-arms.

The northern access to the lists terminated in a similar entrance of thirty feet in breadth, at the extremity of which was a large inclosed space for such knights as might be disposed to enter the lists with the challengers, behind which were placed tents containing refreshments of every kind for their accommodation, with armourers, farriers, and other attendants in readiness to give their services wherever they were necessary.

The exterior of the lists was in part occupied by temporary galleries spread with tapestry and carpets, and accommodated with cushions for the convenience of those ladies and nobles who were expected to attend upon the tournament. A narrow space, betwixt these galleries and the lists, gave accommodation for yeomanry and spectators of a better degree than the mere vulgar, and might be compared to the pit of a theatre. The promiscuous multitude arranged themselves upon large banks of turf prepared for the purpose, which, aided by the natural elevation of the ground, enabled them to look over the galleries and obtain a fair view into the lists. Besides the accommodation which these stations afforded, many hundreds had perched themselves on the branches of the trees which surrounded the meadow, and even the steeple of a country church, at some distance, was crowded with spectators.

It only remains to notice respecting the general arrangement, that one gallery in the very centre of the eastern side of the lists, and consequently exactly opposite to the spot where the shock of the combat must take place, was raised higher than the others, more richly decorated, and graced by a sort of throne and canopy, on which the royal arms were emblazoned. Squires, pages, and yeomen in rich liveries, waited around this place of honour, which was designed for Prince John and his attendants. Opposite to this royal gallery was another, elevated to the same height on the western side of the lists; and more gaily, if less sumptuously decorated, than that destined for the Prince himself. A train of pages and of young maidens, the most beautiful who could be selected, gaily dressed in fancy habits of green and pink, surrounded a throne decorated with the same colours. Among pennons and flags bearing wounded hearts, burning hearts, bleeding hearts, bows and quivers, and all the common-place emblems of the triumphs of Cupid, a blazoned inscription informed the spectators that this seat of honour was designed for *La Royne de la Beaulté et des Amours*. But who the Queen of Beauty and of Love was to prove, no one was prepared to guess.

Meanwhile, spectators of every description thronged forwards to occupy their respective stations, and not without many quarrels concerning those which they were entitled to hold. Some of these were settled by the men-at-arms with brief ceremony; the shafts of their battle-axes, and pummels of their swords, being readily employed as arguments to convince the most refractory. Others, which involved the rank of more elevated persons, were determined by the heralds, or by the two marshals of the field, William de Wyvil, and Stephen de Martival, who, armed at all points, rode up and down the lists to enforce and preserve good order among the spectators.

Gradually the galleries became filled with knights and nobles, in their robes of peace, whose long and rich-tinted mantles were contrasted with the gayer and more splendid habits of the ladies, that, in a greater proportion than even the men themselves, thronged to witness a sport, which one would have thought too bloody and dangerous to afford them much pleasure. The lower and interior space was soon filled by substantial yeomen and burghers, and such of the lesser gentry, as, from modesty, poverty, or dubious title, durst not assume any higher place. It was of course amongst these that the most frequent disputes for precedence occurred.

"Dog of an unbeliever," said an old man, whose thread-bare tunic bore witness to his poverty, as his sword and dagger and golden chain intimated his pretensions to rank,—"whelp of a she-wolf! darest thou press upon a Christian, and a Norman gentleman of the blood of Montdidier?"

This rough expostulation was addressed to no other than our acquaintance Isaac, who, richly and even magnificently dressed in a gaberdine ornamented with lace and lined with fur, endeavoured to make place in the foremost row beneath the gallery for his daughter, the beautiful Rebecca, who had joined him at Ashby, and who was now hanging on her father's arm, not a little terrified for the displeasure which seemed generally excited by her parent's presumption. But Isaac, though we have seen him sufficiently timid upon other occasions, knew well that upon the present he had nothing to fear. It was not in places of general resort, or where their equals were assembled, that any avaricious or malevolent noble durst offer him injury. On such occasions the Jews were under the protection of the general law; and if that proved a weak assurance, it usually happened that there were among the persons assembled some barons, who, for their own interested motives, were ready to act as their protectors. On the present occasion, Isaac felt more than usually confident, being aware that Prince John was even then in the very act of negociating a large loan from the Jews of York, to be secured upon certain jewels and lands. Isaac's own share in this transaction was considerable, and he well knew that the Prince's eager desire to bring it to a conclusion would insure him his protection in the dilemma in which he stood.

Emboldened by these considerations, the Jew pursued his point, and jostled the Norman Christian, without respect either to his descent, quality, or religion. The complaints of the old man, however, excited the indignation of the byestanders. One of these, a stout well-set yeoman, arrayed in Lincoln green, having twelve arrows in his belt, with a baldric and badge of silver, and a bow of six feet length in his hand, turned short round, and while his countenance, which constant exposure to weather had rendered brown as a hazel nut, grew darker with anger, he advised the Jew to remember that all the wealth he had acquired by sucking the blood of his miserable victims had but swelled him like a bottled spider, which might be overlooked while it kept in a corner, but would be crushed if it ventured into the light. This intimation, delivered in Norman-English with a firm voice and a stern aspect, made the Jew shrink back, and he would have probably withdrawn himself altogether from a vicinity so dangerous, had not the attention of every one been called to the sudden entrance of Prince John, who even then entered the lists, attended by a numerous and gay train, consisting partly of laymen, partly of churchmen, as light in their dress, and as gay in their demeanour as their companions. Among the latter was the Prior of Jorvaulx, in the most gallant trim which a dignitary of the church could exhibit. Fur and gold was not spared in his garments; and the points of his boots, out-heroding the preposterous fashion of the time, turned up so very far, as to be attached, not to his knees merely, but to his very girdle, and effectually prevented him from putting his foot into the stirrup. This, however, was a slight inconvenience to the gallant Abbot, who, perhaps, even rejoiced in the opportunity to display his accomplished horsemanship before so many spectators, especially of the fair sex. The rest of Prince John's retinue consisted of the favourite leaders of his mercenary troops, some marauding barons and profligate attendants upon the court, with several Knights Templars and Knights of St John.

It may be here remarked, that the knights of these two orders were accounted hostile to King Richard, having adopted the side of Philip of France in the long train of disputes which took place betwixt that monarch and the lion-hearted King of England. It was the well-known consequence of this discord that Richard's repeated victories were rendered fruitless, his romantic attempts to besiege Jerusalem were disappointed, and the fruit of all the glory which he had acquired dwindled into an uncertain truce with the Sultan Saladin. With the same policy which had dictated the conduct of their brethren in the Holy Land, the Templars and Hospitalars in England and Normandy attached themselves to the faction of Prince John, having little reason to desire the return of Richard to England, or the succession of

Arthur, his legitimate heir. For the opposite reason, Prince John hated and contemned the few Saxon families of consequence which subsisted in England, and omitted no opportunity of mortifying and affronting them; being conscious that his person and pretensions were disliked by them, as well as by the greater part of the English commons, who feared farther innovation upon their rights and liberties from a sovereign of John's licentious and tyrannical disposition.

Attended by this gallant equipage, himself well mounted, and splendidly dressed in crimson and in gold, bearing upon his hand a falcon, and having his head covered by a rich fur bonnet, adorned with a circle of precious stones, from which his long curled hair escaped and overspread his shoulders, Prince John, upon a grey and high-mettled palfrey, caracoled within the lists at the head of his jovial party, laughing loud with his train, and eyeing with all the boldness of royal criticism the beauties who adorned the lofty galleries.

Those who remarked in the countenance of the Prince a dissolute audacity, mingled with extreme haughtiness and indifference to the feelings of others, could not yet deny to his countenance that sort of comeliness which belongs to an open set of features, well formed by nature, modelled by art to the usual rules of courtesy, yet so far frank and honest that they seemed as if they disclaimed to conceal the natural workings of the soul. Such an expression is often mistaken for manly frankness, when in truth it arises from the reckless indifference of a libertine disposition, conscious of superiority of birth, of wealth, or of some other adventitious advantage, totally unconnected with personal merit. To those who did not think so deeply, and they were the greater number by a hundred to one, the splendour of Prince John's *rheno*, (*i.e.* fur tippet,) of his cloak lined with the most costly sables, his maroquin boots and golden spurs, together with the grace with which he managed his palfrey, were sufficient to merit their clamorous applause.

In his joyous caracole round the lists, the attention of the Prince was called by the commotion, not yet subsided, which had attended the ambitious movement of Isaac towards the higher places of the assembly. The quick eye of Prince John instantly recognised the Jew, but was much more agreeably attracted by the beautiful daughter of Zion, who, terrified by the tumult, clung close to the arm of her aged father.

The figure of Rebecca might indeed have compared with the proudest beauties of England, even though it had been judged by as shrewd a connoisseur as Prince John. Her form was exquisitely symmetrical, and was shewn to advantage by a sort of Eastern dress, which she wore according to the fashion of the females of her nation. Her turban of yellow silk suited well with the darkness of her complexion. The brilliancy of her eyes, the superb arch of her eyebrows, her well-formed aquiline nose, her teeth as white as pearl, and the profusion of her sable tresses, which, each arranged in its own little spiral of twisted curls, fell down upon as much of a snow-white neck and bosom as a simarre of the richest Persian silk, exhibiting flowers in their natural colours embossed upon a purple ground, permitted to be visible—all these constituted a combination of loveliness, which yielded not to the loveliest of the maidens who surrounded her. It is true, that of the golden and pearl-studded clasps, which closed her vest from the throat to the waist, the three uppermost were left unfastened on account of the heat, which something enlarged the prospect to which we allude. A diamond necklace, with pendants of inestimable value, were by this means also made more conspicuous. The feather of an ostrich, fastened in her turban by an agraffe set with brilliants, was another distinction of the beautiful Jewess, scoffed and sneered at by the proud dames who sat above her, but secretly envied by those who affected to deride them.

"By the bald scalp of Abraham," said Prince John, "yonder Jewess must be the very model of that perfection, whose charms drove frantic the wisest king who ever lived. What say'st thou, Prior Aymer? —By the Temple, which my wiser brother Richard proved unable to recover, she is the very Bride of the Canticles!"

"The rose of Sharon and the lily of the valley," answered the Prior in a sort of snuffling tone; "but your Grace must remember she is still but a Jewess."

"Ay!" added Prince John, without heeding him, "and there is my Mammon of unrighteousness too—the Marquis of Marks, the Baron of Byzants, contesting for place with pennyless dogs, whose thread-bare cloaks have not a single cross in their pouches to keep the devil from dancing there. By the body of St Mark, my prince of supplies, with his lovely Jewess, shall have a place in the gallery—What is she, Isaac? Thy wife or thy daughter, that Eastern houri that thou lockest under thy arm?"

"My daughter Rebecca, so please your grace," answered Isaac, with a low congee, nothing embarrassed by the Prince's salutation, in which, however, there was at least as much mockery as courtesy.

"The wiser man thou," said John, with a peal of laughter, in which his gay followers obsequiously joined. "But, daughter or wife, she should be preferred according to her beauty and thy merits.—Who sits above there?" he continued, bending his eye on the gallery. "Saxon churls!—out upon them!—let them sit close, and make room for my prince of usurers and his lovely daughter. I'll make the hinds know they must share the high places of the synagogue with those whom the synagogue properly belongs to."

Those who occupied the gallery to whom this injurious and unpolite speech was addressed, were the family of Cedric the Saxon, with that of his ally and kinsman Athelstane of Coningsburgh, a personage, who, on account of his descent from the last Saxon monarchs of England, was held in the highest respect by all the Saxon natives of the north of England. But with the blood of this ancient royal race, many of their infirmities had descended to Athelstane. He was comely in countenance, bulky and strong in person, and in the flower of his age —yet inanimate in expression, dull-eyed, heavy-browed, inactive and sluggish in all his motions, and so slow in resolution, that the soubriquet of one of his ancestors was conferred upon him, and he was very generally called Athelstane the Unready. His friends, and he had many, who, as well as Cedric, were passionately attached to him, contended that this sluggish temper arose not from want of courage, but from mere want of decision; others alleged that his hereditary vice of drunkenness had obscured his faculties, never of a very acute order, and that the passive courage and meek good-nature which remained behind, were merely the dregs of a temper that might have been valuable, but of which all the valuable parts had flown off in the progress of a long course of brutal debauchery.

It was to this person, such as we have described him, that the Prince addressed his imperious command to make place for Isaac and Rebecca. Athelstane, utterly confounded at an order which the manners and feelings of the times held so injuriously insulting, unwilling to obey, yet undetermined how to resist, opposed only the *vis inertiæ* to the will of John; and, without stirring or making any motion whatsoever of obedience, opened his large grey eyes, and stared at the Prince with an astonishment which had in it something extremely ludicrous. But the impatient John regarded it in no such light.

"The Saxon porker," he said, "is either asleep or minds me not—Prick him with your lance, Bracy," speaking to a knight who rode near him, the leader of a band of free companions, or Condottieri, that is, of mercenaries belonging to no particular nation, but attached for the time to any prince by whom they were paid. There was a murmur even among the attendants of Prince John; but Bracy, whose profession freed him from all scruples, extended his long lance over the space which separated the gallery from the lists, and would have executed the commands of the Prince before Athelstane the Unready had recovered presence of mind sufficient even to draw back his person from the weapon, had not Cedric, as prompt as his companion was tardy, unsheathed, with the speed of lightning, the short sword which he wore, and at a single blow severed the point of the lance from the handle. The blood rushed into the countenance of Prince John. He swore one of his deepest oaths, and was about to utter some threat corresponding in violence, when he was diverted from his purpose, partly by his own attendants, who gathered around him conjuring him to be patient, partly by a general exclamation of the crowd uttered in loud applause of the spirited conduct of Cedric. The Prince rolled his eyes in indignation, as if to select some safe and easy victim; and chancing to encounter the firm glance of the same archer whom we have already noticed, and who seemed to persist in his gesture of applause, in spite of the frowning aspect which the Prince bent upon him, he demanded his reason for clamouring thus.

"I always add my hollo," said the yeoman, "when I see a good shot, or a gallant blow."

"Say'st thou?" answered the Prince; "then thou can'st hit the white thyself, I'll warrant."

"A woodsman's mark, and at woodsman's distance, I can hit," answered the yeoman.

"And Wat Tyrrell's mark, at a hundred yards," said a voice from behind, but by whom uttered could not be discerned.

This allusion to the fate of William Rufus, his grandfather, at once incensed and alarmed Prince John. He satisfied himself, however, with commanding the men-at-arms, who surrounded the lists, to keep an eye on that braggart, pointing to the yeoman.

"By St Grizzel," he added, "we will try his own skill, who is so ready to give his voice to the feats of others."

"I shall not fly the trial," said the yeoman, with the composure which marked his whole deportment.

"Meanwhile, stand up, ye Saxon churls," said the fiery Prince; "for, by the light of heaven, since I have said it, the Jew shall have his seat amongst ye!"

"By no means, an it please your grace—it is not fit for such as us to sit with the rulers of the land," said the Jew, whose ambition for precedence, though it had led him to dispute place with the extenuated and impoverished descendant of the line of Montdidier, by no means urged him to an intrusion upon the privileges of the wealthy Saxons.

"Up, infidel dog, when I command you," said Prince John, "or I will have thy swarthy hide stript off, and tanned for horse-furniture."

Thus urged, the Jew began to ascend the steep and narrow steps which led up to the gallery.

"Let me see," said the Prince, "who dare stop him," fixing his eye on Cedric, whose attitude intimated his intention to hurl the Jew down headlong.

The catastrophe was prevented by the clown Wamba, who, springing betwixt his master and Isaac, and exclaiming, in answer to the Prince's defiance, "Marry, that will I," opposed to the beard of the Jew a shield of brawn, which he plucked from beneath his cloak, and with which, doubtless, he had furnished himself, lest the tournament should have proved longer than his appetite could endure abstinence. Finding the abomination of his tribe opposed to his very nose, while the Jester, at the same time, flourished his wooden sword above his head, the Jew recoiled, missed his footing, and rolled down the steps, —an excellent jest to the spectators, who set up a loud laughter, in which Prince John and his attendants heartily joined.

"Deal me the prize, cousin Prince," said Wamba; "I have vanquished my foe in fair fight with sword and shield," he added, brandishing the brawn in one hand and the wooden sword in the other.

"Who, and what art thou, noble champion?" said Prince John, still laughing.

"A fool by right of descent," answered the Jester; "I am Wamba, the son of Witless, who was the son of Weatherbrain, who was the son of an Alderman."

"Make room for the Jew in front of the lower ring," said Prince John, not unwilling perhaps to seize an apology to desist from his original purpose; "to place the vanquished beside the victor were false heraldry."

"Knave upon fool were worse," answered the Jester, "and Jew upon bacon worst of all."

"Gramercy! good fellow," cried Prince John, "thou pleasest me—Here, Isaac, lend me a handful of byzants."

As the Jew, stunned by the request, afraid to refuse, and unwilling to comply, fumbled in the furred bag which hung by his girdle, and was perhaps endeavouring to ascertain how few coins might pass for a handful, the Prince stooped from his jennet and settled Isaac's doubts by snatching the pouch itself from his side; and flinging to Wamba a couple of the gold pieces which it contained, he pursued his career round the lists, leaving the Jew to the derision of those around him, and himself receiving as much applause from the spectators as if he had done some honest and honourable action.

Chapter Eight

At this the challenger with fierce defy
His trumpet sounds; the challenged makes reply:
With clangour rings the field, resounds the vaulted sky;
Their visors closed, their lances in the rest,
Or at the helmet pointed or the crest,
They vanish from the barrier, speed the race,
And spurring see decrease the middle space.
Palamon and Arcite.

IN THE MIDST of Prince John's cavalcade, he suddenly stopt, and, appealing to the Prior of Jorvaulx, declared the principal business of the day had been forgotten.

"By my halidom," said he, "we have forgotten, Sir Prior, to name the fair sovereign of Love and of Beauty, by whose white hand the palm is to be distributed. For my part, I am liberal in my ideas, and I care not if I give my vote for the black-eyed Rebecca."

"Holy Virgin," answered the Prior, turning up his eyes in horror, "a Jewess!—We should deserve to be stoned out of the lists; and I am not yet old enough to be a martyr. Besides, I swear by my patron saint, that she is far inferior to the lovely Saxon, Rowena."

"Saxon or Jew," answered the Prince, "Saxon or Jew, dog or hog, what matters it? I say, name Rebecca, were it only to mortify the Saxon churls."

A murmur arose even among his own immediate attendants.

"This passes a jest, my lord," said Bracy; "no knight here will lay lance in rest if such an insult is attempted."

"It is the mere wantonness of insult," said one of the oldest of Prince John's followers, Waldemar Fitzurse; "and if your grace attempt it, cannot but prove ruinous to your projects."

"I entertained you, sir," said John, reining up his palfrey haughtily, "for my follower, but not for my counsellor."

"Those who follow your grace in the paths which you tread," said Waldemar, but speaking in a low voice, "acquire the right of counsellors; for your interest and safety are not more deeply gaged than theirs."

From the tone in which this was spoken, John saw the necessity of acquiescence. "I did but jest," he said; "and you turn upon me like so many adders. Name whom you will, in the fiend's name, and please yourselves."

"Nay, nay," said Bracy, "let the fair sovereign's throne remain unoccupied, until the conqueror shall be named, and then let him choose the lady by whom it shall be filled. It will add another grace to his triumph, and teach fair ladies to prize the love of valiant knights, who can exalt them to such distinction."

"If Brian de Bois-Guilbert gain the prize," said the Prior, "I will gage my rosary that I name the Sovereign of Love and Beauty."

"Bois-Guilbert," answered Bracy, "is a good lance; but there are others around these lists, Sir Prior, who will not fear to encounter him."

"Silence, sirs," said Waldemar, "and let the Prince assume his seat. The knights and spectators are alike impatient, the time advances, and highly fit it is that the sport should commence."

Prince John, though not yet a monarch, had in Waldemar Fitzurse all the inconveniences of a favourite minister, who, in serving his sovereign, must always do so in his own way. He complied, however, although his disposition was precisely of that kind, which is apt to be obstinate upon trifles, and, assuming his throne, and being surrounded by his followers, gave signal to the heralds to proclaim the laws of the tournament, which were briefly as follows.

First, the five challengers were to undertake all comers.

Secondly, any knight proposing to combat, might, if he pleased, select a special antagonist from among the challengers, by touching his shield. If he did so with the reverse of his lance, the trial of skill was made with what were called the arms of courtesy, that is, lances at whose extremity a piece of round flat board was fixed, so that no danger was encountered, save from the shock of the horses and spears. But if the shield was touched with the sharp end of the lance, the combat was understood to be at *outrance*, that is, the knights were to fight with sharp weapons, as in actual battle.

Thirdly, when the knights present had accomplished their vow, by each of them breaking five lances, the Prince was to declare the victor in the first day's tourney, who should receive as prize a war-horse of exquisite beauty and matchless strength; and in addition to this reward of valour, it was now announced, he should have the peculiar honour of naming the Queen of Love and Beauty, by whom the prize should be given on the ensuing day.

Fourthly, it was announced, that, on the second day, there should be a general tournament, in which all the knights present, who were desirous to win praise, might take part; and being divided into two bands of equal numbers, might fight it out manfully, until the signal was given by Prince John to cease the combat. The elected Queen of Love and Beauty was then to crown the knight whom the Prince should adjudge to have borne himself best in this second day, with a coronet composed of thin gold plate, cut into the shape of a laurel crown. On this second day, the knightly games ceased. But on that which followed, feats of archery, of bull-baiting, and other popular amusements, were to be practised for the more immediate amusement of the populace. In this manner did Prince John endeavour to lay the foundation of a popularity, which he was perpetually throwing down by some inconsiderate act of wanton aggression upon the feelings and prejudices of the people.

The lists now presented a most splendid spectacle. The sloping galleries were crowded with all that was noble, great, wealthy, and beautiful in the northern and midland parts of England; and the contrast of the various dresses of these dignified spectators, rendered the view as gay as it was rich, while the interior and lower space, filled with the substantial burgesses and yeomen of merry England, formed, in their more plain attire, a dark fringe, or border, around this circle of brilliant embroidery, relieving, and, at the same time, setting off its splendour.

The heralds ceased their proclamation with their usual cry of "Largesse, largesse, gallant knights;" and gold and silver pieces were showered on them from the galleries, it being a high point of chivalry to exhibit liberality towards those whom the age accounted the secretaries at once, and historians of honour. The bounty of the spectators was acknowledged by the customary shouts of "Love of Ladies—Death of Champions—Honour to the Generous—Glory to the Brave!" To which the more humble spectators added their acclamations, and a numerous band of trumpeters the flourish of their martial instruments. When these sounds had ceased, the heralds withdrew from the lists in gay and glittering procession, and none remained within them save the marshals of the field, who, armed cap-a-pee, sat on horseback, motionless as statues, at the opposite ends of the lists. Meantime, the enclosed space at the northern extremity of the lists, large as it was, was now completely crowded with knights desirous to prove their skill against the challengers, and, when viewed from the galleries, presented the appearance of a sea of waving plumage, intermixed with glistening helmets, and tall lances, to the extremities of which were, in many cases, attached small pennons of about a span's-breadth, which, fluttering in the air as the breeze caught them, joined with the restless motion of the feathers to add liveliness to the scene.

At length the barriers were opened, and five knights, chosen by lot, advanced slowly into the area; a single champion riding in front, and the other four following in pairs. All were splendidly armed, and my Saxon authority (in the Wardour Manuscript,) records at great length their devices, their colours, and the embroidery of their horse trappings. It is unnecessary to be particular on these subjects. To borrow lines from a contemporary poet, who has written but too little—

> The knights are dust,
> And their good swords are rust,
> Their souls are with the saints, we trust.

Their escutcheons have long mouldered from the walls of their castles. Their castles themselves are but green mounds and shattered ruins—the place that once knew them, knows them no more—nay, many a race since theirs has died out and been forgotten in the very land which they occupied, with all the authority of feudal proprietors and feudal lords. What then would it avail the reader to know their names, or the evanescent symbols of their martial rank!

Now, however, no whit anticipating the oblivion which awaited their names and feats, the champions advanced through the lists, restraining their fiery steeds, and compelling them to move slowly, while, at the same time, they exhibited their paces, together with the grace and dexterity of the riders. As the procession entered the lists, the sound of a wild Barbaric music was heard from behind the tents of the challengers, where the performers were concealed. It was of eastern origin, having been brought from the Holy Land; and the mixture of the cymbals and bells seemed to bid welcome at once, and defiance, to the knights as they advanced. With the eyes of an immense concourse of spectators fixed upon them, the five knights advanced up to the platform upon which the tents of the challengers stood, and there separating themselves, each touched slightly, and with the reverse of his lance, the shield of the antagonist to whom he wished to oppose himself. The lower orders of spectators in general—nay, many of the higher, and it is even said several of the ladies, were rather disappointed at the champions choosing the arms of courtesy. For the same sort of persons, who, in the present day, applaud most highly the deepest tragedies, were then interested in a tournament exactly in proportion to the danger incurred by the champions engaged.

Having intimated their more pacific purpose, the champions retreated to the extremity of the lists, where they remained drawn up in a line; while the challengers, sallying each from his pavilion, mounted their horses, and headed by Brian de Bois-Guilbert, descended from the platform, and opposed themselves individually to the knights who had touched their respective shields.

At the flourish of clarions and trumpets, they started out against each other at full gallop, and such was the superior dexterity or good fortune of the challengers, that those opposed to Bois-Guilbert, Malvoisin, and Front-de-Bœuf, rolled on the ground. The antagonist of Grantmesnil, instead of bearing his lance-point fair against the crest or the shield of his enemy, swerved so much from the direct line as to break his weapon athwart the person of his opponent—a circumstance which was accounted more disgraceful than being actually unhorsed; because the one might happen from accident, whereas the other evinced awkwardness and want of management of the weapon and of the horse. The fifth knight alone maintained the honour of his party, and parted fairly with the Knight of St John, both splintering their lances without advantage on either side.

The shouts of the multitude, together with the acclamations of the heralds, and the clangour of the trumpets, announced the triumph of the victors and the defeat of the vanquished. The former retreated to their pavilions, and the latter, gathering themselves up as they could, withdrew from the lists in disgrace and dejection, to agree with their victors concerning the redemption of their arms and their horses, which, according to the laws of the tournament, they had forfeited. The fifth of their number alone tarried in the lists long enough to be greeted with the applauses of the spectators, amongst which he retreated, to the aggravation, doubtless, of his companions' mortification.

A second and a third party of knights took the field; and although they had various success, yet, upon the whole, the advantage decidedly remained with the challengers, not one of whom lost his seat or swerved from his charge—misfortunes which befel one or two of their antagonists in each encounter. The spirits, therefore, of those opposed to them, seemed to be considerably damped by their continued success. Three knights only appeared on the fourth entry, who, avoiding the shields of Bois-Guilbert and Front-de-Bœuf, contented themselves with touching those of the three other knights, who had not altogether manifested the same strength and dexterity. This politic selection did not alter the luck of the field, the challengers were still successful: one of their antagonists was overthrown, and both the others failed in the *attaint*, that is, in striking the helmet and shield of their antagonist firmly and strongly, with the lance held in a direct line, so that the weapon might break, unless the champion was overthrown.

After this fourth encounter, there was a considerable pause; nor did it appear that any one was very desirous of renewing the encounter. The spectators murmured among themselves; for, among the challengers, Malvoisin and Front-de-Bœuf were unpopular from their characters, and the others, except Grantmesnil, as strangers and foreigners.

But none shared the general feeling of dissatisfaction so keenly as Cedric the Saxon, who saw, in each advantage gained by the Norman challengers, a repeated triumph over the honour of England. His own education had taught him no skill in the games of chivalry, although, with the arms of his Saxon ancestors, he had manifested himself, on many occasions, a brave and determined soldier. He looked anxiously to Athelstane, who had learned the accomplishments of the age, as if desiring that he should make some personal effort to recover the victory which was passing into the hands of the Templar and his associates. But, though both stout of heart and strong of person, Athelstane had a disposition too inert and unambitious to make the exertions which Cedric seemed to expect from him.

"The day is against England, my lord," said Cedric, in a marked tone; "are you not tempted to take the lance?"

"I shall tilt to-morrow," answered Athelstane, "in the *melée*; it is not worth while to arm myself to-day."

Two things displeased Cedric in this speech. It contained the Norman word *melée*, (to express the general conflict,) and it evinced some indifference to the honour of the country; but it was spoken by Athelstane, whom he held in such profound respect, that he would not trust himself to canvass his motives or his foibles. Moreover, he had no time to make any remark, for Wamba thrust in his word, observing, "It was better to be the best man among a hundred, than the best man of two."

Athelstane took the observation as a serious compliment; but Cedric, who better understood the Jester's meaning, darted at him a severe and menacing look; and lucky it was for the Jester, perhaps, that the time and place prevented his receiving, notwithstanding his place and service, more sensible marks of his master's resentment.

The pause in the tournament was still uninterrupted, excepting by the voices of the heralds exclaiming—"Love of ladies, splintering of lances! stand forth, gallant knights, fair eyes look upon your deeds."

The music also of the challengers breathed from time to time wild bursts expressive of triumph or defiance, while the clowns grudged a holiday which seemed to pass away in inactivity; and old knights and nobles lamented in whispers the decay of martial spirit, spoke of the triumph of their younger days, but agreed that the land did not now supply dames of such transcendent beauty as had animated the jousts of former times. Prince John began to talk to his attendants about making ready the banquet, and the necessity of adjudging the prize to Brian de Bois-Guilbert, who had, with a single spear, overthrown two knights, and foiled a third.

At length, as the Saracenic music of the challengers concluded one of those long and high flourishes with which they had broken the silence of the lists, it was answered by a solitary trumpet, which breathed a note of defiance from the northern extremity. All eyes were turned to see the new champion which these sounds announced, and no sooner were the barriers opened than he paced into the lists. As far as could be judged of a man sheathed in armour, the new adventurer did not greatly exceed the middle size, and seemed to be rather slender than strongly made. His suit of armour was formed of steel, richly inlaid with gold, and the device on his shield was a young oak-tree pulled up by the roots, with the Spanish word *Desdichado*, signifying Disinherited. He was mounted on a gallant black horse, and as he passed through the lists he gracefully saluted the Prince and the ladies by lowering his lance. The dexterity with which he managed his horse, and something of youthful grace which he displayed in his manner, won him the favour of the multitude, which some of the lower classes expressed by crying, "Touch Ralph de Vipont's shield—touch the Hospitaller's shield; he has the least sure seat, he is your cheapest bargain."

The champion, moving onward amid these well-meant hints, ascended the platform by the sloping alley which led to it from the lists, and, to the astonishment of all present, riding straight up to the central pavillion, struck with the sharp end of his spear the shield of Brian de Bois-Guilbert until it rung again. All stood astonished at his presumption, but none more than the redoubted Knight whom he had thus defied to mortal combat.

"Have you confessed yourself, brother," said the Templar, "and have you heard mass this morning, that you peril your life so frankly?"

"I am fitter to meet death than thou art," answered the Disinherited Knight, for by this name the stranger had recorded himself in the books of the tourney.

"Then take your place in the lists," said De Bois-Guilbert, "and look your last upon the sun; for this night thou shalt sleep in paradise."

"Gramercy for thy courtesy," replied the Disinherited Knight, "and to requite it, I advise thee to take a fresh horse and a new lance, for by my honour you will need both."

Having expressed himself thus confidently, he reined his horse backwards down the slope which he had ascended, and compelled him in the same manner to move backwards through the lists, till he reached the northern extremity, where he remained stationary, in expectation of his antagonist. This feat of horsemanship again attracted the applause of the multitude.

However incensed at his adversary for the precautions which he recommended, Brian de Bois-Guilbert did not neglect his advice; for his honour was too nearly concerned, to permit his neglecting any means which might ensure victory over his presumptuous opponent. He changed his horse for a fresh one of great strength and spirit. He chose a new and tough spear, lest the wood of the former might have been strained in the previous encounters he had sustained. Lastly, he laid aside his shield, which had received some little damage, and received another from his squires. His first had only borne the general device of his order, representing two knights riding upon one horse, an emblem expressive of the original humility and poverty of the Templars, qualities which they had since exchanged for the arrogance and wealth that finally occasioned their suppression. Bois-Guilbert's new shield bore a raven in full flight, holding in its claws a skull, and bearing the motto *Gare le Corbeau*.

When the two champions stood opposed to each other at the two extremities of the lists, the public expectation was strained to the highest pitch. Few augured the possibility that the encounter could terminate well for the Disinherited Knight, yet his courage and gallantry secured the general good wishes of the spectators.

The trumpets had no sooner given the signal, than the champions vanished from their posts with the speed of lightning, and closed in the centre of the lists with the shock of a thunder-bolt. The lances burst into shivers up to the very grasp, and it seemed at the moment that both knights had fallen, for the shock had made each horse recoil backwards upon its hams. The address of the riders recovered their steeds by use of the bridle and spur, and having glared on each other for an instant with eyes which seemed to flash fire through the bars of their visors, each made a demi-volte, and retiring to the extremity of the lists, received a fresh lance from the attendants.

A loud shout from the spectators, waving of scarfs and handkerchiefs, and general acclamations, attested the interest taken by the spectators in this encounter; the most equal, as well as the best performed, which had graced the day. But no sooner had the knights resumed their station, than the clamour of applause was hushed into a silence, so deep and so dead, that it seemed the multitude were afraid even to breathe.

A few minutes pause having been allowed, that the combatants and their horses might recover breath, Prince John with his truncheon signed to the trumpets to sound the onset. The champions a second time sprung from their stations, and closed in the centre of the lists, with the same speed, the same dexterity, the same violence, but not the same equal fortune as before.

In this second encounter, the Templar aimed at the centre of his antagonist's shield, and struck it so fair and forcibly that his spear went to shivers, and the Disinherited Knight reeled in his saddle. On the other hand, that champion had, in the beginning of his career, directed the point of his lance towards Bois-Guilbert's shield, but, changing his aim almost in the moment of encounter, he addressed it to the helmet, a mark more difficult to hit, but which, if attained, rendered the shock more irresistible. Yet, even at this disadvantage, the Templar sustained his high reputation; and had not the girths of his saddle burst, he might not have been unhorsed. As it chanced, however, saddle, horse, and man, rolled on the ground under a cloud of dust.

To extricate himself from the stirrups and fallen steed, was to the Templar scarce the work of a moment; and stung with madness, both at his disgrace and at the acclamations with which it was hailed by the spectators, he drew his sword and waved it in defiance of his conqueror. The Disinherited Knight sprung from his steed, and also unsheathed his sword. The marshals of the field, however, spurred their horses between them, and reminded them, that the laws of the tournament did not, on the present occasion, permit this species of encounter.

"We shall meet again, I trust," said the Templar, casting a resentful glance at his antagonist; "and where there are none to separate us."

"If we do not," said the Disinherited Knight, "the fault shall not be mine. On foot or horseback, with spear, with axe, or with sword, I am alike ready to encounter thee."

More and angrier words would have been exchanged, but the marshals, crossing their lances betwixt them, compelled them to separate. The Disinherited Knight returned to his first station, and Bois-Guilbert to his tent, where he remained for the rest of the day in an agony of despair.

Without alighting from his horse, the conqueror called for a bowl of wine, and opening the beaver or lower part of his helmet, announced that he quaffed it "To all true English hearts, and to the confusion of foreign tyrants." He then commanded his trumpet to sound a defiance to the challengers, and desired a herald to announce to them, that he should make no election, but was willing to encounter them in the order in which they pleased to advance against him.

The gigantic Front-de-Bœuf, armed in sable armour, was the first who took the field. He bore on a white shield a black bull's head, half defaced by the numerous encounters which he had undergone, and bearing the arrogant motto, *Cave, Adsum*. Over this champion the Disinherited Knight obtained a slight but decisive advantage. Both champions broke their lances fairly, but Front-de-Bœuf, who lost a stirrup in the encounter, was adjudged to have the disadvantage.

In the stranger's third encounter with Sir Philip Malvoisin, he was equally successful; striking that baron so forcibly on the casque, that the laces of the helmet broke, and Malvoisin, only saved from falling by being unhelmed, was declared vanquished like his companions.

In his fourth encounter with De Grantmesnil, the Disinherited Knight shewed as much courtesy as he had hitherto evinced courage and dexterity. De Grantmesnil's horse, which was young and violent, reared and plunged in the course of the career so as to disturb the rider's aim, and the stranger, declining to take the advantage which this accident afforded him, raised his lance, and passing his antagonist without touching him, wheeled his horse and rode again to his own end of the lists, offering his antagonist, by a herald, the chance of a second encounter. This De Grantmesnil declined, avowing himself vanquished as much by the courtesy as by the address of his opponent.

Ralph de Vipont summed up the list of the stranger's triumphs, being hurled to the ground with such force, that the blood gushed from his nose and his mouth, and he was borne senseless from the lists.

The acclamations of thousands applauded the unanimous award of the Prince and Marshals, announcing that day's honours to the Disinherited Knight.

Chapter Nine

————In the midst was seen
A lady of a more majestic mien,
By stature and by beauty mark'd their sovereign queen.
* * * * * * *
And as in beauty she surpass'd the choir,
So nobler than the rest was her attire;
A crown of ruddy gold enclosed her brow,
Plain without pomp, and rich without a shew;
A branch of agnus castus in her hand,
She bore aloft her symbol of command.

The Flower and the Leaf.

WILLIAM DE WYVIL and Stephen de Martival, the marshals of the field, were the first to offer their congratulations to the victor, praying him, at the same time, to suffer his helmet to be unlaced, or, at least, that he would raise his visor ere they conducted him to receive the prize of the day's tournay from the hands of Prince John. The Disinherited Knight, with all knightly courtesy, declined their request, alleging, that he could not at this time suffer his face to be seen, for reasons which he had assigned to the heralds when he entered the lists. The marshals were perfectly satisfied with this reply, for amidst the capricious vows by which knights were accustomed to bind themselves in those days of chivalry, there was none more common than those by which they engaged to remain incognito for a certain space, or until some particular adventure was atchieved. The marshals, therefore, pressed no farther into the mystery of the Disinherited Knight, but announcing to Prince John the conqueror's desire to remain unknown, they requested permission to bring him before his grace, in order that he might receive the reward of his valour.

John's curiosity was excited by the mystery observed by the stranger; and, being already displeased with the issue of the tournament, in which the challengers whom he favoured had been successively defeated by one knight, he answered haughtily to the marshals, "By the light of Our Lady's brow, this same knight hath been disinherited, as well of his courtesy as of his lands, since he desires to appear before us without uncovering his face.—Wot ye, my lords," he said, turning round to his train, "who this gallant can be, that bears himself thus proudly?"

"I cannot guess," answered De Bracy, "nor did I think there had been within the four seas that girth Britain a champion that could bear down these five knights in one day's jousting. By my faith, I shall never forget the force with which he shocked De Vipont. The poor Hospitaller was hurled from his saddle like a stone from a sling."

"Boast not of that," said a Knight of St John, who was present; "your Temple champion had no better luck. I saw Bois-Guilbert roll thrice over, grasping his hands full of sand at every turn."

Bracy, being attached to the Templars, would have replied, but was prevented by Prince John. "Silence, sirs!" he said; "what unprofitable debate have we here?"

"The victor," said De Wyvil, "still waits the pleasure of your highness."

"It is our pleasure," answered John, "that he do so wait until we learn whether there is not some one who can at least guess at his name and quality. Should he remain there till night, he has had work enough to keep him warm."

"Your grace," said Waldemar Fitzurse, "will do less than due honour to the victor, if you compel him to wait till we tell your highness that which we cannot know; at least *I* can form no guess—unless he be one of the good lances who accompanied King Richard, and who are now straggling homeward from the Holy Land."

"It may be the Earl of Salisbury," said Bracy; "he is about the same pitch."

"Sir Thomas de Multon, the knight of Gilsland rather," said Fitzurse; "Salisbury is bigger in the bones." A whisper arose among the train, but by whom first suggested could not be ascertained. "It might be the King—it might be Richard Cœur de Lion himself."

"Over God's forbode!" said Prince John, involuntarily turning at the same time as pale as death, and shrinking as if blighted by a flash of lightning; "Waldemar!—Bracy! brave knights and gentlemen, remember your promises and stand truly by me."

"Here is no danger impending," said Waldemar Fitzurse; "are you so little acquainted with the gigantic limbs of your father's son, as to think they can be held within the circumference of yonder suit of armour?—De Wyvil and Martival, you will best serve the Prince by bringing forward the victor to the throne, and ending an error that has conjured all the blood from his cheeks.—Look at him more closely," he continued, "your highness will see that he wants three inches of King Richard's height, and twice as much of his shoulder-breadth. The very horse he backs, could not have carried King Richard through a single course."

While he was yet speaking, the marshals brought forward the Disinherited Knight to the foot of a wooden flight of steps which formed the ascent from the lists to Prince John's throne. Still discomposed with the idea that his brother, so much injured, and to whom he was so much indebted, had suddenly arrived in his native kingdom, even the distinctions pointed out by Fitzurse did not altogether remove the Prince's apprehensions; and while, with a short and embarrassed eulogy upon his valour, he caused to be delivered to him the war-horse assigned as the prize, he trembled lest from the barred visor of the mailed form before him, an answer might be returned in the deep and awful accents of Richard the Lion-hearted.

But the Disinherited Knight spoke not a word in reply to the compliment of the Prince, which he only acknowledged by a profound obeisance.

The horse was led into the lists by two grooms richly dressed, the animal itself being fully accoutred with the richest war-furniture; which, however, scarcely added to its value in the eyes of those who were judges. Laying one hand upon the pummel of the saddle, the Disinherited Knight vaulted at once upon the back of the steed without making use of the stirrup, and, brandishing aloft his lance, rode twice around the lists, exhibiting the points and paces of the animal with the skill of a perfect horseman.

The appearance of vanity, which might otherwise have been attributed to this display, was removed by the propriety shewn in exhibiting to the best advantage the princely reward with which he had been just honoured, and the Knight was again greeted by the acclamations of all present.

In the meanwhile the bustling Prior of Jorvaulx had reminded Prince John, in a whisper, that the victor must now display his good judgment, instead of his valour, by selecting from among the beauties who graced the galleries a lady, who should fill the throne of the Queen of Beauty and of Love, and deliver the prize of the tourney upon the ensuing day. The Prince accordingly made a sign with his truncheon, as the Knight passed him in his second career around the lists. The Knight turned towards the throne, and sinking his lance, until the point was within a foot of the ground, remained motionless, as if expecting John's commands; while all admired the sudden dexterity with which he instantly reduced his fiery steed from a state of violent motion and high excitation to the stillness of an equestrian statue.

"Sir Disinherited Knight," said Prince John, "since that is the only title by which we can address you, it is now your duty, as well as privilege, to name the fair lady, who, as Queen of Honour and of Love, is to preside over next day's festival. If, as a stranger in our land, you should require the aid of other judgment to guide your own, we can only say that Alicia, daughter of our gallant knight Waldemar Fitzurse, has at our court been long held the first in beauty as in place. Nevertheless, it is your undoubted prerogative to confer on whom you please this crown, by the delivery of which to the lady of your choice the election of to-morrow's Queen will be formal and complete.—Raise your lance."

The Knight obeyed, and Prince John placed upon its point a coronet of green satin, having around its edge a circlet of gold, the upper edge of which was relieved by arrow points and hearts placed interchangeably, like the strawberry leaves and balls upon a ducal crown.

In the broad hint which he dropped respecting the daughter of Waldemar Fitzurse, John had more than one motive, each the offspring of a mind, which was a strange mixture of carelessness and presumption with low artifice and cunning. He wished to banish from the minds of the chivalry around him his own indecent and unacceptable jest respecting the Jewess Rebecca; he was desirous of conciliating Alicia's father Waldemar, of whom he stood in awe, and who had more than once shewn himself dissatisfied during the course of the day's proceedings. He had also a wish to establish himself in the good graces of the lady; for John was at least as licentious in his pleasures as profligate in his ambition. But besides all these reasons, he was desirous to raise up against the Disinherited Knight (towards whom he already entertained a strong dislike) a powerful enemy in the person of Waldemar Fitzurse, who was likely, he thought, highly to resent the injury done to his daughter, in case, as was not unlikely, the victor should make another choice.

And so indeed it proved. For the Disinherited Knight passed the gallery close to that of the Prince, in which the Lady Alicia was seated in the full pride of triumphant beauty, and, pacing forwards as slowly as he had hitherto rode swiftly around the lists, he seemed to exercise his right of examining the numerous fair faces which adorned that splendid circle.

It was worth while to see the different conduct of the beauties who underwent this examination, during the time it was going forward. Some blushed, some assumed an air of pride and dignity, some looked straight forward, and essayed to seem utterly unconscious of what was going on, some endeavoured to forbear smiling, and there were two or three who laughed outright. There were also some who dropped their veils over their charms; but, as the Wardour Manuscript says these were beauties of ten years standing, it may be supposed that, having had their full share of such vanities, they were willing to withdraw their claim, in order to give a fair chance to the rising beauties of the age.

At length the champion paused beneath the balcony in which the Lady Rowena was placed, and the expectation of the spectators was excited to the utmost.

It must be owned, that if an interest displayed in his success could have bribed the Disinherited Knight, the part of the lists before which he paused had merited his predilection. Cedric the Saxon, overjoyed at the discomfiture of the Templar, and still more so at the miscarriage of his two malevolent neighbours, Front-de-Bœuf and Malvoisin, had, with half his body stretched over the balcony, accompanied the victor in each course, not with his eyes only, but with his whole heart and soul. The Lady Rowena had watched the progress of the day with equal attention, though without betraying the same intense interest. Even the unmoved Athelstane had shewn symptoms of shaking off his apathy, when, calling for a huge goblet of muscadine, he quaffed it to the health of the Disinherited Knight.

Another group, stationed under the gallery occupied by the Saxons, had shewn no less interest in the fate of the day.

"Father Abraham!" said Isaac of York, when the first course was run betwixt the Templar and the Disinherited Knight, "how fiercely that Gentile rides! Ah, the good horse that was brought all the long way from Barbary, he takes no more care of him than if he were a wild ass's colt—and the noble armour, that was worth so many sequins to Joseph Pareira, the armourer of Milan, besides seventy in the hundred of profits, he cares for it as little as if he had found it in the highways!"

"If he risks his own person and limbs, father," said Rebecca, "in doing such a dreadful battle, he can scarce be expected to save his horse and armour."

"Child!" replied Isaac, somewhat heated, "thou knowest not what thou speakest—His neck and limbs are his own, but his horse and armour belong to——Holy Jacob! what was I about to say!—Nevertheless, it is a good youth—See, Rebecca! see, he is again about to go up to battle against the Philistine—Pray, child—pray for the safety of the good youth,—and of the speedy horse, and the rich armour.—God of my fathers!" he again exclaimed, "he hath conquered, and the uncircumcised Philistine hath fallen before his lance,—even as Ogg the King of Bashan, and Sihon, King of the Amorites, fell before the sword of our fathers!—Surely he shall take their gold and their silver, and their war-horses, and their armour of brass and of steel, for a prey and for a spoil."

The same anxiety did the worthy Jew display during every course that was run, seldom failing to hazard a hasty calculation concerning the value of the horse and armour which was forfeited to the champion upon each new success. There had been therefore no small interest taken in the success of the Disinherited Knight, by those who occupied the part of the lists before which he now paused.

Whether from indecision or some other motive of hesitation, the champion of the day remained stationary for more than a minute, while the eyes of the silent audience were rivetted upon his motions; and then, gradually and gracefully sinking the point of his lance, he deposited the coronet which it supported at the feet of the fair Rowena. The trumpets instantly sounded, while the heralds proclaimed the Lady Rowena the Queen of Beauty and of Love for the ensuing day, menacing with suitable penalties those who should be disobedient to her authority. They then repeated their cry of Largesse, to which Cedric, in the height of his joy, replied by an ample donative, and to which Athelstane, though less promptly, added one equally large.

There was some murmuring among the damsels of Norman descent, who were as much unused to see the preference given to a Saxon beauty, as the nobles were to sustain defeat in the games of chivalry which they themselves had introduced. But these sounds of disaffection were drowned by the popular shout of "Long live the Lady Rowena, the chosen and lawful Queen of Love and of Beauty!" to which many added, "Long live the Saxon Princess! long live the race of the immortal Alfred!"

However unacceptable these sounds might be to Prince John, and to those around him, he saw himself nevertheless obliged to confirm the nomination of the victor; and accordingly calling to horse, he left his throne, and mounting his jennett, accompanied by his train, he again entered the lists. The Prince paused a moment beneath the gallery of the Lady Alicia, to whom he paid his compliments, observing, at the same time, to those around him—"By my halidome, sirs! if the Knight's feats in arms have shewn that he hath limbs and sinews, his choice hath no less proved that his eyes are none of the clearest."

It was on this occasion, as during his whole life, John's misfortune not perfectly to understand the characters of those whom he wished to conciliate. Waldemar Fitzurse was rather offended than pleased at the Prince stating thus broadly an opinion that his daughter had been slighted.

"I know no right of chivalry," he said, "more precious or inalienable than that of each free knight to choose his lady-love by his own judgment. My daughter courts distinction from no one; and in her own character, and in her own sphere, will never fail to receive the full proportion of that which is her due."

Prince John replied not; but, spurring his horse, as if to give vent to his vexation, he made the animal bound forward to the gallery where Rowena was seated, with the crown still at her feet.

"Assume," he said, "fair lady, the mark of your sovereignty, to which none vows homage more sincerely than ourself; and if it please you to-day, with your noble sire and friends, to grace our banquet in the Castle of Ashby, we shall learn to know the empress to whose service we devote to-morrow."

Rowena remained silent, and Cedric answered for her in his native Saxon.

"The Lady Rowena," he said, "possesses not the language in which to reply to your courtesy, or to sustain her part in your festival. I also, and the noble Athelstane of Coningsburgh, speak only the language, and practise only the manners of our fathers. We therefore decline with thanks your courteous invitation to the banquet. To-morrow the Lady Rowena will take upon her the state to which she has been called by the free election of the victor Knight, confirmed by the acclamations of the people."

So saying, he lifted the coronet, and placed it upon Rowena's head, in token of her acceptance of the temporary authority assigned to her.

"What says he?" said Prince John, affecting not to understand the Saxon language, in which, however, he was well skilled. The purport of Cedric's speech was repeated to him in French. "It is well," he said; "to-morrow we will ourself conduct this mute sovereign to her seat of dignity.—You, at least, Sir Knight," he added, turning to the victor, who had remained near the gallery, "will this day share our banquet."

The Knight, speaking for the first time, in a low and hurried voice, excused himself by pleading fatigue, and the necessity of preparing for to-morrow's encounter.

"It is well," said Prince John haughtily; "although unused to such refusals, we will endeavour to digest our banquet as we may, though ungraced by the most successful in arms, and his elected Queen of Beauty."

So saying, he left the lists with his glittering train, and his departure was the signal for the breaking up and dispersion of the spectators.

Yet, with the vindictive memory proper to offended pride, especially when combined with conscious want of desert, John had hardly proceeded three paces, ere, turning around, he fixed an eye of stern resentment upon the yeoman who had displeased him in the early part of the day, and issued his commands to the men-at-arms who stood near—"On your life, suffer not that fellow to escape."

The yeoman stood the angry glance of the Prince with the same unvaried steadiness which had marked his former deportment, saying, with a smile, "I have no intention to leave Ashby until the day after to-morrow—I must see how Staffordshire and Leicestershire can draw their bows—Needwood and Charnwood must rear good archers."

"I," said Prince John to his attendants, but not in direct reply, "I will see how he can draw his own; and woe betide him unless his skill should prove some apology for his insolence."

"It is full time," said Bracy, "that the *outrecuidance* of these peasants should be restrained by some striking example."

Waldemar Fitzurse, who probably thought his patron was not taking the readiest road to popularity, shrugged up his shoulders and was silent. Prince John resumed his retreat from the lists, and the dispersion of the multitude became general.

In various routes, according to the different quarters from which they came, and in groups of various numbers, the spectators were seen retreating over the plain. By far the most numerous part streamed towards the town of Ashby, where many of the distinguished persons were lodged in the castle, and where others found accommodation in the town itself. Among these were most of the knights who had already appeared in the tournament, or who proposed to fight there the ensuing day, and who, as they rode slowly along, talking over the events of the day, were greeted with loud shouts by the populace. The same acclamations were bestowed upon Prince John, although he was indebted for them rather to the splendour of his appearance and train, than to the popularity of his character.

A more sincere and more general, as well as a better-merited acclamation, attended the victor of the day, until, anxious to withdraw himself from popular notice, he accepted the accommodation of one of those pavilions pitched at the extremities of the lists, the use of which was courteously tendered him by the marshals of the field.

Upon his retiring to his tent, many who had lingered in the lists, to look upon and form conjectures concerning him, also dispersed.

The signs and sounds of a tumultuous concourse of men lately crowded together in one place, and agitated by the same passing events, were now exchanged for the distant hum of voices of different groups retreating in all directions, and these speedily died away in silence. No other sounds were heard save the voices of the menials who stripped the galleries of their cushions and tapestry, in order to put them in safety for the night, and wrangled among themselves for the half-used bottles of wine and reliques of the refreshments which had been served round to the spectators.

Beyond the precincts of the lists more than one forge was erected; and these now began to glimmer through the twilight, announcing the toil of the armourers, which was to continue through the whole night, in order to repair or alter the armour which was to be used to-morrow.

A strong guard of men-at-arms, which was renewed at intervals, from two hours to two hours, surrounded the lists, and kept watch during the night.

Chapter Ten

> Thus, like the sad presaging raven, that tolls
> The sick man's passport in her hollow beak,
> And in the shadow of the silent night
> Doth shake contagion from her sable wings;
> Vex'd and tormented, runs poor Barrabas,
> With fatal curses towards these Christians.
>
> *Jew of Malta.*

THE DISINHERITED KNIGHT had no sooner reached his pavilion, than squires and pages in abundance tendered their services to disarm him, to bring fresh attire, and to offer him the refreshment of the bath. Their zeal on this occasion was perhaps sharpened by curiosity, since every one desired to know who the knight was that had gained so many laurels, yet had refused to lift his visor or to name his name. But their officious inquisitiveness was not gratified. The Disinherited Knight refused all other assistance save that of his own squire, or rather yeoman—a clownish-looking man, who, wrapt in a cloak of dark-coloured felt, and having his head and face half-buried in a Norman bonnet made of black fur, seemed to affect the incognito as much as his master. All others being excluded from the tent, this attendant relieved his master from the more burthensome parts of his armour, and placed food and wine before him, which the exertions of the day had rendered very acceptable.

He had scarcely finished a hasty meal, ere his menial announced to him that five men, each leading a barbed steed, desired to speak with him. The Disinherited Knight had exchanged his armour for the long robe usually worn by those of his condition, which, being furnished with a hood, concealed the features, when such was the pleasure of the wearer, almost as completely as the visor of the helmet itself; but the twilight, which was now fast darkening, would of itself have rendered a disguise unnecessary, unless to persons to whom the face of an individual chanced to be particularly well known.

The Disinherited Knight, therefore, stept boldly forth to the front of his tent, and found the squires of the challengers, whom he easily knew by their russet and black dresses, each of whom led his master's charger, loaded with the armour in which he had that day fought.

"According to the laws of chivalry," said the foremost of these men, "I, Baldwin de Oyley, squire to the redoubted Knight Brian de Bois-Guilbert, make offer to you, styling yourself the Disinherited Knight, of the horse and armour used by the said Brian de Bois-Guilbert in this day's passage of arms, leaving it with your nobleness to retain or to ransom the same, according to your pleasure; for such is the law of arms."

The other squires repeated nearly the same formula, and then stood to await the decision of the Disinherited Knight.

"To you, four sirs," replied the Knight, addressing those who had last spoken, "and to your honourable and valiant masters, I have one common reply. Commend me to the noble Knights, your masters, and say, I should do ill to deprive them of steeds and arms which can never be used by braver cavaliers.—I would I could here end my message to these gallant knights; but being, as I term myself, in truth and earnest, the Disinherited, I must be thus far bound to your masters, that they will, of their courtesy, be pleased to ransom their armour, since that which I wear I can hardly term mine own."

"We stand commissioned," answered the squire of Reginald Front-de-Bœuf, "to offer each a hundred zecchins in ransom of these horses and suits of armour."

"It is sufficient," said the Disinherited Knight. "Half the sum my present necessities compel me to accept; of the remaining half, distribute one moiety among yourselves, sir squires, and divide the other half betwixt the heralds and the pursuivants, and minstrels, and attendants."

The squires, with cap in hand, and low reverences, expressed their deep sense of a courtesy and generosity not often practised, at least upon a scale so extensive. The Disinherited Knight then addressed his discourse to Baldwin, the squire of Brian de Bois-Guilbert. "From your master," said he, "I will accept neither arms nor ransom. Say to him in my name, that our strife is not ended—no, not till we have fought as well with swords as with lances—as well on foot as on horseback. To this mortal quarrel he has himself defied me, and I shall not forget the challenge.—Meantime, let him be assured, that I hold him not as one of his companions, with whom I can with pleasure exchange courtesies; but rather as one with whom I stand upon terms of mortal defiance."

"My master," answered Baldwin, "knows how to requite scorn with scorn, and blows with blows, as well as courtesy with courtesy. Since you disdain to accept from him any share of the ransom at which you have rated the arms of the other knights, I must leave his armour and his horse here, being well assured that he will never mount the one nor wear the other."

"You have spoken well, good squire," said the Disinherited Knight, "well and boldly, as it beseemeth him to speak who answers for an absent master. Leave not, however, the horse and armour here. Restore them to thy master; or, if he scorns to accept them, retain them, good friend, for thine own use. So far as they are mine, I bestow them upon you freely."

Baldwin made a deep obeisance, and retired with his companions; and the Disinherited Knight entered the pavilion.

"Thus far, Gurth," said he, addressing his attendant, "the reputation of English chivalry hath not suffered in my hands."

"And I," said Gurth, "for a Saxon swine-herd, have not ill played the personage of a Norman squire-at-arms."

"Yea, but," answered the Disinherited Knight, "thou hast ever kept me in anxiety lest thy clownish bearing should discover thee."

"Tush!" said Gurth, "I fear discovery from none, saving my playfellow, Wamba the jester, of whom I could never discover whether he were most knave or fool. Yet I could scarce choose but laugh, when my old master passed so near to me, dreaming all the while that Gurth was keeping his porkers many a mile off, in the thickets and swamps of Rotherwood. If I am discovered——"

"Enough," said the Disinherited Knight, "thou knowest my promise."

"Nay, for that matter," said Gurth, "I will never fail my friend for fear of my skin-cutting. I have a tough hide, that will bear the scourge as well as any boar's hide in my herd."

"Trust me, I will requite the risk you run for my love, Gurth," said the Knight. "Meanwhile, I pray you to accept these ten pieces of gold."

"I am richer," said Gurth, putting them into his pouch, "than ever was swine-herd or bondsman."

"Take this bag of gold to Ashby," continued his master, "and find out Isaac the Jew of York, and let him pay himself for the horse and arms with which his credit supplied me."

"Nay, by St Dunstan," replied Gurth, "that I will not do."

"How, knave," replied his master, "wilt thou not obey my commands?"

"So they be honest, reasonable, and Christian commands," replied Gurth; "but this is none of these. To suffer the Jew to pay himself would be dishonest, for it would be cheating my master; and unreasonable, for it were the part of a fool; and unchristian, since it would be plundering a believer to enrich an infidel."

"See him contented, however, thou varlet," said the Disinherited Knight.

"I will do so," said Gurth, taking the bag under his cloak and leaving the apartment; "and it will go hard," he muttered, "but I content him with one-fourth of his own asking." So saying, he departed, and left the Disinherited Knight to his own perplexed ruminations; which, upon more accounts than it is now possible to communicate to the reader, were of a nature peculiarly agitating and painful.

We must now change the scene to the village of Ashby, or rather to a country house in its vicinity belonging to a wealthy Israelite, with whom Isaac, his daughter, and retinue, had taken up their quarters; the Jews, it is well known, being as liberal in exercising the duties of hospitality and charity among their own people, as they were alleged to be reluctant and churlish in extending them to others.

In an apartment, small indeed, but richly furnished with decorations of an Oriental taste, Rebecca was seated on a heap of embroidered cushions, which, piled along a low platform that surrounded the apartment, served like the estrada of the Spaniards, instead of chairs and stools. She was watching the motions of her father with a look of anxious and filial affection, while he paced the apartment with a dejected mien and disordered step; sometimes clasping his hands together—sometimes casting his eyes to the roof of the apartment, as one who laboured under great mental tribulation. "O, Jacob!" he exclaimed—"O all ye twelve Holy Fathers of our tribe! what a losing venture is this for one who hath duly kept every jot and tittle of the law of Moses.—Fifty zecchins wrenched from me at one clutch, and by the talons of a tyrant!"

"But, father," said Rebecca, "you seemed to give the gold to Prince John willingly."

"Willingly? the blotch of Egypt upon him!—Willingly, saidst thou? —Ay, as willingly as when, in the Gulph of Lyons, I flung over my merchandise to lighten the ship, while she laboured in the tempest—robed the seething billows in my choice silks—perfumed their briny foam with myrrh and aloes—enriched their caverns with gold and silver work! And was not that an hour of unutterable misery, though my own hands made the sacrifice?"

"But it was to save our lives, father," answered Rebecca, "and the God of our fathers has since blessed your store and your gettings."

"Ay," answered Isaac, "but if the tyrant lays hold on them as he did to-day, and compels me to smile while he is robbing me—O daughter, disinherited and wandering as we are, the worst evil that befalls our race is, that when we are wronged and plundered, all the world laughs around, and we are compelled to suppress our sense of injury, and to smile tamely, when we should revenge bravely."

"Think not thus of it, my father," said Rebecca; "we also have advantages. These Gentiles, cruel and oppressive as they are, are in some sort dependent on the dispersed children of Zion, whom they despise and persecute. Without the aid of our wealth, they could neither furnish forth their hosts in war, nor their triumphs in peace; and the gold which we lend them returns with increase to our coffers. We are like the herb which flourisheth most when it is most trampled. Even this day's pageant had not proceeded without the consent of the despised Jew, who furnished the means."

"Daughter," said Isaac, "thou hast harped upon another string of sorrow. The goodly steed and the rich armour, equal to the full profit of my adventure with our Kirjath Jairam of Leicester—there is a dead loss too, swallows up the gains of a week; ay, of the space between two Sabaoths—and yet it may end better than I now think, for 'tis a good youth."

"Assuredly," said Rebecca, "you shall not repent you of requiting the good deed received of the stranger knight."

"I trust so, daughter," said Isaac, "and I trust too in the rebuilding of Zion; but as well do I hope with my own bodily eyes to see the walls and battlements of the new Temple, as to see a Christian, yea, the very best of Christians, repay a debt to a Jew, unless under the awe of the judge and the jailor."

So saying, he resumed his discontented walk through the apartment; and Rebecca, perceiving that her attempts at consolation only served to awaken new subjects of complaint, wisely desisted from her unavailing efforts—a prudential line of conduct, and we recommend to all who set up for comforters and advisers, to follow it in the like circumstances.

The evening was now becoming dark, when a Jewish servant entered the apartment, and placed upon the table two silver lamps, fed with perfumed oil; the richest wines, and the most delicate refreshments, were at the same time displayed by another Israelitish domestic on a small ebony table, inlaid with silver; for, in the interior of their houses, the Jews refused themselves no expensive indulgences. At the same time the servant informed Isaac, that a Nazarene (so they termed Christians, while conversing among themselves,) desired to speak with him. He that would live by traffic, must hold his time at the disposal of every one claiming business with him. Isaac at once replaced on the table the untasted glass of Greek wine which he had just raised to his lips, and saying hastily to his daughter, "Rebecca, veil thyself," commanded the stranger to be admitted.

Just as Rebecca had dropped over her fine features a screen of silver gauze which reached to her feet, the door opened, and Gurth entered, wrapt in the ample fold of his Norman mantle. His appearance was rather suspicious than prepossessing, especially as, instead of doffing his bonnet, he pulled it still deeper over his rugged brow.

"Art thou Isaac the Jew of York?" said Gurth in Saxon.

"I am," replied Isaac, in the same language, (for his traffic had rendered every tongue spoken in Britain familiar to him)—"and who art thou?"

"That is not to the purpose," answered Gurth.

"As much as my name is to thee," replied Isaac; "for without knowing thine, how can I hold intercourse with thee?"

"Easily," answered Gurth; "I, being to pay money, must know that I deliver it to the right person; thou, who art to receive it, will not, I think, care very greatly by whose hands it is delivered."

"O," said the Jew, "you are come to pay monies—Holy Father Abraham! that altereth our relation to each other. And from whom dost thou bring it?"

"From the Disinherited Knight," said Gurth, "victor in this day's tournament. It is the price of the armour supplied to him by Kirjath Jairam of Leicester, on thy recommendation. The steed is restored to thy stable. I desire to know the amount of the sum which I am to pay for the armour."

"I said he was a good youth!" exclaimed Isaac with joyful exultation. "A cup of wine will do thee no harm," he added, filling and handing to the swine-herd a richer draught than he had ever before tasted. "And how much money," continued Isaac, "hast thou brought with thee?"

"Holy Virgin," said Gurth, setting down the cup, "what nectar these unbelieving dogs drink, while true Christians are fain to quaff ale as muddy and thick as the draff we give to hogs!—What money have I brought with me?" continued the Saxon, when he had finished this uncivil ejaculation, "even but a small sum; something in hand the whilst. What, Isaac, thou must bear a conscience, though it be a Jewish one."

"Nay, but," said Isaac, "thy master has won goodly steeds and rich armours with the strength of his lance, and of his right hand—but 'tis a good youth—the Jew will take these in present payment, and render him back the surplus."

"My master has disposed of them already," said Gurth.

"Ah! that was wrong," said the Jew, "that was the part of a fool. No Christians here could buy so many horses and armour—no Jew except myself would give him half the values. But thou hast a hundred zecchins with thee in that bag," said Isaac, prying under Gurth's cloak, "it is a heavy one."

"I have heads for cross-bow bolts in it," said Gurth readily.

"Well then," said Isaac, "if I should say that I should take eighty zecchins for the good steed and the rich armour, which leaves me not a guilder's profit, have you money to pay me?"

"Barely," said Gurth, "and it will leave my master nigh pennyless. Nevertheless, if such be your least offer, I must be content."

"Fill thyself another goblet of wine," said the Jew. "Ah! eighty zecchins is too little. It leaveth no profit for the usages of the moneys; and, besides, the good horse may have suffered wrong in this day's encounter. O, it was a hard and a dangerous meeting; man and steed rushing on each other like wild bulls of Bashan. The horse cannot but have had wrong."

"And I say," replied Gurth, "he is sound, wind and limb; and you may see him now, in your stable. And I say, over and above, that seventy zecchins is enough for the armour, and I hope a Christian's word is as good as a Jew's. If you will not take seventy, I will carry this bag (and he shook it till the contents jingled) back to my master."

"Nay, nay!" said Isaac; "lay down the talents—the shekels—the eighty zecchins, and thou shalt see I will consider thee liberally."

Gurth complied, and telling out eighty zecchins upon the table, the Jew delivered out to him an acquittance for the suit of armour. The Jew's hand trembled for joy as he wrapped up the first seventy pieces of gold. The last ten he told over with much deliberation, pausing, and saying something as he took each piece from the table, and dropt it into his purse. It seemed as if his avarice was struggling with his better nature, and compelling him to pouch zecchin after zecchin, while his generosity urged him to restore some part at least to his benefactor. His whole speech ran nearly thus:

"Seventy-one—seventy-two; thy master is a good youth—seventy-three, an excellent youth—seventy-four—that piece hath been clipt within the ring—seventy-five—and that looketh light of weight—

seventy-six—when thy master wants money, let him come to Isaac of York—seventy-seven—that is with reasonable security." Here he made a considerable pause, and Gurth had good hope that the last three pieces might escape the fate of their comrades; but the enumeration proceeded.—"Seventy-eight—thou art a good fellow—Seventy-nine—and deservest something for thyself——"

Here the Jew paused again, and looked at the last zecchin, intending, doubtless, to bestow it upon Gurth. He weighed it upon the tip of his finger, and made it ring by dropping it upon the table. Had it rung too flat, or had it felt a hair's-breadth too light, generosity had carried the day; but, unhappily for Gurth, the chime was full and true, the zecchin plump, newly-coined, and a grain above weight. Isaac could not find in his heart to part with it, so dropt it into his purse as if in absence of mind, with the words, "Eighty completes the tale, and I trust thy master will reward thee handsomely. Surely," he added, looking earnestly at the bag, "thou hast more coins in that pouch?"

Gurth grinned, which was his nearest approach to a laugh, as he replied, "About the same quantity which thou hast just told over so carefully." He then folded the quittance, and put it under his cap, adding,—"Peril of thy beard, Jew, see that this be full and ample." He filled himself, unbidden, a third goblet of wine, and left the apartment without ceremony.

"Rebecca," said the Jew, "that Ishmaelite hath gone somewhat beyond me. Nevertheless his master is a good youth—ay, and I am well pleased that he hath gained shekels of gold and shekels of silver, even by the speed of his horse and by the strength of his lance, which, like that of Goliath the Philistine, might vie with a weaver's beam."

As he turned to receive Rebecca's answer, he observed, that during his chaffering with Gurth, she had left the apartment unperceived.

In the meanwhile, Gurth had descended the stair, and, having reached the dark anti-chamber or hall, was puzzling about to discover the entrance, when a figure in white, shewn by a small silver lamp which she held in her hand, beckoned him into a side apartment. Gurth had some reluctance to obey the summons. Rough and impetuous as a wild boar, where only earthly force was to be apprehended, he had all the characteristic terrors of a Saxon respecting fawns, forest-fiends, white women, and the whole of superstition which they brought with them from the wilds of Germany. He remembered, moreover, that he was in the house of a Jew, a people, who, besides the other unamiable qualities which popular report ascribed to them, were supposed to be profound necromancers and cabalists. Nevertheless, after a moment's pause, he obeyed the beckoning summons of the apparition, and followed her into the apartment which she indicated.

"My father did but jest with thee, good fellow," said Rebecca; "he owes thy master deeper kindness than these arms and steed could pay, were their value tenfold. What sum didst thou pay my father even now?"

"Eighty zecchins," said Gurth, surprised at the question.

"In this purse," said Rebecca, "thou wilt find an hundred. Restore to thy master that which is his due, and enrich thyself with the remainder. Haste—begone—stay not to render thanks! and beware how you pass through this crowded town, where thou may'st easily lose both thy burden and thy life.—Reuben," she added, clapping her hands together, "light forth this stranger, and fail not to draw lock and bar behind him."

Reuben, a dark-brow'd and black-bearded Israelite, obeyed her summons, with a torch in his hand; undid the outward door of the house, and conducting Gurth across a paved court, let him out through a wicket in the entrance-gate, which he closed behind him with such bolts and chains as would well have become that of a prison.

"By St Dunstan," said Gurth, as he stumbled up the dark avenue, "this is no Jewess, but an angel from heaven! Ten zecchins from my brave young master—twenty from this pearl of Zion—Oh! happy day! —Such another, Gurth, will redeem thy bondage, and make thee a brother as free of thy guild as the best. And then do I lay down my swine-herd's horn and staff, and take the freeman's sword and buckler, and follow my young master to the death, without hiding either my face or my name."

Chapter Eleven

1 *Outlaw*. Stand, sir, and throw us that you have about you;
If not, we'll make you sit, and rifle you.
Speed. Sir, we are undone! these are the villains
That all the travellers do fear so much.
Val. My friends,——
1 *Out*. That's not so, sir, we are your enemies.
2 *Out*. Peace! we'll hear him.
3 *Out*. Aye, by my beard, will we;
For he's a proper man.

Two Gentlemen of Verona.

THE NOCTURNAL adventures of Gurth were not yet concluded; indeed he himself became partly of that mind, when, after passing one or two straggling houses which stood in the outskirts of the village, he found himself in a deep lane, running between two banks overgrown with hazle and holly, while here and there a dwarf oak flung its arms altogether across the path. The lane was moreover much rutted and broken up by the carriages which had recently transported articles of various kinds to the place of the tournament; and it was dark, for the banks and bushes intercepted the light of a fair summer moon.

From the village were heard the distant sounds of revelry, mixed occasionally with loud laughter, sometimes broken by screams, and sometimes by wild strains of distant music. All these sounds, intimating the disorderly state of the town, crowded with military nobles, and their dissolute attendants, gave Gurth some uneasiness. "The Jewess was right," he said to himself. "By heaven and St Dunstan, I would I were safe at my journey's end with all this treasure! Here are such numbers, I will not say of arrant thieves, but of errant knights and errant squires, errant monks and errant minstrels, errant jugglers and errant jesters, that a man with a single merk would be in danger, much more a poor swine-herd with a whole bagful of zecchins. Would I were out of the shade of those infernal bushes, that I might at least see any of St Nicholas's clerks before they spring on my shoulders."

Gurth accordingly hastened his pace, in order to gain the open common to which the lane led, but was not so fortunate as to accomplish his object. Just as he had attained the upper end of the lane, where the underwood was thickest, four men sprung upon him, even as his fears had anticipated, two from each side of the road, and seized him so fast, that resistance, if practicable, would have been too late—"Surrender your charge!" said one of them; "we are the deliverers of the commonwealth, who ease every man of his burthen."

"You should not ease me of mine so lightly," muttered Gurth, whose surly honesty could not be tamed even by the pressure of immediate violence,—"had I it but in my power to give three strokes in its defence."

"We shall see that presently," said the robber; and, speaking to his companions, he added, "bring along the knave. I see he would have his head broken, as well as his purse cut, and so be let blood in two veins at once."

Gurth was hurried along agreeably to this mandate, and having been dragged somewhat roughly over the bank, on the left-hand side of the lane, found himself in a straggling thicket, which lay betwixt it and the open common. He was compelled to follow his rough conductors into the very depth of this cover, where, unexpectedly, they stopt in an irregular open space, free in a great measure from trees, and on which, therefore, the beams of the moon fell without much interruption from boughs and leaves. Here his captors were joined by two other persons, apparently belonging to the gang. They had short swords by their sides, and quarter-staves in their hands, and Gurth could now observe that all six wore visors, which rendered their occupation a matter of no question, even had their former proceedings left it in doubt.

"What money hast thou, churl?" said one of the thieves.

"Thirty zecchins of my own property," answered Gurth, doggedly.

"A forfeit—a forfeit," shouted the robbers; "a Saxon hath thirty zecchins, and returns sober from a village! An undeniable and unredeemable forfeit of all he hath about him."

"I hoarded it to purchase my freedom," said Gurth.

"Thou art an ass," replied one of the thieves; "three quarts of double ale had rendered thee as free as thy master, ay, and freer too, if he be a Saxon like thyself."

"A sad truth," replied Gurth; "but if the thirty zecchins will buy my freedom from you, unloose my hands, and I will pay them to you."

"Hold," said one who seemed to exercise some authority over the others; "this bag which thou bearest, as I can feel through thy cloak, contains more coin than thou hast told us of."

"It is the good knight my master's," answered Gurth, "of which, assuredly, I would not have spoken a word, had you been satisfied with working your will upon mine own property."

"Thou art an honest fellow," replied the robber, "I warrant thee; and we worship not St Nicholas so devoutly but what thy thirty zecchins may yet escape, if thou deal uprightly with us. Meantime render up thy trust for the time." So saying, he took from Gurth's breast the large leathern pouch, in which the purse given him by Rebecca was enclosed, as well as the rest of the zecchins, and then continued his interrogation.—"Who is thy master?"

"The Disinherited Knight," said Gurth.

"Whose good lance," replied the robber, "won the prize in to-day's tournay. What is his name and lineage?"

"It is his pleasure," answered Gurth, "that they be concealed; and from me, assuredly, you will learn nought of them."

"What is thine own name and lineage?"

"To tell that," said Gurth, "might reveal my master's."

"Thou art a saucy groom," said the robber, "but of that anon. How comes thy master by this gold? is it of his inheritance, or by what means hath it accrued to him?"

"By his good lance," answered Gurth.—"These bags contain the ransom of four good horses, and four good suits of armour."

"How much is there?" demanded the robber.

"Two hundred zecchins."

"Only two hundred zecchins!" said the bandit; "your master hath dealt liberally by the vanquished, and put them to a cheap ransom. Name those who paid the gold?"

Gurth did so.

"The armour and horse of the Templar Brian de Bois-Guilbert, at what ransom were they held?—Thou see'st thou can'st not deceive me."

"My master," replied Gurth, "will take nought from the Templar save his life's-blood. They are on terms of mortal defiance, and cannot hold courteous intercourse together."

"Indeed!" repeated the robber, and paused after he had said the word. "And what wert thou now doing at Ashby with such a charge in thy custody?"

"I went thither to render to Isaac the Jew of York," replied Gurth, "the price of a suit of armour with which he fitted my master for this tournament."

"And how much did'st thou pay to Isaac?—Methinks, to judge by weight, there is still two hundred zecchins in this pouch."

"I paid to Isaac," said the Saxon, "eighty zecchins, and he restored me a hundred in lieu thereof."

"How! what!" exclaimed all the robbers at once; "darest thou trifle with us, that thou tellest such improbable lies!"

"What I tell you," said Gurth, "is as true as the moon is in heaven. You will find the just sum in a silken purse separate from the rest of the gold."

"Bethink thee, man," said the Captain, "thou speakest of a Jew—of an Israelite,—as unapt to restore gold as the dry sand of his desarts to return the cup of water which the pilgrim spills upon them."

"There is no more mercy in them," said another of the banditti, "than in an unbribed sheriff's officer."

"It is, however, as I say," said Gurth.

"Strike a light instantly," said the Captain; "I will examine this said purse; and if it be as this fellow says, the Jew's bounty is little less miraculous than the stream which relieved his fathers in the wilderness."

A light was procured accordingly, and the robber proceeded to examine the purse. The others crowded around him, and even two who had hold of Gurth relaxed their grasp while they stretched their necks to see the issue of the search. Availing himself of their negligence, by a sudden exertion of strength and activity, Gurth shook himself free of their hold, and might have escaped could he have resolved to leave his master's property behind him. But such was no part of his intention. He wrenched a quarter-staff from one of the fellows, struck down the Captain, who was altogether unaware of his purpose, and had well nigh repossessed himself of the pouch and treasure. The thieves, however, were too nimble for him, and again secured both the bag and the trusty Gurth.

"Knave!" said the Captain, getting up, "thou hast broken my head; and with other men of our sort thou would'st fare the worse for thy insolence. But thou shalt know thy fate instantly. First let us speak of thy master; the knight's matters must go before the squire's, according to the due order of chivalry. Stand thou fast in the meantime—if thou stir again, thou shalt have that will make thee quiet for thy life.—Comrades!" he then said, addressing his gang, "This purse is embroidered with Hebrew characters, and I well believe the yeoman's tale is true. The errant knight, his master, must needs pass us toll-free. He is too like ourselves for us to make booty of him, since dogs should not worry dogs where wolves and foxes are to be found in abundance."

"Like us?" answered one of his gang; "I should like to hear how that is made good."

"Why, thou fool," answered the Captain, "is he not poor and disinherited as we are?—Doth he not win his substance at the sword's point as we do?—Hath he not beaten Front-de-Bœuf and Malvoisin, even as we would beat them if we could? Is he not the enemy to life and death of Brian de Bois-Guilbert, whom we have so much reason to fear? And were all this otherwise, wouldst thou have us show a worse conscience than an unbeliever, an Hebrew Jew?"

"Nay, that were a shame," muttered the other fellow; "and yet, when I served in the band of stout old Gandelyn, we had no such scruples of conscience. And this insolent peasant,—he too, I warrant me, is to be dismissed scatheless?"

"Not if *thou* canst scathe him," replied the Captain. "Here, fellow," continued he, addressing Gurth, "canst thou use the staff, that thou starts to it so readily?"

"I think," said Gurth, "thou should be best able to reply to that question."

"Nay, by my troth, thou gavest me a round knock," replied the Captain; "do as much for this fellow, and thou shalt pass scot-free; and if thou dost not—why, by my faith, as thou art such a sturdy knave, I think I must pay thy ransom myself.—Take thy staff, Miller," he added, "and keep thy head; and do you others let the fellow go, and give him a staff—there is light enough to lay on load by."

The two champions being alike armed with quarter-staves, stepped forward into the centre of the open space, in order to have the full benefit of the moon-light; the thieves in the meantime laughing, and crying to their comrade, "Miller! beware thy toll-dish." The Miller, on the other hand, holding his quarter-staff by the middle, and making it flourish round his head after the fashion which the French call *moulinet*, exclaimed boastfully, "Come on, churl, an thou darest: thou shalt feel the strength of a miller's thumb!"

"If thou beest a miller," answered Gurth, undauntedly, making his weapon play around his head with equal dexterity, "thou art doubly a thief; and I, as a true man, bid thee defiance."

So saying, the two champions closed together, and for a few minutes they displayed great equality in strength, courage, and skill, intercepting and returning the blows of their adversary with the most rapid dexterity, while, from the continued clatter of their weapons, a person at a distance might have supposed that there were at least six persons engaged upon each side. Less obstinate, and even less dangerous combats, have been described in good heroic verse; but that of Gurth and the Miller must remain unsung, for want of a sacred poet to do justice to its eventful progress. Yet, though quarter-staff play be out of date, what we can in prose we will do for these bold champions.

Long they fought equally, until the Miller began to lose temper at finding himself so stoutly opposed, and hearing the laughter of his companions, who, as usual in such cases, enjoyed his vexation. This was not a state of mind favourable to the noble game of quarter-staff, in which, as in ordinary cudgel-playing, the utmost coolness is requisite; and it gave Gurth, whose temper was steady, though surly, the opportunity of acquiring a decided advantage, in availing himself of which he displayed great mastery.

The Miller pressed furiously forward, dealing blows with either end of his weapon alternately, and striving to come to half-staff distance, while Gurth defended himself against the attack, keeping his hands about a yard asunder, and covering himself by shifting his weapon with great celerity, so as to protect his head and body. Thus did he maintain the defensive, making his eye, foot, and hand keep true time, until, observing his antagonist to lose wind, he darted the staff at his face with his left hand; and, as the Miller endeavoured to parry the thrust, he slid his right hand down to his left, and with the full swing of the weapon struck his antagonist on the left side of the head, who instantly measured his length upon the green sward.

"Well and yeomanly done!" shouted the robbers; "fair play and Old England for ever! The Saxon hath saved both his purse and his hide, and the Miller has met his match."

"Thou may'st go thy ways, my friend," said the Captain, addressing Gurth, in special confirmation of the general voice, "and I will cause two of my comrades to guide thee by the best way to thy master's pavilion, and to guard thee from night-walkers that might have less tender consciences than ours; for there is many one of them upon the amble in such a night as this. Take heed, however," he added sternly; "remember thou hast refused to tell thy name—ask not after ours, nor endeavour to discover who or what we are; for, if thou makest such an attempt, thou wilt come by worse fortune than has yet befallen thee."

Gurth thanked the Captain for his courtesy, and promised to attend to his recommendation. Two of the outlaws taking up their quarter-staves, and desiring Gurth to follow close in the rear, walked roundly forward along a bye-path, which traversed the thicket and the broken ground adjacent to it. On the very verge of the thicket two men spoke to his conductors, and receiving an answer in a whisper, withdrew into the wood, and suffered them to pass unmolested. This circumstance induced Gurth to believe both that the gang was strong in numbers, and that they kept regular guards around their place of rendezvous.

When they arrived on the open heath, where Gurth might have had some trouble in finding his road, the thieves guided him straight forward to the top of a little eminence, whence he could see, spread beneath him in the moonlight, the palisades of the lists, the glimmering pavilions pitched at either end, with the pennons which adorned them fluttering in the moon-beam, and from which could be heard the hum of the song with which the centinels were beguiling their night-watch.

Here the thieves stopt.

"We go with you no farther," said they; "it were not safe that we should do so.—Remember the warning you have received—keep secret what has this night befallen you, and you will have no room to repent it—neglect what is now told you, and the Tower of London shall not protect you against our revenge."

"Good night to you, kind sirs," said Gurth; "I shall remember your orders, and trust that there is no harm in wishing you a safer and an honester trade."

Thus they parted, the outlaws returning in the direction from whence they had come, and Gurth proceeding to the tent of his master, to whom, notwithstanding the injunction he had received, he communicated the whole adventures of the evening.

The Disinherited Knight was filled with astonishment, no less at the generosity of Rebecca, by which, however, he resolved he would not profit, than at that of the robbers, to whose profession such a quality seemed totally foreign. His course of reflections upon these singular circumstances was, however, interrupted by the necessity for taking repose, which the fatigue of the preceding day, and the propriety of refreshing himself for the morrow's encounter, rendered alike indispensable.

The knight, therefore, stretched himself for repose upon a rich couch with which the tent was provided; and the faithful Gurth, extending his hardy limbs upon a bear-skin which formed a sort of carpet to the pavilion, laid himself across the opening of the tent, so that no one could enter without awakening him.

Chapter Twelve

The heralds left their pricking up and down.
Now ringen trumpets loud and clarion.
There is no more to say, but east and west,
In go the spears sadly in the rest,
In goth the sharp spur into the side,
There see men who can just and who can ride;
There shiver shaftes upon shieldes thick,
He feeleth through the heart-spone the prick;
Up springen speares, twenty feet in height,
Out go the swordes as the silver bright;
The helms they to-hewn and to-shred;
Out burst the blood with stern streames red.

CHAUCER.

MORNING arose in unclouded splendour, and ere the sun was much above the horizon, the idlest or the most eager of the spectators appeared on the common, moving to the lists as to a general centre, in order to secure a favourable situation for viewing the expected games.

The marshals and their attendants appeared next on the field, together with the heralds, for the purpose of receiving the names of the knights who intended to just, with the side which each chose to espouse. This was a necessary precaution, in order to secure some equality betwixt the two bodies who should be opposed to each other.

According to due formality, the Disinherited Knight was to be considered as leader of the one body, while Brian de Bois-Guilbert, who had been rated as having done second-best in the preceding day, was named first champion of the other band. Those who had concurred in the challenge adhered to his party of course, excepting only Ralph De Vipont, whom his fall had rendered unfit so soon to put on his armour. There was no want of distinguished and noble candidates to fill up the ranks on either side.

In fact, although the general tournament, in which all knights fought at once, was more dangerous than single encounters, they were, nevertheless, more frequented and practised by the chivalry of the age. Many knights, who had not sufficient confidence in their own skill to defy a single adversary of high reputation, were, nevertheless, desirous of displaying their valour in the general combat, where they might meet others with whom they were more upon an equality. On the present occasion, about fifty knights were inscribed as desirous of combating upon each side, when the marshals declared that no more could be admitted, to the disappointment of several who were too late in preferring their claim to be included.

About the hour of ten o'clock, the whole plain was crowded with horsemen, horsewomen, and foot-passengers, hastening to the tournament; and shortly after a grand flourish of trumpets announced Prince John and his retinue, attended by many of those knights who meant to take share in the game, as well as others who had no such intention.

About the same time arrived Cedric the Saxon, with the Lady Rowena, unattended, however, by Athelstane. This baron had arrayed his tall and strong person in armour, in order to take his place among the combatants; and, considerably to the surprise of Cedric, had chosen to enlist himself on the part of the Knight Templar. The Saxon, indeed, had remonstrated strongly with his friend upon the injudicious choice he had made of his party; but he had only received that sort of answer usually given by those who are more obstinate in following their own course, than strong in justifying it.

His best, if not his only reason, for adhering to the party of Brian de Bois-Guilbert, Athelstane had the prudence to keep to himself. Though his apathy of disposition prevented his taking any means to recommend himself to the Lady Rowena, he was, nevertheless, by no means insensible to her charms, and considered his union with her as a matter already fixed beyond doubt, by the assent of Cedric and her other friends. It had therefore been with smothered displeasure that he beheld the victor of the preceding day select Rowena as the object of that honour which it became his privilege to confer. In order to punish him for a preference which seemed to interfere with his own suit, Athelstane, confident of his strength, and to whom his flatterers, at least, ascribed great skill in arms, had determined not only to deprive the Disinherited Knight of his powerful succour, but, if an opportunity should offer, to make him feel the weight of his battle-axe.

Bracy, and other knights attached to Prince John, in obedience to a hint from him, had joined the party of the challengers, John being desirous to secure, if possible, the victory to that side. On the other hand, many other knights, both English and Norman, natives and strangers, took part against the challengers, the more readily that the opposite band was to be led by so distinguished a champion as the Disinherited Knight had approved himself.

So soon as Prince John observed that the destined queen of the day had arrived upon the field, assuming that air of courtesy which sat well upon him when he was so pleased, he rode forward to meet her, doffed his bonnet, and dismounting from his horse, assisted the Lady Rowena from her saddle, while his followers uncovered at the same time, and one of the most distinguished dismounted to hold her palfrey.

"It is thus," said Prince John, "that we set the dutiful example of loyalty to the Queen of Love and Beauty, and are ourselves her guide to the throne which she must this day occupy.—Ladies," he said, "attend your Queen, as you wish to be distinguished by like honours."

So saying, the Prince marshalled Rowena to the seat of honour opposite his own, while the fairest and most distinguished ladies present crowded after her to obtain places as near as possible to their temporary sovereign.

No sooner was Rowena seated, than a burst of music, half-drowned by the shouts of the multitude, greeted her new dignity. Meantime, the sun shone fierce and bright upon the polished arms of the knights of either side, who crowded the opposite extremities of the lists, and held eager conference together concerning the best mode of arranging their line of battle, and supporting the conflict.

The heralds then proclaimed silence until the laws of the tourney should be rehearsed. These were calculated in some degree to abate the dangers of the day; a precaution the more necessary, as the conflict was to be maintained with sharp swords and pointed lances.

The champions were therefore prohibited to thrust with the sword, and were confined to striking. A knight, it was announced, might use a mace or battle-axe at pleasure, but the dagger was a prohibited weapon. A knight unhorsed might renew the fight on foot with any other on the opposite side in the same predicament; but mounted horsemen were in that case forbidden to assail him. When any knight could force his antagonist to the extremity of the lists, so as to touch the palisade with his person or arms, such opponent was obliged to yield himself vanquished, and his armour and horse were placed at the disposal of the conqueror. A knight thus overcome was not permitted to take further share in the combat. If any knight was struck down, and unable to recover his feet, his squire or page might enter the lists and drag his master out of the press; but in that case the knight was adjudged vanquished, and his arms and horse declared forfeited. The combat was to cease as soon as Prince John should throw down his leading-staff, or truncheon; another precaution usually taken to prevent the unnecessary effusion of blood by the too long endurance of a sport so desperate. Any knight breaking the rules of the tournament, or otherwise transgressing the rules of honourable chivalry, was liable to be stript of his arms, and, having his shield reversed, to be placed in that posture astride upon the bars of the palisade, and exposed to public derision, in punishment of his unknightly conduct. Having announced these precautions, the heralds concluded with an exhortation to each good knight to do his duty, and to merit favour from the Queen of Beauty and of Love.

This proclamation having been made, the heralds withdrew to their stations. The knights, entering at either end of the lists in long procession, arranged themselves in a double file, precisely opposite to each other, the leader of each party being in the centre of the foremost rank; a post which he did not occupy until each had carefully arranged the ranks of his party, and stationed every one in his place.

It was a goodly, and at the same time an anxious sight, to behold so many gallant champions mounted bravely, and armed richly, stand ready prepared for an encounter so formidable, seated on their war-saddles like so many pillars of iron, and awaiting the signal of encounter with the same ardour as their generous steeds, which, by neighing and pawing the ground, gave signal of their impatience.

As yet the knights held their long lances upright, their bright points glancing to the sun, and the streamers with which they were decorated fluttering over the plumage of the helmets. Thus they remained while the marshals of the field surveyed their ranks with the utmost exactness, lest either party had more or fewer than the appointed number. The tale was found exactly complete. The marshals then withdrew from the lists, and William de Wyvil, with a voice of thunder, pronounced the signal words—*Laissez aller!* The trumpets sounded as he spoke—the spears of the champions were at once lowered and placed in the rests—the spurs were dashed into the flanks of the horses, and the two foremost ranks of either party rushed upon each other in full gallop, and met in the middle of the lists with a shock, the sound of which was heard at a mile's distance.

The consequences of the encounter were not instantly seen, for the dust raised by the trampling of so many steeds darkened the air, and it was a minute ere the anxious spectators could see the fate of the encounter. When the fight became visible, half the knights on each side were dismounted, some by the dexterity of their adversary's lance,—some by the superior weight, which had broke down both horse and man,—some lay stretched on earth as if never more to rise—some had already gained their feet, and were closing hand to hand with those of the enemy who were in the same predicament—and two or three, who had received wounds by which they were disabled, were stopping their blood by their scarfs, and endeavouring to extricate themselves from the tumult. The mounted knights, whose lances had been almost all broken by the fury of the encounter, were now closely engaged with their swords, shouting their war-cries, and exchanging buffets, as if honour and life depended on the issue of the combat.

The tumult was presently increased by the advance of the second rank on either side, which, acting as a reserve, now rushed on to aid their companions. The followers of Brian de Bois-Guilbert shouted —"*Ha! Beau-seant! Beau-seant!**—for the Temple—for the Temple." The opposite party shouted in answer—"*Desdichado! Desdichado!*"—which watch-word they took from the motto upon their leader's shield.

The champions thus encountering each other with the utmost fury, and with alternate success, the tide of battle seemed to flow now toward the southern, now toward the northern extremity of the lists, as the one or the other party prevailed. Meantime the clang of the blows, and the shouts of the combatants, mixed fearfully with the sound of the trumpets, and drowned the groans of those who fell, and lay rolling defenceless beneath the feet of the horses. The splendid armour of the combatants was now defaced with dust and blood, and gave way at every stroke of the sword and battle-axe. The gay plumage, shorn from the crests, drifted upon the breeze like snow-flakes. All that was beautiful and graceful in the martial array had disappeared, and what was now visible was only calculated to awake terror or compassion.

Yet such is the force of habit, that not only the vulgar spectators, who are naturally attracted by sights of horror, but even the ladies who crowded the galleries, saw the conflict with a thrilling interest certainly, but without a wish to withdraw their eyes from a sight so terrible. Here and there, indeed, a fair cheek might turn pale, or a faint scream might be heard, as a lover, a brother, or a husband was struck from his horse. But, in general, the ladies around encouraged the combatants, not only by clapping their hands, but even by exclaiming, "Brave lance! Good sword!" when any successful thrust or blow took place under their observation.

Such being the interest taken by the fair sex in this bloody game, that of the men is more easily understood. It shewed itself in loud acclamations upon every change of fortune, while all eyes were so rivetted on the lists, that the spectators seemed as if they themselves dealt and received the blows which were there so freely bestowed. And between every pause was heard the voice of the heralds, exclaiming, "Fight on, brave knights! Man dies, but glory lives!—Fight on—death is better than defeat!—Fight on, brave knights! for bright eyes behold your deeds!"

* *Beau-seant* was the name of the Templars' banner, which was half black, half white, to intimate, it is said, that they were candid and fair towards Christians, but black and terrible towards infidels.

Amid the varied fortunes of the combat, the eyes of all endeavoured to discover the leaders of each band, who, mingling in the thick of the fight, encouraged their companions both by voice and example. Both displayed great feats of gallantry, nor did either Bois-Guilbert or the Disinherited Knight find in the ranks opposed to them a champion who could be termed their unquestioned match. They repeatedly endeavoured to single out each other, spurred by mutual animosity, and aware that the fall of either leader might be considered as decisive of victory. Such, however, was the crowd and confusion, that, during the earlier part of the conflict, their efforts to meet were unavailing, and they were repeatedly separated by the eagerness of their followers, each of whom were anxious to win honour, by measuring their strength against the leader of the opposite party.

But when the field became thin by the numbers on either side, who, having yielded themselves vanquished, had been compelled to the extremity of the lists, or had been otherwise rendered incapable of continuing the strife, the Templar and the Disinherited Knight at length encountered hand to hand, with all the fury that mortal animosity, joined to rivalry of honour, could inspire. Such was the address of each in parrying and striking, that the spectators broke forth into an unanimous and involuntary shout, expressive of their delight and admiration.

But at this moment the party of the Disinherited Knight had the worst; the gigantic arm of Front-de-Bœuf on the one flank, and the ponderous strength of Athelstane on the other, bearing down and dispersing those immediately exposed to them. Finding themselves freed from their immediate antagonists, it seems to have occurred to both these knights at the same instant, that they would render the most decisive advantage to their party, by aiding the Templar in his contest with his rival. Turning their horses, therefore, at the same moment, the Norman spurred towards him on the one side, and the Saxon on the other. It was utterly impossible that the object of this unequal and unexpected assault could have sustained it, had he not been warned by a general cry from the spectators, who could not but take interest in one exposed to such disadvantage.

"Beware! beware! Sir Disinherited Knight!" was shouted so universally, that the knight became aware of his danger, and striking a full blow at the Templar, he reined back his steed in the same moment, so as to escape the career of Athelstane, and Front-de-Bœuf; these knights, therefore, their aim being thus eluded, rushed from opposite sides betwixt the object of their attack and the Templar, almost running their horses against each other ere they could stop their career. Recovering their horses, however, and wheeling them round, the whole three pursued their purpose of bearing to the earth the Disinherited Knight.

Nothing could have saved him except the remarkable strength and activity of the noble horse which he had won on the preceding day.

This stood him in the more stead, as the horse of Bois-Guilbert was wounded, and those of Front-de-Bœuf and Athelstane were both tired with the weight of their gigantic masters, clad in complete armour, and with the preceding exertions of the day. The complete horsemanship of the Disinherited Knight, and the activity of the noble animal which he mounted, enabled him for a few minutes to keep at sword's point his three antagonists, turning and wheeling with the agility of a hawk upon the wing, keeping his enemies as far separate as he could, and rushing now against the one, now against the other, dealing sweeping blows with his sword, without waiting to receive those which were aimed at him in return.

But although the lists rung with the applauses of his dexterity, it was evident that he must at last be overpowered; and those around Prince John implored him with one voice to throw down his warder, and to save so brave a knight from the disgrace of being overcome by odds.

"Not I, by the light of Heaven!" answered Prince John; "this same springal, who conceals his name, and despises our proffered hospitality, hath already gained one prize, and may now let others have their turn." As he spoke thus, an unexpected incident changed the fortune of the day.

There was among the ranks of the Disinherited Knight a champion in black armour, mounted on a black horse, large of size, tall, and to all appearance powerful and strong. This knight, who bore on his shield no device of any kind, had hitherto evinced very little interest in the event of the fight, beating off with seeming ease those knights who attacked him, but neither pursuing his advantages, nor himself assailing any one. In short, he acted the part rather of a spectator than of a party in the tournament, a circumstance which procured him among the spectators the name of *Le Noir Faineant*, or the Black Sluggard.

At once this knight seemed to throw aside his apathy, when he discovered the leader of his party so hard bestead; for, setting spurs to his horse, which was quite fresh, he came to his assistance like a thunderbolt, exclaiming, in a voice like a trumpet-call, "*Desdichado*, to the rescue!" It was high time; for, while the Disinherited Knight was pressing upon the Templar, Front-de-Bœuf had got nigh to him with his uplifted sword; but ere the blow could descend, the Sable Knight encountered him, and Front-de-Bœuf rolled on the ground, both horse and man. *Le Noir Faineant* then turned his horse upon Athelstane of Coningsburgh; and his own sword having been broken in his encounter with Front-de-Bœuf, he wrenched from the hand of the bulky Saxon the battle-axe which he wielded, and dealt him such a blow upon the crest, that Athelstane also lay senseless on the field. Having achieved this feat, for which he was the more highly applauded that it was totally unexpected from him, the knight seemed to resume the sluggishness of his character, returning calmly to the northern extremity of the lists, leaving his leader to cope as he best could with Brian de Bois-Guilbert. This was no longer matter of so much difficulty as formerly. The Templar's horse had bled much, and gave way under the shock of the Disinherited Knight's charge. Brian de Bois-Guilbert rolled on the field, incumbered with the stirrup, from which he was unable to draw his foot. His antagonist sprung from horseback, and commanded him to yield himself, when Prince John, more moved by the Templar's dangerous situation than he had been by that of his rival, saved him the mortification of confessing himself vanquished, by casting down his warder, and putting an end to the conflict.

It was, indeed, only the reliques and embers of the fight which continued to burn; for of the few knights who still continued in the lists, the greater part had, by tacit consent, forborne the conflict for some time, leaving it to be determined by the strife of the leaders.

The squires, who had found it a matter of danger and difficulty to attend their masters during the engagement, now thronged into the lists to pay their dutiful attendance to the wounded, who were removed with the utmost care and attention to the neighbouring pavilions, or to the quarters prepared for them in the adjoining village.

Thus ended the memorable field of Ashby-de-la-Zouche, one of the most gallantly contested tournaments of that age; for although only four knights, including one who was smothered by the heat of his armour, had died upon the field, yet upwards of thirty were desperately wounded, four or five of whom never recovered. Several more were disabled for life; and those who escaped best carried the marks of the conflict to the grave with them. Hence it is always mentioned in the old records, as the Gentle and Free Passage of Arms of Ashby.

It being now the duty of Prince John to name the knight who had done best, he determined that the honour of the day remained with the knight whom the popular voice had termed *Le Noir Faineant*. It was pointed out to the Prince, in impeachment of this decree, that the victory had been in fact won by the Disinherited Knight, who, in the course of the day, had overcome six champions with his own hand, and who had finally unhorsed and struck down the leader of the opposite party. But Prince John adhered to his own opinion, on the ground that the Disinherited Knight and his party had lost the day, but for the powerful assistance of the Knight of the Black Armour, to whom, therefore, he persisted in awarding the prize.

To the surprise of all present, however, the knight thus preferred was nowhere to be found. He had left the lists immediately when the conflict ceased, and had been observed by some spectators to move down one of the forest glades with the same slow pace and listless and indifferent manner which had procured him the epithet of the Black Sluggard. After he had been summoned twice by sound of trumpet, and proclamation of the heralds, it became necessary to name another to receive the honours which had been assigned to him. Prince John had now no further excuse for resisting the claim of the Disinherited Knight, whom, therefore, he named the champion of the day.

Through a field slippery with blood, and incumbered with broken armour and the bodies of slain and wounded horses, the marshals of the lists again conducted the victor to the foot of Prince John's throne.

"Disinherited Knight," said Prince John, "since by that only title you will consent to be known to us, we a second time award to you the honours of this tournament, and announce to you your right to claim and receive from the hands of the Queen of Love and Beauty, the Chaplet of Honour which your valour has justly deserved." The Knight bowed low and gracefully, but returned no answer.

While the trumpets sounded, while the heralds strained their voices in proclaiming honour to the brave and glory to the victor—while ladies waved their silken kerchiefs and embroidered veils, and while all ranks joined in a clamorous shout of exultation, the marshals conducted the Disinherited Knight across the lists to the foot of that throne of honour which was occupied by the Lady Rowena.

On the lower step of this throne the champion was made to kneel down. Indeed his whole action since the fight had ended seemed rather to have been upon the impulse of those around him than from his own free will; and it was observed that he tottered as they guided him the second time across the lists. Rowena, descending from her station with a graceful and dignified step, was about to place the chaplet which she held in her hand upon the helmet of the champion, when the marshals exclaimed with one voice, "It must not be thus—his head must be bare." The knight muttered faintly a few words, which were lost in the hollow of his helmet, but their purport seemed to be a desire that his casque might not be removed.

Whether from love of form or from curiosity, the marshals paid no attention to his expressions of reluctance, but unhelmed him by cutting the laces of his casque, and undoing the fastening of his gorget. When the helmet was removed, the well-formed, yet sun-burnt features of a young man of twenty-five were seen, amidst a profusion of short fair hair. His countenance was as pale as death, and marked in one or two places with streaks of blood.

Rowena had no sooner beheld him than she uttered a faint shriek; but at once summoning up the energy of her disposition, and compelling herself, as it were, to proceed, while her frame yet trembled with the violence of sudden emotion, she placed upon the drooping head of the victor the splendid chaplet which was the destined reward of the day, and pronounced, in a clear and distinct tone, these words: "I bestow on thee this chaplet, Sir Knight, as the meed of valour assigned to this day's victor:" Here she paused a moment, and then firmly added; "And upon brows more worthy could a wreath of chivalry never be placed!"

The knight stooped his head, and kissed the hand of the lovely sovereign by whom his valour had been rewarded; and then, sinking yet farther forward, lay prostrate at her feet.

There was a general consternation. Cedric, who had been struck mute by the sudden appearance of his banished son, now rushed forward, as if to separate him from Rowena. But this had been already accomplished by the marshals of the field, who, guessing the cause of Ivanhoe's swoon, had hastened to disarm him, and found that the head of a lance had penetrated his breast-plate, and inflicted a wound upon his side.

Chapter Thirteen

"Heroes, approach!" Atrides thus aloud,
"Stand forth distinguish'd from the circling crowd,
Ye who by skill or manly force may claim,
Your rivals to surpass and merit fame.
This cow, worth twenty oxen, is decreed,
For him who farthest sends the winged reed."
Iliad.

THE NAME of Ivanhoe was no sooner pronounced than it flew from mouth to mouth, with all the celerity with which eagerness could convey and curiosity receive it. It was not long ere it reached the circle of the Prince, whose brow darkened as he heard the news. Looking around him, however, with an air of scorn, "My lords," said he, "and especially you, Sir Prior, what think ye of the doctrine the learned tell us, concerning innate attractions and antipathies? Methinks that I felt the presence of my brother's minion, even when I least guessed whom yonder suit of armour enclosed."

"Front-de-Bœuf must prepare to restore his fief of Ivanhoe," said Bracy, who, having discharged his part honourably in the tournament, had laid his shield and helmet aside, and again mingled with the Prince's retinue.

"Ay," answered Waldemar Fitzurse, "this gallant is likely to reclaim the castle and manor which Richard assigned to him, and which your Highness's generosity has since given to Front-de-Bœuf."

"Front-de-Bœuf," replied John, "is a man more willing to swallow three manors such as Ivanhoe, than to disgorge one of them. For the rest, sirs, I hope none here will deny my right to confer the fiefs of the crown upon the faithful followers who are around me, and ready to perform the usual military service, in the room of those who have wandered to foreign countries, and can neither render homage nor service when called upon."

The audience were too much interested in the question not to pronounce the Prince's assumed right altogether indubitable. "A generous Prince!—a most noble Lord, who thus takes upon himself the task of rewarding his faithful followers."

Such were the words which burst from the train, expectants all of them of similar grants at the expence of King Richard's followers and favourites, if indeed they had not as yet received such. Prior Aymer also assented to the general proposition, observing, however, "That the blessed Jerusalem could not indeed be termed a foreign country. She was *communis mater*—the mother of all Christians. But he saw not," he declared, "how the Knight of Ivanhoe could plead any advantage from this, since he (the Prior) was assured, that the crusaders, under Richard, had never proceeded much farther than Ascalon, which, as all the world knew, was a town of the Philistines, and entitled to none of the privileges of the Holy City."

Waldemar, whose curiosity had led him towards the place where Ivanhoe had fallen to the ground, now returned. "The gallant," said he, "is likely to give your Highness little disturbance, and to leave Front-de-Bœuf in the quiet possession of his gains—he is severely wounded."

"Whatever becomes of him," said Prince John, "he is victor of the day; and were he tenfold our enemy, or the devoted friend of our brother, which is perhaps the same, his wounds must be looked to—our own physician shall attend him."

A stern smile curled the Prince's lip as he spoke. Waldemar Fitzurse hastened to reply, that Ivanhoe was already removed from the lists, and in the custody of his friends.

"I was somewhat moved," he said, "to see the grief of the Queen of Love and Honour, whose sovereignty of a day this event has changed into mourning. I am not a man to be moved by a woman's lament for her lover, but this same Lady Rowena suppressed her sorrow with such dignity of manner, that it could only be discovered by her folded hands, and her tearless eye, which trembled as it remained fixed on the lifeless form before her."

"Who is this Lady Rowena," said Prince John, "of whom we have heard so much?"

"A Saxon heiress of large possessions," replied the Prior Aymer; "a rose of loveliness, and a jewel of wealth; the fairest among a thousand, a bundle of myrrh, and a cluster of camphire."

"We shall cheer her sorrows," said Prince John, "and amend her blood by wedding her to a Norman. She seems a minor, and must therefore be at our royal disposal in marriage.—How say'st thou, De Bracy? What think'st thou of gaining fair lands and livings, by wedding a Saxon, after the fashion of the followers of the Conqueror?"

"If the lands are to my liking, my lord," answered Bracy, "it will be hard to displease me with a bride; and deeply will I hold myself bound to your highness for a good deed, which will fulfill all promises made in favour of your servant and vassal."

"We will not forget it," said Prince John; "and that we may instantly go to work, command our seneschal presently to order the attendance of the Lady Rowena and her company—that is, the rude churl her guardian, and the Saxon ox whom the Black Knight struck down in the tournament, upon this evening's banquet.—De Bigot," he added to his seneschal, "thou wilt word this our second summons so courteously, as to gratify the pride of these Saxons, and make it impossible for them again to refuse; although, by the bones of Becket, courtesy to them is casting pearls before swine."

Prince John had proceeded thus far, and was about to give the signal for retiring from the lists, when a small billet was put into his hand.

"From whence?" said Prince John, looking at the person by whom it was delivered.

"From foreign parts, my lord, but from whence I know not," replied his attendant. "A Frenchman brought it hither, who said, he had ridden night and day to put it into the hands of your highness."

The Prince looked narrowly at the superscription, and then at the seal, placed so as to secure the flox-silk with which the billet was surrounded, and which bore the impression of three fleurs-de-lis. John then opened the billet with apparent agitation, which visibly increased when he had perused the contents, which were expressed in these words—

"*Take heed to yourself, for the devil is unchained.*"

The Prince turned as pale as death, looked first on the earth and then up to heaven, like a man who has received news of sentence of death having been passed upon him. Recovering from the first effects of his surprise, he took Waldemar Fitzurse and Bracy aside, and put the billet into their hands successively.

"This may be a false alarm, or a forged letter," said Bracy.

"It is France's own hand and seal," replied Prince John.

"It is time then," said Fitzurse, "to draw our party to a head, either at York, or some other centrical place. A few days later, and it will be indeed too late. Your highness must break short this present mummery."

"The yeomen and commons," said Bracy, "must not be dismissed discontented, for lack of their share in the sports."

"The day," said Waldemar, "is not yet very far spent—let the archers shoot a few rounds at the target, and the prize be adjudged. This will be an abundant fulfilment of the Prince's promises, so far as this herd of Saxon serfs is concerned."

"I thank thee, Waldemar," said the Prince; "thou remindest me, too, that I have a debt to pay to that insolent peasant who yesterday insulted our person. Our banquet also shall go forward to-night as we proposed. Were this my last hour of power, it should be an hour sacred to revenge and to pleasure—let new cares come with to-morrow's new day."

The sound of the trumpets soon recalled those spectators who had already begun to leave the field; and proclamation was made that Prince John, suddenly called by high and peremptory public duties, held himself obliged to discontinue the entertainments of to-morrow's festival: Nevertheless, that unwilling so many good yeomen should depart without a trial of skill, he was pleased to appoint them, before leaving the ground, presently to execute the competition of archery intended for the morrow. To the best archer a prize was to be awarded, being a bugle-horn, mounted with silver, and a silken baldrick richly ornamented, with a medallion of St Hubert, the patron of sylvan sport.

More than thirty yeomen at first presented themselves as competitors, several of whom were rangers and under-keepers in the royal forests of Needwood and Charnwood. When, however, the archers understood with whom they were to be matched, upwards of twenty withdrew themselves from the contest, unwilling to encounter the dishonour of almost certain defeat. For in these days the skill of each celebrated marksman was as well known for many miles round him, as the qualities of a horse trained at Newmarket are known to those who frequent that celebrated meeting.

The diminished list of competitors for sylvan fame still amounted to eight. Prince John stepped from his royal seat to view more nearly the persons of these chosen yeomen, several of whom wore the royal livery. Having satisfied his curiosity by this investigation, he looked for the object of his resentment, whom he observed standing in the same spot, and with the same composed countenance which he had exhibited upon the preceding day.

"Fellow," said Prince John, "I guessed by thy insolent babble thou wert no true lover of the long-bow, and I see thou darest not adventure thy skill among such merry-men as stand yonder."

"Under favour, sir," replied the yeoman, "I have another reason for refraining to shoot, besides the fearing discomfiture and disgrace."

"And what is thy other reason," said Prince John, who, for some cause which perhaps he could not himself have explained, felt a painful curiosity respecting this individual.

"Because," replied the woodsman, "I know not if these yeomen and I are used to shoot at the same marks; and because, moreover, I know not how your grace might relish the winning of a third prize by one who has unwittingly fallen under your displeasure."

Prince John coloured as he put the question, "What is thy name, yeoman?"

"Locksley," answered the yeoman.

"Then, Locksley," said Prince John, "thou shalt shoot in thy turn, when these yeomen have displayed their skill. If thou carriest the prize, I will add to it twenty nobles; but if thou losest it, thou shalt be stript of thy Lincoln green, and scourged out of the lists with bow-strings, for a wordy and insolent braggart."

"And how if I refuse to shoot on such a wager?" said the yeoman.—"Your grace's power, supported, as it is, by so many men-at-arms, may indeed easily strip and scourge me, but cannot compel me to bend or to draw my bow."

"If thou refusest my fair proffer," said the Prince, "the Provost of the lists shall cut thy bow-string, break thy bow and arrows, and expel thee from the presence as a faint-hearted craven."

"This is no fair chance you put on me, proud Prince," said the yeoman, "to compel me to peril myself against the best archers of Leicester and Staffordshire, under the penalty of infamy if they should overshoot me. Nevertheless, I will obey your will."

"Look to him close, men-at-arms," said Prince John, "his heart is sinking; I am jealous lest he attempt to escape the trial. And do you, good fellows, shoot boldly round; a buck and a butt of wine are ready for your refreshment in yonder tent, when the prize is won."

A target was placed at the upper end of the southern avenue which led to the lists. The contending archers took their stance in turn, at the bottom of the southern access; the distance between that station and the mark allowing full distance for what was called a shot at rovers. The archers, having previously determined by lot their order of precedence, were to shoot each three shafts in succession. The sports were regulated by an officer of inferior rank, termed the Provost of the games; for the high rank of the marshals of the lists would have been held degraded, had they condescended to superintend the games of the yeomanry.

One by one the archers, stepping forward, delivered their shafts yeomanlike and bravely. Of twenty-four arrows, shot in succession, ten were fixed in the target, and the others ranged so near it, that, considering the distance of the mark, it was accounted good archery. Of the ten shafts which hit the target, two within the inner ring were shot by Hubert, a forester in the service of Malvoisin, who was accordingly pronounced victorious.

"Now, Locksley," said Prince John to the devoted yeoman, with a bitter smile, "wilt thou try conclusions with Hubert, or wilt thou yield up bow, baldrick, and quiver to the Provost of the sports?"

"Sith it may be no better," said Locksley, "I am content to try my fortune; on condition that when I have shot two shafts at yonder mark of Hubert's, he shall be bound to shoot one at that which I shall propose."

"That is but fair," answered Prince John, "and it shall not be refused thee.—If thou dost beat this braggart, Hubert, I will fill the bugle with silver-pennies for thee."

"A man can but do his best," answered Hubert; "but my great-grandsire drew a good long bow at Hastings, and I trust not to dishonour his memory."

The former target was now removed, and a fresh one of the same size placed in its room. Hubert, who, as victor in the first trial of skill, had the right to shoot first, took his aim with great deliberation, long measuring the distance with his eye, while he held in his hand his bended bow, with the arrow placed on the string. At length he made a step forward, and raising the bow at the full stretch of his left-arm, till the centre or grasping-place was nigh level with his face, he drew the bow-string to his ear. The arrow whistled through the air, and lighted within the inner-ring of the target, but not exactly in the centre.

"You have not allowed for the wind, Hubert," said his antagonist, bending his bow, "or that had been a better shot."

So saying, and without showing the least anxiety to pause upon his aim, Locksley stept to the appointed station, and shot his arrow as carelessly in appearance as if he had not even looked at the mark. He was speaking almost at the instant that the shaft left the bow-string, yet it alighted in the target two inches nearer to the white spot which marked the centre than that of Hubert.

"By the light of heaven!" said Prince John to Hubert, "an thou suffer that runagate knave to overcome thee, thou art worthy of the gallows."

Hubert had but one set speech for all occasions. "An your highness were to hang me," he said, "a man can but do his best. Nevertheless, my grandsire drew a good bow"——

"The foul fiend on thy grandsire and all his generation," interrupted John; "shoot, knave, and shoot thy best, or it shall be the worse for thee."

Thus exhorted, Hubert resumed his place, and not neglecting the caution which he had received from his adversary, he made the necessary allowance for a very light air of wind, which had just arisen, and shot so successfully that his arrow alighted in the very centre of the target.

"A Hubert! a Hubert!" shouted the populace, more interested in a known person than in a stranger. "In the clout!—in the clout!—a Hubert for ever!"

"Thou can'st not mend that shot, Locksley," said the Prince, with an insulting smile.

"I will notch his shaft for him, however," replied Locksley.

And letting fly his arrow with a little more precaution than before, it lighted right upon that of his competitor, which it split to shivers. The people who stood around were so astonished at his wonderful dexterity, that they could not even give vent to their surprise in their usual clamour. "This must be the devil, and no man of flesh and blood," whispered the yeomen to each other; "such archery was never seen since a bow was first bent in Britain."

"And now," said Locksley, "I crave your grace's permission to plant such a mark as is used in the north country; and welcome every brave yeoman who shall try a shot at it to win a smile from the bonny lass he loves best."

He then turned to leave the lists. "Let your guards attend me," he said, "if you please—I go but to cut a rod from the next willow bush."

Prince John made a signal that some attendants should follow him in case of his escape; but the cry of "Shame! shame!" which burst from the multitude, induced him to alter his ungenerous purpose.

Locksley returned almost instantly with a willow wand about six feet in length, perfectly straight, and rather thicker than a man's thumb. He began to peel this with great composure, observing, at the same time, that to ask a good woodsman to shoot at a target so broad as had hitherto been used, was to put shame upon his skill. "For his own part," he said, "and in the land where he was bred, men would as soon take for their mark King Arthur's round-table, which held sixty knights around it. A child of seven years old," he said, "might hit it with a headless shaft; but," added he, walking deliberately to the other end of the lists, and sticking the willow wand upright in the ground, "he that hits that rod at five-score yards, I call him an archer fit to bear both bow and quiver before a king, an it were the stout King Richard himself."

"My grandsire," said Hubert, "drew a good bow at the battle of Hastings, and never shot at such a mark in his life—and neither will I. If this yeoman can cleave that rod, I give him the bucklers—or rather, I yield to the devil that is in his jerkin, and not to any human skill; a man can but do his best, and I will not shoot where I am sure to miss. I might as well shoot at the edge of our parson's whittle, or at a wheat straw, or at a sun-beam, as at a twinkling white streak which I can hardly see."

"Cowardly dog!" said Prince John.—"Sirrah Locksley, do thou shoot; but, if thou hittest such a mark, I will say thou art the first man ever did so. Howe'er it be, thou shalt not crow over us with a mere shew of superior skill."

"I will do my best, as Hubert says," answered Locksley; "no man can do more."

So saying, he again bent his bow, but on the present occasion looked with attention to his weapon, and changed the string, which he thought was no longer truly round, having been a little frayed by the two former shots. He then took his aim with some deliberation, and the multitude awaited the event in breathless silence. The archer vindicated their opinion of his skill: his arrow split the willow rod against which it was aimed. A jubilee of acclamations followed; and even Prince John, in admiration of Locksley's skill, lost his dislike to his person. "These twenty nobles," he said, "which, with the bugle, thou hast fairly won, are thine own; we will make them fifty, if thou wilt take livery and service with us as a yeoman of our body guard, and be near to our person. For never did so strong a hand bend a bow, or so true an eye direct a shaft."

"Pardon me, noble Prince," said Locksley; "but I have vowed, that if ever I take service, it should be with your royal brother, King Richard. These twenty nobles I leave to Hubert, who has this day drawn as brave a bow as his grandsire did at Hastings. Had his modesty not refused the trial, he would have hit the wand as well as I."

Hubert shook his head as he received with reluctance the bounty of the stranger; and Locksley, anxious to escape further observation, mixed with the crowd, and was seen no more.

The victorious archer would not perhaps have escaped John's

attention so easily, had not that Prince had other subjects of anxious and more important meditation pressing upon his mind at that instant. He called upon his chamberlain as he gave the signal for retiring from the lists, and commanded him instantly to gallop to Ashby, and seek out Isaac the Jew. "Tell the dog," he said, "to send me, before sundown, two thousand crowns. He knows the security; but thou mayest shew him this ring for a token. The rest of the money must be paid at York within six days. If he neglects, I will have the unbelieving villain's head. Look that thou pass him not on the way; for the circumcised slave was displaying his stolen finery amongst us."

So saying, the Prince resumed his horse, and returned to Ashby, the whole crowd breaking up and dispersing upon his retreat.

Chapter Fourteen

In rough magnificence array'd,
When ancient Chivalry display'd
The pomp of her heroic games,
And crested chiefs and tissued dames
Assembled, at the clarion's call,
In some proud castle's high-arched hall.
WARTON.

PRINCE JOHN held his high festival in the Castle of Ashby. This was not the same building of which the stately ruins still interest the traveller, and which was erected at a later period by the Lord Hastings, High Chamberlain of England, one of the first victims of the tyranny of Richard the Third, and yet better known as one of Shakespeare's characters than by his historical fame. The castle and town of Ashby, at this time, belonged to Roger de Quincy, Earl of Winchester, who, during the period of our history, was absent in the Holy Land. Prince John, in the meanwhile, occupied his castle, and disposed of his domains without scruple; and seeking at present to dazzle men's eyes by his hospitality and magnificence, had given orders for great preparations, in order to render the banquet as splendid as possible.

The purveyors of the Prince, who exercised, upon this and other occasions, the full authority of royalty, had swept the country of all that could be collected which was esteemed fit for their master's table. Guests also were invited in great numbers; and in the necessity in which he presently found himself of courting popularity, Prince John had extended these to a few distinguished Saxon and Danish families, as well as to the Norman nobility and gentry of the neighbourhood. However despised and degraded on ordinary occasions, the great numbers of the Anglo-Saxons must necessarily render them formidable in the civil commotions which seemed approaching, and it was an obvious point of policy to secure popularity with their leaders.

It was accordingly the Prince's intention, which he for some time maintained, to treat these unwonted guests with a courtesy to which they had been little accustomed. But although no man with less scruple made his ordinary habits and feelings bend to his interest, it was the misfortune of this Prince, that his levity and petulance were perpetually breaking out, and undoing all that had been gained by his previous dissimulation.

Of this fickle temper he gave a memorable example in Ireland, when sent thither by his father, Henry the Second, with the purpose of buying golden opinions of the inhabitants of that new and important acquisition to the English crown. Upon this occasion the Irish chieftains contended which should first offer to the young Prince their loyal homage and the kiss of peace. But, instead of receiving their salutations with courtesy, John and his petulant attendants could not resist the temptation of pulling the long beards of the Irish chieftains, a conduct which, as might have been expected, was highly resented by these insulted dignitaries, and produced fatal consequences to the English domination in Ireland. It is necessary to keep these inconsistencies of John's character in view, that the reader may understand his conduct during the present evening.

In execution of the resolution which he had formed during his cooler moments, Prince John received Cedric and Athelstane with distinguished courtesy, and expressed his disappointment, without resentment, when the indisposition of Rowena was alleged by the former as a reason for her not attending upon his gracious summons. Cedric and Athelstane were both dressed in the ancient Saxon garb, which, although not unhandsome in itself, and in the present instance composed of costly materials, was so remote in shape and appearance from that of the other guests, that Prince John took great credit to himself with Waldemar Fitzurse for refraining from laughter at a sight which the fashion of the day rendered so ridiculous. Yet, in the eye of sober judgment, the short close tunic and long mantle of the Saxons was a more graceful, as well as a more convenient dress, than the garb of the Normans, whose under garment was a long doublet, so loose as to resemble a shirt or waggoner's frock, covered by a cloak of scanty dimensions, neither fit to defend the wearer from cold or from rain, and the only purpose of which seemed to be to display as much fur, embroidery, and jewellery work, as the ingenuity of the tailor could contrive to lay upon it. The Emperor Charlemagne seems to have been very sensible of the inconveniencies arising from the fashion of this garment. "In heaven's name," said he, "to what purpose serve these abridged cloaks? If we are in bed they are no covering, on horseback they are no protection from the wind and rain, and when seated, they do not protect our legs from the damp or the frost."

Nevertheless, spite of this imperial objurgation, the short cloaks continued in fashion down to the time of which we treat, and particularly among the princes of the house of Anjou. They were therefore in universal use among Prince John's courtiers; and the long mantle, which formed the upper garment of the Saxons, was held in proportional derision.

The guests were seated at a table which groaned under the quantity of good cheer. The numerous cooks who attended on the Prince's progress, having exerted all their art in varying the forms in which the ordinary provisions were served up, had succeeded almost as well as the modern professors of the culinary art in rendering them perfectly unlike their natural appearance. Besides these dishes of domestic origin, there were various delicacies brought from foreign parts, and a quantity of rich pastry, as well as of the simnel-bread and wastle cakes, which were only used at the tables of the highest nobility. The banquet was crowned with the richest wines, both foreign and domestic.

But, though luxurious, the Norman nobles were not, generally speaking, an intemperate race. While indulging themselves in the pleasures of the table, they aimed at delicacy, but avoided excess, and were apt to object gluttony and drunkenness to the vanquished Saxons, as vices peculiar to their inferior strain. Prince John, indeed, and those who courted his pleasure by imitating his foibles, were apt to indulge to excess in the pleasures of the trencher and the goblet; and indeed it is well known that his death was occasioned by a surfeit upon peaches and new ale. His conduct, however, was an exception to the general manners of his countrymen.

With sly gravity, interrupted only by private signs to each other, the Norman knights and nobles beheld the ruder demeanour of Athelstane and Cedric at a banquet, to the form and fashion of which they were unaccustomed. And while their demeanour was thus the subject of sarcastic observation, the untaught Saxons unwittingly transgressed several of the arbitrary rules established for the regulation of society. Now, it is well known that a man may with more impunity be guilty of an actual breach either of real good breeding or of good morals, than appear ignorant of the most minute point of fashionable etiquette. Thus Cedric, who dried his hands upon a towel, instead of suffering the moisture to exhale by waving them gracefully in the air, incurred more ridicule than his companion Athelstane, when he swallowed to his own single share the whole of a large pasty composed of the most exquisite foreign delicacies, and termed at that time a

Karum-pie. When, however, it was discovered, by a serious cross-examination, that the Thane of Coningsburgh (or Franklin, as the Normans termed him,) had no idea what he had been devouring, and that he had taken the contents of the Karum-pie for larks and pigeons, whereas they were in fact beccaficoes and nightingales, his ignorance brought him in for an ample share of the ridicule which would have been more justly bestowed on his gluttony.

The long feast had at length its end; and, while the goblet circulated freely, men talked of the feats of the preceding tournament,—of the unknown victor in the archery game,—of the Black Knight, whose self-denial had induced him to withdraw from the honours he had won,—and of the gallant Ivanhoe, who had so dearly bought the honours of the day. The topics were treated with military frankness, and the jest and laugh went round the hall. The brow of Prince John alone was overclouded during these discussions; some overpowering care seemed agitating his mind, and it was only when he received occasional hints from his attendants that he seemed to take interest in what was passing around him. On such occasions he would start up, quaff off a cup of wine as if to raise his spirits, and then mingle in the conversation by some observation made abruptly or at random.

"We drink this beaker," said he, "to the health of Wilfred of Ivanhoe, champion of this passage of arms, and grieve that his wound renders him absent from our board—Let all fill to the pledge, and especially Cedric of Rotherwood, the worthy father of a son so promising."

"No, my lord," replied Cedric, standing up, and placing on the table his untasted cup, "I yield not the name of son to the disobedient youth, who at once despises my commands, and relinquishes the manners and customs of his fathers."

"'Tis impossible," cried Prince John, with well-feigned astonishment, "that so gallant a knight should be an unworthy or disobedient son."

"Yet, my lord," answered Cedric, "so it is with this Wilfred. He left my homely dwelling to mingle with the gay nobility of your brother's court, where he learned to do those tricks of horsemanship which you prize so highly. He left it contrary to my wish and command; and in the days of Alfred that would have been termed disobedience—ay, and a crime severely punishable."

"Alas!" replied Prince John, with a deep sigh of affected sympathy, "since your son was a follower of my unhappy brother, it need not be enquired where or from whom he learned the lesson of filial disobedience."

Thus spoke Prince John; wilfully forgetting that of all the sons of

Henry the Second, though no one was free from the charge, he himself had been most distinguished for rebellion and ingratitude to his father.

"I think," said he, after a moment's pause, "that my brother proposed to confer upon his favourite the rich manor of Ivanhoe."

"He did endow him with it," answered Cedric; "nor is it my least quarrel against my son, that he stooped to hold, as a feudal vassal, the very domains which his fathers possessed in free and independent right."

"We shall then have your willing sanction, good Cedric," said Prince John, "to confer this fief upon a person whose dignity will not be diminished by holding land of the British crown. Sir Reginald Front-de-Bœuf," he said, turning towards that Baron, "I trust you will so keep the goodly Barony of Ivanhoe, that Sir Wilfred shall not incur his father's farther displeasure by again entering upon that fief."

"By St Anthony!" answered the black-brow'd giant, "I will consent that your highness shall hold me a Saxon, if either Cedric or Wilfred, or the best that ever bore English blood, shall wrench from me the gift with which your highness has graced me."

"Whoever shall call thee Saxon, Sir Baron," replied Cedric, offended at a mode of expression by which the Normans frequently expressed their habitual contempt of the English, "will do thee an honour as great as it is undeserved."

Front-de-Bœuf would have replied, but Prince John's petulance and levity got the start.

"Assuredly," said he, "my lords, the noble Cedric speaks truth; and his race may claim precedence over us as much in the length of their pedigrees as in the longitude of their cloaks."

"They go before us indeed in the field—as deer before dogs," said Malvoisin.

"And with good right may they go before us—forget not," said the Prior Aymer, "the superior decency and decorum of their manners."

"Their singular abstemiousness and temperance," said Bracy, forgetting the plan which promised him a Saxon bride.

"Together with the courage and conduct," said Brian de Bois-Guilbert, "by which they distinguished themselves at Hastings and elsewhere."

While, with smooth and smiling cheek, the courtiers, each in turn, followed their Prince's example, and aimed a shaft of ridicule at Cedric, the face of the Saxon became inflamed with passion, and he glanced his eyes fiercely from one to another, as if the quick succession of so many injuries had prevented his replying to them in turn; or, like a baited bull, who, surrounded by his tormentors, is at a loss to choose from among them the immediate object of his revenge. At length he spoke, with a voice half choked with passion; and, addressing himself to Prince John as the head and front of the offence which he had received, "Whatever," he said, "have been the follies and vices of our race, a Saxon would have been held *nidering*,* (the most emphatic term for abject worthlessness,) who should, in his own hall, and while his own wine-cup passed, have treated an unoffending guest as your highness has this day beheld me used; and whatever was the misfortune of our fathers on the field of Hastings, those may at least be silent," here he looked at Front-de-Bœuf and the Templar, "who have within these few hours once and again lost saddle and stirrup before the lance of a Saxon."

"By my faith, a biting jest," said Prince John. "How like you it, sirs? —Our Saxon subjects rise in spirit and courage; become shrewd in wit, and bold in bearing, in these unsettled times—What say ye, my lords?—By this good light, I hold it best to take our galleys, and return to Normandy in time."

"For fear of the Saxons?" said Bracy, laughing; "we should need no weapon but our hunting spears to bring these boars to bay."

"A truce with your raillery, Sir Knights," said Fitzurse; "and it were well," he added, addressing the Prince, "that your highness should assure the worthy Cedric there is no insult intended him by jests which must sound but harshly in the ear of a stranger."

"Insult?" answered Prince John, resuming his courtesy of demeanour; "I trust it will not be thought that I could mean, or permit any, to be offered in my presence. Here! I fill my cup to Cedric himself, since he refuses to pledge his son's health."

The cup went round amid the well-dissembled applause of the courtiers, which, however, failed to make the impression on the mind of the Saxon which had been designed. He was not naturally acute of perception, but those too much undervalued his understanding who deemed that this flattering compliment would obliterate his sense of the prior insult. He was silent, however, when the royal pledge again passed round, "To Sir Athelstane of Coningsburgh."

The knight made his obeisance, and shewed his sense of the honour by draining a huge goblet in answer to it.

"And now, sirs," said Prince John, who began to be warmed with the wine which he had drank, "having done justice to our Saxon

*There was nothing accounted so ignominious among the Saxons as to merit this disgraceful epithet. Even William the Conqueror, hated as he was by them, continued to draw a considerable army of Anglo-Saxons to his standard, by threatening to stigmatize those that staid at home as *Nidering*. Bartholinus, I think, mentions a similar phrase which had like influence on the Danes. L. T.

guests, we will pray of them some requital to our courtesy. Worthy Thane," he continued, addressing Cedric, "may we pray you to name to us some Norman whose name may least sully your mouth, and to wash down with a goblet of wine all bitterness which the sound may leave behind it?"

Fitzurse arose while Prince John spoke, and, gliding behind the seat of the Saxon, whispered to him not to omit the opportunity of putting an end to unkindness betwixt the two races, by naming Prince John. The Saxon replied not to this politic insinuation, but, rising up, and filling his cup to the brim, he addressed Prince John in these words: "Your highness has required that I should name a Norman deserving to be remembered at our banquet. This, perchance, is a hard task, since it calls on the slave to sing the praises of the master—upon the vanquished, while pressed by all the evils of conquest, to sing the praises of the conqueror. Yet I *will* name a Norman—the first in arms and in place—the best and the noblest of his race. And the lips that shall refuse to pledge me to his well-earned fame, I term false and dishonoured, and will so maintain them with my life.—I quaff this goblet to the health of Richard the Lion-hearted!"

Prince John, who had expected that his own name would have closed the Saxon's speech, started when that of his injured brother was so unexpectedly introduced. He raised mechanically the wine-cup to his lips, then instantly set it down, to view the demeanour of the company at this unexpected proposal, which many of them felt it as unsafe to oppose as to comply with. Some of them, ancient and experienced courtiers, closely imitated the example of the Prince himself, raising the goblet to their lips, and again replacing it before them. There were many who, with a more generous feeling, exclaimed, "Long live King Richard! and may he be speedily restored to us!" And some few, among whom were Front-de-Bœuf and the Templar, in sullen disdain suffered their goblets to stand untasted before them. But no man ventured directly to gainsay a pledge filled to the health of the reigning monarch.

Having enjoyed his triumph for about a minute, Cedric said to his companion, "Up, noble Athelstane! we have remained here long enough, since we have requited the hospitable courtesy of Prince John's banquet. Those who wish to know further of our rude Saxon manners must henceforth seek us in the homes of our fathers, since we have seen enough of royal banquets, and enough of Norman courtesy."

So saying, he arose and left the banqueting room, followed by Athelstane, and by several other guests, who, partaking of the Saxon lineage, held themselves insulted by the sarcasms of Prince John and his courtiers.

"By the bones of St Thomas," said Prince John, as they retreated, "the Saxon churls have borne off the best of the day, and have retreated with triumph."

"*Conclamatum est, poculatum est*," said Prior Aymer; "we have drunk and we have shouted,—it were time we left our wine flagons."

"The monk hath some fair penitent to shrive to-night, that he is in such a hurry to depart," said De Bracy.

"Not so, Sir Knight," replied the Abbot; "but I must move several miles forward this evening upon my homeward journey."

"They are breaking up," said the Prince in a whisper to Fitzurse; "their fears anticipate the event, and this coward Prior is the first to shrink from me."

"Fear not, my lord," said Waldemar; "I will shew him such reasons as shall induce him to join us to hold our meeting at York.—Sir Prior," he said, "I must speak with you in private, before you mount your palfrey."

The other guests were now fast dispersing, with the exception of those immediately attached to Prince John's faction, and his retinue.

"This, then, is the result of your advice," said the Prince, turning an angry countenance upon Fitzurse; "that I should be bearded at my own board by a drunken Saxon churl, and that, on the mere sound of my brother's name, men should fall off from me as if I had the leprosy."

"Have patience, sir," replied his counsellor; "I might retort your accusation, and blame the inconsiderate levity which foiled my design, and misled your own better judgment. But this is no time for recrimination. Bracy and I will instantly go among these cowards, and convince them they have gone too far to recede."

"It will be in vain," said Prince John, pacing the apartment with disordered steps, and expressing himself with an agitation to which the wine he had drank partly contributed—"It will be in vain—they have seen the hand-writing on the wall—they have marked the paw of the lion in the sand—they have heard his approaching roar shake the wood—nothing will re-animate their courage."

"Would to God," said Fitzurse to Bracy, "that aught could re-animate his own! His brother's very name is an ague to him. Unhappy are the counsellors of a Prince, who wants fortitude and perseverance alike in good and in evil."

END OF VOLUME FIRST

IVANHOE

VOLUME II

Chapter One

And yet he thinks,—ha, ha, ha, ha,—he thinks
I am the tool and servant of his will.
Well, let it be; through all the maze of trouble
His plots and base oppression must create,
I'll shape myself a way to higher things,
And who will say 'tis wrong?

Basil, a Tragedy.

NO SPIDER ever took more pains to repair the shattered meshes of his web, than did Waldemar Fitzurse to reunite and combine the scattered members of Prince John's cabal. Few of these were attached to him from inclination, and none from personal attachment. It was therefore necessary, that Fitzurse should open to them new prospects of advantage, and remind them of those which they at present enjoyed. To the young and wild nobles, he held out the prospect of unpunished license and uncontrouled revelry; to the ambitious, that of power, and to the covetous, that of increased wealth and extended domains. The leaders of the mercenaries received a donation in gold; an argument the most persuasive to their minds, and without which all others would have proved in vain. Promises were still more liberally distributed than money by this active agent; and, in fine, nothing was left undone that could determine the wavering, or animate the disheartened. The return of King Richard he spoke of as an event altogether beyond the reach of probability; yet, when he observed, from the doubtful looks and uncertain answers which he received, that this was the apprehension by which the minds of his accomplices were most haunted, he boldly treated that event, should it really take place, as one which ought not to alter their political calculations.

"If Richard returns," said Fitzurse, "he returns to enrich his needy and impoverished crusaders at the expence of those who did not follow him to the Holy Land. He returns to call to a fearful accounting, those who, during his absence, have done aught that can be construed offence or encroachment upon either the laws of the land or the privileges of the crown. He returns to avenge upon the Orders of the Temple and the Hospital, the preference which they shewed to Philip of France during the wars in the Holy Land. He returns, in fine, to punish as a rebel every adherent of his brother Prince John. Are ye afraid of his power?" continued the artful confidant of that prince; "we acknowledge him a strong and valiant knight, but these are not the days of King Arthur, when a champion could encounter an army. If Richard indeed comes back, it must be alone,—unfollowed—unfriended. The bones of his gallant army have whitened the sands of Palestine. The few of his followers who have returned, have straggled hither like this Wilfred of Ivanhoe, beggared and broken men. And what talk ye of Richard's right of birth?" he continued, in answer to those who objected scruples on that head. "Is Richard's title of primogeniture more decidedly certain than that of Duke Robert of Normandy, the Conqueror's eldest son? And yet William the Red, and Henry, his second and third brothers, were successively preferred to him by the voice of the nation. Robert had every merit which can be pleaded for Richard; he was a bold knight, a good leader, generous to his friends and to the church, and, to crown the whole, a crusader and a conqueror of the Holy Sepulchre; and yet he died a blind and miserable prisoner in the Castle of Cardiffe, because he opposed himself to the will of the people, who chose not that he should rule over them. It is our right," he said, "to choose from the blood royal the prince who is best qualified to hold the supreme power—that is," said he, correcting himself, "him whose election will best promote the interests of the nobility. In personal qualifications," he said, "it was possible that Prince John might be inferior to his brother Richard; but when it was considered that the latter returned with the sword of vengeance in his hands, while the former held out rewards, immunities, privileges, wealth and honours, it could not be doubted which was the king whom in wisdom the nobility were called on to support."

These, and many more arguments, some adapted to the peculiar circumstances of those whom he addressed, had the expected weight with the nobles of Prince John's faction. Most of them consented to attend upon the proposed meeting at York, for the purpose of making general arrangements for placing the crown upon the head of Prince John.

It was late at night, when, worn out and exhausted with his various exertions, however gratified with the result, Fitzurse, returning to the

Castle of Ashby, met with De Bracy, who had exchanged his banqueting garments for a short green kirtle, with hose of the same cloth and colour, a leathern cap or head-piece, a short sword, a horn slung over his shoulder, a long bow in his hand, and a bundle of arrows stuck into his belt. Had Fitzurse met this figure in an outer apartment, he would have passed him without notice, as one of the yeomen of the guard; but finding him in the inner-hall, he looked at him with more attention, and recognized the Norman knight in the dress of an English yeoman.

"What mummery is this, De Bracy?" said Fitzurse, somewhat angrily; "is this a time for Christmas gambols and quaint maskings, when the fate of our master, Prince John, is on the very verge of decision? Why hast thou not been, like me, among these heartless cravens, whom the very name of King Richard terrifies, as it is said to do the children of the Saracens?"

"I have been minding mine own business," said De Bracy calmly, "as you, Fitzurse."

"I minding mine own business!" echoed Waldemar; "I have been engaged in that of Prince John, our joint patron."

"As if thou hadst any other reason for that, Waldemar," said De Bracy, "than the promotion of thine own individual interest. Come, Fitzurse, we know each other—ambition is thy pursuit, pleasure is mine, and they become our different ages. Of Prince John thou thinkest as I do; that he is too weak to be a determined monarch, too tyrannical to be an easy monarch, too insolent and presumptuous to be a popular monarch, and too fickle and timid to be long a monarch of any kind. But he is a monarch by whom Fitzurse and Bracy hope to rise and thrive; and therefore you aid him with your policy, and I with the lances of my Free Companions."

"A hopeful auxiliary," said Fitzurse impatiently; "playing the fool in the very moment of utter necessity.—What on earth dost thou purpose by this absurd disguise at a moment so urgent?"

"To get me a wife," answered Bracy coolly, "after the manner of the tribe of Benjamin."

"The tribe of Benjamin?" said Fitzurse, "I comprehend thee not."

"Wert thou not in presence yester-even," said De Bracy, "when we heard the Prior Aymer tell us a tale, in reply to the romance which was sung by the Minstrel?—He told how, long since in Palestine, a deadly feud arose between the clan of Benjamin and the rest of the Israelitish nation; and how they cut to pieces well nigh all the chivalry of that clan; and how they swore by our Blessed Lady that they would not permit those who remained to marry in their lineage; and how they became grieved for their vow, and sent to consult his holiness the Pope how they might be absolved from it; and how, by the advice of the Holy Father, the youth of the tribe of Benjamin carried off from a superb tournament all the ladies who were there present, and thus won them wives without the consent either of their brides or their brides' families."

"I have heard the story," said Fitzurse, "though either the Prior or thou hast made some singular alterations in date and circumstances."

"I tell thee," said De Bracy, "that I mean to purvey me a wife after the fashion of the tribe of Benjamin; which is as much as to say, that in this same equipment I will fall upon that herd of Saxon bullocks, who have this night left the castle, and carry off from them the lovely Rowena."

"Art thou mad, De Bracy?" said Fitzurse. "Bethink thee that, though the men be Saxons, they are rich and powerful, and regarded with the more respect by their countrymen, that wealth and honour are but the lot of few of Saxon descent."

"And should belong to none," said De Bracy; "the work of the Conquest should be completed."

"This is no time for it at least," said Fitzurse; "the approaching crisis renders the favour of the multitude indispensable, and Prince John cannot refuse justice to any one who injures their favourites."

"Let him grant it, if he dare," said De Bracy; "he will soon see the difference betwixt the support of such a lusty lot of spears as mine, and that of a heartless mob of Saxon churls. Yet I mean no immediate discovery of myself. Seem I not in this garb as bold a forester as ever blew horn? The blame of the violence shall rest with the outlaws of the Yorkshire forests. I have sure spies on the Saxons' motions—To-night they sleep in the convent of Saint Wittol, or Withold, or whatever they call that churl of a Saxon Saint at Burton-on-Trent. Next day's march brings them within our reach, and falcon-ways we swoop on them at once. Presently after I will appear in mine own shape, play the courteous knight, rescue the unfortunate and afflicted fair one from the hands of the rude ravishers, conduct her to Front-de-Bœuf's castle, or to Normandy, if it should be necessary, and produce her not again to her kindred until she be the bride and dame of Maurice de Bracy."

"A marvellously sage plan," said Fitzurse, "and, as I think, not entirely of thine own device—Come, be frank, De Bracy, who aided thee in the invention? and who is to assist in the execution? for, as I think, thine own band lies as far off as York."

"Marry, if thou must needs know," said De Bracy, "it was the Templar Brian de Bois-Guilbert that shaped out the enterprize which the adventure of the men of Benjamin suggested to me. He is to aid me in the onslaught, and he and his followers will personate the outlaws, from whom my valorous arm is, after changing my garb, to rescue the lady."

"By my halidome," said Fitzurse, "the plan was worthy of your united wisdom; and thy prudence, De Bracy, is most especially manifested in thy project of leaving the lady in the hands of thy worthy confederate. Thou may'st, I think, succeed in taking her from her Saxon friends, but how thou wilt rescue her afterwards from the clutches of Bois-Guilbert seems considerably more doubtful—He is a falcon well accustomed to pounce on a partridge, and to hold his prey fast."

"He is a Templar," said De Bracy, "and cannot therefore rival me in my plan of wedding this heiress;—and to attempt aught dishonourable against the intended bride of De Bracy—By Heaven! were he a whole Chapter of his Order in his single person, he dared not do me such an injury!"

"Then since nought that I can say," said Fitzurse, "will put this folly from thy imagination (for well I know the obstinacy of thy disposition), at least waste as little time as possible—let not thy folly be lasting as well as untimely."

"I tell thee," answered De Bracy, "that it will be the work of a few hours, and I shall be at York at the head of my daring and valorous fellows, as ready to support any daring design as thy policy can be to form one—But I hear my comrades assembling, and the steeds stamping and neighing in the outer-court—Farewell.—I go, like a true knight, to win the smiles of beauty."

"Like a true knight?" repeated Fitzurse, looking after him; "like a natural fool, I should say, or like a child, who will leave the most serious and needful occupation, to chase the down of the thistle that drives past him—But it is with such tools that I must work, and for whose advantage?—for that of a Prince as unwise as he is profligate, and as likely to be an ungrateful master as he has already proved a rebellious son and an unnatural brother.—But he—he, too, is but one of the tools with whom I labour; and, proud as he is, should he presume to separate his interest from mine, this is a secret which he shall soon learn."

The meditations of the statesman were here interrupted by the voice of the Prince from an interior apartment, calling out, "Noble Waldemar Fitzurse!" and, with bonnet doffed, the future Chancellor, for to such high preferment did the hopes of the wily Norman aspire, hastened to receive the orders of the future sovereign.

Chapter Two

Far in a wild, unknown to public view,
From youth to age a reverend hermit grew;
The moss his bed, the cave his humble cell,
His food the fruits, his drink the crystal well;
Remote from man, with God he pass'd his days,
Prayer all his business—all his pleasure praise.
PARNELL.

THE READER cannot have forgotten that the event of the tournament was decided by the exertions of an unknown knight, whom, on account of the passive and indifferent conduct which he had manifested on the former part of the day, the spectators had entitled, *Le Noir Faineant*. This knight had left the field abruptly when the victory was achieved; and when he was called upon to receive the reward of his valour, he was no where to be found. In the meantime, while summoned by heralds and by trumpets, the knight was holding his course northward, avoiding all frequented paths, and taking the shortest course through the woodlands. He paused for the night at a small hostelry lying out of the ordinary route, where, however, he obtained from a wandering minstrel news of the event of the tourney.

On the next morning the knight departed early, with the purpose of making a long journey; the condition of his horse, which he had carefully spared during the preceding morning, being such as enabled him to travel far without the necessity of much repose. Yet his purpose was baffled by the devious paths through which he rode, so that when evening closed upon him, he only found himself on the frontiers of the West Riding of Yorkshire. By this time both horse and man required refreshment, and it became necessary moreover to look out for some place in which they might spend the night, which was now fast approaching.

The place where the traveller found himself seemed unpropitious for finding either shelter or refreshment, and he was likely to be reduced to the usual expedient of knights errant, who, on such occasions, turned their horses to graze, and laid themselves down to meditate on their lady-mistress, with an oak-tree for a canopy. But the Black Knight either had no mistress to meditate upon, or, as indifferent in love as he seemed to be in war, was not sufficiently occupied by passionate reflections upon her beauty and cruelty, to be able to parry the effects of fatigue and hunger, and suffer love to act as a substitute for the solid comforts of a bed and supper. He felt dissatisfied, therefore, when, looking around, he found himself deeply involved in woods, through which indeed there were many open glades, and some paths, but such as seemed only formed by the numerous herds of cattle which grazed in the forest, or by the animals of chase and the hunters who made prey of them.

The sun, by which the knight had chiefly directed his course, was now sunk behind the Derbyshire hills on his left, and every effort which he might make to pursue his journey was as likely to lead him out of his road as to advance him on his journey. After having in vain endeavoured to select the most beaten path, in hopes it might lead to the cottage of some herdsman, or the sylvan lodge of some forester, and having repeatedly found himself totally unable to determine on a choice, the knight resolved to trust to the sagacity of his horse; experience having, on former occasions, made him acquainted with the wonderful talent possessed by these animals for extricating themselves and their riders upon such emergencies.

The good horse, grievously fatigued with so long a day's journey under a rider cased in mail, had no sooner found, by the slackened reins, that he was abandoned to his own guidance, than he seemed to assume new strength and spirit; and whereas formerly he had scarce replied to the spur, otherwise than by a groan, he now, as if proud of the confidence reposed in him, pricked up his ears, and assumed of his own accord a more lively motion. The path which the animal adopted rather turned off from the course pursued by the knight during the day; but, as the horse seemed confident in his choice, the rider abandoned himself to his discretion.

He was justified by the event; for the footpath soon after appeared a little wider and more worn, and the tinkle of a small bell gave the knight to understand that he was in the vicinity of some chapel or hermitage.

Accordingly, he soon reached an open plat of turf, on the opposite side of which a rock, rising abruptly from a gently sloping plain, offered its grey and weather-beaten front to the traveller. Ivy mantled its sides in some places, and in others oaks and holly bushes, whose roots found nourishment in the cliffs of the crag, waved over the precipice below, like the plumage of the warrior over his steel helmet, giving grace to that whose chief expression was terror. At the bottom of the rock, and leaning as it were against it, was constructed a rude hut, built chiefly of the trunks of trees felled in the neighbouring forest, and secured against the weather by having its crevices stuffed with moss mingled with clay. The stem of a young fir-tree, lopped of its branches, with a piece of wood tied across near the top, was planted upright near the door, as a rude emblem of the holy cross. At a little distance on the right hand, a fountain of the purest water trickled out of the rock, and was received in a hollow stone, which labour had formed into a rustic basin. Escaping from thence, the stream murmured down the descent by a channel which its course had long worn, and so wandered through the little plain to lose itself in the neighbouring wood.

Beside this fountain were the ruins of a very small chapel, of which the roof had partly fallen in. The building, when entire, had never been above sixteen feet long by twelve feet in breadth, and the roof, low in proportion, rested upon four concentric arches which sprung from the four corners of the building, each supported upon a short and heavy pillar. The ribs of two of these arches remained, though the roof had fallen down betwixt them; over the others it remained entire. The entrance to this ancient place of devotion was under a very low round arch, ornamented by several courses of that zig-zag moulding, resembling shark's teeth, which appears so often in the more ancient Saxon churches. A belfry rose above the porch on four small pillars, within which hung the green and weather-beaten bell, the feeble sounds of which had been sometime since heard by the Black Knight.

The whole peaceful and quiet scene lay glimmering in twilight before the eyes of the traveller, giving him good assurance of lodging for the night; since it was a special duty of those hermits who dwelt in the woods to exercise hospitality towards benighted or bewildered passengers.

Accordingly, the knight took no time to consider minutely the particulars which we have detailed, but thanking Saint Julian (the patron of travellers) who had sent him good harbourage, he leaped from his horse and assailed the door of the hermitage with the butt of his lance, in order to arouse attention and gain admittance.

It was sometime before he obtained any answer, and the reply, when made, was unpropitious.

"Pass on, whosoever thou art," was the answer given by a deep hoarse voice from within the hut, "and disturb not the servant of God and St Dunstan in his evening devotions."

"Worthy father," answered the knight, "here is a poor wanderer bewildered in these woods, who gives thee the opportunity of exercising your charity and hospitality."

"Good brother," replied the inhabitant of the hermitage, "it has pleased our Lady and St Dunstan to destine me for the object of those virtues, instead of the exercise thereof. I have no provisions here which even a dog would share with me, and a horse of any tenderness of nurture would despise my couch—pass therefore on thy way, and God speed thee."

"But how," replied the knight, "is it possible for me to find my way through such a wood as this, when darkness is coming on? I pray you, reverend father, as you are a Christian, to undo your door, and at least point out to me my road."

"And I pray you, good Christian brother," replied the anchorite, "to disturb me no more. You have already interrupted one *pater*, two *aves*, and a *credo*, which I, miserable sinner that I am, should, according to my vow, have said before moonrise."

"The road—the road!" vociferated the knight, "if I am to expect no more from thee."

"The road," replied the hermit, "is easy to hit. The path from the wood leads to a morass, and from thence to a ford, which, as the rains have abated, may now be passable. When thou hast crossed the ford, thou wilt take care of thy footing up the left bank, as it is somewhat precipitous; and the path, which hangs over the river, has lately, as I learn, (for I seldom leave the duties of my chapel,) given way in sundry places. Thou wilt then keep straight forward"——

"A broken path—a precipice—a ford, and a morass!" said the knight, interrupting him,—"Sir Hermit, if you were the holiest that ever wore beard or told bead, you shall scarce prevail on me to hold this road to-night. I tell thee, that thou, who livest by the charity of the country—ill deserved, as I doubt it is—hast no right to refuse shelter to the wayfarer when in distress. Either open the door quickly, or, by the rood, I will beat it down and make entry for myself."

"Friend wayfarer," replied the hermit, "be not importunate; if thou puttest me to use the carnal weapon in mine own defence, it will be e'en the worse for you."

At this moment a distant noise of barking and growling, which the traveller had for some time heard, became extremely loud and furious, and made the knight suppose that the hermit, alarmed by his threat of making forcible entry, had called the dogs who made this clamour to aid him in his defence, out of some distant recess in which they had been kennelled. Incensed at this preparation on the hermit's part for making good his inhospitable purpose, the knight struck the door so furiously with his foot, that posts as well as staples shook with violence.

The anchorite, not caring again to expose his door to a similar shock, now called out aloud, "Patience, patience—spare thy strength, good traveller, and I will presently undo the door, though, it may be, my doing so will be little to thy pleasure."

The door accordingly was opened; and the hermit, a large, strong-built man, in his sackcloth gown and hood, girt with a rope of rushes, stood before the knight. He had in one hand a lighted torch, or link, and in the other a baton of crab-tree, so thick and heavy, that it might well be termed a club. Two large shaggy dogs, half greyhound half mastiff, stood ready to rush upon the traveller so soon as the door should be opened. But when the torch glanced upon the armour of the knight, who stood without, the hermit, altering probably his original intentions, repressed the rage of his auxiliaries, and, changing his tone to a sort of churlish courtesy, invited the knight to enter his lodge, making excuse for his unwillingness to open his lodge after sun-set, by alleging the multitude of robbers and outlaws who were abroad, and who gave no honour to our Lady or St Dunstan, nor to those holy men who spent life in their service.

"The poverty of your cell, good father," said the knight, looking around him, and seeing nothing but a bed of leaves, a crucifix rudely carved in oak, a missal, with a rough-hewn table and two stools, and one or two clumsy articles of furniture—"the poverty of your cell should seem a sufficient defence against any risk of thieves, not to mention the aid of two trusty dogs, large and strong enough, I think, to pull down a stag, and, of course, to match with most men."

"The good keeper of the forest," said the hermit, "hath allowed me the use of these animals, to protect my solitude until the times shall mend."

Having said this, he fixed his torch in a twisted branch of iron which served for a candlestick; and placing the oaken trivet before the embers of the fire, which he refreshed with some dry wood, he placed a stool upon one side of the table, and beckoned to the knight to do the same upon the other.

They sat down, and gazed with great gravity at each other; each thinking in his heart that he had seldom seen a stronger or more athletic figure than was placed opposite to him.

"Reverend hermit," said the knight, after looking long and fixedly at his host, "were it not to interrupt your devout meditations, I would pray to know three things of your holiness; first, where I am to put my horse?—secondly, what I can have for supper?—thirdly, where I am to take up my couch for the night?"

"I will reply to you," said the hermit, "with my finger, it being against my rule to speak by words where signs can answer the purpose." So saying, he pointed successively to two corners of the hut. "Your stable," said he, "is there—your bed there; and," reaching down a platter with two handfuls of parched pease upon it from the neighbouring shelf, and placing it upon the table, he added, "your supper is there."

The knight shrugged his shoulders, and leaving the hut, brought in his horse, (which in the interim he had fastened to a tree,) unsaddled him with much attention, and spread upon the steed's weary back his own mantle.

The hermit was apparently somewhat moved to compassion by the anxiety as well as address which the stranger displayed in tending his horse; for, muttering something about provender left for the keeper's palfrey, he dragged out of a recess a bundle of forage, which he spread before the knight's charger, and immediately afterwards shook down a quantity of dried fern in the corner which he had assigned for the rider's couch. The knight returned him thanks for his courtesy; and, this duty done, both resumed their seats by the table, whereon stood the trencher of pease placed between them. The hermit, after a long grace, which had once been Latin, but of which original language few traces remained, excepting here and there the long rolling termination of some word or phrase, set example to his guest, by modestly putting into a very large mouth, furnished with teeth which might have ranked with those of a boar both in sharpness and whiteness, some three or four dried peas,—a miserable grist as it seemed for so large and able a mill.

The knight, in order to follow so laudable an example, laid aside his helmet, his corslet, and the greater part of his armour, and showed to the hermit a head thick-curled with yellow hair, high features, blue eyes, remarkably bright and sparkling, a mouth well formed, having an upper lip clothed with mustachios darker than his hair, and bearing altogether the look of a bold, daring, and enterprizing man, with which his strong form well corresponded.

The hermit, as if wishing to answer to the confidence of his guest, threw back his cowl, and shewed a round bullet-head belonging to a man in the prime of life. His close-shaven crown, surrounded by a circle of stiff curled black hair, had something the appearance of a parish pinfold begirt by its high hedge. The features expressed nothing of monastic austerity, or of ascetic privations; on the contrary, it was a bold bluff countenance, with broad black eyebrows, a well-turned forehead, and cheeks as round and vermilion as those of a trumpeter, from which descended a long and curly black beard. Such a visage, joined to the brawny form of the holy man, spoke rather of sirloins and haunches, than of peas and pulse. This incongruity did not escape the guest. After he had with great difficulty accomplished the mastication of a mouthful of the dried peas, he found it absolutely necessary to request his pious entertainer to furnish him with some liquor; who replied to his request by placing before him a large cann of the purest water from the fountain.

"It is from the well of St Dunstan," said he, "in which, betwixt sun and sun, he baptized five hundred heathen Danes and Britons—blessed be his name!" And applying his black beard to the pitcher, he took a draft much more moderate in quantity than his encomium seemed to warrant.

"It seems to me, reverend father," said the knight, "that the small morsels which you eat, together with this holy, but somewhat thin beverage, have thriven with you marvellously. You appear a man more fit to win the ram at a wrestling match, or the ring at a bout at quarter-staff, or the bucklers at a sword-play, than to linger out your time in this desolate wilderness, saying masses and living upon parched pease and cold water."

"Sir Knight," answered the hermit, "your thoughts, like those of the ignorant laity, are according to the flesh. It has pleased our Lady and my patron saint to bless the pittance to which I restrain myself, even as the pulse and water was blessed to the children Shadrach, Meshech, and Abednego, who drank the same rather than defile themselves with the wine and meats which were appointed them by the King of the Saracens."

"Holy father," said the knight, "upon whose countenance it hath pleased Heaven to work such a miracle, permit a sinful layman to crave thy name?"

"Thou may'st call me," answered the hermit, "the Clerk of Copmanhurst, for so am I termed in these parts—They add, it is true, the epithet holy, but I stand not upon that, as being unworthy of such addition.—And now, valiant knight, may I pray ye for the name of my honourable guest?"

"Truly," said the knight, "Holy Clerk of Copmanhurst, men call me in these parts the Black Knight,—many, sir, add to it the epithet of Sluggard, whereby I am no way ambitious to be distinguished."

The hermit could scarcely forbear from smiling at his guest's reply.

"I see," said he, "Sir Sluggish Knight, that thou art a man of prudence and of counsel; and moreover, I see that my poor monastic fare likes thee not, accustomed, perhaps, as thou hast been, to the licence of courts and of camps, and the luxuries of cities; and now I bethink me, Sir Sluggard, that when the charitable keeper of this forest-walk left these dogs for my protection, and also those bundles of forage, he left me also some food, which, being unfit for my use, the very recollection of it had escaped me amid my more weighty meditations."

"I dare be sworn he did so," said the knight, "I was convinced that there was better food in the cell, Holy Clerk, since you first doffed your cowl.—Your keeper is ever a jovial fellow; and none who beheld thy grinders contending with these peas, and thy throat flooded with this ungenial element, could see thee doomed to such horse-provender and horse-beverage," (pointing to the provisions upon the table,) "and refrain from mending thy cheer.—Let us see the keeper's bounty therefore without delay."

The hermit cast a wistful look upon the knight, in which there was a sort of comic expression of hesitation, as if uncertain how far he should act prudently in trusting his guest. There was, however, as much of bold frankness in the knight's countenance as was possible to be expressed by features. His smile, too, had something in it irresistibly comic, and gave an assurance of faith and loyalty, with which his host could not refrain from sympathising.

After exchanging a mute glance or two, the hermit went to the further side of the hut, and opened a hatch, which was concealed with great care and some ingenuity. Out of the recesses of a dark closet, into which this aperture gave admittance, he brought a large pasty, baked in a pewter platter of unusual dimensions. This mighty dish he placed before his guest, who, using his poniard to cut it open, lost no time in making himself acquainted with its contents.

"How long is it since the good keeper has been here?" said the knight to his host, after having swallowed several hasty morsels of this reinforcement to the hermit's good cheer.

"About two months," answered the father hastily.

"By the true Lord," answered the knight, "every thing in your hermitage is miraculous, Holy Clerk; for I would have been sworn that the fat buck which furnished this venison had been running on foot within the week."

The hermit was somewhat discountenanced by this observation; and, moreover, he made but a poor figure while gazing on the diminution of the pasty, on which his guest was making desperate inroads; a warfare in which his previous professions of abstinence left him no pretext for joining.

"I have been in Palestine, Sir Clerk," said the knight, stopping short of a sudden, "and I bethink me it is a custom there that every host who entertains a guest shall assure him of the wholesomeness of his food, by partaking of it along with him. Far be it from me to suspect so holy a man of aught inhospitable; nevertheless I will be highly bound to you would you comply with this eastern custom."

"To ease your unnecessary scruples, Sir Knight, I will for once depart from my rule," replied the hermit. And as there were no forks in these days, his clutches were instantly in the bowels of the pasty.

The ice of ceremony being once broken, it seemed matter of rivalry between the guest and the entertainer which should display the best appetite; and although the former had probably fasted longest, yet the hermit fairly surpassed him.

"Holy Clerk," said the knight, when his hunger was appeased, "I would gage my good horse yonder against a zecchin, that that same honest keeper to whom we are obliged for the venison has left thee a stoup of wine, or a runlet of canary, or some such trifle, by way of ally to this noble pasty. This would be a circumstance, doubtless, totally unworthy to dwell in the memory of so rigid an anchorite; yet, I think, were you to search yonder crypt once more, you would find that I am right in my conjecture."

The hermit only replied by a grin; and, returning to the hatch, he produced a leathern bottle, which might contain about four quarts. He also brought forth two large drinking cups, made out of the horn of the urus, and hooped with silver. Having made this goodly provision for washing down the supper, he seemed to think no further ceremonious scruple necessary on his part; but, filling both cups, and saying, in the Saxon fashion, "*Waes hael*, Sir Sluggish Knight!" he emptied his own at a draught.

"*Drink hael!* Holy Clerk of Copmanhurst," answered the warrior, and did his host reason in a similar brimmer.

"Holy Clerk," said the stranger, after the first cup was thus swallowed, "I cannot but marvel that a man, possessed of such thews and sinews as thine, and who therewithal shews the talents of so goodly a trencher-man, should think of abiding by himself in this wilderness. In my judgment, you are fitter to keep a castle or a fort, eating of the fat and drinking of the strong, than to live here upon pulse and water, or even upon the charity of the keeper. At least, were I as thee, I should find myself both disport and plenty out of the king's deer. There is many a goodly herd in these forests, and a buck will never be missed that goes to the use of Saint Dunstan's chaplain."

"Sir Sluggish Knight," replied the Clerk, "these are dangerous words, and I pray you to forbear them. I am true hermit to the king and law, and were I to spoil my liege's game, I should be sure of the prison, and, an my gown saved me not, were in some peril of hanging."

"Nevertheless, were I as thou," said the knight, "I would take my walk by moonlight, when foresters and keepers were warm in bed, and ever and anon,—as I pattered my prayers,—I would let fly a shaft among the herds of dun deer that feed in the glades—Resolve me, Holy Clerk, hast thou never practised such a pastime?"

"Friend Sluggard," answered the hermit, "thou hast seen all that can concern thee of my housekeeping, and something more than he deserves who takes up his quarters by violence. Credit me, it is better to enjoy the good which God sends thee, than to be impertinently curious how it comes. Fill thy cup, and welcome; and do not, I pray thee, by further impertinent enquiries, put me to shew that thou couldst hardly have made good thy lodging had I been earnest to oppose thee."

"By my faith," said the knight, "thou makest me more curious than ever! Thou art the most mysterious hermit I ever met; and I will know more of thee ere we part. As for thy threats, know, holy man, thou speakest to one whose trade it is to find out danger wherever it is to be met with."

"Sir Sluggish Knight, I drink to thee," said the hermit; "respecting thy valour much, but deeming wondrous slightly of thy discretion. If thou wilt take equal arms with me, I will give thee, in all friendship and brotherly love, such sufficient penance and complete absolution, that thou shalt not for the next twelve months sin the sin of excess of curiosity."

The knight pledged him, and desired him to name his weapons.

"There is none," replied the hermit, "from the scissars of Dalilah and the tenpenny nail of Jael, to the scymitar of Goliath, at which I am not a match for thee—But, if I am to make the election, what say'st thou, good friend, to these trinkets?"

Thus speaking, he opened another hatch, and took out from it a couple of broad-swords and bucklers, such as were used by the yeomanry of the period. The knight, who watched his motions, observed that this second place of concealment was furnished with two or three good long bows, a cross-bow, a bundle of bolts for the latter, and half-a-dozen sheaves of arrows for the former. A harp, and other matters of a very uncanonical appearance, were also visible when this dark recess was opened.

"I promise thee, brother Clerk," said he, "I will ask thee no more offensive questions. The contents of that cupboard are an answer to all my enquiries; and I see a weapon there (here he stooped and took out the harp) on which I would more gladly prove my skill with thee, than at the sword and buckler."

"I hope, Sir Knight," said the hermit, "thou hast given no good reason for thy sirname of the Sluggard. I do promise thee I suspect thee grievously. Nevertheless, thou art my guest, and I will not put thy manhood to the proof without thine own free will. Sit thee down, then, and fill thy cup; let us drink, sing, and be merry. If thou knowest ever a good lay, thou shalt be welcome to a nook of pasty at Copmanhurst so long as I serve the chapel of St Dunstan, which, please God, shall be till I change my grey covering for one of green turf.—But come, fill a flagon, for it will crave some time to tune the harp; and nought pitches the voice and sharpens the ear like a stoup of wine. For my part, I love to feel the grape at my very finger-ends before they make the harp-strings tinkle."

Chapter Three

At eve, within yon studious nook,
I ope my brass-embossed book,
Pourtray'd with many a holy deed
Of martyrs crown'd with heavenly meed;
Then, as my taper waxes dim,
Chaunt, ere I sleep, my measured hymn.
* * * * * * *
Who but would cast his pomp away,
To take my staff and amice gray,
And to the world's tumultuous stage,
Prefer the peaceful HERMITAGE.

WARTON.

NOTWITHSTANDING the prescription of the genial hermit, with which his guest willingly complied, he found it no easy matter to bring the harp to harmony.

"Methinks, holy father," said he, "the instrument wants one string, and the rest have been somewhat misused."

"Ay, mark'st thou that?" replied the hermit; "that shews thee a master of the craft. Wine and wassel," he added, gravely, casting up his eyes—"all the fault of wine and wassel! I told Allan-a-Dale, the northern minstrel, that he would damage the harp if he touched it after the seventh cup, but he would not be controuled—Friend, I drink to thy successful performance."

So saying, he took off his cup with much gravity, at the same time shaking his head at the intemperance of the northern minstrel.

The knight, meantime, had brought the strings into some order, and after a short prelude, asked his host whether he would choose a *sirvente* in the language of *oc*, or a *lai* in the language of *oui*, or a *virelai*, or a ballat in the vulgar English.

"A ballad, a ballad," said the hermit, "against all the *ocs* and *ouis* of France. Downright English am I, Sir Knight, and downright English was my patron St Dunstan, and scorned *oc* and *oui*, as he would have scorned the parings of the devil's hoof—downright English alone shall be sung in this cell."

"I will assay then," said the knight, "a ballad composed by a Saxon glee-man, whom I knew in Holy Land."

It speedily appeared, that if the knight was not a complete master of the minstrel art, his taste for it had at least been cultivated under the best instructors. Art had taught him to soften the faults of a voice which had little compass, and was naturally rough, rather than mellow, and, in short, had done all that art can do in supplying natural deficiences. His performance, therefore, might have been termed very respectable by abler judges than the hermit, especially as the knight threw into the notes now a degree of spirit, and now of plaintive enthusiasm, which gave force and energy to the verses which he sung.

THE CRUSADER'S RETURN.

1.

High deeds atchieved of knightly fame,
From Palestine the champion came;
The cross upon his shoulders borne,
Battle and blast had dimm'd and torn.
Each dint upon his batter'd shield
Was token of a foughten field;
And thus, beneath his lady's bower,
He sung as fell the twilight hour:

2.

"Joy to the fair!—thy knight behold,
Return'd from yonder land of gold;
No wealth he brings, nor wealth can need,
Save his good arms and battle steed;
His spurs, to dash against a foe,
His lance and sword to lay him low;
Such all the trophies of his toil,
Such—and the hope of Tekla's smile!

3.

"Joy to the fair! whose constant knight
Her favour fired to feats of might;
Unnoted shall she not remain
Where meet the bright and noble train;
Minstrel shall sing and herald tell—
'Mark yonder maid of beauty well,
'Tis she for whose bright eyes was won
The listed field at Ascalon!

4.

"'Note well her smile!—it edged the blade
Which fifty wives to widows made,
When, vain his strength and Mahound's spell,
Iconium's turban'd soldan fell.
See'st thou her locks, whose sunny glow
Half shows, half shades, her neck of snow?
Twines not of them one golden thread,
But for its sake a Paynim bled.'

5.

"Joy to the fair!—my name unknown,
Each deed, and all its praise, thine own;
Then, oh! unbar this churlish gate,
The night-dew falls, the hour is late.
Inured to Syria's glowing breath,
I feel the north breeze chill as death;

Let grateful love quell maiden shame,
And grant him bliss who brings thee fame."

During this performance, the hermit demeaned himself much like a first-rate critic of the present day at a new opera. He reclined back upon his seat, with his eyes half shut; now folding his hands and twisting his thumbs, he seemed absorbed in attention, and anon, balancing his expanded palms, he gently flourished them in time to the music. At one or two favourite cadences, he threw in a little assistance of his own, where the knight's voice seemed unable to carry the air so high as his worshipful taste approved. When the song was ended, the anchorite emphatically declared it a good one, and well sung.

"And, yet," said he, "I think my Saxon countryman had herded long enough with the Normans, to fall into the tone of their melancholy ditties. What took the honest knight from home? or what could he expect but to find his mistress agreeably engaged with a rival on his return, and his serenade, as they call it, as little regarded as the caterwauling of a cat in the gutter? Nevertheless, Sir Knight, I drink this cup to thee, to the success of all true lovers—I fear you are none," he added, on observing that the knight (whose brain began to be heated with these repeated draughts,) qualified his flagon from the water pitcher.

"Why," said the knight, "did you not tell me that this water was from the well of your blessed patron, St Dunstan?"

"Ay, truly," said the hermit, "and many a hundred of pagans did he baptize there, but I never heard that he drank any of it. Every thing should be put to its proper use in the world. St Dunstan knew, as well as any one, the prerogatives of a jovial friar."

And so saying, he reached the harp, and entertained his guest with the following characteristic song, to a sort of derry-down chorus, appropriate to an old English ditty.*

THE BAREFOOTED FRIAR.

1.

I'll give thee, good fellow, a twelvemonth or twain,
To search Europe through, from Byzantium to Spain;
But ne'er shall you find, should you search till you tire,
So happy a man as the Barefooted Friar.

2.

Your knight for his lady pricks forth in career,
And is brought home at even-song prick'd through with a spear;

* It may be proper to remind the reader, that the chorus of "derry down" is supposed to be as ancient, not only as the times of the Heptarchy, but as those of the Druids, and to have furnished the chorus to the hymns of these venerable persons when they went to the wood to gather misseltoe.

I confess him in haste—for his lady desires
No comfort on earth save the Barefooted Friar's.

3.

Your monarch?—Pshaw! many a prince has been known
To barter his robes for our cowl and our gown,
But which of us e'er felt the idle desire
To exchange for a crown the grey hood of a Friar!

4.

The Friar has walk'd out, and where'er he has gone,
The land and its fatness is mark'd for his own;
He can roam where he lists, he can stop when he tires,
For every man's house is the Barefooted Friar's.

5.

He's expected at noon, and no wight till he comes
May profane the great chair, or the porridge of plumbs;
For the best of the cheer, and the seat by the fire,
Is the undenied right of the Barefooted Friar.

6.

He's expected at night, and the pasty's made hot,
They broach the brown ale and they fill the black pot,
And the good-wife would wish the good-man in the mire,
Ere he lack'd a soft pillow, the Barefooted Friar.

7.

Long flourish the sandal, the cord, and the cope,
The dread of the devil and trust of the Pope;
For to gather life's roses, unscathed by the briar,
Is granted alone to the Barefooted Friar!

"By my troth," said the knight, "thou hast sung well and lustily, and in high praise of thine order. And, talking of the devil, Holy Clerk, are you not afraid that he may pay you a visit during some of your uncanonical pastimes?"

"I uncanonical!" answered the hermit; "I scorn the charge—I scorn it with my heels.—I serve the duty of my chapel duly and truly—Two masses daily, morning and evening, primes, noons, and vespers, *aves*, *credos*, *paters*"——

"Excepting moon-light nights, when the venison is in season," said his guest.

"*Exceptis excipiendis*," replied the hermit, "as our old abbot taught me to say when impertinent laymen should ask me if I kept every punctilio of my order."

"True, holy father," said the knight; "but the devil is apt to keep an eye on such exceptions; he goes about, thou knowest, like a roaring lion."

"Let him roar here if he dares," said the friar; "a touch of my cord will make him roar as loud as the tongs of St Dunstan himself did. I never feared man, and I as little fear the devil and his imps.—Saint Dunstan, Saint Dubric, Saint Winibald, Saint Winifred, Saint Swibert, Saint Willick, not forgetting Saint Thomas a Kent, and my own poor merits to speed, I defy every devil of them, come cut and long tail. —But to let you into a secret, I never speak upon such subjects, my friend, until after morning vespers."

He changed the conversation; fast and furious grew the mirth of the parties, and many a song was exchanged betwixt them, when their revels were interrupted by a loud knocking at the door of the hermitage.

The occasion of this interruption we can only explain by resuming the adventures of another set of our characters; for, like old Ariosto, we do not pique ourselves upon continuing uniformly to keep company with any one personage of our drama.

Chapter Four

Away! our journey lies through dell and dingle,
Where the blythe fawn trips by its timid mother,
Where the broad oak, with intercepting boughs,
Chequers the sun-beam in the green-sward alley—
Up and away!—for lovely paths are these
To tread, when the glad Sun is on his throne;
Less pleasant and less safe when Cynthia's lamp
With doubtful glimmer lights the dreary forest.

Ettrick Forest.

WHEN CEDRIC the Saxon saw his son drop senseless down in the lists at Ashby, his first impulse was to order him into the custody and care of his own attendants, but the words choked in his throat. He could not bring himself to acknowledge, in presence of such an assembly, the son whom he had renounced and disinherited. He ordered, however, Oswald to keep an eye upon him; and directed that officer, with two of his serfs, to convey Ivanhoe to Ashby so soon as the crowd was dispersed. Oswald, however, was anticipated in his good office. The crowd dispersed indeed, but the knight was nowhere to be seen.

It was in vain that Cedric's cup-bearer looked around for his young master—he saw the bloody spot on which he had lately sunk down, but himself he saw no longer; it seemed as if the fairies had conveyed him from the spot. Perhaps Oswald (for the Saxons were very superstitious) might have adopted some such hypothesis, to account for Ivanhoe's disappearance, had he not suddenly cast his eye upon a person attired like a squire, in whom he recognized the features of his fellow-servant Gurth. Anxious concerning his master's fate, and in despair at his sudden disappearance, the translated swine-herd was searching for him everywhere, and had neglected in doing so the concealment on which his own safety depended. Oswald deemed it his duty to secure Gurth, as a fugitive of whose fate his master was to judge.

Renewing his enquiries concerning the fate of Ivanhoe, the only information which the cup-bearer could collect from the bystanders was, that the knight had been raised with care by certain well-attired grooms, and placed in a litter belonging to a lady among the spectators, which had immediately transported him out of the press. Oswald, on receiving this intelligence, resolved to return to his master for farther instructions, carrying along with him Gurth, whom he considered in some sort as a deserter from the service of Cedric.

The Saxon had been under very intense and agonizing apprehensions concerning his son, for Nature had asserted her rights, in spite of the patriotic stoicism which laboured to disown her. But no sooner was he informed that Ivanhoe was in careful, and probably in friendly hands, than the paternal anxiety which had been excited by the dubiety of his fate gave way anew to the feeling of injured pride and resentment at what he termed Wilfred's filial disobedience. "Let him wander his way," said he—"let those leech his wounds for whose sake he encountered them. He is fitter to do the juggling tricks of the Norman chivalry than to maintain the fame and honour of his English ancestry with the glaive and brown-bill, the good old weapons of his country."

"If to maintain the honour of ancestry," said Rowena, who was present, "it is sufficient to be wise in council and brave in execution—to be boldest among the bold, and gentlest among the gentle, I know no voice, save his father's——"

"Be silent, Lady Rowena!—on this subject only I hear you not. Prepare yourself for the Prince's festival: we have been summoned thither with unwonted circumstance of honour and of courtesy, such as the haughty Normans have rarely used to our race since the fatal day of Hastings. Thither will I go, were it only to shew these proud Normans how little the fate of a son, who could defeat their bravest, can affect a Saxon."

"Thither," said Rowena, "do I NOT go; and I pray you to beware, lest what you mean for courage and constancy shall be accounted hardness of heart."

"Remain at home then, ungrateful lady," answered Cedric; "thine is the hard heart, which can sacrifice the weal of an oppressed people to an idle and unauthorized attachment. I seek the noble Athelstane, and with him attend the banquet of John of Anjou."

He went accordingly to the banquet, of which we have already mentioned the principal events. Immediately upon retiring from the castle, the Saxon thanes, with their attendants, took horse; and it was during the bustle which attended their doing so, that Cedric, for the first time, cast his eyes upon the deserter Gurth. The noble Saxon had returned from the banquet, as we have seen, in no very placid humour, and wanted but a pretext for wreaking his anger upon some one. "The gyves!" he said, "the gyves!—Oswald—Hundibert!—Dogs and villains!—why leave ye the knave unfettered?"

Without daring to remonstrate, the companions of Gurth bound him with a halter, as the readiest cord which occurred. He submitted to the operation without remonstrance, except that, darting a reproachful look at his master, he said, "This comes of loving your flesh and blood better than mine own."

"To horse, and forward!" said Cedric.

"It is indeed full time," said the noble Athelstane; "for, if we ride not the faster, the worthy Abbot Waltheoff's preparations for a rere-supper* will be altogether spoiled."

The travellers, however, used such speed as to reach the convent of St Withold's before the apprehended evil took place. The Abbot, himself of ancient Saxon descent, received the noble Saxons with the profuse and exuberant hospitality of their nation, wherein they indulged to a late, or rather an early hour; nor did they take leave of their reverend host the next morning until they had shared with him a sumptuous refection.

As the cavalcade left the court of the monastery, an incident happened somewhat alarming to the Saxons, who, of all people of Europe, were most addicted to a superstitious observance of omens, and to whose opinions can be traced most of those notions upon such subjects, still to be found among our popular antiquities. For the Normans being a mixed race, and better informed according to the information of the times, had lost most of the superstitious prejudices which their ancestors had brought from Scandinavia, and piqued themselves upon thinking freely upon such topics.

In the present instance, the apprehension of impending evil was inspired by no less respectable a prophet than a large lean black dog, which, sitting upright, howled most piteously as the foremost riders left the gate, and presently afterwards, barking wildly, and jumping to and fro, seemed bent upon attaching itself to the party.

"I like not that music, father Cedric," said Athelstane; for by this

*A rere-supper was a night-meal, and sometimes signified a collation, which was given at a late hour, after the regular supper had made its appearance. L. T.

title of respect he was accustomed to address him.

"Nor I either, uncle," said Wamba; "I greatly fear we shall have to pay the piper."

"In my mind," said Athelstane, upon whose memory the Abbot's good ale, (for Burton was already famous for that genial liquor,) had made a favourable impression, "in my mind we had better turn back, and abide with the Abbot until the afternoon—it is unlucky to travel where your path is crossed by a monk, a hare, or a howling dog, until you have eaten your next meal."

"Away!" said Cedric, impatiently; "the day is already too short for our journey. For the dog, I know it to be the cur of the run-away slave Gurth, a useless fugitive like its master."

So saying, and rising at the same time in his stirrups impatient at the interruption of his journey, he launched his javelin at poor Fangs—for Fangs it was, who, having traced his master thus far upon his stolen expedition, had here lost him, and was now in his uncouth way rejoicing at his reappearance. The javelin inflicted a wound upon the animal's shoulder, and narrowly missed pinning him to the earth; and Fangs fled howling, from the presence of the enraged thane. Gurth's heart swelled within him, for he felt this meditated slaughter of his faithful adherent in a degree much deeper than the harsh treatment he had himself received. Having in vain attempted to raise his hand to his eyes, he said to Wamba, who, seeing his master's ill humour, had prudently retreated to the rear, "I pray thee, do me the kindness to wipe my eyes with the skirt of thy mantle; the dust offends me, and these bonds will not let me help myself one way or another."

Wamba did him the service he required, and they rode side by side for some time, during which Gurth maintained a moody silence. At length he could repress his feelings no longer.

"Friend Wamba," said he, "of all those who are fools enough to serve Cedric, thou alone hast dexterity enough to make thy folly acceptable to him. Go to him, therefore, and tell him that neither for love nor fear will Gurth serve him longer. He may strike the head from me—he may scourge me—he may load me with irons—but henceforth he shall never compel me either to love or to obey him. Go to him then, and tell him that Gurth the son of Beowolf renounces his service."

"Assuredly," said Wamba, "fool as I am, I shall not do your fool's errand. Cedric hath another javelin stuck into his girdle, and thou knowest he does not always miss his mark."

"I care not," replied Gurth, "how soon he makes a mark of me. Yesterday he left Wilfred, my young master, in his blood. To-day he has striven to kill before my face the only other living creature that ever shewed me kindness. By St Edmund, St Dunstan, St Withold, St Edward the Confessor, and every other Saxon saint in the calendar, (for Cedric never swore by any that was not of Saxon lineage, and all his household had the same limited devotion,) I will never forgive him."

"To my thinking now," said the Jester, who was frequently wont to act as peace-maker in the family, "our master did not propose to hurt Fangs, but only to affright him. For, if you observed, he rose in his stirrups, as thereby meaning to over-cast the mark; and so he would have done, but Fangs happening to bound up at the very moment, received a scratch, which I will be bound to heal with a penny's breadth of tar."

"If I thought so," said Gurth—"if I could but think so—but no—I saw the javelin was well aimed—I heard it whizz through the air with all the wrathful malevolence of him who cast it, and it quivered after it had pitched in the ground, as if with regret for having missed its mark. By the hog dear to St Anthony, I renounce him!"

And the indignant swine-herd resumed his sullen silence, which no efforts of the Jester could again induce him to break.

Meanwhile Cedric and Athelstane, the leaders of the troop, conversed together on the state of the land, on the dissensions of the royal family, on the feuds and quarrels among the Norman nobles, and on the chance which there was that the oppressed Saxons might be able to free themselves from the yoke of the Normans, or at least to elevate themselves into consequence and independence, during the civil convulsions which were likely to ensue. On this subject Cedric was all animation. The restoration of the independence of his race was the idol of his heart, to which he had willingly sacrificed domestic happiness and the interests of his own son. But, in order to achieve this great revolution in favour of the native English, it was necessary they should be united among themselves, and act under an acknowledged head. The necessity of choosing their chief from the Saxon blood-royal was not only evident in itself, but had been made a solemn condition by those whom Cedric had entrusted with his secret plans and hopes. Athelstane had this quality at least; and though he had few mental accomplishments or talents to recommend him as a leader, he had still a goodly person, was no coward, had been accustomed to martial exercises, and seemed willing to defer to the advice of counsellors more wise than himself. Above all, he was known to be liberal and hospitable, and believed to be good-natured. But whatever pretensions Athelstane had to be considered as head of the Saxon confederacy, many of that nation were disposed to prefer to his the title of the Lady Rowena, who drew her descent from Alfred, and whose father had been a chief renowned for wisdom, courage, and generosity, whose memory was highly honoured by his oppressed countrymen.

It would have been no difficult thing for Cedric, had he been so disposed, to have placed himself at the head of a third party, as formidable at least as any of the others. To counterbalance their royal descent, he had courage, activity, energy, and, above all, that devoted attachment to the cause which had procured him the epithet of THE SAXON, and his birth was inferior to none, excepting only that of Athelstane and his ward. These qualities, however, were unalloyed by the slightest shade of selfishness; and, instead of dividing yet farther his weakened nation by forming a faction of his own, it was a leading part of Cedric's plan to extinguish that which already existed, by promoting a marriage betwixt Rowena and Athelstane. An obstacle occurred to this his favourite project, in the mutual attachment of his ward and his son, and hence the original cause of the banishment of Wilfred from the house of his father.

This stern measure Cedric had adopted, in hopes that, during Wilfred's absence, Rowena might relinquish her preference, but in this hope he was disappointed; a disappointment which might be attributed in part to the mode in which his ward had been educated. Cedric, to whom the name of Alfred was as that of a deity, had treated the sole remaining scion of that great monarch with a degree of observance, such as, perhaps, was in these days scarce paid to an acknowledged princess. Rowena's will had been in almost all cases a law to his household; and Cedric himself, as if determined that her sovereignty should be fully acknowledged within that little circle at least, seemed to take a pride in acting as the first of her subjects. Thus trained in the exercise, not only of free will, but despotic authority, Rowena was, by her previous education, disposed both to resist and to resent any attempt to controul her affections, or dispose of her hand contrary to her inclinations, and to assert her independence in a case in which even those females who have been trained up to obedience and subjection, are not infrequently apt to dispute the authority of guardians and parents. The opinions which she felt strongly she avowed boldly; and Cedric, who could not free himself from his habitual deference to her opinions, felt totally at a loss how to enforce his authority of guardian.

It was in vain that he attempted to dazzle her with the prospect of a visionary throne. Rowena, who possessed strong sense, neither considered his plan as possible, nor as desirable, so far as she was concerned, could it have been achieved. Without attempting to conceal her avowed preference of Wilfred of Ivanhoe, she declared that, were that favoured knight out of question, she would rather take refuge in a convent, than share a throne with Athelstane, whom, having always despised, she now began, on account of the trouble she received on his account, thoroughly to detest.

Nevertheless, Cedric, whose opinion of women's constancy was far from strong, persisted in using every means in his power to bring about the proposed match, in which he conceived he was rendering an important service to the Saxon cause. The sudden and romantic appearance of his son in the lists at Ashby, he had justly regarded as being almost a death's blow to his hopes. His paternal affection, it is true, had for an instant gained the victory both over pride and patriotism; but both had returned in full force, and under their joint operation, he was now bent upon making a determined effort for the union of Athelstane and Rowena, together with expediting those other measures which seemed necessary to forward the restoration of Saxon independence.

On this last subject, he was now labouring with Athelstane, not without having reason, every now and then, to lament, like Hotspur, that he should have moved such a dish of skimmed milk to so honourable an action. Athelstane, it is true, was vain enough, and loved to have his ears tickled with tales of his high descent, and of his right by inheritance to homage and sovereignty. But his petty vanity was sufficiently gratified by receiving this homage at the hands of his immediate attendants, and of the Saxons who approached him. If he had the courage to encounter danger, he at least hated the trouble of going to seek it; and while he agreed in the general principles laid down by Cedric, concerning the claim of the Saxons to independence, and was still more easily convinced of his own title to reign over them when that independence should be attained, yet when the means of asserting these rights came to be discussed, he was still "Athelstane the Unready," slow, irresolute, procrastinating, and uninterprizing. The warm and impassioned exhortations of Cedric had as little effect upon his impassive temper, as red-hot balls alighting in the water, which produce a little sound and smoke, and are instantly extinguished.

If, leaving this task, which might be compared to spurring a tired jade, or to hammering upon cold iron, Cedric fell back to his ward Rowena, he received little more satisfaction from conferring with her. For, as his presence interrupted the discourse between the lady and her favourite attendant upon the gallantry and fate of Wilfred, Elgitha failed not to revenge both her mistress and herself, by recurring to the overthrow of Athelstane in the lists, the most disagreeable subject which could greet the ears of Cedric. To this sturdy Saxon, therefore, the day's journey was fraught with all manner of displeasure and discomfort; so that he more than once cursed internally the tournament, and him who had proclaimed it, together with his own folly in ever going thither.

At noon, upon the motion of Athelstane, the travellers paused in a woodland shade by a fountain, to repose their horses and partake of some provisions, with which the hospitable Abbot had loaded a sumpter mule. Their repast was a pretty long one, and these several interruptions rendered it impossible for them to hope to reach Rotherwood without travelling all night, a conviction which induced them to proceed on their way at a more hasty pace than they had hitherto used.

Chapter Five

A train of armed men, some noble dame
Escorting, (so their scattered words discovered,
As unperceived I hung upon their rear)
Are close at hand, and mean to pass the night
Within the castle.

Orra, a Tragedy.

THE TRAVELLERS had now reached the verge of the wooded country, and were about to plunge into its recesses, held dangerous at that time from the number of outlaws whom oppression and poverty had driven to despair, and who occupied the forests in such large bands as could easily bid defiance to the feeble police of the period. From these rovers, however, notwithstanding the lateness of the hour, Cedric and Athelstane accounted themselves secure, as they had in attendance ten servants, besides Wamba and Gurth, whose aid could not be counted upon, the one being a jester and the other a captive. It may be added, that in travelling thus late through the forest, Cedric and Athelstane relied on their descent and character, as well as their courage. The outlaws, whom the severity of the forest laws had reduced to this roving and desperate mode of life, were chiefly peasants and yeomen of Saxon descent, and were generally supposed to respect the persons and property of their countrymen.

As the travellers journeyed on their way, they were alarmed by repeated cries for assistance; and when they rode up to the place from whence they came, they were surprised to find a horse-litter placed upon the ground, beside which sat a young woman, richly dressed in the Jewish fashion, while an old man, whose yellow cap proclaimed him to belong to the same nation, walked up and down with gestures expressive of the deepest despair, and wrung his hands as if affected by some strange disaster.

To the enquiries of Athelstane and Cedric the old Jew could for some time only answer by invoking the protection of all the patriarchs of the Old Testament successively against the sons of Ishmael, who were coming to smite them, hip and thigh, with the edge of the sword. When he began to come to himself out of this agony of terror, Isaac of York (for it was our old friend) became at length able to explain, that he had hired a body guard of six men at Ashby, together with mules for carrying the litter of a sick friend. This party had undertaken to escort him as far as Doncaster. They had come thus far in safety; but having received information from a wood-cutter that there was a strong band of outlaws lying in wait in the woods before them, Isaac's mercenaries had not only taken flight, but had carried off with them the horses which bore the litter, and left the Jew and his daughter without the means either of defence or of retreat, to be plundered, and probably murdered, by the banditti whom they expected every moment would bring down upon them. "Would it but please your valours," added Isaac, in a tone of deep humiliation, "to permit the poor Jews to travel under your safeguard, I swear by the tables of our law, that never has favour been conferred upon a child of Israel since the days of our captivity which shall be more gratefully acknowledged."

"Dog of a Jew!" said Athelstane, whose memory was of that petty kind which stores up trifles of all kinds, but particularly trifling offences, "dost not remember how thou didst beard us in the gallery at the tilt-yard? Fight or flee, or compound with the outlaws as thou dost list, ask neither aid nor company from us; and if they rob only such as thee, who rob all the world, I, for mine own share, shall hold them right honest folks."

Cedric did not assent to the severe proposal of his companion. "We will do better," said he, "to leave them two of our attendants and two horses to convey them back to the next village. It will diminish our strength but little; and, with your good sword, noble Athelstane, and the aid of those who remain, it will be light work for us to face twenty of these runagates."

Rowena, somewhat alarmed by the mention of outlaws in force, and so near them, strongly seconded the proposal of her guardian. But Rebecca, suddenly quitting her dejected posture, and making her way through the attendants to the palfrey of the Saxon lady, knelt down, and, after the Oriental fashion in addressing superiors, kissed the hem of Rowena's garment. Then rising, and throwing back her veil, she implored her in the great name of the God whom they both worshipped, and by that revelation of the Law in which they both believed, that she would have compassion upon them, and suffer them to go forward under their safeguard. "It is not for myself that I pray this favour," said Rebecca; "nor is it even for that poor old man. I know, that to wrong and to spoil our nation is a light fault, if not a merit, with the Christians; and what is it to us whether it be done in the city, in the desert, or in the field? But it is in the name of one dear to many, and dear even to you, that I beseech you to let this sick person be transported with care and tenderness under your protection. For, if evil chance him, the last moment of your life would be embittered with regret for denying that which I ask of you."

The noble and solemn air with which Rebecca made this appeal, gave it double weight with the fair Saxon.

"The man is old and feeble," she said to her guardian, "the maiden young and beautiful, their friend sick and in peril of his life—Jews though they be, we cannot as Christians leave them in this extremity. Let them unload two of the sumpter-mules, and put the baggage behind two of the serfs. The mules may transport the litter, and we have led horses for the old man and his daughter."

Cedric readily assented to what she proposed, and Athelstane only added the condition, "that they should travel in the rear of the whole party, where Wamba," he said, "might attend them with his shield of boar's brawn."

"I have left my shield in the tilt-yard," answered the Jester, "as has been the fate of many a better knight than myself."

Athelstane coloured deeply, for such had been his own fate on the last day of the tournament; while Rowena, who was pleased in the same proportion, as if to make amends for the brutal jest of her unfeeling suitor, requested Rebecca to ride by her side.

"It were not fit I should do so," answered Rebecca, with proud humility, "where my society might be held a disgrace to my protectress."

By this time the change of baggage was hastily achieved, for the single word "outlaws" rendered every one sufficiently alert, and the approach of twilight made the sound yet more impressive. Amid the bustle, Gurth was taken from horseback, in the course of which removal he prevailed upon the Jester to slack the cord with which his arms were bound. It was so negligently refastened, perhaps intentionally on the part of Wamba, that Gurth found no difficulty in freeing his arms altogether from bondage, and then gliding into the thicket he made his escape from the party.

The bustle had been considerable, and it was some time before Gurth was missed; for, as he was to be placed for the rest of the journey behind a servant, every one supposed that some other of his companions had him under his custody, and when it began to be whispered among them that Gurth had actually disappeared, they were under such immediate expectation of an attack from the outlaws, that it was not held convenient to pay much attention to the circumstance.

The path upon which the party travelled was now so narrow, as not to admit, with any sort of convenience, above two riders abreast, and began to descend into a dingle, traversed by a brook whose banks were broken, swampy, and overgrown with dwarf willows. Cedric and Athelstane, who were at the head of their retinue, saw the risk of being attacked at this pass; but neither of them having had much practice in war, no better mode of preventing the danger occurred to them than that they should hasten on as fast as possible. Advancing, therefore, without much order, they had just crossed the brook with a part of their followers, when they were assailed in front, flank, and rear at once, with an impetuosity to which, in their confused and ill-prepared condition, it was impossible to offer effectual resistance. The shout of "A white dragon!—a white dragon!—Saint George for merry England!" war-cries adopted by the assailants, as belonging to their assumed character of Saxon outlaws, was heard on every side, and on every side enemies appeared with a rapidity of advance and attack which seemed to multiply their numbers.

Both the Saxon chiefs were made prisoners at the same moment, and each under circumstances expressive of his character. Cedric, the instant that an enemy appeared, launched at him his remaining javelin, which, taking better effect than that which he had hurled at Fangs, nailed the man against an oak-tree that happened to be close behind him. Thus far successful, Cedric spurred his horse against a second, drawing his sword at the same time, and striking with such inconsiderate fury, that his weapon encountered a thick branch which hung over him, and he was disarmed by the violence of his own blow. He was instantly made prisoner, and pulled from his horse by two or three of the banditti who crowded around him. Athelstane shared his captivity, his bridle having been seized, and he himself forcibly dismounted, long before he could draw his weapon, or assume any posture of effectual defence.

The attendants, embarrassed with baggage, surprised and terrified at the fate of their masters, fell an easy prey to the assailants; while the Lady Rowena, in the centre of the cavalcade, and the Jew and his daughter in the rear, experienced the same misfortune.

Of all the train none escaped except Wamba, who showed upon the occasion much more courage than those who pretended to greater sense. He possessed himself of a sword belonging to one of the domestics, who was just drawing it with a tardy and irresolute hand, laid about him like a lion, drove back several who approached him, and made a brave though ineffectual attempt to succour his master.

Finding himself overpowered, the Jester at length threw himself from his horse, plunged into the thicket, and, favoured by the general confusion, escaped from the scene of action.

Yet the valiant Jester, so soon as he found himself safe, hesitated more than once whether he should not turn back, and share the captivity of a master to whom he was sincerely attached.

"I have heard men talk of the blessings of freedom," said he to himself, "but I wish any wise man would teach me what use to make of it now that I have it."

As he pronounced these words aloud, a voice very near him called out in a low and cautious tone, "Wamba!" and, at the same time, a dog, which he recognized to be Fangs, jumped up and fawned upon him. "Gurth!" answered Wamba, with the same caution, and the swine-herd immediately stood before him.

"What is the matter?" said he eagerly; "what mean these cries, and that clashing of swords?"

"Only a trick of the times," said Wamba; "they are all prisoners."

"Who are prisoners?" exclaimed Gurth, impatiently.

"My lord, and my lady, and Athelstane, and Hundibert, and Oswald."

"In the name of God!" said Gurth, "how came they prisoners?—And to whom?"

"Our master was too ready to fight," said the Jester; "and Athelstane was not ready enough, and no other person was ready at all. And they are prisoners to green cassocks, and black vizors. And they lie all tumbled about on the green, like the crab-apples that you shake down to your swine. And I would laugh at it," said the honest Jester, "if I could for weeping." And he shed tears of unfeigned sorrow.

Gurth's countenance kindled—"Wamba," he said, "thou hast a weapon, and thy heart was ever stronger than thy brain,—we are only two—but a sudden attack from men of resolution will do much—follow me."

"Whither?—and for what purpose?" said the Jester.

"To rescue Cedric."

"But you have renounced his service but now," said Wamba.

"That," said Gurth, "was but while he was fortunate—follow me."

As the Jester was about to obey, a third person suddenly made his appearance, and commanded them both to halt. From his dress and arms, Wamba would have conjectured him to be one of those outlaws who had just assailed his master; but, besides that he wore no masque, the glittering baldric across his shoulder, with the rich bugle-horn which it supported, as well as the calm and commanding expression of his voice and manner, made him, notwithstanding the twilight, recognize Locksley the yeoman, who had been victorious, under such disadvantageous circumstances, in the contest for the prize of archery.

"What is the meaning of all this," said he, "or who is it that rifle, and ransom, and make prisoners, in these forests?"

"You may look at their cassocks close by," said Wamba, "and see whether they be thy children's coats or no—for they are as like thine own, as one green pea-cod is to another."

"I will learn that presently," answered Locksley; "and I charge ye, on peril of your lives, not to stir from the place where ye stand, until I have returned. Obey me, and it shall be the better for you and your masters.—Yet stay, I must render myself as like these men as possible."

So saying, he unbuckled his baldric with the bugle, took a feather from his cap, and gave them to Wamba; then drew a vizard from his pouch, and, repeating his charges to them to stand fast, went to execute his purpose of reconnoitring.

"Shall we stand fast, Gurth?" said Wamba; "or shall we e'en give him leg bail? In my foolish mind, he had all the equipage of a thief too much in readiness, to be himself a true man."

"Let him be the devil," said Gurth, "an he will. We can be no worse of waiting his return. If he belong to that party, he must already have given them the alarm, and it will avail nothing either to fight or fly. Besides, I have late experience, that arrant thieves are not the worst men in the world to have to deal with."

The yeoman returned in the course of a few minutes.

"Friend Gurth," he said, "I have mingled among yon men, and have learnt to whom they belong, and whither they are bound. There is, I think, no chance that they will proceed to any actual violence against their prisoners. For three men to attempt them at this moment, were little less than madness, for they are good men of war, and have as such placed centinels to give the alarm when any one approaches. But I trust soon to gather such a force, as may act in defiance of all their precautions; you are both servants, and, as I think, faithful servants, of Cedric the Saxon, the friend of the rights of Englishmen. He shall not want English hands to help him in this extremity. Come then with me, until I gather more aid."

So saying, he walked through the wood at a great pace, followed by the jester and the swine-herd. It was not consistent with Wamba's humour to travel long in silence.

"I think," said he, looking at the baldric and bugle which he still carried, "that I saw the arrow shot which won this gay prize, and that not so long since as Christmas."

"And I," said Gurth, "could take it on my haly-dome, that I have heard the voice of the good yeoman who won it, by night as well as by day, and that the moon is not three days older since I did so."

"Mine honest friends," replied the yeoman, "who, or what I am, is little to the present purpose; should I free your master, you will have reason to think me the best friend you have ever had in your lives. And whether I am known by one name or another—or whether I can draw a bow as well or better than a cow-keeper, or whether it is my pleasure to walk in sunshine or by moonlight, are matters, which, as they do not concern you, so neither need ye busy yourselves respecting them."

"Our heads are in the lion's mouth," said Wamba, in a whisper to Gurth, "get them out how we can."

"Hush—be silent," said Gurth, "offend him not by thy folly, and I trust sincerely that all will do well."

Chapter Six

When autumn nights were long and drear,
  And forest walks were dark and dim,
How sweetly on the pilgrim's ear
  Was wont to steal the hermit's hymn.

Devotion borrows Music's tone,
  And Music took Devotion's wing;
And, like the bird that hails the sun,
  They soar to heaven, and soaring sing.
    The Hermit of St Clement's Well.

IT WAS AFTER three hours good walking that the servants of Cedric, with their mysterious guide, arrived at a small opening in the forest, in the centre of which grew an oak-tree of enormous magnitude, throwing its twisted branches in every direction. Beneath this tree four or five yeomen lay stretched on the ground, while another, as sentinel, walked to and fro in the moonlight shade.

Upon hearing the sound of feet approaching, the watch instantly gave the alarm, and the sleepers as suddenly started up and bent their bows. Six arrows placed on the string were pointed towards the quarter from which the travellers approached, when their guide, being recognized, was welcomed with every token of respect and attachment, and all signs and fears of a rough reception at once subsided.

"Where is the Miller?" was his first question.

"On the road towards Rotherham."

"With how many?" demanded the leader, for such he seemed to be.

"With six men, and good hope of booty, if it please St Nicholas."

"Devoutly spoken," said Locksley; "and where is Allan-a-Dale?"

"Walked up towards the Watling-street to watch for the Prior of Jorvaulx."

"That is well thought on also," replied the Captain;—"and where is the friar?"

"In his cell."

"Thither will I go," said Locksley. "Disperse and seek your companions. Collect what force you can, for there's game afoot that must be hunted hard, and will turn to bay. Meet me here by day break.—And stay," he added, "I have forgotten what is most necessary of the whole—Two of you take the road quickly towards Torquilstone, the castle of Front-de-Bœuf. A set of gallants, who have been masquerading in such guise as our own, are carrying a band of prisoners thither—Watch them closely, for even if they reach the castle before we collect our force, our honour is concerned to punish them, and we will find means to do so.—Keep a close watch on them therefore; and dispatch one of your comrades, the lightest of foot, to bring the news of the yeomen's whereabout."

They promised implicit obedience, and departed with alacrity on their different errands. In the meanwhile their leader and his two companions, who now looked upon him with great respect, as well as some fear, pursued their way to the chapel of Copmanhurst.

When they had reached the little moon-light glade, having in front the reverend, though ruinous chapel, and the rude hermitage, so well suited to ascetic devotion, Wamba whispered to Gurth, "If this be the habitation of a thief, it makes good the old proverb, The nearer the church the farther from God.—And by my cockscomb," he added, "I think it be even so—Hearken but to the black sanctus which they are singing in the hermitage!"

In fact the anchorite and his guest were performing, at the full extent of their very powerful lungs, an old drinking song, of which this was the burthen:—

"Come, trowl the brown bowl to me,
  Bully boy, bully boy,
Come, trowl the brown bowl to me:
  Ho! jolly Jenkin, I spy a knave in drinking,
Come, trowl the brown bowl to me."

"Now, that is not ill sung," said Wamba, who had thrown in a few of his own flourishes to help out the chorus. "But who, in the saint's name, ever expected to have heard such a jolly chaunt come from out a hermit's cell at midnight?"

"Marry, that should I," said Gurth, "for the jolly Clerk of Copmanhurst is a known man, and kills half the deer that are stolen in this walk. Men say that the keeper has complained to his official, and that he will be stripped of his cowl and cope altogether, if he keep not better order."

While they were thus speaking, Locksley's loud and repeated knocks had at length disturbed the anchorite and his guest. "By my beads," said the hermit, stopping short in a grand flourish, "here come more benighted guests. I would not for my cowl that they found us in this goodly exercise. All men have their enemies, good Sir Sluggard; and there be those malignant enough to construe the hospitable refreshment which I have been offering to you, a weary traveller, for the matter of three short hours, into sheer drunkenness and debauchery, vices alike alien to my profession and my disposition."

"Base calumniators!" replied the knight; "I would I had the chastising of them. Nevertheless, Holy Clerk, it is true that all have their enemies; and there be those in this very land whom I would rather speak to through the bars of my helmet than barefaced."

"Get thine iron pot on thy head then, friend Sluggard, as quickly as thy nature will permit," said the hermit, "while I remove these pewter flagons, whose late contents run strangely in mine own pate; and to drown the clatter—for, in faith, I feel somewhat unsteady—strike into the tune which thou hearest me sing; it is no matter for the words—I scarce know them myself."

So saying, he struck up a thundering *De profundis clamavi*, under cover of which he removed the apparatus of their banquet; while the knight, laughing heartily, and arming himself all the while, assisted his host with his voice from time to time as his mirth permitted.

"What devil's mattins are you after at this hour?" said a voice from without.

"Heaven forgive you, sir traveller!" said the hermit, whose own noise, and perhaps his nocturnal potations, prevented him from recognizing accents which were tolerably familiar to him—"Wend on your way, in the name of God and Saint Dunstan, and disturb not the devotions of me and my holy brother."

"Mad priest," answered the voice from without, "open to Locksley."

"All's safe—all's right," said the hermit to his companion.

"But who is he?" said the Black Knight; "it imports me much to know."

"Who is he?" answered the hermit; "I tell thee he is a friend."

"But what friend?" answered the knight; "for he may be friend to thee and none of mine."

"What friend?" replied the hermit; "that, now, is one of the questions that is more easily asked than answered. What friend?—why, he is, now that I bethink me a little, the very same honest keeper I told thee of a while since."

"Ay, as honest a keeper as thou art a pious hermit," replied the knight, "I doubt it not. But undo the door to him before he beat it from its hinges."

The dogs, in the meantime, which had made a dreadful baying at the commencement of the disturbance, seemed now to recognize the voice of him who stood without; for, totally changing their manner, they scratched and whined at the door, as if interceding for his admission. The hermit speedily unbolted his portal, and admitted Locksley, with his two companions.

"Why, hermit," was the yeoman's first question so soon as he beheld the knight, "what boon companion hast thou here?"

"A brother of our order," replied the friar, shaking his head; "we have been at our orisons all night."

"He is a monk of the church militant, I think," answered Locksley; "and there be more of them abroad. I tell thee, friar, thou must lay down the rosary and take up the quarter-staff; we shall need every one of our merry men, whether clerk or layman.—But," he added, taking him a step aside, "art thou mad? to give admittance to a knight thou dost not know? Hast thou forgot our articles?"

"Not know him!" replied the friar boldly, "I know him as well as the beggar knows his dish."

"And what is his name then?" demanded Locksley.

"His name," said the hermit—"his name is Sir Anthony of Scrablestone—as if I would drink with a man, and did not know his name!"

"Thou hast been drinking more than enough, friar," said the woodsman, "and, I fear, prating more than enough too."

"Good yeoman," said the knight, coming forward, "be not wroth with my merry host. He did but afford me the hospitality which I would have compelled from him if he had refused it."

"Thou compel!" said the friar; "wait but till I have changed this grey gown for a green cassock, and if I make not a quarter-staff ring twelve upon thy pate, I am neither true clerk nor good woodsman."

While he spoke thus, he stript off his gown, and appeared in a close black buckram doublet and drawers, over which he speedily did on a cassock of green, and hose of the same colour. "I pray thee truss my points," said he to Wamba, "and thou shalt have a cup of sack for thy labour."

"Gramercy for thy sack," said Wamba; "but think'st thou it is lawful for me to aid you to transmew thyself from a holy hermit into a sinful forester?"

"Never fear," said the hermit; "I will but confess the sins of my green cloak to my grey-friar's frock, and all shall be well again."

"Amen!" answered the Jester; "a broadcloth penitent should have a sackcloth confessor, and your frock may absolve my motley doublet into the bargain."

So saying, he accommodated the friar with his assistance in tying the endless number of points, as the laces which attached the hose to the doublet were then termed.

While they were thus employed, Locksley led the knight a little apart, and addressed him thus. "Deny it not, Sir Knight—you are he who decided the victory to the advantage of the English against the strangers on the second day of the tournament at Ashby."

"And what follows if you guess truly, good yeoman?" replied the knight.

"I should in that case hold you," replied the yeoman, "a friend to the weaker party."

"Such is the duty of a true knight at least," replied the Black Champion; "and I would not willingly that there were reason to think otherwise of me."

"But for my purpose," said the yeoman, "thou shouldst be as well a good Englishman as a good knight; for that, which I have to speak of, concerns, indeed, the duty of every honest man, but is more especially that of a true-born native of England."

"You can speak to no one," replied the knight, "to whom England, and the life of every Englishman, can be dearer than to me."

"I would willingly believe so," said the woodsman, "for never had this country such need to be supported by those who love her. Hear me, and I will tell thee of an enterprize, in which, if thou be'st really that which thou seemest, thou may'st take an honourable part. A band of villains, in the disguise of better men than themselves, have made themselves master of the person of a noble Englishman, called Cedric the Saxon, together with his daughter and his friend Athelstane of Coningsburgh, and have transported them to a castle in this forest called Torquilstone. I ask of thee, as a good knight and a good Englishman, wilt thou aid in their rescue?"

"I am bound by my vow to do so," replied the knight; "but I would willingly know who you are, who request my assistance in their behalf?"

"I am," said the forester, "a nameless man; but I am the friend of my country, and of my country's friends—With this account of me you must for the present remain satisfied, the more especially since you yourself desire to continue unknown—Believe, however, that my word, when pledged, is as inviolate as if I wore golden spurs."

"I willingly believe it," said the knight; "I have been accustomed to study men's countenances, and I can read in thine honesty and resolution—I will, therefore, ask thee no further questions, but aid thee in setting at freedom these oppressed captives; which done, I trust we shall part better acquainted, and well satisfied with each other."

"So," said Wamba to Gurth,—for the friar being now fully equipped, the jester, having approached to the other side of the hut, had heard the conclusion of the conversation,—"So we have got a new ally—I trust the valour of the knight will be truer metal than the religion of the hermit, or the honesty of the yeoman; for this Locksley looks like a born deer-stealer, and the priest like a lusty hypocrite."

"Hold thy peace, Wamba," said Gurth; "it may all be as thou dost guess,—but were the horned devil to rise and proffer me his assistance to set at liberty Cedric and the Lady Rowena, I fear I should hardly have religion enough to refuse the foul fiend's offer, and bid him get behind me."

The friar was now completely accoutered as a yeoman, with sword and buckler, bow and quiver, and a strong partisan over his shoulder. He left his cell at the head of the party, and, having carefully locked the door, deposited the key under the threshold.

"Art thou in condition to do good service, friar," said Locksley, "or does the brown bowl still run in thy head?"

"Not more than a draught of St Dunstan's fountain will allay," answered the priest; "something there is of a whizzing in my brain, and of instability in my legs, but you shall presently see both pass away."

So saying, he stepped to the stone basin, in which the waters of the fountain as they fell formed bubbles which danced in the white moonlight, and took as long a draught as if he had meant to exhaust the spring.

"When didst thou drink as deep a draught of water before, Holy Clerk of Copmanhurst?" said the Black Knight.

"Never since my wine-butt leaked, and let out its liquor by an illegal vent," replied the friar, "and so left me nothing to drink but my patron's bounty here."

Then plunging his hands and head into the fountain, he washed from them all marks of the midnight revel.

Thus refreshed and sobered, the jolly priest twirled his heavy partizan round his head with three fingers, as if he had been balancing a reed, exclaiming at the same time, "Where be those false ravishers, who carry off wenches against their will? May the foul fiend fly off with me, if I am not man enough for a dozen of them."

"Swearest thou, Holy Clerk?" said the Black Knight.

"Clerk me no clerks," replied the transformed priest; "by Saint

George and the Dragon, I am no longer a shaveling than while my frock is on my back—When I am cased in my green cassock, I will drink, swear, and woo a lass, with any blithe forester in the West Riding."

"Come on, Jack Priest," said Locksley, "and be silent; thou art as noisy as a whole convent on a holy eve, when the father abbot has gone to bed.—Come on you too, my masters, tarry not to talk of it—I say, come on, we must collect all our forces, and few enough we shall have, if we are to storm the castle of Reginald Front-de-Bœuf."

"What! is it Front-de-Bœuf," said the Black Knight, "who has stopt on the king's highway the king's liege subjects?—Is he turned thief and oppressor?"

"Oppressor he ever was," said Locksley.

"And for thief," said the priest, "I doubt if ever he were even half so honest a man as many a thief of my acquaintance."

"Move on, priest, and be silent," said the yeoman; "it were better you led the way to the place of rendezvous, than say what should be left unsaid, both in decency and prudence."

Chapter Seven

Alas, how many hours and years have past,
Since human forms have round this table sate,
Or lamp, or taper, on its surface gleam'd!
Methinks I hear the sound of time long pass'd
Still murmuring o'er us, in the lofty void
Of these dark arches, like the ling'ring voices
Of those who long within their graves have slept.

Orra, a Tragedy.

WHILE these measures were taking in behalf of Cedric and his companions, the armed men by whom the latter had been seized, hurried their captives along towards the place of security, where they intended to imprison them. But darkness came on fast, and the paths of the wood seemed but imperfectly known to the marauders. They were compelled to make several long halts, and once or twice to return on their road to resume the direction which they wished to pursue. The summer morn had dawned upon them ere they could travel in full assurance that they held the right path. But confidence returned with light, and the cavalcade now moved rapidly forward. Meanwhile, the following dialogue took place between the two leaders of the banditti.

"It is time thou should'st leave us, Sir Maurice," said the Templar to Bracy, "in order to prepare the second part of thy mystery. Thou art next, thou knowest, to act the Knight Deliverer."

"I have thought better of it," said Bracy; "I will not leave thee till the prize is fairly deposited in Front-de-Bœuf's castle. There will I appear before the Lady Rowena in mine own shape, and trust that she will set down to the vehemence of my passion, the violence of which I have been guilty."

"And what has made thee change thy plan, De Bracy?" replied the Knight Templar.

"That concerns thee nothing," answered his companion.

"I would hope, however, Sir Knight," said the Templar, "that this alteration of measures arises from no suspicion of my honourable meaning, such as Fitzurse endeavoured to instil into thee."

"My thoughts are my own," answered De Bracy; "the fiend laughs, they say, when one thief robs another; and we know, that were he to spit fire and brimstone instead, it would never prevent a Templar from following his bent."

"Or the leader of a Free Company," answered the Templar, "from dreading at the hands of a comrade and friend, the injustice he does to all mankind."

"This is unprofitable and perilous recrimination," answered De Bracy; "suffice it to say, I know the morals of the Temple-Order, and I will not give thee the power of cheating me out of the fair prey for which I have run such risks."

"Psha," replied the Templar, "what hast thou to fear?—Thou knowest the vows of my order."

"Right well," said De Bracy, "and also how they are kept. Come, Sir Templar, the laws of gallantry have a liberal interpretation in Palestine, and this is a case in which I will trust nothing to your conscience."

"Hear the truth then," said the Templar. "I care not for your blue-eyed beauty. There is in that train, one who will make me a better mate."

"What! would'st thou stoop to the waiting damsel?" said De Bracy.

"No, Sir Knight," said the Templar, haughtily. "To the waiting-woman will I not stoop. I have a prize among the captives, as lovely as thine own."

"By the mass, thou meanest the fair Jewess," said De Bracy.

"And if I do," said Bois-Guilbert, "who shall gainsay me?"

"No one that I know," said De Bracy, "unless it be your vow of celibacy, or a check of conscience for an intrigue with a Jewess."

"For my vow," said the Templar, "our grand master hath granted me a dispensation. And for my conscience, a man that has slain three hundred Saracens, need not reckon up every little failing, like a village girl at her first confession upon Good Friday eve."

"Thou knowest best thine own privileges," said De Bracy. "Yet, I would have sworn thy thought had been more on the old usurer's money bags, than on the black eyes of the daughter."

"I can admire both," answered the Templar; "besides, the old Jew is but half prize. I must share his spoils with Front-de-Bœuf, who will not lend us the use of his castle for nothing. I must have something that I can term exclusively my own by this foray of ours, and I have fixed on the lovely Jewess as my peculiar prize. But, now thou knowest my drift, thou wilt resume thine own original plan, wilt thou not?—Thou hast nothing, thou see'st, to fear from my interference."

"No," replied De Bracy, "I will remain beside my prize—what thou say'st is passing true, but I like not the privileges acquired by the dispensation of the grand master, and the merit acquired by the slaughter of three hundred Saracens. You have too good a right to a free pardon, to render you very scrupulous about peccadilloes."

While this dialogue was proceeding, Cedric was endeavouring to wring out of those who guarded him an avowal of their character and purpose. "You should be Englishmen," said he; "and yet, sacred heaven! you prey upon your countrymen as if you were very Normans. You should be my neighbours, and, if so, my friends; for which of my English neighbours have reason to be otherwise? I tell ye, yeomen, that even those among ye who have been branded with outlawry have had from me protection; for I have pitied their miseries, and curst the oppression of their tyrannic nobles. What, then, would you have of me? or in what can this violence serve ye?—Ye are worse than brute beasts in your actions, and will ye imitate them in their very dumbness?"

It was in vain that Cedric expostulated with his guards, who had too many good reasons for their silence to be induced to break it either by his wrath or his expostulations. They continued to hurry him along, travelling at a very rapid rate, until, at the end of an avenue of huge trees, arose Torquilstone, now the hoary and ancient castle of Reginald Front-de-Bœuf. It was a fortress of no great size, consisting of a donjon, or large and high square tower, surrounded by buildings of inferior height, which were encircled by an inner court-yard. Around the exterior wall was a deep moat, supplied with water from a neighbouring rivulet. Front-de-Bœuf, whose character placed him often at feud with his enemies, had made considerable additions to the strength of his castle, by building towers upon the outward wall, so as to flank it at every angle. The access, as usual in castles of the period, lay through an arched barbican, or outwork, which was terminated and defended by a small turret at each corner.

Cedric no sooner saw the turrets of Front-de-Bœuf's castle raise their grey and moss-grown battlements, glimmering in the morning sun above the wood by which they were surrounded, than he instantly augured more truly concerning the cause of his misfortune.

"I did injustice," he said, "to the thieves and outlaws of these woods, when I supposed such banditti to belong to their bands; I might as justly have confounded the foxes of these brakes with the ravening wolves of France. Tell me, dogs—is it my life or my wealth that your master aims at? Is it too much that two Saxons, myself and the noble Athelstane, should hold land in the country which was once the patrimony of our race?—Put us then to death, and complete your tyranny by taking our lives, as you began with our liberties. If the Saxon Cedric cannot rescue England, he is willing to die for her. Tell your tyrannical master, I do only beseech him to dismiss the Lady Rowena in honour and safety. She is a woman, and he need not dread her; and with us will die all who dare fight in her cause."

The attendants remained as mute to this address as to the former, and they now stood before the gate of the castle. Bracy winded his horn three times, and the archers and cross-bow men, who had manned the wall upon seeing their approach, hastened to lower the drawbridge and admit them. The prisoners were compelled to alight by their guards, and conducted to an apartment, where a hasty repast was offered them, of which none but Athelstane felt any inclination to partake. Neither had the descendant of the Confessor much time to do justice to the good cheer placed before them, for their guards gave him and Cedric to understand that they were to be imprisoned in a chamber apart from Rowena. Resistance was vain; and they were compelled to follow to a large room, which, rising on clumsy Saxon pillars, resembled those refectories and chapter houses which may be still seen in the most ancient parts of our most ancient monasteries.

The Lady Rowena was next separated from her train, and conducted, with courtesy indeed, but still without consulting her inclination, to a distant apartment. The same alarming distinction was conferred on Rebecca, in spite of her father's entreaties, who offered even money, in this extremity of distress, that she might be permitted to abide with him. "Base unbeliever," answered one of his guards, "when thou hast seen thy lair thou wilt not wish thy daughter to partake it." And, without farther discussion, the old Jew was forcibly dragged off in a different direction from the other prisoners. The domestics, after being carefully searched and disarmed, were confined in another part of the castle; and Rowena was refused even the comfort she might have derived from the attendance of her handmaiden Elgitha.

The apartment in which the Saxon chiefs were confined, for to them we turn our first attention, although at present used as a sort of guard-room, had formerly been the great hall of the castle. It was now abandoned to meaner purposes, because the present lord, among other additions to the convenience, security, and beauty of his baronial residence, had erected a new and noble hall, whose vaulted roof was supported by lighter and more elegant pillars, and fitted up with that higher degree of ornament, which the Normans had already introduced into architecture.

Cedric paced the apartment, filled with indignant reflections upon the past and of the present, while the apathy of his companion served, instead of patience and philosophy, to defend him against every thing save the inconvenience of the present moment; and so little did he feel even these last, that he was only from time to time roused to a reply by Cedric's animated and impassioned appeal to him.

"Yes," said Cedric, half speaking to himself, and half addressing himself to Athelstane, "it was in this very hall that my father feasted with Torquil Wolfganger, when he entertained the valiant and unfortunate Harold, then advancing against the Norwegians, who had united themselves to the rebel Tosti.—It was in this hall that Harold returned the magnanimous answer to the ambassador of his rebel brother. Oft have I heard my father kindle as he told the tale. The envoy of Tosti was admitted, when this ample room could scarce contain the crowd of noble Saxon leaders, who were quaffing the blood red wine around their monarch."

"I hope," said Athelstane, somewhat moved by this part of his friend's discourse, "they will not forget to send us some wine and refections at noon—we had scarce a breathing-space allowed to break our fast, and I never have the benefit of my food when I eat immediately after dismounting from horseback, though the leaches recommend that practice."

Cedric went on with his story without noticing this interjectional observation of his friend.

"The envoy of Tosti," he said, "moved up the hall, undismayed by the frowning countenances of all around him, until he made his obeisance before the throne of King Harold.

'What terms,' he said, 'Lord King, hath thy brother Tosti to hope, if he should lay down his arms, and crave peace at thy hands?'

'A brother's love,' cried the generous Harold, 'and the fair earldom of Northumberland.'

'But should Tosti accept these terms,' continued the envoy, 'what lands shall be assigned to his faithful ally, Hardrada King of Norway?'

'Seven feet of English ground,' answered Harold, fiercely, 'or, as Hardrada is said to be a giant, perhaps we may allow him twelve inches more.'

"The hall rung with acclamations, and cup and horn was filled to the Norwegian, who should be speedily in possession of his English territory."

"I could have pledged them with all my soul," said Athelstane, "for my tongue cleaves to my palate."

"The baffled envoy," continued Cedric, pursuing with animation his tale, though it interested not the listener, "retreated, to carry to Tosti and his ally the ominous answer of his injured brother. It was then that the walls of Stamford, and the fatal Welland renowned in prophecy,* beheld that direful conflict, in which, after displaying the most undaunted valour, the King of Norway, and Tosti, both fell with ten thousand of their bravest followers. Who would have thought that upon the proud day when this battle was won, the very gale which waved the Saxon banners in triumph, was filling the Norman sails, and impelling them to the fatal shores of Sussex?—Who would have thought that Harold, within a few brief days, would himself possess no more of his kingdom, than the share which he allotted in his wrath to the Norwegian invader?—Who would have thought that you, noble Athelstane—that you, descended of Harold's blood, and that I, whose father was not the worst defender of the Saxon crown, should be prisoners to a vile Norman, in the very hall in which our ancestors held such high festival!"

"It is sad enough," replied Athelstane; "but I trust they will hold us to a moderate ransom—At any rate it cannot be their purpose to starve us outright; and yet, although it is high noon, I see no preparations for serving dinner—Look up at the window, noble Cedric, and judge by the sun-beams if it is not on the verge of noon."

"It may be so," answered Cedric; "but I cannot look on that stained lattice without its awakening other reflections than those which concern the passing moment, or its privations. When that window was wrought, my noble friend, our hardy fathers knew not the art of making glass, or of staining it—The pride of Wolfganger's father brought an artist from Normandy to adorn his hall with this new species of emblazonment, that breaks the golden light of God's blessed day into so many fantastic hues. The foreigner came here, poor, beggarly, cringing, and subservient, ready to doff his cap to the

*Close by Stamford, was fought, in 1066, the bloody battle in which Harold defeated his rebel brother Tosti, and the Norwegians, only a few days before his fall at Hastings. The bridge over the Welland was furiously contested. One Norwegian long defended it by his single arm, and was at length pierced with a spear thrust through the planks from a boat beneath. Spencer and Drayton, both allude to the prophecies current concerning the fatal Welland:—

"Which to that ominous flood much fear and reverence wan."

Poly-Olbion.

L. T.

meanest native of the household. He returned pampered and proud, to tell his rapacious countrymen of the wealth and the simplicity of the Saxon nobles—a folly, oh Athelstane, foreboded of old, as well as foreseen, by those descendants of Hengist and his hardy tribes who retained the simplicity of their manners. We made these strangers our bosom friends, our confidential servants; we borrowed their artists and their arts, and despised the honest simplicity and hardihood with which our brave ancestors supported themselves, and we became enervated by Norman arts long ere we fell under Norman arms. Far better was our homely diet, eaten in peace and liberty, than the luxurious dainties, the love of which hath delivered us as bondsmen to the foreign conqueror."

"I should," replied Athelstane, "hold very humble diet a luxury at present; and it astonishes me, noble Cedric, that you can bear so truly in mind the memory of past deeds, when it appeareth you forget the very hour of dinner."

"It is time lost," muttered Cedric apart and impatiently, "to speak to him of aught else but that which concerns his appetite. The soul of Hardicanute hath taken possession of him, and he hath no pleasure save to fill, to swill, and to call for more.—Alas!" said he, looking at Athelstane with compassion, "that so dull a spirit should be lodged in so goodly a form! Alas! that such an enterprize as the regeneration of England should turn on a hinge so imperfect! Wedded to Rowena, indeed, her nobler and more generous soul may yet awake the better nature which is torpid within him. Yet how should this be, while Rowena, Athelstane, and I myself, remain the prisoners of this brutal marauder, and have been made so perhaps from a sense of the dangers which our liberty might bring to the usurped power of his nation?"

While the Saxon was plunged in these painful reflections, the door of their prison opened, and gave entrance to a sewer, holding his white rod of office. This important person advanced into the chamber with a grave pace, followed by four attendants, bearing in a table covered with dishes, the sight and smell of which seemed to be an instant compensation to Athelstane for the inconvenience he had undergone. All the persons who attended on the feast were masked and cloaked.

"What mummery is this?" said Cedric; "think you that we are ignorant whose prisoners we are, when we are in the castle of your master? Tell him," he continued, willing to use this opportunity to open a negociation for his freedom,—"Tell your master, Reginald Front-de-Bœuf, that we know no reason he can have for withholding our liberty, excepting his unlawful desire to enrich himself at our expence. Tell him that we yield to his rapacity, as in similar circumstances we should do to that of a literal robber. Let him name the ransom at which he rates our liberty, and it shall be paid, providing the exaction is suited to our means."

The sewer made no answer, but bowed his head.

"And tell Sir Reginald Front-de-Bœuf," said Athelstane, "that I send him my mortal defiance, and challenge him to combat with me, on foot or horseback, at any secure place, within eight days after our liberation, which, if he be a true knight, he will not, under these circumstances, venture to refuse or to delay."

"I shall deliver to the knight your defiance," answered the sewer; "meanwhile I leave you to your food."

The challenge of Athelstane was delivered with no good grace; for a large mouthful, which required the exercise of both jaws at once, added to a natural hesitation, considerably damped the effect of the bold defiance it contained. Still, however, his speech was hailed by Cedric as an incontestible token of reviving spirit in his companion, whose previous indifference had begun, notwithstanding his respect for Athelstane's descent, to wear out his patience. But he now cordially shook hands with him in token of his approbation, and was somewhat grieved when Athelstane observed, "that he would fight a dozen such men as Front-de-Bœuf, if, by so doing, he could hasten his departure from a dungeon where they put so much garlick into their pottage." Notwithstanding this intimation of a relapse into the apathy of sensuality, Cedric placed himself opposite to Athelstane, and soon shewed, that if the distresses of his country could banish the recollection of food while the table was uncovered, yet no sooner were the victuals put there, than he proved that the appetite of his Saxon ancestors had descended to him along with their other qualities.

The captives had not long enjoyed their refreshment, however, ere their attention was disturbed even from this most serious occupation by the blast of a horn winded before the gate. It was repeated three times, with as much violence as if it had been blown before an enchanted castle by the destined knight, at whose summons halls and towers, barbican and battlement, were to roll off like a morning vapour. The Saxons started from the table, and hasted to the window. But their curiosity was disappointed; for these outlets only looked upon the court of the castle, and the sound came from beyond its precincts. The summons, however, seemed of importance, for a considerable degree of bustle seemed instantly to take place in the castle.

Chapter Eight

My daughter—O my ducats—O my daughter!
————O my Christian ducats!
Justice—the Law—my ducats, and my daughter!
Merchant of Venice.

LEAVING the Saxon chiefs to return to their banquet so soon as their ungratified curiosity should permit them to attend to the calls of their half-satiated appetite, we have to look in upon the yet more severe imprisonment of Isaac of York. The poor Jew had been hastily thrust into a dungeon-vault of the castle, the floor of which was deep beneath the level of the ground, and very damp, being lower than even the moat itself. The only light was received through one or two loop-holes far above the reach of the captive's hand. These apertures admitted, even at mid-day, but a dim and uncertain light, which was changed for utter darkness long before the rest of the castle had lost the blessing of day. Chains and shackles, which had been the portion of former captives, from whom active exertions at escape had been apprehended, hung rusted and empty on the walls of the prison; and in the rings of one of those sets of fetters there remained two mouldering bones, which seemed to have been once those of the human leg, as if some prisoner had been left not only to perish there, but to be consumed to a skeleton.

At one end of this ghastly apartment was a large fire-grate, over the top of which were stretched some transverse iron bars, half devoured with rust.

The whole appearance of the dungeon might have appalled a stouter heart than that of Isaac, who, nevertheless, was more composed under the imminent pressure of danger, than he had seemed to be while affected by terrors, of which the cause was as yet remote and contingent. The lovers of the chase say that the hare feels more agony during the pursuit of the greyhounds, than when she is absolutely struggling in their fangs.* And thus it is probable, that the Jews, by the very frequency of their fear on all occasions, had their minds in some degree prepared for every effort of tyranny which could be practised upon them; so that no aggression, when it had taken place, could bring with it that surprise which is the most disabling quality of terror. Neither was it the first time that Isaac had been placed in circumstances so dangerous. He had therefore experience to guide him, as well as hope, that he might again, as formerly, be delivered as a prey

* *Nota Bene.*—We by no means warrant the accuracy of this piece of natural history, which we give on the authority of the Wardour MS. L. T.

from the fowler. Above all, he had upon his side the unyielding obstinacy of his nation, and that unbending resolution, with which they have been frequently known to submit to the uttermost evils which power and violence can inflict upon them, rather than gratify their oppressors by granting their demands.

In this humour of passive resistance, and with his garment collected beneath him to keep his limbs from the wet pavement, Isaac sat in a corner of his dungeon, where his folded hands, his dishevelled hair and beard, his furred cloak and high cap, seen by the wiry and broken light, would have afforded a study for Rembrandt, had that celebrated painter existed at the period. The Jew remained, without altering this position, for nearly three hours, at the expiry of which steps were heard on the dungeon stair. The bolts screamed as they were withdrawn—the hinges creaked as the wicket opened, and Reginald Front-de-Bœuf, followed by the two Saracen slaves of the Templar, entered the prison.

Front-de-Bœuf, a tall and strong man, whose life had been spent in public war or in private feuds and broils, and who had hesitated at no means of extending his feudal power, had features corresponding to his character, and which strongly expressed the fiercer and more malignant passions of the mind. The scars with which his visage was seamed would, on features of a different cast, have excited the sympathy and veneration due to the marks of honourable valour; but, in the peculiar case of Front-de-Bœuf, they only added to the ferocity of his countenance, and to the dread which his presence inspired. This formidable baron was clad in a leathern doublet, fitted close to his body, which was frayed and soiled with the stains of his armour. He had no weapon, excepting a poniard at his belt, which served to counterbalance the weight of the bunch of rusty keys that hung at his right side.

The black slaves who attended Front-de-Bœuf were stripped of their gorgeous apparel, and attired in jerkins and trowsers of coarse linen, their sleeves being tucked up above the elbow, like those of butchers when about to exercise their function in the slaughter-house. Each had in his hand a small panier; and, when they entered the dungeon, they stopt at the door until Front-de-Bœuf himself carefully locked and double-locked it. Having taken this precaution, he advanced slowly up the apartment towards the Jew, upon whom he kept his eye fixed, as if he wished to paralize him with his glance, as some animals are said to fascinate their prey. It seemed indeed as if the sullen and malignant eye of Front-de-Bœuf possessed some portion of that supposed power over his unfortunate prisoner. The Jew sate a-gape, his eyes fixed on the savage baron with such earnestness of terror, that his frame seemed literally to shrink together, and to diminish in size under his fixed and baleful gaze. The unhappy Isaac was deprived not only of the power of rising to make the obeisance which his terror dictated, but he could not even doff his cap, or utter any word of supplication, so strongly was he agitated by the conviction that tortures and death were impending over him.

On the other hand, the stately form of the Norman appeared to dilate in magnitude, like that of the eagle, which ruffles up its plumage when about to pounce on its defenceless prey. He paused within three steps of the corner in which the unfortunate Jew had now as it were coiled himself up into the smallest possible space, and made a sign for one of the slaves to approach. The black satellite came forward accordingly, and, producing from his basket a large pair of scales and several weights, he laid them at the feet of Front-de-Bœuf, and again retired to the respectful distance, at which his companion had already taken his station.

The motions of these men were slow and solemn, as if there impended over their souls some preconception of horror and of cruelty. Front-de-Bœuf himself opened the scene by thus addressing his ill-fated captive.

"Most accursed dog of an accursed race," he said, awaking with his deep and sullen voice the sullen echoes of his dungeon vault, "seest thou these scales?"

The unhappy Jew returned a feeble affirmative.

"In these very scales shalt thou weigh me out," said the relentless Baron, "a thousand silver pounds, after the just measure and weight of the Tower of London."

"Holy Abraham!" returned the Jew, finding voice through the very extremity of his danger, "heard man ever such a demand?—Who ever heard, even in a minstrel's tale, of such a sum as a thousand pounds of silver?—What human sight was ever blessed with the vision of such a mass of treasure?—Not within the walls of York, ransack my house and that of all my tribe, wilt thou find the huge sum of silver that thou speakest of."

"I am reasonable," answered Front-de-Bœuf, "and if silver be scant, I refuse not gold—At the rate of a mark of gold for each six pounds of silver, thou shalt free thy unbelieving carcase from such punishment as thy heart has never even conceived."

"Have mercy on me, noble knight!" said Isaac, "I am old, and poor, and helpless. It were unworthy to triumph over me—It is a poor deed to crush a worm."

"Old thou may'st be," replied the knight; "more shame to their folly who have suffered thee to grow grey in usury and knavery—Feeble thou may'st be, for when had a Jew either heart or hand—But rich it is well known thou art."

"I swear to you, noble knight," said the Jew, "by all which I believe, and by all which we believe in common"——

"Perjure not thyself," said the Norman, interrupting him, "and let not thine obstinacy seal thy doom, until thou hast seen and well considered the fate that awaits thee. Think not I speak to thee only to excite thy terror, and practise on the base cowardice thou hast derived from thy tribe—I swear to thee by that which thou dost NOT believe, by the gospel which our church teaches, and by the keys which are given her to bind and to loose, that my purpose is deep and peremptory. This dungeon is no place for trifling. Prisoners ten thousand times more distinguished than thou have died within these walls, and their fate hath never been known. But for thee is reserved a long and lingering death, to which theirs were luxury."

He again made a signal for the slaves to approach, and spoke to them apart, in their own language, for he also had been in Palestine, where, perhaps, he had learnt his lesson of cruelty. The Saracens produced from their baskets a quantity of charcoal, a pair of bellows, and a flask of oil. While the one struck a light with a flint and steel, the other disposed the charcoal in the large rusty grate which we have already mentioned, and exercised the bellows until the fuel came to a red glow.

"Seest thou, Isaac," said Front-de-Bœuf, "the range of iron bars above that glowing charcoal?—on that warm couch thou shalt lie, stripped of thy clothes as if thou wert to rest on a bed of down. One of these slaves shall maintain the fire beneath thee, while the other shall anoint thy wretched limbs with oil, lest the roast should burn.—Now, choose betwixt such a scorching bed and the payment of a thousand pounds of silver; for, by the head of my father, thou hast no other option."

"It is impossible," said the unfortunate Jew, "it is impossible that your purpose can be real! The good God of nature never made a heart capable of exercising such cruelty."

"Trust not to that, Isaac," said Front-de-Bœuf, "it were a fatal error. Doest thou think that I, who have seen a town sacked, in which thousands of my Christian countrymen perished by sword, by flood, and by fire, will blench from my purpose for the outcries or screams of one single wretched Jew?—or think'st thou that these swarthy slaves, who have neither law, country, nor conscience, but their master's will —who use the poison or the stake, or the poniard, or the cord, at his slightest wink—thinkest thou that they will have mercy, who do not even understand the language in which it is asked?—Be wise, old man; discharge thyself of a portion of thy superfluous wealth; repay to the hands of a Christian a part of what thou hast acquired by the usury thou hast practised on those of his religion. Thy cunning may soon swell out once more thy shrivelled purse, but neither leach nor medicine can restore thy scorched hide and flesh wert thou once stretched on these bars. Tell down thy ransom, I say, and rejoice that at such a rate thou can'st redeem thee from a dungeon, the secrets of which few have returned to tell. I waste no more words with thee—choose between thy dross and thy flesh and blood, and as thou choosest, so shall it be."

"So may Abraham, Jacob, and all the fathers of our people assist me," said Isaac, "I cannot make the choice, because I have not the means of satisfying your exorbitant demand."

"Seize him, and strip him, slaves," said the Knight, "and let the fathers of his race assist him if they can."

The assistants, taking their directions more from the Baron's eye and his hand than his tongue, once more stepped forward, laid hands on the unfortunate Isaac, plucked him up from the ground, and holding him between them, waited the hard-hearted Baron's farther signal. The unhappy Jew eyed their countenances and that of Front-de-Bœuf, in hope of discovering some symptoms of relenting; but that of the Baron exhibited the same cold, half-sullen, half-sarcastic smile which had been the prelude to his cruelty; and the savage eye of the Saracens, rolling gloomy under their dark brows, acquiring a yet more sinister expression by the whiteness of the circle which surrounds the pupil, evinced rather the secret pleasure which they expected from the approaching scene, than any reluctance to be its directors or agents. The Jew then looked at the glowing furnace, over which he was presently to be stretched, and, seeing no chance of his tormentor's relenting, his resolution gave way.

"I will pay," he said, "the thousand pounds of silver—That is," he added, after a moment's pause, "I will pay it with the help of my brethren, for I must beg as a mendicant at the door of our synagogue ere I make up so unheard of a sum.—When and where must it be delivered?"

"Here," replied Front-de-Bœuf, "here it must be delivered—weighed it must be—weighed and told down on this very dungeon floor.—Thinkest thou I will part with thee until thy ransom is secure?"

"And what is to be my surety," said the Jew, "that I shall be at liberty after this ransom is paid?"

"The word of a Norman noble, thou pawn-broking slave,"

answered Front-de-Bœuf; "the faith of a Norman nobleman, more pure than the gold and silver of thee and all thy tribe."

"I crave pardon, noble lord," said Isaac timidly, "but wherefore should I rely wholly on the word of one who will trust nothing to mine?"

"Because thou can'st not help it, Jew," said the knight, sternly. "Wert thou now in thy treasure-chamber at York, and were I craving a loan of thy shekels, it would be thine to dictate the time of payment, and the pledge of security. This is *my* treasure-chamber. Here I have thee at advantage, nor will I again deign to repeat the terms on which I grant thee liberty."

The Jew groaned deeply.—"Grant me," he said, "at least, with my own liberty, that of the companions with whom I travel. They scorned me as a Jew, yet they pitied my desolation, and because they tarried to aid me by the way, a share of my evil hath come upon them; moreover, they may contribute in some sort to my ransom."

"If thou meanest yonder Saxon churls," said Front-de-Bœuf, "their ransom will depend upon other terms than thine. Mind thine own concerns, Jew, I warn thee, and meddle not with those of others."

"I am then," said Isaac, "only to be set at liberty, together with mine wounded friend?"

"Shall I twice recommend it," said Front-de-Bœuf, "to a son of Israel, to meddle with his own concerns, and leave those of others alone?—Since thou hast made thy choice, it remains but that thou pay'st down thy ransom, and that at a short day."

"Yet hear me," said the Jew—"for the sake of that very wealth which thou would'st obtain at the expence of thy"——Here he stopt short, afraid of irritating the savage Norman. But Front-de-Bœuf only laughed, and himself filled up the blank at which the Jew had hesitated. "At the expence of my conscience, thou would'st say, Isaac, speak it out—I tell thee, I am reasonable. I can bear the reproaches of a loser, even when that loser is a Jew. Thou wert not so patient, Isaac, when thou did'st invoke justice against Jacques Fitzdotterel, for calling thee a usurious blood-sucker, when thy exactions had devoured his patrimony."

"I swear by the Talmud," said the Jew, "that your valour has been misled in that matter. Fitzdotterel drew his poniard upon me in mine own chamber, because I craved him for mine own silver. The term of payment was due at the Passover."

"I care not what he did," said Front-de-Bœuf; "the question is, when shall I have mine own?—when shall I have the shekels, Isaac?"

"Let my daughter Rebecca go forth to York," answered Isaac, "with your safe conduct, noble knight, and so soon as man and horse can return, the treasure"——Here he groaned deeply, but added, after the pause of a few seconds,—"The treasure shall be told down on this very floor."

"Thy daughter!" said Front-de-Bœuf, as if surprised,—"By heavens, Isaac, I would I had known of this. I deemed that yonder black-browed girl had been thy concubine, and I gave her to be a handmaiden to Sir Brian de Bois-Guilbert, after the fashion of patriarchs and heroes of the days of old, who set us in these matters a wholesome example."

The yell which Isaac raised at this unfeeling communication made the very vault to ring, and astounded the two Saracens so much that they let go their hold of the Jew. He availed himself of his enlargement to throw himself on the pavement, and clasp the knees of Front-de-Bœuf.

"Take all that you have asked," said he, "Sir Knight—take ten times more—reduce me to ruin and to beggary, if thou wilt,—nay, pierce me with thy poniard, broil me on that furnace, but spare my daughter, deliver her in safety and honour!—As thou art born of woman, spare the honour of a helpless maiden—She is the image of my deceased Rachael, she is the last of six pledges of her love—Will you deprive a widowed husband of his sole remaining comfort?—Will you reduce a father to wish that his only living child was laid beside her dead mother, in the tomb of our fathers?"

"I would," said the Norman, somewhat relenting, "that I had known of this before. I thought your race had loved nothing save their money-bags."

"Think not so humbly of us," said Isaac, eager to improve the moment of apparent sympathy; "the hunted fox, the tortured wild-cat, loves its young—the despised and persecuted race of Abraham love their children."

"Be it so," said Front-de-Bœuf; "I will believe it in future, Isaac, for thy very sake—But it aids us not now, I cannot help what has happened, or what is to follow; my word is passed to my comrade in arms, nor would I break it for ten Jews and Jewesses to boot. Besides, why shouldst thou think evil is to come to the girl, even if she became Bois-Guilbert's booty?"

"There will, there must," exclaimed Isaac, wringing his hands in agony; "when did Templars breathe aught but cruelty to men and dishonour to women?"

"Dog of an infidel," said Front-de-Bœuf, with sparkling eyes, and not sorry, perhaps, to seize a pretext for working himself into a passion, "blaspheme not the Holy Order of the Temple of Zion, but take thought instead to pay me the ransom thou hast promised, or woe betide thy Jewish throat."

"Robber and villain!" said the Jew, retorting the insults of his oppressor with passion, which, however impotent, he now found it impossible to bridle, "I will pay thee nothing—not one silver penny will I pay thee, unless my daughter is delivered to me."

"Art thou in thy senses, Israelite?" said the Norman, sternly—"Has thy flesh and blood a charm against heated iron and scalding oil?"

"I care not!" said the Jew, rendered desperate by paternal affection; "do thy worst. My daughter is my flesh and blood, dearer to me a thousand times than those limbs which thy cruelty threatens. No silver will I give thee, unless I were to pour it molten down thy avaricious throat—no, not a silver penny will I give thee, Nazarene, were it to save thee from the deep damnation thy whole life has merited! Take my life if thou wilt, and say, the Jew, amidst his tortures, knew how to disappoint the Christian."

"We shall see that," said Front-de-Bœuf, "for by the blessed rood, which is the abomination of thy accursed tribe, thou shalt feel the extremities of fire and steel.—Strip him, slaves, and chain him down upon the bars."

In spite of the feeble struggles of the old man, the Saracens had already torn from him his upper garment, and were proceeding totally to disrobe him, when the sound of a bugle twice winded without the castle, penetrated even to the recesses of the dungeon, and immediately after, voices were heard calling for Sir Reginald Front-de-Bœuf. Unwilling to be found engaged in his hellish occupation, the savage Baron gave the slaves a signal to restore Isaac's garment, and, quitting the dungeon with his attendants, he left the Jew to thank God for his own deliverance, or to lament over his daughter's captivity, and probable fate, as his personal or parental feelings might prove strongest.

Chapter Nine

Nay, if the gentle spirit of moving words
Can no way move you to a milder form,
I'll woo you, like a soldier, at arm's end,
And love you 'gainst the nature of love.
Two Gentlemen of Verona.

THE APARTMENT to which the Lady Rowena had been introduced was fitted up with some rude attempts at ornament and magnificence, and her being placed there might be considered as a peculiar mark of respect not offered to the other prisoners. But the wife of Front-de-

Bœuf, for whom it had been originally furnished, was long dead, and decay and neglect had impaired the few ornaments with which her taste had adorned it. The tapestry hung down from the walls in many places, and in others was tarnished and faded under the effects of the sun, or tattered and decayed by age. Desolate, however, as it was, this was the apartment of the castle which had been judged most fitting for the accommodation of the Saxon heiress; and here she was left to meditate upon her fate, until the actors in this nefarious drama had arranged the several parts which each of them was to perform. This had been settled in a council held by Front-de-Bœuf, Bracy, and the Templar, in which, after a long and warm debate concerning the several advantages which each insisted upon deriving from his peculiar share in this audacious enterprize, they had at length determined the fate of their unhappy prisoners.

It was about the hour of noon, therefore, when De Bracy, for whose advantage the expedition had been first planned, appeared, to prosecute his views upon the hand and possessions of the Lady Rowena.

The interval had not entirely been bestowed in holding council with his confederates, for De Bracy had found leisure to decorate his person with all the foppery of the times. His green cassock and vizard were now flung aside. His long luxuriant hair was trained to flow in quaint tresses down his richly furred cloak. His beard was closely shaved, his doublet reached to the middle of his leg, and the girdle which secured it, and at the same time supported his ponderous sword, was embroidered and embossed with gold work. We have already noticed the extravagant fashion of the shoes at this period, and the points of Maurice De Bracy's might have challenged the prize of extravagance with the gayest, being turned up and twisted like the horns of a ram. Such was the dress of a gallant of the period; and in the present instance, that effect was aided by the handsome person and good demeanour of the wearer, whose manners partook alike of the grace of a courtier, and the frankness of a soldier.

He saluted Rowena by doffing his velvet bonnet, garnished with a golden broach, representing St Michael trampling down the Prince of Evil. With this, he gently motioned the lady to a seat; and, as she still retained her standing posture, the knight ungloved his right hand, and proffered to conduct her thither. But Rowena declined, by her gesture, the proffered compliment, and replied, "If I be in the presence of my jailor, Sir Knight—nor will circumstances allow me to think otherwise—it best becomes his prisoner to remain standing till she learns her doom."

"Alas! fair Rowena," returned De Bracy, "you are in presence of your captive, not your jailor, and it is from your fair eyes that De Bracy must receive that doom which you fondly expect from him."

"I know you not, sir," said the lady, drawing herself up with all the pride of offended rank and beauty; "I know you not—and the insolent familiarity with which you apply to me the jargon of a troubadour, forms no apology for the violence of a robber."

"To thyself, fair maid," answered De Bracy, in his former tone—"to thine own charms be ascribed whate'er I have done which passed the respect due to her, whom I have chosen queen of my heart and loadstar of my eyes."

"I repeat to you, Sir Knight, that I know you not, and that no man wearing chain and spurs ought thus to intrude himself upon the presence of an unprotected lady."

"That I am unknown to you," said De Bracy, "is indeed my misfortune; yet let me hope that De Bracy's name has not been always unspoken, when minstrels or heralds have praised deeds of chivalry, whether in the lists or in the battle-field."

"To heralds and to minstrels, then, leave thy praise, Sir Knight," replied Rowena, "more suiting for their mouths than for thine own; and tell me which of them shall record in song, or in book of tournay, the memorable conquest of this night, a conquest obtained over an old man, followed by a few timid hinds; and its booty, an unfortunate maiden, transported against her will to the castle of a robber."

"You are unjust, Lady Rowena," said the knight, biting his lips in some confusion, and speaking in a tone more natural to him than that of affected gallantry, which he had at first adopted; "yourself free from passion, you can allow no excuse for the frenzy of another, although caused by your own beauty."

"I pray you, Sir Knight," said Rowena, "to cease a language so commonly used by strolling minstrels, that it becomes not the mouth of knights or nobles. Certes, you constrain me to sit down, since you enter upon such common-place terms, of which each vile crowder hath a stock that might last from hence to Christmas."

"Proud damsel," said De Bracy, incensed at finding his gallant style procured him nothing but contempt—"proud damsel, thou shalt be as proudly encountered. Know then, that I have supported my pretensions to your hand in the way that best suited thy character. It is meeter for thy humour to be wooed with bow and bill, than in set terms, and in courtly language."

"Courtesy of tongue," said Rowena, "when it is used to veil churlishness of deed, is but a knight's girdle around the breast of a base clown. I wonder not that the restraint appears to gall you—more it were for your honour to have retained the dress and language of an outlaw, than to veil the deeds of one under an affectation of gentle language and demeanour."

"You counsel well, lady," said De Bracy; "and in the bold language which best justifies bold actions, I tell thee, thou shalt never leave this castle, or thou shalt leave it as Maurice De Bracy's wife. I am not wont to be baffled in my enterprizes, nor needs a Norman noble scrupulously vindicate his conduct to the Saxon maiden whom he distinguishes by the offer of his hand. Thou art proud, Rowena, and thou art the fitter to be my wife. By what other means couldst thou be raised to high honour and to princely place, saving by my alliance? How else wouldst thou escape from the mean precincts of a country grange, where Saxons herd with the swine which form their wealth, to take thy seat, honoured as thou shouldst be, amid all in England that is distinguished by beauty, or dignified by power?"

"Sir Knight," replied Rowena, "the grange which you contemn hath been my shelter from infancy; and, trust me, when I leave it—should that day ever arrive—it shall be with one who has not learnt to despise the dwelling and manners in which I have been brought up."

"I guess your meaning, lady," said De Bracy, "though you may think it lies too obscure for my apprehension. But dream not, that Richard Cœur de Lion will ever resume his throne, far less that Wilfred of Ivanhoe, his minion, will ever lead thee to his footstool, to be there welcomed as the bride of a favourite. Another suitor might feel jealousy while he touched this string; but my firm purpose cannot be changed by a passion so childish and so hopeless. Know, lady, that this rival is in my power, and that it rests but with me to betray the secret of his being within the castle to Front-de-Bœuf, whose jealousy will be more fatal than mine."

"Wilfred, here?" said Rowena, in disdain; "that is as true as that Front-de-Bœuf is his rival."

De Bracy looked at her steadily for an instant; "Wert thou really ignorant of this?" said he; "didst thou not know that he travelled in the litter of the Jew?—a meet conveyance for the crusader, whose doughty arm was to reconquer the Holy Sepulchre!" And he laughed scornfully.

"And if he is here," said Rowena, compelling herself to a tone of indifference, though trembling with an agony of apprehension which she could not suppress, "in what is he the rival of Front-de-Bœuf? or what has he to fear beyond a short imprisonment, and an honourable ransom, according to the use of chivalry?"

"Rowena," said De Bracy, "art thou, too, deceived by the common error of thy sex, who think there can be no rivalry but that respecting their own charms? Knowest thou not there is a jealousy of ambition and of wealth, as well as of love; and that this our host, Front-de-Bœuf, will push from his road him who opposes his claim to the fair barony of Ivanhoe, as readily, eagerly, and unscrupulously, as if he were preferred to him by some blue-eyed damsel? But smile on my suit, lady, and the wounded champion shall have nothing to fear from Front-de-Bœuf, whom else thou may'st mourn for, as in the hands of one who has never shewn compassion."

"Save him, for the love of Heaven!" said Rowena, her firmness giving way under terror for her lover's impending fate.

"I can—I will—it is my purpose," said De Bracy; "for, when Rowena consents to be the bride of De Bracy, who is it shall dare to put forth a violent hand upon her kinsman—the son of her guardian—the companion of her youth? But it is thy love must buy his protection. I am not romantic fool enough to further the fortune, or avert the fate, of one who is likely to be a successful obstacle between me and my wishes. Use thine influence with me in his behalf, and he is safe,—refuse to employ it, Wilfred dies, and thou thyself art not the nearer to freedom."

"Thy language," answered Rowena, "hath in its indifferent bluntness something which cannot be reconciled with the horrors it seems to express. I believe not that thy purpose is so wicked, or thy power so great."

"Flatter thyself, then, with that belief," said De Bracy, "until time shall prove it false. Thy lover lies wounded in this castle—thy preferred lover. He is a bar betwixt Front-de-Bœuf and that which Front-de-Bœuf loves better than either ambition or beauty. What will it cost beyond the blow of a poniard, or the thrust of a javelin, to silence his opposition for ever? Nay, were Front-de-Bœuf afraid to justify a deed so open, let the leach but give his patient a wrong draught—let the chamberlain, or the nurse who tends him, but pluck the pillow from his head, and Wilfred, in his present condition, is sped without the effusion of blood. Cedric also——"

"And Cedric also," said Rowena, repeating his words; "my noble—my generous guardian! I deserved the evil I have encountered, for forgetting his fate even in that of his son."

"Cedric's fate also depends upon thy determination," said De Bracy; "and I leave thee to form it."

Hitherto, Rowena had sustained her part in this trying scene with undismayed courage, but it was because she had not considered the danger as serious and imminent. Her disposition was naturally that which physiognomists consider as proper to fair complexions, mild, timid, and gentle; but it had been tempered, and, as it were, hardened, by the circumstances of her education. Accustomed to see the will of all, even of Cedric himself, (sufficiently arbitrary with others) give way before her wishes, she had acquired that sort of courage and self-confidence which arises from the habitual and constant deference of the circle in which we move. She could scarce conceive the possibility of her will being opposed, far less that of its being treated with total disregard.

Her haughtiness and habit of domination was, therefore, a fictitious character, induced over that which was natural to her, and it deserted her when her eyes were opened to the extent of her own danger, as well as that of her lover and her guardian, and when she found her will, the slightest expression of which wont to command respect and attention, was now placed in opposition to that of a man of a strong, fierce, and determined mind, who possessed the advantage over her, and was resolved to use it.

After casting her eyes around, as if to look for the aid which was nowhere to be found, and after a few broken interjections, she raised her hands to heaven, and burst into a passion of uncontroled vexation and sorrow. It was impossible to see so beautiful a creature in such extremity without feeling for her, and De Bracy was not unmoved, though he was yet more embarrassed than touched. He had, in truth, gone too far to recede; and yet, in Rowena's present condition, she could not be acted on either by argument or threats. He paced the apartment to and fro, now vainly exhorting the terrified maiden to compose herself, now hesitating concerning his own line of conduct.

If, thought he, I should be moved by the tears and sorrow of this disconsolate damsel, what would I reap but the loss of those fair hopes for which I have encountered so much risk, and the ridicule of Prince John and his jovial comrades? "And yet," he said to himself, "I feel myself ill framed for the part which I am playing. I cannot look on so fair a face while it is disturbed with agony, or on those eyes when they are drowned in tears. I would she had retained her original haughtiness of disposition, or that I had a larger share of Front-de-Bœuf's thrice-tempered hardness of heart."

Agitated by these thoughts, he could only bid the unfortunate Rowena be comforted, and assure her, that as yet she had no reason for the excess of despair to which she was now giving way. But in this task of consolation De Bracy was interrupted by the horn, "hoarse-winded blowing far and keen," which had at the same time alarmed the other inmates of the castle, and interrupted their several plans of avarice and of licence. Of them all, perhaps, De Bracy least regretted the interruption; for his conference with the Lady Rowena had arrived at a point, where he found it equally difficult to prosecute or to resign his enterprize.

And here we cannot but think it necessary to offer some better proof than the incidents of an idle tale, to vindicate the melancholy representation of manners which has been just laid before the reader. It is grievous to think that those valiant barons, to whose stand against the crown the liberties of England were indebted for their existence, should themselves have been such dreadful oppressors, and capable of excesses contrary not only to the laws of England, but to those of nature and humanity. But, alas! we have only to extract from the industrious Henry one of those numerous passages which he has collected from contemporary historians, to prove that fiction itself can hardly reach the dark reality of the horrors of the period.

The description given by the author of the Saxon Chronicle of the cruelties exercised in the reign of King Stephen by the great barons and lords of castles, who were all Normans, affords a strong proof of the excesses of which they were capable when their passions were inflamed. "They grievously oppressed the poor people by building castles; and when they were built, they filled them with wicked men, or rather devils, who seized both men and women who they imagined had any money, threw them into prison, and put them to more cruel tortures than the martyrs ever endured. They suffocated some in mud, and suspended others by the feet, or the head, or the thumbs, kindling fires below them. They squeezed the heads of some with knotted cords till they pierced their brains, while they threw others into dungeons swarming with serpents, snakes, and toads." But it would be cruel to put the reader to the pain of perusing the remainder of this description.*

As another instance of these bitter fruits of conquest, and perhaps the strongest that can be quoted, we may mention, that the Empress Matilda, though a daughter of the King of Scotland, and afterwards both Queen of England and Empress of Germany, the daughter, the wife, and the mother of monarchs, was obliged, during her early residence for education in England, to assume the veil of a nun, as the only means of escaping the licentious pursuit of the Norman nobles. This excuse she stated before a great council of the clergy of England, as the sole reason for her having taken the religious habit. The assembled clergy admitted the validity of the plea, and the notoriety of the circumstances upon which it was founded; giving thus an indubitable and most remarkable testimony to the existence of that disgraceful licence by which that age was stained. It was a matter of public knowledge, they said, that after the conquest of King William, his Norman followers, elated by so great a victory, acknowledged no law but their own wicked pleasure, and not only despoiled the conquered Saxons of

*Henry's Hist. edit. 1805, vol. vii. p. 346.

their lands and their goods, but invaded the honour of their wives and of their daughters with the most unbridled licence; and hence it was then common for matrons and maidens of noble families to assume the veil, and take shelter in convents, not as called thither by the vocation of God, but solely to preserve their honour from the unbridled wickedness of man.

Such and so licentious were the times, as announced by the public declaration of the assembled clergy, recorded by Eadmer; and we need add nothing more to vindicate the probability of the scenes which we have detailed, and are about to detail, upon the more apocryphal authority of the Wardour MS.

Chapter Ten

I'll woo her as the lion wooes his bride.
Douglas.

WHILE THE SCENES we have described were passing in other parts of the castle, the Jewess Rebecca awaited her fate in a distant and sequestered turret. Hither she had been led by two of her disguised ravishers, and on being thrust into the little cell, she found herself in the presence of an old sybil, who kept murmuring to herself a Saxon rhyme, as if to beat time to the revolving dance which her spindle was performing upon the floor. The hag raised her head as Rebecca entered, and scowled at the fair Jewess with the malignant envy with which old age and ugliness, when united with evil conditions, are apt to look upon youth and beauty.

"Thou must up and away, old house-cricket," said one of the men; "our noble master commands it—Thou must leave this chamber to a fairer guest."

"Ay," grumbled the hag, "even thus is service requited. I have known when my bare word would have cast the best man-at-arms among ye out of saddle and out of service; and now must I up and away at the command of every groom such as thou."

"Good Dame Urfried," said the other man, "stand not to reason on it, but up and away. Lords' hests must be listened to with a quick ear. Thou hast had thy day, old dame, but thy sun has long been set. Thou art now the very emblem of an old war-horse turned out on the barren heath—thou hast had thy paces in thy time, but now a broken amble is the best of them—Come, amble off with thee."

"Ill omens dog ye both!" said the old woman; "and a kennel be your burying-place! May the evil demon Zernebock tear me limb from limb, if I leave my own cell ere I have spun out the hemp on my distaff."

"Answer it to our lord, then, old house-fiend," said the man, and retired; leaving Rebecca in company with the old woman, upon whose presence she had been thus unwillingly forced.

"What devil's deed have they now in the wind?" said the old hag, murmuring to herself, yet from time to time casting a sidelong and malignant glance at Rebecca; "but it is easy to guess—Bright eyes, black locks, and a skin like paper, ere the priest stains it with his black unguent—Ay, it is easy to guess why they send her to this lone turret, whence a shriek could no more be heard than at the depth of five hundred fathoms beneath the earth. Thou wilt have owls for thy neighbours, fair one; and their screams will be heard as far, and as much regarded as thine own. Outlandish, too," she said, marking the dress and turban of Rebecca—"What country art thou of?—a Saracen? or an Egyptian?—Why dost not answer?—thou can'st weep, can'st thou not speak?"

"Be not angry, good mother," said Rebecca.

"Thou need'st say no more," replied Urfried; "men know a fox by the train, and a Jewess by her tongue."

"For the sake of mercy," said Rebecca, "tell me what I am to expect as the conclusion of the violence which hath dragged me hither! Is it my life they seek, to atone for my religion? I will lay it down cheerfully."

"Thy life, minion?" answered the sybil; "what would taking thy life pleasure them?—Trust me thy life is in no peril. Such usage shalt thou have as was once thought good enough for a noble Saxon maiden. And shall a Jewess, like thee, repine because she hath no better? Look at me—I was as young and twice as fair as thou when Front-de-Bœuf, father of this Reginald, and his Normans, stormed this castle. My father and his seven sons defended their inheritance from storey to storey, from chamber to chamber—There was not a room, not a step of the stair, that was not slippery with their blood. They died—they died every man; and ere their bodies were cold, and ere their blood was dried, I had become the prey and the scorn of the conqueror!"

"Is there no help?—Are there no means of escape?" said Rebecca —"Richly, richly would I requite thine aid."

"Think not of it," said the hag; "from hence there is no escape but through the gates of death; and it is late, late," she added, shaking her grey head, "ere these open to us—Yet it is comfort to think that we leave behind us on earth those who shall be wretched as ourselves. Fare thee well, Jewess!—Jew or Gentile, thy fate would be the same;

for thou hast to do with them that have neither scruple nor pity. Fare thee well, I say. My thread is spun out—thy task is yet to begin."

"Stay! stay! for Heaven's sake!" said Rebecca; "stay, though it be to curse and to revile me—thy presence is yet some protection."

"The presence of the mother of God were no protection," answered the old woman. "There she stands," pointing to a rude image of the Virgin Mary, "see if she can avert the fate that awaits thee."

She left the room as she spoke, her features writhed into a sort of sneering laugh, which made them seem even more hideous than their habitual frown. She locked the door behind her, and Rebecca might hear her curse every step for its steepness, as slowly and with difficulty she descended the turret-stair.

Rebecca was now to expect a fate even more dreadful than that of Rowena; for what probability was there that either softness or ceremony would be used towards one of her oppressed race, whatever shadow of these might be preserved towards a Saxon heiress? Yet had the Jewess this advantage, that she was better prepared by habits of thought, and by natural strength of mind, to encounter the dangers to which she was exposed. Of a strong and observing character, even from her earliest years, the pomp and wealth which her father displayed within his walls, or which she witnessed in the houses of other wealthy Hebrews, had not been able to blind her to the precarious circumstances under which they were enjoyed. Like Damocles at his celebrated banquet, Rebecca perpetually beheld, amid that gorgeous display, the sword which was suspended over the heads of her people by a single hair. These reflections had tamed and brought down to a pitch of sounder judgment a temper, which, under other circumstances, might have waxed haughty, supercilious, and obstinate.

From her father's example and injunctions, Rebecca had learnt to bear herself courteously towards all who approached her. She could not indeed imitate his excess of subservience, because she was a stranger to the meanness of mind, and to the constant state of timid apprehension, by which it was dictated; but she bore herself with a proud humility, as if submitting to the evil circumstances in which she was placed as the daughter of a despised race, while she felt in her mind the consciousness that she was entitled to hold a higher rank from her merit, than the arbitrary despotism of religious prejudice permitted her to aspire to.

Thus prepared to expect adverse circumstances, she had acquired the firmness necessary for acting under them. Her present situation required all her presence of mind, and she summoned it up accordingly.

Her first care was to inspect the apartment; but it afforded few hopes either of escape or protection. It contained neither secret passage nor trap-door, and unless where the door by which she had entered joined the main building, seemed to be circumscribed by the round exterior wall of the turret. The door had no inside bolt or bar. The single window opened upon an embattled space surmounting the turret, which gave Rebecca, at first sight, some hopes of escaping; but she soon found it had no communication with any other part of the battlements, being an isolated bartisan or balcony, secured, as usual, by a parapet, with embrasures, at which a few archers might be stationed, for defending the turret and flanking with their shot the wall of the castle on that side.

There was therefore no hope but in passive fortitude, and in that strong reliance on heaven natural to great and generous characters. Rebecca, however erroneously taught to interpret the promises of Scripture to the chosen people of heaven, did not err in supposing the present to be their hour of trial, or in trusting that the children of Zion would be one day called in with the fulness of the Gentiles. In the mean while, all around her showed that their present state was that of punishment and probation, and that it was their especial duty to suffer without sinning. Thus prepared to consider herself as the victim of misfortune, Rebecca had early reflected upon her own state, and school'd her mind to meet the dangers which she had probably to encounter.

The prisoner trembled, however, and changed colour, when a step was heard on the stair, and the door of the turret chamber slowly opened, and a tall man, dressed as one of those banditti to whom they owed their misfortune, slowly entered, and shut the door behind him; his cap, pulled down upon his brows, concealed the upper part of his face, and he held his mantle in such a manner as to muffle the rest. In this guise, as if prepared for the execution of some deed at the thought of which he was himself ashamed, he stood before the affrighted prisoner; yet, ruffian as his dress bespoke him, he seemed at a loss to express what purpose had brought him thither, so that Rebecca, making an effort upon herself, had time to anticipate his explanation. She had already unclasped two costly bracelets and a collar, which she hastened to proffer to the supposed outlaw, concluding naturally that to gratify his avarice was to bespeak his favour.

"Take these," she said, "good friend, and for God's sake be merciful to me and to my aged father! These ornaments are of value, yet are they trifling to what he would bestow to obtain our dismissal from this castle, free and uninjured."

"Fair flower of Palestine," replied the outlaw, "these pearls are orient, but they yield in whiteness to your teeth; the diamonds are brilliant, but they cannot match your eyes; and ever since I have taken up this wild trade, I have made a vow to prefer beauty to wealth."

"Do not do yourself such wrong," said Rebecca; "take ransom and have mercy!—Gold will purchase you pleasure,—to misuse us, could only bring thee remorse. My father will willingly satiate thy utmost wishes; and if thou wilt act wisely, thou may'st purchase with our spoils thy restoration to civil society—may'st obtain pardon for past errors, and be placed beyond the necessity of committing more."

"It is well spoken," replied the outlaw in French, finding it difficult probably to sustain in Saxon a conversation which Rebecca had opened in that language; "but know, bright lily of the vale of Bacca! that thy father is already in the hands of a powerful alchemist, who knows how to convert into gold and silver even the rusty bars of a dungeon grate. The venerable Isaac is subjected to an alembic, which will distil from him all he holds dear, without any assistance from my requests or thy entreaty. Thy ransom must be paid by love and beauty, and in no other coin will I accept it."

"Thou art no outlaw," said Rebecca, in the same language in which he addressed her; "no outlaw had refused such offers. No outlaw in this land uses the dialect in which thou hast spoken. Thou art no outlaw, but a Norman—a Norman, noble perhaps in birth—O be so in thy actions, and cast off this fearful masque of outrage and violence!"

"And thou, who canst guess so truly," said Brian de Bois-Guilbert, dropping the mantle from his face, "art no true daughter of Israel, but in all, save youth and beauty, a very witch of Endor. I am not an outlaw, then, fair rose of Sharon. And I am one who will be more prompt to hang thy neck and arms with pearls and diamonds, which so well become them, than to deprive thee of those ornaments."

"What would'st thou have of me," said Rebecca, "if not my wealth? —We can have nought in common between us—you are a Christian —I am a Jewess.—Our union were contrary to the laws, alike of the church, and the synagogue."

"It were so indeed," replied the Templar, laughing; "wed with a Jewess? *Despardieux!*—Not if she were the queen of Sheba. And know, besides, sweet daughter of Zion, that were the most Christian king to offer me his most Christian daughter with Languedoc for a dowry, I could not wed her. It is against my vow to love any maiden, otherwise than *par amours*, as I will love thee. I am a Templar. Behold the cross of my holy order."

"Darest thou appeal to it," said Rebecca, "on an occasion like the present?"

"And if I do so," said the Templar, "it concerns not thee, who art no believer in the blessed sign of our salvation."

"I believe as my fathers taught," said Rebecca; "and may God forgive my belief if erroneous! But you, Sir Knight, what is *yours*, when you appeal without scruple to that which you deem most holy, even while you are about to transgress the most solemn of your vows as a knight, and as a man of religion?"

"It is gravely and well preached, O daughter of Sirach!" answered the Templar; "but, gentle Ecclesiastica, thy narrow Jewish prejudices make thee blind to our high privilege. Marriage were an enduring crime on the part of a Templar; but what lesser folly I may practise, I shall speedily be absolved from at the next Preceptory of our Order. Not the wisest of monarchs, not his father, whose examples you must needs allow are weighty, claimed wider privileges than we poor soldiers of the Temple of Zion have won by our zeal in its defence. The protectors of Solomon's Temple may claim licence by the example of Solomon."

"If thou readest the Scripture," said the Jewess, "and the lives of the saints, only to justify thine own license and profligacy, thy crime is like that of him who extracts poison from the most healthful and necessary herbs."

The eyes of the Templar flashed fire at this reproof—"Hearken," he said, "Rebecca; I have hitherto spoke mildly to thee, but now my language shall be that of a conqueror. Thou art the captive of my bow and spear—subject to my will by the laws of all nations, nor will I abate an inch of my right, or abstain from taking by violence what thou refusest to entreaty or necessity."

"Stand back," said Rebecca—"stand back, and hear me ere thou offerest to commit a sin so deadly! My strength thou may'st indeed overpower, for God made women weak, and trusted their defence to man's generosity. But I will proclaim thy villainy, Templar, from one end of Europe to the other. I will owe to the superstition of thy brethren what their compassion might refuse me. Each Preceptory—each Chapter of thy Order, shall learn, that, like a heretic, thou hast sinned with a Jewess. Those who tremble not at thy crime, will hold thee accursed for having so far dishonoured the cross thou wearest, as to follow a daughter of my people."

"Thou art keen-witted, Jewess," replied the Templar, well aware of the truth of what she spoke, and that the rules of his Order condemned in the most positive manner, and under high penalties, such intrigues as he now prosecuted, and that, in some instances, even degradation had followed upon it—"thou art sharp-witted," he said, "but loud must be thy voice of complaint, if it is heard beyond the iron walls of this castle; within these, murmurs, laments, appeals to justice, and screams for help, die alike silent away. One thing only can save thee, Rebecca. Submit to thy fate—embrace our religion, and thou shalt go forth in such state, that many a Norman lady shall yield as well in pomp as in beauty to the favourite of the best lance among the defenders of the Temple."

"Submit to my fate!" said Rebecca—"and, sacred Heaven! to what fate?—embrace thy religion! and what religion can it be that harbours such a villain?—*thou* the best lance of the Templars!—craven Knight!—forsworn Priest! I spit at thee, and I defy thee.—The God of Abraham's promise hath opened an escape to his daughter—even from this abyss of infamy."

As she spoke, she threw open the latticed window which led to the bartizan, and in an instant after, stood on the very verge of the parapet, with not the slightest screen between her and the tremendous depth below. Unprepared for such a desperate effort, for she had hitherto stood perfectly motionless, Bois-Guilbert had neither time to intercept nor to stop her. As he offered to advance, she exclaimed, "Remain where thou art, proud Templar, or at thy choice advance!—one foot nearer, and I plunge myself from the precipice; my body shall be crushed out of the very form of humanity upon the stones of that courtyard, ere it becomes the victim of thy brutality."

As she spoke this, she clasped her hands and extended them towards Heaven, as if imploring mercy on her soul before she made the final plunge. The Templar hesitated, and a resolution which had never yielded to pity or distress, gave way to his admiration of her fortitude. "Come down," he said, "rash girl!—I swear by earth, and sea, and sky, I will offer thee no offence."

"I will not trust thee, Templar," said Rebecca; "thou hast taught me better how to estimate the virtues of thine Order. The next Preceptory would grant thee absolution for an oath, the keeping of which concerned nought but the honour or the dishonour of a miserable Jewish maiden."

"You do me injustice," said the Templar; "I swear to you by the name which I bear—by the cross on my bosom—by the sword on my side—by the ancient crest of my fathers do I swear, I will do thee no injury whatsoever. If not for thyself, yet for thy father's sake forbear. I will be his friend, and in this castle he will need a powerful one."

"Alas!" said Rebecca, "I know it but too well—dare I trust thee?"

"May my arms be reversed, and my name dishonoured," said Brian de Bois-Guilbert, "if thou shalt have reason to complain of me! Many a law, many a commandment have I broken, but my word never."

"I will then trust thee," said Rebecca, "thus far," and she descended from the verge of the battlement, but remained standing close by one of the embrasures, or *machicolles*, as they were then called.—"Here," she said, "I take my stand. Remain where thou art, and if thou shalt attempt to diminish by one step the distance now between us, thou shalt see that the Jewish maiden will rather trust her soul with God, than her honour to the Templar."

While Rebecca spoke thus, her high and firm resolve, which corresponded so well with the expressive beauty of her countenance, gave to her looks, air, and manner, a dignity that seemed more than mortal. Her glance quailed not, her cheek blanched not, for the fear of a fate so instant and so horrible; on the contrary, the thought that she had her fate at her command, and could escape at will from infamy to death, gave a yet deeper colour of carnation to her complexion, and a yet more brilliant fire to her eye. Bois-Guilbert, proud himself and high-spirited, thought he had never beheld beauty so animated and so commanding.

"Let there be peace between us, Rebecca," he said.

"Peace, if thou wilt," answered Rebecca—"Peace—but with this space between."

"Thou need'st no longer fear me," said Bois-Guilbert.

"I fear thee not," replied she; "thanks to him that reared this dizzy tower so high, that nought could fall from it and live—thanks to him, and to the God of Israel!—I fear thee not."

"Thou dost me injustice," said the Templar; "by earth, sea, and sky, thou dost me injustice. I am not naturally that which you have seen me, hard, selfish, and relentless. It was woman that taught me cruelty, and on woman therefore I have exercised it; but not upon such as thou. Hear me, Rebecca—Never did knight take lance in his hand with a heart more devoted to the lady of his love than Brian de Bois-Guilbert. She, the daughter of a petty baron, who boasted for all his domains but a ruinous tower and an unproductive vineyard, and some few leagues of the barren Landes of Bourdeaux, her name was known wherever deeds of arms were done, known wider than that of many a lady's that had a county for a dowery.—Yes," he continued, pacing up and down the little platform with an animation in which he seemed to lose all consciousness of Rebecca's presence—"Yes, my deeds, my danger, my blood, made the name of Adelaide De Montemare known from the court of Castile to that of Byzantium. And how was I requited?—When I returned with my dear-bought honours, purchased by toil and blood, I found her wedded to a Gascon squire, whose name was never heard beyond the limits of his own paltry domain! Truly did I love her, and bitterly did I revenge me of her broken faith. But my vengeance has recoiled on myself. Since that day I have separated myself from life and its ties—My manhood must know no domestic home—must be soothed by no affectionate wife—My age must know no kindly hearth—My grave must be solitary, and no offspring must outlive me, to bear the ancient name of Bois-Guilbert. At the feet of my Superior I have laid down the right of self-action—the privilege of independence. The Templar, a serf in all but the name, can possess neither lands nor goods, and lives, moves, and breathes, but at the will and pleasure of another."

"Alas!" said Rebecca, "what advantages could compensate for such an absolute sacrifice?"

"The power of vengeance, Rebecca," replied the Templar, "and the prospects of ambition."

"An evil recompense," said Rebecca, "for the surrender of the rights which are dearest to humanity."

"Say not so, maiden," answered the Templar; "revenge is a feast for the gods! And if they have reserved it, as priests tell us, to themselves, it is because they hold it an enjoyment too precious for the possession of mere mortals.—And ambition? it is a temptation which could disturb even the bliss of heaven itself."—He paused a moment, and then added, "Rebecca! she who could prefer death to dishonour, must have a proud and a powerful soul. Mine thou must be!—Nay, start not," he added, "it must be with thine own consent, and on thine own terms. Thou must consent to share with me hopes more extended than can be viewed from the throne of a monarch——Hear me ere you answer, and judge ere you refuse. The Templar loses, as thou hast said, his social rights, his power of free agency, but he becomes a member and a limb of a mighty body before which thrones already tremble; even as the single drop of rain which mixes with the sea becomes an individual part of that resistless ocean, which undermines rocks and ingulphs royal armadas. Such a swelling flood is that powerful league. Of this mighty Order I am no mean member, but already one of the Chief Commanders, and may well aspire one day to hold the baton of Grand Master. The poor soldiers of the Temple will not alone place their foot upon the necks of kings—a hemp-sandall'd monk can do that. Our mailed step shall ascend their throne—our gauntlet shall wrench the sceptre from their gripe. Not the reign of your vainly-expected Messias offers such power to your dispersed tribes as my ambition may aim at. I have sought but a kindred spirit to share it, and I have found such in thee."

"Sayest thou this to one of my people?" answered Rebecca. "Bethink thee"——

"Answer me not," said the Templar, "by urging the difference of our creeds; within our secret conclaves we hold these nursery tales in derision. Think not we long remained blind to the ideotical folly of our founders, who forswore every delight of life for the pleasure of dying martyrs by hunger, by thirst, and by pestilence, and by the swords of savages, while they vainly strove to defend a barren desert, valuable only in the eyes of superstition. Our Order soon adopted bolder and wider views, and found out a better indemnification for our sacrifices. Our immense possessions in every kingdom of Europe, our high military fame, which brings within our circle the flower of chivalry from every Christian clime—these are dedicated to ends of which our pious founders little dreamed, and which are equally concealed from such weak spirits as embrace our Order on the ancient principles, and whose superstition makes them our passive tools. But I will not further withdraw the veil of our mysteries. That bugle-sound announces something which may require my presence. Think on what I have said.—Farewell!—I do not say forgive me the violence I have threatened, for it was necessary to the display of thy character. Gold can be only known by the application of the touchstone. I will soon return and hold further conference with thee."

He re-entered the turret-chamber, and descended the stair, leaving Rebecca scarce more terrified at the prospect of the death to which she had been so lately exposed, than at the furious ambition of the bold bad man in whose power she found herself so unhappily placed. When she entered the turret-chamber, her first duty was to return thanks to the God of Jacob for the protection which he had afforded her, and to implore its continuance for her and for her father. Another name glided into her petition—it was that of the wounded Christian, whom fate had placed in the hands of blood-thirsty men, his avowed enemies. Her heart indeed checked her, as if, even in communing with the Deity in prayer, she mingled in her devotions the recollection of one with whose fate hers could have no alliance—a Nazarene, and an enemy to her faith. But the petition was already breathed, nor could all the narrow prejudices of her sect induce Rebecca to wish it recalled.

Chapter Eleven

A damn'd cramp piece of penmanship as ever I saw in my life.

She Stoops to Conquer.

WHEN THE TEMPLAR reached the hall of the castle, he found De Bracy already there. "Your love-suit," said De Bracy, "hath, I suppose, been disturbed, like mine, by this obstreperous summons. But you have come later and more reluctantly, and therefore I presume your interview has proved more agreeable than mine."

"Has your suit, then, been unsuccessfully paid to the Saxon heiress?" said the Templar.

"By the bones of Thomas a Becket," answered De Bracy, "the Lady Rowena must have heard that I cannot endure the sight of women's tears."

"Away!" said the Templar; "thou a leader of a Free Company, and regard a woman's tears! A few drops sprinkled on the torch of love, make the flame blaze the brighter."

"Gramercy for the few drops of thy sprinkling," replied De Bracy; "but this damsel hath wept enough to extinguish a beacon-light. Never was such wringing of hands and such overflowing of eyes, since the days of St Niobe,* of whom Prior Aymer told us. A water-fiend hath possessed the fair Saxon."

"A legion of fiends hath occupied the bosom of the Jewess," replied the Templar; "for, I think no single one, not even Apollyon himself, could have inspired such indomitable pride and resolution.—But where is Front-de-Bœuf? That horn is sounded more and more clamorously."

"He is negociating with the Jew, I suppose," replied De Bracy, coolly; "probably the howls of Isaac have drowned the blast of the bugle. Thou may'st know, by experience, Sir Brian, that a Jew parting with his treasures on such terms as our friend Front-de-Bœuf is like to offer, will raise a clamour loud enough to be heard over twenty bugles and trumpets to boot. But we will make the vassals call him."

They were soon after joined by Front-de-Bœuf, who had been disturbed in his tyrannic cruelty in the manner with which the reader is acquainted, and had only tarried to give some necessary directions.

"Let us see the cause of this cursed clamour," said Front-de-Bœuf —"here is a letter, and, if I mistake not, it is in Saxon."

He looked at it, turning it round and round, as if he had had really some hopes of coming at the meaning by inverting the position of the paper, and then handed it to De Bracy.

"It may be magic spells for aught I know," said De Bracy, who possessed his full proportion of the ignorance which characterized the chivalry of the period. "Our chaplain attempted to teach me to write," he said, "but all my letters were formed like spear-heads, and sword-blades, and so the old shaveling gave up the task."

"Give it me," said the Templar. "We have that of the priestly character, that we have some knowledge to enlighten our valour."

*I wish the Prior had also informed them when Niobe was sainted. Probably during that enlightened period when

"Pan to Moses lent his pagan horn."

L. T.

"Let us profit by your most reverend knowledge, then," said De Bracy; "what says the scroll?"

"It is a formal letter of defiance," answered the Templar; "but, by our Lady of Bethlehem, if it be not a foolish jest, it is the most extraordinary cartel that ever was sent across the draw-bridge of a baronial castle."

"Jest!" said Front-de-Bœuf, "I would gladly know who dares jest with me in such a matter!—Read it, Sir Brian."

The Templar accordingly read as follows:—

"I, Wamba the son of Witless, Jester to a noble and free-born man, Cedric of Rotherwood, called the Saxon.—And I, Gurth the son of Beowolf, the swine-herd——"

"Thou art mad," said Front-de-Bœuf, interrupting the reader.

"By St Luke, it is so set down," answered the Templar. Then resuming his task, he went on. "I, Gurth, the son of Beowolf, swine-herd unto the said Cedric, with the assistance of our allies and confederates, who make common cause with us in this our feud, namely, the good knight, called for the present *Le Noir Faineant*, do you, Reginald Front-de-Bœuf, and your allies and accomplices whomsoever, to wit, that whereas you have, without cause given or feud declared, wrongfully and by mastery seized upon the person of our lord and master the said Cedric; also upon the person of a noble and free-born damsel, the Lady Rowena of Hargottstandstede; also upon the person of a noble and free-born man, Athelstane of Coningsburgh; also upon the persons of certain free-born men, their *cnichts;* also upon certain serfs their born bondsmen; also upon a certain Jew, named Isaac of York, together with his daughter, a Jewess, and certain horses and mules: Which noble persons, with their *cnichts* and slaves, and also with the horses and mules, Jew and Jewess beforesaid, were all in peace with his majesty, and travelling as liege subjects upon the king's highway; therefore we require and demand that the said noble persons, namely, Cedric of Rotherwood, Rowena of Hargottstandstede, Athelstane of Coningsburgh, with their servants, *cnichts*, and followers, also the horses and mules, Jew and Jewess aforesaid, together with all goods and chattels to them pertaining, be, within an hour after the delivery hereof, delivered to us, or to those whom we shall appoint to receive the same, and that untouched and unharmed in body and goods. Failing of which, we do pronounce to you, that we hold ye as robbers and traitors, and will wager our bodies against ye in battle, siege, or otherwise, and do our utmost to your annoyance and destruction. Wherefore may God have you in his keeping.—Signed by us upon the eve of St Withold's day, under the great trysting oak in the Harthill-walk, the above being written by an holy man, Clerk to God, our Lady, and St Dunstan, in the Chapel of Copmanhurst."

At the bottom of this document was scrawled, in the first place, a rude sketch of a cock's head and comb, with a legend expressing this hieroglyphic to be the sign-manual of Wamba, son of Witless. Under this respectable emblem stood a cross, stated to be the mark of Gurth, the son of Beowolf. Then was written, in rough bold characters, the words, *Le Noir Faineant*. And, to conclude the whole, an arrow, neatly enough drawn, was described as the mark of the yeoman Locksley.

The knights heard this uncommon document read from end to end, and then gazed on each other in silent amazement, as being utterly at a loss to know what it could portend. De Bracy was the first to break silence by an uncontroulable fit of laughter, wherein he was joined, though with more moderation, by the Templar. Front-de-Bœuf, on the contrary, seemed impatient of their ill-timed mirth.

"I give you plain warning," he said, "fair sirs, that you had better consult how to bear yourselves under these circumstances, than give way to such ill-timed merriment."

"Front-de-Bœuf has not recovered his temper since his late overthrow," said De Bracy to the Templar; "he is cowed at the very idea of a cartel, though it come but from a fool and a swine-herd."

"By St Michael," answered Front-de-Bœuf, "I would thou couldst stand the whole brunt of this adventure thyself, De Bracy. These fellows dared not have acted with such inconceivable impudence, had they not been supported by some strong bands. There are enough of outlaws in this forest to resent my protecting the deer. I did but tie one fellow, who was taken redhanded and in the fact, to the horns of a wild stag, which gored him to death in five minutes, and I had as many arrows shot at me as there were launched against yonder target at Ashby.—Here, fellow," he added, to one of his attendants, "hast thou sent out to see by what force this precious challenge is to be supported?"

"There are at least two hundred men assembled in the woods," answered a squire who was in attendance.

"Here is a proper matter!" said Front-de-Bœuf; "this comes of lending you the use of my castle, that cannot manage your undertaking quietly, but you must bring this nest of hornets about my ears."

"Of hornets?" said De Bracy, "of stingless drones rather; a band of lazy knaves, who take to the wood and destroy the venison rather than labour for their maintenance."

"Stingless!" replied Front-de-Bœuf; "fork-headed shafts of a cloth-yard in length, and these shot within the breadth of a French crown, are sting enough."

"For shame, Sir Knight!" said the Templar. "Let us summon our people, and sally forth upon them. One knight—ay, one man-at-arms, were enough for twenty such peasants."

"Enough, and too much," said De Bracy; "I should only be ashamed to couch lance against them."

"True," answered Front-de-Bœuf; "were they black Turks or Moors, Sir Templar, or the craven peasants of France, most valiant De Bracy; but these are English yeomen, over whom we shall have no advantage, save what we may derive from our arms and horses, which will avail us little in the glades of the forest. Sally, saidst thou? we have scarce men enough to defend the castle. The best of mine are at York, so is all your band, De Bracy; and we have scarcely twenty, besides the handful that were engaged in this mad business."

"Thou dost not fear," said the Templar, "that they can assemble in force sufficient to attempt the castle?"

"Not so, Sir Brian," answered Front-de-Bœuf. "These outlaws have indeed a daring captain; but without machines, scaling ladders, and experienced leaders, my castle may defy them."

"Send to thy neighbours," said the Templar; "let them assemble their people, and come to the rescue of three knights, besieged by a jester and a swine-herd in the baronial castle of Reginald Front-de-Bœuf!"

"You jest, Sir Knight," answered the baron; "but to whom should I send?—Malvoisin is by this time at York with his retainers, and so are my other allies; and so should I have been, but for this infernal enterprize."

"Then send to York, and recall our people," said De Bracy. "If they abide the shaking of my standard, or the sight of my Free Companions, I will give them credit for the boldest outlaws ever bent bow in green-wood."

"And who shall bear such a message?" said Front-de-Bœuf; "they will beset every path, and rip the errand out of his bosom.—I have it," he said, after pausing for a moment—"Sir Templar, thou canst write as well as read, and if we can but find the writing materials of my chaplain, who died a twelvemonth since in the midst of his Christmas carousals——"

"So please ye," said the squire, who was still in attendance, "I think old Urfried has them somewhere in keeping, for love of the confessor. He was the last man, I have heard her say, who ever said aught to her, which man ought in courtesy to say to maid or matron."

"Go, search them out, Engelred; and then, Sir Templar, thou shalt return an answer to this bold challenge."

"I would rather do it at the sword's point than at that of the pen," said Bois-Guilbert; "but be it as you will."

He sat down accordingly, and indited, in the French language, an epistle of the following tenor:—

"Sir Reginald Front-de-Bœuf, with his noble and knightly allies and confederates, receive no defiances at the hands of slaves, bondsmen, or fugitives. If the person calling himself the Black Knight have indeed a claim to the honours of chivalry, he ought to know that he stands degraded by his present association, and has no right to ask reckoning at the hands of good men of noble blood. Touching the prisoners we have made, we do in Christian charity require you to send a man of religion, to receive their confession and reconcile them with God; since it is our fixed intention to execute them this morning before noon, so that their heads being placed on the battlements, shall show to all men how lightly we esteem those who have bestirred themselves in their rescue. Wherefore, as above, we require you to send a priest to reconcile them to God, in doing which you shall render them the last earthly service."

This letter being folded, was delivered to the squire, and by him to the messenger who waited without, as the answer to that which he had brought.

The yeoman having thus accomplished his mission, returned to the head-quarters of the allies, which were for the present established under a venerable oak-tree, about three arrow's flight distant from the castle. Here Wamba and Gurth, with their allies the Black Knight, and Locksley, and the jovial hermit, awaited with impatience an answer to their summons. Around, and at a distance from them, were seen many a bold yeoman, whose sylvan dress and weather-beaten countenances showed the ordinary nature of their occupation. More than two hundred had already assembled, and others were fast coming in. Those whom they obeyed as leaders were only distinguished from the others by a feather in the cap, their dress, arms, and equipments being in all other respects the same.

Besides these bands, a less orderly and a worse armed force, consisting of the Saxon inhabitants of the neighbouring township, as well as many bondsmen and servants from Cedric's extensive estate, had already arrived, for the purpose of assisting in his rescue. Few of these were armed otherwise than with such rustic weapons as necessity sometimes converts to military purposes. Boar-spears, scythes, flails, and the like, were their chief arms; for the Normans, with the usual policy of conquerors, were jealous of permitting to the conquered Saxons the possession or the use of arms. These circumstances rendered the assistance of the Saxons far from being so formidable to the besieged, as the strength of the men themselves, their superior numbers, and the animation inspired by a just cause, might otherwise well have made them. It was to the leaders of this motley army that the letter of the Templar was now delivered.

Reference was at first made to the chaplain for an exposition of its contents.

"By the crook of St Dunstan," said that worthy ecclesiastic, "which hath brought more sheep within the sheepfold than the crook of e'er another saint in paradise, I swear that I cannot expound unto you this jargon, which, whether it be French or Arabic, is beyond my guess."

He then gave the letter to Gurth, who shook his head gruffly and passed it to Wamba. The Jester looked at each of the four corners of the paper with such a grin of affected intelligence as a monkey is apt to assume upon similar occasions, then cut a caper, and gave the letter to Locksley.

"If the long letters were bows, and the short letters arrows, I might know something of the matter," said the honest yeoman; "but as the matter stands, the meaning is as safe, for me, as the stag that's at twelve miles distance."

"I must be clerk, then," said the Black Knight; and taking the letter from Locksley, he first read it over to himself, and then explained the meaning in Saxon to his confederates.

"Execute the noble Cedric!" exclaimed Wamba; "by the rood, thou must be mistaken, Sir Knight."

"Not I, my worthy friend," replied the knight, "I have explained the words as they are here set down."

"Then, by St Thomas of Canterbury," replied Gurth, "we will have the castle, should we tear it down with our hands."

"We have nothing else to tear it with," replied Wamba, "but mine are scarce fit to make mammocks of free-stone and mortar."

"'Tis but a contrivance to gain time," said Locksley; "they dare not do a deed for which I could exact a fearful penalty."

"I would," said the Black Knight, "there were some one among us who could obtain admission into the castle, and discover how the case stands with the besieged. Methinks, as they require a confessor to be sent, this holy hermit might at once exercise his pious vocation, and procure us the information we desire."

"A plague on thee, and thy advice," said the good hermit; "I tell thee, Sir Slothful Knight, that when I doff my friar's frock, my priesthood, my sanctity, my very Latin are put off along with it; and when in my green jerkin I can better kill twenty deer than confess one Christian."

"I fear," said the Black Knight, "I fear greatly, there is no one here that is qualified to take upon him, for the nonce, this same character of father confessor?"

All looked on each other, and were silent.

"I see," said Wamba, after a short pause, "that the fool must be still the fool, and put his neck in the venture which wise men shrink from. You must know, my dear cousins and countrymen, that I wore russet before I wore motley, and was bred to be a friar ere I found I had wit enough to be a fool. I trust, with the assistance of the good hermit's frock, together with the priesthood, sanctity, and learning which are stitched into the cowl of it, I shall be found qualified to administer both worldly and ghostly comfort to our worthy master Cedric, and his companions in adversity."

"Hath he sense enough, think'st thou?" said the Black Knight, addressing Gurth.

"I know not," said Gurth; "but if he hath not, it will be the first time he hath wanted wit to turn his folly to account."

"On with the frock then, good fellow," quoth the Knight, "and let thy master send us an account of their situation within the castle. Their numbers must be few, and it is five to one they may be accessible by a sudden and bold attack. Time wears—away with thee."

"And, in the meantime," said Locksley, "we will beset the place so closely, that not so much as a fly shall carry news from thence. So that, my good friend," he continued, addressing Wamba, "thou may'st assure these tyrants, that whatsoever violence they exercise on the persons of their prisoners, shall be most severely repaid upon their own."

"*Pax vobiscum*," said Wamba, who was now muffled in his religious disguise.

And so saying, he imitated the solemn and stately deportment of a friar, and departed to execute his mission.

Chapter Twelve

The hottest horse will oft be cool,
The dullest will shew fire;
The friar will often play the fool,
The fool will play the friar.
Old Song.

WHEN THE JESTER, arrayed in the cowl and frock of the hermit, and having his knotted cord twisted around his middle, stood before the portal of the castle of Front-de-Bœuf, the warder demanded of him his name and errand.

"*Pax vobiscum*," answered the Jester, "I am a poor brother of the Order of St Francis, who come hither to do my office to certain unhappy prisoners now secured within this castle."

"Thou art a bold friar," said the warder, "to come hither, where, saving our own drunken confessor, a cock of thy feather hath not crowed these twenty years."

"Yet, I pray thee, do mine errand to the lord of the castle," answered the pretended friar; "trust me it will find good acceptance with him, and the cock shall crow, that the whole castle shall hear him."

"Gramercy," said the warder; "but if I come to shame for leaving my post upon thine errand, I will try whether a friar's grey gown be proof against a grey-goose shaft."

With this threat he left his turret, and carried to the hall of the castle the unwonted intelligence, that a holy friar stood before the gate and demanded instant admission. With no small surprise he received his master's commands to admit the holy man immediately; and, having previously manned the entrance to guard against surprise, he obeyed, without further scruple, the commands which he had received. The hair-brained self-conceit which had emboldened Wamba to undertake this dangerous office, was scarce sufficient to support him when he found himself in the presence of a man so dreadful, and so much dreaded, as Reginald Front-de-Bœuf, and he brought out his *pax vobiscum*, to which he, in a good measure, trusted for supporting his character, with more anxiety and hesitation than had hitherto accompanied it. But Front-de-Bœuf was accustomed to see men of all ranks tremble in his presence, so that the timidity of the supposed father did not give him any cause of suspicion. "Who and whence art thou, priest?" said he.

"*Pax vobiscum*," reiterated the Jester, "I am a poor servant of St Francis, who, travelling through this wilderness, have fallen among thieves, (as Scripture hath it), *quidam viator incidit in latrones*, which thieves have sent me unto this castle in order to do mine ghostly office on two persons condemned by your honourable justice."

"Ay, right," answered Front-de-Bœuf; "and canst thou tell me, holy father, the number of those banditti?"

"Gallant sir," answered the Jester, "*nomen illis legio*, their name is legion."

"Tell me in plain terms what numbers there are? or, priest, thy cloak and cord will ill protect thee."

"Alas!" said the supposed friar, "*cor meum eructavit*, that is to say, I was like to burst with fear! but I conceive they may be—what of yeomen—what of commons, at least five hundred men."

"What!" said the Templar, who came into the hall that moment, "muster the wasps so thick here? it is time to stifle such a mischievous brood." Then taking Front-de-Bœuf aside, "Knowest thou the priest?"

"He is a stranger from a distant convent," said Front-de-Bœuf; "I know him not."

"Then trust him not with thy purpose in words," answered the Templar. "Let him carry a written order to Bracy's company of Free Companions, to repair instantly to their master's aid. In the meantime, and that the shaveling may suspect nothing, permit him to go freely about his task of preparing these Saxon hogs for the slaughter-house."

"It shall be so," said Front-de-Bœuf. And he forthwith appointed a domestic to conduct Wamba to the apartment where Cedric and Athelstane were confined.

The impatience of Cedric had been rather enhanced than diminished by his confinement. He walked from one end of the hall to the other, with the attitude of one who advances to charge an enemy, or to storm the breach of a beleaguered place, sometimes ejaculating to himself, sometimes addressing Athelstane, who stoutly and stoically awaited the issue of the adventure, digesting, in the meantime, with great composure, the liberal meal which he had made at noon, and not greatly interesting himself about the duration of his captivity, which he concluded, would, like all earthly evils, find an end in Heaven's good time.

"*Pax vobiscum*," said the Jester, entering; "the blessing of St Dunstan, St Dennis, St Duthoc, and all other saints whatsoever, be upon ye and about ye."

"*Salvete et vos*," answered Cedric to the supposed friar, "with what intent art thou come hither?"

"To bid you prepare yourself for death," answered the Jester.

"It is impossible," replied Cedric, starting. "Fearless and wicked as they are, they dare not attempt such open and gratuitous cruelty."

"Alas!" said the Jester, "to restrain them by their sense of humanity, is the same as to stop a runaway horse with a bridle of silk thread. Bethink thee, therefore, noble Cedric, and you also, gallant Athelstane, what crimes you have committed in the flesh; for this very day will ye be called to answer at a higher tribunal."

"Hearest thou this, Athelstane?" said Cedric; "we must rouse up our hearts to this last action, since better it is we should die like men, than live like slaves."

"I am ready," answered Athelstane, "to stand the worst of their malice, and shall walk to my death with as much composure as ever I did to my dinner."

"Let us then unto our holy gear, father," said Cedric.

"Wait yet a moment, good uncle," said the Jester, in his natural tone; "better look long before ye leap in the dark."

"By my faith," said Cedric, "I should know that voice."

"It is that of your trusty slave and jester," answered Wamba, throwing back his cowl. "Had you taken a fool's advice formerly, you would not have been here at all. Take a fool's advice now, and you will not be here long."

"How mean'st thou, knave?" answered the Saxon.

"Even thus," replied Wamba; "take thou this frock and cord, which are all the orders I ever had, and march quietly out of the castle, leaving me your cloak and girdle to take the long leap in thy stead."

"Leave thee in my stead!" said Cedric, astonished at the proposal; "why, they would hang thee, my poor knave."

"E'en let them do as they are permitted," said Wamba; "I trust—no disparagement to your birth—that the son of Witless may hang in a chain with as much gravity as the chain hung upon his ancestor the alderman."

"Well, Wamba," answered Cedric, "for one thing will I grant thy request. And that is, if thou wilt make the exchange of garments with Lord Athelstane instead of me."

"No, by St Dunstan," answered Wamba; "there were little reason in that. Good right there is, that the son of Witless should suffer to save the son of Hereward; but little wisdom there were in his dying for the benefit of one whose fathers were strangers to his."

"Villain," said Cedric, "the fathers of Athelstane were monarchs of England."

"They might be whomsoever they pleased," replied Wamba; "but my neck stands too straight upon my shoulders to have it twisted for their sake. Wherefore, good my master, either take my proffer yourself, or suffer me to leave this dungeon as free as I entered."

"Let the old tree wither," continued Cedric, "so the stately hope of the forest be preserved. Save the noble Athelstane, my trusty Wamba! it is the duty of each who has Saxon blood in his veins. Thou and I will abide together the utmost rage of our injurious oppressors, while he, free and safe, shall rouse the awakened spirits of our countrymen to avenge us."

"Not so, father Cedric," said Athelstane, grasping his hand, for, when roused to think or act, his deeds and sentiments were not unbecoming his high race—"Not so," he continued, "I would rather remain in this hall for a week without food save the prisoner's stinted loaf, or drink save the prisoner's measure of water, than embrace the opportunity of escape which this slave's untaught kindness has purveyed for his master."

"You are called wise men, sirs," said the Jester, "and I a crazed fool. But, uncle Cedric, and cousin Athelstane, the fool shall decide this controversy for ye, and save ye the trouble of straining courtesies any further. I am like John-a-Duck's mare, that let no man mount her but John-a-Duck. I came to save my master, and if he will not consent —basta—I can but go away home again—kind service cannot be chucked from hand to hand like a shuttlecock or stool-ball. I'll hang for no man but my own born master."

"Go, then, noble Cedric," said Athelstane; "neglect not this opportunity. Your presence without may encourage friends to our rescue—your remaining here would ruin us all."

"And is there any prospect, then, of rescue from without?" said Cedric, looking to the Jester.

"Prospect, indeed!" echoed Wamba; "let me tell you. When you fill my cloak, you are wrapped in a general's cassock. Five hundred men are there without, and I was this morning one of their chief leaders. My fool's-cap was a casque, and my bauble a truncheon. Well, we will see what good they shall make by exchanging a fool for a wise man. Truly, I fear they will lose in valour what they may gain in discretion. And so farewell, master, and be kind to poor Gurth and his dog Fangs; and let my cockscomb hang in the hall at Rotherwood, in memory that I flung away my life for my master, like a faithful—— fool."

The last word came out with a sort of double expression, betwixt jest and earnest. The tears stood in Cedric's eyes.

"Thy memory shall be preserved," he said, "while fidelity and affection have honour upon earth. But that I trust I will find the means of saving Rowena, and thee Athelstane, and thee, my poor Wamba, thou shouldst not overbear me in this matter."

The exchange of dress was now accomplished, when a sudden doubt struck Cedric.

"I know no language," he said, "but my own, and a few words of their mincing Norman. How shall I bear myself like a reverend brother?"

"The spell lies in two words," replied Wamba—"*Pax vobiscum* answers all queries. If you go or come, eat or drink, bless or ban, *Pax vobiscum* carries you through it all—it is as useful to a friar as a broomstick to a witch, or a wand to a conjuror. Speak it but thus, in a deep grave tone,—*Pax vobiscum!*—it is irresistible—Watch and ward, knight and squire, foot and horse, it acts as a charm upon them all. I think, if they bring me out to be hanged to-morrow, as is much to be doubted they may, I will try its weight upon the finisher of the sentence."

"If such prove the case," said his master, "my religious orders are easily taken—*Pax vobiscum*. I trust I shall remember the pass-word.—Noble Athelstane, farewell; and farewell, my poor boy, whose heart might make amends for a weaker head—I will save you, or return and die with you—the royal blood of our Saxon kings shall not be spilled while mine beats in my veins; nor shall one hair fall from the head of the kind knave who risked himself for his master, if Cedric's peril can prevent it.—Farewell."

"Farewell, noble Cedric," said Athelstane; "remember it is the true part of a friar to accept refreshment, if you are offered any."

"Farewell, uncle," added Wamba; "and remember *Pax vobiscum*."

Thus exhorted, Cedric sallied forth upon his expedition; and it was not long ere he had occasion to try the force of that spell which his Jester had recommended as omnipotent. In a low-arched and dusky passage, by which he endeavoured to make his way to the hall of the castle, he was interrupted by a female form.

"*Pax vobiscum!*" said the pseudo-friar, and was endeavouring to hurry past, when a soft voice replied, "*Et vobis—quæso, domine reverendissime, pro misericordia vestra.*"

"I am somewhat deaf," answered Cedric in good Saxon, and at the same time muttered to himself, "A curse on the fool and his *Pax vobiscum!* I have lost my javelin at the first cast."

It was, however, no unusual thing for a priest of those days to be deaf of his Latin ear, and this the person who now addressed Cedric knew right well.

"I pray you of dear love, reverend father," she replied in his own language, "that you will deign to visit with your ghostly comfort a wounded prisoner of this castle, and have such compassion upon him and us as thy holy office teaches—Never shall good deed so highly advantage thy convent."

"Daughter," answered Cedric, much embarrassed, "my time in this castle will not permit me to exercise the duties of mine office—I must presently forth—there is life and death upon my speed."

"Yet, father, let me entreat you by the vow you have taken on you," replied the suppliant, "not to leave the oppressed and endangered without counsel or succour."

"May the fiend fly away with me, and land me in Ifrin with the souls of Odin and of Thor!" answered Cedric impatiently, and would probably have proceeded in the same tone of total departure from his spiritual character, when their colloquy was interrupted by the harsh voice of Urfried, the old crone of the turret.

"How, minion," said she to the female speaker, "is this the manner in which you requite the kindness which permitted thee to leave thy prison-cell yonder and to watch the couch of thy wounded gallant?—Puttest thou the reverend man to use ungracious language to free himself from the importunities of a Jewess?"

"A Jewess!" said Cedric, availing himself of the information to get clear of their interruption.—"Let me pass, woman! stop me not at your peril. I am fresh from my holy office, and would avoid pollution."

"Come this way, father," said the old hag; "thou art a stranger in this castle, and canst not leave it without a guide. Come hither, for I would speak with thee—and you, daughter of an accursed race, go to the sick man's chamber, and tend him till my return; and woe betide you if you again quit it without my permission!"

Rebecca retreated. Her importunities had prevailed on Urfried to suffer her to quit the turret, and Urfried had employed her services where she herself would most gladly have paid them, by the bed-side of the wounded Ivanhoe. With an understanding awake to their dangerous situation, and prompt to avail herself of each means of safety which occurred, Rebecca had hoped something from the presence of a man of religion, who, she learned from Urfried, had penetrated into this godless castle. She watched the return of the supposed ecclesiastic, with the purpose of addressing him, and interesting him in favour of the prisoners; with what imperfect success the reader has been just acquainted.

Chapter Thirteen

Fond wretch! and what canst thou relate,
  But deeds of sorrow, shame, and sin?
Thy deeds are proved—thou know'st thy fate;
  But come, thy tale—begin—begin.

\- - - - - - - -

But I have griefs of other kind,
  Troubles and sorrows more severe;
Give me to ease my tortured mind,
  Lend to my woes a patient ear;
And let me, if I may not find
  A friend to help—find one to hear.

CRABBE'S *Hall of Justice.*

WHEN URFRIED had with clamours and menaces driven Rebecca back to the apartment from which she had sallied, she proceeded to conduct the unwilling Cedric into a small apartment, the door of which she heedfully secured. Then fetching from a cupboard a large stoup of wine and two flagons, she placed them on the table, and said, in a tone rather asserting a fact than asking a question, "Thou art a Saxon, father—Deny it not," she continued, observing that Cedric hastened not to reply; "the sounds of my native language are sweet in mine ears, though seldom heard save from the tongues of the wretched and degraded serfs, on whom the proud Normans impose the meanest drudgery of this dwelling. Thou art a Saxon, father, a Saxon and a free man, save as thou art a servant of God—thine accents are sweet in mine ear."

"Do no Saxon priests visit this castle, then?" replied Cedric; "it were, methinks, their duty to comfort the outcast and oppressed children of the soil."

"They come not—or if they come, better love to revel at the boards of their conquerors," answered Urfried, "than to hear the groans of their countrymen—so, at least, report speaks of them—of myself, I can say little. This castle, for ten years, has opened to no priest save the debauched Norman chaplain who partook the nightly revels of Front-de-Bœuf, and he has been long gone to render an account of his stewardship.—But thou art a Saxon—a Saxon priest, and I have one question to ask at thee."

"I am a Saxon," answered Cedric, "but unworthy, surely, of the name of priest. Let me be gone on my way—I swear I will return, or send one of our fathers more worthy to hear your confession."

"Stay yet a while," said Urfried; "the accents of the voice which thou hearest now, will be soon choaked with the cold earth, and I would not descend to it like the beast I have lived. But wine must give me strength to tell the horrors of my tale." She poured forth a cup, and drank it with a frightful avidity, which seemed desirous of draining the very last drop in the goblet. "It stupifies," she said, looking upwards as she finished her draught, "but it cannot cheer—Partake it, father, if you would hear my tale without sinking down upon the pavement." Cedric would have avoided pledging her in this ominous conviviality, but the sign which she made to him expressed impatience and despair. He complied with her request, and answered her challenge in a large wine cup; she then continued her story, as if appeased by his compliance.

"I was not born," said she, "father, the wretch that thou now see'st me. I was free, was happy, was honoured, loved, and was beloved. I am now a slave, miserable and degraded—the sport of my masters' passions while I had yet beauty—the subject of their contempt, scorn, and hatred, when it has passed away.—Doest thou wonder, father, that I should hate mankind, and, over all, the race that has wrought this change in me? Can the wrinkled, decrepit hag before thee, whose wrath must vent itself in impotent curses, forget she was once the daughter of the noble Thane of Torquilstone, before whose frown a thousand vassals trembled?"

"Thou the daughter of Torquil Wolfganger!" said Cedric, recoiling as he spoke; "thou—thou—the daughter of that noble Saxon, my father's friend and companion in arms!"

"Thy father's friend!" echoed Urfried; "then Cedric called the Saxon stands before me, for the noble Hereward of Rotherwood had but one son, whose name is well known among his countrymen. But if thou art Cedric of Rotherwood, why this religious dress. Hast thou too despaired of saving thy country, and sought refuge from oppression in the shade of the convent?"

"It matters not who I am," said Cedric; "proceed, unhappy woman, with thy tale of horror and guilt!—guilt there must be—there is guilt even in thy living to tell it."

"There is—there is," answered the wretched woman, "deep, black, damning guilt—guilt, that lies like a load in my breast—guilt, that all the penitential fires of hereafter cannot cleanse.—Yes, in these halls, stained with the noble and pure blood of my father and my brethren—in these very halls, to have lived the paramour of their murderer, the slave at once and the partaker of his pleasures, was to render every breath which I drew of vital air, a crime and a curse."

"Wretched woman!" exclaimed Cedric. "And while the friends of thy father—while each true Saxon heart, as it breathed a requiem for his soul and those of his valiant sons, forgot not in their prayers the murdered Ulrica—while all mourned and honoured thee dead, thou hast lived to merit our hate and execration—lived to unite thyself with the vile tyrant who murdered thy nearest and dearest—who shed the blood even of infancy, rather than a male of the noble house of Torquil Wolfganger should survive—with him hast thou lived to unite thyself, and in the bands of lawless love!"

"In lawless bands indeed, but not in those of love," answered the hag; "love will sooner visit the regions of eternal doom, than these unhallowed vaults.—No, with that at least I cannot reproach myself—hatred to Front-de-Bœuf and his race gnawed my soul most deeply, even in the hours of his guilty endearment."

"You hated him, and yet you lived," replied Cedric; "wretch! was there no poniard—no knife—no bodkin?—Well was it for thee, since thou did'st prize such an existence, that the secrets of a Norman castle are like those of the grave, for had I but dreamed of the daughter of Torquil living in foul communion with the murderer of her father, the sword of a true Saxon had found thee out even in the very arms of thy paramour."

"Wouldst thou indeed have done this justice to the name of Torquil?" said Ulrica, for we may now lay aside her assumed name of Urfried; "thou art then the true Saxon which report speaks thee! for even within these accursed walls, where, as thou well say'st, guilt shrouds itself in inscrutable mystery, even there has the name of Cedric been sounded—and I, wretched and degraded, have rejoiced to think that there yet breathed an avenger of our unhappy nation.—I also have had my hours of vengeance. I have fomented the quarrels of our foes, heated drunken revelry into murderous broil—I have seen their blood flow—I have heard their dying groans!—Look on me, Cedric—are there not still left on this foul and faded face some traces of Torquil's features?"

"Ask me not of them, Ulrica," replied Cedric, in a tone of grief mixed with abhorence; "these traces form such a resemblance as arises from the grave of the dead, when a fiend has animated the lifeless corpse."

"Be it so," answered Ulrica; "yet wore these fiendish features the mask of a spirit of light when they were able to set at variance the elder Front-de-Bœuf and his son Reginald—the darkness of hell should hide what followed, but Revenge must lift the veil, and darkly intimate what it would raise the dead to speak aloud. Long had the smouldering fire of discord glowed between the tyrant father and his savage son—long had I nursed, in secret, the unnatural hatred—it blazed forth in an hour of drunken wassail, and at his own board fell my oppressor by the hand of his own son. Such are the secrets these vaults conceal!—rend asunder, ye accursed arches," she added, looking up towards the roof, "and bury in your fall all who are conscious of the hideous mystery!"

"And thou, creature of guilt and misery," said Cedric, "what became thy lot on the death of thy ravisher?"

"Guess it, but ask it not.—Here have I dwelt, till age, premature age, has stamped its ghastly features on my countenance—scorned and insulted where I was once obeyed, and compelled to limit the revenge which had once such ample scope, to the efforts of petty malice of a discontented menial, or the vain, unheeded curses of an impotent hag—condemned to hear from my lonely turret the sounds of revelry in which I once partook, or the shrieks and groans of new victims of oppression."

"Ulrica," said Cedric, "with a heart which still, I fear, regrets the lost reward of thy crimes, as much as the deeds by which thou didst acquire that meed, how didst thou dare to address thee to one who wears this robe? Consider, unhappy woman, what could the sainted Edward himself do for thee, were he here in bodily presence? The royal Confessor was endowed by Heaven with power to cleanse the ulcers of the body, but only God himself can cure the leprosy of the soul."

"Yet, turn not from me, stern prophet of wrath," she exclaimed, "but tell me if thou canst, in what shall terminate these new and awful feelings which burst on my solitude—Why do deeds, long since done, rise now before me dressed in new and irresistible terrors? What fate is prepared beyond the grave for her, to whom God has assigned on earth a lot of such unspeakable wretchedness? Better had I turn to Woden, Hertha, and Zernebock—to Mista, and to Skogula, the gods of our yet unbaptized ancestors, than endure the dreadful anticipations which have of late haunted my waking and my sleeping hours."

"I am no priest," said Cedric, turning with disgust from this miserable picture of guilt, wretchedness, and despair; "I am no priest, though I wear a priest's garment."

"Priest or layman," answered Ulrica, "thou art the first I have seen for twenty years, by whom God was feared or man regarded; and dost thou bid me despair?"

"I bid thee repent," said Cedric. "Seek to prayer and penance, and may'st thou find acceptance! But I cannot, I will not, longer abide with thee."

"Stay yet a moment," said Ulrica; "son of my father's friend, leave me not now, lest the demon who has governed my life should tempt me to avenge myself of thy hard-hearted scorn.—Think'st thou, if Front-de-Bœuf found Cedric the Saxon in his castle, in such a disguise, that thy life would be a long one?—already his eye has been upon thee like a falcon on its prey."

"And be it so," said Cedric; "and let him tear me with beak and talons, ere my tongue say one word which my heart doth not warrant. I will die a Saxon, true in word, open in deed—I bid thee avaunt!—touch me not, stay me not!—the sight of Front-de-Bœuf himself is less odious to me than thine, degraded and degenerate as thou art."

"Be it so," said Ulrica, no longer interrupting him; "go thy way, and forget, in the insolence of thy superiority, that the wretch before thee is the daughter of thy father's friend.—Go thy way—If I am separated from mankind by my sufferings—separated from those whose aid I might most justly expect—not less will I be separated from them in my revenge!—No man shall aid me, but the ears of all men shall tingle to hear of the deed which I shall dare to do!—Farewell!—thy scorn has burst the last tie which seemed yet to unite me to my kind—a thought that my woes might claim the compassion of my people."

"Ulrica," said Cedric, softened by this appeal, "hast thou borne up and endured to live through so much guilt and so much misery, and wilt thou now yield to despair when thine eyes are opened to thy guilt, and when repentance were thy fitter occupation?"

"Cedric," answered Ulrica, "thou little knowest the human heart.

To act as I have acted, to think as I have thought, requires the maddening love of pleasure mingled with the keen appetite of revenge, the proud consciousness of power; draughts too intoxicating for the human heart to bear, and yet retain the power to repent. Their fever has long passed away—Age has no pleasure, wrinkles have no influence, revenge itself dies away in impotent curses—then comes remorse with all its vipers, mixed with vain regrets for the past and despair for the future!—then, when all other strong impulses have ceased, we become like the fiends in hell, who may feel remorse, but never repentance—but thy words have awakened a new soul within me—Well hast thou said, all is possible to those who dare to die!—thou hast shown me the means of revenge, and be assured I will embrace them—it has hitherto shared this wasted bosom with other and with rival passions—henceforward it shall possess me wholly, and thou thyself shalt say, that, whatever was the life of Ulrica, her death well became the daughter of the noble Torquil. There is a force without beleaguering this accursed castle—hasten to lead them to the attack, and when thou shalt see a red flag wave from the turret on the eastern angle of the donjon, press the Normans hard—they will then have enough to do within, and you may win the wall in spite both of bow and mangonel.—Begone, I pray thee—follow thine own fate, and leave me to mine."

Cedric would have inquired further into the purpose which she thus darkly announced, but the stern voice of Front-de-Bœuf was heard, exclaiming, "Where tarries this loitering priest? By the scallop-shell of Compostella, I will make a martyr of him, if he loiters here to hatch treason amongst my domestics."

"What a true prophet," said Ulrica, "is an evil conscience! But heed him not. Out and to thy people—Cry your Saxon *onslaught*, and let them sing their war-song of Rollo, if they will. Vengeance shall bear a burthen to it."

As she thus spoke, she vanished through a private door, and Reginald Front-de-Bœuf entered the apartment. Cedric, with some difficulty, compelled himself to make obeisance to the haughty Baron, who returned his courtesy with a slight inclination of the head.

"Thy penitents, father, have made a long shrift—it is the better for them, since it is the last they shall make. Hast thou prepared them for death?"

"I found them," answered Cedric in such French as he could command, "expecting the worst, from the moment they knew into whose power they had fallen."

"How now, Sir Friar," replied Front-de-Bœuf hastily, "thy speech, methinks, smacks of a Saxon tongue?"

"I was bred in the convent of St Withold of Burton," answered Cedric.

"Ay?" said the Baron, "it had been better for thee to have been a Norman, and better for my purpose too; but need has no choice of messengers. That St Withold's of Burton is a howlet's nest worth the harrying. The day will soon come that the frock shall protect the Saxon as little as the mail-coat."

"God's will be done," said Cedric, in a voice tremulous with passion, which Front-de-Bœuf imputed to fear.

"I see," said he, "thou dreamest already that our men-at-arms are in thy refectory and thy ale-vaults. But do me one cast of thine holy office, and, come what list of others, thou shalt sleep as safe in thy cell as a snail within his shell of proof."

"Speak your commands," said Cedric with suppressed emotion.

"Follow me through this passage, then, that I may dismiss thee by the postern."

And as he strode on his way before the supposed friar, Front-de-Bœuf thus schooled him in the part which he desired he should act.

"Thou seest, Sir Friar, yon herd of Saxon swine, who have dared to environ this castle of Torquilstone—Tell them whatever thou canst devise of the weakness of this fortalice, or aught else that can detain them before it for twenty-four hours. Meantime bear thou this scroll—but soft—canst read, Sir Priest?"

"Not a jot I," answered Cedric, "save on my breviary; and then I know the characters, because I have the holy service by heart, praised be our Lady and St Withold."

"The fitter messenger for my purpose—carry thou this scroll to the castle of Philip de Malvoisin. Say it cometh from me, and is written by the Templar Brian de Bois-Guilbert, and that I pray him to send it to York with all the speed man and horse can make. Meanwhile, tell him to doubt nothing that he shall find us whole and sound behind our battlements—Shame on it that we should be compelled to hide thus by a pack of runagates, who are wont to fly even at the flash of our pennons and the tramp of our horses! I say to thee, priest, on thy life contrive some cast of thine art to keep the knaves where they are, until our friends bring up their lances. My vengeance is awake, and she is a falcon that slumbers not till she has been gorged."

"By my patron saint," said Cedric, with deeper energy than became his character, "and by every saint who has lived and died in England, your commands shall be obeyed! Not a Saxon shall stir from before these walls, if I have art and influence to detain them there."

"Ha!" said Front-de-Bœuf, "thou changest thy tone, Sir Priest, and speakest brief and bold, as if thy heart were in the slaughter of the

Saxon herd; and yet thou art thyself of kindred to the swine?"

Cedric was no ready practiser of the art of dissimulation, and would at this moment have been much the better of a hint from Wamba's more fertile brain. But necessity, according to the ancient proverb, sharpens invention, and he muttered something under his cowl concerning the men without being excommunicated outlaws both to church and to kingdom.

"*Despardieux*," answered Front-de-Bœuf, "thou hast spoken the very truth—I forgot that the knaves can strip a fat abbot, as well as if they had been born south of yonder salt channel. Was it not he of St Ives whom they tied to an oak tree, and compelled to sing a mass while they were rifling his mails and his wallets?—No, by our Lady—that jest was played by Gualtier of Middleton, one of our own companions-at-arms. But they were Saxons who robbed the chapel at St Bees of cup, candlestick, and chalice, were they not?"

"They were godless men," answered Cedric.

"Ay, and they drank out all the good wine and ale that lay in store for many a secret carousal, when ye pretend ye are but busied with vigils and primes—Priest, thou art bound to revenge such sacrilege."

"I am indeed bound to vengeance," murmured Cedric; "Saint Withold knows my heart."

Front-de-Bœuf, in the meanwhile, led the way to a postern, where, passing the moat on a single plank, they reached a small barbican, or exterior defence, which communicated with the open field by a well defended sally-port.

"Begone then; and if thou wilt do mine errand, and return hither when it is done, thou shalt see Saxon flesh cheap as ever was hog's in the shambles of Sheffield. And, hark thee, thou seemest to be a jolly confessor—come hither after the onslaught, and thou shalt have as much Malvoisie as would drench thy whole convent."

"Assuredly we shall meet again," answered Cedric.

"Something in hand the whilst," continued the Norman; and, as they parted at the sally-port, he thrust into Cedric's reluctant hand a gold bezant, adding, "Remember, I will flay off both cowl and skin, if thou failest me in thy purpose."

"And free leave shall I give thee to do both," answered Cedric, leaving the sally-port, and striding forth over the free field with a joyful step, "if, when we meet next, I deserve not better at thine hand."—Turning then back towards the castle, he threw the piece of gold to the donor, exclaiming at the same time, "False Norman, thy money perish with thee!"

Front-de-Bœuf heard the words imperfectly, but the action was suspicious—"Archers," he called to the warders on the outward battlements, "send me an arrow through yon monk's frock—yet stay," he said, as his retainers were bending their bows, "it avails not—we must thus far trust him since we have no better shift. I think he dares not betray me. At the worst I can but treat with these Saxon dogs whom I have safe in kennel.—Ho! Giles jailor, let them bring Cedric of Rotherwood before me, and the other churl, his companion—him I mean of Coningsburgh—Athelstane there, or what call they him? Their very names are an incumbrance to a Norman knight's mouth, and have, as were, a flavour of rusted bacon—Give me a stoup of wine, as jolly Prince John said, that I may wash away the relish—place it in the armoury, and thither lead the prisoners."

His commands were obeyed; and, upon entering that Gothic apartment, hung with many spoils won by his own valour and that of his father, he found a flagon of wine on the massive oaken table, and the two Saxon captives under the guard of four of his dependants. Front-de-Bœuf took a long draught of wine, and then addressed his prisoners;—for the manner in which Wamba drew the cap over his face, the change of dress, the gloomy and broken light, and the Baron's imperfect acquaintance with the features of Cedric, (who avoided his Norman neighbours, and seldom stirred beyond his own domains,) prevented him from discovering that the most important of his captives had made his escape.

"Gallants of England," said Front-de-Bœuf, "how relish ye your entertainment at Torquilstone?—Are ye yet aware what your *surquedy* and *outrecuidance** merit, for scoffing at the entertainment of a prince of the house of Anjou?—have ye forgotten how ye requited the unmerited hospitality of the royal John? By God and St Dennis, an ye pay not the richer ransom, I will hang ye up by the feet from the iron bars of these windows, until the kites and hooded crows have made skeletons of you!—Speak out, ye Saxon dogs—what bid ye for your worthless lives?—How say you, you of Rotherwood?"

"Not a doit, I," answered poor Wamba—"and for hanging up by the feet, my brain has been topsy turvy, they say, ever since the biggin was bound first round my head; so turning me upside down may peradventure restore it again."

"Saint Genevieve!" said Front-de-Bœuf, "what have we got here?"

And with the back of his hand he struck Cedric's cap from the head of the Jester, and, throwing open his tunic, discovered the fatal badge of servitude, the silver collar round his neck.

"Giles—Clement—dogs and vassals!" exclaimed the furious Norman, "what have you brought me here?"

* *Surquedy* and *outrecuidance*—insolence and presumption.

"I think I can tell you," said De Bracy, who just entered the apartment. "This is Cedric's clown, who fought so manful a skirmish with Isaac of York about a question of precedence."

"I shall settle it for them both," replied Front-de-Bœuf; "they shall hang on the same gallows, unless his master and this boar of Coningsburgh will pay well for their lives. Their wealth is the least they can surrender; they must also carry off with them the swarms that are besetting my castle, subscribe a surrender of their pretended immunities, and live under us as serfs and vassals; too happy if, in the new world which is about to begin, we leave them the breath of their nostrils.—Go," said he, to two of his attendants, "fetch me the right Cedric hither, and I pardon your error for once; the rather that you only mistook a fool for a Saxon Franklin."

"Aye, but," said Wamba, "your chivalrous excellency will find there are more fools than Franklins amongst us."

"What means the knave?" said Front-de-Bœuf, looking towards his followers, who, lingering and loath, faultered forth their belief, that if this were not Cedric who was there in presence, they knew not what was become of him.

"Saints of Heaven," exclaimed De Bracy, "he must have escaped in the monk's garments!"

"Fiends of hell," echoed Front-de-Bœuf, "it was then the boar of Rotherwood whom I ushered to the postern, and dismissed with my own hands! And thou," he said to Wamba, "whose folly could overreach the wisdom of ideots yet more gross than thyself—I will give thee holy orders—I will shave thy crown for thee!—Here, let them tear the scalp from his head, and then pitch me him headlong from the battlements—Thy trade is to jest, canst thou jest now?"

"You deal with me better than your word, noble knight," whimpered forth poor Wamba, whose habits of buffoonery were not to be overcome even by the immediate prospect of death; "if you give me the red cap you purpose, out of a simple monk you will make a cardinal of me."

"The poor patch," said De Bracy, "is resolved to die in his vocation. Front-de-Bœuf, you shall not slay him. Give him to me, to make sport for my Free Companions.—How say'st thou, knave? Wilt thou take heart of grace, and go to the wars with me?"

"Ay, with my master's leave," said Wamba, "for, look you, I must not slip collar, (and he touched that which he wore) without his permission."

"Oh, a Norman saw will soon cut a Saxon collar," said De Bracy.

"Ay, noble sir," replied Wamba, "and thence goes the proverb—

'Norman saw on English oak,
On English neck a Norman yoke;
Norman spoon in English dish,
And England ruled as Normans wish;
Blithe world in England ne'er will be more
Till England's rid of all the four.'"

"Thou doest well, De Bracy," said Front-de-Bœuf, "to stand there listening to a fool's jargon, when destruction is gaping for us. Seest thou not we are over-reached, and that our purposed mode of communicating with our friends without, has been disconcerted by this same motley gentleman thou art so fond to brother? What terms have we to expect but instant storm?"

"To the battlements then," said De Bracy; "when didst thou ever see me the graver for the thoughts of battle? Call the Templar yonder, and let him fight but half as well for his life as he has done for his Order—make thou to the walls thyself with thy huge body—let me do my poor endeavour in my own way, and I tell thee the Saxon outlaws may as soon attempt to scale the clouds, as the castle of Torquilstone; or, if you will treat with the banditti, why not employ the mediation of this worthy Franklin, who seems in such deep contemplation of the wine-flagon?—Here, Saxon," he continued, addressing Athelstane, and handing the cup to him, "rinse thy throat with that noble liquor, and rouse up thy soul to say what thou wilt do for thy liberty."

"What a man of mould may," answered Athelstane, "providing it be what a man of manhood ought.—Dismiss me free, with my companions, and I will pay a ransom of a thousand marks."

"And wilt moreover assure us the retreat of that scum of mankind who are swarming around the castle, contrary to God's peace and the king's?" said Front-de-Bœuf.

"In so far as I can," answered Athelstane, "I will withdraw them; and I fear not but that my father Cedric will do his best to assist me."

"We are agreed then," said Front-de-Bœuf—"thou and thine are to be set at freedom, and peace is to be on both sides, for payment of a thousand marks. It is a trifling ransom, Saxon, and thou wilt owe gratitude to the moderation which accepts of it in exchange for your persons. But mark, this extends not to the Jew Isaac."

"Nor to the Jew Isaac's daughter," said the Templar, who had now joined them.

"Neither," said Front-de-Bœuf, "belong to this Saxon's company."

"I were unworthy to be called Christian, if they did," replied Athelstane: "deal with the unbelievers as you list."

"Neither does the ransom include the Lady Rowena," said De

Bracy. "It shall never be said I was scared out of a fair prize without striking a blow for it."

"Neither," said Front-de-Bœuf, "does our treaty refer to this wretched Jester, whom I retain, that I may make him an example to every knave who turns jest into earnest."

"The Lady Rowena," answered Athelstane, with the most steady countenance, "is my affianced bride. I will be drawn by wild horses before I consent to part with her. The slave Wamba has this day saved the life of my father Cedric. I will lose mine ere a hair of his head be injured."

"Thy affianced bride? the Lady Rowena the affianced bride of a vassal like thee?" said De Bracy; "Saxon, thou dreamest that the days of thy seven kingdoms are returned again. I tell thee, the princes of the House of Anjou confer not their wards on men of such lineage as thine."

"My lineage, proud Norman," replied Athelstane, "is drawn from a source more pure and ancient than that of a beggarly Frenchman, whose living is won by selling the blood of the thieves whom he assembles under his paltry standard. Kings were my ancestors, strong in war and wise in council, who every day feasted in their hall more hundreds than thou canst number individual followers; whose names have been sung by minstrels, and their laws recorded by Wittenagemotes; whose bones were interred amid the prayers of saints, and over whose tombs minsters have been builded."

"Thou hast it, De Bracy," said Front-de-Bœuf, well pleased with the rebuff which his companion had received; "the Saxon hath hit thee fairly."

"As fairly as a captive can strike," said De Bracy, with apparent carelessness; "for he whose hands are tied should have his tongue at freedom.—But thy glibness of reply, comrade," rejoined he, speaking to Athelstane, "will not win the freedom of the Lady Rowena."

To this Athelstane, who had already made a longer speech than was his custom to do on any topic, however interesting, returned no answer. The conversation was interrupted by the arrival of a menial, who announced that a monk demanded admittance at the postern gate.

"In the name of Saint Bennet, the prince of these bull-beggars," said Front-de-Bœuf, "have we a real monk this time, or another imposture? Search him, slaves—for an ye suffer a second impostor to be palmed upon you, I will have your eyes torn out, and hot coals put into the sockets."

"Let me endure the extremity of your anger, my lord," said Giles, "if this be not a real shaveling. Your squire Jocelyn knows him well, and will vouch him to be brother Ambrose, a monk in attendance upon the Prior of Jorvaulx."

"Admit him," said Front-de-Bœuf; "most likely he brings us news from his jovial master. Surely the devil keeps holiday, and the priests are released from duty, that they are strolling thus wildly through the country. Remove these prisoners; and, Saxon, think on what thou hast heard."

"I claim," said Athelstane, "an honourable imprisonment, with due care of my board and of my couch, as becomes my rank, and as is due to one who is in treaty for ransom. Moreover, I hold him that deems himself the best of you, bound to answer to me with his body for this aggression on my freedom. This defiance hath already been sent to thee by thy sewer; thou underliest it, and art bound to answer me. There lies my glove."

"I answer not the challenge of my prisoner," said Front-de-Bœuf; "nor shalt thou, Maurice De Bracy.—Giles," he continued, "hang the Franklin's glove upon the tine of yonder branchy antlers. There shall it remain until he is a free man. Should he then presume to demand it, or to affirm that he was unlawfully made my prisoner, by the belt of Saint Christopher, he will speak to one who hath never refused to meet a foe on foot or on horseback, alone or with his vassals at his back."

The Saxon prisoners were accordingly removed, just as they introduced the monk Ambrose, who appeared to be in great perturbation.

"This is the real *Deus vobiscum*," said Wamba, as he passed the reverend brother; "the others were but counterfeits."

"Holy Mother!" said the monk, as he addressed the assembled knights, "Am I at last safe and in Christian keeping?"

"Safe thou art," replied De Bracy; "and for Christianity, here is the stout Baron Reginald Front-de-Bœuf, whose utter abomination is a Jew; and the good Knight Templar, Brian de Bois-Guilbert, whose trade it is to slay Saracens—If these are not good marks of Christianity, I know no other which they bear about them."

"Ye are friends and allies of our reverend father in God, Aymer, Prior of Jorvaulx," said the monk, without noticing the tone of De Bracy's reply; "ye owe him aid both by knightly faith and holy charity, —for what sayeth the blessed Saint Augustin, in his treatise *De Civitate Dei*"——

"What saith the devil!" interrupted Front-de-Bœuf; "or rather what dost *thou* say, Sir Priest? We have little time to hear texts from the holy fathers."

"*Sancta Maria!*" ejaculated Father Ambrose, "how prompt to ire are these unhallowed laymen!—But be it known to you, brave knights, that certain murtherous caitiffs, casting behind them fear of God, and reverence of his church, and not regarding the bull of the Holy See, *Si quis, suadente Diabolo*,"——

"Brother priest," said the Templar, "all this we know or guess at—tell us plainly, is thy master, the Prior, made prisoner, and to whom?"

"Surely," said Ambrose, "he is in the hands of the men of Belial, infesters of these woods, and contemners of the holy text, 'Touch not thou mine anointed, and do my prophets nought of evil.'"

"Here is a new argument for our swords, sirs," said Front-de-Bœuf, turning to his companions; "and so, instead of reaching us any assistance, the Prior of Jorvaulx requests aid at our hands: a man is well helped of these lazy churchmen when he hath most to do. But speak out, priest, and speak at once. What doth thy master expect from us?"

"So please you," said Ambrose, "violent hands having been imposed on my reverend superior, contrary to the holy ordinance which I did already quote, and the men of Belial having rifled his mails and budgets, and stripped him of two hundred marks of pure refined gold, they do yet demand of him a large sum beside, ere they will suffer him to depart from their uncircumcised hands. Wherefore the reverend father in God prays you, as his dear friends and allies, to rescue him, either by paying down the ransom at which they hold him, or by force of arms, at your best discretion."

"The foul fiend quell the Prior!" said Front-de-Bœuf; "his morning's draught has been a deep one. When did thy master ever hear of a Norman baron unbuckling his purse to relieve a churchman, whose bags are ten times as weighty as ours?—And how can we do aught by valour, that are cooped up here by ten times our number, and expect an assault every moment?"

"And that was what I was about to tell you," said the monk, "had your hastiness allowed me time. But, God help me, I am old, and these foul onslaughts distract an old man's brain. Nevertheless it is of verity that they assemble a camp, and raise a bank against the walls of this castle."

"To the battlements!" cried De Bracy, "and let us mark what these knaves do without;" and so saying, he opened a latticed window which led to a sort of bartizan or projecting balcony, and immediately called from thence to those in the apartment—"Saint Dennis, but the old monk hath brought true tidings: they bring forward mantelets and pavisses,* and the archers muster on the skirts of the wood like a

*Mantelets were temporary and moveable defences formed of planks, under cover of which the assailants advanced to the attack of fortified places of old. Pavisses were a species of large shields covering the whole person, employed on the same occasions.

dark cloud before a hail-storm."

Reginald Front-de-Bœuf also looked out upon the field, and immediately snatched his bugle; and, after winding a long and loud blast, commanded his men to their posts on the walls.

"De Bracy, look to the eastern side, where the walls are lowest—Noble Bois-Guilbert, thy trade hath well taught thee how to attack and defend, look thou to the western side—I myself will take post at the barbican. Yet, do not confine your exertions to any one spot, noble friends!—we must this day be everywhere, and multiply ourselves, were it possible, so as to carry by our presence succour and relief wherever the attack is hottest. Our numbers are few, but activity and courage may supply that defect, since we have only to do with rascal clowns."

"But, noble knights," exclaimed Father Ambrose, amid the bustle and confusion occasioned by the preparations for defence, "will none of ye hear the message of the reverend Father in God Aymer, Prior of Jorvaulx?—I beseech thee to hear me, noble Sir Reginald!"

"Go patter thy petitions to heaven," said the fierce Norman, "for we on earth have no time to listen to them—Ho there! Anselm! see that seething pitch and oil are ready to pour on the heads of these audacious traitors—Look that the cross-bowmen lack not bolts*—Fling abroad my banner with the old bull's head—the knaves shall soon find with whom they have to do this day."

"But, noble sir," continued the monk, persevering in his endeavour to draw attention, "consider my vow of obedience, and let me discharge myself of my superior's errand."

"Away with this prating dotard, fellows," said Front-de-Bœuf, "lock him up in the chapel, to bid his beads till the broil be over. It will be a new thing to the saints in Torquilstone to hear aves and paters; they have not been often so honoured, I trow, since they were cut out of stone."

"Blaspheme not the holy saints, Sir Reginald," said De Bracy, "we shall have need of their aid to-day before yon rascal rout disband."

"I expect little aid from their hand," said Front-de-Bœuf, "unless we were to hurl them from the battlements on the heads of the villains. There is a huge lumbering Saint Christopher yonder, sufficient to bear a whole company to the earth."

The Templar in the meantime had been looking out on the proceedings of the besiegers, with rather more attention than the brutal Front-de-Bœuf, or his giddy companion.

* The bolt was the arrow peculiarly fitted to the cross-bow, as that of the long-bow was called the shaft. Hence the English proverb—"I will either make a shaft or bolt of it," signifying a determination to make one use or other of the thing spoken of.

"By the faith of mine order," he said, "these men approach with more touch of discipline than could have been judged, howsoever they come by it. See ye how dexterously they avail themselves of every cover which a tree or bush affords, and shun exposing themselves to the shot of our cross-bows? I spy neither banner nor pennon amongst them, and yet will I gage my golden chain, that they are led on by some noble or gentleman, skilful in the practice of wars."

"I espy him," said De Bracy; "I see the waving of a knight's crest, and the gleam of his armour. See yon tall man in the black mail, who is busied marshalling the farther troop of the rascaille yeomen—By Saint Dennis, I hold him to be the same whom we called *Le Noir Faineant*, who overthrew thee, Front-de-Bœuf, in the lists at Ashby."

"So much the better," said Front-de-Bœuf, "that he comes here to give me my revenge. Some hilding fellow he must be, who dared not stay to assert his claim to a prize which chance had assigned him. I should have in vain sought for him where knights and nobles seek their foes, and right glad am I he hath here shewn himself among yon villain yeomanry."

The demonstrations of the enemy's immediate approach cut off all farther discourse. Each knight repaired to his post, and at the head of the few followers whom they were able to muster, and who were in numbers inadequate to defend the whole circuit of the walls, they awaited with calm determination the threatened assault.

Chapter Fourteen

This wandering race, severed from other men,
Boast yet their intercourse with human arts;
The seas, the woods, the deserts which they haunt,
Find them acquainted with their secret treasures;
And unregarded herbs, and flowers, and blossoms,
Display undream'd of powers when gathered by them.

The Jew.

OUR HISTORY must needs retrograde for the space of a few pages, to inform the reader of certain passages material to his understanding the rest of this important narrative. His own intelligence may indeed have easily anticipated that, when Ivanhoe sunk down, and seemed abandoned by all the world, it was the importunity of Rebecca which prevailed on her father to have the gallant young warrior transported from the lists to the house which for the time the Jews inhabited in the suburbs of Ashby.

It would not have been difficult to have persuaded Isaac to this step in any other circumstances, for his disposition was kind and grateful.

But he had also the prejudices and scrupulous timidity of his persecuted people, and those were to be conquered.

"Holy Abraham!" he exclaimed, "it is a good youth, and my heart bleeds to see the gore trickle down his rich embroidered hacqueton, and his corselet of goodly price—but to carry him to our home!—damsel, hast thou well considered?—he is a Christian, and by our law we may not deal with the stranger and Gentile, save for the advantage of our commerce."

"Speak not so, my dear father," replied Rebecca; "we may not indeed mix with them in banquet and in jollity; but in wounds and in misery, the Gentile becometh the Jew's brother."

"I would I knew what the Rabbi Jacob Ben Tudela would opine on it," replied Isaac;—"nevertheless, the good youth must not bleed to death. Let Seth and Reuben bear him to Ashby."

"Nay, let them place him in my litter," said Rebecca, "I will mount one of the palfreys."

"That were to expose thee to the gaze of these dogs of Ishmael and of Edom," whispered Isaac, with a suspicious glance towards the crowd of knights and squires. But Rebecca was already busied in carrying her charitable purpose into effect, and listed not what he said, until Isaac, seizing the sleeve of her mantle, again exclaimed in a hurried voice—"Beard of Aaron!—what if the youth perish!—if he die in our custody, shall we not be held guilty of his blood, and torn to pieces by the multitude?"

"He will not die, my father," said Rebecca, gently extricating herself from the grasp of Isaac—"he will not die unless we abandon him, and if so, we were indeed answerable for his blood to God and to man."

"Nay," said Isaac, releasing his hold, "it grieveth me as much to see the drops of his blood, as if they were so many golden bezants from mine own purse; and I well know, that the lessons of Miriam, daughter of the Rabbi Manasses of Byzantium, whose soul is in Paradise, have made thee skilful in the art of healing, and that thou knowest the craft of herbs, and the force of elixirs. Therefore do as thy mind giveth it thee—thou art a good damsel, and a blessing, and a crown, and a song of rejoicing unto me and unto my house, and unto the people of my fathers."

The apprehensions of Isaac, however, were not ill founded; and the generous and grateful benevolence of his daughter exposed her, on her return to Ashby, to the unhallowed gaze of Brian de Bois-Guilbert. The Templar twice passed and repassed them on the road, fixing his bold and ardent look on the beautiful Jewess; and we have already seen the consequences of the admiration which her charms excited, when accident threw her into the power of that unprincipled voluptuary.

Rebecca lost no time in causing the patient to be transported to their temporary dwelling, and proceeded with her own hands to examine and to bind up his wounds. The youngest reader of romances and romantic ballads, must recollect how often the females, during the dark ages as they are called, were initiated into the mysteries of surgery, and how frequently the gallant knight submitted the wounds of his person to her cure, whose eyes had yet more deeply penetrated his heart.

But the Jews, both male and female, possessed and practised the medical science in all its branches, and the monarchs and powerful barons of the time frequently committed themselves to the charge of some experienced sage among this despised people, when wounded or in sickness. The aid of the Jewish physicians was not the less eagerly sought after, though a general belief prevailed among the Christians, that the Jewish Rabbins were deeply acquainted with the occult sciences, and particularly with the cabalistical art, which had its name and origin in the studies of the sages of Israel. Neither did the Rabbins disown such acquaintance with supernatural arts, which added nothing (for what could add aught) to the hatred with which their nation was regarded, while it diminished the contempt with which that malevolence was mingled. A Jewish magician might be the subject of equal abhorrence with a Jewish usurer, but he could not be equally despised. It is, besides, probable, considering the wonderful cures they are said to have performed, that the Jews possessed some secrets of the healing art peculiar to themselves, and which, with the exclusive spirit arising out of their condition, they took great care to conceal from the Christians amongst whom they dwelt.

The beautiful Rebecca had been heedfully brought up in all the knowledge proper to her nation, which her apt and powerful mind had retained, arranged, and enlarged, in the course of a progress beyond her years, her sex, and even the age in which she lived. Her knowledge of medicine and of the healing art had been acquired under an aged Jewess, the daughter of one of their most celebrated doctors, who loved Rebecca as her daughter, and was believed to have communicated to her secrets, which had been left to herself by her sage father. The fate of Miriam had indeed been to fall a sacrifice to the fanaticism of the times; but her secrets had survived in her apt pupil.

Rebecca, thus endowed with knowledge as with beauty, was universally revered and admired by her own tribe, who almost regarded her as one of those gifted women mentioned in the sacred history. Her father himself, out of a sort of reverence for her talents, which involuntarily mingled itself with his unbounded affection, permitted the maiden a greater liberty than was usually indulged to those of her sex by the habits of their people, and was, as we have just seen, frequently guided by her opinion, even in preference to his own.

When Ivanhoe reached the habitation of Isaac, he was still in a state of unconsciousness, owing to the profuse loss of blood which had taken place during his exertions in the lists. Rebecca examined the wound, and having applied to it such vulnerary remedies as her art prescribed, informed her father that if fever could be averted, of which the great bleeding rendered her little apprehensive, and if the healing balsam of Miriam retained its virtue, there was nothing to fear for his guest's life, and that he might with safety travel to York with them on the ensuing day. Isaac looked a little blank at this annunciation: his charity would willingly have stopped short at Ashby, or, at most, would have left the wounded Christian to be tended in the house where he was residing at present, with an assurance to the Hebrew to whom it belonged, that all expences should be duly discharged. To this, however, Rebecca opposed many reasons, of which we shall only mention two that had peculiar weight with Isaac. The one was, that she would on no account put her phial of precious balsam into the hands of another physician even of her own tribe, lest that valuable mystery should be discovered; the other, that this wounded knight, Wilfred of Ivanhoe, was an intimate favourite of Richard Cœur de Lion, and that, in case the monarch should return, Isaac, who had supplied his brother John with treasure to prosecute his rebellious purposes, would stand in no small need of a powerful protector who enjoyed Richard's favour.

"Thou art speaking but sooth, Rebecca," said Isaac, giving way to these weighty arguments—"it were an offending of Heaven to betray the secrets of the blessed Miriam; for the good which Heaven giveth us, is not rashly to be squandered upon others, whether it be talents of gold and shekels of silver, or whether it be the secret mysteries of a wise physician—assuredly they should be preserved to those to whom Providence hath vouchsafed them. And him whom the Nazarenes of England call the Lion's Heart, assuredly it were better for me to fall into the hands of a strong lion of Idumea than into his, if he shall have assurance of my dealing with his brother. Wherefore I will lend ear to thy counsel, and this youth shall journey with us unto York, and our house shall be as a home to him until his wounds shall be healed. And if he of the Lion's Heart shall return to the land, as is now noised abroad, then shall this Wilfred of Ivanhoe be unto me as a wall of defence, when the king's displeasure shall burn high against thy father. And if he doth not return, this Wilfred may natheless repay us our charges when he shall gain treasure by the strength of his spear and of his sword, even as he did yesterday and this day also. For the youth is a good youth, and keepeth the day which he appointeth, and restoreth that which he borroweth, and succoureth the Israelite, even the child of my father's house, when he is encompassed by strong thieves and sons of Belial."

It was not until evening was nearly closed that Ivanhoe was restored to consciousness of his situation. He awakened from a broken slumber, under the confused impressions which are naturally attendant on the recovery from a state of insensibility. He was unable for some time to recall exactly to memory the circumstances which had preceded his fall in the lists, or to make out any connected chain of the events in which he had been engaged upon the yesterday. A sense of wound and injury, joined to great weakness and exhaustion, was mingled with the recollection of blows dealt and received, of steeds rushing upon each other, overthrowing and overthrown—of shouts and clashing of arms, and all the heady tumult of a confused fight. An effort to draw aside the curtain of his couch was in some degree successful, although rendered difficult by the pain of his wound.

To his great surprise he found himself in a room magnificently furnished, but having cushions instead of chairs to rest upon, and in other respects partaking so much of oriental costume, that he began to doubt whether he had not been, during his sleep, transported back again to the land of Palestine. The impression was increased, when, the tapestry being drawn aside, a female form, dressed in a rich habit, which partook more of the eastern taste than that of Europe, glided through the door which it concealed, and was followed by a swarthy domestic.

As the wounded knight was about to address this fair apparition, she imposed silence by placing her slender finger on her ruby lip, while the attendant approaching him proceeded to uncover Ivanhoe's side, and the lovely Jewess satisfied herself that the bandage was in its place, and the wound doing well. She performed her task with a graceful and dignified simplicity and modesty, which might, even in more civilized days, have served to redeem it from whatever might seem repugnant to female delicacy. The idea of so young and beautiful a person engaged in attendance on the sick-bed, and in dressing the wound of one of a different sex, was melted away and lost in that of a beneficent being contributing her effectual aid to relieve pain, and to avert the stroke of death. Rebecca's few and brief directions were given in the Hebrew language to the old domestic; and he, who had been frequently her assistant in similar cases, obeyed them without reply.

The accents of an unknown tongue, however harsh they might have sounded when uttered by another, had, coming from the beautiful Rebecca, the romantic and pleasing effect which fancy ascribes to the charms pronounced by some beneficent fairy, unintelligible indeed to the ear, but, from the sweetness of utterance, and benignity of aspect which accompany them, touching and affecting to the heart. Without, then, making an attempt at further question, Ivanhoe suffered them in silence to take the measures they thought most proper for his recovery; and it was not until these were completed and his kind physician about to retire, that his curiosity could no longer be suppressed.—"Gentle maiden," he began in the Arabian tongue, with which his eastern travels had rendered him familiar, and which he thought most likely to be understood by the turban'd and caftan'd damsel who stood before him, "I pray you, gentle maiden, of your courtesy"——

But here he was interrupted by his fair physician, a smile which she could scarce suppress dimpling for an instant a face, whose general expression was that of contemplative melancholy. "I am of England, Sir Knight, and speak the English tongue, although my dress and my lineage belong to another climate."

"Noble damsel,"—again the Knight of Ivanhoe began; and again Rebecca hastened to interrupt him.

"Bestow not on me, Sir Knight," she said, "the epithet of noble. It is well you should speedily know that your hand-maiden is a poor Jewess, the daughter of that Isaac of York, to whom you were so lately a good and a kind lord. It well becomes him, and those of his household, to render to you such careful tendance as your present state necessarily demands."

I know not whether the fair Rowena would have been altogether satisfied with the species of emotion with which her devoted knight had hitherto gazed on the beautiful features, and fair form, and lustrous eyes, of the lovely Rebecca; eyes whose brilliancy was shaded, and as it were mellowed, by the shade of her long dark silken eyelashes, and which a minstrel would have compared to the evening star darting its rays through a bower of jessamine. But Ivanhoe was too good a Catholic to retain the same class of feelings towards a Jewess. This Rebecca had foreseen, and for this very purpose she had hastened to mention her father's name and lineage. Yet, for the fair and wise daughter of Isaac was not without a touch of female weakness, she could not but sigh internally when the glance of respectful admiration, not altogether unmixed with tenderness, with which Ivanhoe had hitherto regarded his unknown benefactress, was exchanged at once for a manner cold, composed, and collected, and fraught with no deeper feeling than that which expressed a grateful sense of courtesy received from an unexpected quarter and one of an inferior race. It was not that Ivanhoe's former carriage expressed more than that general devotional homage which youth always pays to beauty; yet it was mortifying that one word should operate as a spell to remove poor Rebecca, who could not be supposed altogether ignorant of her title to such homage, to a degraded class, to whom it could not be honourably rendered.

But the gentleness and candour of Rebecca's nature imputed no fault to Ivanhoe for sharing in the universal prejudices of his age and religion. On the contrary, the fair Jewess, though sensible her patient now regarded her as one of a race of reprobation, with whom it was disgraceful to hold any beyond the most necessary intercourse, ceased not to pay the same patient and devoted attention to his safety and convenience. She informed him of the necessity they were under of removing to York, and of her father's resolution to transport him thither, and tend him in his own house until his health should be restored. Ivanhoe expressed great repugnance to this plan, which he grounded on unwillingness to give farther trouble to his benefactors.

"Was there not," he said, "in Ashby, or near it, some Saxon Franklin, or even some wealthy peasant, who would endure the burthen of a wounded countryman's residence with him until he should be again able to bear his armour?—Was there no convent of Saxon endowment, where he could be received?—Or could he not be transported as far as Burton, where he was sure to find hospitality with Waltheoff, the Abbot of St Withold's, to whom he was related?"

"Any, the worst of these harbourages," said Rebecca, with a melancholy smile, "would unquestionably be more fitting for your residence than the abode of a despised Jew; yet, Sir Knight, unless you would dismiss your physician, you cannot change your lodging. Our nation, as you well know, can cure wounds, though we deal not in inflicting them; and in our own family, in particular, are secrets which have been handed down since the days of Solomon, and of which you have already in part experienced the advantage. No Nazarene—I crave your forgiveness—no Christian leach, within the four seas of Britain, could enable you to bear your corslet within a month."

"And how soon wilt thou enable me to brook it?" said Ivanhoe impatiently.

"Within eight days, if thou wilt be patient and conformable to my directions," replied Rebecca.

"By our Blessed Lady," said Wilfred, "if it be not a sin to name her here, it is no time for me or any true knight to be bedridden; and if thou accomplish thy promise, maiden, I will pay thee with my casque full of crowns, come by them as I may."

"And I will accomplish my promise," said Rebecca. "And thou shalt bear thine armour on the eighth day from hence, if thou wilt grant me but one boon in the stead of the silver thou dost promise me."

"If it be within my power, and such as a true Christian knight may grant to one of thy people," replied Ivanhoe, "I will grant thy boon blithely and thankfully."

"Nay," answered Rebecca, "I will but pray of thee to believe henceforward that a Jew may do good service to a Christian, without other guerdon than the blessing of the Great Father, who made both Jew and Gentile."

"It were sin to doubt it, maiden," replied Ivanhoe; "and I repose myself on thy skill without further doubt or question, well trusting you will enable me to bear my corslet on the eighth day. And now, my kind leach, let me inquire of the news abroad. What of the noble Saxon Cedric and his household?—what of the lovely Lady"—he stopt, as if unwilling to speak Rowena's name in the house of a Jew—"of her, I mean, who was named Queen of the tournament?"

"And who was selected by you, Sir Knight, to hold that dignity, with judgment which was admired as much as your valour," replied Rebecca.

The blood which Ivanhoe had lost did not prevent a flush from crossing his cheek, feeling that he had incautiously betrayed the interest he had in Rowena by the awkward attempt he had made to conceal it.

"It was less of her I would speak," said he, "than of Prince John; and I would fain know somewhat of a faithful squire, and why he now attends me not?"

"Let me use my authority as a leach," answered Rebecca, "and enjoin you to keep silence, and avoid agitating reflections, whilst I apprise you of what you desire to know. Prince John hath broken off the tournament, and set forward in all haste towards York, with the nobles, knights, and churchmen of his party, after collecting such sums as they could wring, by fair means or foul, from those who are esteemed the wealthy of the land. It is said he designs to assume his brother's crown."

"Not without a blow struck in its defence," said Ivanhoe, raising himself on the couch, "if there were but one true subject in England. I will fight for Richard's title with the best of them—ay, one to two in his just quarrel."

"But that you may be able to do so," said Rebecca, touching his shoulder with her hand, "you must now observe my directions and remain quiet."

"True, maiden," said Ivanhoe, "as quiet as these disquieted times will permit—And of Cedric and his household?"

"His steward came but brief while since," said the Jewess, "panting with haste, to ask my father for certain monies, the price of wool the growth of Cedric's flocks, and from him I learned that Cedric and Athelstane of Coningsburgh had left the Prince's banquet in high displeasure, and were about to set forth on their return homeward."

"Went any lady with them to the banquet?" said Wilfred.

"The Lady Rowena," said Rebecca, answering the question with more precision than it had been asked—"The Lady Rowena went not to the Prince's feast, and, as the steward reported to us, she is now on her journey back to Rotherwood, with her guardian Cedric. And touching your faithful squire Gurth"——

"Ha!" exclaimed the knight, "knowest thou his name?—But thou dost," he immediately added, "and well thou may'st, for it was from thy hands, and, as I think, from thine own generosity of spirit, that he received but yesterday an hundred zecchins."

"Speak not of that," said Rebecca, blushing deeply; "I see how easy it is for the tongue to betray what the heart would blithely conceal."

"But this sum of gold," said Ivanhoe gravely, "my honour is concerned in repaying it to your father."

"Let it be as thou wilt," said Rebecca, "when eight days have passed away; but think not, and speak not now, of aught that may retard thy recovery."

"Be it so, kind maiden," said Ivanhoe, "I were most ungrateful to dispute thy commands. But one word of the fate of poor Gurth, and I have done with questioning thee."

"I grieve to tell thee, Sir Knight," answered the Jewess, "that he is in custody by the orders of Cedric."—And then observing the distress which her communication gave to Wilfred, she instantly added, "But the steward Oswald said, that if nothing occurred to renew his master's displeasure against him, he was sure that Cedric would pardon Gurth, a faithful serf, and one who stood high in favour, and who had but committed this error out of the love that he bore to Cedric's son. And he said, moreover, that he and his comrades, and especially Wamba the Jester, were resolved to warn Gurth to make his escape by the way, in case Cedric's ire against him could not be mitigated."

"Would to God they may keep their purpose!" said Ivanhoe; "but it seems as if I were destined to bring ruin on whomsoever hath shewn kindness to me—My king, by whom I was honoured and distinguished, thou see'st that the brother most indebted to him is raising his arm to grasp his crown;—my regard hath brought restraint and trouble on one the fairest of her sex;—and now my father in his mood may slay this poor bondsman, but for his love and loyal service to me—

Thou see'st, maiden, what an ill-fated wretch thou dost labour to assist; be wise, and let me go, ere the misfortunes which track my footsteps like slot-hounds, shall involve thee also in their pursuit."

"Nay," said Rebecca, "thy weakness and thy grief, Sir Knight, make thee unjustly miscalculate the purposes of Heaven. Thou hast been restored to thy country when it most needed the assistance of a strong hand and a true heart—thou hast humbled the pride of thine enemies, and those of thy king, when their horn was most highly exalted—and for the evil which thou hast sustained, see'st thou not that Heaven has raised thee a helper and physician, even among the most despised of the land?—Therefore be of good courage, and trust that thou art preserved for some marvel which thine arm shall work before this people. Adieu and having taken the medicine which I shall send thee by the hand of Reuben, compose thyself again to rest, that thou may'st be the more able to endure the journey on the succeeding day."

Ivanhoe was convinced by the reasoning, and obeyed the directions of Rebecca. The draught which Reuben administered was of a sedative and narcotic quality, and secured the patient sound and undisturbed slumbers. In the morning his kind physician found him entirely free from feverish symptoms, and fit to undergo the fatigue of a journey.

He was deposited in the horse-litter which had brought him from the lists, and every precaution taken for his travelling with ease. In one circumstance only even the entreaties of Rebecca were unable to secure sufficient attention to the accommodation of the wounded traveller. Isaac, like the enriched traveller of Juvenal's tenth satire, had ever the fear of robbery before his eyes, conscious that he would be alike accounted fair game by the marauding Norman noble and by the Saxon outlaw. He therefore journeyed at a great rate, and made short halts, and shorter repasts, so that he passed by Cedric and Athelstane, who had several hours the start of him, but had been delayed by their protracted feasting at the convent of Saint Withold's. Yet such was the virtue of Miriam's balsam, or such the strength of Ivanhoe's constitution, that he did not sustain from the hurried journey that inconvenience which his kind physician had apprehended.

In another point of view, however, the Jew's haste proved somewhat more than good speed. The rapidity with which he insisted upon travelling, bred several disputes betwixt him and the party whom he had hired to attend him as a guard. These men were Saxons, and not free by any means from the national love of ease and good living which the Normans stigmatized as laziness and gluttony. Reversing Shylock's position, they had accepted the employment in hopes of feeding upon the wealthy Jew, and were very much displeased when they found themselves disappointed, by the rapidity with which he insisted on their proceeding. They remonstrated also upon the risk of damage to their horses by these forced marches. Finally there arose betwixt Isaac and his satellites a deadly feud, concerning the quantity of wine and ale to be allowed for consumption at each meal. And thus it happened, that when the alarm of danger approached, and that which Isaac feared was likely to come upon him, he was deserted by the discontented mercenaries on whose protection he had relied, without using the means necessary to secure their attachment.

In this deserted condition the Jew, with his daughter and her wounded patient, was found by Cedric, as has already been noticed, and soon afterwards fell into the power of De Bracy and his confederates. Little notice was at first taken of the horse-litter, and it might have remained behind but for the curiosity of De Bracy, who looked into it under the impression that it might contain the object of his enterprize, for Rowena had not unveiled herself. But De Bracy's astonishment was considerable, when he discovered that the litter contained a wounded man, who, conceiving himself to have fallen into the power of Saxon outlaws, with whom his name might be a protection for himself and his friends, frankly avowed himself to be Wilfred of Ivanhoe.

The ideas of chivalrous honour, which, amidst his wildness and levity, never utterly abandoned De Bracy, prohibited him from doing the knight any injury in his defenceless condition, and equally interdicted his betraying him to Front-de-Bœuf, who would have no scruples to put to death, under any circumstances, the rival claimant of the feof of Ivanhoe. On the other hand, to liberate a rival preferred by the Lady Rowena, as the events of the tournament, and indeed Wilfred's previous banishment from his father's house, had made matter of notoriety, was a pitch far above the flight of De Bracy's generosity. A middle course betwixt good and evil was all which he found himself capable of adopting, and he commanded two of his own squires to keep close by the litter, and to suffer no one to approach it. If questioned, they were directed by their master to say, that the empty litter of the Lady Rowena was employed to transport one of their comrades who had been wounded in the scuffle. On arriving at Torquilstone, while the Knight Templar and the lord of that castle were each intent upon their own schemes, the one on the Jew's treasure and the other on his daughter, De Bracy's squires conveyed Ivanhoe, still under the name of a wounded comrade, to a distant apartment. This was accordingly returned by De Bracy's squires to Front-de-Bœuf, when he questioned them why they did not make for the battlements upon the alarm.

"A wounded companion!" he replied in great wrath and astonishment. "No wonder that churls and yeomen wax so presumptuous as even to lay leaguer before castles, and that clowns and swine-herds send defiances to nobles, since men-at-arms have turned sick men's nurses, and Free Companions are grown keepers of dying folk's curtains, when the castle is about to be assailed.—To the battlements, ye loitering villains!" he exclaimed, raising his stentorian voice till the arches around rung again, "to the battlements, or I will splinter your bones with this truncheon!"

The men sulkily replied, "that they desired nothing better than to go to the battlements, providing Front-de-Bœuf would bear them out with their master, who had commanded them to tend the dying man."

"The dying man, knaves!" rejoined the Baron; "I promise thee we shall all be dying men an we stand not to it the more stoutly. But I will relieve the guard upon this caitiff companion of yours.—Here, Urfried—hag—fiend of a Saxon witch—hearest thou not?—tend me this bed-ridden fellow, since he must needs be tended, whilst these knaves use their weapons.—Here be two arblasts, comrade, with windlaces and quarrells*—to the barbican with you, and see you drive each bolt through a Saxon brain."

The men, who, like most of their description, were fond of enterprize, and detested inaction, went joyfully to the scene of danger as they were commanded, and thus the charge of Ivanhoe was transferred to Urfried, or Ulrica. But she, whose brain was burning with remembrance of injuries and with hopes of vengeance, was readily induced to devolve upon Rebecca the care of her patient.

Chapter Fifteen

Ascend the watch-tower yonder, valiant soldier,
Look on the field, and say how goes the battle.
SCHILLER'S *Maid of Orleans.*

A MOMENT of peril is often also a moment of open-hearted kindness and affection. We are thrown off our guard by the general agitation of our feelings, and betray the intensity of those, which, at more tranquil moments, our prudence at least conceals if it cannot altogether suppress them. In finding herself once more by the side of Ivanhoe, Rebecca was astonished at the keen sensation of pleasure which she experienced, even in a moment when all around them both was danger, if not despair. As she felt his pulse and enquired after his health,

*The arblast was a steel cross-bow, the windlace the machine used in bending that weapon, and the quarrell, so called from its square or diamond shaped head, was the bolt adapted to it.

there was a softness in her touch and in her accents, implying a kinder interest than she would herself have been pleased to have voluntarily expressed. Her voice faultered and her hand trembled, and it was only the cold question of Ivanhoe, "Is it you, gentle maiden?" which recalled her to herself, and reminded her the sensations which she felt were not and could not be mutual. A sigh escaped, but it was scarce audible, and the questions which she put to the knight concerning his state of health, were put in the tone of calm friendship. Ivanhoe answered her hastily that he was, in point of health, as well and better than he could have expected—"Thanks," he said, "dear Rebecca, to thy helpful skill."

"He calls me dear Rebecca," said the maiden to herself, "but it is in the cold and careless tone which ill suits the word. His war-horse—his hunting hound, were dearer to him than the despised Jewess."

"My mind, gentle maiden," continued Ivanhoe, "is more disturbed by anxiety, than my body with pain. From the speeches of these men who were my warders just now, I learn that I am a prisoner, and, if I judge aright of the loud hoarse voice which even now dispatched them hence on some military duty, I am in the castle of Front-de-Bœuf—If so, how will this end, or how can I protect Rowena and my father?"

"He names not the Jew or Jewess," said Rebecca, internally; "yet what is our portion in him, and how justly am I punished by Heaven for letting my thoughts dwell upon him!" She hastened after this brief self-accusation to give Ivanhoe what information she could; but it amounted only to this, that the Templar Bois-Guilbert, and the Baron Front-de-Bœuf, were commanders within the castle; that it was beleaguered from without, but by whom she knew not. She added, that there was a Christian priest within the castle who might be possessed of more information.

"A Christian priest," said the knight, joyfully; "fetch him hither, Rebecca, if thou canst—say a sick man desires his ghostly counsel—say what thou wilt, but bring him—something I must do or attempt, but how can I determine until I know how matters stand without?"

Rebecca, in compliance with the wishes of Ivanhoe, made that attempt to bring Cedric into the wounded Knight's chamber, which was defeated as we have already seen by the interference of Urfried, who had been also on the watch to intercept the supposed monk. Rebecca retired to communicate to Ivanhoe the failure of her errand.

They had not much leisure to regret the failure of this source of intelligence, or to contrive by what means it might be supplied; for the noise within the castle, occasioned by the defensive preparations which had been considerable for some time, now increased into tenfold bustle and clamour. The heavy yet hasty step of the men-at-arms, traversed the battlements, or resounded on the narrow and winding passages and stairs which led to the various bartizans and points of defence. The voices of the knights were heard, animating their followers or directing measures of defence, while their commands were often drowned in the clashing of armour, or the clamorous shouts of those whom they addressed. Tremendous as these sounds were, and yet more terrible from the awful event which they presaged, there was a sublimity mixed with them, which Rebecca's high-toned mind could feel even in that moment of terror. Her eye kindled, although the blood fled from her cheeks; and there was a strange mixture of fear and of a thrilling sense of the sublime, as she repeated, half whispering to herself, half speaking to her companion, the sacred text,—"The quiver rattleth—the glittering spear and the shield—the noise of the captains and the shouting."

But Ivanhoe was like the war-horse of that sublime passage, glowing with impatience at his inactivity, and with his ardent desire to mingle in the affray of which these sounds were the introduction. "If I could but drag myself," he said, "to yonder window, that I might see how this brave game is like to go—if I had but bow to shoot a shaft, or battle-axe to strike were it but a single blow for our deliverance!—it is in vain—it is in vain—I am alike nerveless and weaponless."

"Fret not thyself, noble knight," answered Rebecca, "the sounds have ceased of a sudden—it may be they join not battle."

"Thou knowest nought of it," said Wilfred, impatiently; "this dead pause only shews that the men are at their posts on the walls, and expecting an instant attack; what we have heard was but the distant muttering of the storm—it will burst anon in all its fury.—Could I but reach yonder window!"

"Thou wilt but injure thyself by the attempt, noble knight," replied his attendant. Observing his extreme solicitude, she firmly added, "I myself will stand at the lattice, and describe to you as I can what passes without."

"You must not—you shall not!" exclaimed Ivanhoe; "each lattice, each aperture, will be soon a mark for the archers; some random shaft"——

"It shall be welcome," murmured Rebecca, as with firm pace she ascended two or three steps which led to the window of which they spoke.

"Rebecca, dear Rebecca!" exclaimed Ivanhoe, "this is no maiden's pastime—do not expose thyself to wounds and death, and render me for ever miserable for having given the occasion; at least, cover thyself with yonder ancient buckler, and shew as little of your person at the lattice as may be."

Following with wonderful promptitude the directions of Ivanhoe, and availing herself of the protection of the large ancient shield, which she placed against the lower part of the window, Rebecca, with tolerable security to herself, could witness part of what was passing without the castle, and report to Ivanhoe the preparations which the assailants were making for the storm. Indeed the situation which she thus obtained was peculiarly favourable for this purpose, because, being placed in an angle of the main building, Rebecca could not only see what passed beyond the precincts of the castle, but also commanded a view of the outwork likely to be the first object of the meditated assault. It was an exterior fortification of no great height or strength, intended to protect the postern-gate, through which Cedric had been recently dismissed by Front-de-Bœuf. The castle moat divided this species of barbican from the rest of the fortress, so that, in case of its being taken, it was easy to cut off the communication with the main building, by withdrawing the temporary bridge. In the outwork was a sally-port corresponding to the postern of the castle, and the whole was surrounded by a strong palisade. Rebecca could observe, from the number of men placed for the defence of this post, that the besieged entertained apprehensions for its safety; and from the mustering of the assailants in a direction nearly opposite to the outwork, it seemed no less plain that it had been selected as a vulnerable point of attack.

These appearances she hastily communicated to Ivanhoe, and added, "The skirts of the wood seem lined with archers, although only a few are advanced from its dark shadow."

"Under what banner?" asked Ivanhoe.

"Under no ensign of war which I can observe," answered Rebecca.

"A selcouth novelty," muttered the knight, "to advance to storm such a castle without pennon or banner displayed.—See'st thou who they be that act as leaders?"

"A knight, clad in sable armour, is the most conspicuous," said the Jewess; "he alone is armed from head to heel, and seems to assume the direction of all around him."

"What device does he bear on his shield?" replied Ivanhoe.

"Something resembling a bar of iron with a padlock painted blue on the black shield."

"A fetterlock and shacklebolt azure," said Ivanhoe; "I know not who may bear that device—but well I ween it might now be mine own. Canst thou not see the motto?"

"Scarce the device itself at this distance," replied Rebecca; "but when the sun glances fair upon his shield, it seems as I tell you."

"Seem there no other leaders?" continued the anxious enquirer.

"None of mark and distinction that I can behold from this station," said Rebecca, "but, doubtless, the other side of the castle is also assailed. They seem even now preparing to advance.—God of Zion, protect us!—What a dreadful sight!—Those who advance first bear huge shields, and defences made of plank—the others follow, bending their bows as they come on.—They raise their bows!—God of Moses, forgive the creatures thou hast made!"

Her description was here suddenly interrupted by the signal for assault, which was given by the blast of a shrill bugle, and at once answered by a flourish of the Norman trumpets from the battlements, which, mingled with the deep and hollow clang of the nakers (a species of kettle-drum), retorted in notes of defiance the challenge of the enemy. The shouts of both parties augmented the fearful din, the assailants crying, "Saint George for England!" and the Normans answering them with cries of "*En avant De Bracy!—Beau-seant! Beau-seant!—Front-de-Bœuf a la rescousse!*" according to the war-cries of their different commanders.

It was not, however, by clamour that the contest was to be decided, and the desperate efforts of the assailants were met by an equally vigorous defence on the part of the besieged. The archers, trained by their woodland pastimes to the most effective use of the long bow, shot, to use the appropriate phrase of the time, so "wholly together," that no point at which a defender could shew the least part of his person escaped their cloth-yard shafts. By this heavy discharge, which continued as thick and sharp as hail, while, notwithstanding, every arrow had its individual aim, and flew by scores together against each embrasure and opening in the parapets, as well as at every window where a defender either actually had post or might be suspected to be stationed,—by this sustained discharge, two or three of the garrison were slain, and several others wounded. But, confident in their armour of proof, and in the cover which their situation afforded, the followers of Front-de-Bœuf, and his allies, shewed an obstinacy in defence proportioned to the fury of the attack; replied with the discharge of their large cross-bows, as well as with long bows, slings, and other missiles, to the close and continued shower of arrows; and, as the assailants were necessarily but indifferently protected, did considerably more damage than they received at their hand. The whizzing of shafts and of missiles, on both sides, was only interrupted by the shouts which arose when either side inflicted or sustained some notable loss.

"And I must lie here like a bedridden monk," exclaimed Ivanhoe, "while the game that gives me freedom or death is played out by the hand of others!—Look from the window once again, kind maiden, but beware that you are not marked by the archers beneath—Look out once more, and tell me if they yet advance to the storm."

With patient courage, strengthened by the interval which she had employed in mental devotion, Rebecca again took post at the lattice, sheltering herself, however, so as not to be visible from beneath.

"What dost thou see, Rebecca?" again demanded the wounded knight.

"Nothing but the cloud of arrows, flying so thick as to dazzle mine eyes, and to hide the bowmen who shoot them."

"That cannot endure," said Ivanhoe; "if they press not right on to carry the castle by pure force of arms, the archery may avail but little against stone walls and bulwarks. Look for the knight of the fetterlock, fair Rebecca, and see how he bears himself; for as the leader is, so will his followers be."

"I see him not," said Rebecca.

"Foul craven!" exclaimed Ivanhoe; "does he blench from the helm when the wind blows highest?"

"He blenches not! he blenches not!" said Rebecca, "I see him now; he heads a body of men close under the outer barrier of the barbican.* —They pull down the piles and palisades; they hew down the barriers with axes—His high black plume floats abroad over the throng, like a raven over the field of the slain.—They have made a breach in the barriers—they rush in—they are thrust back!—Front-de-Bœuf heads the defenders, I see his gigantic form above the press. They throng again to the breach, and the pass is disputed hand to hand and man to man. God of Jacob! it is the meeting of two fierce tides—the conflict of two oceans moved by adverse winds."

She turned her head from the lattice, as if unable longer to endure a sight so terrible.

"Look forth again, Rebecca," said Ivanhoe, mistaking the cause of her retiring; "the archery must in some degree have ceased, since they are now fighting hand to hand—Look again, there is now less danger."

Rebecca again looked forth, and almost immediately exclaimed, "Holy prophets of the law! Front-de-Bœuf and the Black Knight fight hand to hand on the breach, amid the roar of their followers, who watch the progress of the strife—Heaven strike with the cause of the oppressed and of the captive!" She then uttered a loud shriek, and exclaimed, "He is down!—he is down!"

*Every Gothic castle and city had, beyond the outer-walls, a fortification composed of palisades, called the barriers, which were often the scene of severe skirmishes, as these must necessarily be carried before the walls themselves could be approached. Many of those valiant feats of arms which adorn the chivalrous pages of Froissart took place at the barriers of besieged places.

"Who is down?" cried Ivanhoe; "for our dear Lady's sake, tell me which has fallen?"

"The Black Knight," answered Rebecca, faintly; then instantly again shouted with joyful eagerness—"But no—but no!—The name of the Lord of Hosts be blessed!—He is on foot again, and fights as if there were twenty men's strength in his single arm—his sword is broken—he snatches an axe from a yeoman—he presses Front-de-Bœuf with blow on blow—the giant stoops and totters like an oak under the steel of the woodman—he falls—he falls!"

"Front-de-Bœuf!" exclaimed Ivanhoe.

"Front-de-Bœuf," answered the Jewess; "his men rush to the rescue, headed by the haughty Templar—their united force compels the champion to pause—they drag Front-de-Bœuf within the walls."

"The assailants have won the barriers, have they not?" said Ivanhoe.

"They have—they have—and they press the besieged hard upon the outer wall; some plant ladders, some swarm like bees, and endeavour to ascend upon the shoulders of each other—down go stones, beams, and trunks of trees upon their heads, and as fast as they bear the wounded to the rear, fresh men supply their place in the assault—Great God! hast thou given men thine own image, that it should be thus cruelly defaced by the hands of their brethren!"

"Think not of that," replied Ivanhoe; "this is no time for such thoughts.—who yield?—who push their way?"

"The ladders are thrown down," replied Rebecca, shuddering; "the soldiers lie grovelling under them like crushed reptiles—the besieged have the better."

"Saint George strike for us," said the Knight; "do the false yeomen give way?"

"No!" exclaimed Rebecca, "they bear themselves right yeomanly—The Black Knight approaches the postern with his huge axe. The thundering blows which he deals, you may hear them above all the din and shouts of the battle—stones and beams are hailed down on the bold champion—he regards them no more than if they were thistle-down or feathers."

"By Saint John of Acre," said Ivanhoe, raising himself joyfully on his couch, "methought there was but one man in England that might do such a deed."

"The postern gate shakes," continued Rebecca; "it crashes—it is splintered by his blows—it is broken down—they rush in—the out-work is won—Oh God!—they hurl the defenders from the battlements—they drive them into the moat—O men, if ye be indeed men, spare them that can resist no longer!"

"The bridge—the bridge which communicates with the castle—have they won that pass?" exclaimed Ivanhoe.

"No," replied Rebecca, "the Templar has destroyed the plank on which they crossed—few of the defenders escaped with him into the castle—the shrieks and cries which you hear tell the doom of the others—Alas! I see that it is still more difficult to look upon victory than upon battle."

"What do they now, maiden?" said Ivanhoe; "look forth yet again—this is no time to faint at bloodshed."

"It is over for the time," said Rebecca; "our friends strengthen themselves within the out-work which they have mastered, and it affords them so good a shelter from the foemen's shot, that the garrison only bestow a few bolts on it from interval to interval, as if rather to disquiet than effectually injure them."

"Our friends," said Wilfred, "will surely not abandon an enterprize so gloriously begun and an advantage so happily attained.—O no! I will put my faith in the good knight whose axe has rent heart-of-oak and bars of iron.—Singular," he again muttered to himself, "if there be two who can do a deed of such *derring-do**—a fetter-lock, and a shackle-bolt on a field sable—what may that mean?—seest thou nought else, Rebecca, by which the Black Knight may be distinguished?"

"Nothing," replied the Jewess; "all about him is black as the wing of the night raven. Nothing can I spy that may mark him further. But having once seen him put forth his strength in battle, methinks I could know him again among a thousand warriors—he rushes to the fray as if he were summoned to a banquet—there is more than mere strength, there seems as if the whole soul and spirit of the champion were given to every blow which he deals upon his enemies. God assoilzie him of the sin of bloodshed!—it is fearful, yet magnificent, to behold how the arm and heart of one man can triumph over hundreds."

"Rebecca," said Ivanhoe, "thou hast painted a hero. Surely they rest but to refresh their force, or to purvey the means of crossing the moat. Under such a leader as thou hast spoken this knight to be, there are no craven fears, no cold-blooded delays, no yielding up a gallant emprize; since the difficulties which render it arduous render it also glorious. I swear by the honour of my house—I vow by the name of my bright lady-love, I would endure ten years of captivity to fight for one day by that good knight's side in such a quarrel as this!"

"Alas!" said Rebecca, leaving her station at the window, and approaching the couch of the wounded knight, "this impatient yearning after action—this struggling with and repining at your present

* *Derring-do*—desperate courage.

weakness, will not fail to injure your returning health—How couldst thou hope to inflict wounds on others, ere that be healed which thou thyself hast received?"

"Rebecca," he replied, "thou knowest not how impossible it is for one trained to actions of chivalry, to remain passive as a priest, or a woman, when they are acting deeds of honour around him. The love of battle is the food upon which we live—the dust of the mellay is the breath of our nostrils!—we live not—we wish to live no longer than while we are victorious and renowned—Such, maiden, are the laws of chivalry to which we are sworn, and to which we offer all that we hold dear."

"Alas!" said the fair Jewess, "and what is it, valiant knight, save an offering of sacrifice to a demon of vain-glory, and a passing through the fire to Moloch?—what remains to you as the prize of all the blood you have spilled, of all the travail and pain you have endured, of all the tears which your deeds have caused, when death hath broken the strong man's spear, and overtaken the speed of his war-horse?"

"What remains?" echoed Ivanhoe; "Glory, maiden, glory! which gilds our sepulchre and embalms our name."

"Glory?" continued Rebecca; "alas, is the rusted mail which hangs as a hatchment over the champion's dim and mouldering tomb—is the defaced sculpture of the inscription which the ignorant monk can hardly read to the inquiring pilgrim—are these sufficient rewards for the sacrifice of every kindly affection, for a life spent miserably that ye make others miserable? Or is there such virtue in the rude rhymes of a wandering bard, that domestic love, kindly affection, peace and happiness, are so wildly bartered, to become the hero of these ballads which vagabond minstrels sing to drunken churls over their evening ale?"

"By the soul of Hereward!" replied the knight impatiently, "thou speakest, maiden, of thou knowest not what. Thou wouldst quench the pure light of chivalry, which alone distinguishes the noble from the base, the gentle knight from the churl and the savage; which rates our life far, far beneath the pitch of our honour; raises us victorious over pain, toil, and suffering, and teaches us to fear no evil but disgrace. Thou art no Christian, Rebecca; and to thee are unknown those high feelings which swell the bosom of a noble maiden when her lover hath done some deed of emprize which sanctions his flame. Chivalry!—why, maiden, it is the nurse of pure and high affection—the stay of the oppressed, the redresser of grievances, the curb of the power of the tyrant—nobility were but an empty name without her, and liberty finds the best protector in her lance and sword."

"I am, indeed," said Rebecca, "sprung from a race whose courage was distinguished in the defence of their own land, but who warred not, even while yet a nation, save at the command of the Deity, or in defending their country from oppression. The sound of the trumpet wakes Judah no longer, and her dispersed children are now but the unresisting victims of hostile and military oppression. Well hast thou spoken, Sir Knight,—until the God of Jacob shall raise up for his chosen people a second Gideon, or a new Maccabæus, it ill beseemeth the Jewish damsel to speak of battle or of war."

The high-minded maiden concluded the argument in a tone of sorrow, which deeply expressed her sense of the degradation of her people, embittered perhaps by the idea that Ivanhoe considered her as one not entitled to entertain, or capable of expressing, sentiments of honour and generosity.

"How little he knows this bosom," she said, "to imagine that cowardice and meanness of soul must needs be its guests, because I have censured the fantastic chivalry of the Nazarenes! Would to heaven that the shedding of mine own blood, drop by drop, could redeem the captivity of Judah! Nay, would to God it could avail to set free my father, and this his benefactor, from the chains of the oppressor! The proud Christian should then see whether the daughter of God's chosen people dared not to die as bravely as the proudest Nazarene maiden, that boasts her descent from some petty chieftain of the rude and frozen north!"

She then looked towards the couch of the wounded knight.

"He sleeps," she said; "nature exhausted by sufferance and by the waste of spirits, his wearied frame embraces the first moment of temporary relaxation to sink into slumber. Alas! is it a crime that I should look upon him, when it may be for the last time?—When yet but a short space, and those fair features will be no longer animated by the bold and buoyant spirit which forsakes them not even in sleep!—when the nostril shall be distended, the mouth agape, the eyes fixed and blood-shot; and when the proud and noble knight may be trodden on by the lowest caitiff of this accursed castle, yet stir not when the heel is lifted up against him!—And my father!—oh, my father! evil is it with his daughter, when his grey hairs are not remembered because of the golden locks of youth!—What know I but that these evils are the messengers of Jehovah's wrath to the unnatural child, who thinks of a stranger's captivity before a parent's? who forgets the desolation of Judah, and looks upon the comeliness of a Gentile and a stranger?—But I will tear this folly from my heart, though every fibre bleed as I rend it away!"

She wrapped herself closely in her veil, and sat down at a distance from the couch of the wounded knight, with her back turned towards it, fortifying or endeavouring to fortify her mind, not only against the impending evils from without, but also against those treacherous feelings which assailed her from within.

Chapter Sixteen

Approach the chamber, look upon his bed.
His is the passing of no peaceful ghost,
Which, as the lark arises to the sky,
Mid morning's sweetest breeze and softest dew,
Is wing'd to heaven by good men's sighs and tears!—
Anselm parts otherwise.

Old Play.

DURING the interval of quiet which followed the first success of the besiegers, while the one party was preparing to follow their advantage, and the other to strengthen their means of defence, the Templar and De Bracy held brief council together in the hall of the castle.

"Where is Front-de-Bœuf?" said the latter, who had superintended the defence of the fortress on the other side; "men say he hath been slain."

"He lives," said the Templar coolly, "lives as yet; but had he worn the bull's head of which he bears the name, and ten plates of iron to fence it withal, he must have gone down before yonder fatal axe. Yet a few hours, and Front-de-Bœuf is with his fathers—a powerful limb lopped off Prince John's enterprize."

"And a brave addition to the kingdom of Satan," said De Bracy; "this comes of reviling saints and angels, and ordering images of holy things and holy men to be flung down on the heads of these rascaille yeomen."

"Go to—thou art a fool," said the Templar; "thy superstition is upon a level with Front-de-Bœuf's want of faith; neither of you can render a reason for your belief or unbelief."

"Benedicite, Sir Templar," replied De Bracy, "I pray you to keep better rule with your tongue when I am the theme of it. By the Mother of Heaven, I am a better Christian man than thou and thy fellowship; for the *bruit* goeth shrewdly out, that the most holy Order of the Temple of Zion nurseth not a few heretics within its bosom, and that Sir Brian de Bois-Guilbert is of the number."

"Care not thou for such reports," said the Templar; "but let us think of making good the castle.—How fought these villain yeomen on thy side?"

"Like fiends incarnate," said De Bracy. "They swarmed close up to the walls, headed, as I think, by the knave who won the prize at the archery, for I knew his horn and baldrick. And this is old Fitzurse's boasted policy, encouraging these malapert knaves to rebel against us! Had I not been armed in proof, the villain had marked me down seven times with as little remorse as if I had been a buck in season. He told every rivet on my armour with a cloth-yard shaft, that rapped against my ribs with as little remorse as if my bones had been of iron—But that I wore a shirt of Spanish mail under my plate-coat, I had been fairly sped."

"But you maintained your post," said the Templar. "We lost the outwork on our part."

"That is a shrewd loss," said De Bracy; "the knaves will find cover there to assault the castle more closely, and may, if not well watched, gain some unguarded corner of a tower, or some forgotten window, and so break in upon us. Our numbers are too few for the defence of every point, and the men complain that they can nowhere shew themselves, but they are a mark for as many arrows as a parish-butt on a holy-day even. Front-de-Bœuf is dying too, so we shall receive no more aid from his bull's head and brutal strength. How think you, Sir Brian, were we not better make a virtue of necessity, and compound with the rogues by delivering up our prisoners?"

"How?" exclaimed the Templar; "deliver up our prisoners, and stand an object alike of ridicule and execration, as the doughty warriors who dared by a night attack to possess themselves of the persons of a party of defenceless travellers, yet could not make good a strong castle against a vagabond troop of outlaws, led by swine-herds, jesters, and the very refuse of mankind?—Shame on thy counsel, Maurice de Bracy!—The ruins of this castle shall bury both my body and my shame, ere I tamely consent to such base and dishonourable composition."

"Let us to the walls, then," said De Bracy carelessly; "that man never breathed, be he Turk or Templar, who holds life at lighter rate than I do. But I trust there is no dishonour in wishing I had here some two scores of my gallant troop of Free Companions?—Ah, my brave lances! if ye knew but how hard your captain was this day bestad, how soon would I see my banner at the head of your clump of spears! and how short while would these rabble villains stand to endure your encounter!"

"Wish for whom thou wilt," said the Templar, "but let us make what defence we can with the soldiers who remain—They are chiefly Front-de-Bœuf's followers, hated by the English for a thousand acts of insolence and oppression."

"The better," replied De Bracy; "the rugged slaves will defend themselves to the last drop of blood, ere they encounter the vengeance of the peasants without. Let us up and be doing, then, Brian de Bois-Guilbert; and, live or die, thou shalt see Maurice de Bracy bear himself this day as a gentleman of blood and lineage."

"To the walls!" answered the Templar; and they both ascended the battlements to do all which skill could dictate, and manhood accomplish, in defence of the place. They readily agreed that the point of greatest danger was that opposite to the out-work, of which the assailants had possessed themselves. The castle indeed was divided from that barbican by the moat, and it was impossible that the besiegers could assail the postern door, with which the out-work corresponded, without surmounting that obstacle; but it was the opinion both of the Templar and De Bracy, that they would endeavour, by a formidable assault, to draw the chief part of the defenders' observations to this point, and take measures to avail themselves of every negligence which might take place in the defence elsewhere. To guard against such an evil, their numbers only permitted the knights to place centinels from space to space along the walls in communication with each other, who might give the alarm whenever danger was threatened. Meanwhile, they agreed that De Bracy should command the defence at the postern, and the Templar should keep with him a score of men or thereabouts as a body of reserve, ready to rush to any other point which might be suddenly threatened. The loss of the barbican had also this unfortunate effect, that, notwithstanding the superior height of the castle walls, the besieged could not see from them, with the same precision as before, the operations of the enemy; for some straggling underwood approached so near the sally-port of the out-work, that the assailants might introduce into it whatever force they thought proper, not only under cover, but even without the knowledge of the defenders. Utterly uncertain, therefore, upon what point the storm was to burst, De Bracy and his companion were under the necessity of providing against every possible contingence, and their followers, however brave, experienced the anxious dejection of mind incident to men inclosed by enemies, who possessed the power of chusing their time and mode of attack.

Meanwhile, the lord of the beleaguered and endangered castle lay upon a bed of bodily pain and mental agony. He had not the usual resource of bigots in that superstitious period, most of whom were wont to atone for the crimes they were guilty of by liberality to the Church, stupifying by this means their remorse by the idea of atonement and forgiveness; and although the repose which sinners thus purchased no more resembled the peace of mind which follows on sincere repentance, than the turbid stupefaction procured by opium resembles healthy and natural slumbers, it was still a state of mind preferable to the agonies of awakened remorse. But among the vices of Front-de-Bœuf, a hard and gripple man, avarice was predominant; and he preferred setting church and churchmen at defiance, to purchasing from them pardon and absolution at the price of treasure and of manors. Nor did the Templar, an infidel of another stamp, justly characterize his associate, when he said Front-de-Bœuf could assign no cause for his unbelief and contempt for the established faith; for the Baron would have alleged that the Church sold her wares too dear, that the spiritual freedom which she put up to sale was only to be bought like that of the chief captain at Jerusalem, "with a great sum," and Front-de-Bœuf preferred denying the virtue of the medicine, to paying the expense of the physician. But the moment had now arrived when earth and all its treasures were gliding from before his eyes, and when his heart, though hard as a nether millstone, became appalled as he gazed forward into the waste darkness of futurity. The fever of his body aided the impatience and agony of his mind, and his death-bed exhibited a mixture of the newly awakened feelings of remorse, combating with the fixed and inveterate reprobacy of his disposition;—a fearful state of mind, only to be equalled in those tremendous regions, where there are complaints without hope, remorse without repentance, a horrid sense of present agony, and a presentiment that it cannot cease or be diminished!

"Where be these dog-priests now," growled the Baron, "who set such price on their ghostly mummery?—Where be all those unshod Carmelites, for whom old Front-de-Bœuf founded the convent of St Anne's, robbing his heir of many a fair rood of meadow, and many a fat field and close—Where be the greedy hounds now?—swilling, I warrant me, at the ale, or playing their juggling tricks at the bed-side of some miserly churl.—Me, the heir of their founder—me, whom their foundation binds them to pray for—me—ungrateful villains as they are!—they suffer to die like the houseless hare on yonder common, unshriven and unhouseled!—Tell the Templar to come hither—he is a priest, and may do something—But no!—as well confess myself to the devil as to Brian de Bois-Guilbert, who recks neither of heaven nor of hell.—I have heard old men talk of prayer—prayer by their own voice—such need not to court or to bribe the false priest—But I—I dare not!"

"Lives Reginald Front-de-Bœuf," said a broken yet shrill voice close to his bed-side, "to say there is that which he dares not!"

The evil conscience and the shaken nerves of Front-de-Bœuf heard, in this strange interruption to his soliloquy, the voice of one of those demons, who, as the superstition of the times believed, beset the beds of dying men, to distract their thoughts, and turn them from the meditations and duties which concerned their eternal welfare. He shuddered and drew himself together; but, instantly summoning up his wonted resolution, exclaimed, "Who is there?—what art thou, that darest to echo my words in a tone like that of the night-raven?—Come before my couch that I may see thee."

"I am thine evil angel, Reginald Front-de-Bœuf," replied the voice.

"Let me behold thee then in thy bodily shape, if thou be'st indeed a fiend," replied the dying knight; "think not that I will blench from thee!—By the eternal dungeon, could I but grapple with these horrors that hover around me as I have done with mortal dangers, heaven nor hell should say that I shrunk from the conflict!"

"Think on thy sins, Reginald Front-de-Bœuf—on rebellion, on murder, on rapine!—Who stirred up the licentious John to war against his grey-headed father—against his generous"——

"Man or fiend, priest or devil," replied Front-de-Bœuf, "thou liest in thy throat!—Not I stirred John to rebellion—not I alone—there were fifty knights and barons, the flower of the midland counties—better men never laid lance in rest—And must I answer for the fault done by fifty?—False fiend, I defy thee! Depart, and haunt my couch no more—let me die in peace if thou be mortal—if thou be indeed a demon, thy time is not yet come."

"In peace thou shalt NOT die," repeated the voice; "even in death shalt thou think on thy murders—on the groans which this castle has echoed—on the blood that is ingrained in its walls!"

"Thou canst not shake me by thy petty malice," answered Front-de-Bœuf with a ghastly and constrained laugh. "The infidel Jew—it was merit with heaven to deal with him as I did, else wherefore are men canonized who dip their hands in the blood of Saracens?—The Saxon porkers, whom I have slain, they were the foes of my country, and of my lineage, and of my liege lord.—Ho! ho! thou see'st there is no crevice in my coat of plate—Art thou fled?—art thou silenced?"

"No, foul parricide!" replied the voice; "think of thy father!—think of his death!—think of his banquet-room, flooded with his gore, and by the hand of a son!"

"Nay!" answered the Baron, after a long pause, "an thou knowest that, thou art indeed the author of evil, and as omniscient as the monks call thee!—That secret I deemed locked in my own breast, and in that of one beside—the temptress, the partaker of my guilt.—Go, leave me, fiend! and seek the Saxon witch Ulrica, who alone could tell thee what she and I alone witnessed—Go, I say, to her, who washed the wounds, and straighted the corpse, and gave to the slain man the outward show of one parted in time and in the course of nature

—Go to her—she was my temptress, the foul provoker, the more foul rewarder of the deed—let her, as well as I, taste of the tortures which anticipate hell!"

"She already tastes them," said Ulrica, stepping before the couch of Front-de-Bœuf; "she hath long drunken of this cup, and its bitterness is sweetened to see that thou dost partake it.—Grind not thy teeth, Front-de-Bœuf—roll not thine eyes—clench not thy hand, nor shake it at me with that gesture of menace!—The hand which this morning could, like that of the renowned ancestor who gained thy name, have broken with one stroke the skull of a mountain-bull, is now unnerved and powerless as mine own!"

"Vile murderous hag!" replied Front-de-Bœuf, "detestable screech-owl! is it then thou art come to exult over the ruins thou hast assisted to lay low?"

"Ay, Reginald Front-de-Bœuf," answered she, "it is Ulrica!—it is the daughter of the murdered Torquil Wolfganger!—it is the sister of his slaughtered sons!—it is she who demands of thee, and of thy father's house, father and kindred, name and fame, body and soul—all that she has lost by the name of Front-de-Bœuf!—Think of my wrongs, Front-de-Bœuf, and answer me if I speak not truth. Thou hast been my evil angel, and I will be thine—I will dog thee till the very instant of dissolution."

"Detestable fury!" answered Front-de-Bœuf, "that moment shalt thou never witness—Ho! Giles, Clement, and Eustace! Saint Maur and Stephen! seize this damned witch, and hurl her from the battlements headlong—she has betrayed us to the Saxon.—Ho! Saint Maur! Clement! false-hearted knaves, where tarry ye?"

"Call on them again, valiant Baron," said the hag, with a smile of grisly mockery; "summon thy vassals around thee, doom them that loiter to the scourge and the dungeon—But know, mighty chief," she continued, suddenly changing her tone, "thou shalt have neither answer, nor aid, nor obedience at their hands.—Listen to these horrid sounds," for the din of the recommenced assault and defence now rung fearfully loud from the battlements of the castle; "in that war-cry is the downfall of thy house—The blood-cemented fabric of Front-de-Bœuf's power totters to the foundation, and before the foes he most despised!—The Saxon, Reginald!—the scorned Saxon assails thy walls!—Why liest thou here, like a worn-out hind, when the Saxon storms thy place of strength?"

"Gods and fiends!" exclaimed the wounded knight; "O for one moment's strength, to drag myself to the mellay, and perish as becomes my name!"

"Think not of it, valiant warrior!" replied she; "thou shalt die no soldier's death, but perish like the fox in his den, when peasants have set fire to the cover around it."

"Hateful hag! thou liest," exclaimed Front-de-Bœuf; "my followers bear them bravely—my walls are strong and high—my comrades in arms fear not a whole host of Saxons, were they headed by Hengist and Horsa!—The war-cry of the Templar and of the Free Companions rises high over the conflict! And by mine honour, when we kindle the blazing beacon, for joy of our defence, it shall consume thee, body and bones; and I shall live to hear thou art gone from earthly fires to those of that hell, which never sent forth an incarnate fiend more utterly diabolical!"

"Hold thy belief," replied Ulrica, "till the proof teach thee—But, no!" she said, interrupting herself, "thou shalt know, even now, the doom, which all thy power, strength, and courage is unable to avert, though it is prepared for thee by this feeble hand.—Markest thou the smouldering and suffocating vapour which already eddies in sable folds through the chamber?—Didst thou think it was but the darkening of thy bursting eyes—the difficulty of thy cumbered breathing?—No! Front-de-Bœuf, there is another cause—Rememberest thou not the magazine of fuel that is stored beneath these apartments?"

"Woman!" he exclaimed with fury, "thou hast not set fire to it?—By heaven thou hast, and the castle is in flames!"

"They are fast rising at least," said Ulrica, with frightful composure; "and a signal shall soon wave to warn the avengers to press hard those who would extinguish them.—Farewell, Front-de-Bœuf!—May Mista, Skogula, and Zernebock, gods of the ancient Saxons—fiends, as the priests now call them—supply the place of comforters at your dying bed, which Ulrica now relinquishes!—Yet know, if it will give thee comfort to know it, that Ulrica is bound to the same dark coast with thyself, the companion of thy punishment as the companion of thy guilt.—And now, parricide, farewell for ever!—May each stone of this vaulted roof find a tongue to echo that title into thine ear!"

So saying, she left the apartment; and Front-de-Bœuf could hear the crash of the ponderous key as she locked and double-locked the door behind her, thus cutting off the most slender chance of escape. In the extremity of agony he shouted upon his servants and allies—"Stephen and Saint Maur!—Clement and Giles!—I burn here unaided!—To the rescue—to the rescue, brave Bois-Guilbert, valiant De Bracy—it is Front-de-Bœuf who calls!—It is your master, ye traitor squires!—Your ally—your brother in arms, ye perjured and faithless knights!—All the curses due to traitors upon your recreant heads, do you abandon me to perish thus miserably!—They hear me not—they cannot hear me—my voice is lost in the din of battle.—The smoke rolls thicker and thicker—the fire has caught upon the floor below—O for one draught of the air of heaven, were it to be purchased by instant annihilation!" And in the mad phrenzy of despair, the wretch now shouted with the shouts of the fighters, now muttered curses on himself, on mankind, and on Heaven itself.—"The red fire flashes through the thick smoke!" he exclaimed; "the demon marches against me under the banner of his own element—Foul spirit, avoid!—I go not with thee without my comrades—all, all are thine, that garrison these walls—thinkest thou, Front-de-Bœuf will be singled out to go alone?—No—the infidel Templar—the licentious De Bracy—Ulrica, the foul murthering strumpet—the men who aided my enterprizes—the dog Saxons and accursed Jews, who are my prisoners—all, all shall attend me—a goodly fellowship as ever took the downward road—Ha, ha, ha!" and he laughed in his frenzy till the vaulted roof rung again. "Who laughed there!" exclaimed Front-de-Bœuf, in altered mood, for the noise of the conflict did not prevent the echoes of his own frenzied laughter from returning upon his ear—"Who laughed there?—Ulrica, was it thou?—Speak, witch, and I forgive thee—for, only thou or the fiend of hell himself could have laughed at such a moment. Avaunt—avaunt!"——

But it were impious to trace any farther the picture of the blasphemer and parricide's death-bed.

END OF VOLUME SECOND

IVANHOE

VOLUME III

Chapter One

> Once more unto the breach, dear friends, once more,
> Or close the wall up with our English dead.
> ———————And you, good yeomen,
> Whose limbs were made in England, shew us here
> The mettle of your pasture—let us swear
> That you are worth your breeding.
>
> *King Henry V.*

CEDRIC, after his liberation from captivity, was received with loud shouts of gratulation by the friendly bands which had assembled for his assistance, and for that of his companions in misfortune. But the emergency did not leave time for much greeting, and he was quickly engaged with the principal leaders of the besiegers in serious discussion of the measures which were to be adopted. The Saxon failed not, by every argument he could suggest, to encourage the others to persevere in the attack on the place. He described the hazardous position of those whom he had left in the power of Front-de-Bœuf and his confederates and, although not greatly confiding in Ulrica's message, omitted not to communicate her promise to the Black Knight and Locksley. They were well pleased to find that they had a friend within the place, who might, in the moment of need, be able to facilitate their entrance, and readily agreed with the Saxon that a storm, under whatever disadvantages, ought to be attempted, as the only means of liberating the prisoners now in the hands of the cruel Front-de-Bœuf.

"The royal blood of Alfred is endangered," said Cedric.

"The honour of a noble lady is in peril," said the Black Knight.

"And, by the Saint Christopher at my baldric," said the good yeoman, "were there no other cause than the safety of that poor faithful knave, Wamba, I would jeopard a joint ere a hair of his head were hurt."

"And so would I," said the Friar; "what, sirs! We are not all born to be clerks—I trust well that a fool—I mean, d'ye see me, sirs, a fool that is free of his guild and master of his craft, and, with all his jests, gibes and quiddities, can give as much relish and savour to a cup of wine as ever a flitch of bacon can—I say, brethren, such a fool shall never want a wise clerk to pray for or fight for him at a strait, while I can say a mass or flourish a partizan."

And with that he made his heavy halbert to play around his head as a shepherd boy flourishes his little crook.

"True, Holy Clerk," said the Black Knight; "true as if Saint Dunstan himself had said it.—And now, good Locksley, were it not well that noble Cedric should assume the direction of this assault?"

"Not a jot, I," returned Cedric; "I have never been wont to study either how to take in or how to hold out those abodes of tyrannic power, which the Normans have erected in this groaning land. I will fight among the foremost; but my honest neighbours well know I am not a trained soldier in the discipline of wars, or the attack of strongholds."

"Since it stands thus with noble Cedric," said Locksley, "I am most willing to take on me the direction of the archery; and ye shall hang me up on my own Trysting-tree, an the defenders be permitted to shew themselves over the walls without being stuck with as many shafts as there are cloves in a gammon of bacon at Christmas."

"Well said, stout yeoman, for the honour of the long bow," said the Black Knight; "and if I be thought worthy to have a charge in this matter, and can find among these brave men as many as are willing to follow a true knight, for so I may call myself, I am ready, with such skill as my experience has taught me, to lead them to the attack of these walls."

The parts being thus distributed to the leaders, they commence l the first assault, of which the reader already has heard the issue.

When the barbican was carried, the Sable Knight sent notice of the happy event to Locksley, requesting him, at the same time, to keep such an observation on the castle as might prevent the defenders from combining their force for a sudden sally, and recovering the out-work that they had lost. This the knight was chiefly desirous of avoiding, conscious that the men whom he led, being hasty and untrained voluntaries, imperfectly armed and unaccustomed to discipline, must upon any sudden attack fight at great disadvantage with the veteran soldiers of the Norman knights, who were well provided with arms both defensive and offensive; and who, to match the zeal and high spirit of the besiegers, had all the confidence which arises from perfect discipline and the habitual use of weapons.

The knight employed this interval in causing to be constructed a sort of floating bridge or long raft, by means of which he hoped to cross the moat in despite of the resistance of the enemy. This was a work of some time, which the leaders the less regretted, as it gave Ulrica time to execute her plan of a diversion in their favour, whatever that might be.

But when the raft was completed, "It avails not waiting here longer," said the Black Knight; "the sun is descending to the west—and I have that upon my hands which will not permit me to tarry with you another day. Besides, it is a marvel if the horsemen come not upon us from York, unless we speedily accomplish our purpose. Wherefore, one of ye go to Locksley, and bid him commence a discharge of arrows on the opposite side of the castle, and move forward as if about to assault it; and you, true English hearts, stand by me, and be ready to thrust the raft endlong across the moat whenever the postern on our side is thrown open. Follow me boldly across, and aid me to burst yon sally-port in the main wall of the castle. As many of you as like not this service, or are but ill armed to meet it, do you man the top of the outwork, draw your bow-strings to your ears, and mind you quell with your shot whatever shall appear to man the rampart—Noble Cedric, wilt thou take the direction of those which remain?"

"Not so, by the soul of Hereward!" said the Saxon; "lead I cannot; but may posterity curse me in my grave, if I follow not with the foremost wherever thou shalt point the way—The quarrel is mine, and well it becomes me to be in the van of the battle."

"Yet, bethink thee, noble Saxon!" said the knight, "thou hast neither hauberk nor corslet, nor aught but that light helmet, target, and sword."

"The better!" answered Cedric; "I shall be the lighter to climb these walls. And, forgive the boast, Sir Knight, thou shalt this day see the naked breast of a Saxon as boldly presented to the battle as ever ye beheld the steel corslet of a Norman."

"In the name of God, then," said the knight, "fling open the door, and launch the floating bridge."

The portal, which led from the inner-wall of the barbican to the moat, and which corresponded with a sally-port in the main wall of the castle, was now suddenly opened; the temporary bridge was then thrust forward, and soon flashed in the waters, extending its length between the castle and outwork, and furnishing a slippery and precarious passage for two men abreast to cross the moat. Well aware of the importance of taking the foe by surprise, the Black Knight, closely followed by Cedric, threw himself upon the bridge, and reached the opposite side. Here he began to thunder with his axe on the gate of the castle, protected in part from the shot and stones cast by the defenders by the ruins of the former drawbridge, which the Templar had demolished in his retreat from the barbican, leaving the counterpoize still attached to the upper part of the portal. The followers of the knight had no such shelter; two were instantly shot with cross-bow bolts, and two more fell into the moat; the others retreated back into the barbican.

The situation of Cedric and of the Black Knight was now truly dangerous, and would have been still more so, but for the constancy of the archers in the barbican, who ceased not to shower their arrows upon the battlements, distracting the attention of those by whom they were manned, and thus affording a respite to their two chiefs from the storm of missiles by which they must have been otherwise overwhelmed. But their situation was eminently perilous, and was becoming more so with every moment.

"Shame on ye all!" cried De Bracy to the soldiers around him; "do ye call yourselves cross-bowmen, and let these two dogs keep their station under the walls of the castle?—Heave over the coping stones from the battlements, an better may not be—Get pick-axe and levers, and down with that huge pinnacle," pointing to a heavy piece of stone carved-work that projected from the parapet.

At this moment the besiegers caught sight of the red flag upon the angle of the tower which Ulrica had described to Cedric. The good yeoman Locksley was the first who was aware of it, as he was hasting to the outwork, impatient to see the progress of the assault.

"Saint George!" he cried, "Merry Saint George for England!—To the charge, bold yeomen!—why leave ye the good knight and the noble Cedric to storm the pass alone?—Make in, mad Priest, show thou canst fight for thy rosary—make in, brave yeomen!—the castle is ours, we have friends within—See yonder flag, it is the appointed signal—Torquilstone is ours!—think of honour, think of spoil—one effort, and the place is ours."

With that he bent his good bow, and sent a shaft right through the breast of one of the men-at-arms, who, under De Bracy's direction, was loosening a fragment from one of the battlements to precipitate on the heads of Cedric and the Black Knight. A second soldier caught from the hands of the dying man the iron crow, with which he heaved at and had loosened the stone pinnacle, when, receiving an arrow through his head-piece, he dropped from the battlements into the moat a dead man. The men-at-arms were daunted, for no armour seemed proof against the shot of this tremendous archer.

"Do you give ground, base knaves!" said De Bracy; "*Mount joye Saint Dennis!*—Give me the lever."

And, snatching it up, he again assailed the loosened pinnacle, which was of weight enough, if thrown down, not only to have destroyed the remnant of the drawbridge, which sheltered the two foremost assailants, but also to have sunk the rude float of planks over which they had crossed. All saw the danger, and the boldest, even the stout Friar himself, avoided setting foot on the raft. Thrice did Locksley bend his shaft against De Bracy, and thrice did his arrow bound back from the knight's armour of proof.

"A curse on thy Spanish steel-coat!" said Locksley, "had English smith forged it, these arrows had gone through, an as it had been silk or sendal." He then began to call out, "Comrades! friends! noble Cedric! bear back, and let the ruin fall."

His warning voice was unheard, for the din which the knight himself occasioned by his strokes on the postern would have drowned twenty war-trumpets. The faithful Gurth indeed sprung forwards on the planked bridge to warn Cedric of his impending fate, or to share it with him. But his warning would have come too late; the massive pinnacle already tottered, and De Bracy would have accomplished his purpose, had not the voice of the Templar sounded in his ear.

"All is lost, De Bracy, the castle burns."

"Thou art mad to say so," replied the knight.

"It is all in a light flame on the western side. I have striven in vain to extinguish it."

With the stern coolness which formed the basis of his character, Brian de Bois-Guilbert communicated this hideous intelligence, which was not so calmly received by his astounded comrade.

"Saints of paradise!" said De Bracy; "what is to be done? I vow to Saint Nicholas of Limoges a candlestick of pure gold"——

"Spare thy vow," said the Templar, "and mark me. Lead thy men down, as if to a sally; throw the postern gate open—There are but two men who occupy the float, fling them into the moat, and push across for the barbican. I will sally from the main-gate, and attack the barbican on the outside; and if we can regain that post, be assured we shall defend ourselves until we are relieved, or at least they grant us fair quarter."

"It is well thought upon," said De Bracy; "I will play my part—Templar, thou wilt not fail me?"

"Hand and glove, I will not!" said Bois-Guilbert. "But haste thee, in the name of God!"

De Bracy hastily drew his men together, and rushed down to the postern gate, which he caused instantly to be thrown open. But scarce was this done ere the portentous strength of the Black Knight forced his way inward in despite of De Bracy and his followers. Two of the foremost instantly fell, and the rest gave way in despite of their leader's efforts to stop them.

"Dogs!" said De Bracy, "will ye let *two* win our only pass for safety?"

"He is the devil!" said a veteran man-at-arms, bearing back from the blows of their sable antagonist.

"And if he be the devil," replied De Bracy, "would you fly from him into the mouth of hell?—The castle burns behind us, villains!—let despair give you courage, or let me forward, I will cope with this champion myself."

And well and chivalrously did De Bracy that day maintain the fame he had acquired in the civil wars of that dreadful period. The vaulted passage to which the postern gave entrance, and in which these two redoubted champions were now fighting hand to hand, rung with the furious blows which they dealt each other, De Bracy with his sword, the Black Knight with his ponderous axe. At length the Norman received a blow, which, though its force was partly parried by his shield, for otherwise never more would De Bracy have moved limb, descended yet with such violence on his crest, that he measured his length on the paved floor.

"Yield thee, De Bracy," said the Black Champion, stooping over him, and holding against the bars of his helmet the fatal poniard with which the knights dispatched their adversaries, (and which was called the dagger of mercy),—"yield thee, Maurice De Bracy, rescue or no rescue, or thou art but a dead man."

"I will not yield," replied De Bracy faintly, "to an unknown conqueror. Tell me thy name, or work thy pleasure on me—it shall never be said that Maurice De Bracy was prisoner to a nameless churl."

The Black Knight whispered something into the ear of the vanquished.

"I yield me to be true prisoner, rescue or no rescue," answered the Norman, exchanging his tone of stern and determined obstinacy for one of the deepest submission.

"Go to the barbican," said the victor, in a tone of authority, "and there wait my further orders."

"Yet first, let me say," said De Bracy, "what it imports thee to know. Wilfred of Ivanhoe is wounded and a prisoner, and will perish in the burning castle without present help."

"Wilfred of Ivanhoe!" exclaimed the Black Knight—"prisoner, and perish!—the life of every man in the castle shall answer it if a hair of his head be singed—Shew me his chamber."

"Ascend yonder winding stair—it leads to his apartment—Wilt thou not accept my guidance?"

"No. To the barbican, and there wait my orders. I trust thee not, De Bracy."

During this combat and the brief conversation which ensued, Cedric, at the head of a body of men, among whom the Friar was conspicuous, pushed across the bridge so soon as they saw the postern open, and drove back the dispirited and despairing followers of De Bracy, of whom some asked quarter, some offered vain resistance, and the greater part fled towards the court-yard. De Bracy himself arose from the ground, and cast a sorrowful glance after his conqueror. "He trusts me not," he repeated; "but have I deserved his trust?" He then lifted his sword from the floor, took off his helmet in token of submission, and, going to the barbican, gave up his sword to Locksley, whom he met by the way.

As the fire augmented, symptoms of it became soon apparent in the chamber, where Ivanhoe was watched and tended by the Jewess Rebecca. He had been awakened from his brief slumber by the noise of the battle; and his attendant was, at his anxious desire, again placed at the window to watch and report to him the fate of the attack, which for some time prevented either from observing the increase of the smouldering and stifling vapour. At length the volumes of smoke which rolled into the apartment—the cries for water, which were heard even above the din of the battle, made them sensible of the progress of this new danger.

"The castle burns," said Rebecca; "it burns!—What can we do to save ourselves?"

"Fly, Rebecca, and save thine own life," said Ivanhoe, "for no human aid can avail me."

"I will not fly," said Rebecca, "we will be saved or perish together—And yet, great God!—my father, my father—what will be his fate!"

At this moment the door of the apartment flew open, and the Templar presented himself,—a ghastly figure, for his gilded armour was both broken and bloody, and the plume was partly shorn away, partly burned from his casque. "I have found thee," said he to Rebecca; "thou shalt prove I will keep my word to share weal and woe with thee—There is but one path to safety, I have cut my way through fifty dangers to point it to thee—up, and instantly follow me."

"Alone," answered Rebecca, "I will not follow thee. If thou wert born of woman—if thou hast but a touch of human charity in thee—if thy heart be not hard as thy breast-plate—save my aged father—save this wounded knight."

"A knight," answered the Templar, with his characteristic calmness, "a knight, Rebecca, must encounter his fate whether it meet him in the shape of sword or of flame—and who recks how or where a Jew meets with his?"

"Savage warrior," replied Rebecca, "rather will I perish in the flames than accept safety from thee!"

"Thou shalt not chuse, Rebecca—once didst thou foil me, but never mortal did so twice."

So saying, he seized on the terrified maiden, who filled the air with her shrieks, and bore her out of the room in his arms in spite of her cries, and without regarding the menaces and defiance which Ivanhoe thundered against him. "Hound of the Temple, stain to thine Order—set free the damsel! Traitor of Bois-Guilbert, it is Ivanhoe commands thee!—Villain, I will have thy heart's-blood."

"I had not found thee, Wilfred," said the Black Knight, who at that instant entered the apartment, "but for thy shouts."

"If thou be'st true knight," said Wilfred, "think not of me—pursue yon ravisher—save the Lady Rowena—look to the noble Cedric."

"In their turn," answered he of the Fetterlock, "but thine is first."

And seizing on Ivanhoe, he bore him off with as much ease as the Templar had carried off Rebecca, rushed with him to the postern, and having there delivered his burthen to the care of two yeomen, he again entered the castle to assist in the rescue of the other prisoners.

One turret was now in bright flames, which flashed out furiously from window and shot-hole. But in other parts, the great thickness of the walls and the vaulted roofs of the apartments, resisted the progress of the flames, and there the rage of man still triumphed, as the scarce more dreadful element held mastery elsewhere; for the besiegers pursued the defenders of the castle from chamber to chamber, and satiated in their blood the vengeance which had long animated them against the soldiers of the tyrant Front-de-Bœuf. Most of the garrison resisted to the uttermost—few of them asked quarter—none received it. The air was filled with groans and clashing of arms—the floors were slippery with the blood of despairing and expiring wretches.

Through this scene of confusion, Cedric rushed in quest of Rowena, while the faithful Gurth, following him closely through the mellay, neglected his own safety while he strove to avert the blows which were aimed at his master. The noble Saxon was so fortunate as to reach his ward's apartment just as she had abandoned all hope of safety, and, with a crucifix clasped in agony to her bosom, sate in expectation of instant death. He committed her to the charge of Gurth, to be conducted in safety to the barbican, the road to which was now cleared of the enemy, and not yet interrupted by the flames. This accomplished, the loyal Cedric hastened in quest of his friend Athelstane, determined at every risk to himself to save that last scion of Saxon royalty. But ere Cedric penetrated as far as the old hall in which he had himself been a prisoner, the inventive genius of Wamba had procured liberation for himself and his companion in adversity.

When the noise of the conflict announced that it was at the hottest, the Jester began to shout, with the utmost power of his lungs, "Saint George and the dragon!—Bonny Saint George for merry England!—The castle is won!" And these sounds he rendered yet more fearful, by banging against each other two or three pieces of rusty armour which lay scattered around the hall.

A guard, which had been stationed in the outer, or ante-room of the old hall, and whose spirits were already in a state of alarm, took fright at Wamba's clamour, and, leaving the door open behind them, ran to tell the Templar that foemen had won the old hall. Meanwhile the prisoners found no difficulty in making their escape into the ante-room, and from thence into the court of the castle, which was now the last scene of contest. Here sat the fierce Templar, mounted on horseback, surrounded by several of the garrison both on horse and foot, who had united their strength to that of this renowned leader, in order to secure the last chance of safety and retreat which remained to them. The draw-bridge had been lowered by his orders, but the passage was beset; for the archers, who had hitherto only annoyed the castle on that side by their missiles, no sooner saw the flames breaking out, and the bridge lowered, than they thronged to the entrance, as well to prevent the escape of the garrison, as to secure their own share of booty ere the castle should be burned down. On the other hand, those of the besiegers who had entered by the postern were now issuing out into the court-yard, and attacking with fury the remnant of the defenders, who were thus attacked on both sides at once.

Animated, however, by despair, and supported by the example of their indomitable leader, the remaining soldiers of the castle fought with the utmost valour; and, being well armed, succeeded more than once in driving back the assailants, though much inferior in numbers. Rebecca, placed on horseback before one of the Templar's Saracen slaves, was in the midst of the little party; and Bois-Guilbert, notwithstanding the confusion of the bloody fray, shewed every attention to her safety. Repeatedly he was by her side, and, neglecting his own defence, held before her the fence of his triangular steel-plated shield; and anon starting from her side, he cried his war-cry, dashed forward, struck to earth the most forward of the assailants, and was in the same instant once more at her bridle rein.

Athelstane, who, as the reader knows, was slothful, but not cowardly, beheld the female form whom the Templar protected thus sedulously, and doubted not that it was Rowena that the knight was carrying off, in despite of all resistance which could be offered.

"By the soul of Saint Edward," he said, "I will rescue her from yonder over-proud knight, and he shall die by my hand!"

"Think what you do," said Wamba; "the hasty hand catches frog for fish—By my bauble, yonder is none of my Lady Rowena—see but her long dark locks!—nay, an ye will not know black from white, ye may be leader, but I will be no follower—no bones of mine shall be broken unless I know for whom.—And you without armour too!—Bethink you, silk bonnet never kept out steel blade—Nay, then, if wilful will to water, wilful must drench.—*Deus vobiscum*, most doughty Athelstane"—he concluded, loosening the hold which he had hitherto kept upon the Saxon's tunic.

To snatch a mace from the pavement, on which it lay beside one whose dying grasp had just relinquished it—to rush on the Templar's band, and to strike in quick succession to the right and left, levelling a warrior at each blow, was, for Athelstane's great strength, now animated with unusual fury, but the work of a single moment. He was now within two paces of Brian de Bois-Guilbert, whom he defied in his loudest tone.

"Turn, false-hearted Templar!—let go her whom thou art unworthy to touch—turn, cursed limb of a band of murthering robbers!"

"Dog!" said the Templar, grinding his teeth, "I will teach thee to blaspheme the holy order of the Temple of Zion." And with these words, half-wheeling his steed, he made a demi-courbette towards the Saxon, and rising in the stirrups, so as to take full advantage of the descent of the horse, he discharged a fearful blow upon the head of Athelstane.

Well said Wamba, that silken bonnet keeps out no steel blade. So trenchant was the Templar's weapon, that it shore asunder, as if it had been a willow twig, the tough and plaited handle of the mace, which the ill-fated Saxon reared to parry the blow, and, descending on his head, levelled him with the earth.

"*Ha! Beau-seant!*" exclaimed Bois-Guilbert, "thus be it to the maligners of the Temple-knights!" Taking advantage of the dismay which was spread by the fall of Athelstane, and calling aloud, "Those who would save themselves, follow me!" he pushed over the drawbridge, dispersing the archers who would have intercepted them. He was followed by his Saracens, and some five or six men-at-arms, who had mounted their horses. The Templar's retreat was rendered perilous by the numbers of arrows shot off at him and his party; but this did not prevent him from galloping round to the barbican, of which, according to his previous plan, he supposed it possible De Bracy might have been in possession.

"De Bracy! De Bracy!" he shouted, "art thou there?"

"I am here," replied De Bracy, "but I am a prisoner."

"Can I rescue thee?" cried Bois-Guilbert.

"No," replied De Bracy; "I have rendered me, rescue or no rescue. I will be true prisoner. Save thyself—there are hawks abroad—put the seas betwixt you and England—I dare not say more."

"Well," answered the Templar, "an thou wilt tarry there, remember I have redeemed word and glove. Be the hawks who they will, methinks the walls of the Preceptory of Templestowe will be cover sufficient, and thither will I, like heron to her haunt."

Having thus spoken, he galloped off, with his followers.

Those of the castle who had not gotten to horse, still continued to fight desperately against the besiegers, after the departure of the Templar, but rather in despair of quarter than that they entertained any hope of escape. The fire was spreading rapidly through all parts of the castle, when Ulrica, who had first kindled it, appeared on a turret, in the guise of one of the ancient Furies, yelling forth a war-song, such as was of yore chaunted on the field of battle by the scalds of the yet heathen Saxons. Her long dishevelled grey hair flew back from her uncovered head; the inebriating delight of gratified vengeance contended in her eyes with the fire of insanity; and she brandished the distaff which she held in her hand, as if she had been one of the Fatal Sisters, who spin and abridge the thread of human life. Tradition has preserved some wild strophes of the barbarous hymn which she chaunted wildly amid that scene of fire and of slaughter:—

1.

Whet the bright steel,
Sons of the White Dragon!
Kindle the torch,
Daughters of Hengist!
The steel glimmers not for the carving of the banquet,
It is hard, broad, and sharply pointed;
The torch goeth not to the bridal chamber,
It steams and glitters blue with sulphur.
Whet the steel, the raven croaks!
Light the torch, Zernebock is yelling!
Whet the steel, sons of the Dragon!
Kindle the torch, daughters of Hengist!

2.

The black cloud is low over the thane's castle;
The eagle screams—he rides on its bosom.
Scream not, grey rider of the sable cloud,
Thy banquet is prepared!
The maidens of Valhalla look forth,
The race of Hengist will send them guests.
Shake your black tresses, maidens of Valhalla!
And strike your loud timbrels for joy!
Many a haughty step bends to your halls,
Many a helmed head.

3.

Dark sits the evening upon the thane's castle,
The black clouds gather round;
Soon shall they be red as the blood of the valiant!
The destroyer of forests shall shake his red crest against them,
He, the bright consumer of palaces,
Broad waves he his blazing banner,
Red, wide, and dusky,
Over the strife of the valiant:
His joy is in the clashing swords and the broken bucklers;
He loves to lick the hissing blood as it bursts warm from the
wound!

4.

All must perish!
The sword cleaveth the helmet;
The strong armour is pierced by the lance;
Fire devoureth the dwelling of princes,
Engines break down the fences of the battle.
All must perish!
The race of Hengist is gone—
The name of Horsa is no more!
Shrink not then from your doom, sons of the sword!
Let your blades drink blood like wine;
Feast ye in the banquet of slaughter,
By the light of the blazing halls!
Strong be your swords while your blood is warm,
And spare neither for pity nor fear,
For vengeance hath but an hour;
Strong hate itself shall expire!
I also must perish.

The towering flames had now surmounted every obstruction, and rose to the evening skies one huge and burning beacon, seen far and wide through the adjacent country. Tower after tower crashed down, with blazing roof and rafter; and the combatants were driven from the court-yard. The vanquished, of whom very few remained, scattered and escaped into the neighbouring wood. The victors, assembling in large bands, gazed with wonder, not unmixed with fear, upon the flames, in which their own ranks and arms glanced dusky red. The maniac figure of the Saxon Ulrica was for a long time visible on the lofty stand she had chosen, tossing her arms abroad with gestures of wild exultation, as if she reigned empress of the conflagration which she had raised. At length, with a terrific crash, the whole turret gave way, and she perished in the flames which had consumed her seducer. An awful pause of horror silenced each murmur of the armed spectators, who, for the space of several minutes, stirred not a finger, save to sign the cross. The voice of Locksley was then heard, "Shout, yeomen!—the den of tyrants is no more! Let each bring his spoil to our chosen place of rendezvous at the Trysting-tree in the Harthill-walk; for there at break of day will we make just partition among our own bands, together with our worthy allies in this great deed of vengeance."

Chapter Two

Trust me each state must have its policies:
Kingdoms have edicts, cities have their charters;
Even the wild outlaw, in his forest-walk,
Keeps yet some touch of civil discipline.
For not since Adam wore his verdant apron,
Hath man with man in social union dwelt,
But laws were made to draw that union closer.
Old Play.

THE DAY-LIGHT dawned merrily upon the glades of the oak forest. The green boughs glittered with all their pearls of dew. The hind led her fawn from the covert of high fern to the more open walks of the green-wood; and no huntsman was there to watch or intercept the stately hart, as he paced at the head of the antler'd herd.

The outlaws were all assembled around the Trysting-tree in the Harthill-walk, where they had spent the night in refreshing themselves after the fatigues of the siege, some with wine, some with slumber, many with hearing and recounting the events of the day, and computing the heaps of plunder which their success had placed at the disposal of their Chief.

The spoils were indeed considerable; for, notwithstanding that much was consumed by the fire, a great deal of plate, rich armour, and splendid clothing, had been rescued by the exertions of the dauntless outlaws, who could be appalled by no danger when such rewards were in view. Yet so strict were the laws of their society, that no one ventured to appropriate any part of the booty, which was brought into one common mass to be at the disposal of their leader.

The place of rendezvous was an aged oak; not however the same to which Locksley had conducted Gurth and Wamba in the earlier part of the story, but one which was the centre of a sylvan amphitheatre, within half a mile of the demolished castle of Torquilstone. Here Locksley assumed his seat—a throne of turf erected under the twisted branches of the huge oak, and his sylvan followers were gathered around him. He assigned to the Black Knight a seat on his right hand, and to Cedric a place upon his left.

"Pardon my freedom, noble sirs," he said, "but in these glades I am monarch—they are my kingdom; and these my wild subjects would reck but little of my power, were I, within mine own dominions, to yield place to mortal man.—Now, sirs, who hath seen our chaplain? where is our curtal Friar? A mass amongst Christian men best begins a busy morning."—No one had seen the Clerk of Copmanhurst.—"Over God's forbode," said the outlaw Chief, "I trust the jolly priest hath but abidden by the wine-pot a thought too late. Who saw him since the castle was ta'en?"

"I," quoth the Miller, "marked him busy about the door of a cellar, swearing by each saint in the calendar he would taste the smack of Front-de-Bœuf's Gascogne wine."

"Now, the saints, as many as there be of them," said the Captain, "forefend, lest he has drunk too deep of the wine-butts, and perished by the fall of the castle!—Away, Miller!—Take with you enow of men, seek the place where you last saw him—throw water from the moat on the scorching ruins—I will have them removed stone by stone ere I lose my curtal Friar."

The numbers who hastened to execute this duty, considering that an interesting division of spoil was about to take place, showed how much the troop had at heart the safety of their spiritual father.

"Meanwhile, let us proceed," said Locksley; "for when this bold deed shall be sounded abroad, the bands of De Bracy, of Malvoisin, and other allies of Front-de-Bœuf, will be in motion against us, and it were well that we provide in time for our safety.—Noble Cedric," he said, turning to the Saxon, "that spoil is divided into two portions; do thou make choice of that best suits thee, to recompence thy people who were partakers with us in this adventure."

"Good yeoman," said Cedric, "my heart is oppressed with sadness. The noble Athelstane of Coningsburgh is no more—the last sprout of the sainted Confessor! Hopes have perished with him which can never revive!—A sparkle hath been quenched by his blood, which no human breath can again rekindle! My people, save the few who are now with me, do but tarry my presence to transport his honoured remains to their last mansion. The Lady Rowena is desirous to return to Rotherwood, and must be escorted by a sufficient force. I should, therefore, have ere now left this place; and I waited—not to share the booty, for, so help me God and Saint Withold! as neither I nor any of mine will touch the value of a liard,—I waited but to render my thanks to thee and thy bold yeomen, for the life and honour ye have saved."

"Nay, but," said the chief Outlaw, "we did but half the work at most—take of the spoil what may reward your own neighbours and followers."

"I am rich enough to reward them from mine own wealth," answered Cedric.

"And some," said Wamba, "have been wise enough to reward themselves. They do not march off empty-handed altogether—we do not all wear motley."

"They are welcome," said Locksley; "our laws bind but ourselves."

"But thou, my poor knave," said Cedric, turning and embracing his Jester, "how shall I reward thee, who feared not to give thy body to chains and death in the stead of mine!—All forsook me, when the poor fool was faithful!"

A tear stood in the eye of the rough Thane as he spoke—a mark of feeling which even the death of Athelstane had not extracted; but there was something in the half-instinctive attachment of his clown, that waked his nature more keenly than even grief itself.

"Nay," said the Jester, extricating himself from his master's caress, "if you pay my service with the water of your eye, the Jester must weep for company, and then what becomes of his vocation?—But, uncle, if you would indeed pleasure me, let me pray you to pardon my playfellow Gurth, who stole a week from your service to bestow it on your son."

"Pardon him!" exclaimed Cedric; "I will both pardon and reward him.—Kneel down, Gurth."—The swine-herd was in an instant at his master's feet.—"THEOW and ESNE art thou no longer," said Cedric, touching him with a wand; "FOLK-FREE and SACLESS art thou in town and from town, in the forest as in the field. A hyde of land I give to thee in my steads of Walburghham, from me and mine to thee and thine aye and for ever; and God's malison on his head who this gainsays!"

No longer a serf, but a freeman and a land-holder, Gurth sprung upon his feet, and twice bounded aloft to almost his own height from the ground.

"A smith and a file," he cried, "to do the collar from the neck of a freeman!—Noble master! doubled is my strength by your gift, and doubly will I fight for you!—There is a free spirit in my breast—I am a man changed to myself and all around.—Ha, Fangs!" he continued,—for that faithful cur, seeing his master thus transported, began to jump upon him, to express his sympathy,—"knowest thou thy master still?"

"Ay," said Wamba, "Fangs and I still know thee, Gurth, though we must needs abide by the collar; it is only thou who art likely to forget both us and thyself."

"I shall forget myself indeed ere I forget thee, true comrade," said Gurth; "and were freedom fit for thee, Wamba, the master would not let thee want it."

"Nay," replied Wamba, "never think I envy thee, brother Gurth; the serf sits by the hall-fire when the freeman must forth to the field—And what saith Oldhelm of Malmesbury—Better a fool at a feast than a wise man in a fray."

The tramp of horses was now heard, and the Lady Rowena appeared, surrounded by several riders, and a much stronger party of footmen, who joyfully shook their pikes and clashed their brown-bills for joy of her freedom. She herself, richly attired, and mounted on a dark chesnut palfrey, had recovered all the dignity of her manner, and only an unwonted degree of paleness shewed the sufferings she had undergone. Her lovely brow, though serious, bore on it a cast of reviving hope referring to the future, as well as of grateful thankfulness for the past deliverance—She knew that Ivanhoe was safe, and she knew that Athelstane was dead. The former assurance filled her with the most sincere delight; and if she did not rejoice at the other, she might be pardoned for feeling the full advantage of being freed from further persecution on the only subject in which she had ever been contradicted by her guardian Cedric.

As Rowena bent her steed toward Locksley's seat, that bold yeoman, with all his followers, rose to receive her as if by a general instinct of courtesy. The blood rose to her cheek, as, courteously waving her hand, and bending so low that her beautiful and loose tresses were for an instant mixed with the flowing mane of her palfrey, she expressed in few but apt words her obligations and her gratitude to Locksley and her other deliverers.—"God bless you, brave men," she concluded, "God and Our Lady bless you and requite you for gallantly periling yourselves in the cause of the oppressed!—If any of you should hunger, remember Rowena has food—if you should thirst, she has many a butt of wine and brown ale—and if the Normans drive ye from these walks, Rowena has forests of her own, where her gallant deliverers may range at full freedom."

"Thanks, gentle lady," replied Locksley; "thanks from my company and myself. But, to have saved you requites itself. We who walk the greenwood do many a wild deed, and the Lady Rowena's deliverance may be received as an atonement."

Again bowing from her palfrey, Rowena turned to depart; but, pausing a moment, while Cedric, who was to attend her, was also taking his leave, she found herself unexpectedly close by the prisoner De Bracy. He stood under a tree in deep meditation, his arms crossed upon his breast, and Rowena was in hopes she might pass him unobserved. He looked up, however, and, when aware of her presence, a deep flush of shame suffused his handsome countenance. He stood a moment most irresolute; then, stepping forward, took her palfrey by the rein, and bent his knee before her.

"Will the Lady Rowena deign to cast an eye on a captive knight—on a dishonoured soldier?"

"Sir Knight," answered Rowena, "in enterprizes such as yours, the real dishonour lies not in failure, but in success."

"Conquest, lady, should soften the heart," answered De Bracy; "let me but know that the Lady Rowena forgives the violence occasioned by an ill-fated passion, and she shall soon learn that De Bracy knows how to serve her in nobler ways."

"I forgive you, Sir Knight, but it is as a Christian."

"That means," said Wamba, "that she does not forgive him at all."

"But I can never forget the misery and desolation your madness has occasioned," continued Rowena.

"Unloose your hold on the lady's rein," said Cedric, coming up. "By the bright sun above us, but that it were shame, I would pin thee to the earth with my javelin—but be well assured, thou shalt smart, Maurice De Bracy, for thy share in this foul deed."

"He threatens safely who threatens a prisoner," said De Bracy; "but when had a Saxon any touch of courtesy?"

Then retiring two steps backwards, he permitted the lady to move on.

Cedric, ere they departed, expressed his peculiar gratitude to the Black Champion, and earnestly entreated him to accompany him to Rotherwood.

"I know," he said, "that ye errant knights desire to carry your fortunes on the point of your lance, and reck not of land or goods; but war is a changeful mistress, and a home is sometimes desirable even to those champions whose trade is wandering. Thou hast earned one in the halls of Rotherwood, noble knight. Cedric has wealth enough to repair the injuries of fortune, and all he has is his deliverer's—Come, therefore, to Rotherwood, not as a guest, but as a son or brother."

"Cedric has already made me rich," said the Knight,—"he has taught me the value of Saxon virtue. To Rotherwood will I come, brave Saxon, and that speedily; but, as now, pressing matters of moment detain me from your halls. Peradventure when I come thither, I shall ask such a boon as will put even thy generosity to the test."

"It is granted ere spoken out," said Cedric, striking his ready hand into the gauntletted palm of the Black Knight,—"it is granted already, were it to affect half my fortune."

"Gage not thy promise so lightly," said the Knight of the Fetterlock; "yet well I hope to gain the boon I shall ask—meanwhile adieu."

"I have but to say," added the Saxon, "that, during the funeral rites of the noble Athelstane, I shall be an inhabitant of the halls of his castle of Coningsburgh—They will be open to all who chuse to partake of the funeral banquetting; and—I speak in name of the noble Edith, mother of the fallen prince—they will never be shut against him who laboured so bravely, though unsuccessfully, to save Athelstane from Norman chains and Norman steel."

"Ay, ay," said Wamba, who had resumed his attendance on his master, "rare feeding there will be—pity that the noble Athelstane cannot banquet at his own funeral.—But he," continued the Jester, lifting up his eyes gravely, "is supping in Paradise, and doubtless does honour to the cheer."

"Peace, and move on," said Cedric, his anger at this untimely jest being checked by the recollection of Wamba's recent services. Rowena waved a graceful adieu to him of the Fetterlock—the Saxon bad God speed him, and on they moved through a wide glade of the forest.

They had scarce departed, ere a sudden procession moved from under the greenwood branches, swept slowly round the sylvan amphitheatre, and took the same direction with Rowena and her followers. The priests of a neighbouring convent, in expectation of the ample donation, or *soul-scat*, which Cedric had proposed, attended upon the bier on which the body of Athelstane was laid, and sang hymns as it was sadly and slowly borne on the shoulders of his vassals to his castle of Coningsburgh, to be there deposited in the grave of Hengist, from whom the deceased derived his long descent. Many of his vassals had assembled at the news of his death, and followed the bier with all the external marks, at least, of dejection and sorrow. Again the outlaws arose, and paid the same rude and spontaneous homage to death, which they had so lately rendered to beauty. The slow chaunt and mournful step of the priests, brought back to their remembrance such of their comrades as had fallen in the yesterday's affray. But such recollections dwell not long with those who lead a life of danger and enterprize, and ere the sound of the death-hymn had died on the wind, the outlaws were again busied in the distribution of their spoil.

"Valiant knight," said Locksley to the Black Champion, "without whose good heart and mighty arm our enterprize must have altogether failed, will it please you to take from that mass of spoil whatever may best serve to pleasure you, and to remind you of this my Trysting-tree?"

"I accept the offer," said the Knight, "as frankly as it is given; and I ask permission to dispose of Sir Maurice de Bracy at my own pleasure."

"He is thine already," said Locksley; "and well for him! else the tyrant had graced the highest bough of this oak, with as many of his Free Companions as we could gather, hanging thick as acorns around him.—But he is thy prisoner, and he is safe, had he slain my father."

"Bracy," said the Knight, "thou art free—depart—he whose prisoner thou art scorns to take mean revenge for what is passed. But beware of the future, lest a worse thing befal thee. Maurice de Bracy, I say beware!"

De Bracy bowed low and in silence, and was about to withdraw, when the yeomen burst at once into a shout of execration and derision. The proud knight instantly stopped, turned back, folded his arms, drew up his form to its full height, and exclaimed, "Peace, ye yelping curs! who open upon a cry which ye followed not when the stag was at bay—De Bracy scorns your censure as he would disdain your applause. To your brakes and caves, ye outlawed thieves! and be silent when aught knightly or noble is but spoken within a league of your fox-earths."

This ill-timed defiance might have procured for De Bracy a volley of arrows, but for the hasty interference of the outlaw Chief. Meanwhile the knight caught a horse by the rein, for several which had been taken in the stables of Front-de-Bœuf stood accoutred around, and were a valuable part of the booty. He threw himself into the saddle, and galloped off through the wood.

When the bustle occasioned by this incident was something composed, the chief Outlaw took from his neck the rich horn and baldric which he had recently gained at the strife of archery near Ashby.

"Noble knight," he said to him of the Fetterlock, "if you disdain not to grace by your acceptance a bugle which I have once worn, this I will pray you to keep as a memorial of your gallant bearing. And if ye have aught to do, and as happeneth oft to a brave knight, ye chance to be hard bestad in any forest betwixt Trent and Tees, wind three *mots** upon the horn thus, *Wa-sa-hoa!* and it may well chance ye shall find helpers and rescue."

He then gave breath to the bugle, and winded once and again the call which he described, until the knight had caught the notes.

*The notes on the bugle were anciently called mots, and are distinguished in the old treatises on hunting, not by musical characters, but by written words.

"Gramercy for thy gift, bold yeoman," said the knight; "and better help than thine and thy rangers' would I never seek, were it at my utmost need." And then in his turn he winded the call till all the greenwood rang.

"Well blown and clearly," said the yeoman; "beshrew me an thou knowest not as much of woodcraft as of war!—thou hast been a striker of deer in thy day, I warrant.—Comrades, mark these three mots—it is the call of the Knight of the Fetterlock; and he who hears it, and hastens not to serve him at his need, I will have him scourged out of our band with his own bow-string."

"Long live our leader!" shouted the yeomen, "and long live the Black Knight of the Fetterlock!—May he soon use our service, to prove how readily it will be paid."

Locksley now proceeded to the distribution of the spoil, which he performed with the most laudable impartiality. A tenth part of the whole was set apart for the church, and for pious uses; a portion was next allotted to a sort of public treasury; a part was assigned to the widows and children of those who had fallen, or to be expended in masses for the souls of such as had left no surviving family. The rest was divided amongst the outlaws, according to their rank and merit; and the judgment of the Chief, on all such doubtful questions as occurred, was delivered with great shrewdness, and received with absolute submission. The Black Knight was not a little surprised to find that men, in a state so lawless, were nevertheless amongst themselves so regularly and equitably governed, and all that he observed added to his opinion of the justice and judgment of their leader.

When each had taken his own proportion of the booty, and while the treasurer, accompanied by four tall yeomen, was transporting that belonging to the state to some place of concealment or of security, the portion devoted to the church still remained unappropriated.

"I would," said the leader, "we could hear tidings of our joyous chaplain—he was never wont to be absent when meat was to be blessed, or spoil to be parted; and it is his duty to take charge of these the tithes of our successful enterprize. Also, I have a holy brother of his a prisoner at no great distance, and I would have the Friar to help me to deal with him in due sort—I greatly misdoubt the safety of the bluff priest."

"I were right sorry for that," said the Knight of the Fetterlock, "for I stand indebted to him for the joyous hospitality of a merry night in his cell. Let us to the ruins of the castle; it may be we shall there learn some tidings of him."

While they thus spoke, a loud shout among the yeomen announced the arrival of him for whom they feared, as they learned from the stentorian voice of the Friar himself, long before they saw his burly person.

"Make room, my merry men!" he exclaimed; "room for your ghostly father and his prisoner—Ay, huzza once more.—I come, noble leader, like an eagle, with my prey in my clutch."—And making his way through the ring, amidst the laughter of all around, he appeared in majestic triumph, his huge partizan in one hand, and in the other a halter, one end of which was fastened to the neck of the unfortunate Isaac of York, who, bent double by sorrow and terror, was dragged on by the victorious priest.—"Where is Allan-a-Dale," said the Friar, "to chronicle me in a ballad or a lay?—By Saint Hermangild, the jangling crowder is ever out of the way when there is an apt theme for exalting valour!"

"Curtal Priest," said the Captain, "thou hast been at a wet mass this morning, for as early as 'tis—in the name of Saint Nicholas, whom hast thou got there?"

"A captive to my sword and to my lance, noble Captain," replied the Clerk of Copmanhurst; "to my bow and to my halbert, I would rather say; and yet I have redeemed him by my divinity from a worse captivity. Speak, Jew,—have I not ransomed thee from Sathanas?—have I not taught thee thy creed, thy *pater*, and thine *Ave Maria!*—Did I not spend the whole night in drinking to thee, and in expounding of mysteries?"

"For the love of God!" ejaculated the poor Jew; "will no one take me out of the keeping of this mad—I mean this holy man?"

"How's this, Jew?" said the Friar, with a menacing aspect; "dost thou recant, Jew?—Bethink thee, if thou dost relapse into thine infidelity, though thou art not so tender as a sucking pig—I would I had one to break my fast upon—thou art not too tough to be roasted! Be conformable, Isaac, and repeat the words after me. *Ave Maria!*"——

"Nay, we will have no profanation, mad priest," said Locksley; "let us rather hear where you found this prisoner of thine."

"By Saint Dunstan," said the Friar, "I found him where I sought for better ware. I did step but into the cellarage to see what might be rescued there; for though a cup of burned wine, with spice, be an evening's draught for an Emperor, it were waste, I thought, to let so much good liquor be mulled at once; and I had but caught up one runlet of sack, and was coming to call more aid amongst these lazy knaves, who are ever to seek when a good deed is to be done, when I was avised of a strong door—Aha! thought I, here is the choicest juice of all in this secret crypt; and the knave butler, being disturbed in his vocation, hath left the key in the door—In therefore I went, and found just nought, besides a commodity of rusted chains and this dog of a

Jew, who presently rendered himself my prisoner, rescue or no rescue. I did but refresh myself, after the fatigue of the action, with the unbeliever, with one humming cup of sack, and was proceeding to lead forth my captive, when, crash after crash, as if with wild thunder-dint and levin-fire, down toppled the masonry of an outer tower, (marry beshrew their hands that built it not the firmer!) and blocked up the passage. The roar of one falling tower followed another and I gave up thought of life; and deeming it a dishonour for one of my profession to pass out of this world in company with a Jew, I heaved up my halbert to beat his brains out; but I took ruth on his grey hairs, and deemed it better to lay down the partizan, and take up my spiritual weapons for his conversion. And truly, by the blessing of Saint Dunstan, the seed has been sown in good soil; only that, with speaking to him of mysteries through the whole night (for the few draughts of sack which I sharpened my wits with were not worth marking) my head is well nigh dizzied, I trow.—But I was clean exhausted—Gilbert and Wilibald know in what state they found me—quite and clean exhausted."

"We can bear witness," said Gilbert; "for when we cleared away the ruin, and by Saint Dunstan's help lighted upon the dungeon stair, we found the runlet of sack half empty, the Jew half dead, and the Friar more than half exhausted, as he calls it."

"Ye lie, knave! ye lie!" retorted the offended Friar; "it was you and your gormandizing companions that drank up the sack, and called it your morning draught—I am a pagan, an I kept it not for the Captain's own throat. But what recks it? The Jew is converted, and understands all I have told him, very nearly, if not altogether, as well as myself."

"Jew," said the Captain, "is this true? hast thou renounced thine unbelief?"

"May I so find mercy in your eyes," said the Jew, "as I know not one word which the reverend prelate spake to me all this fearful night. Alas! I was so distraught with agony, and fear, and grief, that had our holy father Abraham come to preach to me, he had found but a deaf listener."

"Thou liest, Jew, and thou knowest thou dost," said the Friar; "I will remind thee but of one word of our conference—thou didst promise to give all thy substance to our holy Order."

"So help me the Promise, fair sirs," said Isaac, more alarmed than even before, "as no such sounds ever crossed my lips!—Alas! I am an aged beggar'd man and now I fear me a childless—Have ruth on me, and let me go!"

"Nay," said the Friar, "if thou dost retract vows made in favour of Holy Church, thou must do penance."

Accordingly he raised his halbert, and would have laid the staff of it lustily on the Jew's shoulders, had not the Black Knight stopped the blow, and thereby transferred the Holy Clerk's resentment to himself.

"By Saint Thomas of Kent," said he, "an I buckle to my gear, I will teach thee to mell with thine own matters, maugre thine iron case there."

"Nay, be not wroth with me," said the knight; "thou knowest I am thy sworn friend and comrade."

"I know no such thing," answered the Friar, "and defy thee for a meddling cocks-comb."

"Nay, but," said the knight, who seemed to take pleasure in provoking his quondam host, "hast thou forgotten that for my sake, (for I say nothing of the temptation of the flagon and the pasty,) thou didst break thy vow of fast and vigil?"

"Truly, friend," said the Friar, clenching his huge fist, "I will bestow a buffet on thee."

"I accept no such presents," replied the knight; "I will repay thee with usury as steep as ever thy prisoner there exacted in his traffic."

"I will prove that presently," said the Hermit.

"Hola!" cried the Captain, "what art thou after, mad Friar? brawling beneath our Trysting-tree?"

"No brawling," replied the knight, "it is but a friendly interchange of courtesies. Friar, strike an thou darest—I will stand thy blow, if thou wilt stand mine."

"Thou hast the vantage with that iron-pot on thy head," said the churchman; "but have at thee—Down thou goest an thou wert Goliah of Gath in his brazen helmet."

The Friar bared his brawny arm up to the elbow, and giving his full strength to the blow, dealt the knight a buffet that might have felled an ox. But his adversary stood as firm as a rock. A loud shout was uttered by all the yeomen around.

"Now, Priest," said the knight, pulling off his gauntlet, "if I had vantage on my head, I will have none on my hand—stand forth as a true man."

"*Genam meam dedi vapulatori*—I have given my cheek to the smiter," said the Priest; "an thou stirrest me from the spot, fellow, I will give thee the Jew's ransom."

So spoke the burly Priest, assuming, on his part, high defiance. But who may resist his fate? The buffet of the knight was given with such strength and good will, that the Friar rolled head over heels upon the plain, to the great amusement of all the spectators. But he arose neither angry nor crest-fallen.

"Brother," said he to the knight, "thou should'st have used thy strength with more discretion. I had mumbled but a lame mass an thou hadst broken my jaw, for the piper plays ill that wants the nether chops. Nevertheless, there is my hand, in friendly witness that I will exchange no more cuffs with thee, having been a loser by the barter. End now all unkindness. Let us put the Jew to ransom, since the leopard will not change his spots, and a Jew he will continue to be."

"The Priest," said Gilbert, "is not half so confident of the Jew's conversion, since he received that buffet on the ear."

"Go to, knave, what pratest thou of conversions?—what, is there no respect?—all masters, and no men?—I tell thee, fellow, I was somewhat totterish when I received the good knight's courtesy, or I had kept my ground under it. But an thou gibest more of it, thou shalt learn I can give as well as take."

"Peace all!" said the Captain.—"And thou, Jew, think of thy ransom: thou needest not be told that thy race are held accursed in all Christian communities, and trust me that we cannot endure thy presence amongst us. Think, therefore, of an offer, while I examine a prisoner of another cast."

"Were many of Front-de-Bœuf's men taken?" demanded the Black Knight.

"None of note enough to be put to ransom," answered the Captain; "a set of hilding fellows there were, whom we dismissed to find them a new master—enough had been done for revenge and profit; the bunch of them were not worth a cardecu. The prisoner I speak of is better booty—a jolly monk riding to visit his leman, an I may judge by his horse-gear and wearing apparel.—Here cometh the worthy prelate, as pert as a pyet." And, between two yeomen, was brought before the sylvan throne of the outlaw Chief, our old friend, Prior Aymer of Jorvaulx.

Chapter Three

——Flower of warriors,
How is't with Titus Lartius?
Marcius. As with a man busied about decrees,
Condemning some to death and some to exile,
Ransoming him or pitying, threatening the other.
Coriolanus.

THE CAPTIVE Prior's features and manner exhibited a whimsical mixture of offended pride, deranged foppery and bodily terror.

"Why, how now, my masters?" said he, with a voice in which all three emotions were blended. "What order is this among ye? Be ye Turks or Christians, that handle a churchman?—Know ye what it is, *manus imponere in servos Domini?* Ye have plundered my mails—torn my cope of curious cut lace, which might have served a cardinal—Another in my place would have been at his *excommunicabo vos;* but I am placable, and if ye order forth my palfrey, release my brethren, and restore my mails, send with all speed an hundred crowns to be expended in masses at the high altar of Jorvaulx Abbey, and make your vow to eat no venison until next Pentecost, it may be you shall hear little more of this mad frolic."

"Holy Father," said the chief Outlaw, "it grieves me to think that you have met with such usage from any of my followers, as calls for your fatherly reprehension."

"Usage!" echoed the Prior, encouraged by the mild tone of the sylvan leader; "it were usage fit for no hound of good race—much less for a Christian—far less for a priest—and least of all for the Prior of the holy community of Jorvaulx. Here is a profane and drunken minstrel, called Allan-a-Dale—*nebulo quidam*—who has menaced me with corporeal punishment—nay, with death itself, an I pay not down five hundred crowns of ransom, to the boot all the treasure of which he hath robbed me—gold chains and gymmal rings to an unknown value; besides what is broken and spoiled among their rude hands, as my pouncet-box and silver crisping-tongs."

"It is impossible that Allan-a-Dale can have thus treated a man of your reverend bearing," replied the Captain.

"It is true as the gospel of Saint Nicodemus," said the Prior; "he swore, with many a cruel north country oath, that he would hang me up on the highest tree in the greenwood."

"Did he so in very deed? Nay, then, reverend father, I think you were better comply with his demands—for Allan-a-Dale is the very man to abide by his word when he has so pledged it."

"You do but jest with me," said the astounded Prior, with a forced laugh; "and I love a good jest with all my heart. But, ha! ha! ha! when the mirth has lasted the live-long night, it is time to be grave in the morning."

"And I am as grave as a father confessor," replied the Outlaw; "you must pay a round ransom, Sir Prior, or your convent is likely to be called to a new election; for your place will know you no more."

"Are ye Christians," said the Prior, "and hold this language to a churchman?"

"Christians! aye, marry are we, and have divinity amongst us to boot," answered the Outlaw. "Let our buxom chaplain stand forth, and expound to this reverend father the texts which concern this matter."

The Friar, half-drunk, half-sober, had huddled a friar's frock over his green cassock, and now summoning together whatever scraps of learning he had learned by rote in former days, "Holy father," said he, "*Deus faciet salvum benignitatem vestrum*—You are welcome to the greenwood."

"What profane mummery is this?" said the Prior; "Friend, if thou be'st indeed of the church, it were a better deed to shew me how I shall escape from these men's hands, than to stand ducking and grinning here like a morris-dancer."

"Truly, reverend brother," said the Friar, "I know but one mode in which thou may'st escape. This is Saint Andrew's day with us, we are taking our tythes."

"But not of churchmen, I trust, my good brother," said the Prior.

"Of church and lay," said the Friar; "and therefore, Sir Prior, *facite vobis amicos de Mammone iniquitatis*—make yourselves friends with the Mammon of iniquity, for no other friendship is like to serve your turn."

"I love a jolly woodsman at heart," said the Prior; "come, ye must not deal too hard with me—I can well of woodcraft, and can wind a horn clear and lustily, and hollo till every oak rings again—Come, ye must not deal too hard with me."

"Give him a horn," said the Outlaw, "we will prove the skill he boasts of."

The Prior Aymer winded a blast accordingly. The Captain shook his head.

"Sir Prior," he said, "this may not ransom thee—we cannot afford, as the legend on a good knight's shield hath it, to set thee free for a blast. Moreover, I have found thee. Thou art one of those, who, with new French quavers and Tra-li-ras, do disturb the ancient English bugle notes.—Prior, that last flourish on the recheat hath added fifty crowns to thy ransom, for corrupting the honest old manly blasts of venerie."

"Well, friend," said the Abbot, peevishly, "thou art ill to please with woodcraft. I pray thee be more conformable in the matter of my ransom. At a word—since I must needs, for once, hold a candle to the devil—what ransom am I to pay for walking on Watling-street, without having fifty men at my back?"

"Were it not well," said the Lieutenant of the gang apart to the Captain, "that the Prior should name the Jew's ransom, and the Jew name the Prior's."

"Thou art a mad knave," said the Captain, "but thy plan transcends!—Here, Jew, step forth—Look at that holy Father Aymer, Prior of the rich Abbey of Jorvaulx, and tell us at what ransom we should hold him?—Thou knowest the income of his convent, I warrant thee."

"O, assuredly," said Isaac. "I have trafficked with the good fathers, and bought wheat and barley, and fruits of the earth, and also much wool. O, it is a rich abbey-stede, and they do live upon the fat, and drink the sweet wine upon the lees, these good fathers of Jorvaulx. Ah, if an out-cast like me had such a home to go to, and such incomings by the year and by the term, I would pay much gold and silver to redeem my captivity."

"Hound of a Jew!" exclaimed the Prior, "no one knows better than thy own cursed self, that our holy house of God is indebted for the finishing of our chancel"——

"And for the storing of your cellars in the last season with the due allowance of Gascon wine," interrupted the Jew; "but it is small matters."

"Hear the infidel dog!—he jangles as if our holy community did come under debt for the wines which we have a license to drink, *propter necessitatem et ad frigus depellendum*. The circumcised villain blasphemeth the holy church, and Christian men listen and rebuke him not!"

"All this helps nothing," said the leader.—"Isaac, pronounce what he may pay, without flaying both hide and hair."

"An six hundred crowns," said Isaac, "the good Prior might well pay to your honoured valours, and never sit less soft in his stall."

"Six hundred crowns," said the leader, gravely; "I am contented—thou hast well spoken, Isaac—Six hundred crowns—it is a sentence, Sir Prior."

"A sentence!—a sentence!" exclaimed the band; "Solomon had not done it better."

"Thou hearest thy doom, Prior," said the leader.

"Ye are mad, my masters," said the Prior; "where am I to find such a sum? If I sell the very pyx and candlesticks on the altar at Jorvaulx, I shall scarce raise the half; and it will be necessary for that purpose that I go to Jorvaulx myself; ye may retain as borrows* my two priests."

"That will be but blind trust," said the Outlaw; "we will retain thee, Prior, and send them to fetch thy ransom. Thou shalt not want a cup of wine and a collop of venison the while; and thou lovest woodcraft, thou shalt see such as your north country never witnessed."

"Or, if so please you," said Isaac, willing to curry favour with the outlaws, "I can send to York for the six hundred crowns, out of certain monies of the good fathers in my hands, if so be that the most reverend

*Borghs or borrows signifies pledges. Hence our word to borrow, because we pledge ourselves to restore what is lent.

Prior here present will grant me a quittance."

"He shall grant thee whatever thou dost list, Isaac," said the Captain; "and thou shalt lay down the redemption money for Prior Aymer as for thyself."

"For myself! ah, courageous sirs," said the Jew, "I am a broken and impoverished man; a beggar's staff must be my portion through life, supposing I were to pay you fifty crowns."

"The Prior shall judge of that matter," replied the Captain; "how say you, father Aymer?—Can the Jew afford a good ransom?"

"*Can* he afford a ransom?" answered the Prior—"Is he not Isaac of York, rich enough to redeem the captivity of the ten tribes of Israel, who were led into Assyrian bondage?—I have seen but little of him myself, but our cellarer and treasurer have dealt largely with him, and report that his house at York is so full of gold and silver as is a shame in any Christian land. Marvel it is to all living Christian hearts that such gnawing adders should be suffered to eat into the bowels of the state, and even of the holy church herself, with foul usuries and extortions."

"Holy father," said the Jew, "mitigate and assuage your choler. I pray of your reverence to remember that I force my monies upon no one. But when churchman and layman, prince and prior, knight and priest, come knocking to Isaac's door, they borrow not his shekels with these uncivil terms. It is then, Friend Isaac, will you pleasure us in this matter, and our day shall be truly kept, so God sa' me?—and kind Isaac, if ever you served man, shew yourself a friend in this need. And when the day comes, and I ask my own, then what hear I but damned Jew, and the curse of Egypt on your tribe, and all that may stir up the rude, uncivil populace against poor strangers?"

"Prior," said the Captain, "Jew though he be, he hath in this spoken well: do thou, therefore, name his ransom, as he named thine, without farther rude terms."

"None but *latro famosus*—the interpretation whereof," said the Prior, "I will give at some other time and tide—would place a Christian prelate and an unbaptized Jew upon the same bench. But since ye require me to put a price on this caitiff, I tell you openly that ye will wrong yourselves if you take from him a penny under a thousand crowns."

"A sentence!—a sentence!" said the chief Outlaw.

"A sentence!—a sentence!" shouted his assessors; "the Christian has shewn his good nurture, and dealt with us more generously than the Jew."

"The God of my fathers help me!" said the Jew; "will ye bear to the ground an impoverished creature?—I am this day childless, and will ye also deprive me of the means of livelihood?"

"Thou wilt have the less to provide for, Jew, if thou art childless," said Aymer.

"Alas! my lord," said Isaac, "your law permits you not to know how the child of our bosom is entwined with the strings of our heart—O Rebecca! daughter of my beloved Rachael! were each leaf on that tree a zecchin, and each zecchin mine own, all that mass of wealth would I give to know whether thou art alive, and escaped the hands of the Nazarene!"

"Was not thy daughter dark-haired?" said one of the outlaws; "and wore she not a veil of crimson sendal, broidered with silver?"

"She did!—she did!" replied the old man, trembling with eagerness, as formerly with fear. "The blessing of Jacob be upon thee! canst thou tell me aught of her safety?"

"It was she, then," said the yeoman, "who was carried off by the proud Templar, when he broke through our ranks on yester-even. I had drawn my bow to send a shaft after him, but spared him even for the sake of the damsel, who I feared might sustain harm from the arrow."

"Oh!" answered the Jew, "I would to God thou hadst shot, though the arrow had pierced her bosom—better the tomb of her fathers than the dishonourable couch of the licentious and savage Templar. Ichabod! Ichabod! the glory hath departed from my house."

"Friends," said the Chief, looking round, "the old man is but a Jew, natheless his grief touches me.—Deal uprightly with us, Isaac—will paying this ransom of a thousand crowns leave thee altogether pennyless?"

Isaac, recalled to think of his worldly goods, the love of which, by dint of inveterate habit, contended even with his parental affection, grew pale, stammered, and could not deny there might be some small surplus.

"Well—go to—what though there be," said the Outlaw, "we will not reckon with thee too closely. Without treasure thou may'st as well hope to redeem thy child from the clutches of Sir Brian de Bois-Guilbert, as to shoot a stag-royal with a headless shaft—We will rate thee at the same ransom with Prior Aymer, or rather at one hundred crowns lower, which hundred crowns shall be mine own particular loss; and so we shall avoid the heinous offence of rating a Jew merchant as high as a Christian prelate, and thou wilt have five hundred crowns remaining to treat for thy daughter's ransom. Templars love the glitter of silver shekels as well as the sparkle of black eyes—Haste to make thy crowns chink in the ear of De Bois-Guilbert, ere worse comes of it. Thou wilt find him, as our scouts have brought notice, at the next Preceptory house of his Order.—Said I well, my merry mates?"

The yeomen expressed their wonted acquiescence in their leader's opinion; and Isaac, relieved of one half of his apprehensions, by learning that his daughter lived, and might possibly be ransomed, threw himself at the feet of the generous Outlaw, and, rubbing his beard against his buskins, sought to kiss the hem of his green cassock. The Captain drew himself back, and extricated himself from the Jew's grasp, not without some marks of contempt.

"Nay, beshrew thee, man, up with thee! I am English-born, and love no such eastern prostrations—Kneel to God, and not to a poor sinner like me."

"Ay, Jew," said Prior Aymer; "kneel to God, as represented in the servant of his altar, and who knoweth, with thy sincere repentance and due gifts to the shrine of Saint Robert, what grace thou mayst acquire for thyself and thy daughter Rebecca? I grieve for the maiden, for she is of fair and comely countenance, I beheld her in the lists at Ashby. Also Brian de Bois-Guilbert is one with whom I may do much—bethink thee how thou canst deserve my good word with him."

"Alas! alas!" said the Jew, "on every hand the spoilers arise against me—I am given as a prey unto the Assyrian, and a booty unto him of Egypt."

"And what else should be the lot of thy accursed race?" answered the Prior; "for what saith holy writ, *verbum Domini projecerunt, et sapientia est nulla in eis*—they have cast forth the word of the Lord, and there is no wisdom in them; *propterea dabo mulieres eorum exteris*—I will give their women to strangers, that is to the Templar, as in the present matter; *et thesauros eorum hæredibus alienis*, and their treasures to others."

Isaac groaned deeply, and began to wring his hands and to relapse into his state of desolation and despair. But the leader of the yeomen led him aside.

"Advise thee well, Isaac, what thou wilt do in this matter; my counsel to thee is to make a friend of this churchman. He is vain, Isaac, and he is covetous, at least he needs money to supply his profusion. Thou canst easily gratify his greed; for think not that I am blinded by thy pretexts of poverty. I know, Isaac, the very iron chest in which thou dost keep thy money-bags—What, know I not the great stone under the appletree, that leads into the vaulted chamber under thy garden at York?" The Jew grew as pale as death—"But fear nothing from me," continued the yeoman, "for we are of old acquainted. Dost thou not remember the sick yeoman whom thy fair daughter Rebecca redeemed from the gyves at York, and kept him in thy house till his health was restored, when thou didst dismiss him recovered, and with a piece of money?—Usurer as thou art, thou didst never place coin at better interest than that poor silver mark, for it has this day saved thee five hundred crowns."

"And thou art he whom we called Diccon Bend-the-Bow?" said Isaac; "I thought ever I knew the accent of thy voice."

"I am Bend-the-Bow," said the Captain, "and Locksley, and have a good name besides all these."

"But thou art mistaken, good Bend-the-Bow, concerning that same vaulted apartment. So help me Heaven, as there is nought in it but some merchandizes which I will gladly part with you—An hundred yards of Lincoln green to make doublets to thy men, and an hundred staves of Spanish yew to make bows, and an hundred silken bow-strings, tough, round, and sound—these will I send thee for thy good-will, honest Diccon, an thou wilt keep silence about the vault, my good Diccon."

"Silent as a dormouse," said the Outlaw; "and never trust me but I am grieved for thy daughter. But I may not help it—the Templars are too strong for my archery—they would scatter us like dust. Had I but known it was Rebecca when she was borne off, something might have been done; but now thou must needs proceed by policy. Come, shall I treat for thee with the Prior?"

"In God's name, Diccon, an thou canst, aid me to recover the child of my bosom."

"Do not thou interrupt me then with thine ill-timed avarice," said the Outlaw, "and I will deal with him in thy behalf."

He then turned from the Jew, who followed him, however, as closely as his shadow.

"Prior Aymer," said the Captain, "come apart with me under this tree. Men say thou dost love wine, and a lady's smile, better than beseems thy Order, Sir Priest; but with that I have nought to do. I have heard, too, thou dost love a brace of good dogs and a fleet horse, and it may well be that thou hatest not a purse of gold. But I have never heard that thou didst love oppression or cruelty.—Now, here is Isaac willing to give thee the means of pleasure and pastime in a bag containing one hundred marks of silver, if thy intercession with thine ally the Templar shall avail to procure the freedom of his daughter."

"In safety and honour, as when taken from me," said the Jew, "otherwise it is no bargain."

"Peace, Isaac," said the Outlaw, "or I give up thine interest.—What say you to this my purpose, Prior Aymer?"

"The matter," quoth the Prior, "is of a mixed condition; for, if I do a good deed on the one hand, yet, on the other, it goeth to the vantage of a Jew, and in so much is against my conscience. Yet, if the Israelite will advantage the Church by giving somewhat over to the building of our *dortour*,* I will take it on my conscience to aid him in the matter of his daughter."

"For a score of marks to the dortour," said the Outlaw,—"Be still, I say, Isaac!—or for a brace of silver candlesticks to the altar, we will not stand with you."

"Nay, but, good Diccon Bend-the-Bow"—said Isaac, endeavouring to interpose.

"Good Jew—good beast—good earth-worm!" said the yeoman, losing patience; "an thou dost go on to put thy filthy lucre in the balance with thy daughter's life and honour, by Heaven, I will strip thee of every maravedi thou hast in the world, before three days are out!"

Isaac shrunk together, and was silent.

"And what pledge am I to have for all this?" said the Prior.

"When Isaac returns successful through your mediation," said the Outlaw, "I swear by Saint Hubert, that I will see that he pays thee the money in good silver, or I will reckon with him for it in such sort, he had better have paid twenty such sums."

"Well then, Jew," said Aymer, "since I must needs meddle in this matter, let me have the use of thy writing tablets—though, hold—rather than use thy pen, I would fast for twenty-four hours, and where shall I find one?"

"If your holy scruples can dispense with using the Jew's tablets, for the pen I can find a remedy," said the yeoman: And, bending his bow, he aimed his shaft at a wild-goose which was soaring over their heads, the advanced-guard of a phalanx of his tribe, which were winging their way to the distant and solitary fens of Holderness. The bird came fluttering down, transfixed with the arrow.

"There, Prior," said the Captain, "are quills enow to supply all the monks of Jorvaulx for the next hundred years, an they take not to writing chronicles."

The Prior sat down, and at great leisure indited an epistle to Brian de Bois-Guilbert, and, having carefully sealed up the tablets, delivered them to the Jew, saying, "This will be thy safe conduct to the Preceptory of Templestowe, and, as I think, is most likely to accomplish the delivery of thy daughter, if it be well backed with proffers of advantage and commodity at thine own hand; for, trust me well, the good Knight Bois-Guilbert is of their confraternity that do nought for nought."

"Well, Prior," said the Outlaw, "I will detain thee no longer here than to give the Jew a quittance for the six hundred crowns at which thy ransom is fixed. I accept of him for my pay-master; and if I hear

***Dortour* or dormitory.

that ye boggle at allowing him in his accompts the sum so paid by him, Saint Mary refuse me, an I burn not the abbey over thine head, though I hang ten years the sooner."

With a much worse grace than that wherewith he had penned the letter to Bois-Guilbert, the Prior wrote an acquittance, discharging the Jew Isaac of York of six hundred crowns, advanced to him in his need for acquittal of his ransom, and faithfully promised to hold true compt with him for that sum.

"And now," said Prior Aymer, "I will pray you of restitution of my mules and palfreys, and the freedom of the reverend brethren attending upon me, and also of the *cimelia*, rings, jewels, and fair vestures, of which I have been despoiled, having now satisfied you for my ransom as a true prisoner."

"Touching your brethren, Sir Prior," said Locksley, "they shall have present freedom, it were unjust to detain them; touching your horses and mules, they shall also be restored, with such spending-money as may enable you to reach York, for it were cruel to deprive you of the means of journeying.—But as concerning rings, jewels, chains, and what else, you must understand that we are men of tender consciences, and will not yield to a venerable man like yourself, who should be dead to the vanities of this life, the strong temptation to break the rule of his foundation by wearing rings, chains, or other vain gauds."

"Think what you do, my masters," said the Prior, "ere you put your hand on the Church's patrimony—These things are *inter res sacras*, and I wot not what judgment may ensue were they to be handled by laical hands."

"I will take care of that, reverend Prior," said the Hermit of Copmanhurst; "for I will wear them myself."

"Friend, or brother," said the Prior, in answer to this solution of his doubts, "if thou hast really taken religious orders, I pray thee to look how thou wilt answer to thine official the share thou hast taken in this day's work."

"Friend Prior," returned the Hermit, "you are to know that I belong to a little diocese, where I am my own diocesan, and care as little for the Bishop of York as I do for the Abbot of Jorvaulx, the Prior, and all the convent."

"Thou art utterly irregular," said the Prior; "one of those disorderly men, who, taking on them the sacred character without due license, profane the holy rites, and endanger the souls of those who seek counsel at their hands; *lapides pro pane condonantes iis*, giving them stones instead of bread, as the Vulgate hath it."

"Nay," said the Hermit, "an my brain-pan could have been broken by Latin, it had not held so long together. I say, that the easing a world of such dandiprat priests as thou art of their jewels and their gimcracks, is a lawful spoiling of the Egyptians."

"Thou liest, Jack Priest," said the Prior, in great wrath, "*excommunicabo vos*."

"Thou liest thyself like a thief and a heretic," said the Friar, equally indignant; "I will pouch up no such affront before my parishioners, as thou thinkest it not shame to put upon me, although I be a reverend brother to thee; *ossa ejus perfringam*, I will break your bones, as the Vulgate hath it."

"Holla," cried the Captain, "come the reverend brethren to such terms?—keep thine assurances—Prior, an thou hast not made thy peace with God, provoke the Friar no further.—Hermit, let the reverend father in God depart in peace, as a ransomed man."

The yeomen separated the incensed priests, who continued to raise their voices, vituperating each other in bad Latin, which the Prior delivered most fluently, and the Hermit with the greater vehemence. The Prior at length recollected himself sufficiently to be aware that he was compromising his dignity, by squabbling with such a hedge-priest as the Outlaw's chaplain, and being joined by his attendants, rode off with considerably less pomp, and in a much more apostolical condition, so far as worldly matters were concerned, than he had exhibited before this rencounter.

It remained that the Jew should produce some security for the ransom which he was to pay on the Prior's account, as well as upon his own. He gave, accordingly, an order sealed with his signet, to a brother of his tribe at York, requiring him to pay to the bearer the sum of a thousand crowns, and to deliver certain merchandizes specified in the note.

"My brother Sheva," he said, groaning deeply, "hath the key of my warehouses."

"And of the vaulted chamber?" whispered Locksley.

"No, no—may heaven forefend!" said Isaac; "evil is the hour that let any one whomsoever into that secret."

"It is safe with me," said the Outlaw, "so be that this thy scroll produce the sum therein nominated and set down.—But what now, Isaac? art dead? art stupified? hath the payment of a thousand crowns put thy daughter's peril out of thy mind?"

The Jew started to his feet—"No, Diccon, no—I will presently set forth.—Fare thee well, thou whom I may not call good, and dare not and will not call evil."

Yet ere Isaac departed, the Outlaw Chief bestowed on him this parting advice:—"Be liberal of thine offers, Isaac, and spare not thy purse for thy daughter's safety. Credit me, that the gold thou shalt spare in her cause, will hereafter give thee as much agony as if it were poured molten down thy throat."

Isaac acquiesced with a deep groan, and set forth on his journey, accompanied by two tall foresters, who were to be his guides, and at the same time his guards through the wood.

The Black Knight, who had seen with no small interest these various proceedings, now took his leave of the Outlaw in turn; nor could he avoid expressing his surprise at having witnessed so much of civil policy amongst persons cast out from all the ordinary protection and influence of the laws.

"Good fruit, Sir Knight," replied the yeoman, "will sometimes grow on a sorry tree; and evil times are not always productive of evil alone and unmixed. Amongst those who are driven into this lawless state, there are, doubtless, numbers who wish to exercise its licence with some moderation, and some who regret, it may be, that they are obliged to follow such a trade at all."

"And to one of these," said the knight, "I am now, I presume, speaking?"

"Sir Knight," said the Outlaw, "we have each our secret. You are welcome to form your judgment of me, and I may use my conjectures touching you, though neither of our shafts may hit the mark they are shot at. But as I do not pray to be admitted into your mystery, be not offended that I preserve mine own."

"I crave pardon, brave Outlaw," said the knight, "your reproof is just. But it may be we shall meet hereafter with less of concealment on either side.—Meanwhile we part friends, do we not?"

"There is my hand upon it," said Locksley; "and I will call it the hand of a true Englishman, though an outlaw for the present."

"And there is mine in return," said the knight; "and I hold it honoured by being clasped with your's. For he that does good, having the unlimited power to do evil, deserves praise not only for the good which he performs, but for the evil which he forbears.—Fare thee well, gallant Outlaw!"

Thus parted that fair fellowship; and He of the Fetterlock, mounting upon his strong war-horse, rode off through the forest.

Chapter Four

King John. I'll tell thee what, my friend,
He is a very serpent in my way;
And wheresoe'er this foot of mine doth tread,
He lies before me.—Doest thou understand me?
King John.

THERE WAS brave feasting in the Castle of York, to which Prince John had invited those nobles, prelates, and leaders, by whose assistance he hoped to carry through his ambitious projects upon his brother's throne. Waldemar Fitzurse, his able and politic agent, was in secret at work amongst them, tempering all to that pitch of courage which was necessary ere making an open declaration of their purpose. But their enterprize was delayed by the absence of more than one main limb of the confederacy. The stubborn and daring, though brutal courage of Front-de-Bœuf; the buoyant spirits and bold bearing of De Bracy; the sagacity, martial experience, and renowned valour of Brian de Bois-Guilbert, were important to the success of their conspiracy; and, while cursing betwixt themselves their unnecessary and unmeaning absence, neither John nor his adviser dared to proceed without them. Isaac the Jew also seemed to have vanished, and with him the hope of certain sums of money, making up the subsidy for which Prince John had contracted with that Israelite and his brethren. This deficiency was likely to prove perilous in an emergency so critical.

It was on the morning after the fall of Torquilstone, that a confused report began to spread abroad in the city of York, that De Bracy and Bois-Guilbert, with their confederate Front-de-Bœuf, had been taken or slain. Waldemar brought the rumour to Prince John, announcing, that he feared its truth the more that they had set out ill-attended, with the purpose of committing an assault on the Saxon Cedric and his attendance. At another time the Prince would have treated this deed of violence as a good jest; but now, that it interfered with and impeded his own plans, he exclaimed against the perpetrators, and spoke of the broken laws, and the infringement of public order and of private property, in a tone which might have become King Alfred.

"The unprincipled marauders!" he said—"were I monarch of England, I would hang such transgressors over the draw-bridges of their own castles."

"But to become monarch of England," said his Achitophel coolly, "it is necessary not only that your Grace should endure the transgressions of these unprincipled marauders, but that you should afford them your protection, notwithstanding your laudable zeal for the laws which they are in the habit of infringing. We shall have been finely holped up, if the churl Saxons should have realized your Grace's vision, of converting feudal draw-bridges into gibbets; and yonder bold-spirited Cedric seemeth one to whom such an imagination might occur. Your Grace is well aware, it will be dangerous to stir without Front-de-Bœuf, De Bracy, and the Templar; and yet we have gone too far to recede with safety."

Prince John struck his forehead with impatience, and then began to stride up and down the apartment.

"The villains," said he, "the base, treacherous villains, to desert me at this pinch!"

"Nay, say rather the feather-pated giddy fools," said Waldemar, "who must be toying with follies when such business was in hand."

"What is to be done?" said the Prince, stopping short before Waldemar.

"I know nothing which can be done," answered his counsellor, "save that which I have already taken order for.—I came not to bewail this evil chance with your Grace, until I had done my best to remedy it."

"Thou art ever my better angel, Waldemar," said the Prince; "and when I have such a chancellor to advise withal, the reign of John will be renowned in our annals.—What hast thou commanded?"

"I have caused Louis Winkelbrand, De Bracy's lieutenant, to cause his trumpets to sound to horse and to display his banner, and set presently forth towards the castle of Front-de-Bœuf, to do what yet may be done for the succour of our friends."

Prince John's face flushed with the pride of a spoilt child, who has undergone what it conceives to be an insult.

"By the face of God!" he said, "Waldemar Fitzurse, much hast thou taken upon thee; and over malapert thou wert to cause trumpet to blow, or banner to be raised, in a town where ourselves were in presence, without our express command."

"I crave your Grace's pardon," said Fitzurse, internally cursing the idle vanity of his patron; "but when time pressed, and even the loss of minutes might be fatal, I judged it better to take this much burthen upon me, in a matter of such importance to your Grace's interest."

"Thou art pardoned, Fitzurse," said the Prince, gravely; "thy purpose hath atoned for thy hasty rashness.—But whom have we here?—De Bracy himself, by the rood!—and in strange guise doth he come before us."

It was indeed De Bracy "bloody with spurring, fiery red with speed." His armour bore all the marks of the late obstinate fray, being broken, defaced, stained with blood in many places, and covered with clay and dust from the crest to the spur. Undoing his helmet, he placed it on the table, and stood a moment as if to collect himself before he told his news.

"De Bracy," said Prince John, "what means this?—Speak, I charge thee!—Are the Saxons in rebellion?"

"Speak, De Bracy," said Fitzurse, almost in the same moment with his master, "thou wert wont to be a man—Where is the Templar?—where Front-de-Bœuf?"

"The Templar is fled," said De Bracy; "Front-de-Bœuf you will never see more. He has found a red grave among the blazing rafters of his own castle, and I alone am escaped to tell you."

"Cold news," said Waldemar, "to us, though you speak of fire and conflagration."

"The worst news is not yet said," answered De Bracy; and, coming up to Prince John, he uttered in a low and emphatic tone the words—"Richard is in England—I have seen and spoken with him."

Prince John turned pale, tottered, and caught at the back of an oaken bench to support himself—much like to a man who receives an arrow in his bosom.

"Thou ravest, De Bracy," said Fitzurse, "it cannot be."

"It is as true as truth itself," said De Bracy; "I was his prisoner, and spoke with him."

"With Richard Plantagenet, sayest thou?" continued Fitzurse.

"With Richard Plantagenet," replied De Bracy, "with Richard Cœur de Lion—with Richard of England."

"And thou wert his prisoner?" said Waldemar; "he is then at the head of a power?"

"No—only a few outlawed yeomen were around him, and to these his person is unknown. I heard him say he was about to depart from them. He joined them but to assist in the storming of Torquilstone."

"Ay," replied Fitzurse, "such is indeed the fashion of Richard—A true knight-errant he, and will wander in wild adventure, trusting the prowess of his single arm, like any Sir Guy or Sir Bevis, while the weighty affairs of his kingdom slumber, and his own safety is endangered.—What dost thou propose to do, De Bracy?"

"I—I offered Richard the service of my Free Lances, and he refused them—I will lead them to Hull, seize on shipping, and embark for Flanders; thanks to the bustling times, a man of action will always find employment. And thou, Waldemar, wilt thou take lance and shield, and lay down thy policies and wend along with me, and share the fate which God sends us?"

"I am too old, Maurice, and I have a daughter," answered Waldemar.

"Give her to me, Fitzurse, and I will maintain her as fits her rank, with the help of lance and stirrup," said De Bracy.

"Not so," answered Fitzurse; "I will take sanctuary in the church of Saint Peter—the Archbishop is my sworn brother."

During this discourse, Prince John had gradually awakened from the stupor into which he had been thrown by the unexpected intelligence, and had become attentive to the conversation which passed betwixt his followers. "They fall off from me," he said to himself, "they hold no more by me than the withered leaf by the branch when a breeze blows on it!—Hell and fiends, can I shape no means for myself when I am deserted by these cravens?"—He paused, and there was an expression of diabolical passion in the constrained laugh with which he at length broke in on their conversation.

"Ha, ha, ha! my good lords, by the light of Our Lady's brow, I held ye sage men, bold men, ready-witted men; yet ye throw down wealth, honour, pleasure, all that our noble game promised you, at the moment it might be won by one bold cast!"

"I understand you not," said De Bracy. "So soon as Richard's return is blown abroad, he will be at the head of an army, and all is then over with us. I would counsel you, my lord, either to fly to France, or take the protection of the Queen Mother."

"I seek no safety for myself," said Prince John, haughtily; "that I could secure by a word spoken to my brother. But although you, De Bracy, and you, Waldemar Fitzurse, are so ready to abandon me, I should not greatly delight to see your heads set on Clifford's gate, yonder. Thinkest thou, Waldemar, that the wily Archbishop will not suffer thee to be taken from the very horns of the altar, would it make his peace with King Richard? And forgettest thou, De Bracy, that Robert Estoteville lies betwixt thee and Hull with all his forces, and that the Earl of Essex is gathering his followers? If we had reason to fear these levies even before Richard's return, trowest thou there is any doubt now which party their leaders will take? Trust me, Estoteville alone has strength enough to drive all thy Free Lances into the Humber."—Waldemar Fitzurse and De Bracy looked in each other's faces with blank dismay.—"There is but one road to safety," continued the Prince, and his brow grew black as midnight; "this object of our terror journeys alone—He must be met withal."

"Not by me," said De Bracy, hastily; "I was his prisoner, and he took me to mercy—I will not harm a feather in his crest."

"Who spoke of harming him?" said Prince John, with a hardened laugh; "the knave will say next that I meant he should slay him!—No

—a prison were better; and whether in Britain or Austria, what matters it? Things will be but as they were when we commenced our enterprize—It was founded on the hope that Richard should remain a captive in Germany—Our uncle Robert lived and died in the castle of Cardiffe."

"Ay, but," said Waldemar, "your grandsire Henry sate more firm on his seat than your Grace can. I say the best prison is that which is made by the sexton—no dungeon like a church-vault! I have said my say."

"Prison or tomb," said De Bracy, "I wash my hands of the whole matter."

"Villain!" said Prince John, "thou wouldest not bewray our counsel?"

"Counsel was never bewrayed by me," said De Bracy, haughtily, "nor must the name of villain be coupled with mine."

"Peace, Sir Knight!" said Waldemar;—"and you, good my lord, forgive the scruples of valiant De Bracy; I trust I shall soon remove them."

"That passes your eloquence, Fitzurse," replied the knight.

"Why, good Sir Maurice," rejoined the wily politician, "start not aside like a scared steed, without, at least, considering the object of your terror.—This Richard—but a day since, and it would have been thy dearest wish to have met him hand to hand in the ranks of battle—an hundred times I have heard thee wish it."

"Ay," said De Bracy, "but that was as thou sayest, hand to hand, and in the ranks of battle! Thou never heardest me breathe a thought of assaulting him alone, and in a forest?"

"Thou art no good knight if thou dost scruple at it," said Waldemar. "Was it in battle that Lancelot de Lac and Sir Tristram won renown? or was it not by encountering gigantic knights under the shade of deep and unknown forests?"

"Ay, but I promise you," said De Bracy, "that neither Tristram nor Lancelot would have been match, hand to hand, for Richard Plantagenet, and I think it was not their wont to take odds against a single man."

"Thou art mad, De Bracy—what is it we propose to thee, a hired and retained captain of Free Companions, whose swords are purchased for Prince John's service, than a surprizal of our enemy. And this thou scruplest, though thy patron's fortunes, those of thy comrades, thine own, and the life and honour of every one amongst us be at stake!"

"I tell you," said De Bracy, sullenly, "that he gave me my life—true, he sent me from his presence, and refused my homage—so far I owe him neither favour nor allegiance—But I will not lift hand against him."

"It needs not—send Louis Winkelbrand and a score of thy lances."

"Ye have sufficient ruffians of your own," said De Bracy; "not one of mine shall budge on such an errand."

"Art thou so obstinate, De Bracy?" said Prince John; "and wilt thou forsake me, after so many protestations of zeal for my service?"

"I mean it not," said De Bracy; "I will abide by you in aught that becomes a knight, whether in the lists or in the camp; but this highway practice comes not within my vow."

"Come hither, Waldemar," said Prince John. "An unhappy prince am I. My father, King Henry, had faithful servants—He had but to say that he was plagued with a factious priest, and the blood of Thomas-a-Becket, saint though he was, stained the steps of his own altar.—Tracy, Morville, Brito,* loyal and daring subjects, your names, your spirit, are extinct! and although Reginald Fitzurse hath left a son, he hath fallen off from his father's fidelity and courage."

"He has fallen off in neither," said Waldemar Fitzurse; "and since it may no better be, I will take on me the conduct of this perilous enterprize. Dearly, however, did my father purchase the praise of a zealous friend; and yet did his proof of loyalty to Henry fall far short of what I am about to afford. For rather would I assail a whole calendar of saints, than put spear in rest against Cœur de Lion.—De Bracy, to thee I must trust to keep up the spirits of the doubtful, and to guard Prince John's person. If you receive such news as I trust to send you, our enterprize will no longer wear a doubtful aspect.—Page," he said, "hie to my lodgings, and tell my armourer to be there in readiness; and bid Stephen Wetheral, Broad Thoresby, and the three spears of Spyinghow, attend me instantly; and let the scout-master, Hugh Bardan, attend me also. Adieu, my Prince, till better times." Thus speaking, he left the apartment.

"He goes to make my brother prisoner," said Prince John to De Bracy, "with as little touch of compunction as if it but concerned the liberty of a Saxon Franklin. I trust he will observe our orders, and use our dear Richard's person with all due respect."

De Bracy only answered by a smile.

"By the light of Our Lady's brow," said Prince John, "our orders to him were most precise—though it may be you heard them not, as we stood together in the oriel window—Most clear and positive was our charge that Richard's safety should be cared for, and woe to

*Reginald Fitzurse, William de Tracy, Hugh de Morville, and Richard Brito, were the gentlemen of Henry the Second's household, who, instigated by some passionate expressions of their sovereign, slew the celebrated Thomas-a-Becket.

Waldemar's head if he transgress it!"

"I had better pass to his lodgings," said De Bracy, "and make him fully aware of your Grace's pleasure; for, as it quite escaped my ear, it may not perchance have reached that of Waldemar."

"Nay, nay," said Prince John impatiently, "I promise thee he heard me; and, besides, I have farther occupation for thee, Maurice. Come hither, let me lean on thy shoulder."

They walked a turn through the hall in this familiar posture, and Prince John, with an air of the most confidential intimacy, proceeded to say, "What thinkest thou of this Waldemar Fitzurse, my De Bracy? —He trusts to be our Chancellor. Surely we will pause ere we give an office so high to one who shows evidently how little he reverences our blood, by his so readily undertaking this enterprize against Richard. Thou dost think, I warrant, that thou hast lost some of our regard, by thy boldly declining this unpleasing task—But no, Maurice! I rather honour thee for thy virtuous constancy. There are things most necessary to be done, the perpetrator of which we neither love nor honour; and there may be refusals to serve us, which shall rather exalt in our estimation those who deny us our request. The arrest of my unfortunate brother forms no such good title to the high office of Chancellor, as thy chivalrous and courageous denial establishes upon the truncheon of High Marshal. Think on this, De Bracy, and begone to thy charge."——

"Fickle tyrant!" murmured De Bracy, as he left the presence of the Prince; "evil luck have they who trust thee. Thy Chancellor, indeed! —He who hath the keeping of thy conscience shall have an easy charge, I trow. But High Marshal of England! that," said he, extending his arm, as if to grasp the baton of office, and assuming a loftier stride along the anti-chamber, "that is indeed a prize worth playing for!"

De Bracy had no sooner left the apartment than Prince John summoned an attendant.

"Bid Hugh Bardan, our scout-master, come hither, so soon as he shall have spoken with Waldemar Fitzurse."

The scout-master arrived after a brief delay, during which John traversed his apartment with unequal and disordered steps, now slowly, now with a rapid, but always with a disordered pace.

"Bardan," said he, "what did Waldemar desire of thee?"

"Two resolved men, well acquainted with these northern wilds, and skilful in tracking the tread of man and horse."

"And thou hast fitted him?"

"Let your Grace never trust me else," answered the master of the spies. "One is from Hexhamshire; he is wont to trace the Tynedale and Teviotdale thieves, as a blood-hound follows the slot of a hurt deer. The other is Yorkshire bred, and has twanged his bow-string right in merry Sherwood. He knows each glade and dingle, copse and high-wood, betwixt this and Richmond."

"'Tis well," said the Prince. "Goes Waldemar forth with them?"

"Instantly," said Bardan.

"With what attendance?" replied John carelessly.

"Broad Thoresby goes with him, and Wetheral, whom they call, for his cruelty, Stephen Steelheart; and three northern men-at-arms that belonged to Ralph Middleton's gang—they are called the Spears of Spyinghow."

"'Tis well," said Prince John; then added, after a moment's pause, "Bardan, it imports our service that thou keep a strict watch on Maurice De Bracy—so that he shall not observe it, however—And let us know of his motions from time to time, with whom he converses, what he proposeth. Fail not in this, as thou wilt be answerable."

Hugh Bardan bowed, and retired.

"If Maurice betrays me," said Prince John—"if he betrays me, as his bearing leads me to fear, I will have his head, were Richard thundering at the gates of York!"

Chapter Five

Arouse the tiger of Hyrcanian deserts,
Strive with the half-starved lion for his prey;
Lesser the risk, than rouse the slumbering fire
Of wild Fanaticism.

Anonymous.

OUR TALE now returns to Isaac of York.—Mounted upon a mule, the gift of the Outlaw Chief, and with two tall yeomen to act as his guard and guide, the Jew had set out for the Preceptory of Templestowe, for the purpose of negociating his daughter's redemption. The Preceptory was but a day's journey from the demolished castle of Torquilstone, and the Jew had hoped to reach it before nightfall; accordingly, having dismissed his guides at the verge of the forest, and rewarded them with a piece of silver, he began to press on with such speed as his weariness permitted him to exert. But his strength failed him totally ere he had reached within four miles of Templestowe; racking pains shot along his back and through his limbs, and the excessive anguish which he felt at heart being now augmented by bodily suffering, he was rendered altogether incapable of proceeding farther than a small market-town, where dwelt a Jewish Rabbi of his tribe, eminent in the medical profession, and to whom Isaac was well known. Nathan Ben

Samuel received his suffering countryman with that kindness which the law prescribed, and which the Jews practised to each other. He insisted on his betaking himself to repose, and used such remedies as were then in most repute to check the progress of the fever, which terror, fatigue, and sorrow, had brought upon the poor old Jew.

On the morrow, when Isaac prepared to arise and renew his journey, Nathan remonstrated against his purpose, both as his host and as his physician. It might cost him, he said, his life. But Isaac replied, that more than life and death depended on his going that morning to Templestowe.

"To Templestowe!" said his host with surprise; again felt his pulse, and then muttered to himself, "His fever is abated, yet seems his mind somewhat alienated and disturbed."

"And why not to Templestowe?" answered his patient. "I grant thee, Nathan, that it is a dwelling of those to whom the despised Children of the Promise are a stumbling-block and an abomination; yet thou knowest that pressing affairs of traffic sometimes carry us amongst these blood-thirsty Nazarene soldiers, and that we visit the Preceptories of the Templars, as well as the Commanderies of the Knights Hospitallers, as they are called."*

"I knew it well," said Nathan; "but wottest thou that Lucas de Beaumanoir, the chief of their Order, and whom they term Grand Master, is now himself at Templestowe?"

"I know it not," said Isaac; "our last letters from our brethren at Paris avised him to be at that city, beseeching Philip for aid against the Sultan Saladin."

"He hath since come to England, unexpected by his brethren; and he cometh among them with a strong and outstretched arm to correct and to punish. His countenance is kindled in anger against those who have departed from the vows which they have made, and great is the fear of those sons of Belial. Thou must have heard of his name?"

"It is well known unto me," answered Isaac; "the Gentiles deliver this Lucas Beaumanoir as a man zealous to slaying for every point of the Nazarene law; and our brethren have termed him a cruel destroyer of the Saracens, and a cruel tyrant to the Children of the Promise."

"And truly have they termed him," said Nathan the physician. "Other Templars may be moved from the purpose of their heart by pleasure, or bribed by promise of gold and silver; but Beaumanoir is

*The establishments of the Knights Templars were called Preceptories, and the title of those who presided in the Order was Preceptor, as the principal Knights of Saint John were termed Commanders, and their houses Commanderies. But these terms were sometimes, it would seem, used indiscriminately.

of a different stamp—hating sensuality, despising treasure, and pressing forward to that which they call the crown of martyrdom—The God of Jacob speedily send it unto him, and over them all!—Specially hath this proud man extended his glove over the children of Judah, as holy David over Edom, holding the murther of a Jew to be an offering of as sweet savour as the death of a Saracen. Impious and false things has he said even of the virtues of our medicines, as if they were the devices of Satan—The Lord rebuke him!"

"Nevertheless," said Isaac, "I must present myself at Templestowe, though he hath made his face like unto an fiery furnace seven times heated."

He then explained to Nathan the pressing cause of his journey. The Rabbi listened with interest, and testified his sympathy after the fashion of his people, rending his clothes, and saying, "Ah, my daughter! —ah, my daughter!—Alas! for the daughter of Zion—Alas! for the captivity of Israel!"

"Thou seest," said Isaac, "how it stands with me, and that I may not tarry. Peradventure, the presence of this Lucas Beaumanoir, being the chief man over them, may turn Brian de Bois-Guilbert from the ill which he doth meditate, and that he may deliver to me my beloved daughter Rebecca."

"Go thou," said Nathan Ben Samuel, "and be wise, for wisdom availed Daniel, even in the den of lions into which he was cast; and may it go well with thee, even as thy heart wisheth. Yet if thou canst keep thee from the presence of the Grand Master, it were better with thee, for to do foul scorn to our people is his morning and evening delight. It may be if thou couldst speak with Bois-Guilbert in private, thou shalt the better prevail with him; for men say that these accursed Nazarenes are not at one together in the Preceptory—May their counsels be confounded and brought to shame! But do thou, brother, return to me as if it were to the house of thy father, and bring me word how it has sped with thee; and well do I hope thou wilt bring with thee Rebecca, even the scholar of the wise Miriam, whose cures the Gentiles slandered as if they had been wrought by nigromancy."

Isaac accordingly bade his friend farewell, and about an hour's riding brought him before the Preceptory of Templestowe.

This establishment of the Templars was seated amidst fair meadows and pastures, which the devotion of the former proprietor had bestowed upon their Order. It was strong and well fortified, a point never neglected by these knights, and which the disordered state of England rendered peculiarly necessary. Two halberdiers, clad in black, guarded the draw-bridge, and others, in the same sad livery, glided to and fro upon the walls with a funereal pace, resembling spectres more than soldiers. The inferior officers of the Order were thus dressed, ever since their use of white garments, similar to those of the knights and esquires, had given rise to a combination of certain false brethren in the mountains of Palestine, terming themselves Templars, and bringing great dishonour on the Order. A knight was now and then seen to cross the court in his long white cloak, his head depressed on his breast, and his arms folded. They passed each other, if they chanced to meet, with a slow, solemn, and mute greeting; for such was the rule of their Order, quoting thereupon the holy texts, *In many words thou shalt not avoid sin*, and *Life and death are in the power of the tongue.* In a word, the stern ascetic rigour of the Temple discipline, which had so long been exchanged for prodigal and licentious indulgence, seemed at once to have revived at Templestowe under the severe eye of Lucas Beaumanoir.

Isaac paused at the gate, to consider how he might seek entrance in the manner most likely to bespeak favour; for he was well aware, that to his unhappy race the reviving fanaticism of the Order was not less dangerous than their unprincipled licentiousness; and that his religion would be the object of hate and persecution in the one case, as his wealth would have exposed him in the other to the extortions of unrelenting oppression.

Meantime Lucas Beaumanoir walked in a small garden belonging to the Preceptory, included within the precincts of its exterior fortification, and held sad and confidential communication with a brother of the Order, who had come in his company from Palestine.

The Grand Master was a man advanced in age, as was testified by his long grey beard, and the shaggy grey eye-brows over-hanging eyes, of which, however, years had been unable to quench the fire. A formidable warrior, his thin and severe features retained the soldier's fierceness of expression; an ascetic bigot, they were no less marked by the emaciation of abstinence, and the spiritual pride of the self-satisfied devotee. Yet, with these sinister traits of physiognomy, there was mixed something striking and noble, arising, doubtless, from the great part which his high office called upon him to act among monarchs and princes, and from the habitual exercise of supreme authority over the valiant and high-born knights, who were united by the rules of the Order. His stature was tall, and his gait, undepressed by age and toil, was erect and stately. His white mantle was shaped with severe regularity, according to the rule of Saint Bernard himself, being composed of what was then called Burrel cloth, justly fitted to the size of the wearer, and bearing on the left shoulder the octangular cross peculiar to their Order, shaped in red cloth. No vair or ermine decked this garment; but in respect of his age, the Grand Master, as permitted by the rules, wore his doublet trimmed and lined with the softest lamb-skin, dressed with the wool outwards, which was the nearest approach he could regularly make to the use of furs, then the greatest luxury of dress. In his hand he bore that singular *abacus*, or staff of office, with which Templars are often represented, having at the upper end a round plate, on which was engraved the cross of the Order, inscribed within a circle or an orle, as heralds term it. His companion, who attended on this great personage, had nearly the same dress in all respects, but his extreme deference towards his superior shewed that no other equality subsisted betwixt them. The Preceptor, for such he was in rank, walked not in a line with the Grand Master, but just so far behind that Beaumanoir could speak to him without turning round his head.

"Conrade," said the Grand Master, "dear companion of my battles and my toils, to thy faithful bosom alone I can confide my sorrows. To thee alone can I tell how oft, since I came to this kingdom, I have desired to be dissolved and to be with the just. Not one object in England hath met mine eye on which it could repose with pleasure, save the tombs of our brethren, beneath the massive roof of our Temple Church in yonder proud capital. O, valiant Robert de Ros! did I exclaim internally, as I gazed upon these good soldiers of the cross, where they lie sculptured on their tombs,—O, worthy William de Mareschal! open your marble cells, and take to your repose a weary brother, who would rather strive with a hundred thousand pagans than witness the decay of our Holy Order!"

"It is but true," answered Conrade Mountfitchet; "it is but too true; and the irregularities of our brethren in England are even more gross than those in France."

"Because they are more wealthy," answered the Grand Master. "Bear with me, brother, though I should something vaunt myself. Thou knowest the life I have led, keeping each point of my Order, striving with devils embodied and disembodied, striking down the roaring lion, who goeth about seeking whom he may devour, like a good knight and a devout priest, wheresoever I met with him—even as blessed Saint Bernard hath prescribed to us in the forty-fifth capital of our rule, *Ut Leo semper feriatur*. But, by the Holy Temple! the zeal which hath devoured my substance and my life, yea, the very nerves and marrow of my bones; by that very Holy Temple I swear to thee, that save thyself, and some few who still retain the ancient severity of our Order, I look upon no brethren whom I can bring my soul to embrace under that holy name. What say our statutes, and how do our brethren observe them? They should wear no vain or worldly ornament, no crest upon their helmet, no gold upon stirrup or bridle-bit;

yet who now go pranked out so proudly and so gaily, as the poor soldiers of the Temple? They are forbidden to take one bird by means of another, to shoot beasts with bow or arblast, to hollo to a hunting-hound, or to spur the horse after game. But now, at hunting and hawking, and each idle sport of wood and river, who so prompt as they in all these fond vanities? They were forbidden to read, save what their Superiors permitted, or what holy thing was read aloud during the hours of refection; and they were commanded to extirpate magic and heresy. Lo! they are charged with studying the accursed cabalistical secrets of the Jews, and the magic of the Paynim Saracens. Simpleness of diet was prescribed to them, roots, pottage, gruels, eating flesh but thrice a-week, because the accustomed feeding on flesh is dishonourable corruption of the body; and behold, their tables groan under delicate fare. Their drink was to be water; and now, to drink like a Templar, is the boast of each jolly boon companion! This very garden, filled as it is with curious herbs and trees sent from the eastern climes, better beseems the haram of an unbelieving Emir, than the plot which Christian monks should devote to raise their pot-herbs.—And O, Conrade! well it were that the relaxation of discipline stopped even here!—Well thou knowest that we were forbidden to receive those devout women, who at the beginning were associated as sisters of our Order, because, saith the fifty-sixth chapter, the Ancient Enemy hath, by female society, withdrawn many from the right path to paradise. Nay, in the last capital, being, as it were, the cope-stone which our blessed founder placed on the pure and undefiled doctrine which he had enjoined, we are prohibited from offering, even to our sisters and our mothers, the kiss of affection—*ut omnium mulierum fugiantur oscula.*—I shame to speak—I shame to think of the corruptions which have rushed in upon us even like a landflood. The souls of our pious founders, the spirits of Hugh de Payen and Godfrey de Saint Omer, and of the blessed Seven who with them first joined in dedicating their lives to the defence of the Temple, are disturbed even in the enjoyment of paradise itself. I have seen them, Conrade, in the visions of the night—their sainted eyes shed tears for the follies and sins of their brethren, and for the foul and shameful luxury in which they wallow. Beaumanoir, they say, thou slumberest—awake! There is a stain in the fabric of the Temple, deep and foul as that left by the streaks of leprosy in the walls of the infected houses of old.* The soldiers of the Cross, who should shun the glance of woman as the eye of a basilisk, live in open sin, not with the females of their own race only, but with the daughters of the accursed heathen and more accur-

* See the 13th chapter of Leviticus.

sed Jew. Beaumanoir, thou sleepest, up, and avenge our cause!—Slay the sinners, male and female!—Take to thee the brand of Phineas!—The vision fled, Conrade, but as I awaked I could still hear the clank of their mail, and see the waving of their white mantles.—And I will do according to their word, I WILL purify the fabric of the Temple! and the unclean stones in which the plague is, will I remove and cast out of the building."

"Yet bethink thee, reverend father," said Mountfitchet, "the stain hath become engrained by time and consuetude; let thy reformation be cautious, as it is just and wise."

"No, Mountfitchet—it must be sharp and sudden—the Order is on the crisis of its fate. The sobriety, self-devotion, and piety of our predecessors, made us powerful friends—our presumption, our wealth, our luxury, have raised up against us mighty enemies.—We must cast away these riches, which are a temptation to princes—we must lay down that presumption, which is an offence to them—we must reform that license of manners, which is a scandal to the whole Christian world! Or—mark my words—the Order of the Temple will be utterly demolished—and the place thereof shall no longer be known among the nations."

"Now may God avert such a calamity!" said the Preceptor.

"Amen," said the Grand Master, with solemnity, "but we must deserve his aid. I tell thee, Conrade, that neither the powers in Heaven nor the powers on earth, will longer endure the wickedness of this generation—My intelligence is sure—the ground on which our fabric is reared is already undermined, and each addition we make to the structure of our greatness will only sink it the sooner in the abyss. We must retrace our steps, and shew ourselves the faithful Champions of the Cross, sacrificing to our calling, not alone our blood and our lives—not alone our lusts and our vices—but our ease, our comforts, and our natural affections, and many a pleasure that may be lawful to others, but is forbidden to the vowed soldier of the Temple."

At this moment a squire, clothed in a thread-bare vestment, (for the aspirants after this holy Order wore during their novitiate the cast-off garments of the knights,) entered the garden, and, bowing profoundly before the Grand Master, stood silent, awaiting his permission ere he presumed to tell his errand.

"Is it not more seemly," said the Grand Master, "to see this Damian, clothed in the garments of Christian humility, thus appear with reverend silence before his Superior, than but two days since, when the fond fool was decked in a painted coat, and jangling as pert and as proud as any popingay?—Speak, Damian, we permit thee—What is thine errand?"

"A Jew stands without the gate, noble and reverend father, who prays to speak with brother Brian de Bois-Guilbert."

"Thou wert right to give me knowledge of it," said the Grand Master; "in our presence a Preceptor is but as a common confrere of our Order, who may not walk according to his own will, but that of his Master—even according to the text, 'In the hearing of the ear he hath obeyed me.'—It imports us especially to know of this Bois-Guilbert's proceedings," said he, turning to his companion.

"Report speaks him brave and valiant," said Conrade.

"And truly is he so spoken," said the Grand Master; "in our valour only we are not degenerated from our predecessors, the heroes of the Cross. But brother Brian came into our Order a moody and disappointed man, stirred, I doubt me, to take our vows and to renounce the world, not in sincerity of soul, but as one whom some touch of light discontent had driven into penitence. Since then, he hath become an active and earnest agitator, a murmurer, and a machinator, and a leader amongst those who impugn our authority; not considering that the rule is given to the Master even by the symbol of the staff and the rod—the staff to support the infirmities of the weak—the rod to correct the faults of delinquents.—Damian," he continued, "lead the Jew to our presence."

The squire departed with a profound reverence, and in a few minutes returned, marshalling in Isaac of York. No naked slave, ushered into the presence of some mighty prince, could approach his judgment-seat with more profound reverence and terror than that with which the Jew drew near to the presence of the Grand Master. When he had approached within the distance of three yards, Beaumanoir made a sign with his staff that he should come no farther. The Jew kneeled down on the earth, which he kissed in token of reverence; then rising, stood before the Templars, his hands folded on his bosom, his head bowed on his breast, in all the submission of oriental slavery.

"Damian," said the Grand Master, "retire, and have a guard ready to await our sudden call; and suffer no one to enter the garden until we shall leave it."—The squire bowed and retreated.—"Jew," continued the haughty old man, "mark me. It suits not our condition to hold with thee long communication, nor do we waste words and time upon any one. Wherefore be brief in thy answers to what questions I shall ask thee, and let thy words be of truth; for if thy tongue doubles with me, I will have it torn from thy misbelieving jaws."

The Jew was about to reply, but the Grand Master went on.

"Peace, unbeliever!—not a word in our presence, save in answer to our questions.—What is thy business with our brother Brian de Bois-Guilbert?"

Isaac gasped with terror and uncertainty. To tell his tale might be interpreted into scandalizing the Order; yet, unless he told it, what hope could he have of achieving his daughter's deliverance? Beaumanoir saw his mortal apprehension, and condescended to give him some assurance.

"Fear nothing," he said, "for thy wretched person, Jew, so thou dealest uprightly in this matter.—I demand again to know from thee thy business with Brian de Bois-Guilbert?"

"I am bearer of a letter," stammered out the Jew, "so please your reverend valour, to that good knight, from Aymer, Prior of the Abbey of Jorvaulx."

"Said I not these were evil times, Conrade?" said the Master. "A Cistercian Prior sends a letter to a soldier of the Temple, and can find no more fitting messenger than a misbelieving Jew.—Give me the letter."

The Jew, with trembling hand, undid the folds of his Armenian cap, in which he had deposited the Prior's tablets for the greater security, and was about to approach, with hand extended and body crouch'd, to place it within the reach of his grim interrogator.

"Back, dog!" said the Grand Master; "I touch not misbelievers, save with the sword.—Conrade, take thou the letter from the Jew, and give it to me."

Beaumanoir, being thus possessed of the tablets, inspected the outside carefully, and then proceeded to undo the packthread which secured its folds. "Reverend Father," said Conrade, interposing, though with much deference, "wilt thou break the seal?"

"And will I not?" said Beaumanoir, with a frown. "Is it not written in the forty-second capital, *De Lectione Literarum*, that a Templar shall not receive a letter, no not from his father, without communicating the same to the Grand Master, and reading it in his presence?"

He then perused the letter in haste, with an expression of surprise and horror; read it over again more slowly; then holding it out to Conrade with one hand, and slightly striking it with the other, exclaimed,—"Here is goodly stuff for one Christian man to write to another, and both members, and no inconsiderable members, of religious professions! When," said he solemnly, and looking upward, "wilt thou come with thy fanners to purge the threshing-floor?"

Mountfitchet took the letter from his superior, and was about to peruse it. "Read it aloud, Conrade," said the Grand Master, "and do thou (to Isaac) attend to the purport of it, for we will question thee concerning it."

Conrade read the letter, which was in these words: "Aymer, by divine grace, Prior of the Cistercian house of Saint Mary's of Jorvaulx, to Sir Brian de Bois-Guilbert, a Knight of the holy Order of the Temple, wisheth health, with the bounties of Bacchus and of my Lady Venus.

"Touching our present condition, dear Brother, we are a captive in the hands of certain lawless and godless men, who have not feared to detain our person, and put us to ransom, whereby we have also learned of Front-de-Bœuf's misfortune, and that thou had escaped with that fair Jewish sorceress, whose black eyes have bewitched thee. We are heartily rejoiced of thy safety; nevertheless, we pray thee to be on thy guard in the matter of this second Witch of Endor. For we are privately assured that your Great Master, who careth not a bean for cherry cheeks and black eyes, comes from Normandy hither to diminish your mirth, and amend your misdoings. Wherefore we pray you heartily to beware, and to be found watching, even as the Holy Text hath it, *Invenientur vigilantes*. And the wealthy Jew her father, Isaac of York, having prayed of me letters in his behalf, I give him these, earnestly advising that you do hold the damsel to ransom, seeing he will pay you from his bags as much as may find fifty damsels upon safer terms, whereof I trust to have my part when we make merry together, as true brothers, not forgetting the wine-cup. For what saith the text, *Vinum laetificat cor hominis;* and again, *Rex delectabitur pulchritudine tua*.

"Till which merry meeting, we wish you farewell. Given from this den of thieves, about the hour of mattins,

"AYMER PR. S. M. JORVOLCIENCIS.

"*Postscriptum*. Truly your golden chain hath not long abidden with me, and will now sustain, around the neck of an outlaw deer-stealer, the whistle wherewith he calleth on his hounds."

"What sayest thou to this, Conrade?" said the Grand Master—"Den of thieves! and a fit residence is a den of thieves for such a Prior. No wonder that the hand of God is upon us, and that in the Holy Land we lose place by place, foot by foot, before the infidels, when we have such churchmen as this Aymer.—And what meaneth he, I trow, by this second Witch of Endor?" said he to his confidant, something apart.

Conrade was better acquainted (perhaps by practice) with the jargon of gallantry, than was his superior; and he expounded the passage which embarrassed the Grand Master, to be a sort of language used by worldly men towards those whom they loved *par amours;* but the explanation did not satisfy the bigotted Beaumanoir.

"There is more in it than thou doest guess, Conrade; thy simplicity is no match for this deep abyss of wickedness. This Rebecca of York was a pupil of that Miriam of whom thou hast heard. Thou shalt hear the Jew own it even now." Then turning to Isaac, he said aloud, "Thy daughter, then, is prisoner with Brian de Bois-Guilbert?"

"Ay, reverend and valorous sir, and whatsoever ransom a poor man may pay for her deliverance"——

"Peace!" said the Grand Master. "This thy daughter hath practised the art of healing, hath she not?"

"Ay, gracious sir; and knight and yeoman, squire and vassal, may bless the goodly gift which Heaven hath assigned to her. Many a one can testify that she hath recovered them by her art when every other human aid had proved vain; but the blessing of the God of Jacob was upon her."

Beaumanoir turned to Mountfitchet with a grim smile. "See, brother," he said, "the deceptions of the devouring enemy! Behold the baits with which he fishes for souls, giving a poor space of earthly life in exchange for eternal happiness hereafter. Well said our blessed rule, *Semper percutiatur leo vorans.*—Upon the lion! Down with the destroyer!" said he, shaking aloft his mystic abacus, as if in defiance of the powers of darkness. "Thy daughter worketh her cures, I doubt not," thus he went on to address the Jew, "by words and sigils, and periapts, and other cabalistical mysteries."

"Nay, reverend and brave Knight," answered Isaac, "but in chief measure by a balsam of marvellous virtue."

"Whence had she that secret?" said Beaumanoir.

"It was derived to her," answered Isaac, reluctantly, "from Miriam, a sage matron of our tribe."

"Ah, false Jew! was it from that witch Miriam, the abomination of whose enchantments has been heard of throughout every Christian land?" exclaimed the Grand Master, crossing himself. "Her body was burned at a stake, and her ashes scattered to the four winds; and so be it with me and mine Order, an I do not as much to her pupil, and more also! I will teach her to throw spell and incantation over the soldiers of the blessed Temple.—There, Damian, spurn this Jew from the gate —shoot him dead if he oppose or turn again. With his daughter we will deal as the Christian law and our own high office best warrant."

Poor Isaac was hurried off accordingly; all his entreaties, and even his offers, unheard and disregarded. He could do no better than return to the house of the Rabbi, and endeavour, through his means, to learn how his daughter was to be disposed of. He had hitherto feared for her honour, he was now to tremble for her life.

Meanwhile, the Grand Master ordered to his presence the Preceptor of Templestowe.

Chapter Six

Say not my art is fraud—all live by seeming.
The beggar begs with it, and the gay courtier
Gains land and title, rank and rule, by seeming;
The clergy scorn it not, and the bold soldier
Will eke with it his service.—All admit it,
All practise it; and he who is content
With shewing what he is shall have small credit
In church, or camp, or state—So wags the world.
Old Play.

ALBERT MALVOISIN, President, or, in the language of the Order, Preceptor of the establishment of Templestowe, was brother to that Philip Malvoisin who has been already occasionally mentioned in this history, and was, like that baron, in close league with Brian de Bois-Guilbert.

Amongst dissolute and unprincipled men, of whom the Temple Order included but too many, Albert of Templestowe might be distinguished; but with this difference from the audacious Bois-Guilbert, that he knew how to throw over his vices and his ambition a dark veil of hypocrisy, and to assume in his exterior the fanaticism which he internally despised. Had not the arrival of the Grand Master been so unexpectedly sudden, he would have seen nothing at Templestowe which might have seemed to argue any relaxation of discipline. And, even although surprised, and to a certain extent detected, Albert Malvoisin listened with such respect and apparent contrition to the rebuke of his Superior, and made such haste to reform the particulars which he censured,—succeeded, in fine, so well in giving the air of ascetic devotion to a family which had been lately devoted to license and pleasure, that Lucas Beaumanoir began to entertain a higher opinion of the Preceptor's morals, than the first appearance of the establishment had inclined him to adopt.

But these favourable sentiments on the part of the Grand Master were greatly shaken by the intelligence that Albert had received within the house of religion the Jewish captive, and, as was to be feared, the paramour of a brother of the Order; and when Albert appeared before him, he was regarded with unwonted sternness.

"There is in this mansion, dedicated to the purposes of the holy Order of the Temple," said the Grand Master, in a severe tone, "a Jewish woman, brought hither by a brother of religion, by your connivance, Sir Preceptor."

Albert Malvoisin was overwhelmed with confusion; for the unfortunate Rebecca had been confined in a remote and secret part of the building, and every precaution used to prevent her residence there from being known. He read in the looks of Beaumanoir ruin to Bois-Guilbert and to himself, unless he should be able to avert the impending storm.

"Why are you mute?" continued the Grand Master.

"Is it permitted to me to reply?" answered the Preceptor, in a tone of the deepest humility, although by the question he only meant to give an instant's space for arranging his ideas.

"Speak! you are permitted," said the Grand Master—"speak, and say, knowest thou the capital of our holy rule,—*De commilitonibus Templi in sancta civitate, qui cum miserimis mulieribus versantur, propter oblectationem carnis?*"

"Surely, most reverend father," answered the Preceptor, "I have not risen to this office in the Order, being ignorant of one of its most important prohibitions."

"How comes it then, I demand of thee once more, that thou hast suffered a brother to bring a paramour, and that paramour a Jewish sorceress, into this holy place, to the stain and pollution thereof?"

"A Jewish sorceress!" echoed Albert Malvoisin; "good angels guard us!"

"Ay, brother, a Jewish sorceress!—Darest thou deny that this Rebecca, the daughter of that wretched usurer Isaac of York, and the pupil of the foul witch Miriam, is now—shame to be thought or spoken!—lodged within this thy Preceptory?"

"Your wisdom, reverend father," answered the Preceptor, "hath rolled away the darkness from my understanding. Much did I wonder that so good a knight as Brian de Bois-Guilbert seemed so fondly besotted on the charms of this female, whom I received into this house merely to place a bar betwixt their growing intimacy, which else had cemented at the expence of the fall of our valiant and religious brother."

"Hath nothing, then, as yet passed betwixt them in breach of his vow?" demanded the Grand Master.

"What! under this roof?" said the Preceptor, crossing himself; "Saint Magdalene and the ten thousand virgins forbid!—No! if I have sinned in receiving her here, it was in the erring thought that I might thus break off our brother's besotted devotion to this Jewess, which seemed to me so wild and unnatural that I could not but ascribe it to some touch of insanity, more to be cured by pity than by reproof. But since your reverend wisdom hath discovered this Jewish quean to be a sorceress, perchance it may account fully for his enamoured folly."

"It doth!—it doth!" said Beaumanoir; "see, brother Conrade, the peril of yielding to the first devices and blandishments of Sathan! We look upon woman only to gratify the lust of the eye, and to take pleasure in what men term her beauty; and the Ancient Enemy obtains power over us, to complete, by talisman and spell, the work which was begun by idleness and folly. It may be that our brother Bois-Guilbert does in this matter deserve rather pity than severe chastisement; rather the support of the staff, than the stripes of the rod; and that our admonitions and prayers may turn him from his folly, and restore him to his brethren."

"It were deep pity," said Conrade Mountfitchet, "to lose to the Order one of its best lances, when the Holy Community most requires the aid of its sons. Three hundred Saracens hath this Brian de Bois-Guilbert slain with his own hand."

"The blood of these accursèd dogs," said the Grand Master, "shall be a sweet and acceptable offering to the saints and angels whom they despise and blaspheme; and with their aid will we counteract the spells and charms with which our brother is entwined as in a net. He shall burst the bands of this Dalilah, as Sampson burst the two new cords with which the Philistines had bound him, and shall slaughter the infidels, even heaps upon heaps. But concerning this foul witch, who hath flung her enchantments over a brother of the Holy Temple, assuredly she shall die the death."

"But the laws of England"—said the Preceptor, who, though delighted that the Grand Master's resentment, thus fortunately averted from himself and Bois-Guilbert, had taken another direction, began now to fear he was carrying it too far.

"The laws of England," said Beaumanoir, "permit and enjoin each judge to execute justice within his own jurisdiction. The most petty baron may arrest, try, and condemn a witch found within his own domain. And shall that power be denied to the Grand Master of the Temple within the Preceptories of his Order?—No!—we will judge and condemn. The witch shall be taken out of the land, and the wickedness thereof shall be forgiven. Prepare the castle-hall for the trial of the sorceress."

Albert Malvoisin bowed and retired,—not to give directions for preparing the hall, but to seek out Brian de Bois-Guilbert, and communicate to him how matters were like to terminate. It was not long ere he found him foaming with indignation at a repulse he had of new sustained from the fair Jewess. "The unthinking," he said, "the ungrateful—Who, amidst blood and flames, would have saved her life at the risk of his own? By Heaven, Malvoisin! I abode till roof and rafter crackled and crashed around me. I was the butt of an hundred arrows; they rattled on mine armour like hail-stones against a latticed casement, and the only use I made of my shield was for her protection. This did I endure for her; and now the self-willed girl upbraids me because I did not leave her to perish, and refuses me not only the slightest proof of gratitude, but even the most distant hopes that she will ever be brought to grant any. The devil, that possessed her race with obstinacy, has concentered its full force in her single person!"

"The devil," said the Preceptor, "hath, I think, possessed you both. How oft have I preached to you caution at least, if not continence? Did I not tell you that there were willing enough Christian damsels to be met with, who would think it sin to refuse so brave a knight *le don d'amoureuse merci?* and you must needs anchor your affection on a wilful, obstinate Jewess? By the mass, I think old Lucas Beaumanoir judges right, when he maintains she hath cast a spell over you."

"Lucas Beaumanoir?" said Bois-Guilbert,—"Are these thy precautions, Malvoisin? Hast thou suffered the dotard to learn that Rebecca is in the Preceptory?"

"How could I help it?" answered the Preceptor. "I neglected nothing that could keep secret your mystery; but it is betrayed, and whether by the devil or no, the devil only can tell. But I have turned the matter as I could; you are safe if you renounce Rebecca. You are pitied—the victim of magical delusion. She is a sorceress, and must suffer as such."

"She shall not, by Heaven!" said Bois-Guilbert.

"By Heaven, she must and will!" said Malvoisin. "Neither you nor any one else can save her. Lucas Beaumanoir hath settled that the death of a Jewess will be a sin-offering sufficient to atone for all the amorous indulgences of the Knights Templars; and thou knowest he hath both the power and will to execute so reasonable and pious a purpose."

"Will future ages believe that such stupid bigotry ever existed?" said Bois-Guilbert, striding up and down the apartment.

"What they may believe, I know not," said Malvoisin, calmly; "but I know well, that in this our day clergy and laymen, take ninety-nine to the hundred, will cry *amen* to the Grand Master's sentence."

"I have it," said Bois-Guilbert. "Albert, thou art my friend—thou must connive at her escape, Malvoisin, and I will transport her to some place of greater security and secrecy."

"I cannot, if I would," replied the Preceptor; "the mansion is filled with the attendants of the Grand Master, and others who are devoted to him. And, to be frank with you, brother, I would not embark with you in this matter, even if I could hope to bring my bark to haven. I have risked enough already for your sake. I have no mind to encounter the risk of degradation, or even to lose my Preceptory, for the sake of a painted piece of Jewish flesh and blood. And you, if you will be guided by my counsel, will give up this wild-goose chase, and fly your hawk at some other game. Think, Bois-Guilbert: thy present rank, thy future honours, all depend on thy place in the Order. Shouldst thou adhere perversely to thy passion for this Rebecca, thou wilt give Beaumanoir the power of expelling thee, and he will not neglect it. He is jealous of the truncheon which he holds in his trembling gripe, and he knows thou stretchest thy bold hand towards it. Doubt not he will ruin thee, if thou affordest him a pretext so fair as thy protection of a Jewish sorceress. Give him his scope in this matter, for thou canst not controul him. When the staff is in thine own firm grasp, thou mayest caress the daughters of Judah, or burn them, as may best suit thine own humour."

"Malvoisin," said Bois-Guilbert, "thou art a cold-blooded"——

"Friend," said the Preceptor, hastening to fill up the blank, in which Bois-Guilbert would probably have placed a worse word. "A cold-blooded friend I am, and therefore more fit to give thee advice. I tell thee once more, that thou canst not save Rebecca. I tell thee once more, thou canst but perish with her. Go hie thee to the Grand Master —throw thyself at his feet and tell him"——

"Not at his feet, by Heaven! but to the dotard's very beard will I say"——

"Say to him then to his beard," continued Malvoisin, coolly, "that you love this captive Jewess to distraction; and the more thou dost enlarge on thy passion, the greater will be his haste to end it by the death of the fair enchantress; while thou, taken in flagrant delict in the avowal of a crime contrary to thine oath, canst hope no aid of thy brethren, and must exchange all thy brilliant visions of ambition and power, to lift perhaps a mercenary spear in some of the petty quarrels between Flanders and Burgundy."

"Thou speakest the truth, Malvoisin," said Brian de Bois-Guilbert, after a moment's reflection. "I will give the hoary bigot no advantage over me; and for Rebecca, she hath not merited at my hand that I should expose rank and honour for her sake. I will cast her off—Yes, I will leave her to her fate, unless"——

"Qualify not thy wise and necessary resolution," said Malvoisin; "women are but the toys which amuse our lighter hours—ambition is the serious business of life—Perish a thousand such frail baubles as this Jewess, before thy manly step pause in the brilliant course which is stretched before thee! For the present we part, nor must we be seen to hold close communication—I must order the hall for his judgment-seat."

"What," said Bois-Guilbert, "so soon?"

"Ay," replied the Preceptor, "trial moves speedily on when the judge has predetermined the sentence."——

"Rebecca," said Bois-Guilbert, when he was left alone, "thou art like to cost me dear—Why cannot I abandon thee to thy fate as this calm hypocrite recommends?—One effort will I make to save thee—but beware of ingratitude, for if I am again repulsed, my vengeance shall equal my love. The life and honour of Bois-Guilbert must not be hazarded, where contempt and reproaches are his only reward."

The Preceptor had hardly given the necessary orders, when he was joined by Conrade Mountfitchet, who acquainted him with the Grand Master's resolution to bring the Jewess to instant trial for sorcery.

"It is surely a dream," said the Preceptor; "we have many Jewish physicians, and we call them not wizards though they work wonderful cures."

"The Grand Master thinks otherwise," said Mountfitchet; "and, Albert, I will be upright with thee—wizard or not, it were better this miserable damsel die, than that Brian de Bois-Guilbert should be lost to the Order, or the Order divided by internal dissention. Thou knowest his high rank, his fame in arms—thou knowest the zeal with which many of our brethren regard him—but all this will not avail him with our Grand Master, should he consider Brian as the accomplice, not the victim, of this Jewess. Were the souls of the twelve tribes in her single body, it were better she suffered alone, than that Bois-Guilbert were partner in her destruction."

"I have been working him even now to abandon her," said Malvoisin; "but still, are there grounds enough to condemn this Rebecca for sorcery?—Will not the Grand Master change his mind when he sees that the proofs are so weak?"

"They must be strengthened, Albert," replied Mountfitchet, "dost thou understand me?—they must be strengthened—the good of the Order requires her death and the honour of the Grand Master must be preserved—he must not appear to decide on slight grounds. Dost thou understand me?"

"I do," said the Preceptor, "nor do I scruple to do aught for advancement of the Order—but there is little time to find engines fitting."

"Malvoisin, they must be found," said Conrade; "well will it advantage both the Order and thee. This Templestowe is a poor Preceptory—that of Maison-Dieu is worth double its value—thou knowest my interest with our old Chief—find those who can carry this matter through, and thou art Preceptor of Maison-Dieu in the fertile Kent—How sayest thou?"

"There is," replied Malvoisin, "among those who come hither with

Bois-Guilbert, two fellows whom I well know; servants they were to my brother Philip de Malvoisin, and passed from his service to that of Front-de-Bœuf—It may be they know something of the witcheries of this woman."

"Away, seek them out instantly—and hark thee—if a bezant or two will sharpen their memory, let it not be wanting."

"They would swear the mother that bore them a sorceress for a zecchin," said the Preceptor.

"Away then," said Mountfitchet; "at noon the affair will proceed. I have not seen our senior in such earnest preparation since he condemned to the stake Hamet Alfagi, a convert who relapsed to the Moslem faith."

The ponderous castle-bell had tolled the point of noon, when Rebecca heard a trampling of feet upon the private stair which led to her place of confinement. The noise announced the arrival of several persons, and the circumstance rather gave her joy; for she was more afraid of the solitary visits of the fierce and passionate Bois-Guilbert than of any evil which could befal her besides. The door of the chamber was unlocked, and Conrade with the Preceptor Albert Malvoisin entered, attended by four warders clothed in black, and bearing halberts.

"Daughter of an accursed race!" said the Preceptor, "arise and follow us."

"Whither," said Rebecca, "and for what purpose?"

"Damsel," answered Conrade, "it is not for thee to question, but to obey. Nevertheless, be it known to thee, that thou art to be brought before the tribunal of the Grand Master of our holy Order, there to answer for thine offences."

"May the God of Abraham be praised!" said Rebecca, folding her hands devoutly; "the name of a judge, though an enemy to my people, is to me as the name of a protector. Most willingly do I follow thee—permit me only to wrap my veil around my head."

They descended the stair with slow and solemn step, traversed a long gallery, and, by a folding pair of doors placed at the end, entered the great hall in which the Grand Master had for the time established his court of justice.

The lower part of this ample apartment was filled with squires and yeomen, who made way not without some difficulty for Rebecca, attended by the Preceptor and Mountfitchet, and followed by the guard of halberdiers, to move forward to the seat appointed for her. As she passed through the crowd, her arms folded and her head depressed, a scrap of paper was thrust into her hand which she received almost unconsciously, and continued to hold without examining its contents. The assurance that she possessed some friend in this awful assembly gave her courage to look around, and to mark into whose presence she had been conducted. She gazed accordingly upon the scene which we shall endeavour to describe in our next chapter.

Chapter Seven

Stern was the law, which bade its vot'ries leave
At human woes with human hearts to grieve;
Stern was the law, which at the winning wile
Of frank and harmless mirth forbade to smile;
But sterner still, when high the iron-rod
Of tyrant power she shook, and call'd that power of God.

The Middle Ages.

THE TRIBUNAL, erected for the trial of the innocent and unhappy Rebecca, occupied the dais or elevated part of the upper end of the great hall—a platform, which we have already described as the place of honour, destined to be occupied by the most distinguished inhabitants or guests of an ancient mansion.

On an elevated seat, directly before the accused, sate the Grand Master of the Temple, in full and ample robes of flowing white, holding in his hand the mystic staff, which bore the symbol of the Order. At his feet was placed a table, occupied by two scribes, chaplains of the Order, whose duty it was to reduce to formal record the proceedings of the day. The black dresses, bare scalps, and demure looks of these churchmen, formed a strong contrast to the warlike appearance of the knights who attended, either as residing in the Preceptory, or as come thither to attend upon their Grand Master. The Preceptors, of whom there were four present, occupied seats lower in height, and somewhat drawn back behind that of their superior; and the Knights, who enjoyed no such rank in the Order, were placed on benches still lower, and preserving the same distance from the Preceptors as these from the Grand Master. Behind them, but still upon the dais or elevated portion of the hall, stood the Esquires of the Order, in white dresses of an inferior quality.

The whole assembly wore an aspect of the most profound gravity; and in the aspect of the knights might be perceived traces of military daring, united with the solemn carriage becoming men of religious profession, and which in the presence of their Grand Master failed not to sit upon every brow.

The remaining and lower part of the hall was filled with guards, holding partizans, and with other attendants whom curiosity had drawn thither, to see at once a Grand Master and a Jewish sorceress.

By far the greater part of these inferior persons were, in one rank or other, connected with the Order, and were accordingly distinguished by their black dresses. But peasants from the neighbouring country were not refused admittance; for it was the pride of Beaumanoir to render the edifying spectacle of the justice which he administered as public as possible. His large blue eyes seemed to expand as he gazed around the assembly, and his countenance appeared dilated by the conscious dignity and imaginary merit of the part which he was about to perform. A psalm, which he himself accompanied with a deep mellow voice, which age had not deprived of its powers, commenced the proceedings of the day; and the solemn sounds, *Venite exultemus Domino*, so often sung by the Templars before engaging with earthly adversaries, was judged by Lucas most appropriate to introduce the approaching triumph, for such he deemed it, over the powers of darkness. The long prolonged notes, raised by an hundred masculine voices accustomed to combine in the choral chaunt, rose to the vaulted roof of the hall, and rolled on amongst its arches with the pleasing yet solemn sound of the rushing of mighty waters.

When the sounds ceased, the Grand Master turned his eyes slowly round the circle, and observed that the seat of one of the Preceptors was vacant. Brian de Bois-Guilbert, by whom it had been occupied, had left his place, and was now standing near the extreme corner of one of the benches occupied by the Knights Companions of the Temple, one hand extending his long mantle, so as in some degree to hide his face; while the other held his cross-handled sword, with the point of which, sheathed as it was, he was slowly drawing lines upon the oaken floor.

"Unhappy man!" said the Grand Master, after favouring him with a glance of compassion. "Thou seest, Conrade, how this holy work distresses him—to this can the light look of woman, aided by the Prince of the powers of this world, bring a valiant and worthy knight! Seest thou he cannot look upon us; he cannot look upon her; and who knows by what impulse from his tormentors his hand forms these cabalistic lines upon the floor? It may be our life and safety are thus aimed at; but we spit and defy the foul enemy.—*Semper Leo percutiatur.*"

This was communicated apart to his confidential follower, Conrade Mountfitchet. The Grand Master then raised his voice, and addressed the assembly.

"Reverend and valiant men, Knights, Preceptors, and Companions of this Holy Order, my brethren and my children!—you also, well-born and pious Esquires, who aspire to wear this holy Cross!—and you also, Christian brethren, of every degree!—Be it known to you, that it is not defect of power in us which hath occasioned the assembling of this congregation. For to us, however unworthy in our person, yet still to us is committed, with this batton, full power to judge and to try all that regards the weal of this our holy Order. Holy Saint Bernard, in the rule of our knightly and religious profession, hath said, in the fifty-ninth capital,* that he would not that brethren be called to assemble in council, save at the will and command of the Master; leaving it free to us, as to those more worthy fathers who have preceded us in this our office, to judge, as well of the occasion as of the time and place in which a chapter of the whole Order, or of any part thereof, may be convoked. Also, in all such chapters, it is our duty to hear the advice of our brethren, and to proceed according to our own pleasure. But when the raging wolf hath made an inroad upon the flock, and carried off one member thereof, it is the duty of the head shepherd to call his comrades together, that with bows and slings they may quell the invader, according to our well-known rule, that the lion is ever to be beaten down. We have therefore, summoned to our presence a Jewish woman, by name Rebecca, daughter of Isaac of York—a woman infamous for sortileges and for witcheries; wherewith she hath maddened the blood and besotted the brain, not of a churl, but of a Knight—not of a secular Knight, but of one devoted to the service of the Holy Temple—not of a Knight Companion, but of a Preceptor of our Order, first in honour as in place. Our brother Brian de Bois-Guilbert is well known to ourselves, and to all degrees who now hear me, as a true and zealous champion of the Cross, by whose arm many deeds of valour have been wrought in the Holy Land, and the holy places purified from pollution by the blood of those infidels who defiled them. Neither have our brother's sagacity and prudence been less patent to his brethren than his valour and discipline; in so much, that knights, both in eastern and western lands, have named De Bois-Guilbert as one who may well be put in nomination as successor to this batton, when it shall please Heaven to release us from the toil of bearing it. If we were told that such a man, so honoured, and so honourable, suddenly casting away regard for his character, his vows, his brethren, and his prospects, had associated to himself a Jewish damsel, wandered in this lewd company through solitary places, defended her person in preference to his own, and, finally, was so utterly blinded and besotted by his folly, as to bring her even to one of our own Preceptories, what should we say but that the noble knight was possessed by some evil demon, or influenced by some wicked spell?—If we could suppose it otherwise, think not rank, valour, high

*The reader is referred to the Rules of the Poor Military Brotherhood of the Temple, which occur in the Works of St Bernard.—L. T.

repute, or any earthly consideration, should prevent us from visiting him with punishment, that the evil thing might be removed, even according to the text, *Auferte malum ex vobis*. For various and heinous are the acts of transgression against the rule of our blessed Order in this lamentable history.—1st, He hath walked according to his proper will, contrary to capital 33, *Quod nullus juxta propriam voluntatem incedat*.—2d, He hath held commune with an excommunicated person, capital 57, *Ut fratres non participent cum excommunicatis*, and hath therefore a portion in *Anathema Maranatha*.—3d, He hath consorted with strange women, contrary to the capital, *Ut fratres non versantur cum extraneis mulieribus*.—4th, He hath not avoided, nay he hath, it is to be feared, solicited, the kiss of woman; by which, saith the last rule of our renowned Order, *Ut Fugiantur oscula*, the soldiers of the Cross are brought into a snare. For which heinous and multiplied guilt, Brian de Bois-Guilbert should be cut off and cast out from our congregation, were he the right hand and right eye thereof."

He paused. A low murmur went through the assembly. Some of the younger part, who had been inclined to smile at the statute *De osculis fugiendis*, became now grave enough, and anxiously waited what the Grand Master was next to propose.

"Such," he said, "and so great should indeed be the punishment of a Knight Templar, who wilfully offended against the rules of his Order in such weighty points. But if, by means of charms and of spells, Satan had obtained dominion over the Knight, perchance because he cast his eyes too lightly upon a damsel's beauty, we are then rather to lament than chastise his backsliding; and, imposing on him only such penance as may purify him from his iniquity, we are to turn the full edge of our indignation upon the accursed instrument, which had so nigh occasioned his utter falling away. Stand forth, therefore, and bear witness, ye who have witnessed these unhappy doings, that we may judge of the form and bearing thereof; and whether our justice may be satisfied with the punishment of this infidel woman, or must proceed, with a bleeding heart, to the further proceeding against our brother."

Several witnesses were called upon to prove the risks to which Bois-Guilbert exposed himself in endeavouring to save Rebecca from the blazing castle, and his neglect of his personal defence in attending to her safety. The men gave these details with the exaggerations common to vulgar minds which have been strongly excited by any remarkable event, and their natural disposition to the marvellous was increased greatly by the satisfaction which their evidence seemed to afford to the eminent person for whose information it had been delivered. Thus the dangers which Bois-Guilbert surmounted, in themselves sufficiently great, became portentous in their narrative. The devotion of the knight to Rebecca's defence was exaggerated beyond the bounds, not only of discretion, but even of the most frantic excess of chivalrous zeal; and his deference to what she said, though her language was often severe and upbraiding, was painted as carried to an excess, which, in a man of his haughty temper, seemed well nigh preternatural.

The Preceptor of Templestowe was then called upon to describe the manner in which Bois-Guilbert and the Jewess arrived at the Preceptory. The evidence of Malvoisin was skilfully guarded. But while he apparently studied to spare the feelings of Bois-Guilbert, he threw in, from time to time, such hints, as seemed to infer that he laboured under some temporary alienation of the mind, so deeply did he appear to be enamoured of the damsel whom he brought along with him. With sighs of penitence, the Preceptor avowed his own contrition for having admitted Rebecca and her lover within the walls of his Preceptory—"But my defence," he concluded, "has been made in my confession to our most reverend father the Grand Master; he knows my motives were not evil, though my conduct may have been irregular. Joyfully will I submit to any penance he shall assign me."

"Thou hast spoken well, Brother Albert," said Beaumanoir; "thy motives were good, since thou didst judge it right to stop thine erring brother in his career of precipitate folly. But thy conduct was wrong; as he who would stop a runaway steed, and seizing him by the stirrup in place of the bridle, receives injury himself instead of accomplishing his purpose. Thirteen pater-nosters are assigned by our pious founder for matins, and nine for vespers; be those services doubled by thee. Thrice a-week are Templars permitted the use of flesh; but do thou keep fast for all the seven days. This do for six months to come, and thy penance is accomplished."

With a hypocritical look of the deepest submission, the Preceptor of Templestowe bowed to the ground before his Superior, and resumed his seat.

"Were it not well, brethren," said the Grand Master, "that we examine something into the life and conversation of this woman, specially that we may discover whether she be one like to use magical charms and spells, since the truths which we have heard may well incline us to suppose, that in this unhappy course our erring brother has been acted upon by some infernal enticement and delusion?"

Herman of Goodalricke was the fourth Preceptor present; the other three were Conrade, Malvoisin, and Bois-Guilbert himself. Herman was an ancient warrior, whose face was marked with the scars inflicted by the sabres of the Moslemah, and had great rank and consideration among his brethren. He arose and bowed to the Grand Master, who instantly granted him licence of speech. "I would crave to know, most Reverend Father, of our valiant brother, Brian de Bois-Guilbert, what he says to these wondrous accusations, and with what eye he himself now regards his unhappy intercourse with this Jewish maiden?"

"Brian de Bois-Guilbert," said the Grand Master, "thou hearest the question which our Brother of Goodalricke desireth thou shouldest answer. I command thee to reply to him."

Bois-Guilbert turned his head towards the Grand Master when thus addressed, but remained silent.

"He is possessed by a dumb devil," said the Grand Master. "Avoid thee, Sathanas!—Speak, Brian de Bois-Guilbert, I conjure thee, by this symbol of our Holy Order."

Bois-Guilbert made an effort to suppress his rising scorn and indignation, the expression of which, he knew well, would little here avail him. "Brian de Bois-Guilbert," he answered, "replies not, most Reverend Father, to such wild and vague charges. If his honour be impeached, he will defend it with his body, and with that sword which has often fought for Christendom."

"We forgive thee, Brother Brian," said the Grand Master. "That thou hast boasted thy warlike achievements before us, is a glorifying of thine own deeds, and cometh of the Enemy, who tempteth us to exalt our own worship. But thou hast our pardon, judging thou speakest less of thine own suggestion than from the impulse of him whom, by Heaven's leave, we will quell and drive forth from our assembly." A glance of disdain flashed from the dark fierce eyes of Bois-Guilbert, but he made no reply.—"And now," pursued the Grand Master, "since our Brother of Goodalricke's question has been thus imperfectly answered, pursue we our quest, brethren, and, with our patron's assistance, we will search to the bottom this mystery of iniquity. Let those who have aught to witness of the life and conversation of this Jewish woman, stand forth before us." There was a bustle in the lower part of the Hall, and when the Grand Master inquired the reason, it was replied, that there was in the crowd a bed-ridden man, whom the prisoner had restored to the perfect use of his limbs, by a miraculous balsam.

The poor peasant, a Saxon by birth, was dragged forward to the bar, terrified at the penal consequences which he might have incurred by the guilt of having been cured of the palsy by a Jewish damsel. Perfectly cured he certainly was not, for he dragged himself forward on crutches to give evidence. Most unwilling was his testimony, and given with many tears; but he admitted that two years since, when residing at York, he was suddenly afflicted with a sore disease, while labouring for Isaac the rich Jew, in his vocation of a joiner; that he had been unable to stir from his bed until the remedies applied by Rebecca's directions, and specially a warming and spicy-smelling balsam had in some degree restored him to health. Moreover, he said she had given him a pot of that precious unguent, and furnished him with a piece of money withal, to return to the house of his father, near to Templestowe. "And may it please your gracious Reverence," said the man, "I cannot think that the damsel meant harm by me, though she hath the ill hap to be a Jewess; for ever when I used her remedy, I said the Pater and the Creed, and it never operated a whit less kindly."

"Peace, slave," said the Grand Master, "and be gone. It well suits brutes like thee to be tampering and trinketting with hellish cures, and to be giving your labour to the sons of misbelief. I tell thee, the fiend can impose diseases for the very purpose of removing them, in order to bring into credit some diabolical fashion of cure. Hast thou that unguent of which thou spokest?"

The peasant, fumbling in his bosom with a trembling hand, produced a small box, bearing some Hebrew characters on the lid, which was, with most of the audience, a sure proof that the devil had stood apothecary. Beaumanoir, after crossing himself, took the box into his hand, and, learned in most of the Eastern tongues, read with ease the motto on the lid,—*The lion of the tribe of Judah hath conquered.* "Strange powers of Sathanas," he said, "which can convert Scripture into blasphemy, mingling poison with our most necessary food!—Is there no leech here who can tell us the ingredients of this mystic unguent?"

Two mediciners, as they termed themselves, the one a monk, the other a barber, appeared and avouched they knew nothing of the materials, excepting that they savoured of myrrh and camphire—oriental herbs. But with true professional hatred to a successful practitioner of their art, they insinuated that, since the medicine was beyond their own knowledge, it must necessarily have been compounded from an unlawful and magical pharmacopeia; since they themselves, though no conjurers, fully understood every branch of their art, so far as it might be exercised with the good faith of a Christian. When this medical research was ended, the Saxon peasant desired humbly to have back the medicine which he had found so salutary; but the Grand Master frowned severely at the request. "What is thy name, fellow?" said he to the cripple.

"Higg, the son of Snell," answered the peasant.

"Then Higg, son of Snell," said the Grand Master, "I tell thee it is better to be bed-ridden, than to accept the benefits of unbelievers that thou mayest arise and walk; better to despoil infidels of their treasure by the strong hand, than to accept of their benevolence gifts, or to do them service for wages. Go, thou, and do as I have said."

"Alack," said the peasant, "an it shall not displease your Reverence, the lesson comes too late for me, for I am but a maimed man; but I will tell my two brethren, who serve the rich Rabbi Nathan Ben Samuel, that your Mastership says it is more lawful to rob him than to render him faithful service."

"Out with the prating villain!" said Beaumanoir, who was not prepared to refute this practical application of his general maxim.

Higg, the son of Snell, withdrew into the crowd, but, interested in the fate of his benefactress, lingered until he should learn her doom, even at the risk of again encountering the frown of that severe judge, the terror of which withered his very heart within him.

At this period of the trial, the Grand Master commanded Rebecca to unveil herself. Opening her lips for the first time, she replied quietly, but with dignity,—"That it was not the wont of the daughters of her people to uncover their faces when alone in an assembly of strangers." The sweet tones of her voice, and the softness of her reply, impressed on the audience a sentiment of pity and sympathy. But Beaumanoir, in whose mind the suppression of each feeling of humanity which could interfere with his imagined duty, was a virtue of itself, repeated his commands that his victim should be unveiled. The guards were about to remove her veil accordingly, when she stood up before the Grand Master and said, "Nay, but for the love of your own daughters—Alas," she said, recollecting herself, "ye have no daughters!—but for the remembrance of your mothers—for the love of your sisters, and of female decency, let me not be mishandled in your presence; it suits not a maiden to be disrobed by such rude grooms. I will obey you," she added, with an expression of patient sorrow in her voice, which had almost melted the heart of Beaumanoir himself; "ye are elders among your people, and at your command I will shew the features of an ill-fated maiden."

She withdrew her veil, and looked on them with a countenance in which bashfulness contended with dignity. Her exceeding beauty excited a murmur of surprise, and the younger knights told each other with their eyes, in stolen correspondence, that Brian's best apology was in the power of her real charms, rather than of her imaginary witchcraft. But Higg, the son of Snell, felt most deeply the effect produced by the sight of the countenance of his benefactress. "Let me go forth," he cried, to the warders at the door of the Hall—"let me go forth!—To look on her again will kill me, as I have had a share in murthering her."

"Peace, poor man," said Rebecca, when she heard his exclamation; "thou hast done me no harm by speaking the truth—thou canst not aid me by thy complaints or lamentations. Peace, I pray thee—go home and save thyself."

Higg was about to be thrust out by the compassion of the warders, who were apprehensive lest his clamorous grief should draw upon them reprehension, and upon himself punishment. But he promised to be silent, and was permitted to remain.

The two men-at-arms, with whom Albert Malvoisin had not failed to communicate upon the import of their testimony, were now called forward. Though both were hardened and inflexible villains, the sight of the captive maiden, as well as her exceeding beauty, at the first appeared to stagger them; but an expressive glance from the Preceptor of Templestowe restored them to their dogged composure; and they delivered, with a precision which would have seemed suspicious to more favourable judges, circumstances either altogether fictitious, or trivial and natural in themselves, but rendered pregnant with suspicion by the exaggerated manner in which they were told, and the sinister commentary which the witnesses added to the facts. The circumstances of their evidence would have been, in modern days, divided into two classes—those which were immaterial, and those which were actually and physically impossible. But both were, in those ignorant and superstitious days, eagerly credited as proofs of guilt.—That Rebecca was heard to mutter to herself in an unknown tongue—that the songs she sung by fits were of a strangely sweet sound, which made the ears of the listener tingle, and his heart throb—that she spoke at times to herself, and seemed to look upward for a reply—that her garments were of a strange and mystic form, unlike those of other women of good—that she had rings impressed with cabalistical devices, and that strange characters were broidered on her veil—all these circumstances, so natural and trivial, were gravely listened to as proofs, or, at least, as affording strong suspicions that Rebecca had unlawful correspondence with mystical powers.

But there was less equivocal testimony, which the credulity of the assembly, or of the greater part, greedily swallowed, however incredible. One of the soldiers had seen her work a cure upon a wounded man, brought with them to the Castle of Torquilstone. She did, he said, make certain signs upon the wound, and repeated certain mysterious words, which he blessed God he understood not, when the iron head of a square cross-bow bolt disengaged itself from the wound, the bleeding was staunched, the wound was closed, and the dying man was, within the quarter of an hour, walking upon the ramparts, and assisting the witness in managing a mangonel, or machine for hurling stones. This legend was probably founded on the fact, that Rebecca had attended on the wounded Ivanhoe when in the castle of Torquilstone. But it was the more difficult to dispute the accuracy of the witness, as, in order to produce real evidence in support of his verbal testimony, he drew from his pouch the very bolt-head, which, according to his story, had been thus miraculously extracted from the wound; and as the iron weighed a full ounce, it completely confirmed the tale, however marvellous.

His comrade had been a witness from a neighbouring battlement of the scene betwixt Rebecca and Bois-Guilbert, when she was upon the point of precipitating herself from the top of the tower. Not to be behind his companion, this fellow stated, that he had seen Rebecca perch herself on the parapet of the turret, and there take the form of a milk-white swan, under which appearance she flitted three times round the castle of Torquilstone, then again settled on the turret, and assumed once more the female form.

Less than one half of this weighty evidence would have been sufficient to convict any old woman, poor and ugly, even though she had not been a Jewess. United with that fatal circumstance, the body of proof was too weighty for Rebecca's youth, even when united with the most exquisite beauty.

The Grand Master had collected the suffrages, and now in a solemn tone demanded of Rebecca what she had to say against the sentence of condemnation, which he was about to pronounce.

"To invoke your pity," said the lovely Jewess, with a voice somewhat tremulous with emotion, "would, I am aware, be as useless as I should hold it mean. To state that to relieve the sick and wounded of another religion, cannot be displeasing to the acknowledged Founder of both our faiths, were also unavailing; to plead that many things which these men (whom may Heaven pardon!) have spoken against me are impossible, would avail me but little, since you believe in their possibility; and still less would it advantage me to explain, that the peculiarities of my dress, language, and manners, are those of my people—I had well nigh said of my country, but alas! we have no country. Nor will I even vindicate myself at the expence of my oppressor, who stands there listening to the fictions and surmises which seem to convert the tyrant into the victim.—God be judge betwixt him and me! but rather would I submit to ten such deaths as your pleasure denounces against me, than listen to the suit which that man of Belial has urged upon me—friendless, defenceless, and his prisoner. But he is of your own faith, and his lightest affirmance would weigh down the most solemn protestations of the distressed Jewess. I will not therefore return to himself the charge brought against me—but to himself

—Yes, Brian de Bois-Guilbert, to thyself I appeal, whether these accusations are not false? as monstrous and calumnious as they are deadly?"

There was a pause; all eyes turned to Brian de Bois-Guilbert. He was silent.

"Speak," she said, "if thou art a man—if thou art a Christian, speak!—I conjure thee, by the cross which thou dost wear, by the name thou didst inherit—by the knighthood thou didst vaunt—by the honour of thy mother—by the tomb and the bones of thy father—I conjure thee to say, are these things true?"

"Answer her, brother," said the Grand Master, "if the Enemy with whom thou dost wrestle will give thee power."

In fact, Bois-Guilbert seemed agitated by contending passions, which almost convulsed his features, and it was with a constrained voice that at length he replied, looking to Rebecca,—"The scroll!—the scroll!"

"Ay," said Beaumanoir, "this is indeed testimony—the victim of her witcheries can only name the fatal scroll, which is, doubtless, the cause of his silence."

But Rebecca put another interpretation on the words extorted as it were from Bois-Guilbert, and glancing her eye upon the slip of parchment which she continued to hold in her hand, she read thereupon in the Arabian character, *Demand a Champion!* The murmuring commentary which ran through the assembly at the strange reply of Bois-Guilbert, gave Rebecca leisure to examine and instantly to destroy the scroll, as she thought unobserved. When the whisper had ceased, the Grand Master spoke.

"Rebecca, thou canst derive no benefit from the evidence of this unhappy knight, for whom, as we well perceive, the Enemy is yet too powerful. Hast thou aught else to say?"

"There is yet one chance of life left to me," said Rebecca, "even by your own fierce laws. Life has been miserable—miserable, at least, of late—but I will not cast away the gift of God, while he affords me the means of defending it. I deny this charge—I maintain my innocence, and I declare the falsehood of this accusation. I challenge the privilege of trial by combat, and will appear by my champion."

"And who, Rebecca," replied the Grand Master, "will lay lance in rest for a sorceress?—who will be the champion of a Jewess?"

"God will raise me up a champion," said Rebecca—"It cannot be that in merry England—the hospitable, the generous, the free, where so many are ready to peril their lives for honour, there shall not be found one to fight for justice. But it is enough that I challenge the trial by combat—there lies my gage."

She took her embroidered glove from her hand, and flung it down before the Grand Master with an air of mingled simplicity and dignity, which excited universal surprise and admiration.

Chapter Eight

——There I throw my gage,
To prove it on thee to the extremest point
Of martial daring.
Richard II.

EVEN LUCAS BEAUMANOIR himself was affected by the mien and appearance of Rebecca. He was not originally a cruel or even a severe man; but with passions by nature cold, and with a high, though mistaken, sense of duty, his heart had been gradually hardened by the ascetic life which he pursued, the supreme power which he enjoyed, and the supposed necessity of subduing infidelity and eradicating heresy, which he conceived peculiarly incumbent on him. His features relaxed in their usual severity as he gazed upon the beautiful creature before him, alone, unfriended, and defending herself with so much spirit and courage. He crossed himself twice, as doubting whence arose the unwonted softening of a heart, which on such occasions was wont to resemble in hardness the steel of his sword. At length he spoke.

"Damsel," he said, "if the pity I feel for thee arise from any practice thine evil arts have made on me, great is thy guilt. But I rather judge it the kinder feelings of nature which grieves that so goodly a form should be a vessel of perdition. Repent, O my daughter—confess thy witchcrafts—turn thee from thine evil faith—embrace this holy emblem, and all shall yet be well with thee here and hereafter. In some sisterhood of the strictest order, shalt thou have time for prayer and fitting penance, and that repentance not to be repented of. This do and live—what has the law of Moses done for thee that thou shouldest die for it?"

"It was the law of my fathers," said Rebecca; "it was delivered in thunders and in storms upon the mountain of Sinai, in cloud and in fire. This, if ye are Christians, ye believe—it is, you say, recalled, but so my teachers have not taught me."

"Let our chaplain," said Beaumanoir, "stand forth, and tell this obstinate infidel"——

"Forgive the interruption," said Rebecca, meekly; "I am a maiden, unskilled to dispute for my religion, but I can die for it, if it be God's will.—Let me pray your answer to my demand of a champion."

"Give me her glove," said Beaumanoir. "This is indeed," he continued, as he looked at the flimsy texture and slender fingers, "a slight and frail gage for a purpose so deadly—Seest thou, Rebecca, as this thin and light glove of thine is to one of our heavy steel gauntlets, so is thy cause to that of the Temple, for it is our Order which thou hast defied."

"Cast my innocence into the scale," answered Rebecca, "and the glove of silk shall outweigh the glove of iron."

"Then thou doest persist in thy refusal to confess thy guilt, and in that bold challenge which thou hast made?"

"I do persist, noble sir," answered Rebecca.

"So be it then, in the name of Heaven," said the Grand Master; "and may God shew the right!"

"Amen," replied the Preceptors around him, and the word was deeply echoed by the whole assembly.

"Brethren," resumed Beaumanoir, "ye are aware that we might well have refused to this woman the benefit of the trial by combat—but though a Jewess and an unbeliever, she is also a stranger and defenceless, and God forbid that she should ask the benefit of our mild laws, and that it should be refused to her. Moreover, we are knights and soldiers as well as men of religion, and shame it were to us, upon any pretence, to refuse proffered combat. Thus, therefore, stands the case. Rebecca, the daughter of Isaac of York, is by many pregnant and suspicious circumstances, defamed of sorcery practised on the person of a noble knight of our holy Order, and hath challenged the combat in proof of her innocence. To whom, reverend brethren, is it your opinion that we should deliver this her gage of battle, naming him, at the same time, to be our champion in the field?"

"To Brian de Bois-Guilbert, whom it chiefly concerns," answered the Preceptor of Goodalricke, "and who, moreover, best knows how the truth stands in this matter."

"But if," said the Grand Master, "our brother Brian be under the influence of a charm or a spell—we speak but for the sake of precaution, for to the arm of none of our holy Order would we more willingly confide this or a more weighty cause."

"Reverend father," answered the Preceptor of Goodalricke, "no spell can affect the champion who comes forward to fight for the judgment of God."

"Thou say'st right, brother," said the Grand Master. "Albert Malvoisin, give this gage of battle to Brian de Bois-Guilbert.—It is our charge to thee, brother," he continued, addressing himself to Bois-Guilbert, "that thou do this battle manfully, nothing doubting that thy good cause shall triumph.—And do thou, Rebecca, attend, that we assign thee the third day from the present to find a champion."

"That is but brief space," answered Rebecca, "for a stranger, and one of another faith, to find one who will do battle, wagering life and honour for her cause."

"We may not extend it," answered the Grand Master; "the field must be foughten in our own presence, and divers weighty causes call us on the fourth day from hence."

"God's will be done!" said Rebecca; "I put my trust in Him, to whom an instant is as effectual to save as a whole age."

"Thou hast spoken well, damsel," replied the Grand Master; "but well know we who can array himself like an angel of light. It remains but to name a convenient and fitting place of combat, and, if it shall so hap, also of execution.—Where is the Preceptor of this house?"

Albert Malvoisin, still holding Rebecca's glove in his hand, was speaking to Bois-Guilbert very earnestly, but in a low voice.

"How!" said the Grand Master, "will he not receive the gage?"

"He will—he doth, most Reverend Father," said Malvoisin, slipping the glove under his own mantle. "And for the place of combat, I hold the fittest to be the lists of Saint George belonging to this Preceptory, and used by us for military exercise."

"It is well," said the Grand Master. "Rebecca, in those lists shalt thou produce thy champion; and if thou failest to do so, or if thy champion shall be discomfited by the judgment of God, thou shalt then die the death of a sorceress, according to doom.—Let this our judgment be recorded, and the record read aloud, that no one may pretend ignorance."

One of the chaplains, who acted as clerks to the chapter, immediately ingrossed the order in a huge volume, which contained the proceedings of the Templar Knights when solemnly assembled upon such occasions; and when he had finished writing, the other read aloud the sentence of the Grand Master, which, when translated from the Norman French, in which it was couched, was expressed as follows:—

"Rebecca, a Jewess, daughter of Isaac of York, being attainted of sorcery, seduction, and other damnable practices, practised on a Knight of the most Holy Order of the Temple of Zion, doth deny the same; and saith, that the testimony delivered against her this day is false, wicked, and disloyal; and that by lawful *essoine** of her body, as being unable to combat in her own behalf, she doth offer, by a gentleman instead thereof, to avouch her case, he performing his loyal *devoir* in all knightly sort, with such arms as to gage of battle do fitly apper-

* *Essoine* signifies excuse, and here relates to the appellant's privilege of appearing by her champion, in excuse of her own person on account of her sex.

tain, and that at her peril and cost. And therewith she proffered her gage. And the gage having been delivered to the noble Lord and Knight, Brian de Bois-Guilbert of the Holy Order of the Temple of Zion, he was appointed to do this battle, in behalf of his Order and himself, as injured and impaired by the practices of the said appellant. Whereupon the most reverend Father and puissant Lord, Lucas, Marquis of Beaumanoir, did allow of the said challenge, and of the said *essoine* of the appellant's body, and assigned the third day for the said combat, the place being the inclosure called the lists of Saint George, near to the Preceptory of Templestowe. And the Grand Master appoints the appellant to appear there by her champion, on pain of doom, as a person convicted of sorcery or seduction; and also the defendant so to appear, under the penalty of being held and adjudged recreant in case of default; and the noble Lord and most reverend Father aforesaid appointeth the battle to be done in his own presence, and according to all that is commendable and profitable in such a case. And may God aid the just cause!"

"Amen!" said the Grand Master; and his word was echoed by all around. Rebecca spoke not, but she looked up to heaven, and, folding her hands, remained for a minute without change of attitude. She then modestly reminded the Grand Master, that she ought to be permitted some opportunity of free communication with her friends, for the purpose of making her condition known to them, and procuring, if possible, some champion to fight in her behalf.

"It is just and lawful," said the Grand Master; "chuse what messenger thou wilt trust, and he shall have free communication with thee in thy prison chamber."

"Is there," said Rebecca, "any one here, who, either for love of a good cause, or for an ample hire, will do the errand of a distressed being?"

All were silent; for none thought it safe, in the presence of the Grand Master, to avow any interest in the calumniated prisoner, lest he should be suspected of a leaning towards Judaism. Not even the prospect of reward, far less any feelings of compassion alone, could surmount this apprehension.

Rebecca stood for a few minutes in indescribable anxiety, and then exclaimed, "Is it really thus?—And, in this English land, am I to be deprived of the poor chance of safety which remains to me, for want of an act of charity which would not be refused to the worst criminal?"

Higg, the son of Snell, at length replied, "I am but a maimed man, but that I can at all stir or move was owing to her charitable assistance. —I will do thine errand," he added, addressing Rebecca, "as well as a crippled object can, and happy were my limbs fleet enough to repair the mischief done by my tongue. Alas! when I boasted of thy charity, I little thought I was leading thee into danger."

"God," said Rebecca, "is the disposer of all. He can turn back the captivity of Judah, even by the weakest instrument. To execute his errand the snail is as sure a messenger as the falcon. Seek out Isaac of York—here is that will pay for horse and man—and let him have this scroll.—I know not if it be of Heaven the spirit which inspires me, but most truly do I judge that I am not to die this death, and that a champion will be raised up for me. Farewell!—Life and death are in thy haste."

The peasant took the scroll, which contained only a few words in Hebrew. Many of the crowd would have dissuaded him from touching a document so suspicious; but Higg was resolute in the service of his benefactress. She had saved his body, he said, and he was confident that she did not mean to peril his soul.

"I will get me," he said, "my neighbour Buthan's good capul, and I will be at York within as brief space as man and beast may."

But as it fortuned, he had no occasion to go so far, for within a quarter of a mile from the gate of the Preceptory he met with two riders, whom, by their dress and their huge yellow caps, he knew to be Jews; and, on approaching more nearly, discovered that one of them was his ancient employer, Isaac of York. The other was the Rabbi Ben Samuel; and both had approached as near to the Preceptory as they dared, on hearing that the Grand Master had summoned a chapter for the trial of a sorceress.

"Brother Ben Samuel," said Isaac, "my soul is disquieted, and I wot not why. This charge of necromancy is right often used for cloaking evil practices on our people."

"Be of good comfort, brother," said the physician; "thou canst deal with the Nazarenes as one possessing the mammon of unrighteousness, and canst therefore purchase immunity at their hands—it rules the savage minds of these ungodly men, even as the signet of the mighty Solomon was said to command the evil genii. But what poor wretch comes hither upon his crutches, desiring, as I think, some speech with me?—Friend," continued the physician, addressing Higg, the son of Snell, "I refuse thee not the aid of mine art, but I relieve not with one asper those who beg for alms on the highway. Out upon thee!—Hast thou the palsy in thy legs? then let thy hands work for thy livelihood; for, albeit thou be'st unfit for a speedy post, or for a careful shepherd, or for the warfare, or for the service of a hasty master, yet there be occupations—How now, brother?" said he, interrupting his harangue to look towards Isaac, who had but glanced at the scroll which Higg offered, when, uttering a deep groan, he fell from his mule like a dying man, and lay for a minute insensible.

The Rabbi now dismounted in great alarm, and hastily applied the remedies which his art suggested for the recovery of his companion. He had even taken from his pocket a cupping apparatus, and was about to proceed to phlebotomy, when the object of his anxious solicitude suddenly revived; but it was to dash his cap from his head, and to throw dust on his grey hairs. The physician was at first inclined to ascribe this sudden and violent emotion to the effects of insanity; and, adhering to his original purpose, began once again to handle his instruments. But Isaac soon convinced him of his error.

"Child of my sorrow," he said, "well shouldst thou be called Benoni, instead of Rebecca! Why should thy death bring down my grey hairs to the grave, till in the bitterness of my heart I curse God and die?"

"Brother," said the Rabbi in great surprise, "art thou a father in Israel, and dost thou utter words like unto these?—I trust that the child of thy house yet liveth?"

"She liveth," answered Isaac; "but it is as Daniel, which was called Belteshazzar, even when within the den of the lions. She is captive unto those men of Belial, and they will wreak their cruelty upon her, sparing neither for her youth nor her comely favour. O! she was as a crown of green palms to my grey locks; and she must wither in a night, like the gourd of Jonah.—Child of my love!—child of my old age!—oh, Rebecca, daughter of Rachael! the darkness of the shadow of death hath encompassed thee."

"Yet read the scroll," said the Rabbi; "peradventure we may yet find out a way of deliverance."

"Do thou read, brother," answered Isaac, "for mine eyes are as fountains of water."

The physician read, but in their native language, the following words:—

"To Isaac, the son of Adonikam, whom the Gentiles call Isaac of York, peace and the blessing of the Promise be multiplied upon thee!—My father, I am as one doomed to die for that which my soul knoweth not—even for the crime of witchcraft. My father, if a strong man can be found to do battle for my cause with sword and spear, according to the custom of the Nazarenes, and that within the lists of Templestowe, on the third day from this time, peradventure our fathers' God will give him strength to defend the innocent, and her who hath none to help her. But if this may not be, let the virgins of our people mourn for me as for one cast off, and for the hart that is stricken by the hunter, and for the flower which is cut down by the scythe of the mower. Wherefore look now what thou doest, and whether there be any rescue. One Nazarene warrior might indeed bear arms in my behalf, even Wilfred, son of Cedric, whom the Gentiles call Ivanhoe. But he may not yet endure the weight of his armour. Nevertheless, send the tidings unto him, my father; for he hath favour among the strong men of his people, and, as he was our companion in the house of bondage, he may find some one to do battle for my sake. And say unto him, even unto him, even unto Wilfred, the son of Cedric, that if Rebecca live, or if Rebecca die, she liveth or dieth wholly free of the guilt she is charged withal. And if it be the will of God that thou shalt be deprived of thy daughter, do not thou tarry, old man, in this land of bloodshed and cruelty; but betake thyself to Cordova, where thy brother liveth in safety, under the shadow of the throne, even of the throne of Boabdil the Saracen; for less cruel are the cruelties of the Moors unto the race of Jacob, than the cruelties of the Nazarenes of England."

Isaac listened with tolerable composure while Ben Samuel read the letter, and then again resumed the gestures and exclamations of oriental sorrow, tearing his garments, besprinkling his head with dust, and ejaculating, "My daughter! my daughter! flesh of my flesh, and bone of my bone!"

"Yet," said the Rabbi, "take courage, for this grief availeth nothing. Girth up thy loins, and seek out this Wilfred, the son of Cedric. It may be he will help thee with counsel or with strength; for the youth hath favour in the eyes of Richard, called of the Nazarenes Cœur de Lion, and the tidings that he hath returned, are constant in the land. It may be that he will obtain his letter, and his signet, commanding these men of blood, who take their name from the Temple to the dishonour thereof, that they proceed not in this purposed wickedness."

"I will seek him out," said Isaac, "for he is a good youth, and hath compassion for the exile of Jacob. But he cannot bear his armour, and what other Christian shall do battle for the oppressed of Zion?"

"Nay, but," said the Rabbi, "thou speakest as one who knoweth not the Gentiles. With gold shalt thou buy their valour, even as with gold thou buyest thine own safety. Be of good courage, and do thou set forward to find out this Wilfred of Ivanhoe. I will also up and be doing, for great sin it were to leave thee in thine calamity. I will hie me to the city of York, where many warriors and strong men are assembled, and doubt not but I will find among them some one who will do battle for thy daughter; for gold is their god, and for riches will they pawn their lives as well as their lands.—Thou wilt fulfil, my brother, such promises as I may make unto them in thy name?"

"Assuredly, brother," said Isaac, "and Heaven be praised that raised me up a comforter in misery. Howbeit, grant them not their full demand at once, for thou shalt find it the quality of this accursed people that they will ask pounds, and peradventure accept of ounces —Nevertheless, be it as thou willest, for I am distracted even in this thing, and what would my gold avail me if the child of my love should perish?"

"Farewell," said the physician, "and may it be to thee as thy heart desires."

They embraced accordingly, and departed on their several routes. The crippled peasant remained for some time looking after them.

"These dog-Jews!" said he; "take no more notice of a free guild-brother, than if I were a bond slave, or a heathen Turk, or a circumcised Hebrew like themselves! They might have flung me a mancus or two, however. I was not obliged to bring their unhallowed scrawls, and to run the risk of being bewitched, as more folks than one told me. And what care I for the bit of gold that the wench gave me, if I am to come to harm from the priest next Easter at confession, and be obliged to give twice as much to make it up with him, and be called the Jew's flying post all my life, it may hap, into the bargain? I think I was bewitched in earnest when I was beside that girl!—But it was always so with Jew and Gentile, whosoever came near her—none could stay when she had an errand to go—And still, whenever I think of her, I would give shop and tools to save her life."

Chapter Nine

O maid, unrelenting and cold as thou art,
My bosom is proud as thine own.
SEWARD.

IT WAS IN the twilight of the day when her trial, if it could be called such, had taken place, that a low knock was heard at the door of Rebecca's prison chamber. It disturbed not the inmate, who was then engaged in the evening prayer recommended by her religion, and which concluded with a hymn we have ventured thus to translate into English.

When Israel, of the Lord beloved,
  Out from the land of bondage came,
Her father's God before her moved,
  An awful guide in smoke and flame.
By day, along the astonish'd lands
  The cloudy pillar glided slow;
By night, Arabia's crimson'd sands
  Return'd the fiery column's glow.

Then rose the choral hymn of praise,
  And trump and timbrel answer'd keen,

And Zion's daughters pour'd their lays,
  With priest's and warrior's voice between.
No portents now our foes amaze,
  Forsaken Israel wanders lone;
Our fathers would not know THY ways,
  And THOU hast left them to their own.

Yet, present still, though now unseen!
  When brightly shines the prosperous day,
Be thoughts of THEE a cloudy screen
  To temper the deceitful ray.
And oh, when stoops on Judah's path
  In shade and storm the frequent night,
Be THOU, long-suffering, slow to wrath,
  A burning and a shining light!

Our harps we left by Babel's streams,
  The tyrant's jest, the Gentile's scorn;
No censer round our altar beams,
  And mute are timbrel, trump, and horn.
But THOU hast said, The blood of goat,
  The flesh of rams, I will not prize;
A contrite heart, a humble thought,
  Are mine accepted sacrifice.

When the sounds of Rebecca's devotional hymn had died away in silence, the low knock at the door was again renewed. "Enter," she said, "if thou art a friend; and if a foe, I have not the means of refusing thy entrance."

"I am," said Brian de Bois-Guilbert, entering the apartment, "friend or foe, Rebecca, as the event of this our interview shall make me."

Alarmed at the sight of this man, whose licentious passion she considered as the root of her misfortunes, Rebecca drew backwards, with a cautious and alarmed, yet not a timorous demeanour, into the farthest corner of the apartment, as if determined to retreat as far as she could, but to stand her ground when retreat became no longer possible. She drew herself into an attitude not of defiance, but of resolution, as one that would avoid provoking assault, yet was resolute to repell it, being offered, to the utmost of her power.

"You have no reason to fear me, Rebecca," said the Templar; "or if I must so qualify my speech, you have at least *now* no reason to fear me."

"I fear you not, Sir Knight," replied Rebecca, although her short-drawn breath seemed to belie the heroism of her accents; "my trust is strong, and I fear thee not."

"You have no cause," answered Bois-Guilbert, gravely; "my former frantic attempts you have not now to dread—within your call is a guard, over whom I have no authority, and they are designed to conduct you to death, Rebecca, yet would not suffer you to be insulted by any one, even by me, were my frenzy—for frenzy it is—to urge me so far."

"May Heaven be praised!" said the Jewess; "death is the least of my apprehensions in this den of evil."

"Ay," replied the Templar, "the idea of death is easily received by the courageous mind, when the road to it is sudden and open—a thrust with a lance, a stroke with a sword, were to me little—to you, a spring from a dizzy battlement, a stroke with a sharp poniard, has no terrors, compared with what either thinks disgrace. Mark me—I say either—perhaps mine own sentiments of honour are not less fantastic, Rebecca, than thine are; but we know alike how to die for them."

"Unhappy man!" said the Jewess; "and art thou then condemned to expose thy life for principles, of which thy sober judgment does not acknowledge the solidity?—surely this is a parting with your treasure for that which is not bread—But deem not so of me—thy resolution may fluctuate on the wild and changeful billows of human opinion, but mine is anchored on the Rock of Ages."

"Silence, maiden," answered the Templar; "such discourse now avails but little—thou art condemned to die not a sudden and easy death, such as misery chuses, and despair allows, but a slow, wretched, protracted course of torture, suited to what the diabolical bigotry of these men calls thy crime."

"And to whom—if such my fate—to whom do I owe this?" said Rebecca; "surely only to him, who, for a most selfish and brutal cause, dragged me hither, and who now, for some unknown purpose of his own, strives to exaggerate the wretched fate to which he has exposed me."

"Think not," said the Templar, "that I have so exposed thee; I would have bucklered thee against such danger with my own bosom, as freely as ever I exposed it to the shafts which had otherwise reached thy life."

"Had thy purpose been the honourable protection of the innocent," said Rebecca, "I had thanked thee for thy care—as it is, thou hast claimed merit for it so often, that I tell thee life is worth nothing to me, preserved at the price which thou wouldst exact for it."

"Truce with thine upbraidings, Rebecca," said the Templar; "I have my own cause of grief, and brook not that thy reproaches should add to it."

"What is thy purpose then, Sir Knight?" said the Jewess; "speak it briefly.—If thou hast aught to do, save to witness the misery thou hast caused, let me know it; and then, if so it please you, leave me to myself

—the step betwixt time and eternity is short but terrible, and I have few moments to prepare for it."

"I perceive, Rebecca," said Bois-Guilbert, "that thou dost continue to burthen me with the charge of distresses, which most fain would I have prevented."

"Sir Knight," said Rebecca, "I would avoid reproaches—But what is more certain than that I owe my death to thine unbridled passion?"

"You err—you err,"—said the Templar hastily, "if you impute what I could neither foresee nor prevent to my purpose or agency.—Could I guess the unexpected arrival of yonder dotard, whom some flashes of frantic valour, and the praises due to the stupid self-torments of an ascetic, have raised for the present above his own merits, above common sense, above me, and above the hundreds of our Order, who think and feel as men free from such silly and fantastic prejudices as are the grounds of his ideas and actions?"

"Yet," said Rebecca, "you sate a judge upon me, innocent—most innocent—as you knew me to be—you concurred in my condemnation, and, if I aright understood, are yourself to appear in arms to assert my guilt, and assure my punishment."

"Thy patience, maiden," replied the Templar.—"No race knows so well as thine own how to submit to the time, and so to trim their bark as to make advantage even of an adverse wind."

"Lamented be the hour," replied Rebecca, "that hath taught such art to the House of Israel—but adversity bends the heart as fire bends the stubborn steel, and those who are no longer their own governors, and denizens of their own free independent state, must crouch before strangers. It is our curse, Sir Knight, deserved, doubtless, by our own misdeeds and those of our fathers; but you—you who boast your freedom as your birthright, how much deeper is your disgrace when you stoop to soothe the prejudices of others, and that against your own conviction?"

"Your words are bitter, Rebecca," said Bois-Guilbert, pacing the apartment with impatience, "but I came not hither to bandy reproaches with thee.—Know that Bois-Guilbert yields not to created man, although circumstances may for a time induce him to alter his plan. His will is the mountain stream, which may indeed be turned for a little space aside by the rock, but fails not to find its course to the ocean. That scroll which warned thee to demand a champion, from whom could'st thou think it came, if not from Bois-Guilbert? In whom else could'st thou have excited such interest?"

"A brief respite from instant death," answered Rebecca, "which will little avail me—is this all thou could'st do for one, on whose head thou hast heaped sorrow, and whom thou hast brought near even to the verge of the tomb?"

"No, maiden," said Bois-Guilbert, "this was not all that I purposed. Had it not been for the accursed interference of yonder fanatical dotard, and the fool of Goodalricke, who, being a Templar, affects to think and judge according to the ordinary rules of humanity, the office of the Champion Defender had devolved, not on a Preceptor, but on a Companion of the Order. Then I myself—such was my purpose—had, on the sounding of the trumpet, appeared in the lists as thy champion, disguised indeed in the fashion of a roving knight, who seeks adventures to prove his shield and spear; and then, let Beaumanoir chuse not one, but two or three of the brethren here assembled, I had not doubted to cast them out of the saddle with my single lance. Thus, Rebecca, should thine innocence have been avouched, and to thine own gratitude would I have trusted for the reward of my victory."

"This, Sir Knight," said Rebecca, "is but idle boasting—a brag of what you would have done had you not found it convenient to do otherwise. You received my glove, and my champion, if a creature so desolate can find one, must encounter your lance in the lists—yet you would assume the air of my friend and protector!"

"Thy friend and protector," said the Templar, gravely, "I will yet be—but mark at what risk, or rather at what certainty, of dishonour, and then blame me not if I make my stipulations, before I offer up all my life has hitherto held dear, to save the life of a Jewish maiden."

"Speak," said Rebecca; "I understand thee not."

"Well, then," said Bois-Guilbert, "I will speak as freely as ever did doating penitent to his ghostly father, when placed in the tricky confessional.—Rebecca, if I appear not in these lists I lose fame and rank—lose that which is the breath of my nostrils, the esteem, I mean, in which I am held by my brethren, and the hopes I have of succeeding to that mighty authority, which is now wielded by the bigotted and dotard Lucas de Beaumanoir. Such is my certain doom, except I appear in arms against thy cause. Accursed be he of Goodalricke, who baited this trap for me! and doubly accursed Albert de Malvoisin, who withheld me from the resolution I had formed, of hurling back the glove at the face of the superstitious and superannuated fool, who listened to a charge so absurd, and against a creature so high in mind and so lovely in form as thou art!"

"And what now avails rant or flattery?" answered Rebecca. "Thou hast made thy choice betwixt causing to be shed the blood of an innocent woman, and thine own earthly state and earthly hopes—What avails it to reckon together?—thy choice is made."

"No, Rebecca," said the knight, in a softer tone, and drawing nearer towards her; "my choice is not made—nay, more, it is thine to make the election. If I appear in the lists, I must maintain my name in arms; and if I do so, championed or unchampioned, thou diest by the stake and faggot, for there lives not the knight who hath coped with me in arms on equal issue, or on terms of vantage, save Richard Cœur de Lion, and his minion of Ivanhoe. Ivanhoe, as thou well knowest, is unable to bear his corslet, and Richard is in a foreign prison. If I appear, then thou diest, even if thy charms should instigate some hot-headed youth to enter the lists in thy defence."

"And what avails repeating this so often?" said Rebecca.

"Much," replied the Templar; "for thou must learn to look at thy fate on every side."

"Well then, turn the tapestry," said the Jewess, "and let me see the other side."

"If I appear," said Bois-Guilbert, "in the fatal lists, thou diest by a slow and cruel death, in pain such as they say is destined to the guilty hereafter. But if I appear not, then am I a degraded and dishonoured knight, accused of witchcraft, and of communion with infidels—the illustrious name which has grown yet more so under my wearing, becomes a hissing and a reproach. I lose fame, I lose power, I lose the prospect of such greatness as scarce emperors attain to—I sacrifice mighty ambition, I destroy schemes built as high as the mountains with which heathens say that their heaven was once nearly scaled—And yet, Rebecca," he added, throwing himself at her feet, "this greatness will I sacrifice, this fame will I renounce, this power will I forego, even now when it is half within my grasp, if thou wilt say, Bois-Guilbert, I receive thee for my lover."

"Think not of such foolishness, Sir Knight," answered Rebecca, "but hasten to the Regent and to Prince John—they cannot, in honour to the crown, allow of the proceedings of your Grand Master. So shall you give me protection without sacrifice on your part, or the pretext of requiring any requital from me."

"With these I deal not," he continued, holding the train of her robe—"it is thee only I address; and what can counterbalance thy choice? Bethink thee, were I a fiend, yet death is a worse, and it is death who is my rival."

"I weigh not these evils," said Rebecca, afraid to provoke the wild knight, yet equally determined neither to endure his passion, nor even feign to endure it. "Be a man, be a Christian! If indeed thy faith recommends that mercy which rather your tongues than your actions pretend, save me from this dreadful death, without seeking a requital which would change thy magnanimity into base barter."

"No, damsel!" said the proud Templar, springing up, "thou shalt not thus impose on me—if I renounce present fame and future ambition, I renounce it for thy sake, and we will escape in company. Listen to me, Rebecca," he added, again softening his tone; "England, nay Europe, is not the world—there are spheres in which we may act, ample enough even for my ambition. We will go to Palestine, where Conrade, Marquis of Montserrat, is my friend—a friend free as myself from the doting scruples which fetter our free-born reason—Rather with Saladin will we league ourselves, than endure the scorn of the bigots whom we contemn.—I will frame new paths to greatness," he continued, again traversing the room with hasty strides—"Europe shall hear the loud step of him she has driven from her sons!—Not the millions whom her crusades send to slaughter, can do so much to defend Palestine—not the sabres of the thousands and ten thousands of Saracens can hew their way so deep into that land for which nations are striving, as the strength and policy of me and of the brethren, who, despite of yonder old bigot, will adhere to me in good and evil. Thou shalt be a queen, Rebecca—on Mount Carmel will we pitch the throne which my valour will gain for you, and I will exchange my long desired batton for a sceptre."

"A dream," said Rebecca; "an empty vision of the night, which, were it a waking reality, affects me not—enough that the power which thou mayest acquire, I will never share; nor hold I so light of country or religious faith, as to esteem him who is willing to barter their ties, and cast away the bonds of the Order of which he is a sworn member, in order to gratify an unruly passion for the daughter of another people.—Put not a price on my deliverance, Sir Knight—sell not a deed of generosity—protect the oppressed for the sake of charity, and not for a selfish advantage—Go to the throne of England, Richard will listen to my appeal from these cruel men."

"Never, Rebecca," said the Templar, fiercely. "If I renounce mine Order, for thee alone will I renounce it—Ambition shall remain mine, if thou refuse me love; I will not be fooled on all hands.—Stoop my crest to Richard?—ask a boon of that heart of pride?—Never, Rebecca, will I place the Order of the Temple at his feet in my person. I may forsake the Order, I will never degrade or betray it."

"Then God be gracious to me," said Rebecca, "for the succour of man is well nigh hopeless!"

"It is indeed," said the Templar; "for proud as thou art, thou hast in me found thy match. If I enter the lists with my spear in rest, think not any human consideration shall prevent my putting forth my strength; and think then upon thine own fate—to die the dreadful death of the worst of criminals—to be consumed upon a blazing pile—dispersed to the elements of which our strange forms are so mystically composed—not a relique left of that graceful frame, from which we could say this lived and moved!—Rebecca, it is not in woman to sustain this prospect—Thou wilt yield to my suit."

"Bois-Guilbert," answered the Jewess, "thou knowest not the heart of woman, or hast only conversed with those who are lost to her best feelings. I tell thee, proud Templar, that not in thy fiercest battles hast thou displayed more of thy vaunted courage, than has been shewn by woman when called upon to suffer by affection and duty. I am myself a woman, tenderly nurtured, naturally fearful of danger, and impatient of pain—yet, when we enter those fatal lists, thou to fight and I to suffer, I feel the strong assurance within me, that my courage shall mount higher than thine. Farewell—I waste no more words on thee; the time that remains on earth to the daughter of Jacob must be otherwise spent—she must seek the Comforter, who may hide his face from his people, but who ever opens his ear to the cry of those who seek him in sincerity and in truth."

"We part then thus," said the Templar, after a short pause; "would to Heaven that we had never met, or that thou hadst been noble in birth and Christian in faith!—Nay, by Heaven! while I gaze on thee, and think when and how we are next to meet, I could even wish myself one of thine own degraded nation; my hand conversant with ingots and shekels, instead of spear and shield; my head bent down before each petty noble, and my look only terrible to the shivering and bankrupt debtor—this could I wish myself, Rebecca, to be near to thee in life, and to escape the fearful share which I must have in thy death."

"Thou hast spoken the Jew," said Rebecca, "as the persecution of such as thou art has made him. Heaven in ire has driven him from his country, but industry has opened to him the only road to power and to influence, which oppression has left unbarred. Read the ancient history of the people of God, and tell me if those, by whom Jehovah wrought such marvels among the nations, were then a people of misers and of usurers!—And know, proud knight, we number names amongst us to which your boasted northern nobility is as the gourd compared with the cedar—names that ascend far back to those high times when the Divine Presence shook the mercy-seat between the cherubim, and which derive their splendour from no earthly prince, but from the awful Voice, which bade their fathers be nearest of the congregation to the Vision—Such were the princes of the House of Jacob."

Rebecca's colour rose as she boasted the ancient glories of her race, but faded as she added, with a sigh, "Such *were* the princes of Judah, now such no more!—They are trampled down like the shorn grass, and mixed with the mire of the ways. Yet are there those amongst them who shame not such high descent, and of such shall be the daughter of Isaac son of Adonikam! Farewell!—I envy not thy blood-won honours—I envy not thy barbarous descent from northern heathens—I envy thee not thy faith, which is ever in thy mouth, but never in thy heart nor in thy practice."

"There is a spell on me, by Heaven!" said Bois-Guilbert. "I well nigh think yon bigotted skeleton spoke truth, and that the reluctance with which I part from thee hath something in it more than is natural.—Fair creature!" he said, approaching near her, but with great respect,—"so young, so beautiful, so fearless of death! yet doomed to die, and with infamy and agony—who would not weep for thee?—the tear, which has been a stranger to these eye-lids for twenty years, moistens them as I gaze on thee. But it must be—nothing may now save thy life. Thou and I are but the blind instruments of some irresistible fatality, that hurries us along, like goodly vessels driving before the storm, which are dashed against each other, and so perish. Forgive me, then, and let us part at least as friends part. I have assailed thy resolution in vain, and mine own is fixed as the adamantine decrees of fate."

"Thus," said Rebecca, "do men throw on fate the issue of their own wild passions. But I do forgive thee, Bois-Guilbert, though the author of my early death. There are noble things which cross over thy powerful mind; but it is the garden of the sluggard, and the weeds have rushed up, and conspired to choak the fair and wholesome blossom."

"Yet," said the Templar, "I am, Rebecca, as thou hast spoken me, untaught, untamed—and proud, that, amidst a shoal of empty fools and crafty bigots, I have retained the pre-eminent fortitude that places me above them. I have been a child of battle from my youth upward, high in my views, steady and inflexible in pursuing them. Such must I remain—proud, inflexible, and unchanging; and of this the world shall have proof.—But thou forgivest me, Rebecca?"

"As freely as ever victim forgave her executioner."

"Farewell, then," said the Templar, and left the apartment.

The Preceptor Albert waited impatiently in an adjacent chamber the return of Bois-Guilbert.

"Thou hast tarried long," he said; "I have been as if stretched on red-hot iron with very impatience. What if the Grand Master, or his spy Conrade, had come hither? I had paid dear for my complaisance. —But what ails thee, brother?—thy step totters, thy brow is as black as night. Art thou well, Bois-Guilbert?"

"Ay," answered the Templar, "as well as the wretch who is doomed to die within an hour.—Nay, by the rood, not half so well—for there be those in such state, who can lay down life like a cast-off garment. By heaven, Malvoisin, yonder girl hath well nigh unmanned me. I am half resolved to go to the Grand Master, abjure the Order to his very teeth, and refuse to act the brutality which his tyranny has imposed on me."

"Thou art mad," answered Malvoisin; "thou mayest thus indeed utterly ruin thyself, but canst not even find a chance thereby to save the life of this Jewess, which seems so precious in thine eyes. Beaumanoir will name another of the Order to defend his judgment in thy place, and the accused will as assuredly perish as if thou hadst taken the duty imposed on thee."

"'Tis false— I will myself take arms in her behalf," answered the Templar, haughtily; "and, should I do so, I think, Malvoisin, that thou knowest not one of the Order, who will keep his saddle before the point of my lance."

"Ay, but thou forgettest thou wilt have neither leisure nor opportunity to execute this mad project. Go to Lucas Beaumanoir, and say thou hast renounced thy vow of obedience, and see how long the despotic old man will leave thee in personal freedom. The words shall scarce have left thy lips, ere thou shalt either be an hundred foot under ground, in the dungeon of the Preceptory, to abide trial as a recreant knight; or, if his opinion holds concerning thy possession, thou shalt be enjoying straw, darkness, and chains, in some distant convent cell, stunned with exorcisms, and drenched with holy water, to expel the foul fiend which hath obtained dominion over thee. Thou must to the lists, Brian, or thou art a lost and dishonoured man."

"I will break forth and fly," said Bois-Guilbert—"fly to some remote land, to which folly and fanaticism have not yet found their way. No drop of the blood of this most excellent creature shall be spilled by my sanction."

"Thou canst not fly," said the Preceptor; "thy ravings have excited suspicion, and thou wilt not be permitted to leave the Preceptory. Go and make the essay—present thyself before the gate, and command the bridge to be lowered, and mark what answer thou shalt receive.—Thou art surprised and offended; but is it not better for thee? Wert thou to fly, what could ensue but the reversal of thy arms, the dishonour of thine ancestry, the degradation of thy rank?—Think on it. Where shall thine old companions in arms hide their heads when Brian de Bois-Guilbert, the best lance of the Templars, is proclaimed recreant, amid the hisses of the assembled people? What grief will be at the Court of France! With what joy will the haughty Richard hear the news, that the knight that set him hard in Palestine, and well nigh darkened his renown, has lost fame and honour for a Jewish girl, whom he could not even save by so costly a sacrifice."

"Malvoisin," said the Knight, "I thank thee—thou hast touched the string at which my heart most readily thrills!—Come of it what may, recreant shall never be added to the name of Bois-Guilbert. Would to God, Richard, or any of his vaunting minions of England, would appear in these lists! But they will be empty—no one will risk to break a lance for the innocent, the forlorn."

"The better for thee, if it prove so," said the Preceptor; "if no champion appears, it is not by thy means that this unlucky damsel shall die, but by the doom of the Grand Master, with whom rests all the blame, and who will count that blame for praise and commendation."

"True," said Bois-Guilbert; "if no champion appears, I am but as a part of the pageant, sitting indeed on horseback in the lists, but having no part in what is to follow."

"None whatsoever," said Malvoisin; "no more than the armed image of Saint George when it makes part of a procession."

"Well, I will resume my resolution. She has despised me—repulsed me—reviled me—And wherefore should I offer up for her whatever of estimation I have in the opinion of others? Malvoisin, I will appear in the lists."

He left the apartment hastily as he uttered these words, and the Preceptor followed, to watch and confirm him in his resolution; for in Bois-Guilbert's fame he had himself a strong interest, expecting much advantage from his being one day at the head of the Order, not to mention the preferment of which Mountfitchet had given him hopes, on condition he could forward the condemnation of the unfortunate Rebecca. Yet although, in combating his friend's better feelings, he possessed all the advantage which a wily, composed, selfish disposition has over a man agitated by strong and contending passions, it required all Malvoisin's art to keep Bois-Guilbert steady to the purpose which he had prevailed on him to adopt. He was obliged to watch him closely to prevent his resuming his purpose of flight, to intercept his communication with the Grand Master, lest he should come to an open rupture with his Superior, and to renew, from time to time, the various arguments by which he endeavoured to shew, that, in appearing as champion on this occasion, Bois-Guilbert, without either accelerating or ensuring the fate of Rebecca, would follow the only course by which he could save himself from degradation and disgrace.

Chapter Ten

Shadows, avaunt!—Richard's himself again.
Richard III.

WHEN THE BLACK KNIGHT—for it becomes necessary to resume the train of his adventures—left the Trysting-tree of the generous Outlaw, he held his way straight to a neighbouring religious house, of small extent and revenue, called the Priory of Saint Botolph, to which the wounded Ivanhoe had been removed when the castle was taken, under the guidance of the faithful Gurth, and the magnanimous Wamba. It is unnecessary at present to mention what took place in the interview betwixt Wilfred and his deliverer; suffice it to say, that after long and grave communication, messengers were dispatched by the Prior in several directions, and that upon the succeeding morning the Black Knight was about to set forth on his journey, accompanied by the jester Wamba, who attended as his guide.

"We will meet," he said to Ivanhoe, "at Coningsburgh, the castle of the deceased Athelstane, since thy father Cedric holds there the funeral feast for his noble relative. I would see your Saxon kindred together, Sir Wilfred, and become better acquainted with them than heretofore. Thou also wilt meet me; and it shall be my task to reconcile thee to thy father."

So saying, he took an affectionate farewell of Ivanhoe, who expressed his anxious desire himself to attend upon his deliverer. But the Black Knight would not listen to the proposal.

"Rest this day; thou wilt have scarce strength enough to travel on the next. I will have no guide with me but honest Wamba, who can play priest or fool as I shall be most in the humour."

"And I," said Wamba, "will attend you with all my heart. I would fain see the feasting at the funeral of Athelstane; for, an it be not full and frequent, he will rise from the dead to rebuke cook, sewer, and cup-bearer; and that were a sight worth seeing. Always, Sir Knight, I will trust your valour for making mine excuse to Cedric, in case my own wit should fail."

"And how should my poor valour succeed, Sir Jester, when thy light wit halts?—resolve me that."

"Wit, Sir Knight," replied the Jester, "may do much—he is a quick, apprehensive knave, who sees his neighbour's blind side, and knows how to take the lee-gage when his passions are blowing high. But Valour is a sturdy fellow, that makes all split—he rows against both wind and tide, and makes way notwithstanding. And, therefore, good

Sir Knight, while I take advantage of the fair weather in our noble master's temper, I will expect you to bestir yourself when it grows rough."

"Sir Knight of the Fetterlock, since it is your pleasure still to be so distinguished," said Ivanhoe, "I fear me you have chosen a talkative and a troublesome fool to be your guide. But he knows every path and alley of the woods as well as e'er a hunter who frequents them; and the poor knave, as thou hast partly seen, is as faithful as steel."

"Nay," said the Knight, "an he have the gift of shewing my road, I shall not grumble with him that he desires to make it pleasant.—Fare thee well, kind Wilfred—I charge thee not to attempt to travel till to-morrow at earliest."

So saying, he extended his hand to Ivanhoe, who pressed it to his lips, took leave of the Prior, mounted his horse, and departed, with Wamba for his companion. Ivanhoe followed them with his eyes, until they were lost in the shades of the surrounding forest, and then returned into the convent.

But shortly after mattin-song, he requested to see the Prior. The old man came in haste, and enquired anxiously after the state of his health.

"It is better," he said, "than my fondest hope could have anticipated; either my wound has been slighter than the effusion of blood led me to suppose, or this wonderful balsam hath wrought a miraculous cure upon it. I feel already as if I could bear my corslet; and so much the better, for thoughts press on my mind which render me unwilling to remain here longer in inactivity."

"Now, the saints forbid," said the Prior, "that the son of the Saxon Cedric should leave our convent ere his wounds were healed! It were shame to our profession should we suffer it."

"Nor would I desire to leave your hospitable roof, venerable father," said Ivanhoe, "did I not feel myself both able to endure the journey, and impelled to undertake it."

"And what can have urged you to such a sudden departure?" said the Prior.

"Have you never, holy father," answered the Knight, "felt an apprehension of approaching evil, for which you in vain attempted to assign a cause?—Have you never found your mind darkened, like the sunny landscape, by the sudden cloud, which augurs a coming tempest?—And thinkest thou not that such impulses are deserving of attention, as being the hints of our guardian spirits, that danger is impending?"

"I may not deny," said the Prior, crossing himself, "that such things have been, and have been of Heaven; but then such communications have had a visibly useful scope and tendency. But thou, wounded as thou art, what avails it thou shouldst follow the steps of him whom thou couldst not aid, were he to be assaulted?"

"Prior," said Ivanhoe, "thou doest mistake—I am stout enough to exchange buffets with any who will challenge me to such a traffic—But were it otherwise, may I not aid him were he in danger, by other means than by force of arms? It is but too well known that the Saxons love not the Norman race, and who knows what may be the issue, if he breaks in upon them when their hearts are irritated with the death of Athelstane, and their heads heated by the carousal in which they will indulge themselves? I hold his entrance among them at such a moment most perilous, and I am resolved to go to share or avert the danger, which, that I may the better do, I would crave of thee the use of some palfrey whose pace may be softer than that of my *destrier*."*

"Surely," said the worthy churchman; "you shall have mine own ambling jennet, and I would it paced as easy for your sake as that of the Abbot of Saint Albans. Yet this will I say for Malkin, for so I call her, that unless you were to borrow a ride on the juggler's steed which prances a hornpipe amongst the eggs, you could not go a journey on a creature so gentle and smooth-paced. I have composed many a homily on her back, to the edification of my brethren of the convent, and many poor Christian souls."

"I pray you, reverend father, let Malkin be got ready instantly, and bid Gurth attend me with mine arms."

"Nay, but fair sir, I pray you to remember that Malkin hath as little skill in arms as her master, and that I warrant not her enduring the sight or weight of your full panoply.—O, Malkin, I promise you, is a beast of judgment, and will contend against any undue weight—I did but borrow the *Fructus Temporum* from the priest of Saint Bees, and I promise you she would not stir from the gate until I had exchanged the huge volume for my breviary."

"Trust me, holy father," said Ivanhoe, "I will not distress her with too much weight; and if she calls a combat with me, it is odds but she has the worst."

This reply was made while Gurth was buckling on the Knight's heels a pair of large gilded spurs, capable of convincing any restive horse that his best safety lay in being conformable to the will of his rider.

The deep and sharp rowels with which Ivanhoe's heels were now armed, began to make the worthy Prior repent of his courtesy, and ejaculate,—"Nay, but fair sir, now I bethink me, my Malkin abideth not the spur—Better it were that you tarry for the mare of our man-

* *Destrier*—war-horse.

ciple down at the Grange, which may be had in little more than an hour, and cannot but be tractable, in respect that she draweth much of our winter fire-wood, and eateth no corn."

"I thank you, reverend father, but will abide by your first offer, as I see Malkin is already led forth to the gate. Gurth shall carry mine armour; and for the rest, rely on it, that as I will not overload Malkin's back, she shall not overcome my patience. And now, farewell!"

Ivanhoe now descended the stairs more hastily and easily than his wound promised, and threw himself upon the jennet, eager to escape the importunity of the Prior, who stuck as closely to his side as his age and fatness would permit, now singing the praises of Malkin, now recommending caution to the Knight in managing her.

"She is at the most dangerous period for maidens as well as mares," said the old man, laughing at his own jest, "being barely in her fifteenth year."

Ivanhoe, who had other web to weave than to stand canvassing a palfrey's paces with its owner, lent but a deaf ear to the Prior's grave advices and facetious jests, and having leapt on the mare, and commanded his squire, for such Gurth now stiled himself, to keep close by him, he followed the track of the Black Knight into the forest, while the Prior stood at the gate of the convent looking after him, and ejaculating,—"Saint Mary! how prompt and fiery be these men of war! I would I had not trusted Malkin to his keeping, for, crippled as I am with the cold rheum, I am undone if aught but good befalls. And yet," said he, recollecting himself, "as I would not spare my own old and disabled limbs in the good cause of Old England, so Malkin must e'en run her hazard on the same venture; and it may be they will think our poor house worthy of some munificent guerdon—or, it may be, they will send the old Prior a pacing nag. And if they do none of these, as great men will forget little men's service, truly I shall hold me well apaid in doing that which is right. And, as I think, it be now well nigh the fitting time to summon the brethren to breakfast in the refectory—Ah! I doubt they obey that call more cheerily than the bells for primes and mattins."

So the Prior of Saint Botolph's hobbled back again into the refectory, to preside over the stock-fish and ale, which was just serving out for the friars' breakfast. Pursy and important, he sat him down at the table, and many a dark word he threw out, of benefits to be expected to the convent, and high deeds of service done by himself, which, at another season, would have attracted much observation. But as the stock-fish was highly salted, and the ale reasonably powerful, the jaws of the brotherhood were too anxiously employed to admit of their making much use of their ears; nor do we read of any of the fraternity, who were tempted to speculate upon the mysterious hints of their Superior, excepting Father Diggory, who was severely afflicted by the tooth-ache, so that he could only eat on one side of his face.

In the meantime, the Black Champion and his guide were pacing at their leisure through the recesses of the forest; the good Knight whiles humming to himself the lay of some enamoured troubadour, sometimes encouraging by questions the prating disposition of his attendant, so that their dialogue formed a whimsical mixture of song and jest, of which we would fain give our readers some idea.

You are then to imagine this Knight, such as we have already described him, strong in person, tall, broad-shouldered, and large of bone, mounted on his mighty black charger, which seemed made on purpose to bear his weight, so easily he paced forward under it, having the visor of his helmet raised, so as to admit freedom of breath, yet keeping the beaver, or under part, closed, so that his features could be but imperfectly distinguished. But his ruddy embrowned cheek-bones could be plainly seen, and the large and bright blue eyes, that flashed with unusual keenness from under the iron shade of the raised visor; and the whole gestures and looks of the champion expressed careless gaiety and fearless confidence—a mind which was unapt to apprehend danger, and prompt to defy it when most imminent—yet with whom danger was a familiar thought, as with one whose trade was war and adventure.

The Jester wore his usual fantastic habit, but late incidents had led him to adopt a good cutting falchion, instead of his wooden sword, with a targe to match it; of both which weapons he had, notwithstanding his profession, shewn himself a skilful master during the storming of Torquilstone. Indeed, the infirmity of Wamba's brain consisted chiefly in a kind of impatient irritability, which suffered him not long to remain patient in any posture, or to adhere to any certain train of ideas, although he was for a few minutes alert enough in performing any immediate task, or in apprehending any immediate topic. On horseback, therefore, he was perpetually swinging himself backwards and forwards, now on the horse's ears, then anon on the very rump of the animal,—now hanging both his legs on one side, and now sitting with his face to the tail, mopping, mowing, and making a thousand apish gestures, until his palfrey took his freaks so much to heart, as fairly to lay him at length on the green grass—an incident which greatly amused the Knight, but compelled his companion to ride more steadily in future.

At the point of their journey at which we take them up, this joyous pair were engaged in singing a *virelai*, as it was called, in which the clown bore a stiff and mellow burthen, to the better instructed Knight of the Fetterlock. And thus run the ditty:—

KNIGHT.

Anna-Marie, love, up is the sun,
Anna-Marie, love, morn is begun,
Mists are dispersing, love, birds singing free,
Up in the morning, love, Anna-Marie.
Anna-Marie, love, up in the morn,
The hunter is winding blythe sounds on his horn,
The echo rings merry from rock and from tree,
'Tis time to arouse thee, love, Anna-Marie.

WAMBA.

O Tybalt, love, Tybalt, awake me not yet,
Around my soft pillow while softer dreams flit;
For what are the joys that in waking we prove,
Compared with these visions, O Tybalt, my love?
Let the birds to the rise of the mist carol shrill,
Let the hunter blow out his loud horn on the hill,
Softer sounds, softer pleasures in slumber I prove,—
But think not I dream'd of thee, Tybalt, my love.

"A dainty song," said Wamba, when they had finished their carol; "and I swear by my bauble, a pretty moral—I used to sing it with Gurth, once my play-fellow, and now, by the grace of God and his master, no less than a free man; and we once came by the cudgel for being so entranced by the melody, that we lay in bed two hours after sun-rise, singing the ditty betwixt sleeping and waking—my bones ache at thinking of the tune ever since. Nevertheless, I have played the part of Anna-Marie, to please you, fair sir."

The Jester next struck into another carol, a sort of comic ditty, to which the Knight, catching up the tune, replied in the like manner.

KNIGHT and WAMBA.

There came three merry men from south, west, and north,
  Ever more sing the roundelay;
To win the Widow of Wycombe-forth,
  And where was the widow might say them nay?

The first was a knight, and from Tynedale he came,
  Ever more sing the roundelay;
And his fathers, God save us, were men of great fame,
  And where was the widow might say him nay?

Of his father the laird, of his uncle the squire,
  He boasted in rhime and in roundelay;
She bade him go bask by his sea-coal fire,
  For she was the widow would say him nay.

WAMBA.

The next that came forth, swore by blood and by nails,
  Merrily sing the roundelay;

Hur's a gentleman, God wot, and hur's lineage was of Wales,
And where was the widow might say him nay?

Sir Davit ap Morgan ap Griffith ap Hugh
Ap Tudor ap Rhice, quoth his roundelay;
She said that one widow for so many was too few,
And she bade the Welshman wend his way.

But there next came a yeoman, a yeoman of Kent,
Jollily rung his roundelay;
He spoke to the widow of living and rent,
And where was the widow could say him nay?

BOTH.

So the knight and the squire were both left in the myre,
There for to sing their roundelay;
For a yeoman of Kent, with his yearly rent,
There never was a widow could say him nay.

"I would, Wamba," said the Knight, "that our host of the Trysting-tree, or the jolly Friar, his chaplain, heard this ditty in praise of our bluff yeoman."

"So would not I," quoth Wamba—"but for the horn that hangs at your baldric."

"Ay," said the Knight,—"this is a pledge of Locksley's good will, though I am not like to need it. Three *mots* on this bugle will, I am assured, bring round us, at our need, a jolly band of yonder honest yeomen."

"I would say, Heaven forefend," said the Jester, "were it not that that fair gift is a pledge they would let us pass peaceably."

"Why, what meanest thou?" said the Knight; "thinkest thou that but for this pledge of fellowship they would assault us?"

"Nay, for me I say nothing," said Wamba; "for green trees have ears as well as stone walls. But canst thou construe me this, Sir Knight —When is thy wine-pitcher and thy purse better empty than full?"

"Why, never, I think," replied the Knight.

"Thou never deservest to have a full one in thine hand, for so simple an answer! Thou hadst best empty thy pitcher ere thou pass it to a Saxon, and leave thy money at home ere thou walk in the green-wood."

"You hold our friends for robbers, then?" said the Knight of the Fetterlock.

"You hear me not say so, fair sir," said Wamba; "it may ease a man's steed to take off his mail when he hath a long journey to make; and certes it may do good to his soul to ease him of that which is the root of evil; therefore will I give no hard name to those who do such services. Only I would wish my mail at home, and my purse in my chamber, when I meet with these good fellows, because it might save them some trouble."

"*We* are bound to pray for them, my friend, notwithstanding the fair character thou dost afford them."

"Pray for them with all my heart," said Wamba; "but in the town, not in the green-wood, like the Abbot of Saint Bees, whom they caused to sing mass with an old hollow oak-tree for his stall."

"Say as thou list, Wamba," replied the Knight, "these yeomen did thy master Cedric yeomanly service at Torquilstone."

"Ay, truly," answered Wamba; "but that was in the fashion of their trade with Heaven."

"Their trade, Wamba! how mean you by that?" replied his companion.

"Marry, thus," said the Jester. "They make up a balanced accompt with Heaven, as our old cellarer use to call his cyphering, as fair as Isaac the Jew keeps with his debitors, and, like him, give out a very little, and take large credit for doing so; reckoning, doubtless, on their own behalf the seven-fold usury which the blessed text hath promised to charitable loans."

"Give me an example of your meaning, Wamba,—I know nothing of cyphers or rates of usage," answered the Knight.

"Why," said Wamba, "an your valour be so dull, you will please to learn that those honest fellows balance a good deed with one not quite so laudable; as a crown given to a begging friar with an hundred bezants taken from a fat abbot, or a wench kissed in the green-wood with the relief of a poor widow."

"Which of these was the good deed, which was the felony?" interrupted the Knight.

"A good gibe! a good gibe!" said Wamba; "keeping witty company sharpeneth the apprehension. You said nothing so well, Sir Knight, I will be sworn, when you held drunken vespers with the bluff Hermit.—But to go on. The merry men of the forest set off the building of a cottage against the burning of a castle,—the thatching of a choir against the robbing of a church,—the setting free a poor prisoner against the murther of a proud sheriff—or, to come nearer our point, the deliverance of a Saxon Franklin against the burning alive of a Norman baron. Gentle thieves they be, in short, and courteous robbers; but it is ever the luckiest to meet with them when they are at the worst."

"How so, Wamba?" said the Knight.

"Why, then they have some compunction, and are for making up matters with Heaven. But when they have struck an even balance, Heaven help them with whom they next open the accompt! The travellers who first met them after their good service at Torquilstone would have a woeful flaying.—And yet," said Wamba, coming close up to the Knight's side, "there be these companions that are far more dangerous for travellers to meet than yonder outlaws."

"And who may these be, for you have neither lions nor wolves, I trow?" said the Knight.

"Marry, sir, but we have Malvoisin's men-at-arms," said Wamba; "and let me tell you, that, in time of civil war, a halfscore of these is worth a band of wolves at any time. They are now expecting their harvest, and are reinforced with the soldiers that escaped from Torquilstone. So that, should we meet a band of them, we are like to pay for our feats at arms.—Now, I pray you, Sir Knight, what would you do if we met two of them?"

"Pin the villains to earth with my lance, Wamba, if they offered us any impediment."

"But what if there were four of them?"

"They should drink of the same cup," answered the Knight.

"What if six," continued Wamba, "and we, as we now are, barely two—would you not remember Locksley's horn?"

"What! sound for aid," exclaimed the Knight, "against a score of such *rascaille* as these, whom one good knight could drive before him, as the wind drives the withered leaves!"

"Nay, then," said Wamba, "I will pray you for a closer sight of that same horn that hath so powerful a breath."

The Knight undid the clasp of the baldrick, and indulged his fellow-traveller, who immediately hung the bugle round his own neck.

"Tra-lira-la," said he, whistling the notes; "nay, I know my gamut as well as another."

"How mean you, knave?" said the Knight; "restore me the bugle."

"Content you, Sir Knight, it is in safe keeping. When Valour and Folly travel, Folly should bear the horn, because she can blow the best."

"Nay but, rogue," said the Black Knight, "this exceedeth thy licence—Beware ye tamper not with my patience."

"Urge me not with violence, Sir Knight," said the Jester, keeping at a distance from the impatient champion, "or Folly will show a clean pair of heels, and leave Valour to find his way through the wood as best he may."

"Nay, thou hast hit me there," said the Knight; "and, sooth to say, I have little time to jangle with thee. Keep the horn an thou wilt, but let us proceed on our journey."

"You will not harm me, then?" said Wamba.

"I tell thee no, thou knave!"

"Ay, but pledge me your knightly word for it," continued Wamba, as he approached with great caution.

"My knightly word I pledge; only come on with thy foolish self."

"Nay, then, Folly and Valour are once more boon comrades," said the Jester, coming up frankly to the Knight's side; "but, in honest truth, I love not such buffets as that you bestowed on the burley Friar, when his holiness rolled on the green like a king of the nine-pins. And, now that Folly wears the horn, let Valour rouse himself, and shake his mane; for, if I mistake not, there are company in yonder brake that are on the look-out for us."

"What makes thee judge so?" said the Knight.

"Because I have twice or thrice noticed the glance of a morrion from amongst the green leaves. Had they been honest men, they had kept the path. But yonder thicket is a choice chapel for the Clerks to Saint Nicholas."*

"By my faith," said the Knight, closing his visor, "I think thou be'st in the right on't."

And in good time did he close it, for three arrows flew at the same instant from the suspected spot against his head and breast, one of which must have penetrated to the brain, had it not been turned aside by the steel visor. The other two were averted by the gorget, and by the shield which hung around his neck.

"Thanks, trusty armourer," said the Knight.—"Wamba, let us close with them,"—and he rode straight to the thicket. He was met by six or seven men-at-arms, who run against him with their lances at full career. Three of the weapons struck against him, and splintered with as little effect as if they had been driven against a tower of steel. The Black Knight's eyes seemed to flash fire even through the apertures of his visor. He raised himself in his stirrups with an air of inexpressible dignity, and exclaimed, "What means this, my masters!"—The men made no other reply than by drawing their swords and attacking him on every side, crying aloud, "Die, tyrant!"

"Ha! Saint Edward! Ha! Saint George!" exclaimed the Black Knight, striking down a man at every invocation; "have we traitors here?"

The assailants, desperate as they were, bore back from an arm which carried death in every blow, and it seemed as if the terror of his single strength was about to gain the battle against such odds, when a knight, in blue armour, who had hitherto kept himself behind the other assailants, spurred forward with his lance, and taking aim, not at the rider but at the steed, wounded the noble animal mortally.

* Robbers were anciently called *Saint Nicholas's clerks*, probably in allusion to Old Nick. They were also called *good fellows*, the reason for which is not so obvious.

"That was a felon stroke!" exclaimed the Black Knight, as the steed fell to the earth, bearing his rider along with him.

And at this moment, Wamba winded the bugle, for the whole had passed so speedily, that he had not time to do so sooner. The sudden sound made the murderers bear back once more, and Wamba, though so imperfectly weaponed, did not hesitate to rush in and assist the Black Knight to arise.

"Shame on you, ye false cowards!" exclaimed the knight, who seemed to lead the assailants; "do you fly from the empty blast of a horn blown by a Jester?"

And animated by his words, they attacked the Knight anew, whose best refuge was now to place his back against an oak, and defend himself with his sword. The felon Knight, who had taken another spear, watching the moment when his formidable antagonist was most closely pressed, galloped against him in hopes to nail him with his lance against the tree, when his purpose was again intercepted by Wamba. The Jester, making up by agility for the want of strength, and little noticed by the men-at-arms who were busied in their more important object, hovered on the skirts of the fight, and effectually checked the fatal career of the Blue Knight, by ham-stringing his horse with a stroke of his sword. Horse and man went to the ground; yet the situation of the Knight of the Fetterlock continued very precarious, as he was pressed close on all sides by men completely armed, and began to be fatigued with the violent exertion necessary to defend himself on so many points at nearly the same moment, when a gray-goose shaft suddenly stretched on the earth one of the most formidable of his assailants, and a band of yeomen broke forth from the glade, headed by Locksley and the jovial Friar, who, taking ready and effectual part in the fray, soon disposed of the assailants, all of whom lay on the spot dead or mortally wounded. The Black Knight thanked his deliverers with a dignity they had not observed in his former bearing, which hitherto seemed rather that of a blunt bold soldier, than of a person of exalted rank.

"It concerns me much," he said, "even before I express my full gratitude to my ready friends, to discover, if I may, who have been my unprovoked enemies.—Open the visor of that Blue Knight, Wamba, who seems the chief of these villains."

The Jester instantly made up to the leader of the assassins, who, bruised by his fall, and entangled under the wounded steed, lay incapable either of flight or resistance.

"Come, valiant sir," said Wamba, "I must be your armourer as well as your equerry—I have dismounted you, and now I will unhelm you."

So saying, with no very gentle hand he undid the helmet of the Blue

Knight, which, rolling to a distance on the grass, displayed to the Knight of the Fetterlock grizzled locks, and a countenance which he did not expect to have seen under such circumstances.

"Waldemar Fitzurse!" he said in astonishment; "what could urge one of thy rank and seeming valour to so felon an undertaking?"

"Richard," said the captive Knight, looking up to him, "thou knowest little of mankind, if thou knowest not to what ambition and revenge can lead every child of Adam."

"Revenge?" answered the Black Knight; "I never wronged thee—On me thou hast nought to avenge."

"My daughter, Richard, whose alliance thou didst scorn—was that no injury to a Norman, whose blood is as noble as thine own?"

"Thy daughter!" replied the Black Knight; "a proper cause of enmity, and followed up to a bloody issue.—Stand back, my masters, I would speak with him alone.—And now, Waldemar Fitzurse, say me the truth—confess who set thee on this traitorous deed."

"Thy father's son," answered Waldemar, "who, in so doing, did but avenge on thee thy disobedience to thy father."

Richard's eyes sparkled with indignation, but his better nature overcame it. He pressed his hand against his brow, and remained for an instant gazing on the face of the humbled baron, in whose features pride was contending with shame.

"Thou dost not ask thy life, Waldemar," said the King.

"He that is in the lion's clutch," answered Fitzurse, "knows it were needless."

"Take it then unasked," said Richard; "the lion preys not on prostrate carcasses—Take thy life, but with this condition, that within three days thou leave England, and go to hide thine infamy in thy Norman castle, and thou wilt never mention the name of John of Anjou as connected with thy felony. If thou art found on English ground after the space I have allotted thee, thou diest—or if thou breathest aught that can attaint the honour of my house, by my patron Saint George! not the altar itself shall be a sanctuary. I will hang thee out to feed the ravens, from the very pinnacle of thine own castle.—Let this knight have a steed, Locksley, for I see your yeomen have caught those which were running loose, and let him depart unharmed."

"But that I judge I listen to a voice whose behests must not be disputed," answered the yeoman, "I would send a shaft after the skulking villain that should spare him the labour of a long journey."

"Thou bearest an English heart, Locksley," said the Black Knight, "and well dost judge thou art the more bound to obey my behest—I am Richard of England!"

At these words, pronounced in a tone of majesty suited to the high rank, and no less distinguished character, of Cœur de Lion, the yeomen at once kneeled down before him, and at the same time tendered their allegiance, and implored pardon for their offences.

"Rise, my friends," said Richard, in a gracious tone, looking on them with a countenance in which his habitual good humour had already conquered the blaze of hasty resentment, and whose features retained no mark of the late desperate conflict, excepting the flush arising from exertion,—"Arise," he said, "my friends!—Your misdemeanours, whether in forest or field, have been atoned by the loyal services you rendered my distressed subjects before the walls of Torquilstone, and the rescue you have this day afforded to your sovereign. Arise, my liegemen, and be good subjects in future.—And thou, brave Locksley"——

"Call me no longer Locksley, my liege, but know me under a name, which, I fear, fame hath blown too widely not to have reached even your royal ears—I am Robin Hood, of Sherwood Forest."

"King of Outlaws, and Prince of good fellows!" said the King, "who hath not heard a name that has been borne as far as Palestine? But be assured, brave Outlaw, that no deed done in our absence, and in the turbulent times to which it hath given rise, shall be remembered to thy disadvantage."

"True says the proverb," said Wamba, interposing his word, but with some abatement of his usual petulance,—

"When the cat is away,
The mice will play."

"What, Wamba, art thou there?" said Richard; "I have been so long of hearing thy voice, I thought thou hadst taken the flight."

"I the flight!" said Wamba; "when do you ever find Folly separated from Valour? There lies the trophy of my sword, that good grey gelding, whom I heartily wish upon his legs again, conditioning his master lay houghed there in his place. It is true, I gave a little ground at first, for motley does not brook lance-heads as a steel doublet will. But if I fought not at sword's point, you will grant me that I sounded the onset."

"And to good purpose, honest Wamba," replied the King. "Thy good service shall not be forgotten."

"*Confiteor! Confiteor!*"—exclaimed, in a submissive tone, a voice near the King's side—"my Latin will carry no farther—but I confess my deadly treason, and pray leave to have absolution before I am led to execution."

Richard looked around, and beheld the jovial Friar on his knees, telling his rosary, while his quarter-staff, which had not been idle during the skirmish, lay on the grass beside him. His countenance was gathered so as he might best express the most profound contrition, his eyes being turned up, and the corners of his mouth drawn down, as Wamba expressed it, like the tassels at the mouth of a purse. Yet this demure affectation of extreme penitence was whimsically belied by a ludicrous meaning which lurked in his huge features, and seemed to pronounce his fear and repentance alike hypocritical.

"For what art thou cast down, mad Priest?" said Richard; "Art thou afraid thy diocesan should learn how truly thou doest serve Our Lady and Saint Dunstan?—Tush, man! fear it not; Richard of England betrays no secrets that pass over the flagon."

"Nay, most gracious sovereign," answered the Hermit, (well known to the curious in penny-histories of Robin Hood, by the name of Friar Tuck,) "it is not the crosier I fear, but the sceptre.—Alas! that my sacrilegious fist should ever have been applied to the ear of the Lord's anointed!"

"Ha! ha!" said Richard, "sits the wind there?—In truth, I had forgotten the buffet, though mine ear sung after it for a whole day as if I had a psaltery in my head. But if the cuff was fairly given, I will be judged by the good men around, if it was not as well repaid—or, if thou thinkest I still owe thee aught, and will stand forth for another counter-buff"——

"By no means," replied Friar Tuck, "I had mine own back, and with usury—may your Majesty ever pay your debts as fully!"

"If I could do so with cuffs," said the King, "my creditors should have little reason to complain of an empty exchequer."

"And yet," said the Friar, resuming his demure hypocritical countenance, "I know not what penance I ought to perform for that most sacrilegious blow!"

"Speak no more of it, brother," said the King; "after having stood so many cuffs from Paynim and misbeliever, I were void of reason to quarrel with the buffet of a clerk so holy as he of Copmanhurst. Yet, mine honest Friar, I think it would be best both for the church and thyself, that I should procure a licence to unfrock thee, and retain thee as a yeoman of our guard, serving in care of our person, as formerly upon the altar of Saint Dunstan."

"My Liege," said the Friar, "I humbly crave your pardon; and you would readily grant my excuse, did you but know how the sin of laziness has beset me. Saint Dunstan—may he be gracious to us!—stands quiet in his niche, though I should forget my orisons in killing a fat buck—I stay out of my cell sometimes a night, doing I wot not what—Saint Dunstan never complains—a quiet master he is, and a peaceful, as ever was made of wood.—But to be a yeoman in attendance on my sovereign the king—the honour is great, doubtless—yet, if I were but to step aside to comfort a widow in one corner, or to kill a deer in another, it would be, 'where is the dog Priest?' says one. 'Who has seen the accursed Tuck?' says another. 'The unfrocked villain destroys more venison than half the country besides,' says one keeper; 'And is hunting after every shy doe in the country!' a second.—In fine, good my Liege, I pray you to leave me as you found me, or, if in aught you desire to extend your benevolence to me, that I may be considered as the poor Clerk of Saint Dunstan's cell in Copmanhurst, to whom any small donation will be most thankfully acceptable."

"I understand thee," said the King, "and the Holy Clerk shall have a grant of vert and venison in my woods of Warncliffe. Mark, however, I will but assign thee three bucks every season; but if that do not prove an apology for thy slaying thirty, I am no Christian knight or true king."

"Your Grace may be well assured," said the Friar, "that, with the grace of Saint Dunstan, I shall find the way of multiplying your most bounteous gift."

"I nothing doubt it, good brother," said the King; "and as venison is but dry food, our cellarer shall have orders to deliver to thee a butt of sack, a runlet of Malvoisie, and three hogsheads of ale of the first strike, yearly—If that will not quench thy thirst, thou must come to court, and become acquainted with my butler."

"But for Saint Dunstan?" said the Friar—

"A cope, a stole, and altar-cloth shalt thou also have," continued the King, crossing himself.—"But we may not turn our game into earnest, lest God punish us for thinking more on our own follies than on his honour and worship."

"I will answer for my patron," said the Priest, joyously.

"Answer for thyself, Friar," said King Richard, something sternly; but immediately stretching out his hand to the Hermit, the latter, somewhat abashed, bent his knee and saluted it. "Thou dost less honour to my extended palm than to my clenched fist," said the Monarch; "thou didst only kneel to the one, and to the other didst prostrate thyself."

But the Friar, afraid perhaps of again giving offence by continuing the conversation in too jocose a style,—a false step to be particularly guarded against by those who converse with monarchs—bowed profoundly, and fell into the rear.

At the same time, two additional personages appeared on the scene.

Chapter Eleven

All hail to the lordings of high degree,
Who live not more happy, though greater than we!
Our pastimes to see,
Under every green tree
In all the gay woodland, right welcome ye be.
MACDONALD.

THE NEW COMERS were Wilfred of Ivanhoe, on the Prior of Saint Botolph's palfrey, and Gurth, who attended him, on the Knight's own war-horse. The astonishment of Ivanhoe was beyond bounds, when he saw his master besprinkled with blood, and six or seven dead bodies lying around in the little glade in which the battle had taken place. Nor was he less surprised to find Richard surrounded by so many sylvan attendants, the outlaws, as they seemed to be, of the forest, and a perilous retinue therefore for a prince. He hesitated whether to address the King as the Black Knight-errant, or in what other manner to demean himself towards him. Richard saw his embarrassment.

"Fear not, Wilfred," he said, "to address Richard Plantagenet as himself, since thou seest him in the company of true English hearts, although it may be they have been urged a few steps aside by warm English blood."

"Sir Wilfred of Ivanhoe," said the gallant Outlaw, stepping forward, "my assurances can add nothing to those of our sovereign; yet, let me say somewhat proudly, that of men who have suffered much, he hath not truer subjects than those who now stand around him."

"I cannot doubt it, brave man," said Wilfred, "since thou art of the number—But what mean these marks of death and danger? these slain men, and the bloody armour of my Prince?"

"Treason hath been with us, Ivanhoe," said the King; "but, thanks to these brave men, treason hath met its meed—But, now I bethink me, thou too art a traitor," said Richard, smiling; "a most disobedient traitor; for were not our orders positive, that thou should'st repose thyself at Saint Botolph's until thy wound was healed?"

"It is healed," said Ivanhoe; "it is not of more consequence than the scratch of a bodkin. But why, oh why, noble Prince, will you thus vex the hearts of thy faithful servants, and expose your life by lonely journies and rash adventures, as if it were of no more value than that of a mere knight-errant, who has no interest on earth save what lance and sword may procure him?"

"And Richard Plantagenet," said the King, "desires no more fame than his good lance and sword may acquire him—and Richard Plantagenet is prouder of achieving an adventure, with only his good sword, and his good arm to speed, than if he led to battle an host of an hundred thousand armed men."

"But your kingdom, my lord," said Ivanhoe, "your kingdom is threatened with dissolution and civil war—your subjects menaced by every species of evil, if deprived of their sovereign in some of these dangers which it is your daily pleasure to incur, and from which you have but this moment narrowly escaped."

"Ho! ho! my kingdom and my subjects?" answered Richard, impatiently; "I tell thee, Sir Wilfred, the best of them are most willing to repay my follies in kind—For example, my faithful servant, Wilfred of Ivanhoe, will not obey my positive commands, and yet reads his king a homily, because he does not walk exactly conformable to his advice. Which of us has most reason to upbraid the other?—Yet forgive me, my faithful Wilfred. The time I have spent, and am yet to spend in concealment, is, as I explained to thee at Saint Botolph's, necessary to give my friends and faithful nobles time to assemble their forces, that when Richard's return is announced, he should be at the head of such a force as enemies shall tremble to face, and thus subdue the meditated treason, without even unsheathing a sword. Estoteville and Bohun will not be strong enough to move forward to York for twenty-four hours. I must have news of Salisbury from the south; and of Beauchamp, in Warwickshire; and of Multon and Percy, in the north. The Chancellor must make sure of London and I must hear the tidings. Too sudden an appearance would subject me to dangers, other than what my sword and lance, though backed by the bow of Bold Robin, the quarter staff of Friar Tuck, and the horn of the sage Wamba, may be able to rescue me from"——

Wilfred bowed in submission, well knowing how vain it was to contend with the wild spirit of chivalry which so often impelled his master upon dangers which he might easily have avoided, or rather, which it was unpardonable in him to have sought out.

Wilfred sighed, therefore, and held his peace; while Richard, rejoicing at having silenced his counsellor, though his heart acknowledged the justice of the charge he had brought against him, went on in conversation with Robin Hood.—"King of Outlaws," he said, "have you no refreshment to offer to your brother sovereign? for these dead knaves have found me both in exercise and appetite."

"In troth," replied the Outlaw, "for I scorn to lie to your Grace, our larder is chiefly supplied with"—— He stopped, and was somewhat embarrassed.

"With venison, I suppose," said Richard, gaily; "better food at need there can be none—and truly, if a king will not remain at home to slay his own game, methinks he should not brawl too loud if he find it killed to his hand."

"If your Grace, then," said Robin, "will again honour with your presence one of Robin Hood's places of rendezvous, the venison shall not be lacking; and a stoup of ale, or it may be a cup of reasonably good wine, to relish it withal."

The Outlaw accordingly led the way, followed by the buxom Monarch, more happy probably in this chance meeting with Robin Hood and his foresters, than he would have been in again assuming his royal state, and presiding over a splendid circle of peers and nobles. Novelty in society and in adventure was the zest of life to Richard Cœur de Lion, and it had its highest relish when enhanced by dangers encountered and surmounted. In the lion-hearted King, the brilliant, but useless character, of a knight of romance, was in great measure realized; and the personal glory which he acquired by his own deeds of arms, was far more dear to his excited imagination than that which a course of policy and wisdom would have spread around his government. Accordingly, his reign was like the course of a brilliant and rapid meteor, which shoots along the face of heaven, shedding around an unnecessary and portentous light, which is instantly swallowed up by universal darkness; his feats of chivalry furnishing themes for bards and minstrels, but affording none of those solid benefits to his country on which history loves to pause, and hold up as an example to posterity. But in his present company, Richard shewed to the greatest imaginable advantage. He was gay, good-humoured, liberal, and fond of manhood in every rank of life.

Beneath a huge oak-tree the sylvan repast was hastily prepared for the King of England, surrounded by men late outlaws to his government, but who now formed his court and his guard. As the flagon passed round, the rough foresters soon lost their awe for the presence of majesty. The song and the jest were exchanged—the stories of former feats were told with advantage; and at length, while boasting of their successful infraction of the laws, no one recollected they were speaking in presence of their natural guardian. The merry King, nothing heeding his dignity any more than the company, laughed, quaffed, and jested amongst the jolly band. The natural and rough sense of Robin Hood led him to be desirous that the scene should be closed ere something should occur to disturb its harmony, the more especially that he observed Ivanhoe's brow clouded with anxiety. "We are honoured," he said to the Baron, apart, "by the presence of our gallant Sovereign; yet I would not that he dallied with time, which the circumstances of his kingdom may render precious."

"It is well and wisely spoken, brave Robin Hood," said the Knight; "and know, moreover, that they who jest with majesty, even in its gayest mood, are but toying with the lion's whelp, which, on slight provocation, uses both fangs and claws."

"You have touched the very cause of my fear," said the Outlaw; "my men are rough by practice and nature, the King is hasty as well as good-humoured; nor know I how soon cause of offence may arise, or how warmly it may be received—it is time this revel were broken off."

"It must be by your management then, gallant yeoman," said Ivanhoe; "for each hint I have essayed to give him serves only to induce him to prolong it."

"Must I so soon risk the pardon and favour of my sovereign?" said Robin Hood, pausing for an instant; "but by Saint Christopher, it shall be so. I were undeserving his grace did I not peril it for his good. —Here, Scathlock, get thee behind yonder thicket, and wind me a Norman blast on thy bugle, and without an instant's delay, on peril of your life."

Scathlock obeyed his captain, and in less than five minutes the revellers were startled by the sound of his horn.

"It is the bugle of Malvoisin," said the Miller, starting to his feet, and seizing his bow—the Friar dropped the flagon, and grasped his quarter-staff—Wamba stopt short in the midst of a jest, and betook himself to sword and target—all the others stood to their weapons.

Men of their precarious course of life change readily from the banquet to the battle; and, to Richard, the exchange seemed but a succession of pleasure. He called for his helmet and the most cumbrous parts of his armour, which he had laid aside; and while Gurth was putting them on, he laid his strict injunctions on Wilfred, under pain of his highest displeasure, not to engage in the skirmish which he supposed was approaching.

"Thou hast fought for me a hundred times, Wilfred,—and I have seen it. Thou shalt this day look on, and see how Richard will fight for his friend and liegeman."

In the meanwhile, Robin Hood had sent off several of his followers in different directions, as if to reconnoitre the enemy; and when he saw the company effectually broken up, he approached Richard, who was now completely armed, and, kneeling down on one knee, craved pardon of his sovereign.

"For what, good yeoman?" said Richard, somewhat impatiently. "Have we not already granted thee a full pardon for all transgressions? Thinkest thou our word is a feather, to be blown backward and forward betwixt us? Thou canst not have had time to commit any new offence since that time?"

"Ay, but I have though," answered the Outlaw, "if it be an offence to deceive my prince for his own advantage. The bugle you have heard was none of Malvoisin's, but was blown by my direction, to break off our banquet, lest it trenched upon hours of dearer import than to be thus dallied with."

He then rose from his knee, folded his arms on his bosom, and, in a manner rather respectful than submissive, awaited the answer of the King,—like one who is conscious he may have given offence, yet is confident in the rectitude of his motive. The blood rushed in anger to the countenance of Richard; but it was the first transient emotion, and his sense of justice instantly subdued it.

"The King of Sherwood," he said, "grudges his venison and his wine-flask to the King of England? It is well, bold Robin!—but when you come to see me in merry London, I trust to be a less niggard host. Thou art right, however, good fellow. Let us therefore to horse and away—Wilfred has been impatient this hour. Tell me, bold Robin, hast thou never a friend in thy band, who, not content with advising, will needs direct thy motions, and look miserable when thou dost presume to act for thyself?"

"Such a one," said Robin, "is my Lieutenant, Little John, who is even now absent on an expedition as far as the borders of Scotland; and I will own to your Majesty, that I am sometimes displeased by the freedom of his councils—but, when I think twice, I cannot be long angry with one who can have no motive for his anxiety save zeal for his master's service."

"Thou art right, good yeoman," answered Richard; "and if I had Ivanhoe, on the one hand, to give grave advice, and recommend it by the sad gravity of his brow, and thee, on the other, to trick me into what thou thinkest my own good, I should have as little the freedom of mine own will as any king in Christendom or Heathenesse.—But, come, sirs, let us merrily on to Coningsburgh, and think no more on't."

Robin Hood assured them that he had detached a party in the direction of the road they were to pass, who would not fail to discover and apprize them of any second ambuscade; and that he had little doubt they would find the ways secure, or, if otherwise, would receive such timely notice of the danger as might enable them to fall back upon a strong troop of archers, with which he himself proposed to follow on the same route.

The wise and attentive precautions adopted for his safety touched Richard's feelings, and removed any slight grudge he might retain on account of the deception which the Outlaw Captain had practised upon him. He once more extended his hand to Robin Hood, assured him of his full pardon and future favour, as well as his firm resolution to restrain the tyrannical exercise of the forest rights, and other oppressive laws, by which so many English yeomen were driven into a state of rebellion. But Richard's good intentions towards the bold Outlaw were frustrated by the King's untimely death; and the Charter of the Forest was extorted from the unwilling hands of King John when he succeeded to his heroic brother. As for the rest of Robin Hood's career, as well as the tale of his treacherous death, they are to be found in those black-letter garlands, once sold at the low and easy rate of one halfpenny,

> "Now cheaply purchased at their weight in gold."

The Outlaw's opinion proved true; and the King, attended by Ivanhoe, Gurth, and Wamba, arrived, without any interruption, within view of the Castle of Coningsburgh, while the sun was yet in the horizon.

There are few more beautiful or striking scenes in England, than are presented by the vicinity of this ancient Saxon fortress. The soft and gentle river Don sweeps through an amphitheatre, in which cultivation is richly blended with woodland, and on a mount, ascending from the river, well defended by walls and ditches, rises this ancient edifice, which, as its Saxon name implies, was, previous to the Conquest, a royal residence of the kings of England. The outer walls have probably been added by the Normans, but the inner keep bears token of very great antiquity. It is situated on a mount at one angle of the inner court, and forms a complete circle of perhaps twenty-five feet in diameter. The wall is of immense thickness, and is propped or defended by six huge external buttresses which project from the circle, and rise up against the sides of the tower as if to strengthen or support it. These massive buttresses are hollowed out towards the top, and terminate in a sort of turrets communicating with the interior of the keep itself. The distant appearance of this huge building, with these singular accompaniments, is as interesting to the lovers of the picturesque, as the interior of the castle is to the eager antiquary, whose imagination it carries back to the days of the Heptarchy. A barrow, in the vicinity of the castle, is pointed out as the tomb of the memorable Hengist; and various monuments, of great antiquity and curiosity, are shewn in the neighbouring church-yard.

When Cœur de Lion and his retinue approached this rude yet stately building, it was not, as at present, surrounded by external fortifications. The Saxon architect had exhausted his art in rendering the main keep defensible, and there was no other circumvallation than a rude barrier of palisades.

A huge black banner, which floated from the top of the tower, announced that the obsequies of its late owner were still in the act of being solemnized. It bore no emblem of the deceased's birth or quality, for armorial bearings were then a novelty among the Norman chivalry themselves, and were totally unknown to the Saxons. But above the gate was another banner, on which the figure of a white horse, rudely painted, indicated the nation and rank of the deceased, by the well known symbol of Hengist and his warriors.

All around the castle was a scene of busy commotion; for such funeral banquets were a time of general and profuse hospitality, which not only every one who could claim the most distant connection with the deceased, but all passengers whatsoever, were invited to partake. The wealth and consequence of the deceased Athelstane occasioned this custom to be observed in the fullest extent.

Numerous parties, therefore, were seen ascending and descending the hill on which the castle was situated; and when the king and his attendants entered the open and unguarded gates of the external barrier, the space within presented a scene not easily reconciled with the cause of the assemblage. In one place cooks were toiling to roast huge oxen, and fat sheep; in another, hogsheads of ale were set abroach, to be drained at the freedom of all comers. Groupes of every description were to be seen devouring the food and swilling the liquor thus abandoned to their discretion. The half-naked Saxon serf was drowning the sense of his half year's hunger and thirst, in one day's gluttony and drunkenness—the more pampered burgess and guild-brother was eating his morsel with gust, or curiously criticizing the quality of the malt and the skill of the brewer. Some few of the poorer Norman gentry might also be seen, distinguished by their shaven chins and short cloaks, and not less so by their keeping together, and looking with great scorn on the whole solemnity, even while condescending to avail themselves of the good cheer which was so liberally supplied.

Mendicants were of course assembled by the score, together with strolling soldiers returned from Palestine (according to their own account at least); pedlars were displaying their wares, travelling mechanics were enquiring after employment, and wandering palmers, hedge-priests, Saxon minstrels, and Welch bards, were muttering prayers, and extracting mistuned dirges from their harps, crowds,* and rotes. One sent forth the praises of Athelstane in a doleful panegyric; another, in a Saxon genealogical poem, rehearsed the uncouth and harsh names of his noble ancestry. Jesters and jugglers were not awanting, nor was the solemnity of the occasion supposed to render

*The crowth or crowd was a species of violin, the rote a sort of guitar, the strings of which were managed by a kind of wheel, from which the instrument took its name.

the exercise of their profession indecorous or improper. Indeed the ideas of the Saxons on such occasions were as natural as they were rude. If sorrow was thirsty, there was drink—if hungry, there was food—if it sunk down upon and saddened the heart, there were the means supplied of mirth, or at least of amusement. Nor did the assistants scorn to avail themselves of those means of consolation, although, every now and then, as if suddenly recollecting the cause which had brought them together, the men groaned in unison, while the females, of whom many were present, raised up their voices and shrieked for very woe.

Such was the scene in the castle-yard at Coningsburgh when it was entered by Richard and his followers. The seneschal or steward, who deigned not to take notice of the groups of inferior guests who were perpetually entering and withdrawing, unless so far as was necessary to preserve order, was struck with the good mien of the Monarch and Ivanhoe, more especially as he imagined the features of the latter were familiar to him. Besides, the approach of two knights, for such their dress bespoke them, was a rare event at a Saxon solemnity, and could not but be regarded as a sort of honour to the deceased and his family.

And in his sable dress, and holding in his hand his white wand of office, this important personage made way through the miscellaneous assemblage of guests, thus conducting Richard and Ivanhoe to the entrance of the tower. Gurth and Wamba speedily found acquaintances in the court-yard, nor presumed to intrude themselves any farther until their presence was required.

Chapter Twelve

I found them winding of Marcello's corpse.
And there was such a solemn melody,
'Twixt doleful songs, tears, and sad elegies,—
Such as old grandames, watching by the dead,
Are wont to outwear the night with.——

Old Play.

THE MODE of entering the great tower of Coningsburgh Castle is very peculiar, and partakes of the rude simplicity of the early times in which it was erected. A flight of steps, so deep and narrow as to be almost precipitous, leads up to a low portal on the south side of the tower, by which the adventurous antiquary may still, or at least could a few years since, gain access to a small stair within the thickness of the main wall of the tower, which leads up to the third storey of the building,—the two lower being dungeons or vaults, which neither receive air nor light, save by a square hole in the third storey, with which they seem to have communicated by a ladder. The access to the upper apartments in the tower, which consists in all of five stories, is given by stairs which are carried up through the external buttresses.

By this difficult and complicated entrance the good King Richard, followed by his faithful Ivanhoe, was ushered into the round apartment which occupies the whole of the third storey from the ground. The latter had time to muffle his face in his mantle, as it had been held expedient that he should not present himself to his father until the King should give him the signal.

There were assembled in this apartment, around a large oaken table, about a dozen of the most distinguished representatives of Saxon families in the adjacent country. These were all old, or, at least, elderly men; for the younger race, to the great disquiet of the seniors, had, like Ivanhoe, broken down many of the barriers which had separated for half a century the Norman victors from the vanquished Saxons. The downcast and sorrowful looks of these venerable men, their silence and their mournful posture, formed a strong contrast to the levity of the revellers on the outside of the castle. Their grey locks and long full beards, together with their antique tunics and loose black mantles, suited well with the singular and rude apartment in which they were seated, and gave the appearance of a band of the ancient worshippers of Woden, recalled to life to mourn over the decay of their national glory.

Cedric, seated in equal rank among his countrymen, seemed yet, by common consent, to act as chief of the assembly. Upon the entrance of Richard (only known to him as the valorous Knight of the Fetterlock) he arose gravely, and gave him welcome by the ordinary salutation, *Waes hael*, raising at the same time a goblet to his head. The King, no stranger to the customs of his English subjects, returned the greeting with the appropriate words, *Drinc hael*, and partook of a cup which was handed to him by the sewer. The same courtesy was offered to Ivanhoe, who pledged his father in silence, supplying the usual speech by an inclination of his head, lest his voice should have been recognized.

When this introductory ceremony was performed, Cedric arose, and, extending his hand to Richard, conducted him into a small and very rude chapel, which was excavated, as it were, out of one of the external buttresses. As there was no opening, saving a very narrow loop-hole, the place would have been nearly quite dark but for two flambeaux or torches, which shewed, by a red and smoky light, the arched roof and naked walls, the rude altar of stone, and the crucifix of the same materials.

Before this altar was placed a bier, and on each side of the bier kneeled three priests, who told their beads, and muttered their prayers, with the greatest signs of external devotion. For this service a splendid *soul-scat* was paid to the convent of Saint Edmund by the mother of the deceased; and, that it might be fully deserved, the whole brethren, saving the lame sacristan, had transferred themselves to Coningsburgh, where, while six of their number, relieved from time to time by their brethren, were constantly engaged in the performance of divine rites beside the bier of Athelstane, the others failed not to take their share of the refreshments and amusements which went on in the castle. In maintaining this pious watch and ward, the good monks were particularly careful not to interrupt their hymns for an instant, lest Zernebock, the ancient Saxon Apollyon, should lay his clutches on the departed Athelstane. Nor were they less careful to prevent any unhallowed layman from touching the pall, which, having been that used at the funeral of Saint Edmund, was liable to be desecrated, if handled by prophane hands. If, in truth, these attentions could be of any use to the deceased, he had some right to expect them at the hands of the brethren of Saint Edmund's, since, besides an hundred mancus's of gold paid down as the soul-ransom, the mother of Athelstane had announced her intention of endowing that foundation with the better part of the lands of the deceased, in order to maintain perpetual prayers for his soul, and that of her departed husband.

Richard and Wilfred followed the Saxon Cedric into this apartment of death, where, as their guide pointed with a solemn air to the untimely bier of Athelstane, they followed his example in devoutly crossing themselves, and muttering a brief prayer for the weal of the departed soul.

This act of pious charity performed, Cedric again motioned them to follow him. Gliding over the stone floor with a noiseless tread; and, after ascending a few steps, he opened with great caution the door of a small oratory, which adjoined to the chapel. It was about eight feet square, hollowed, like the chapel itself, out of the thickness of the wall; but the loop-hole, which enlightened it, being to the west, and widening considerably as it sloped inward, a beam of the setting sun found its way into its dark recess, and shewed a female of a dignified mien, and whose countenance retained the marked remains of majestic beauty. Her long mourning robes, and her flowing wimple of black cypress, enhanced the whiteness of her skin, and the beauty of her light-coloured and flowing tresses, which time had neither thinned nor mingled with silver. Her countenance expressed the deepest sorrow that is consistent with resignation. On the stone table before her stood a crucifix of ivory, beside which was laid a missal, having its pages richly illuminated, and its boards adorned with clasps of gold, and bosses of the same precious metal.

"Noble Edith," said Cedric, after having stood a minute silent, as if to give Richard and Wilfred time to look upon the lady of the manor, "these are worthy strangers, come to take a part in thy sorrows. And this, in especial, is the valiant Knight, who fought so bravely for the deliverance of him for whom we this day mourn."

"His bravery hath my thanks," returned the lady; "although it be the will of Heaven that it should be displayed in vain. I thank, too, his courtesy, and that of his companion, which hath brought them hither to behold the widow of Adeling, the mother of Athelstane, in her deep hour of sorrow and lamentation. To your care, kind kinsman, I entrust them, satisfied that they will want no hospitality which these sad walls can yet afford."

The guests bowed deeply to the mourning parent, and withdrew with their hospitable guide.

Another winding stair conducted them to an apartment of the same size with that they had first entered, occupying indeed the storey immediately above. From this room, ere yet the door was opened, proceeded a low and melancholy strain of vocal music. When they entered, they found themselves in presence of about twenty matrons and maidens of distinguished Saxon lineage. Four maidens, Rowena leading the choir, raised a hymn for the soul of the deceased, of which we have only been able to decypher two or three stanzas:—

Dust unto dust,
To this all must;
The tenant hath resign'd
The faded form
To waste and worm—
Corruption claims her kind.

Through paths unknown
Thy soul hath flown,
To seek the realms of woe,
Where fiery pain
Shall purge the stain
Of actions done below.

In that sad place,
By Mary's grace,
Brief may thy dwelling be!
Till prayers and alms,
And holy psalms,
Shall set the captive free.

While this dirge was sung, in a low and melancholy tone, by the female choristers, the others were divided into two bands, of which one was engaged in bedecking, with such embroidery as their skill and taste could compass, a large silken pall, destined to cover the bier of Athelstane, whilst the others busied themselves in selecting, from baskets of flowers placed before them, garlands, which they destined for the same mournful purpose. The behaviour of the maidens was decorous, if not marked with deep affliction; but now and then a whisper or a smile called forth the rebuke of the severer matrons, and here and there might be seen a damsel apparently more interested in endeavouring to find out how her mourning robe became her, than in the dismal ceremony for which they were preparing. Neither was this propensity (if we must needs confess the truth) at all diminished by the appearance of two stranger knights, which occasioned some looking up, peeping, and whispering. Rowena alone, too proud to be vain, paid her greeting to her deliverer with graceful courtesy. Her demeanour was serious, but not dejected; and it may be doubted whether thoughts of Ivanhoe, and of the uncertainty of his fate, did not claim as great a share in her gravity as the death of her kinsman.

To Cedric, however, who, as we have observed, was not remarkably clear-sighted on such occasions, the sorrows of his ward seemed so much deeper than any of the other maidens, that he deemed it proper to whisper the explanation—"She was the affianced bride of the noble Athelstane."—It may be doubted whether this communication went a far way to increase Wilfred's disposition to sympathise with the mourners of Coningsburgh.

Having thus formally introduced the guests to the various chambers in which the obsequies of Athelstane were celebrated under different forms, Cedric conducted them into a small room, destined, as he informed them, for the exclusive accommodation of honourable guests, whose more slight connection with the deceased might render them unwilling to join those who were immediately affected by the unhappy event. He assured them of every accommodation, and was about to withdraw when the Black Knight took his hand.

"I crave to remind you, noble Thane," he said, "that when we last parted, you promised, for the service which I had the fortune to render you, to grant me a boon."

"It is granted ere named, noble Knight," said Cedric; "yet, at this sad moment"——

"Of that also," said the King, "I have bethought me—but my time is brief—neither does it seem to me unfit, that, when closing the grave on the noble Athelstane, we should deposit therein certain prejudices and hasty opinions."

"Sir Knight of the Fetterlock," said Cedric, colouring and interrupting the King in his turn, "I trust your boon regards yourself and no other; for in that which concerns the honour of my house, it is scarce fitting that a stranger should mingle."

"Nor do I wish to mingle," said the King, mildly, "unless in so far as you will admit me to have an interest. As yet you have known me but as the Black Knight of the Fetterlock—Know me now as Richard Plantagenet!"

"Richard of Anjou!" exclaimed Cedric, stepping backward with the utmost astonishment.

"No, noble Cedric—Richard of England whose dearest interest, whose deepest wish it is to see her sons united with each other.—And, how now, worthy Thane! hast thou no knee for thy prince?"

"To Norman blood," said Cedric, "it hath never bended."

"Reserve thine homage then," said the Monarch, "until I shall prove my right to it by my equal protection of both Normans and English."

"Prince," answered Cedric, "I have ever done justice to thy bravery and thy worth—Nor am I ignorant of thy claim to the crown through thy descent from Matilda, niece to Edgar Atheling, and daughter to Malcolm of Scotland. But Matilda, though of the royal Saxon blood, was not the heir to the monarchy."

"I will not dispute my title with thee, noble Thane; but I will bid thee look around, and see where thou wilt find another which can be put into the scale against it."

"And hast thou ventured hither, Prince, to tell me so?" said Cedric —"To upbraid me with the ruin of my race, ere the grave closed on the last scion of Saxon Royalty?"—His countenance darkened as he spoke.—"It was boldly—it was rashly done!"

"Not so, by the holy-rood!" replied the King; "it was done in the frank confidence which one brave man may repose in another, without a shadow of danger."

"Thou sayest well, Sir King—for King I own thou art, and wilt be, despite of my feeble opposition.—I dare not take the only mode to prevent it, though thou hast placed the strong temptation within my reach!"

"And now to my boon," said the King, "which I ask not with one jot the less confidence, that thou hast refused to acknowledge my lawful sovereignty. I require of thee, as a man of thy word, and on pain of being held faithless, man-sworn, and *nidering*,* to forgive and receive to thy paternal affection the good knight, Wilfred of Ivanhoe. In this reconciliation thou wilt own I have an interest—the happiness of my friend, and the quelling of dissention among my faithful people."

"And this is Wilfred," said the Saxon, pointing to his son.

"My father!—my father!" said Ivanhoe, prostrating himself at Cedric's feet, "grant me thy forgiveness!"

*Infamous.

"Thou hast it, my son," said Cedric, raising him. "The son of Hereward knows how to keep his word, even when it has been passed to a Norman. But let me see thee use the dress and customs of thy English ancestry—no short cloaks, no gay tunics, no fantastic plumage in my decent household. He that would be the son of Cedric must shew himself of English ancestry.—Thou art about to speak," he added, sternly, "and I guess the topic. The Lady Rowena must complete two years of mourning, as for a betrothed husband—all our Saxon ancestors would disown us were we to knit a new union for her ere the grave of him whom she should have wedded—him, so much more worthy of her hand by birth and ancestry—is yet closed. The ghost of Athelstane himself would burst his bloody cerements, and stand before us to forbid such dishonour to his memory."

It seemed as if Cedric's words had raised a spectre; for, scarce had he uttered them ere the door flew open, and Athelstane, arrayed in the garments of the grave, stood before them, pale, hagard, and like something arisen from the dead!

The effect of this apparition on the persons present was utterly appalling. Cedric started back as far as the wall of the apartment would permit, and, leaning against it as one unable to support himself, gazed on the figure of his friend with eyes that seemed fixed, and a mouth which he appeared incapable of shutting. Ivanhoe crossed himself, repeating prayers in Saxon, Latin, and Norman-French, as they occurred to his memory, while Richard alternately said, *Benedicite*, and swore, *Mort de ma vie!*

In the meantime, a horrible noise was heard below stairs, some crying, "Secure the treacherous monks!"—others, "Down with them into the lowest dungeon!"—others, "Pitch them from the highest battlements!"

"In the name of God!" said Cedric, addressing what seemed the spectre of his departed friend, "if thou art mortal, speak!—if a departed spirit, say for what cause thou dost revisit these towers, or if I may do aught that can set thy spirit at repose.—Living or dead, noble Athelstane, speak to Cedric!"

"I will," said the spectre, very composedly, "when I have collected breath, and when you give me time—Alive, saidst thou?—I am as much alive as he can be who has fed on bread and water for three days, which seem three ages—Yes, bread and water, Father Cedric! By heaven, and all saints in it, better food hath not passed my weasand for three livelong days, and by God's providence it is that I am now here to tell it."

"Why, noble Athelstane," said the Black Knight, "I myself saw you struck down by the fierce Templar, towards the end of the storm at

Torquilstone, and as I thought, and Wamba reported, your skull was cloven to the teeth."

"You thought amiss, Sir Knight," said Athelstane, "and Wamba lied. My teeth are in good order, and that my supper shall presently find—No thanks to the Templar though, whose sword turned in his hand, so that the blade struck me flatlings—had my steel-cap been on I had not valued it a rush, and had dealt him such a counter-buff as would have spoilt his retreat. But as it was, down I went, stunned, indeed, but unwounded. Others, of both sides, were beaten down and slaughtered above me, so that I never recovered my senses until I found myself in a coffin—(an open one by good luck)—placed before the high altar of the church of Saint Edmund's. I sneezed repeatedly—groaned—awakened, and would have arisen, when the Sacristan and Abbot, full of terror, came running at the noise, surprised, doubtless, and no way pleased to find the man alive, whose heirs they had proposed themselves to be. I asked for wine—they gave me some, but it must have been highly medicated, for I slept yet more deeply than before, and wakened not for many hours. I found my arms swathed down—my feet tied so fast that mine ankles ache at the very remembrance—the place was utterly dark—the oubliette,* as I suppose, of their accursed convent, and from the close, stifled, damp smell, I conceive it is also used as a place of sepulture. I had strange thoughts of what had befallen me, when the door of my dungeon creaked, and two villain monks entered. They would have persuaded me I was in purgatory, but I knew too well the pursy short-breathed voice of the Father Abbot.—Saint Jeremy! how different from that tone with which he used to ask me for another slice of the haunch!—the dog has feasted with me from Christmas to Twelfth-night."

"Have patience, noble Athelstane," said the King, "take breath—tell your story at leisure—beshrew me but such a tale is as well worth listing to as a romance."

"Ay but, by the rood of Bromeholm, there was no romance in the matter!—a barley loaf and a pitcher of water—that they gave me, the niggardly villains, whom my father and I myself had enriched, when their best resources were the flitches of bacon and measures of corn, out of which they wheedled poor serfs and bondsmen, in exchange for their prayers—the nest of foul ungrateful vipers—barley bread and ditch water to such a patron as I had been! I will smoke them out of their nest, though I be excommunicated."

"But in the name of Our Lady, noble Athelstane," said Cedric,

* *Oubliette* or cell of forgetfulness, in which those were imprisoned who were doomed never to revisit the daylight. Such horrid dungeons were common both in the convents and the feudal castles of former times. L. T.

grasping the hand of his friend, "how didst thou escape this imminent danger?—did their hearts relent?"

"Did their hearts relent!" echoed Athelstane.—"Do rocks melt with the sun? I should have been there still, had not some stir in the Convent, which I find was their procession hitherward to eat my funeral feast, when they well knew how and where I had been buried alive, summoned the swarm out of their hive. I heard them droning out their death-psalms, little judging they were sung in respect for my soul by those who were thus punishing my body. They went, however, and I waited long for food—no wonder—the gouty Sacristan was even too busy with his own provender to mind mine. At length down he came, with an unstable step and a strong flavour of wine and spices about his person. Good cheer had opened his heart, for he left me a nook of pasty and a flask of wine, instead of my former fare. I eat, drank, and was invigorated; when, to add to my good luck, the Sacristan, too totty to discharge his duty of turnkey fitly, locked the door beside the staple, so that it fell ajar—the light, the food, the wine, set my invention to work—the staple to which my chains were fixed, was more rusted than I or the villain Abbot had supposed—even iron could not stand without consuming in the damps of that infernal dungeon."

"Take breath, noble Athelstane," said Richard, "and partake of some refreshment, ere you proceed with a tale so dreadful."

"Partake!" quoth Athelstane; "I have been partaking five times today—and yet a morsel of that savoury ham were not altogether foreign to the matter; and I pray you, fair sir, to do me reason in a cup of wine."

The guests, though still agape with astonishment, pledged their resuscitated landlord, who thus proceeded in his story:—He had indeed now many more auditors than those to whom it was commenced, for Edith having given certain necessary orders for arranging matters within the Castle, had followed the dead-alive up to the strangers' apartment, attended by as many of the guests, male and female, as could squeeze into the small room, while others, crowding the staircase, caught up an erroneous edition of the story, and transmitted it still more inaccurately to those beneath, who again sent it forth to the vulgar without, in a fashion totally irreconcilable to the real fact.

Athelstane, however, went on as follows, with the history of his escape.—"Finding myself freed from the staple, I dragged myself up stairs as well as a man loaded with shackles, and emaciated with fasting, might; and after much groping about, I was at length directed, by the sound of a jolly roundelay, to the apartment where the worthy

Sacristan, an it please ye, was holding a devil's mass with a huge beetle-browed broad-shouldered brother of the grey frock and cord, who looked much more like a thief than a clergyman. I burst in upon them, and the fashion of my grave-clothes, as well as the clanking of my chains, made me more resemble an inhabitant of the other world than of this. Both stood aghast; but when I knocked down the Sacristan with my fist, the other fellow, his pot-companion, fetched a blow at me with a huge quarter-staff."

"This must be our Friar Tuck, for a count's ransom," said Richard, looking at Ivanhoe.

"He may be the devil, an he will," said Athelstane. "Fortunately he missed his aim; and on my approaching to grapple with him, took to his heels and ran for it. I failed not to set my own heels at liberty by means of the fetter-key which hung amongst others at the sexton's belt; and I had thoughts of beating out the knave's brains with the bunch of keys, but the thoughts of the nook of pasty and the flask of wine which the rascal had imparted to my captivity, came over my heart; so, with a brace of hearty kicks, I left him on the floor, pouched some baked meat, and a leathern bottle of wine, with which the two venerable brethren had been regaling, went to the stable, and found in a private stall mine own best palfrey, which, doubtless, had been set apart for the holy father Abbot's particular use. Hither I came with all the speed the beast could compass—man and mother's son flying before me wherever I came, taking me for a spectre, the more especially as, to prevent my being recognized, I drew the corpse-hood over my face. I had not gained admittance into my own castle, had I not been supposed to be the attendant of a juggler who is making the people in the castle-yard very merry, considering they are assembled to celebrate their lord's funeral. I say the sewer thought I was dressed to bear a part in the tregetour's mummery, and so I got admission, and did but disclose myself to my mother, and eat a hasty morsel, ere I came in quest of you, my noble friend."

"And you have found me," said Cedric, "ready to resume our brave projects of honour and liberty. I tell thee, never will dawn a morrow so auspicious as the next, for the deliverance of the noble Saxon race."

"Talk not to me of delivering any one," said Athelstane; "it is well I am delivered myself. I am more intent on punishing that villain Abbot. He shall hang on the top of this Castle of Coningsburgh, in his cope and stole; and if the stairs be too strait to admit his fat carcase, I will have him craned up from without."

"But, my son," said Edith, "consider his sacred office."

"Consider my three days fast," replied Athelstane; "I will have their blood every man of them. Front-de-Bœuf was burned alive for a less matter, for he kept a goodly table for his prisoners, only put too much garlic in his last dish of pottage. But these hypocritical, ungrateful slaves, so often the self-invited flatterers at my board, who gave me neither pottage nor garlic, more or less, they die, by the soul of Hengist!"

"But the Pope, my noble friend," said Cedric——

"But the devil, my noble friend,"—answered Athelstane; "they die, and no more of them. Were they the last monks upon earth, the world would go on without them."

"For shame, noble Athelstane," said Cedric; "forget such wretches in the career of glory which lies open before thee. Tell this Norman prince, Richard of Anjou, that, lion-hearted as he is, he shall not hold undisputed the throne of Alfred, while a male descendant of the Holy Confessor lives to dispute it."

"How!" said Athelstane, "is this the noble King Richard?"

"It is Richard Plantagenet himself," replied Cedric; "yet I need not remind thee that, coming hither a guest of free-will, he may neither be injured nor detained prisoner—thou well knowest thy duty to him as his host."

"Ay, by my faith!" said Athelstane; "and my duty as a subject besides, for here I tender him my allegiance, heart and hand."

"My son," said Edith, "think on thy royal rights."

"Think on the freedom of England, degenerate Prince!" said Cedric.

"Mother and friend," said Athelstane, "a truce to your upbraidings—bread and water and a dungeon are marvellous mortifiers of ambition, and I arise from the tomb a wiser man than I descended into it. One half of those vain follies were puffed into mine ears by that perfidious Abbot Wolfram, and you may now judge if he is a counsellor to be trusted. Since these plots were set in agitation, I have had nothing but hurried journies, indigestions, blows and bruises, imprisonment and starvation; besides that they can only end in the murder of some thousands of quiet folks. I tell you, I will be king in my own domains, and no where else; and my first act of dominion shall be to hang the Abbot."

"And my ward Rowena," said Cedric—"I trust you intend not to desert her?"

"Father Cedric," said Athelstane, "be reasonable. The Lady Rowena cares not for me—she loves the little finger of my kinsman Wilfred's glove better than my whole person. There she stands to avouch it—Nay, blush not, kinswoman, there is no shame in loving a courtly knight better than a country franklin—and do not laugh neither, Rowena, for grave-clothes and a thin visage are, God knows, no matter of merriment—Nay, an thou wilt needs laugh, I will find thee a better jest—Give me thy hand, or rather lend it me, for I but ask it in the way of friendship.—Here, cousin Wilfred of Ivanhoe, in thy favour I renounce and abjure——Hey! by Saint Dunstan, our cousin Wilfred hath vanished!—Yet, unless my eyes are still dazzled with the fasting I have undergone, I saw him stand there but even now."

All now looked around and enquired for Ivanhoe, but he had vanished. It was at length discovered that a Jew had enquired for him; and that, after very brief conference, he had called for Gurth and his armour, and had instantly left the castle.

"Fair cousin," said Athelstane to Rowena, "could I think that this sudden disappearance of Ivanhoe were occasioned by other than the weightiest reasons, I would myself resume"——

But he had no sooner let go her hand, on first observing that Ivanhoe had disappeared, than Rowena, who found her situation extremely embarrassing, had taken the opportunity to escape from the apartment.

"Certainly," quoth Athelstane, "women are the least to be trusted of all animals, monks and abbots excepted. I am an infidel, if I expected not thanks from her, and perhaps a kiss to boot—These cursed grave-clothes have surely a spell on them, every one flies from me. To you I turn, noble King Richard, with the vows of allegiance, which, as a liege-subject"——

But King Richard was gone also, and no one knew whither. At length it was learned that he had hastened to the court-yard, summoned to his presence the Jew who had spoken with Ivanhoe, and after a moment's speech with him, had called vehemently to horse, thrown himself on a steed, compelled the Jew to mount another, and set off at a rate, which, according to Wamba, rendered the old Jew's neck not worth a liard's purchase.

"By my halidome!" said the astounded Athelstane, "it is certain Zernebock hath possessed himself of my castle in my absence. I return in my grave-clothes, a pledge redeemed from the very sepulchre, and every one I speak to vanishes so soon as they hear my voice!—But it skills not talking of it. Come, my friends—such of you as are left, follow me to the banquet-hall, before any more of us disappear—it is, I trust, as yet tolerably furnished, as becomes the obsequies of an ancient Saxon noble; and should we tarry any longer, who knows but the devil may next fly off with the supper?"

Chapter Thirteen

Be Mowbray's sins so heavy in his bosom,
That they may break his foaming courser's back,
And throw the rider headlong in the lists,
A caitiff recreant.——

Richard II.

OUR SCENE now returns to the exterior of the Castle, or Preceptory of Templestowe, about the hour when the bloody die was to be cast for the life or death of Rebecca. It was a scene of bustle and life, as if the whole vicinage had poured forth its inhabitants to a village wake, or rural feast. But the evident desire to look on blood and death, is not peculiar to these dark ages; though in the gladiatorial exercises of single combat and general tourney, they were habituated to the bloody spectacle of brave men falling by each other's hands. Even in our own days, when morals are better understood, an execution, a bruising match between two professors, a riot, or a meeting of radical reformers, collects at considerable hazard to themselves immense crowds of spectators, otherwise little interested, excepting to see how matters are to be conducted, and whether the heroes of the day are, in the heroic language of insurgent tailors, *flints* or *dunghills*.

The eyes, therefore, of a very considerable multitude were bent on the gate of the Preceptory of Templestowe, with the purpose of witnessing the procession; while still greater numbers had already surrounded the tilt-yard belonging to that establishment. This inclosure was formed on a space of ground adjacent to the Preceptory, which had been levelled with care, for the exercise of military and chivalrous sports. It occupied the brow of a soft and gentle eminence, was carefully palisaded around, and, as the Templars willingly invited spectators to be witnesses of their skill in feats of chivalry, was amply supplied with galleries and benches for the use of spectators.

Upon the present occasion, a throne was erected at the eastern end for the Grand Master, surrounded with seats of distinction for the Preceptors and Knights of the Order. Over these floated the sacred standard, called *Le Beau-seant*, which was the ensign, as its name was the battle-cry, of the Templars.

At the opposite end of the lists was a pile of faggots, so arranged around a stake, deeply fixed in the ground, as to leave a space for the victim whom they were destined to consume, to enter within their fatal circle, in order to be chained to the stake by the fetters which hung ready for that purpose. Beside this deadly apparatus stood four black slaves, whose colour and African features, then so little known in

England, appalled the multitude, who gazed on them as on demons employed about their own diabolical exercises. These men stirred not, excepting now and then, under the direction of one who seemed their chief, to shift and replace the ready fuel. They looked not on the multitude. In fact, they seemed insensible of their presence, and of every thing save the discharge of their own horrible duty. And when, in speech with each other, they expanded their blabber lips, and shewed their white fangs, as if they grinned at the thoughts of the expected tragedy, the startled commons could scarcely help believing that they were actually the familiar spirits with whom the witch had convened, and who now, her time being out, stood ready to assist in her dreadful punishment. They whispered with each other, and enumerated all the feats which Satan had performed during that busy and unhappy period, not failing, of course, to give the devil rather more than his due.

"Have you not heard, Father Dennet," quoth one boor to another advanced in years, "that the devil has carried away bodily the great Saxon Thane, Athelstane of Coningsburgh?"

"Ay, but he brought him back though, by the blessing of God and Saint Dunstan."

"How's that?" said a brisk young fellow, dressed in a green cassock, embroidered with gold, and having at his heels a stout lad bearing a harp upon his back, which betrayed his vocation. The Minstrel seemed of no vulgar rank; for, besides the splendour of his newly broidered doublet, he wore around his neck a silver chain, by which hung the *wrest*, or key with which he tuned his harp. On his right arm was a silver plate, which, instead of bearing, as usual, the cognizance or badge of the baron to whose family he belonged, had barely the word SHERWOOD engraved upon it.—"How mean you by that?" said this gay Minstrel, mingling in the conversation of the peasants; "I came to seek one subject for my rhyme, and, by'r Lady, I were glad to find two."

"It is well avouched," said the elder peasant, "that after Athelstane of Coningsburgh had been dead four weeks"——

"That is impossible," said the Minstrel; "I saw him in life at the Passage of Arms at Ashby-de-la-Zouche."

"Dead, however, he was, or else translated," said the younger peasant; "for I heard the Monks of Saint Edmund's singing the death-hymn for him; and, moreover, there was a rich death-meal and dole at the Castle of Coningsburgh, as right was, and thither had I gone but for Mabel Parkins, who"——

"Ay, dead was Athelstane," said the old man, shaking his head, "and the more pity it was, for the old Saxon blood"——

"But, your story, my masters—your story," said the Minstrel, somewhat impatiently.

"Ay, ay—construe us the story," said a burley Friar, who stood beside them, leaning on a pole that hovered in appearance betwixt a pilgrim's staff and a quarter-staff, and probably acted as either when occasion served,—"Your story," said this stalwart churchman; "burn not day-light about it—we have short time to spare."

"An please your reverence," said Dennet, "a drunken priest came to visit the Sacristan at Saint Edmund's"——

"It does not please my reverence," answered the churchman, "that there should be such an animal as a drunken priest, or, if there were, that a layman should so speak him. Be mannerly, my friend, and conclude the holy man only rapt in meditation, which makes the head dizzy and foot unsteady, as if the stomach was filled with new wine—I have felt it myself."

"Well then," answered Father Dennet, "a holy brother came to visit the Sacristan at Saint Edmund's—a sort of a hedge-priest is the visitor, and kills half the deer that are stolen in the forest, who loves the tinkling of a pint-pot better than the sacring-bell, and deems a flitch of bacon worth ten of his breviary; for the rest, a good fellow and a merry, who will flourish a quarter-staff, draw a bow, and dance a Cheshire round with e'er a man in Yorkshire."

"That last part of thy speech, Dennet," said the Minstrel, "has saved thee a rib or twain."

"Tush, man, I fear him not," said Dennet; "I am somewhat old and stiff, but when I fought for the bell and ram at Doncaster"——

"But the story—the story, my friend," again said the Minstrel.

"Why, the tale is but this—Athelstane of Coningsburgh was buried at Saint Edmund's."

"That's a lie, and a loud one," said the Friar, "for I saw him borne to his own Castle of Coningsburgh."

"Nay then, e'en tell the story yourself, my masters," said Dennet, turning sulky at these repeated contradictions; and it was with some difficulty that the boor could be prevailed, by the request of his comrade and the Minstrel, to renew his tale.—"These two *sober* friars," said he at length, "since this reverend man will needs have them such, had continued drinking good ale, and wine, and what not, for the best part of a summer's day, when they were aroused by a deep groan, and a clanking of chains, and the figure of the deceased Athelstane entered the apartment, saying, 'Ye evil shepherds'"——

"It is false," said the Friar hastily, "he never spoke a word."

"So ho! Friar Tuck," said the Minstrel, drawing him apart from the rustics; "we have started a new hare, I find."

"I tell thee, Allan-a-Dale," said the Hermit, "I saw Athelstane of Coningsburgh as much as bodily eyes ever saw a living man. He had his shroud on, and all about him smelt of the sepulchre—A butt of sack will not wash it out of my memory."

"Pshaw!" answered the Minstrel; "thou dost but jest with me?"

"Never believe me," said the Friar, "an I fetched not a knock at him with my quarter-staff that would have felled an ox, and it glided through his body as it might through a pillar of smoke!"

"By Saint Hubert," said the Minstrel, "it is a wonderous tale, and well fit to be put in metre to the ancient tune, 'Sorrow came to the old Friar.'"

"Laugh, if ye list," said Friar Tuck; "but an ye catch me singing on such a theme, may the next ghost or devil carry me off with him headlong! No, no—I instantly formed the purpose of assisting at some good work, such as the burning of a witch, a judicial combat, or the like matter of godly service."

As they thus conversed, the heavy toll of the church of Saint Michael of Templestowe, a venerable building, situated in a hamlet at some distance from the Preceptory, broke short their argument. One by one the sullen sounds fell successively on the ear, leaving but sufficient space for each to die away in distant echo, ere the air was again filled by repetition of the iron knell. These sounds, the signal of the approaching ceremony, chilled with awe the hearts of the assembled multitude, whose eyes were now turned to the Preceptory, expecting the approach of the Grand Master, the champion, and the criminal.

At length the draw-bridge fell, the gates opened, and a knight, bearing the great standard of the Order, sallied from the castle, preceded by six trumpets, and followed by the Knights Preceptors, two and two, the Grand Master coming last, mounted on a stately horse, whose furniture was of the simplest kind. Behind him came Brian de Bois-Guilbert, armed cap-a-pee in bright armour, but without his lance, shield, and helmet, which were borne by his two esquires behind him. His face, though in part hidden by a long plume which flowed down from his basnet-cap, bore a strange and mingled expression of passion, in which pride seemed to contend with irresolution. He looked ghastly pale, as if he had not slept for several nights, yet reined his pawing war-horse with the habitual ease and grace proper to the best lance of the Order of the Temple. His general appearance was grand and commanding; but, on looking at him with attention, men read that in his dark features, from which we willingly withdraw our eyes.

On either side rode Conrade of Mountfitchet, and Albert de Malvoisin, who acted as godfathers to the champion. They were in their robes of peace, the white dress of the Order. Behind them followed other Knights Companions of the Temple, with a long train of esquires and pages, clad in black, aspirants to the honour of being one day Knights of the Order. After these neophites came a guard of warders on foot, in the same sable livery, amidst whose partizans might be seen the pale form of the accused, moving forward with a slow but undismayed step towards the scene of her fate. She was stript of all her ornaments, lest perchance there should have been among them one of those amulets which Satan was supposed to bestow upon his victims, to deprive them of the power of confessing even when under the torture. A coarse white dress, of the simplest form, had been substituted for her oriental garments; yet there was such an exquisite mixture of courage and resignation in her looks, that even in this garb, and with no other ornament than her long black tresses, each eye wept that looked upon her, and even the most hardened bigot regretted the fate that had converted a creature so goodly into a vessel of wrath, and a waged slave of the devil.

A crowd of inferior personages belonging to the Preceptory followed the victim, all moving with the utmost order, with arms folded and looks bent upon the ground.

This slow procession moved up the gentle eminence, on the summit of which was the tilt-yard, and, entering the lists, marched once around them from right to left, and when they had completed the circle, made a halt. There was then a momentary bustle, while the Grand Master and all his attendants, excepting the champion and his godfathers, dismounted from their horses, which were immediately removed out of the lists by the esquires, who were in attendance for that purpose.

The unfortunate Rebecca was conducted to the black chair placed near the pile. On her first glance at the terrible spot where preparations were making for her dying a death alike dismaying to the mind and painful to the body, she was observed to shudder and shut her eyes, praying internally doubtless, for her lips moved though no speech was heard. In the space of a minute she opened her eyes, looked fixedly on the pile as if to familiarize her mind with the object, and then slowly and naturally turned away her eyes.

Meanwhile, the Grand Master had assumed his seat; and when the chivalry of his order was placed around and behind him, each in his due rank, a loud and long flourish of the trumpets announced that the Court were seated for judgment. Malvoisin, then, acting as the godfather of the Champion, stepped forward, and laid the glove of the Jewess, which was the pledge of battle, at the feet of the Grand Master.

"Valorous Lord, and reverend Father," said he, "here standeth the good Knight, Brian de Bois-Guilbert, Knight Preceptor of the Order of the Temple, who, by accepting the gage of battle which I now lay at your reverence's feet, hath become bound to do his devoir in combat this day, to maintain that this Jewish maiden, by name Rebecca, hath justly deserved the doom passed upon her in a Chapter of the most Holy Order of the Temple of Zion, condemning her to die as a sorceress. And here, I say, he standeth such battle to do, knightly and honourably, if such be your noble and sanctified pleasure."

"Hath he made oath," said the Grand Master, "that his quarrel is just and honourable? Bring forward the Crucifix and the *Te igitur*."

"Sir, and most reverend Father," answered Malvoisin, readily, "our brother here present hath already sworn to the truth of his accusation in the hand of the good Knight Conrade de Mountfitchet; and otherwise ought he not to be sworn, seeing that his adverse party is an unbeliever, and may take no oath."

This explanation was satisfactory, to Albert's great joy; for the wily knight had foreseen the great difficulty, or rather impossibility, of prevailing upon Brian de Bois-Guilbert to take such an oath before the assembly, and had invented this excuse to escape the necessity of his doing so.

The Grand Master, having allowed of the apology of Albert de Malvoisin, commanded the herald to stand forth and do his devoir. The trumpets then again flourished, and a herald, stepping forward, proclaimed aloud,—"Oyez, oyez, oyez.—Here standeth the good Knight, Sir Brian de Bois-Guilbert, ready to battle with any knight of free blood, who will sustain the quarrel allowed and allotted to the Jewess Rebecca, to try by champion, in respect of lawful essoyne of her own body. And to such champion the reverend Valour of the Grand Master here present allows a fair field, true and equal partition of sun and wind, and whatever else appertains to a fair combat." The trumpets again sounded, and there was a dead pause of many minutes.

"No champion appears for the appellant," said the Grand Master. "Go, herald, and ask her whether she expects any one to do battle for her in this her cause." The herald went to the chair in which Rebecca was seated, and Bois-Guilbert suddenly turning his horse's head towards that end of the lists, in spite of the hints on either side from Malvoisin and Mountfitchet, was by the side of Rebecca's chair as soon as the herald.

"Is this regular, and according to the laws of combat?" said Malvoisin, looking to the Grand Master.

"Albert de Malvoisin, it is," answered Beaumanoir; "for in this appeal to the judgment of God, we may not prohibit parties from having that communication with each other, which may best tend to bring forth the truth of the quarrel."

In the mean while, the herald spoke to Rebecca in these terms:— "Damsel, the Honourable and Reverend Grand Master demands of thee, if thou art prepared with a champion to do battle this day in thy behalf, or if thou doest yield thee as one justly condemned to a deserved doom?"

"Say to the Grand Master," replied Rebecca, "that I maintain my innocence, and will not yield me as justly condemned, lest I become guilty of mine own blood. Say to him, that I challenge such delay as his forms will permit to see if God, whose opportunity is in man's extremity, will raise me up a deliverer; and when such uttermost space is passed, may His holy will be done!" The herald retired to carry this answer to the Grand Master.

"God forbid," said Lucas de Beaumanoir, "that Jew or Pagan should impeach us of injustice.—Until the shadows be cast from the west to the eastward, will we wait to see if a champion will appear for this unfortunate woman. When the hour of noon is so far passed, let her prepare for death."

The herald communicated the words of the Grand Master to Rebecca, who bowed her head submissively, folded her arms, and, looking up towards heaven, seemed to expect that aid from above which she could scarce promise herself from man.

During this awful pause, the voice of Bois-Guilbert broke on her ear—it was but a whisper, yet it startled her more than the summons of the herald had appeared to do.

"Rebecca," said the Templar, "doest thou hear me?"

"I have no portion in thee, cruel, hard-hearted man," said the unfortunate maiden.

"Ay, but doest thou understand my words?" said the Templar; "for the sound of my voice is frightful in mine own ears. I scarce know on what ground we stand, or for what purpose they have brought us hither—this listed space—that chair—these faggots—I know their purpose, and yet it seems to me something unreal—the fearful picturing of a vision, which appals my sense with hideous fantasies, which convince not my mind."

"My mind and senses keep touch and time," answered Rebecca, "and tell me alike that these faggots are destined to consume my earthly body, and open a painful but a brief passage to a better world."

"Dreams! Rebecca, dreams," answered the Templar; "idle visions, rejected by the wisdom of your own wiser Sadducees. Hear me, Rebecca," he said, proceeding with animation; "a better chance hast thou for life and liberty than yonder knaves and dotard dream of.

Mount thee behind me on my steed—on Zamor, the gallant horse that never failed his rider. I won him in single fight from the Soldan of Trebizond—mount, I say, behind me—in one short hour is pursuit and inquiry far behind—a new world of pleasure opens to thee—to me a new career of fame. Let them speak the doom which I despise, and erase the name of Bois-Guilbert from their list of monastic slaves! I will wash out with blood whatever blot they may dare to cast on my scutcheon."

"Tempter," said Rebecca, "begone!—Not in this last extremity canst thou move me one hair's-breadth from my resting place—surrounded as I am by foes, I hold thee as my worst and most deadly—avoid thee, in the name of God!"

Albert de Malvoisin, alarmed and impatient at the duration of their conference, now advanced to interrupt it.

"Hath the maiden acknowledged her guilt?" he demanded of Bois-Guilbert; "or is she resolute in her denial?"

"She is indeed *resolute*," said Bois-Guilbert.

"Then," said Malvoisin, "must thou, noble brother, resume thy place to attend the issue—The shades are changing on the circle of the dial—Come, brave Bois-Guilbert—come, thou hope of our holy Order, and soon to be its head."

As he spoke in this soothing tone, he laid his hand on the knight's bridle, as if to lead him back to his station.

"False villain! what meanest thou by thy hand on my rein?" said Sir Brian, angrily. And shaking off his companion's grasp, he rode back to the upper end of the lists.

"There is yet spirit in him," said Malvoisin apart to Mountfitchet, "were it well directed—but, like the Greek fire, it burns whatever approaches it."

The Judges had now been two hours in the lists, awaiting in vain the appearance of a champion. It became the general opinion that no one would wage battle for the unhappy maiden.

"And reason good," said Friar Tuck, "seeing she is a Jewess—and yet, by mine Order, it is hard that so young and beautiful a creature should perish without one blow being struck in her behalf. Were she ten times a witch, providing she were but the least bit of a Christian, my quarter-staff should ring noon on the steel cap of yonder fierce Templar, ere he carried the matter off thus."

It was, however, the general belief, that no one could or would appear for a Jewess accused of sorcery, and the knights, instigated by Malvoisin, whispered to each other, that it was time to declare the pledge of Rebecca forfeited. At this instant a knight, urging his horse to speed, appeared on the plain advancing towards the lists.

An hundred voices exclaimed, "A champion! a champion!" And despite the prepossession, and prejudices of the multitude, they shouted unanimously as the knight rode into the tilt-yard. The second glance, however, served to destroy the hope that his timely arrival had excited. His horse, urged for many miles to its utmost speed, appeared to reel from fatigue, and the rider, however undauntedly he presented himself in the lists, either from weakness, weariness, or both, seemed scarce able to support himself in the saddle.

To the summons of the herald, who demanded his rank, his name, and purpose, the stranger knight answered readily and boldly, "I am a good knight and noble, come hither to sustain with lance and sword the just and lawful quarrel of this damsel, Rebecca, daughter of Isaac of York; to uphold the doom pronounced against her to be false and truthless, and to defy Sir Brian de Bois-Guilbert, as a traitor, a murtherer, and a liar; as I will prove in this field with my body against his, by the aid of God, of Our Lady, and of Monseigneur Saint George, the good knight."

"The stranger must first show," said Malvoisin, "that he is good Knight, and of honourable lineage. The Temple sendeth not forth her champions against nameless men."

"My name," said the Knight, raising his helmet, "is better known, my lineage more pure, Malvoisin, than thine own. I am Wilfred of Ivanhoe."

"I will not fight with thee," said the Templar, in a changed and hollow voice. "Get thy wounds healed, purvey thee with a fresh horse, and it may be I will hold it worth my while to scourge out of thee this boyish spirit of bravade."

"Ha! proud Templar," said Ivanhoe, "hast thou forgotten that twice didst thou fall before this lance? Remember the lists at Acre—remember the Passage of Arms at Ashby—remember thy proud vaunt in the halls of Rotherwood, and the gage of your gold chain against my reliquary, that thou wouldst do battle with Wilfred of Ivanhoe, and recover the honour thou hadst lost! By that reliquary, and the holy relique it contains, I will proclaim thee, Templar, a coward in every court of Europe—in every Preceptory of thine Order—unless thou do battle without farther delay."

Bois-Guilbert turned his countenance irresolutely towards Rebecca, and then exclaimed, looking fiercely at Ivanhoe, "Dog of a Saxon sire! take thy lance, and prepare for the death thou hast drawn upon thee!"

"Does the Grand Master allow me the combat?" said Ivanhoe.

"I may not deny what you have challenged," said the Grand Master, "providing the maiden accepts thee as her champion. Yet I would thou wert in better plight to do battle. An enemy of our Order hast thou ever been, yet would I have thee honourably met with."

"Thus—thus as I am, and not otherwise," said Ivanhoe; "it is the judgment of God—to his keeping I commit myself.—Rebecca," said he, riding up to the fatal chair, "doest thou accept of me for thy champion?"

"I do," she said—"I do," fluttered by an emotion which the fear of death had been unable to produce, "I do accept thee as the champion whom Heaven hath sent me. Yet, no—no—thy wounds are uncured—Meet not that proud man—why shouldst thou perish also?"

But Ivanhoe was already at his post, and had closed his visor, and assumed his lance. Bois-Guilbert did the same; and his esquire remarked, that as he clasped his visor, his face, which had, notwithstanding the variety of emotions by which he had been agitated, continued during the whole morning of an ashy paleness, now became suddenly very much flushed.

The herald, then, seeing each champion in his place, uplifted his voice, repeating thrice—*Faites vos devoirs, preux chevaliers*. After the third cry, he withdrew to one side of the lists, and again proclaimed, that none, on peril of instant death, should dare by word, cry, or action, to interfere with or disturb this fair field of combat. The Grand Master, who held in his hand the gage of battle, Rebecca's glove, now threw it into the lists, and pronounced the fatal signal words, *Laissez aller*.

The trumpets sounded, and the knights charged each other in full career. The wearied horse of Ivanhoe, and its no less exhausted rider, went down, as all had expected, before the well aimed lance and vigorous steed of the Templar. This issue of the combat all had expected; but although the spear of Ivanhoe did but, in comparison, touch the shield of Bois-Guilbert, that champion, to the astonishment of all who beheld it, reeled in his saddle, lost his stirrups, and fell in the lists.

Ivanhoe, extricating himself from his fallen horse, was soon on foot, trusting to mend his fortune with his sword; but his antagonist arose not. Wilfred, placing his foot on his breast, and the sword-point to his throat, commanded him to yield him, or die on the spot. Bois-Guilbert returned no answer.

"Slay him not, Sir Knight," cried the Grand Master, "unshriven and unabsolved—kill not body and soul. We allow him vanquished."

He descended into the lists, and commanded them to unhelm the conquered champion. His eyes were closed—the dark red flush was still on his brow—as they looked on him in astonishment, the eyes opened but they were fixed and glazed—the flush passed from his brow, and gave way to the pallid hue of death. Unscathed by the lance of his enemy, he had died a victim to the violence of his own contending passions.

"This is indeed the judgment of God," said the Grand Master, looking upwards—"*Fiat voluntas tua!*"

Chapter Fourteen

So! now 'tis ended, like an old wife's story.
WEBSTER.

WHEN THE FIRST MOMENTS of surprise were over, Wilfred of Ivanhoe demanded of the Grand Master, as judge of the field, if he had manfully and rightfully done his duty in the combat?

"Manfully and rightfully has it been done," said the Grand Master; "I pronounce the maiden free and guiltless—The arms and the body of the deceased knight are at the will of the victor."

"I will not despoil him of his weapons," said the Knight of Ivanhoe, "nor condemn his corpse to shame—he hath fought for Christendom—God's arm, no human hand, hath this day struck him down. But let his obsequies be private, as becomes those of a man who died in an unjust quarrel.—And for the maiden"——

He was interrupted by a clattering of horses' feet, advancing in such numbers, and so rapidly, as to shake the ground before them; and the Black Knight gallopped into the lists. He was followed by a numerous band of men-at-arms, and several knights in complete armour.

"I am too late," he said, looking around him. "I had doomed Bois-Guilbert for mine own property.—Ivanhoe, was this well, to take on thee such a venture, and thou scarce able to keep thy saddle?"

"Heaven, my Liege," answered Ivanhoe, "hath taken this proud man for its victim. He was not to be so honoured in dying as your will had designed."

"Peace be with him," said Richard, looking stedfastly on the corpse, "if it may be so—he was a gallant knight, and has died in his steel harness full knightly. But we must waste no time—Bohun, do thine office!"

A Knight stepped forwards from the King's attendance, and laying his hand on the shoulder of Albert de Malvoisin, said, "I arrest thee of High Treason."

The Grand Master had hitherto stood astonished at the apparition of so many warriors.—He now spoke.

"Who dares to arrest a Knight of the Temple of Zion, within the girth of his own Preceptory, and in the presence of the Grand Master?

and by whose authority is this bold outrage offered?"

"I make the arrest," replied the Knight—"I, Henry Bohun, Earl of Essex, Lord High Constable of England."

"And he arrests Malvoisin," said the King, raising his visor, "by the order of Richard Plantagenet, here present. Conrade Mountfitchet, it is well for thee thou art born no subject of mine.—But for thee, Malvoisin, thou diest with thy brother Philip, ere the world be a week older."

"I will resist thy doom," said the Grand Master.

"Proud Templar," said the King, "thou canst not—look up and behold the Royal Standard of England floats over thy towers instead of thy Temple banner!—Be wise, Beaumanoir, and make no bootless opposition—Thy hand is in the lion's mouth."

"I will appeal to Rome against thee," said the Grand Master, "for usurpation on the immunities and privileges of our Order."

"Be it so," said the King; "but for thine own sake tax me not with usurpation now.—Dissolve thy Chapter, and depart with thy followers to thy next Preceptory, (if thou canst find one) which has not been made the scene of treasonable conspiracy against the King of England—Or, if thou wilt, remain, to share our hospitality, and to behold our justice."

"To be a guest in the house where I should command?" said the Templar; "Never.—Chaplains, raise the Psalm, *Quare fremuerunt Gentes?*—Knights, squires, and followers of the Holy Temple, prepare to follow the banner of *Beau-seant!*"

The Grand Master spoke with a dignity which confronted even that of England's king himself, and inspired courage into his surprised and dismayed followers. They gathered around him like the sheep around the watch-dog, when they hear the baying of the wolf. But they evinced not the timidity of the scared flock—there were dark brows of defiance, and looks which menaced the hostility they dared not to proffer in words. They drew together in a dark line of spears, from which the white cloaks of the knights were visible among the dusky garments of their retainers, like the lighter-coloured edges of a sable cloud. The multitude, who had raised a clamorous shout of reprobation, paused and gazed in silence on the formidable and experienced body to which they had unwarily bade defiance, and shrunk back from their front.

The Earl of Essex, when he beheld them pause in their assembled force, dashed the rowels into his charger's sides, and galloped backwards and forwards to array his followers, in opposition to a band so formidable. Richard alone, as if he loved the danger his presence had provoked, rode slowly along the front of the Templars, calling aloud,

"What, sirs! Among so many gallant knights, will none dare splinter a spear with Richard?—Sirs of the Temple! your ladies are but sun-burned, if they are not worth the shiver of a broken lance."

"The Brethren of the Temple," said the Grand Master, riding forward in advance of their body, "fight not on such idle and profane quarrel—and not with thee, Richard of England, shall a Templar cross lance in my presence. The Pope and Princes of Europe shall judge our quarrel, and whether a Christian prince has done well in bucklering the cause which thou hast to-day adopted. If unassailed, we depart assailing no one. To thine honour we refer the armour and household goods of the Order which we leave behind us, and on thy conscience we lay the scandal and offence thou hast this day given to Christendom."

With these words, and without waiting a reply, the Grand Master gave the signal of departure. Their trumpets sounded a wild march, of an oriental character, which formed the usual signal for the Templars to advance. They changed their array from a line to a column of march, and moved off as slowly as their horses could step, as if to shew it was only the will of their Grand Master, and no fear of the opposing force which compelled them to withdraw.

"By the splendour of Our Lady's brow!" said King Richard, "it is pity of their lives that these Templars are not so trusty as they are disciplined and valiant."

The multitude, like a timid cur which waits to bark till the object of its challenge has turned his back, raised a feeble shout as the rear of the squadron left the ground.

During the tumult which attended the retreat of the Templars, Rebecca saw and heard nothing—she was locked in the arms of her aged father, giddy, and almost senseless, with the rapid change of circumstances around her. But one word from Isaac at length recalled her scattered feelings.

"Let us go," he said, "my dear daughter, my recovered treasure—let us go to throw ourselves at the feet of the good youth."

"Not so," said Rebecca, "O no—no—no—I must not at this moment dare to speak to him—Alas! I should say more than——No, my father, let us instantly leave this evil place."

"But, my daughter," said Isaac, "to leave him who hath come forth like a strong man with spear and shield, holding his life as nothing, so he might redeem thy captivity; and thou, too, the daughter of a people strange unto him and his—this is service to be thankfully acknow-ledged."

"It is—it is—most thankfully—most devoutly acknowledged—it shall be still more so—but not now—for the sake of thy beloved

Rachael, father, grant my request—not now!"

"Nay, but," said Isaac, insisting, "they will deem us more thankless than mere dogs."

"But thou seest, my dear father, that King Richard is in presence, and that"——

"True, my best—my wisest Rebecca!—Let us hence—let us hence!—Money he will lack, for he has just returned from Palestine, and, as they say, from prison—and pretext for exacting it, should he need any, may arise out of my simple traffic with his brother John. Away, away—let us hence!"

And hurrying his daughter in his turn, he conducted her from the lists, and by the means of conveyance which he had provided, transported her safely to the house of the Rabbi Nathan.

The Jewess, whose fortunes had formed the principal interest of the day, had not retired so much unobserved, but for the attention of the populace having been transferred to the Black Knight. They now filled the air with "Long life to Richard with the Lion's Heart, and down with the usurping Templars!"

"Notwithstanding all this lip-loyalty," said Ivanhoe to the Earl of Essex, "it was well the King took the precaution to bring thee with him, noble Earl, and so many of thy trusty followers."

The Earl smiled, and shook his head.

"Gallant Ivanhoe, dost thou know our Master so well, and yet suspect him of taking so wise a precaution? I was drawing towards York, having heard a rumour that Prince John was making a head there, when I met King Richard, like a true knight-errant, gallopping hither to achieve this adventure of the Templar and the Jewess, with his own single arm. I accompanied him with my band almost maugre his consent."

"And what news from York, brave Earl?" said Ivanhoe; "will the rebels bide us there?"

"No more than December's snow will bide July's sun," said the Earl; "they are dispersed; and who should come posting to bring the news, but John himself?"

"The traitor! the ungrateful insolent traitor!" said Ivanhoe; "Did not Richard order him into confinement?"

"O! he received him," replied the Earl, "as if they had met after a hunting-party; and, pointing to me and our men-at-arms, said, Thou seest, brother, I have some angry men with me—thou wert best go to our mother, carry her my duteous affection, and abide with her until men's minds are pacified."

"And this was all he said?" replied Ivanhoe; "would not any one say that this Prince invites to treason by his clemency?"

"Just," replied the Earl, "as the man may be said to invite death, who undertakes to fight a combat with a dangerous wound unhealed."

"I forgive thee the jest, Lord Earl," said Ivanhoe; "but, remember, I hazarded but my own life—Richard, the welfare of his kingdom."

"Those," replied Essex, "who are specially careless of their own welfare, are seldom remarkably attentive to that of others—But let us haste to the castle, for Richard meditates punishing some of the subordinate members of the conspiracy, though he has pardoned their principal."

From the judicial investigations which followed on this occasion, and which are given at length in the Wardour Manuscript, it appears that Maurice de Bracy escaped over seas, and went into the service of Philip of France; while Philip de Malvoisin, and his brother Albert, the Preceptor of Templestowe, were executed, although Waldemar Fitzurse, the soul of the conspiracy, escaped with banishment; and Prince John, for whose behoof it was undertaken, was not even censured by his good-natured brother. No one, however, pitied the fate of the two Malvoisins, who only suffered the death which they had both well deserved, by many acts of falsehood, cruelty, and oppression.

Briefly after the judicial combat, Cedric the Saxon was summoned to the court of Richard, which, for the purpose of quieting the counties that had been disturbed by the ambition of his brother, was then held at York. Cedric tushed and pshawed more than once at the message—but he refused it not. In fact, the return of Richard had quenched every hope he had entertained of restoring a Saxon dynasty in England; for, whatever head the Saxons might have raised in the event of a civil war, it was plain that nothing could be done under the undisputed dominion of Richard, popular as he was by his personal good qualities and military fame, although his administration was wilfully careless, now too indulgent, and now allied to despotism.

But, moreover, it could not escape even Cedric's reluctant observation, that his project for an absolute union among the Saxons, by the marriage of Rowena and Athelstane, was now completely at an end by the mutual dissent of both the parties concerned. This was, indeed, an event which, in his ardour for the Saxon cause, he could not have anticipated, and even when the disinclination of both was broadly and plainly manifested, he could scarce bring himself to believe that two Saxons of royal descent should scruple, on personal grounds, at an alliance so necessary for the public weal of the nation. But it was no less certain: Rowena had always expressed her repugnance to Athelstane, and now Athelstane was no less plain and positive in proclaiming his resolution, never to pursue his addresses to the Lady Rowena. Even the natural obstinacy of Cedric sunk beneath these obstacles, where he, remaining on the point of junction, had the task of dragging a reluctant pair up to it, one with each hand. He made, however, a last vigorous attack on Athelstane, and he found that resuscitated sprout of Saxon royalty engaged, like country squires of our own day, in a furious war with the clergy.

It seems that, after all his deadly menaces against the Abbot of Saint Edmund's, Athelstane's spirit of revenge, what betwixt the natural indolent kindness of his own disposition, what with the prayers of his mother Edith, attached, like most ladies, (of the period) to the clerical order, had terminated in his keeping the Abbot and his monks in the dungeons of Coningsburgh for three days on a meagre diet. For this atrocity the Abbot menaced him with excommunication, and made out a dreadful list of complaints in the bowels and stomach, suffered by himself and his monks, in consequence of the tyrannical and unjust imprisonment they had sustained. With this controversy, and with the means he had adopted to counteract this clerical persecution, Cedric found the mind of his friend Athelstane so fully occupied, that it had no room for another idea. And when Rowena's name was mentioned, the noble Athelstane prayed leave to quaff a full goblet to her health, and that she might soon be the bride of his kinsman Wilfred. It was a desperate case therefore. There was obviously no more to be made of Athelstane; or, as Wamba expressed it, in a phrase which has descended from Saxon times to ours, he was "a cock which would not fight."

There remained betwixt Cedric and the determination to which the lovers desired he should come to, only two obstacles—his own obstinacy, and his dislike of the Norman dynasty. The former feeling gradually gave way before the endearments of his ward, and the pride which he could not help nourishing in the fame of his son. Besides, he was not insensible to the honour of allying his own line to that of Alfred, when the superior claims of the descendant of Edward the Confessor were abandoned for ever. Cedric's aversion to the Norman race of kings was also much undermined,—first, by consideration of the impossibility of ridding England of the new dynasty, a feeling which goes far to create loyalty in the subject; and, secondly, by the personal attentions of King Richard, who delighted in the blunt humour of Cedric, and, to use the language of the Wardour Manuscript, "so dealt with the noble Saxon, that, ere he had been a guest at court for seven days, he had given his consent to the marriage of his ward Rowena and his son Wilfred of Ivanhoe."

The nuptials of our hero, thus finally approved by his father, were celebrated in the most august of temples, the noble Minster of York. The King himself attended, and from the countenance which he afforded on this and other occasions to the distressed and hitherto degraded Saxons, gave them a safer and more certain prospect of attaining their just rights, than they could have rationally hoped from the precarious chance of civil war. The Church gave her full solemnities, graced with all the splendour which She of Rome knows how to apply with such brilliant effect.

Gurth, gallantly apparelled, attended as esquire upon the young master whom he had served so faithfully, and the magnanimous Wamba, decorated with a new cap and a most gorgeous set of silver bells. Sharers of Wilfred's dangers and adversity, they remained, as they had a right to expect, the partakers of his more prosperous career.

But besides this domestic attendance, these distinguished nuptials were celebrated by the attendance of the high-born Normans, as well as Saxons, joined with the universal jubilee of the lower orders, that marked the marriage of two individuals as a type of the future peace and harmony betwixt two races, which, since that period, have been so completely mingled, that the distinction has become utterly invisible. Cedric lived to see this union approximate toward its completion; for as the two nations mixed in society and formed intermarriages with each other, the Normans abated their scorn, and the Saxons were refined from their rusticity. But it was not until the reign of Edward the Third that the mixed language, now termed English, was spoken at the court of London, and that the hostile distinction of Norman and Saxon seems entirely to have disappeared.

It was upon the second morning after this happy bridal, that the Lady Rowena was made acquainted by her hand-maid Elgitha, that a damsel desired admission to her presence, and solicited that their parley might be without witness. Rowena wondered, hesitated, became curious, and ended by commanding the damsel to be admitted, and her attendants to withdraw.

She entered—a noble and commanding figure, the long white veil in which she was shrouded, overshadowing rather than concealing the elegance and majesty of her shape. Her demeanour was that of respect, unmingled by the least shade either of fear, or of a wish to propitiate favour. Rowena, however full of her own rank, was ever ready to acknowledge the claims, and attend to the feelings of others. She arose, and would have conducted the lovely stranger to a seat, but she looked at Elgitha, and again intimated a wish to discourse with the Lady Rowena alone. Elgitha had no sooner retired with unwilling steps, than, to the surprise of the Lady of Ivanhoe, her fair visitant kneeled on one knee, pressed her hands to her forehead, and bending her head to the ground, in spite of Rowena's resistance, kissed the embroidered hem of her tunic.

"What means this?" said the surprised bride; "or why do you offer to me a deference so unusual?"

"Because to you, Lady of Ivanhoe," said Rebecca, rising up and resuming the usual quiet dignity of her manner, "I may lawfully, and without rebuke, pay the debt of gratitude which I owe to Wilfred of Ivanhoe. I am—forgive the boldness which has offered to you the homage of my country—I am the unhappy Jewess, for whom your husband hazarded his life against such fearful odds in the tilt-yard at Templestowe."

"Damsel," said Rowena, "Wilfred of Ivanhoe on that day rendered back but in slight measure your unceasing charity towards him in his wounds and misfortunes. Speak, is there aught remains in which he and I can serve thee?"

"Nothing," said Rebecca, calmly, "unless you will transmit to him my grateful farewell."

"You leave England, then," said Rowena, scarce recovering the surprise of this extraordinary visit.

"I leave it, lady, ere this moon again changes. My father hath a brother high in favour with Mohammed Boabdil, King of Grenada—thither we go, secure of peace and protection, for the payment of such ransom as the Moslem exact from our people."

"And are you not then as well protected in England?" said Rowena. "My husband has favour with the King—the King himself is just and generous."

"Lady," said Rebecca, "I doubt it not—but the people of England are a fierce race, quarreling ever with their neighbours or among themselves, and ready to plunge the sword into the bowels of each other. Such is no safe abode for the children of my people. Ephraim is an heartless dove—Issachar an over-laboured drudge, which stoops between two burthens. Not in a land of war and blood, surrounded by hostile neighbours, and distracted by internal factions, can Israel hope to rest during her wanderings."

"But you, maiden," said Rowena—"you surely can have nothing to fear. She who nursed the sick-bed of Ivanhoe," she continued, rising with enthusiasm—"she can have nothing to fear in England, where Saxon and Norman will contend who shall most do her honour."

"Thy speech is fair, lady," said Rebecca, "and thy purpose fairer; but it may not be—there is a gulph betwixt us. Our breeding, our faith, alike forbid either to pass over it. Farewell—yet, ere I go, indulge me one request. The bridal-veil hangs over thy face; raise it, and let me see the features of which fame speaks so highly."

"They are scarce worthy of being looked upon," said Rowena; "but, expecting the same from my visitant, I remove the veil."

She took it off accordingly, and partly from the consciousness of beauty, partly from bashfulness, she blushed so intensely, that cheek, brow, neck, and bosom, were suffused with crimson. Rebecca blushed also, but it was a momentary feeling; and, mastered by higher emotions, past slowly from her features like the crimson cloud, which changes colour when the sun sinks beneath the horizon.

"Lady," she said, "the countenance you have deigned to shew me will long dwell in my remembrance. There reigns in it gentleness and goodness; and if a tinge of the world's pride or vanities may mix with an expression so lovely, how may we chide that which is of earth for bearing some colour of its original? Long, long will I remember your features, and bless God that I leave my noble deliverer united with"——

She stopped short—her eyes filled with tears. She hastily wiped them, and answered to the anxious enquiries of Rowena—"I am well, lady—well. But my heart swells when I think of Torquilstone and the lists at Templestowe.—Farewell. One, the most trifling part of my duty, remains undischarged. Accept this casket—startle not at its contents."

Rowena opened the small silver-chased casket, and perceived a carcanet, or necklace, with ear-jewels, of diamonds, which were visibly of immense value.

"It is impossible," she said, tendering back the casket. "I dare not accept a gift of such consequence."

"Yet keep it, lady," returned Rebecca.—"You have power, rank, command, and influence; we have wealth, the source alike of our strength and weakness. The value of these toys, ten times multiplied, would not influence half so much as your slightest wish. To you, therefore, the gift is of little value—and to me, what I part with is of much less. Let me not think you deem so wretchedly ill of my nation as your commons believe. Think ye that I prize these sparkling fragments of stone above my liberty? or that my father values them in comparison to the honour of his only child? Accept them, lady—to me they are valueless. I will never wear jewels more."

"You are then unhappy," said Rowena, struck with the manner in which Rebecca uttered the last words. "O, remain with us—the counsel of holy men will wean you from your unhappy law, and I will be a sister to you."

"No, lady," answered Rebecca, the same calm melancholy reigning in her soft voice and beautiful features—"that may not be. I may not change the faith of my fathers like a garment unsuited to the climate in which I seek to dwell, and unhappy, lady, I will not be. He, to whom I dedicate my future life, will be my comforter, if I do His will."

"Have you then convents, to one of which you mean to retire?" asked Rowena.

"No, lady," said the Jewess; "but among our people, since the time of Abraham downward, have been women who have devoted their thoughts to Heaven, and their actions to works of kindness to men, tending the sick, feeding the hungry, and relieving the distressed. Among these will Rebecca be numbered. Say this to thy lord, should he enquire after the fate of her whose life he saved."

There was an involuntary tremor in Rebecca's voice, and a tenderness of accent, which perhaps betrayed more than she would willingly have expressed. She hastened to bid Rowena adieu.

"Farewell," she said. "May He, who made both Jew and Christian, shower down on you his choicest blessings! The bark that wafts us hence will be under weigh ere we can reach the port."

She glided from the apartment, leaving Rowena surprised as if a vision had passed before her. The fair Saxon related the singular conference to her husband, on whose mind it made a deep impression. He lived long and happily with Rowena, for they were attached to each other by the bonds of early affection, and they loved each other the more, from recollection of the obstacles which had impeded their union. Yet it would be enquiring too curiously to ask, whether the recollection of Rebecca's beauty and magnanimity did not recur to his mind more frequently than the fair descendant of Alfred might altogether have approved.

Ivanhoe distinguished himself in the service of Richard, and was graced with farther marks of the royal favour. He might have risen still higher, but for the premature death of the heroic Cœur de Lion, before the Castle of Chaluz, near Limoges. With the life of that generous, but rash and romantic monarch, perished all the projects which his ambition and his generosity had formed; and to him may be applied, with a slight alteration, the lines composed by Johnson for Charles of Sweden—

> His fate was destined to a "foreign" strand,
> A petty fortress and a "humble" hand;
> He left the name at which the world grew pale,
> To point a moral, or adorn a TALE.

THE END

HISTORICAL NOTE

Historical Setting. Despite Scott's informing us very early in the novel that it is set 'towards the end of the reign of Richard I.' (15.31) it is quite clearly set in the very middle of his ten year reign (1189–99), in 1194, the year of his return to England. Richard left England almost immediately after succeeding to the throne and in 1190 embarked on the Third Crusade along with the French King, Philip Augustus. Their combined force recaptured Acre but Richard's relations with Philip deteriorated badly and Philip returned to France later in the same year and began plotting against Richard. Richard scored some major victories in Palestine but was unable to fulfil the Crusaders' main goal, the retaking of Jerusalem from Saladin, although he and his army reached Beit-Nuba, only twelve miles from the city. After receiving news that his brother John was undermining his position at home Richard concluded a truce with Saladin which left the coastal strip in Christian hands and allowed Christians and Muslims free passage through the whole of Palestine. He sailed for England in October 1192 but storms and a shipwreck forced him to change his route. Trying to cross Germany in disguise he was recognised and arrested near Vienna and imprisoned by Leopold, Duke of Austria. After payment of a large ransom to the emperor, Henry VI, he was finally freed in March 1194 and arrived in England later the same month. His long absence had allowed his brother John ample time to intrigue against him, latterly in league with Philip Augustus. Together they had offered the emperor bribes to keep Richard in prison but John had retreated to France when it became clear that Richard would indeed return. On Richard's arrival he found various castles holding out against him in John's name. The revolt was quickly crushed but Richard himself soon left to defend his French possessions, never to return to England. In France, not in England as Scott relates it, John sought his pardon and was generously forgiven.

Although *Ivanhoe* is set in the 1190s it looks both backwards to the time of the Norman Conquest in 1066 and the earlier Anglo-Saxon period and forwards to the time when Anglo-Saxons and Normans finally blended together in one race. Scott portrays a world divided between the dominant Norman ruling class and the conquered English only a few of whom have retained any prominent rank in society. The influential nineteenth-century historian Edward Freeman criticised Scott for painting a picture of late twelfth-century England in which 'there was a broadly marked line, recognized on both sides, between "Normans" and "Saxons"' and claimed that 'long before the twelfth century was out, the man of Norman descent born on English soil had learned to call himself an Englishman'[1] but the co-existence within the country of two languages (the Norman-French of the conquerors and the English of the conquered) along with memories of the Conquest itself must have kept alive some sense of two disparate races. On the other hand it might be argued that the ruling class, whether of English or Norman descent, had by the late twelfth century become French-speaking in language and Norman in attitude, but in this respect too Scott's picture is defensible: the few remaining prominent Anglo-Saxon families in *Ivanhoe* are already beginning to assimilate to Norman ways and Cedric the Saxon's insistence on preserving the purity of Anglo-Saxon customs is unusual amongst his contemporaries and not followed by his son. What is more problematic is Scott's portrayal of his 'Saxons' as preserving unchanged the clothing, hairstyles and eating habits of pre-Conquest England. In describing these features of Cedric and Rowena he drew closely on historians describing the customs of the Anglo-Saxons (see notes to 30.40, 44.4–6, 44.11–12, 44.14–18) although, interestingly, for his description of the clothing of the Saxon thrall Gurth he drew for some, but not all details, on Strutt's description of the dress of peasants of the Norman period (see notes to 18.13–23, 18.24). In the matter of religion, too, Scott is anachronistic in showing the Saxon Ulrica as a believer in the Germanic gods and even Cedric as naming his dog after the Norse god Balder. Finally, the tournament which plays such an important part in the first volume of the novel is more fourteenth-century than twelfth-century in character (see note to 30.34).

With his usual interest in linguistic matters Scott accurately describes the Saxons and Normans as speaking two separate languages but, with less justification, he sees the two languages, English and Norman-French, as already merging to form what he variously describes as 'the lingua Franca, or mixed language in which Norman and Saxon races conversed with each other' (27.9–10), although he does go on to say that 'it was not until the reign of Edward the Third that the mixed language, now termed English, was spoken at the court of London' (398.21–23). Some such lingua franca or pidgin may have existed (although we have no evidence of it) but it is not the origin of modern English which is more accurately described as a descendant of the English of the Anglo-Saxon period with a very strong admixture of French (and other) vocabulary. Moreover this invasion of French words, one case of which is so memorably described in Wamba's discussion of the names of animals in the field and on the table, mostly took place somewhat later, although it had begun in this period. On the other hand Scott is correct in asserting that the English language was not widely used at court until the fourteenth century.

Principal Historical Characters. The central characters of *Ivanhoe* are fictional, including Rowena and Athelstane, the supposed descendants of the Anglo-Saxon kings, but the historical Richard I and Prince John and the possibly historical Robin Hood play important subsidiary roles. Minor roles are also assigned to other historical characters, mostly members of the nobility, and these are discussed in the notes.

The portrait of Richard parallels in many respects the one offered by the historians of Scott's own time. Robert Henry (see note to 8.16) tells us that 'His understanding was excellent, his memory retentive, his imagination lively, and his courage so undaunted, that it procured him the surname of *Coeur de Lion*, or *the Lion-hearted*' and that 'In his conversation he was pleasant and facetious' but that 'though on some occasions he acted in a noble manner, especially to his prostrate enemies, he was in general haughty, cruel, covetous, passionate and sensual, an undutiful son, an unfaithful husband, and a most pernicious king, having by his long absence and continual wars, drained his English dominions both of men and money' (Henry, 3.163–4).[2] Scott softens or ignores some of Richard's vices but most of these characteristics are found in his portrait. However, he added another side of Richard drawn from literary sources. In his 1830 introduction he explained that the meeting of the disguised king with Friar Tuck was based on a medieval romance which relates a similar story of a 'King Edward' meeting a hermit (see note to 140.31). Beginning with the hint of this friendly encounter (narrated originally of another king), he expanded it to a whole picture of Richard as a ruler committed to the welfare of his English subjects and an upholder of their rights against Norman aggression. In fact, Richard seems to have been more interested in the Crusades and in his French possessions than in England and it is very probable that he was not fluent in English, if indeed he spoke it at all, as Scott more or less admitted in a Magnum note: having said that Richard could imitate both northern and southern French literature, he adds it is 'less likely that he should have been able to compose or sing an English ballad; yet so much do we wish to assimilate Him of the Lion Heart to the band of warriors whom he led, that the anachronism, if there be one, may readily be forgiven' (Magnum, 16.262). An alternative explanation is that Scott was influenced by David Hume's assertion that Richard 'seems to have been much beloved by his English subjects; and he is remarked to have been the first prince of the Norman line that bore any sincere regard to them'.[3] On the other hand the mixture of impetuous anger and generosity which Scott portrayed in his Richard is based on historical events and, if he sometimes adopts a more favourable view of Richard than historians like Henry, his attitude to him remains at best equivocal: in the end he sees him as fulfilling 'the brilliant, but useless character, of a knight of romance' and as more concerned with personal glory than with the good of his kingdom (365.14–19).

The almost totally unfavourable picture of John is more thoroughly in line with the view of him taken by Scott's contemporaries; Henry, for instance, has nothing good to say of John's character (Henry, 3.186–87). With John there was no favourable romance to counterbalance the condemnation of historians although here too Scott was influenced, though less strongly, by a literary text of a later period, in this case Shakespeare's *King John*. Scott consciously admits the debt by placing a motto from *King John* at the head of a chapter which parallels events in the play (294) and subconsciously perhaps by a tendency in the manuscript to refer to him as 'King' rather than 'Prince'. But he also works much actual historical detail into the text as in the dramatic scene where John receives Philip Augustus' message 'Take heed to yourself, for the devil is unchained' (see note to 119.41) or when he remembers John's liking for fine horses and hawks (see note to 71.8–10).

The historicity of Robin Hood is open to doubt but a case can certainly be made for his being a real historical figure.[4] As to the date at which he lived, the rule is perhaps *quot homines, tot sententiae* but Scott's placement of him in the late twelfth century agrees with the best scholarly opinion of his time as embodied in the work of Joseph Ritson and has recently received some new, though tentative, support (see note to 6.24).

Sources. In the Dedicatory Epistle to the novel Scott, speaking in the persona of Laurence Templeton, names some of his principal historical sources. Amongst his own contemporaries he names three historians, Robert Henry (see note to 8.16), Joseph Strutt (see note to 6.16) and Sharon Turner (see note to 8.17). Of these Strutt was the most important. From him Scott took details about Saxon and Norman dress and hair-styles, and tournaments (see note to 68.7–8). Also from Strutt, at least partly, came Gurth's collar, one of the best known details in the novel (see note to 18.39–43). The main evidence for metal collars being worn by slaves in the Anglo-Saxon period was Strutt's very questionable interpretation of a manuscript illustration but Scott accepted this striking symbol and worked it thoroughly into his story. In the fourth volume of Turner's history of the Anglo-Saxons, Scott found information about the beliefs of the pagan Anglo-Saxons, including a passage claiming, erroneously, that they and/or the continental Saxons worshipped the Slavonic god Czarnabog (see note to 193.40), and various Anglo-Saxon personal names (see notes to 38.10 and 325.41). Henry provided quotations from the Anglo-Saxon Chronicle (see note to 192.12), erroneous information about the abusive term *nidering* (see note to 130.5) and details (not always correct) about Anglo-Saxon and Norman money (see notes to 53.20, 181.36, 337.12). Either Henry or Strutt could have been the source for the inaccurate information that English Jews were obliged to wear yellow caps (see note to 47.31–33).

Another, somewhat earlier, historian that Scott may have used is Richard Verstegan although he is not mentioned in the Dedicatory Epistle. Scott owned a copy of Verstegan's quaintly named *A Restitution of Decayed Intelligence*, first published in 1628, but Verstegan was pillaged by later writers and Scott could, for instance, have read full versions of the story of Rowena in both Verstegan and Strutt (see note to 29.14). He may, however, be Scott's source for Hengist's white horse standard (see note to 369.5–6).

Scott (via Templeton) mentions only two medieval historical sources in the Dedicatory Epistle, 'Ingulphus' (see note to 12.20–21) and 'Geoffrey de Vinsauf', that is, the *Itinerarium Peregrinorum et Gesta Regis Ricardi* (see note to 12.21–22). No evidence of Scott's use of Ingulf has been found, and, even if some of Scott's information about the Third Crusade may ultimately come from the *Itinerarium*, there is nothing which is not also mentioned in other sources (see, however, note to 363.37–38). Scott had other medieval sources in his library, including Matthew Paris, Roger de Hoveden, and William of Malmesbury but here again there is no irrefutable evidence of Scott going directly to these original sources in writing *Ivanhoe*. The novel does include the mistake about *nidering* which demonstrably comes ultimately from the edition of William of Malmesbury which Scott actually possessed but the same mistake is repeated in Henry (see note to 130.5). Similarly the story about the devil being unchained is told by Hoveden but Scott's wording again suggests that Henry is his source (see note to 119.41). There is, however, one clear case where Scott uses a contemporary original source and that is the Templar Rule, which dates from the early twelfth century (see note to 304.39), and is his major source of information on the Templars. In a footnote (321) he refers his readers to the works of St Bernard for a copy of the Rule but his own source clearly was *The Theatre of Honour and Knight-Hood* (1623), translated from the French of André Favine (see list of often-cited works, 503). This book offered him information about the significance of their standard, Beau-Seant, which is followed almost word for word in Scott's footnote on the subject (see note to 112.6). The only text commonly printed in St Bernard's works that may have had an influence on the novel is *De Laude Novae Militiae*, a tract in praise of the Templars which could have suggested to Scott the use of a particular biblical text by the Grand Master (see note to 305.17). Yet if Scott made good and proper use of these contemporary documents, his picture of the Templars is also strongly influenced by the accusations made against them at the time of their dissolution more than a hundred years later (see note to 201.42–43). From all of this it will be evident that Scott had access (direct or indirect) to some reasonably reliable historical sources.

In the fourteenth-century *Richard Coeur de Lion* (see 8.35–37) he was dealing with a text of a quite different nature. This is an out-and-out romance including such absurdities as portraying Richard as a cannibal, a practice which the writer seems to consider as perfectly admirable behaviour. Rejecting such ridiculous material as this, Scott nevertheless took from this romance the idea for the interchange of blows between Richard and Friar Tuck, as he pointed out in a note to the Magnum (17.170), and some names for the tournament at Acre in which Ivanhoe had distinguished himself (see notes to 50.43, 51.1, 51.3, 51.8).

Scott found much of interest in such sources as these but he did not have for the twelfth century the kind of intimate knowledge of both spoken and written sources which he had been able to bring to his Scottish novels. While, as Jerome Mitchell has shown,[5] he was widely read in those medieval romances which were available to him, they did not always contain what Laurence Templeton calls 'All those minute circumstances belonging to private life and domestic character, all that gives verisimilitude to a narrative and individuality to the persons introduced' (6.39–41). Furthermore they all dated from later than the twelfth century. Chaucer, of course, did provide some of these 'minute circumstances' but he, too, belonged to a later period than the novel's setting. This difficulty Scott surmounted by the simple expedient of having Laurence Templeton offer the disarming admission that 'it is extremely probable that I may have confused the manners of two or three centuries, and introduced, during the reign of Richard the First, circumstances appropriated to a period either considerably earlier, or a good deal later than that era' (12.8–12). Here the first edition actually reads 'Richard the Second'; while clearly a mistake, it may represent a subconscious recognition of the importance, as a source for his novel, of Chaucer, a poet of Richard II's reign. Indeed, the opening chapters could well be called Scott's General Prologue, not only because they introduce most of the main characters of the novel but because of their debt to Chaucer. Scott has taken hints for his Prior or Abbot (he uses both titles) Aymer from the Monk (see note to 23.22–23) and models his picture of the 'yeoman' Locksley on Chaucer's Yeoman (see note to 70.5). Scott's Friar Tuck also owes something to Chaucer's Monk. Moreover there is a sense in which Chaucer's Knight, who had also been on Crusades, was an antitype for that very different crusader, Brian de Bois-Guilbert. Chaucer's 'Knight's Tale' is quoted, in Dryden's version, at the beginning of the description of the tournament at Ashby-de-la-Zouche and seems to have contributed to Scott's conception of what a tournament was like. Numerous other smaller historical and linguistic features attest to Chaucer's influence throughout the book.

The other major literary influence is Shakespeare, always prominent in Scott's work: he is even more remote from the twelfth century than Chaucer but *The Merchant of Venice* offers hints for the portrayal of Isaac the Jew (see note to 53.13, 53.24–25, 98.27), and the Old Testament in the Authorised Version is an even greater influence on Isaac's language. Scott also drew on the Bible, both in Latin and English, for other characters, this being one of his traditional sources that it was appropriate to carry over from the Scottish novels. He took a number of small details, mainly about tournaments, from French literature, particularly the fifteenth-century romance *Jehan de Saintré*, a work which he had referred to in his 'Essay on Chivalry' (*Prose Works*, 6.7–9, 29–32, 40–41). A rather different kind of literary resource to Chaucer and Shakespeare are the ballads and specifically the Robin Hood ballads. As well as general information about Robin Hood's life, Scott found in the ballad 'Robin Hood and Allen a Dale' hints for his portrait of Allan-a-Dale at the trial by combat (see note to 148.21–22) and took the description of Friar Tuck as a 'curtal friar' from 'Robin Hood and the Curtal Friar' (see note to 361.14). Both these occur in Joseph Ritson's collection of Robin Hood material and from Ritson's editorial matter Scott seems to have taken up the notion of Robin as a king in his own domains (see note to 272.8–9).

The picture of twelfth-century England in *Ivanhoe* is accurate in many respects and inaccurate in others. But it is a remarkably vivid narrative, that draws upon the whole range of imaginative and historical sources open to an author in the early nineteenth century. It reveals once more that in the exploration of the past Walter Scott is monarch in these glades: 'they are my kingdom; and these my wild subjects would reck but little of my power, were I, within mine own dominions, to yield place to mortal man'.[6]

NOTES

1 *The History of the Norman Conquest*, 6 vols (Oxford, 1867–79), 5.825.
2 For the abbreviated forms of reference used here see 502–04.
3 *The History of England*, 8 vols (Edinburgh, 1810), 2.35.
4 The number of books on Robin Hood is legion, but a convenient starting point (especially for those interested in the literary development of the story) is R. B. Dobson and J. Taylor, *Rymes of Robyn Hood: An Introduction to the English Outlaw* (London and Pittsburgh, 1976; reprinted with a new foreword, Gloucester and Wolfboro, 1989). It contains an edition of most of the Robin Hood material known to Scott.
5 See *Scott, Chaucer, and Medieval Romance* (Lexington, 1987).
6 *Ivanhoe*, 272.9–11.

EXPLANATORY NOTES

In these notes a comprehensive attempt is made to identify Scott's sources, and all quotations, references, historical events, and historical personages, to explain proverbs, and to translate difficult or obscure language. (Phrases are explained in the notes while single words are treated in the glossary.) When a quotation has not been traced this is stated: any new information from readers will be welcomed. When quotations reproduce their sources accurately, the reference is given without comment; verbal differences in the source are indicated by a prefatory 'see'. References are to standard editions or to the editions Scott himself owned. For Scott's novels a reference is given to the EEWN text by page and line number where possible, and otherwise to the volume, page and line numbers of the first edition. Books in the Abbotsford Library are identified by reference to the appropriate page of the *Catalogue of the Library at Abbotsford* (*CLA*), preceded by the word 'see' if Scott had a different edition to the one cited. Biblical quotations, unless otherwise stated, are from the Authorised Version. Plays by Shakespeare are cited without authorial ascription and references are to *William Shakespeare: The Complete Works*, edited by Peter Alexander (London and Glasgow, 1951, frequently reprinted).

The following publications are distinguished by abbreviations, or are given without the names of their authors, in the notes and essays:

AV The Authorised Version, or King James Bible (1611).

Berners's Froissart Jean Froissart, *Cronycles*, trans. John Bourchier, Lord Berners, 2 vols (London, 1523–25); see *CLA*, 29.

The Canterbury Tales Geoffrey Chaucer, *The Canterbury Tales* (written *c.* 1387–1400), in *The Riverside Chaucer*, 3rd edn, ed. Larry D. Benson (Oxford, 1988); see *CLA*, 42, 154, 155, 172, 239.

Child Francis James Child, *The English and Scottish Popular Ballads*, 5 vols (Boston and New York, 1882–98)

CLA [J. G. Cochrane], *Catalogue of the Library at Abbotsford* (Edinburgh, 1838).

de Curzon Henri de Curzon, *La Règle du Temple* (Paris, 1886). This work contains both the original Rule of the Templars and the supplementary rules: see Rule below.

Dress and Habits Joseph Strutt, *A Complete View of the Dress and Habits of the People of England*, 2 vols (London, 1796–99); *CLA*, 154.

Du Cange Charles de Fresne, Seigneur Du Cange, *Glossarium Mediae et Infimae Latinitatis*, 10 vols (Niort, 1883–87); Scott's edition 6 vols, Paris, 1733–36: *CLA*, 251.

Ellis George Ellis, *Specimens of Early English Metrical Romances*, 3 vols (London, 1805); *CLA*, 105.

Favine Andrew Favine, *The Theater of Honour and Knight-Hood*, 2 vols in 1 (London, 1623). This work was originally written in French by Favine, and published in Paris in 1619. It was probably translated into English by William Jaggard; *CLA*, 270.

Henry Robert Henry, *The History of Great Britain, from the First Invasion of it by the Romans under Julius Caesar*, 6 vols (London, 1771–93); see *CLA*, 28.

Horda Joseph Strutt, *Horda Angel-cynnan*, 3 vols (London, 1775–76); *CLA*, 154.

Hoveden Roger of Hoveden, *Chronica Magistri Rogeri de Houedene*, ed. William Stubbs, 4 vols (London, 1868–71); see *CLA*, 27.

Itinerarium *Itinerarium Peregrinorum et Gesta Regis Ricardi* in *Chronicles and Memorials of the Reign of Richard I*, ed. William Stubbs, 2 vols (London, 1864–65); see *CLA*, 27.

Jehan de Saintré Antoine de la Sale, *Jehan de Saintré*, ed. Jean Misrahi and Charles A. Knudson (Geneva, 1965).

Journal *The Journal of Sir Walter Scott*, ed. W. E. K. Anderson (Oxford, 1972).

Letters *The Letters of Sir Walter Scott*, ed. H. J. C. Grierson and others, 12 vols (London, 1932–37).

Lockhart J. G. Lockhart, *Memoirs of the Life of Sir Walter Scott, Bart.*, 7 vols (Edinburgh, 1837).

Magnum *Waverley Novels*, 48 vols (Edinburgh, 1829–33).

Morte D'Arthur Sir Thomas Malory, *Le Morte D'Arthur*, 2 vols (London, 1906); see *CLA*, 275. This edition derives, like any edition Scott would have used, from Caxton's edition, rather than the standard modern text edited by Vinaver which is based on the original manuscript, but, for easy reference to Vinaver, Caxton's book and chapter numbers are given as they are included in Vinaver's text.

ODEP *The Oxford Dictionary of English Proverbs*, 3rd edn, rev. F. P. Wilson (Oxford, 1977).

ODECN *The Oxford Dictionary of English Christian Names*, 3rd edn, ed. E. G. Withycombe (Oxford, 1970).

OED *The Oxford English Dictionary*, 2nd edn, ed. J. A. Simpson and E. S. C. Weiner, 20 vols (Oxford, 1989).

Percy Thomas Percy, *Reliques of Ancient English Poetry*, 3 vols (London, 1765); see *CLA*, 172.

Poetical Works *The Poetical Works of Sir Walter Scott, Bart.*, ed. J. G. Lockhart, 12 vols (Edinburgh, 1833–34).

Proofs The surviving proofs of *Ivanhoe*; NLS MS 3401.

Prose Works *The Prose Works of Sir Walter Scott, Bart.*, 28 vols (Edinburgh, 1834–36).

Rule The original Rule of the Templars in its Latin form. The rules of the Templars fall into two parts. Scott had access to the original Rule in Favine's *Theater of Honour and Knight-Hood* (see above), which contains a late 12th-century Latin version (Paris, Bibliothèque Nationale, MS 15045), the only Latin version known in Scott's time. This appears as *Regulae Pauperum Commilitonum Templi* (Rules of the Poor Military Brotherhood of the Temple) on unnumbered pages between 2.406–07 in Favine, and is cited as Rule. An English translation follows, also on the unnumbered pages; it is not clear whether the translation (probably by William Jaggard: see Favine, above) is directly of the Latin text, or of Favine's translation of the Latin text into French. The Templar Rule as translated into English in the English version of Favine is cited as 'Rule in English'. There was a further set of supplementary rules in French, which are included in de Curzon (see above), but there is no evidence that Scott had direct knowledge of them.

Ritson Joseph Ritson, *Robin Hood: A Collection of All the Ancient Poems, Songs, and Ballads*, 2 vols (London, 1795): *CLA*, 174.

Rymes of Robyn Hood R. B. Dobson and J. Taylor, *Rymes of Robyn Hood: An Introduction to the English Outlaw* (Gloucester, 1989).

Sports and Pastimes Joseph Strutt, *Sports and Pastimes of the People of England* (London, 1801); *CLA*, 154.

Turner Sharon Turner, *The History of the Anglo-Saxons*, 4 vols (London, 1799–1805); see *CLA*, 235.

Vulgate *Biblia Sacra juxta Vulgatum Clementinam* (Rome, 1927). The Vulgate Latin version of the Bible.

William of Malmesbury William of Malmesbury, *De Gestis Regum Anglorum*, ed. William Stubbs, 2 vols (London, 1887–89); see *CLA*, 27.

In compiling these notes the following editions have been particularly helpful: the World's Classics edition of *Ivanhoe*, ed. Ian Duncan (Oxford, 1996); Penguin English Library edition, ed. A. N. Wilson (Harmondsworth, 1982); The Dryburgh Edition, 25 vols (London, 1892–94), Vol. 9; The Border Edition, ed. Andrew Lang, 24 vols (London, 1898–99), Vol. 9. Information has also come from: Jerome Mitchell, *Scott, Chaucer, and Medieval Romance* (Lexington, 1987); James Anderson, *Sir Walter Scott and History* (Edinburgh, 1981); Patricia Christine Hodgell, *The Nonsense of Ancient Days: Sources of Scott's 'Ivanhoe'* (Unpublished PhD dissertation, University of Minnesota, 1987). Roland Abramczyk's *Über die Quellen zu Walter Scotts Roman 'Ivanhoe'* (Leipzig, 1903), though full of inaccuracies, has also been useful.

Title page motto Matthew Prior, 'The Thief and the Cordelier' (1718), lines 23–24. Scott added a footnote in the Magnum explaining that the motto 'alludes to the Author returning to the stage repeatedly after having taken leave'.

5.3 Dr Dryasdust fictitious antiquary who appears first in *The Antiquary* (1816: EEWN 3, 282.2), is the addressee in the 'Introductory Epistle' to *The Fortunes of Nigel* (1822), and is the nominal author of the 'Prefatory Letter' to *Peveril of the Peak* (1822), and of the 'Conclusion' to *Redgauntlet* (1824: EEWN 17, 378–80).

5.3 F.A.S. Fellow of the Antiquarian Society, now generally known as the Society of Antiquaries, founded in 1717.

5.13–14 Horn of King Ulphus . . . Lands bestowed ivory drinking horn, presented to York Minster before 1042, and still preserved there as a token of a large gift of land by the 11th-century thegn Ulf. Made of ivory, it was probably produced by Islamic artisans in Sicily or Southern Italy. Its story is told in William Camden's *Britannia* (ed. Richard Gough, 4 vols (London, 1806), 3.306), and it is mentioned in *The Antiquary* (EEWN 3, 281.42–43).

5.14–15 patrimony of St Peter historically, a name for the Papal States, the territory ruled by the Pope in Italy; more generally, the material wealth and estates of the Church. In this case, it refers specifically to the lands given by Ulf to the cathedral in York which was dedicated to St Peter.

5.18 Detur digniori *Latin* let it be given to the worthier one.

5.29 Mr Oldbuck of Monkbarns the antiquary in Scott's novel *The Antiquary* (1816), who describes Dr Dryasdust as 'a literary friend at York, with whom I have long corresponded on the subject of the Saxon horn that is preserved in the Minster there' (EEWN 3, 281.41–42).

5.36 M'Pherson James Macpherson (1736–96) who published between 1760 and 1763 what he claimed to be translations of ancient Gaelic poetry by Ossian. There was much controversy at the time about their authenticity but it is now clear that they were partly based on Gaelic tradition but with much extra material of Macpherson's own.

6.6–7 as simple and as patriarchal . . . Iroquois the Mohawks were one of the five original tribes which made up the League of the Iroquois. They fought as allies of the English against the French in the 17th century, and in the American Revolution also sided with the British. Their social organisation was not, in fact, patriarchal but Scott perhaps uses the word to mean 'characteristic of ancient times, as in the time of the biblical Patriarchs'.

6.12–13 Queen Anne Queen of Great Britain and Ireland 1702–14.

6.22 Kendal green green cloth of comparable quality to Lincoln Green (see note to 70.5), which was manufactured at Kendal in Westmorland but not until the 14th century. The term 'Kendal Green' first appears in the early 16th century and is associated with Robin Hood as early as the mid-17th century 'Playe of Robyn Hoode, verye proper to be played in Maye Games', known to Scott from Ritson (2.192–203). See also *1 Henry IV*, 2.4.225.

6.24 Robin Hood opinions vary as to the date and location of the English outlaw Robin Hood. Scott possessed a chapbook entitled 'A True Tale of Robin Hood . . . who lived and died A.D. 1198'. According to Joseph Ritson (1752–1803), the outlaw was born in about 1160 (Ritson, 1.iv, xvi). In giving this date Ritson was following John Major, writing in 1521, who believed that Robin flourished in the reign of Richard I (*Historia Majoris Britanniae*, ed. R. Freebairn (Edinburgh, 1740), 128). Dobson and Taylor in their original 1976 introduction to their edition of the Robin Hood ballads claimed that there was no evidence whatever for this dating (*Rymes of Robyn Hood*, 16) but their 1989 Foreword to a new edition suggests that a recently discovered reference ('Willelmi Robehod fugitivi') in Berkshire in 1262 may render a late 12th-century date just conceivable (*Rymes*, xxi–ii). See also note to 121.20.

6.24–25 if duly conjured with, should raise a spirit see *Julius Caesar*, 1.2.146–47: 'Conjure with 'em:/ "Brutus" will start a spirit as soon as "Caesar"'.

6.25 Rob Roy Rob Roy MacGregor (1671–1734), famous Scottish outlaw and a central character in Scott's *Rob Roy* (1818).

6.27 Bruces and Wallaces Scottish heroes. Robert Bruce (1274–1329) was one of those who fought to free Scotland from English conquest. He was inaugurated as King of Scots in 1306, was forced into exile, but slowly regained power and defeated the English at Bannockburn in 1314. Sir William Wallace (*c.* 1270–1305), was in 1297–98 the first champion of the Scottish people in their struggle for independence. He was captured by the English in 1305, taken to London and executed.

6.31–32 patriotic Syrian . . . all the rivers of Israel! Naaman; see 2 Kings 5.12.

7.7 Scottish magician Scott, referred to in the satirical 'Chaldee MS' by James Hogg and others as 'the great magician who dwelleth in the old fastness, hard by the river Jordan, which is by the Border' (*Blackwood's Edinburgh Magazine*, 2 (October 1817), 91); he was called 'The Wizard' in 1820 and the 'wizard of Abbotsford' in 1821 (*Memoir and Correspondence of Mrs Grant of Laggan*, 3 vols (London, 1844), 2.274, 289) and 'The Wizard of the North' (*The Literary Gazette* (14 July 1821), 444).

7.7 Lucan's witch in the *Pharsalia* by Lucan (AD 39–65), Pompey consults the Thessalian witch Erictho, who brings to life a corpse chosen from the battle-field (see note to 7.14–16).

7.14–16 gelidas . . . in corpore quærit *Latin* 'prying into the inmost parts cold in death, till she finds the substance of the stiffened lungs unwounded and still firm, and seeking the power of utterance in a corpse': Lucan, *Pharsalia*, 6.629–31, trans. J. D. Duff (London, 1928), 351.

7.18 Northern Warlock see note to 7.7.

7.20–21 nothing was to be found . . . Jehoshaphat for the vision of the valley of dry bones see Ezekiel 37.1–14. For 'valley of Jehoshaphat' see Joel 3.12: 'Let the heathen be wakened, and come up to the valley of Jehoshaphat: for there will I sit to judge all the heathen round about'. Scott has conflated the two passages.

7.43 hinds here used in the Scottish and northern English sense of a skilled farm-worker who played a responsible part in running the farm. Elsewhere in the novel it means an ordinary farm-worker, a servant, or, used abusively, a boor.

8.12–13 vie privée *French* private life.

8.16 Dr Henry Rev. Dr Robert Henry (1718–90), author of *The History of Great Britain, from the Invasion of it by the Romans under Julius Caesar* (1771–93); he laid strong emphasis on social aspects of history. Scott owned his work (*CLA*, 28) and used it extensively in *Ivanhoe.*

8.16 Mr Strutt Joseph Strutt (1749–1802), author, antiquary, artist and engraver, who wrote *Horda Angel-cynnan or a Compleat View of the Manners, Customs, Arms, Habits etc. of the Inhabitants of England* (1775–76: *CLA*, 154), *Dress and Habits of the People of England* (1796–99: *CLA*, 154) and *Sports and Pastimes of the People of England* (1801: *CLA*, 154). His works contributed many social history details to *Ivanhoe.*

8.17 Mr Sharon Turner (1768–1847), author of *The History of the Anglo-Saxons from the Earliest Period to the Norman Conquest* (1799–1805), an important source of background material for *Ivanhoe,* in particular the fourth volume which deals with social history. In 1805 Scott had written to Turner's publishers, Longman's, that the '4th volume of Turners history is come safe and gave me great pleasure' (*Letters*, 1.270) although the Abbotsford library catalogue includes only a copy of the 1821 edition (*CLA*, 235).

8.34 Horace Walpole . . . goblin tale Horace Walpole (1717–97) wrote the Gothic novel *The Castle of Otranto* (1765).

8.35–37 George Ellis . . . Abridgement of the Ancient Metrical Romances George Ellis (1753–1815), was a friend of Scott's. His *Specimens of Early English Metrical Romances* (3 vols, London, 1805: *CLA*, 105) combines excerpts from the texts with summaries of the stories and includes the 14th-century romance *Richard Coeur de Lion* (2.171–279) on which Scott drew in writing *Ivanhoe.*

9.8–9 Caxton or Wynken de Worde William Caxton (1422–91), the first English printer and Jan van Wynkyn, nicknamed Wynkyn de Worde (d. 1534 or 1535), apprenticed to Caxton and later a successful printer in his own right.

9.14 Mr Galland's first translation of the Arabian Tales *The Arabian Nights' Entertainments, or The Thousand and One Nights*, a collection of tales from Arabic, Indian and Persian sources, was first made known in Europe by Antoine Galland between 1704 and 1717 in a free rendering of the oldest known manuscript (1548), and aroused considerable interest. Scott possessed reprints of some of Galland's translations (*CLA*, 44).

9.33 Mr Strutt . . . Queen-Hoo-Hall Strutt's unfinished novel, set in the 15th century in the time of Henry VI, was completed by Scott and published in 1808. In his General Preface to the Waverley Novels, Scott says that *Queen-Hoo Hall* was written 'to illustrate the manners, customs, and language of the people of England during that period', but that its lack of success was due to Strutt's 'rendering his language too ancient, and displaying his antiquarian knowledge too liberally' (Magnum, 1.xv–xvi).

10.3 Chaucer Geoffrey Chaucer (*c.* 1340–1400). Scott possessed various copies of his works (*CLA*, 41, 154, 155, 172, 239).

10.13 well of English undefiled Edmund Spenser, *The Faerie Queene*, Bk 4 (1596), Canto 2, stanza 32. The reference is to Chaucer.

10.15 the age of Cressy and of Poictiers at Crécy (1346) and at Poitiers (1356) the English defeated the French. Geoffrey Chaucer (*c.* 1340–1400) was too young to be writing in 1346 but until recent times was believed to have been born in 1328.

10.21 Chatterton Thomas Chatterton (1752–70) forged poems that he claimed to be by a 15th-century priest, Thomas Rowley. He largely took his vocabulary from words marked as 'O.' (old) in a dictionary.

10.38–41 they had "eyes, hands, organs . . . the same winter and summer" see *The Merchant of Venice*, 3.1.50–54.

11.26–27 cypress trees upon Inch-Merrin Inch-Murrin, or Inch-

Marrin, an island in Loch Lomond. The cypress tree requires a warm, temperate or sub-tropical climate.

11.27–28 **Persepolis** ancient ruined city of Persia, about 35 miles (56 kms) NE of Shiraz in SW Iran.

12.5 **keeping and costume** technical terms from painting: keeping is the maintenance of harmony between the parts and costume the appropriate fashions and customs for the period or place in which a work is set.

12.14 **modern Gothic** much 18th-century Gothic architecture was simply Gothic ornamentation, often of mixed styles, on buildings which were basically classical in conception. From about 1830 there was a greater demand for authenticity and adherence to the style of a chosen period of Gothic rather than mixing features from different periods.

12.20–21 **Ingulphus . . . Monk of Croydon** the *Historia Monasterii Croylandensis*, printed by Henry Savile (London, 1596: *CLA*, 27) and once attributed to Ingulf (d. 1109), abbot of Croyland in Lincolnshire, is now considered to be a forgery, probably compiled in the early 15th century. Scott's 'Croydon' is a mistake.

12.21–22 **Geoffrey de Vinsauff** Vinsauf (fl. 1190–1200) wrote the *Ars Poetica*, a treatise on the rules of poetical composition, which was very popular in the Middle Ages. Scott probably refers to *Itinerarium Peregrinorum et Gesta Regis Ricardi*, which gives an eye-witness account of Richard I's involvement in the Third Crusade, and was for long attributed to him (although he is not now thought to be the author). See *CLA*, 27, under 'Hist. Galfridi Vinesalvi', also cited in Henry under Vinsauf's name.

12.24 **Froissart** Jean Froissart (c. 1337–c. 1410) described by Scott as 'the most picturesque of historians' (*Letters*, 4.214). His *Chronicles* provide a history of the Hundred Years' War. Scott made particular use (e.g. see note to 80.31) of Lord Berners's translation of 1523–25 of which he owned a modern reprint (London, 1812: *CLA*, 29) but he also possessed the modern translation of Johnes (Hafod, 1803–05: *CLA*, 28).

12.27 **minstrel coronet** Du Cange quotes a passage about a silver crown given in 1367 to the king of the minstrels (Du Cange, under *ministelli*), a title given to the chief minstrel of the country (see W. Chappell, *Popular Music of the Olden Time*, 2 vols (London, 1859), 1.28–29). Originally the term *minstrel* referred to various kinds of entertainer but by Scott's time it was restricted to mean a medieval musician or singer who sang or recited poetry while playing an accompaniment on a stringed instrument.

12.28 **Bristol stones** rock-crystal, a cheap alternative to diamonds, found in the limestone at Clifton, near Bristol.

12.33 **Anglo-Norman MS. . . . Sir Arthur Wardour** Sir Arthur Wardour is a character in Scott's *The Antiquary* (1816), and the manuscript is, of course, fictitious.

12.40 **the Bannatyne MS.** celebrated manuscript collection of old Scottish poetry, compiled by the Edinburgh merchant George Bannatyne (1545–1608) in 1568.

12.40 **the Auchinleck MS.** manuscript dated about 1330 containing, among other items, a fragment of the metrical romance *Richard Coeur de Lion* (see note to 8.35–37). It had belonged to Lord Auchinleck, whose signature, with the date 1740, appears on the inside fly-leaf but by this time was in the Advocates' Library in Edinburgh (now the National Library of Scotland). Scott knew it well; he took the text for his edition of *Sir Tristrem* from it and included a catalogue of its contents in his introduction (see *Poetical Works*, 5.107–27).

13.1 **printer's devil** errand boy in a printing office, so called because of his being blackened by the printer's ink.

13.10–11 **the Wall . . . Habitancum** Hadrian's Wall, running from

Wallsend to Bowness, in the N of England, built in AD 122–28 to protect the Roman settlers from attack by the northern tribes. Habitancum (present-day Risingham, near the hamlet of West Woodburn in the N of Northumberland) was an outpost fort.

13.13 **Robin of Redesdale** the pseudonym of the leader of an uprising in Yorkshire in 1469. In Scott's day a rock near Risingham (see note above), carved with the figure of a hunter known as Robin of Redesdale, attracted so much public attention that the farmer on whose land it stood broke it into pieces and cut it up for gate-posts.

13.17 **fit of the stone** Scott himself had gall-stones at the time of writing *Ivanhoe*. However, this unfriendly thought probably refers to another painful kind of stone, as Scott wrote to J.B.S. Morritt in 1816 about the same incident, saying, 'I wish the fragments were in his bladder with all my heart' (*Letters*, 4.271).

13.19 **Tell this not in Gath** 2 Samuel 1.20.

13.21 **Arthur's oven** dome-shaped Roman building near Falkirk, Stirlingshire, demolished in 1743 by its owner, Sir Michael Bruce, who used its stones to repair a mill-dam. Its association with Arthur may have been due to the nearby Roman town of Camelon being thought to be Camlann, the site of King Arthur's last battle. It is also referred to in *Waverley* (1.109.17–22).

13.28–29 **Secretary to the Antiquarian Society** James Skene (1775–1864), Laird of Rubislaw, in Aberdeen, who was secretary to the Society of Antiquaries of Scotland, founded in 1780. A close friend of Scott's, he published *Sketches of the existing Localities alluded to in the Waverley Novels*, drawn and etched by himself (1829–31) in 21 volumes, simultaneously with the publication of the Magnum.

13.33 **besom of destruction** Isaiah 14.23.

13.33–14.1 **John Knox . . . Reformation** the protests of John Knox (*c.* 1512–72) and his followers against idolatry and corruption in the Church led to the rioting of 1559 in Perth when churches and monasteries were gutted, altars torn down, and ornamentation and images destroyed, and to the establishment of a Protestant state in Scotland in 1560.

13.36–37 **gentleman . . . post-office** Sir Francis Freeling (1764–1836), Secretary to the Post Office 1797–1836, member of the Roxburghe and Bannatyne clubs and a Fellow of the Society of Antiquaries. Scott's correspondence includes a number of references to Freeling's generosity in franking (allowing free carriage) of letters for Scott and his friends (see A. R. B. Haldane, *Three Centuries of Scottish Posts* (Edinburgh, 1971), 244–45).

14.1 **vale tandem, non immemor mei** *Latin* farewell, finally, and do not forget me: a variation on a standard farewell in letters in Latin.

14.6 **Egremont** small town in Cumberland near Whitehaven.

15 **motto** Pope's translation of Homer's *Odyssey* (1725–26), 14.453–56.

15.10–11 **In . . . the river Don** most of the action of *Ivanhoe* takes place between Sheffield and Doncaster, in Yorkshire.

15.11 **a large forest** in Norman England forests covered much of the area of Yorkshire. At the time of the Domesday Survey (1084–86), 'the forest of Sherwood extended from the banks of the rivers Aire and Calder, southward, to the neighbourhood of Sheffield and Rotherham, and far beyond the southern boundaries of Yorkshire, covering great parts of the neighbouring counties of Nottingham and Derby' (Thomas Baines, *Yorkshire, Past and Present*, 2 vols (London, 1871–77), 1.424).

15.14–15 **noble seats of Wentworth, of Warncliffe Park** Wentworth Park, near Rotherham, seat of Earl Fitzwilliam, and Wharncliffe Park which belonged to the Wortleys, later Earls of Wharncliffe; both contained extensive woodland.

15.16 Dragon of Wantley subject of a humorous ballad of about the 17th century: see Percy, 3.277. 'Wantley' was a local variation of Wharncliffe. For conjectures about the origins of the dragon story see Lockhart, 1.396–97.
15.16–17 many of the most desperate battles . . . wars of the Roses the area in which *Ivanhoe* is set lies between the battlefields of Wakefield (1460) and Towton (1461) to the NW, and Bosworth Field (1485) to the S, battles fought in the course of the thirty-year struggle (1455–85) for the English crown.
15.18–19 bands of gallant outlaws . . . song Robin Hood and his outlaw band. See note to 6.24.
15.21 towards the end of the reign of Richard I see Historical Note, 403.
15.25 Stephen King of England (reigned 1135–54).
15.26 Henry the Second King of England (reigned 1154–89).
15.28–29 the English Council of State there was no body of this name at the time; possibly Scott has in mind Walter de Coutances and his advisors who were governing England in the absence of Richard; see also note to 342.30.
16.3 Franklins land-owners of free birth, with holdings smaller than the feudal gentry, but larger than the middle class of villagers. They paid rent for their land and did not owe military service or labour to their lords.
16.7 petty kings the great feudal lords of England.
16.24 conquest by Duke William of Normandy in 1066.
16.24–29 Four generations . . . defeat Henry (see note to 8.16) makes much of the animosity between the Normans and the English, citing Giraldus Cambrensis that 'when a Norman was accused of any thing which he thought dishonourable, and chose to deny, he commonly said,—*What! do you imagine I am an Englishman?*—or—*May I become an Englishman if I did it*' (3.557). Giraldus (*Opera*, ed. J. S. Brewer, James F. Dimock, and George F. Warner, 8 vols (London, 1861–91), 4.424) is quoting the words of Richard I's unpopular chancellor William de Longchamp. Scott would also have known the contrary view of David Hume that by the late 12th century the Normans had been 'entirely incorporated with' the Anglo-Saxons (*History of England*, 8 vols (Edinburgh, 1810), 1.465–66: see *CLA*, 28). See also Historical Note, 495–96.
16.32–35 whole race of Saxon princes . . . inferior classes by the time the Domesday Book was compiled twenty years after the Conquest only two of the king's leading tenants were of English descent and only about eight per cent of the land remained in the possession of the surviving members of the Anglo-Saxon aristocracy.
16.40 laws of the chase according to Blackstone's *Commentaries* which Scott knew well, 'Richard the first, a brave and magnanimous prince, was a sportsman as well as a soldier; and therefore enforced the forest laws with some rigour' (William Blackstone, *Commentaries on the Laws of England*, 8th edn, 4 vols (Oxford, 1778), 4.423: see *CLA*, 296).
17.2–5 Norman French . . . justice Henry writes: 'the Norman or French was the language of the court of England, of the nobility, and of all who wished to be thought persons of rank and fashion, for about three centuries after the conquest' (Henry, 4.582). Some of the ruling class, such as Richard I's chancellor, William de Longchamp, who was born in Normandy, did not speak English at all (see Hoveden, 3.146: *CLA*, 27).
17.4–5 chivalry a term covering knights and their activities. Originally applied to a group of knights or mounted soldiers of the Middle Ages it came to mean 'knights as a class', then, specifically, 'brave and gallant knights' and 'knighthood as a rank in society'. It further extended to cover knightly behaviour and came to mean 'the knightly code of conduct', 'knightly bravery and

honourable conduct' and 'knightly skill in arms'. Each of these meanings is found in *Ivanhoe.*

17.9–10 dialect . . . Anglo-Saxon see Historical Note, 403.

17.21 reign of William the Second William II (reigned 1087–1100), faced with a plot by the Norman barons to dethrone him, called for the 'Englishmen', as distinct from the Normans, to help him quell the rebellion (see note to 130.5). Scott would have read about this in Henry (3.363) who quotes William of Malmesbury (see William of Malmesbury, 2.361–62) as his source. Scott had a copy of Savile's 1596 edition of William (*CLA*, 27).

17.24 Edward the Third reigned 1327–77.

17.42 rites of Druidical superstition the ancient Celtic Druids performed their religious ceremonies in oak groves. In the late 17th century the antiquary John Aubrey associated the stone circle at Stonehenge with them, and by the 19th century the theory of the druidic origins of stone circles had gained general acceptance.

18.13–23 His garment . . . shirt Scott took the details of Gurth's clothing from Strutt's description of the dress of Norman peasants (*Dress and Habits*, 1.88, citing 12th-century manuscripts; *Horda*, 1.46).

18.23 hauberk defensive armour, usually of ring or chain mail. Originally it was to protect the head and shoulders, but by the 12th century it had come to be a coat reaching to about the knees, and slit in front and behind for convenience in the saddle.

18.24 a sort of roll of thin leather see *Dress and Habits*, Vol. 1, Plate XXX, entitled 'Norman Rustics of the Eleventh Century', which includes a figure whose leg coverings fit the description given here.

18.33–34 Sheffield whittle large knife made in Sheffield. The miller in 'The Reeve's Tale' (*The Canterbury Tales*, 1 (A), 3933) carries a Sheffield whittle.

18.39–43 brass ring . . . use of the file see *Horda*, 1.107–08, note to Plate XIII.8: 'this figure has a collar round his neck, which bears the evident marks of the antient Saxon custom, viz. putting a collar of iron round the necks of those who were accounted bondsmen; the youth also wore a ring of iron in token of bondage, till by their bravery they had it taken off with honour'. The German custom of wearing an iron ring as a voluntary badge of slavery is described by Tacitus in *Germania* (A.D. 98), Ch. 31; Scott refers to Tacitus's observation in his 'Essay on Chivalry' (*Prose Works*, 6.7), but here describes it as an iron ring upon the arm. The idea of a brass collar as distinct from an iron one may have been suggested by the brass collar found in the Firth of Forth and donated to the Society of Antiquaries of Scotland, the description on which reads: 'ALEXr. STEUART, found guilty of death, for theft at Perth, the 5th of December 1701, and gifted by the justiciars as a perpetual servant to Sir John Areskine of Alva' (see William Smellie, *Account of the Institution and Progress of the Society of Antiquaries of Scotland*, Part Second (Edinburgh, 1784), 122). It thus served, like Gurth's collar, as a mark of servitude. Slavery was common amongst the Anglo-Saxons though it rapidly became uncommon after the Conquest.

18.43 Saxon in accordance with the practice of his time, Scott uses this term for the people, language and period we now refer to as Anglo-Saxon or, in the case of the language, Old English. The Saxons were one of the three Germanic tribes, Angles, Saxons and Jutes, which invaded Britain in the 5th and 6th centuries but even before the Norman Conquest they had all come to refer to themselves as 'English'. The term *Saxon* was reintroduced in Middle English from French and was applied from the 14th century to the Anglo-Saxons and their language.

19.1 Gurth this name is probably taken from Gyrth or Gurth (d. 1066), brother of King Harold and Earl of East Anglia.

19.1 Beowolf this was not a common Anglo-Saxon name. Scott would have known it from the Old English poem, called *Beowulf* by modern editors, of which a somewhat inaccurate description appears in Turner (4.398–408).

19.2 thrall this meant either a serf (see note to 19.41) or a slave; possibly here a slave, since Scott gives Gurth the neck-ring Turner believed to be a mark of slavery (see note to 18.39–43).

19.2 Cedric name coined by Scott for this novel; it is possibly a mistake for Cerdic, the name, Celtic rather than Germanic in origin (*ODECN*, 61), of a king of the West Saxons (d. 543).

19.2 Rotherwood fictitious place imagined as near to the real town of Rotherham in South Yorkshire.

19.7 more fantastic appearance medieval fools were traditionally attired in motley (see note to 169.3) or other fantastic apparel with an eared hood and coxcomb. Sandra Billington (*A Social History of the Fool* (Brighton, 1984), 4) shows from pictures in Psalters and Bibles that the fool was shown as a 'naked or semi-naked figure with bauble and occasionally a bell on his eared hood' before 1350 but finely costumed and decorated from 1380.

19.16 Wamba the name possibly comes from Wamba, King of the Goths (reigned 672–80), who figures in legends about St Giles.

19.35–36 class whom . . . edge-tools proverbially it is both children and fools who should not be allowed to play with edge-tools (see *ODEP*, 120, 411).

19.37–38 sword of lath . . . modern stage make-believe weapon of wood. Harlequin the clown, in the popular pantomimes of Scott's time, had a magic wand, a modification of his traditional bat.

19.41 serf an unfree person; in modern times the term is often understood as referring to someone who was attached to a particular piece of land so that when ownership of the land changed he was transferred to the new owner, whereas a slave was the personal property of his owner, unattached to the land. However, the distinction between serfdom and slavery in late Anglo-Saxon and Norman England was by no means clear cut (see F. Barlow, *The Feudal Kingdom of England 1042–1216* (London, 1961), 15–16; H. W. C. Davis, *England Under the Normans and Angevins*, 11th edn (London, 1937), 39; F. W. Maitland, *Domesday Book and Beyond* (Cambridge, 1921), 26–29).

20.14 curse of St Withold St Withold may not have been a real saint, but in his poem 'St Swithin's Chair' in *Waverley* (1.188.15–190.8), which clearly draws on the St Withold (Swithold in early editions) of *King Lear*, Scott seemingly identifies him with the historical St Swithin (d. 862). Gurth may be referring to St Withold's powers of protection against the night-mare (see *King Lear*, 3.4.118–19), a female spirit or monster which visited people during the night.

20.23 true man an honest man, as opposed to a criminal.

20.29 malice prepense intention of doing wrong, an Anglo-French legal phrase, often anglicised as 'malice aforethought'.

20.31–33 ranger of the forest . . . trade in a Magnum note Scott writes that a 'most sensible grievance of those aggrieved times were the Forest Laws. . . . The disabling dogs, which might be necessary for keeping flocks and herds, from running at the deer, was called *lawing*, and was in general use' (Magnum, 16.17).

20.34–35 when thou'st got the weather-gage when you have got to the windward of them.

21.6–28 Why, how call you . . . matter of enjoyment to Ballantyne's objection that he did not understand this Scott replied, 'Surely the strongest possible badge of the Norman conquest exists in the very curious fact that while an animal remaind alive under the charge of the Saxon slaves it retained the

Saxon name *Sow Ox* or *calf*—when it was killd & became flesh which was only eaten by the Normans the Sow became Porc the ox *boeuf* or beef the calf *veau* or veal. So that we still have the peculiarity of having two words one to denominate the animal alive another his flesh when dead and served up to table. The circumstance shows that the Saxon bondsmen kept the herds & flock, the Norman baron eats the flesh. A thousand volumes cannot speak the condition of the country more strongly' (Proofs, 1.50–51).

21.10 flayed skinned; human beings were often flayed alive, as were, at this time, one of the assassins of Conrad of Montferrat (Hoveden, 3.181) and the archer whose cross-bow bolt led to the death of Richard I (Hoveden, 4.83).

21.10 drawn, and quartered disembowelled and divided into quarters; until replaced by hanging in 1870, the legal punishment for high treason in England (and in Scotland from 1708) was to be hanged, drawn and quartered.

21.22 Alderman in Old English this denoted the king's deputy in a part of the country; in Middle English it meant the head man of a guild or, later, a member of a municipal council.

21.25–26 Mynheer Calve . . . Monsieur de Veau *mijn heer* is the equivalent of 'mister' in Dutch. Scott uses it in the absence of any known Anglo-Saxon equivalent. By contrast *Monsieur de Veau* suggests a French noble title; *veau* is French for 'calf'.

21.29 St Dunstan an important Anglo-Saxon churchman, a leader of monastic reform, and Archbishop of Canterbury 960–88.

21.37 standing in the gap see 'The Knight's Tale': 'Right as the hunters . . . That stondeth at the gappe with a spere' (*The Canterbury Tales*, 1 (A), 1638–9).

21.38 Front-de-Bœuf the name means 'bull-brow' in French. See 256.8–11 for a story explaining the origin of his name. As Scott explains in the Magnum introduction (16.xx), 'a roll of Norman warriors, occurring in the Auchinleck Manuscript, gave him the formidable name of Front-de-Bœuf'. The list is mentioned in Scott's edition of *Sir Tristrem* (*Poetical Works*, 5.117).

22.2 Malvoisin literally 'bad neighbour', which is no doubt why Scott chose it, but it does occur in history as the name given to two castles (Hoveden, 1.150; Berners's Froissart, Vol. 2, Chs 23–24), and to a catapult used at the siege of Acre (*Itinerarium*, Bk 3, Ch. 7; 1.218).

22.3–4 thou art but a cast-away swine-herd compare *The Tempest*, 4.1.202: 'Thou wert but a lost monster'.

22.15–16 riders . . . Oberon in Scott's essay 'On the Fairies of Popular Superstition', he notes that fairies often ride in invisible procession (*Minstrelsy of the Scottish Border*, ed. T. F. Henderson, 4 vols (Edinburgh, 1902), 2.354). The reference to Oberon, however, is an anachronism, as he appeared first in English literature in 1534 in Berners's translation of Huon of Bordeaux, later being popularised in Shakespeare's *A Midsummer Night's Dream*.

22.27 Eumæus Odysseus's faithful swineherd in Homer's *Odyssey*, Bk 14.

22 motto partly modernised from the 'General Prologue' to *The Canterbury Tales*, 1 (A), 165–72.

23.9 Cistercian originally 'Benedictine' in MS, but changed by Scott in proof. Founded by Robert of Molesme at Cîteaux in 1098, the Cistercian order of monks established their first English house in 1129. Their habits being made of undyed wool, they were called the 'white monks'.

23.16 pent-house of his eye see *Macbeth*, 1.3.20, and John Dryden, *King Arthur* (1691), 3.313.

23.22–23 rich furs . . . golden clasp compare the Monk in the 'General Prologue' to *The Canterbury Tales* who wore expensive squirrel fur on his sleeves and a 'ful curious pyn' of gold under his chin (1 (A), 194–96), ornaments inconsistent with the monk's vow of poverty.

23.31 bells Chaucer's monk likewise had bells on his bridle (see motto, 22).

23.38 jennets small Spanish horses. The first recorded English use of the word in the *OED* is from the mid-15th century, about the time when the monks of the Carthusian order in Spain began to breed the fine Andalusian horses.

24.10 scarlet cap said by T. D. Fosbrooke, one of Scott's sources in *The Monastery*, to have been worn by Templars (*British Monachism* (London, 1817), 385) but not mentioned by Favine (see note to 24.30).

24.30 scarlet the Templar Rule required that the knights' garments be of one colour only; and strongly recommended white material (Rule, Chs 20–22; de Curzon, 27–29, 67–68) which became normal. On it they wore a red cross as authorised by Pope Eugenius III (d. 1153). Scott may have been thinking of Knights Hospitallers who by the mid-13th century wore a red surcoat with a white cross.

24.31–32 four regular orders of monks the Benedictine 'black monks'; the Cluniacs, attached to the influential monastery of Cluny, who also wore black; the Cistercian 'white monks' (see note to 23.9); and the Carthusians, whose garments were also white and made of a coarse cloth.

24.33 cross of a peculiar form see note to 40.25.

24.39–40 feet . . . steel according to the supplementary rules, Templar knights wore iron shoes without uppers (de Curzon, 112) as this made walking easier.

25.6–7 Damascene carving designs cut into the surface and filled with gold or silver.

25.12 small triangular shield by this time the curved sides of the kite-shaped shield of the Norman Conquest had flattened to give a triangular shape.

25.13–14 covered with a scarlet cloth Laurent Daillez, in *Les Templiers et les Règles de l'Ordre du Temple* (Paris, 1972) notes that their shields were covered with wood and leather, and without any mark, only the Master having the right to bear the black and silver arms of the Order (101, n. 47).

25.15 two squires the original Templar Rule allowed a knight one squire (Rule, Ch. 31; de Curzon, 54) but the supplementary rules permitted a Preceptor like Bois-Guilbert (see notes to 305.10 and 308.3) to have two (de Curzon, 107).

25.15–17 two attendants . . . eastern country in a note in the Magnum (16.38) Scott defends his inclusion of the two black slaves in the absence of positive proof of their existence in England at this time. 'What can be more natural, than that the Templars, who, we know, copied closely the luxuries of the Asiatic warriors with whom they fought, should use the service of the enslaved Africans, whom the fate of war transferred to new masters?' He also relates a story from a medieval romance of how a minstrel painted himself black and 'succeeded in imposing himself on the king, as an Ethiopian minstrel'. From this he concludes that 'negroes, therefore, must have been known in England in the dark ages'.

25.20 silver collars round their throats, and bracelets compare note to 18.39–43.

25.30 Saracens originally applied by the Greeks to the nomadic tribes of the Arabian peninsula, this term, when adopted into English, was applied to any Muslims, especially Arabs and Turks, and finally to any heathen of any period.

25.31 El Jerrid this game took its name from the wooden javelin, or jerid, about five feet long, used by Turkish, Arabian and Persian horsemen.

25.39 coursers fast horses or racers, the normal meaning since the 17th century. Originally it meant a large, powerful cavalry horse, such as would carry a knight in battle or in a tournament as in the chapter mottoes taken from Dryden's version of Chaucer's 'The Knight's Tale' (see 65 motto) and from Shakespeare (see 382 motto).

25.43 Prior Scott refers to Aymer at different times as 'prior' and as 'abbot'. Strictly speaking, an abbot was the head of a monastery and the prior his second in command, but in cathedral monasteries, where the bishop took the place of the abbot, the prior was effectively the head of the establishment. The resident head of a subsidiary monastery was also called a prior. In using the terms interchangeably Scott was following the view of T. D. Fosbrooke, one of his sources, that they 'are usually considered, except in Cathedrals . . . synonymous terms' (*British Monachicism* (London, 1817), 126).

25.43 Jorvaulx Abbey Jervaulx, a Cistercian Abbey, founded at Fors, in Wensleydale, but moved to Witton, near Middleham (15 kms SW of Richmond), in 1156; destroyed in 1537. Its ruins were cleared and traced out in 1807.

26.1 the chase hunting. Strutt noted that 'the bishops and abbots of the middle ages hunted with great state, having a large train of retainers and servants; and some of them are recorded for their skill in this fashionable pursuit' (*Sports and Pastimes*, 9).

26.5 Aymer a name current in France and England at about this time but also providing a pun on the French verb *aimer*, to love. Scott may be remembering Henry III's half-brother Aymer de Valence (d. 1260), appointed bishop of Winchester against much opposition from the Church because of his youth, ignorance and his not being a priest.

26.14–16 The Prior . . . North Riding the Monk in the 'General Prologue' to *The Canterbury Tales*, with a similar love of hunting, had greyhounds 'as swift as fowel in flight' (1 (A), 190).

26.26–27 charity . . . sins see 1 Peter 4.8: 'For charity shall cover the multitude of sins'; here *charity* means 'love' but Scott uses it with its modern meaning.

26.41 benedicite, mes filz *Latin* bless you; *French* my sons.

27.9 lingua Franca a mixed language for communication between people of different tongues, a pidgin. See Historical Note, 403.

27.25 Brinxworth Brinsworth, between Sheffield and Rotherham.

27.28 Copmanhurst a fictitious name, possibly derived from Copmanthorpe, a village about 6 kms SW of York.

27.33–34 Clericus clericum non decimat *Latin* one clergyman does not exact tithes from another. For tithes see note to 278.15.

27.39 bear the bells see note to 19.7 but *bear the bell* means 'take first place'.

27.40–41 charity . . . begin at home proverbial: *ODEP*, 115.

28.2 Saxon not a normal 12th-century term for an Englishman (see note to 18.43); moreover Cedric lives in an originally Angle (not Saxon) area.

28.24–25 holy Church . . . loveth see Hebrews 12.6: 'whom the Lord loveth he chasteneth'.

28.29–30 Saracen head such images were used in heraldry, and as a target in tilting.

28.34 Holy Sepulchre the rock cave in Jerusalem where, according to early tradition, Christ was buried and rose from the dead. Jerusalem had been captured by the Muslim Saladin (d. 1193) in 1187.

28.35 Knights Templars crusading order, so called from their original residence within the precincts of the Temple of Solomon in Jerusalem, initiated in 1118 to defend pilgrims on their journey to the Holy Land.

28.43 cubit ancient unit of measurement, based on the length of the forearm; about 45 cms.

29.14 Rowena Scott took this name from the story of Vortigern, a British ruler who, according to the 9th-century writer Nennius, welcomed the Saxon exiles Hengist and Horsa on their arrival in Britain in the 5th century. Infatuated by Hengist's daughter, Vortigern gave the kingdom of Kent to the Saxons in order to marry her. Nennius does not name the woman but Geoffrey of Monmouth in the 12th century (see note to 45.11) calls her *Renwein*. Layamon, writing about 1200, calls her *Ronwen* or *Rowen* (*Brut*, ed. G. L. Brook and R. F. Leslie, 2 vols, Early English Text Society, OS 250, 277 (London, 1963 and Oxford, 1978), line 7114) and Verstegan (*A Restitution of Decayed Intelligence* (London, 1628), 127) uses the latinised form *Rowena* which was taken up by Strutt (*Horda*, 1.48) and other historians. Scott had a copy of Verstegan (London, 1673: *CLA*, 26). The name was popularised by Scott's use of it in this novel (*ODECN*, 259).

29.15–16 hear and see and say nothing proverbial: *ODEP*, 362.

29.26–27 a fool speaking according to his folly see Proverbs 26.4.

29.34 Odin in Norse mythology, the greatest of the gods; known as Woden to the Anglo-Saxons but sometimes referred to in Scott's time by his Norse name even in Anglo-Saxon contexts (e.g. Turner, 4.19).

29.40–41 every land . . . fashions compare 'Every land has its laugh, and every corn has its chaff': see *ODEP*, 441; and James Kelly (*A Complete Collection of Scotish Proverbs* (London, 1721), 92: *CLA*, 169) whose explanation reads: 'Every Country hath its own Laws, Customs, and Usages'. *Laugh* is a variant of 'laich', an area of low-lying ground.

30.6 Hereward Hereward the Wake, a Lincolnshire squire who held the Isle of Ely against William the Conqueror in 1070–71, and thus a popular hero of the Anglo-Saxons.

30.6 Heptarchy name given by 16th-century historians to the seven kingdoms (Northumbria, Mercia, Wessex, East Anglia, Essex, Sussex and Kent) of Anglo-Saxon England in the 6th and 7th centuries which they erroneously thought of as 'making but one Body and one State' (Rapin de Thoyras, *The History of England*, trans. and ed. N. Tindal, 2nd edn, 4 vols (London, 1732), 1.46).

30.9 vae victis *Latin* woe to the conquered. According to Livy (59 BC–AD 17) these were the words of the Gaulish chief Brennus as he threw his sword into the balance when settling on a ransom for the Romans (*Ab Urbe Condita*, Bk 5, Ch. 48). Scott uses the phrase to mean the sufferings inflicted on the vanquished.

30.12 troubadour lyric poet singing chiefly about love and chivalry. The troubadour movement arose in Provence and flourished in the 12th and 13th centuries.

30.13 arrests authoritative sentences or decrees made by a court. In Provence in the Middle Ages there were *cours d'amour* (courts of love) established to discuss and judge questions of love. See Scott's 'Essay on Chivalry' of 1818 (*Prose Works*, 6.114).

30.16 churl in the Anglo-Saxon period applied simply to a man or, more specifically, a freeman, not of noble birth, recognised by law to have certain rights and obligations. Following the Norman Conquest most of these lost their freedom and became serfs (see note to 19.41) and the word came to mean an ill-bred, ill-mannered person.

30.24 Mahound short form for Mohammed (*c.* 570–632), prophet of Islam. Many medieval Christians erroneously thought the Muslims worshipped him as a god.

30.26–27 weighed in the balance . . . wanting in Daniel 5.27, the meaning of the word *TEKEL* in Belshazzar's dream: see also note to 132.34.

30.28 Chian from the island of Chios in the Ægean, famous since Roman and Byzantine times for its fine wines.

30.34 lists palisades, or other barriers, around an area used for holding tournaments and jousts; it also was applied to the area so enclosed. However, the term belongs to the later Middle Ages and 12th-century tournaments were generally rough contests between two sides, not unlike real battles, ranging over the countryside between two towns (see next note) rather than confined to a specific plot of land.

30.35 **Ashby-de-la-Zouche** 25 kms NW of Leicester. It was not one of the 5 places appointed by Richard I for tournaments (see note to 38.1), which were 'between Sarum and Wilton;—between Warwick and Kenelworth;—between Stamford and Wallingford;—between Brakely and Mixeburg;—and between Blie and Tykehill' (*Sports and Pastimes*, 104n).

30.38 **file your tongue** see the Pardoner in the 'General Prologue' to *The Canterbury Tales* who 'moste preche and wel affile his tonge/ To wynne silver' (1 (A), 712–13). Shakespeare also uses the phrase, in *Love's Labour's Lost* (5.1.9) and in *The Passionate Pilgrim* (18.8).

31.9–10 **as meekly as a maiden** the Knight in *The Canterbury Tales* was 'of his port as meeke as is a mayde' (1 (A), 69).

33 **motto** James Thomson, *Liberty* (1735–36), 4.668–70.

33.10 **German Ocean** North Sea.

34.16 **The Dividers of Bread** the word *lord* derives from the OE *hlaf-weard*, or 'bread-keeper', shortened to *hlaford*. *Lady* comes from the OE *hlæf-dige* from *hlaf*, 'loaf' and the root *dig-*, to knead. Verstegan, however, sees *hlaford* as meaning 'provider or afforder of bread', and *hlafdige* as 'bread-server' (*Restitution of Decayed Intelligence* (London, 1628), 316–18).

34.20 **thane** originally meaning 'servant' or 'attendant', by the 12th century it had come to mean a nobleman and holder of land, whose service to his lord (normally the king) was in military and peace-keeping matters. Alternatively it simply denoted someone in rank between an ealdorman (see note to 21.22) and a churl (see note to 30.16). In this sense, the term fell out of use in the 12th century (as Scott indicates at 41.19), and was replaced by *baron* and *knight*. Franklins (see note to 16.3) did not exactly equate with thanes since they had no military responsibilities attendant on their land tenure.

34.34–38 **His long yellow hair . . . shoulders** Strutt records that in Anglo-Saxon drawings men's hair 'is parted upon the middle of the head, and flows on either side the face upon the shoulders' (*Dress and Habits*, 1.11).

34.40 **minever** literally 'little vair', *vair* being in French usage the fur of the *petit-gris*, a variety of the common squirrel; but it is not certain which kind of fur was being referred to in the early (14th-century) use of the word in England. Miniver, described as 'plain White Furr' by Randle Holme (*The Academy of Armory, or, a Storehouse of Armory and Blazon* (Chester, 1688), 3.50), was popular as trimming or lining for ceremonial clothing.

35.3 **bracelets of gold** an Anglo-Saxon rather than Norman ornament. Strutt says that William of Malmesbury, 'complaining of the luxury of the English in the time of the Confessor, tells us, that "they adorned their arms with massie bracelets of gold"' (*Horda*, 1.47; see William of Malmesbury, 2.305).

35.6 **sword** not normally worn as a part of civil attire in the Middle Ages (see Francis M. Kelly and Randolph Schwabe, *A Short History of Costume and Armour*, 2 vols (London, 1931), 1.10).

35.23 **now called terriers** the term was used as early as the mid-15th century.

35.29 **wolf-dog** large hunting dog, like Scott's own favourite Maida.

35.33 **Balder** Balder 'the good', a god of Norse mythology, associated with light, summer, beauty and wisdom; Jacob Grimm notes that the names of Germanic gods were given to dogs (*Teutonic Mythology*, trans. James Steven Stallybrass, 4 vols (London, 1880–88), 4.1282) but this is still a rather unlikely name for a dog in the 12th century.

35.36–37 evening mass in the Middle Ages the mass was normally celebrated in the morning although it was celebrated in the early evening on fast days.
36.20 kirtle term applied to garments for both sexes: a woman's long gown, sometimes worn as an outer garment over a smock, and a man's tunic reaching to the knees or lower.
36.31 warders the term usually means a guard at an entrance, or a watchman on a tower, but, as explained, it is here used with a special meaning which might be expressed as 'retainer'.
36.33–36 curfew... tyrannical bastard the enforced covering of all fires at an early hour of the evening indicated by the ringing of a bell. It was probably introduced to reduce the risk of fire at night, but at least as early as Richard Grafton's *Chronicle* of 1568 it was believed to have been introduced by William the Conqueror as an oppressive measure against the English (edn of 1809, 1.161; *CLA*, 28). See also William Blackstone's *Commentaries on the Laws of England* (8th edn (London, 1778), 4.419) but Henry's view is that 'this opinion does not seem to be well founded' (Henry, 3.567).
36.35 The foul fiend the devil; see *King Lear*, 3.4.45 etc.
36 footnote this could have been taken from Turner (4.178–82), but he makes no mention of cnichts ever being bondsmen.
36.43 chevalier a Central French term; the Anglo-Norman equivalent was *chevaler*.
37.3 William the Bastard William the Conqueror (1027–87) was the illegitimate son of Robert I, Duke of Normandy, and Herleva, daughter of a tanner of Falaise.
37.4 Hastings the site of the battle of 1066 at which William of Normandy defeated the English king, Harold.
37.16 great council the *magnum concilium*, an assembly of the great feudal lords and ecclesiastics of the realm.
37.22 Wilfred name originating from the Old English *Wilfrith*, latinised as *Wilfridus*, and made famous by St Wilfrid of York (634–709). It did not survive the Norman Conquest but appears again in the 16th century (*ODECN*, 293) and became quite popular in the 19th due to the success of *Ivanhoe* and to the Tractarian movement's interest in the saint.
37.38 hership *Scots* raiding.
37.41–42 Brian de Bois-Guilbert Brian is a name of Irish origin but was well-known in medieval France from its use in romances. Bois-Guilbert (Gilbert-wood) is a real name, borne, for example, by Pierre de Boisguilbert (1646–1714), an early French economist.
38.1 tournament mock combat with real or blunted weapons between a number of armed knights according to prescribed rules. Banned under Henry II because they were so dangerous, they were reintroduced under Richard I in 1194. See also note to 30.35.
38.6 impeached called in question, discredited. Henry cites various authorities for his claim that 'Hospitality may be justly reckoned among the national virtues of the Anglo-Saxons' (2.551).
38.10 Hundebert taken from Turner's list of Anglo-Saxon names (Turner, 4.48).
38.26 Middleham 25 kms NE of Ripon.
39.1 morat drink made from honey and flavoured with mulberries. Henry (2.595–96), followed by Turner (4.69), apparently adapted the word from the mediaeval Latin *moratum*, from *morus*, meaning 'mulberry'.
39.3 Elgitha Elgiva, queen of King Edwy, is mentioned by Henry (2.192) and Turner tells her story at some length (3.155–60); her name is a latinisation of the common Old English name Æthelgifu (*ODECN*, 98) but Scott seems to

have combined it with Githa, a Norse name found in England in the 11th century (*ODECN*, 135).

39.11–12 thy tongue outruns thy discretion compare 'Your tongue runs before your wit', known in various forms from the 14th century (*ODEP*, 830).

39.13 descendant of Alfred i.e. Rowena, supposedly descended from Alfred the Great (reigned 871–99).

40 motto Pope's translation of Homer's *Odyssey* (1725–26), 20.314–17, 322–24.

40.17–18 beard trimmed ... possibly permit in fact, Cistercians were clean-shaven, unlike the Knights Templars who wore beards.

40.25 eight-pointed cross the Templars originally adopted the Patriarchal Cross, with two cross bars (Favine, 2.401) but in about 1182 they rejected this, 'taking one Blacke with eight Points; like to that of the *Hospitallers of Saint John*, with an *Urle and Bordure White*' (Favine, 2.402). An urle or orle is a narrow band following the outline of a shield or escutcheon without touching the edge of it.

40.37 hussar in July 1819, while Scott was writing *Ivanhoe*, his son Walter joined the 18th regiment of Hussars.

40.38 Sclaveyn or Slavonian pilgrim's mantle, a recognised part of the pilgrim's attire. The term appears in English from the 13th century and derives either from *sclavus* ('slave') or, as Scott's explanation 'Slavonian' suggests he believed, from *Sclavus* ('slav'). In the romance *Richard Coeur de Lion* Richard and his companions set off for the Holy Land equipped 'With pike, and with sclavyn,/ As palmers wear in Paynim' (Ellis, 2.190) and Ritson has a long note on the *sclaveyn* in his *Ancient Engleish Metrical Romanceës*, 3 vols (London, 1802), 3.278.

40.39 a broad and shadowy hat this feature of a pilgrim's dress did not come into use until 'probably in the middle of the 13th century' (Jonathan Sumption, *Pilgrimage: An Image of Medieval Religion* (London, 1975), 172).

40.39 cockle-shells worn as a badge by pilgrims who had visited the shrine of St James the Greater at Compostella, in N Spain. Although called 'cockle-shells', they were in fact scallop-shells.

40.41 a branch of palm traditionally carried by a pilgrim who had returned from the Holy Land to signify this. In the romance *Richard Coeur de Lion* Richard travels disguised as a palmer (Ellis, 2.190; see note to 40.38) and Jerome Mitchell cites a number of other parallels in medieval literature (see *Scott, Chaucer, and Medieval Romance* (Lexington, 1987), 127–28).

41.19 Thane ... antiquated see note to 34.20.

41.21 horns Jewish altars in biblical times had projections, or horns, at each corner to which animals for sacrifice could be tied; see Psalm 118.27.

41.25 odour of sanctity literally, a sweet aroma believed to be given off by the bodies of great saints after their death; figuratively, a reputation for holiness.

41.27 Hilda of Whitby Hilda (614–80) who founded a monastery for men and women at Whitby in 657.

42.23 hang up hang on a gallows; also used in imprecations as in 'Hang up Philosophy' (*Romeo and Juliet*, 3.3.57).

42.25 uncle Scott imitates Shakespeare's use of 'nuncle' (from 'mine uncle') in *King Lear* (e.g. 1.4.103) as a way for a fool or jester to address his superior.

42.25–26 on the bow-hand 16th and 17th-century expression meaning literally 'off the target to the left' (the bow being held in the left hand) and figuratively 'wide of the mark'.

42.37–38 disforested ... Forest Charter William I and his successors set aside large areas as forest for their exclusive use. From 1204 some of the land was returned to the people, or 'disforested', but this had not begun in 1194. The Forest Charter of 1217 disforested the land made forest by Henry II, Richard and John and reduced penalties.

43.3–14 The feast . . . drinking horns see Plate 16, fig. 1, in *Horda*, 1.48.

43.12–14 goblet . . . drinking horns 'we are told, that the northern nations were much addicted to hard drinking, which may be the reason that at their banquets they seem much better provided with drinking horns than with plates and dishes' (*Horda*, 1.49).

43.34 sultanas originally denoting the wife or concubine of a sultan, the word was by the 19th century applied in English to any mistress or concubine or simply a beautiful woman.

44.4–6 Her profuse hair . . . nature in the Anglo-Saxon period, according to Henry, 'young ladies before their marriage wore their hair uncovered, and untied, flowing in ringlets over their shoulders' (2.583–84) and Turner cites a description by Aldhelm (*c.* 640–709) of a wife's 'twisted hairs delicately curled with the iron of those adorning her' (Turner, 4.75). Young girls still wore their hair loose at the end of the 12th century but older women had theirs parted in the middle and arranged in two long braids.

44.7–8 worn at full length . . . maiden see *Dress and Habits*, 1.42: 'none but the nobility of the first class, and princes of the blood royal, were permitted to wear their hair at its full length'. But Strutt also says that this rule 'does not seem to have ever taken place among the Anglo-Saxons'.

44.11–12 long loose robe . . . sleeves see *Horda*, 1.47: Anglo-Saxon women 'were habited in a long loose robe reaching down to the ground, and large loose sleeves'. For more detail see *Dress and Habits*, 1.16.

44.14–18 veil of silk . . . shoulders see *Horda*, 1.47: Anglo-Saxon women, 'added a hood (or vail) over the head, which falling down before, was wrapped round the neck with great order'. Strutt uses *vail* in its original sense of a piece of material covering the hair and shoulders but not the face: women are shown in Plates 7, 13 and 15 wearing hoods, but in no case does it cover their faces or appear as if it would do so. Scott uses *vail* ('veil') in its modern meaning of a light covering for the face.

44.42 Athelstane popular Old English name which did not survive the Norman Conquest (*ODECN*, 35).

44.42 Coningsburgh castle about mid-way between Rotherham and Doncaster, now called Conisbrough. In 1194 it belonged to Hamlin, the illegitimate half-brother of Henry II. See also note to 368.16.

45.4–7 acid preparation of milk . . . lac dulce . . . lac acidum see Turner, 4.63: 'Lac acidum, perhaps butter-milk or whey, was used in a monastery . . . from Hokeday [2nd Tuesday after Easter Sunday] to Michaelmas [29 September], and lac dulce from Michaelmas to Martinmas [11 November]'.

45.11 wassail salutation when drinking or offering a drink. See *Horda*, 1.48: 'The old health by historians reported to have been drank by Rowena (the daughter or niece of Hengest) to Vortergren, (king of the Britons) was after this fashion: She came into the room where the king and his guests were sitting, making a low obedience to him, she said, Waes Heal, Hlaford Cinning, (*be of health lord king*) then having drank, she presented it on her knees to the king, who (being told the meaning of what she had said, together with the custom) took the cup, saying drinc heal (*I drink* your *health*) and drank also'. The ultimate source of this story is Geoffrey of Monmouth (d. 1155), *Historia Regum Britannie* (ed. Neil Wright (Cambridge, 1985), 67: see *CLA*, 27) but the use of the name Rowena suggests that Scott's source was Verstegan (see note to 29.14) or Strutt.

45.14 Vortigern see note to 29.14.

45.22–23 truce with Saladin three-year truce signed before Richard left

Acre in October 1192. An-Nasir Salah-ad-Din Yusuf ibn-Aiyub (*c.* 1137–1193), known in the West as Saladin, was Sultan of Egypt and Syria (comprising modern Syria, Lebanon and Israel) from 1174; he united the greater part of Islam against the Christian enclave in Jerusalem. He defeated a Christian army near Tiberias, and captured the Christian Jerusalem itself in 1187, thus provoking the Third Crusade (1189–92) under the Holy Roman Emperor, Richard I of England and Philip II of France. Their initial success against Saladin led to the truce of 1192.

45.37 **Go to** used either with its original meaning 'come on then', or 'get on with it', or in its later usage, familiar to us from Shakespeare, to express remonstrance or incredulity.

46 **motto** *The Merchant of Venice*, 3.1.50–54.

46.37 **Jews' inheritance** in this case the land of Israel, which is often described as an 'inheritance' in the Bible (e.g. Deuteronomy 21.23, Joshua 11.23, 1 Kings 8.36).

46.40 **stiff-necked** stubborn; a term applied a number of times in the Bible to the Hebrews, e.g. Deuteronomy 9.13, 'I have seen this people, and, behold, it is a stiffnecked people'.

47.8 **Termagaunt** imaginary god, believed in the Middle Ages to be worshipped by the Muslims, and portrayed as a violent character in the morality plays of the 14th and 15th centuries.

47.31–33 **He wore . . . from Christians** at the fourth Lateran Council of 1215 it was decreed that both Jews and Saracens were to wear distinctive clothing. Customs differed throughout Europe. In England in 1218 all Jews were ordered to wear a white cloth badge with a representation of the two tablets of the Law given to Moses (see Exodus 32.15). Du Cange outlines the different forms of identification used in Europe, including the yellow cap worn in Poland (Du Cange, under *Judæi*). Henry (3.584) and Strutt (*Dress and Habits*, 1.99) quote Du Cange as saying that the Jews 'were obliged to wear square caps, of a yellow colour', not observing that this applied only in Poland.

48.14–15 **like his people . . . resting place** partly refers to the exodus of the Israelites from Egypt, when for forty years they wandered 'from nation to nation' (1 Chronicles 16.20) without a land of their own, and partly to the dispersal of the Jews after the destruction of Jerusalem in AD 70.

48.20–21 **mess of pottage** dish of boiled vegetables or soup. The expression is often associated with the biblical story of Jacob and Esau (Genesis 25.28–34) because several of the early Bibles (1537, 1539 and the 1560 Geneva Bible) headed Chapter 25 'Esau selleth his birthright for a mess of potage'.

48.42 **wood-craft** skill in matters relating to the forests, especially in hunting. Probably Scott's source for this word, which went out of use for several centuries before re-emerging in Scott's time, was Chaucer's comment on the Yeoman in the 'General Prologue' to *The Canterbury Tales*: 'Of wodecraft wel koude he al the usage' (1 (A), 110).

49.8 **new-fangled jargon** in a note to the Magnum Scott writes: 'the objects of their pursuit, whether bird or animal, changed their name each year, and there were a hundred conventional terms, to be ignorant of which was to be without one of the distinguishing marks of a gentleman . . . As the Normans reserved the amusement of hunting strictly to themselves, the terms of this formal jargon were all taken from the French language' (Magnum, 16.68–69).

49.8 **curée** the part of the deer given to the hounds. In his notes to *Sir Tristrem* Scott explains: 'the heart, liver, *lights* (lungs), and blood . . . being arranged on the hide, and eaten there by the hounds, formed the *quirré*, or quarry. This operation was called by the French huntsman, *fairre la curee*' (*Poetical Works*, 5.385).

49.8 arbor gullet, or wind-pipe; sometimes also the heart, liver and lungs. Scott may not have fully understood the word since he took the phrase *to make the arber* to mean disembowelling the animal (*Poetical Works*, 5.387) whereas it is in fact only the first stage of this process.

49.8 nombles in Norman French and in English this term was applied to the edible viscera of animals, especially deer, but Scott, in his notes to *Sir Tristrem*, claims that they 'seem to have included the midriff, and the dowsets, or testicles' (*Poetical Works*, 5.387).

49.9 Sir Tristrem one of the principal knights in the story of King Arthur. In his edition of *Sir Tristrem*, Scott notes that 'Tristrem is uniformly represented as the patron of the chase, and the first who reduced hunting to a science' (*Poetical Works*, 5.377) and quotes Malory's comment that Tristrem 'began good measures of blowyng of beasts of venery, and beasts of chase, and all manner of vermin, and all these terms we have yet of hawking and hunting' (*Morte D'Arthur*, 1.242: Bk 8, Ch. 3).

49.18–19 Northallerton . . . Holy Standard at Cowton Moor near Northallerton in 1138 the Scots were defeated by the English, who carried with them 'a tall mast, having at the top a pix and a cross, from which were suspended the banners of St Peter, St John of Beverley, and St Wilfred' (John Mayhall, *Annals of Yorkshire* (Leeds, 1861), 18–19). From this the fight was named 'The Battle of the Standard'.

49.20 cri de guerre *French* war-cry.

49.25–28 A Saxon bard . . . clamour of a bridal Scott's knowledge of Anglo-Saxon poetry was limited and the language used here is not a close imitation of Old English poetic diction.

49.39 Knights Hospitallers an order of military monks who took their name from the hospital which was their headquarters at the end of the 11th century. They cared for pilgrims and crusaders in the Holy Land and grew to be a wealthy community with a strong military organisation.

49.42–43 Richard of the Lion's Heart the name *Coeur de Lion* ('Lion-Heart') has traditionally been given to Richard I and the romance *Richard Coeur de Lion* (see note to 8.35–37) purports to tell the origin of this name. The king of Almain, wishing to dispose of Richard, at that time his prisoner, had a hungry lion taken to Richard's cell. However 'the hero, seizing his opportunity when the monster's jaws were extended, suddenly darted on him, drove his arm down the throat, and, grasping the heart, forcibly tore it out through the mouth together with a part of the entrails'. Going to the hall where the king was dining, he dipped the heart in salt and ate it. Much impressed by this feat, the king christened him 'Richard Coeur de Lion' (Ellis, 2.200–01).

50.17–18 a tournament after the taking of St John-de-Acre the ancient seaport in northern Israel now called Akko was known during the Crusades as St Jean d'Acre. Taken by Saladin in 1187, it was recaptured in 1191 by Richard I of England and Philip II of France. No contemporary reference to a tournament after the fall of the city has been found, but Ellis's version of *Richard Coeur de Lion* refers to 'a fortnight spent in feasts and rejoicing' after the taking of the city (Ellis, 2.261). Other details come from an earlier incident in the poem, a tournament held at Salisbury in the first year of Richard's reign: see note to 51.1.

50.43 Earl of Leicester the crusader Robert Fitz-Parnel of Beaumont (d. 1204), son of Robert de Beaumont (d. 1190), invested with the earldom of Leicester by Richard I at Messina in 1191. He figures quite prominently in Ellis's version of *Richard Coeur de Lion* (Ellis, 2.240, 242, 252, 270).

51.1 Sir Thomas Multon Ellis's account of *Richard Coeur de Lion*, tells how Richard held a tournament at Salisbury for the purpose of discovering 'the stoutest knights in his dominions'. Sir Thomas de Multon, 'a knight whose prowess was deservedly held in the highest estimation', and Sir Fulk Doyley proved themselves worthy companions for the king, and they became 'brothers in arms' and commanders of divisions of Richard's army (Ellis, 2.186–89, 204). Thomas de Multon of 1194 was a real person but no evidence that he went on the crusade with Richard has been found; he had apparently died by 1201. Scott later portrayed Sir Thomas Multon in *The Talisman* as Richard's Master of the Horse.

51.3 Sir Foulk Doilly see previous note. Foulk Doilly may have been a younger son of Henry I d'Oilly (d. 1163) or Henry II d'Oilly (d. 1196) of Hook Norton, but it is highly likely that the details of a 14th-century romance are not historically accurate.

51.8 Sir Edwin Turneham Stephan de Turneham was among those listed in Holinshed's *Chronicles* for their 'high valiancie' in the Holy Land (Raphael Holinshed, *Chronicles of England, Scotland, and Ireland*, 6 vols (London, 1807–08), 2.232: see *CLA*, 29). Ellis's version of *Richard Coeur de Lion* refers frequently to a Sir Robert Turnham or Tourneham (Ellis, 2.212, 240, 250, 260, 270, 278) and once to a Sir Thomas Tourneham (Ellis, 2.255). Apparently Scott combined the surname Turneham with the Anglo-Saxon first name Edwin, in order to provide a 'genuine Saxon' for the list.

51.9 Hengist together with his brother Horsa, Hengist (d. 488) founded the English kingdom of Kent. See also note to 29.14.

51.20 Ivanhoe in his 1830 Introduction to *Ivanhoe*, Scott writes: 'The name of Ivanhoe was suggested by an old rhyme . . . recording three names of the manors forfeited by the ancestor of the celebrated Hampden, for striking the Black Prince a blow with his racket, when they quarrelled at tennis;— "Tring, Wing, and Ivanhoe,/ For striking of a blow,/ Hampden did forego,/ And glad he could escape so." The word suited the author's purpose . . . for, first, it had an ancient English sound; and secondly, it conveyed no indication whatever of the nature of the story.' (Magnum, 16.xviii–xix).

51.34 Mount Carmel mountainous promontory near Acre, the retreat of anchorites from early times and site of the first Carmelite monastery, founded in the later 12th century.

51.35 pater noster the Lord's Prayer in Latin, so named from its first two words.

51.37 vailing his bonnet taking off his cap as a sign of respect. It is not clear what kind of headgear Scott has in mind: Bois-Guilbert is no longer wearing his high cap (see 40.26–27).

51.41–42 the four seas of Britain the North Sea, the Irish Sea, the English Channel and the Atlantic Ocean.

52.33 rood of Bromholme the cross of Bromholme, in Norfolk, reputed to be part of the true cross, and brought from Constantinople to Bromholme in 1223. It is referred to in *Piers Plowman* (*c.* 1362–*c.* 1387: see B-text, 5.229) and in 'The Reeve's Tale', *The Canterbury Tales* (1 (A), 4286).

53.13 Unbelieving dog Shylock, in *The Merchant of Venice*, is called 'misbeliever, cut-throat dog' (1.3.106) and the references to Isaac as a 'dog Jew' echo the same play (see 2.8.14).

53.18 usury lending money at interest, a practice allowed at this period to the Jews but forbidden by the Church for Christians.

53.20 halfling Henry (2.488, 505) claims this was the name of an Anglo-Saxon coin equal to half a penny and that it is 'mentioned in the Saxon gospels' (2.505) but its use in this sense has not been traced in either Old or Middle English.

53.21 God of Abraham common biblical phrase: e.g. Genesis 31.42, Exodus 3.6, Psalm 47.9. Abraham was the founder of the Hebrew nation.

53.23 Exchequer of the Jews following the riots of 1190 (see note to

69.38–39) in which so many Jews were killed and many more impoverished, two officials of the King's Exchequer were, in 1194, designated to supervise their affairs. This expanded into an institution known as the Exchequer of the Jews.

53.23–24 **Father Jacob** father of the twelve sons whose families became the twelve tribes of Israel. See also note to 96.36.

53.24–25 **gaberdine** loose smock of coarse material. Perhaps because of Shylock's reference to 'my Jewish gaberdine' in *The Merchant of Venice* (1.3.107), the word came to mean, in the 19th century, a garment worn by Jews.

53.25 **Tadcaster** village 15 kms SW of York.

54 **motto** *The Merchant of Venice*, 1.3.163–65.

54.38–39 **apartment of the Lady Rowena** see the description of Anglo-Saxon houses in Turner, 4.87–90.

55.38 **French faction . . . Templars** when the Crusaders came near to Jerusalem, 'the Templars, Hospitallers, and Pisans, joining with the French, opposed the besieging of it . . . and obliged Richard to return with his army towards Ascalon' (Henry, 3.147–48). However, although Henry cites the *Itinerarium* as his source, it makes no mention of the French in this context (see *Itinerarium*, Bk 5, Ch. 1; 1.308–09); it does however record that the French king occupied the Templars' palace in Acre after it fell (*Itinerarium*, Bk. 3, Ch. 18; 1.234) and Roger of Hoveden tells us that they had helped the French in the siege of that city (Hoveden, 3.116).

56.26 **sleeping cup** drink to induce sleep.

57.6–7 **child of circumcision . . . tribe** according to the covenant made between God and Abraham (Genesis 17.10–14), every male Jewish child was circumcised on the eighth day, and thus the Jewish people were sometimes known as the 'children of the circumcision'.

57.7 **abomination of his tribe** pigs. Jewish law did not permit Jews to eat or touch pig's flesh (see Leviticus 11.7–8).

57.34 **Norman-English** see Historical Note, 403.

58.32 **Moses . . . Aaron** Moses led his people out of slavery in Egypt on their journey to the land of Canaan, the Promised Land. Aaron, his brother, acted as his spokesman and later became High Priest.

58.35–36 **saws and harrows . . . Ammon** in laying waste the country of the Ammonites, David sacked the city of Rabbah and 'brought out the people that were in it, and cut them with saws, and with harrows of iron, and with axes' (1 Chronicles 20.3).

58.39–41 **you have cause . . . princes and nobles** see 62.3–7.

59.15 **Lazarus** see Luke 16.20–21: Lazarus sat at the gate of a rich man, 'full of sores, And desiring to be fed with the crumbs which fell from the rich man's table'. Isaac, though a Jew, refers to Christ's parable.

59.18 **Israelite** descendant of Jacob, also known as Israel. Terms like 'Israelite', 'Children of Israel' or 'Men of Israel' are the normal Old Testament ways of referring to the whole body of God's chosen people.

59.19 **Ishmaelite** term applied in the Bible to the nomadic tribes of northern Arabia, believed to be descended from Ishmael (the son of Abraham by his slave, Hagar; see Genesis, Chs 16–21) and seen as traditional enemies of the Israelites.

59.33 **gird up our loins** common biblical phrase (e.g. see 2 Kings 4.29) implying preparing for action by drawing in one's clothes in a belt to allow unimpeded movement.

59.42 **Eumæus in Ithaca** Eumæus was Odysseus's faithful swineherd in Homer's *Odyssey*, Bk 14; Ithaca was the island-kingdom of Odysseus.

61.11 **en croupe** *French* on the rear part of the horse's back.

61.34 **flying fish** see Richard Hakluyt, *Principal Navigations* (1589), 542, and Christopher Marlowe, *Edward II* (written 1591–92; published 1594), 2.2.23–28. The *Encyclopedia Britannica* of 1797 says that the flying fish 'seems to lead a most miserable life. In its own element, it is perpetually harassed by the dorados and other fish of prey. If it endeavours to avoid them by having recourse to the air, it either meets its fate from the gulls or the albatross, or is forced down again into the mouth of the inhabitants of the water' (see under *exocoetus*).

62.3 well-known story of King John related in Holinshed's *Chronicles of England, Scotland, and Ireland* (6 vols (London, 1807–08), 2.301) and by Henry (3.526–29).

62.16 Jews' Exchequer see note to 53.23.

62.17–18 Jews increased, multiplied see Exodus 1.7.

62.19 bills of exchange written orders requiring someone to pay the drawer (i.e. the person writing the bill) or a third party a certain sum on a specified day.

62.39–40 May the wheels . . . drive heavily see Exodus 14.25: the Egyptians are prevented from pursuing the people of Israel through the Red Sea.

63.16 Zareth see Marlowe, *The Jew of Malta* (first performed *c.* 1592), 1.1.176; see also note to 64.26. Marlowe probably took the name from Joshua 13.19, where the town of Zareth-shahar is listed as part of the inheritance given by Moses to the descendants of Reuben.

63.33 in thy danger at your mercy: see *The Merchant of Venice*, 4.1.175.

64.9 take the staff and sandal as a sign of going on pilgrimage a pilgrim received a staff and wallet (or bag) as Richard did in 1190 before setting out for the Holy Land (Hoveden, 3.36).

64.9–10 walk afoot . . . dead men go on pilgrimage.

64.15 knight's chain and spurs of gold the chain is a knight's girdle (see note to 188.41); golden spurs were fixed to the heels of a young man when he was dubbed knight, and distinguished him from a squire as Scott recorded in his 'Essay on Chivalry' (*Prose Works*, 6.64).

64.26 Kirjath Jairam name of a border town in Palestine, also used as a personal name, in the form 'Kirriah Jairim', in Marlowe, *The Jew of Malta*, 1.1.126. Its transference from place name to personal name can probably be attributed to 1 Chronicles 2.50–53, where it is used in a way which makes it appear to be the name of one of the Jewish patriarchs. See also note to 63.16.

64.27 Milan harnesses suits of armour made in Milan. By at least the 13th century Milan had numerous master smiths making coats of mail and later in the Middle Ages there are frequent references in English texts to armour made in Milan.

64.39 blessing of our Father i.e. of Abraham.

64.40 rod of Moses the rod which God changed into a serpent (Exodus 4.2–5), by means of which Moses was able to call down plagues upon the Egyptians (Exodus Chs 7–10) and bring forth water out of a rock (Exodus 17.6; Numbers 20.11).

65.1–2 nothing for nothing proverbial: *ODEP*, 579.

65 motto John Dryden, 'Palamon and Arcite' (1699), 3.453–463.

65.30–31 King Richard . . . Austria Richard was held first by the Duke of Austria in the castle of Durrenstein and then handed over to the emperor, Henry VI, appearing before him at Ratisbon and then Treves.

65.35 Prince John the title is an anachronism (albeit one found in Scott's sources: see Henry, 3.149), and was not used by the younger sons of the English kings until the reign of James I. Contemporary sources refer to John as 'lord John' (Latin *dominus*; e.g. Hoveden, 3.14) or 'earl John' (Latin *comes*; e.g. Hoveden, 3.139).

65.35–38 Prince John . . . favours while Richard was held prisoner negotiations were conducted with the emperor. Philip and John, anxious to strengthen their own positions in England and Normandy, offered the emperor (rather than the Duke of Austria) bribes to keep Richard prisoner. Richard had treated John generously and granted him a number of earldoms before leaving for the Crusade (Henry, 3.137; Hoveden, 3.6).

65.40 Arthur b. 1187 and apparently murdered at Rouen in 1203, probably at John's instigation. John became king at Richard's death in 1199; usurpation is perhaps too strong a term for this as Richard had named him as his heir and the strict rule of primogeniture was not yet established.

66.4 lawless resolutes *Hamlet*, 1.1.98.

66.19–20 consuming cankers *I Henry VI*, 2.4.71.

66.36 Passage of Arms tournament in which a group of knights take on all challengers; this was not a recognised Middle English term. Scott seems to have been the first to use this phrase in English, apparently basing it on the French *pas d'armes* (see 'Essay on Chivalry', *Prose Works*, 6.45), the name given to a stylised representation of the defence of a passage or cross-roads against all comers.

67.7 lists . . . strong palisades see note to 30.34.

67.18 On a platform the layout and organisation of this tournament are influenced by the Jousts of St Inglebert as described by Froissart (Berners's Froissart, Vol. 2, Chs 162, 168; see also Scott's 'Essay on Chivalry', *Prose Works*, 6.82–85).

67.24 savage or sylvan man in the 16th century a *savage man*, both in pageants and heraldry, was a stylised depiction of a wild man, naked or dressed only in leaves.

67.25–26 character . . . game knights taking part in tournaments sometimes adopted the guise of characters from literature or legend. Philip of Novara (*Mémoires* (Paris, 1913), 7.134) describes a tournament in Arthurian dress in 1223 in Cyprus and such events continued throughout the Middle Ages (see R. S. Loomis, 'Chivalric and Dramatic Imitations of the Arthurian Romance', in *Medieval Studies in Memory of A. K. Loomis*, ed. A. Henry (Cambridge, Mass., 1939), 79).

67.33 Hugh de Grantmesnil Hugh de Grantmesnil (d. 1094) followed William the Conqueror to England and was given several grants of land in Leicestershire and Nottinghamshire. By 1194 his estate had passed to the Beaumont family (see note to 50.43). He does not appear to have been Lord High Steward of England.

67.35 Ralph de Vipont probably Robert de Vipont, or Vieuxpont (d. 1228), one of King John's most trusted followers.

67.36 Knight of St John of Jerusalem Knight Hospitaller: see note to 49.39. But there is no evidence that de Vipont was one.

67.37 Heather 7 kms SE of Ashby-de-la-Zouche.

68.7–8 The exterior of the lists . . . carpets see *Sports and Pastimes*, 111: 'the lists were superbly decorated, and surrounded by the pavilions belonging to the champions ornamented with their arms, banners, and banerolls; the scaffolds for the reception of the nobility of both sexes who came as spectators, and those especially appointed for the royal family, were hung with tapestry and embroideries of gold and silver'.

68.36 Cupid god of love in Roman mythology.

68.37–38 La Royne de la Beaulté et des Amours *French* the Queen of Beauty and Love. In fact, there is only one French tournament of the period in which ladies were recorded as being spectators, that at Joigni and their involvement in English tournaments stems from the end of the 13th century: see N. Denholm-Young, 'The Tournament in the Thirteenth Century', in *Studies in Medieval History presented to Frederick Maurice Powicke*, ed. R. W. Hunt and others (Oxford, 1948), 242, 265.

69.4–5 William de Wyvil, and Stephen de Martival fictitious characters.

69.20–21 Norman gentleman . . . Montdidier the name perhaps comes from Ralph of Montdidier, step-father of Philip I of France.

69.38–39 Prince John was even then . . . York in fact, the Jewish community in York had been virtually wiped out by a massacre in 1190. An 1194 record of arrangements made to raise Richard's ransom, which lists the Jewish communities in England, does not mention York: see Cecil Roth, *A History of the Jews in England*, 3rd edn (Oxford, 1964), 24.

70.5 yeoman see Glossary. The word was frequently used in the Robin Hood ballads to describe Robin Hood and his followers. Dobson and Taylor consider that a significant part of Robin Hood's appeal lay in his being 'a hero who was neither a knight nor a peasant or "husbonde" but something in between' (*Rymes of Robyn Hood*, 34) but J. C. Holt makes the case that Robin may have come from the 'yeoman officer' rank of the feudal household rather than being a 'yeoman landholder' (*Robin Hood* (London, 1982), 116–27). The description which follows shares a number of features with that of Chaucer's Yeoman: green clothing, arrows at the belt, very large bow, baldric, silver badge (later shown to be St Christopher: see 259.30 and note), brown face. See the 'General Prologue' to *The Canterbury Tales*, 1 (A), 101–17.

70.5 Lincoln green green cloth made at Lincoln from the later Middle Ages onwards. It has been associated with Robin Hood since at least the 15th century when it is referred to in 'A Lytell Geste of Robyn Hode' (Ritson, 1.74, Fytte 8, line 17: Child, 117). See also note to 6.22.

70.7 turned short round turned around abruptly.

70.11 bottled spider *Richard III*, 1.3.242 and 4.4.81.

70.22 points of his boots Strutt claims that the fashion of lengthening the toes of the shoes and bringing them forward to a sharp point was first introduced in the reign of William Rufus (1087–1100): 'Soon after, a courtier . . . improved upon the first idea by filling the vacant part of the shoe with tow, and twisting it round in the form of a ram's horn'. They were 'inveighed against by the clergy, and strictly forbidden to be worn by the religious orders. So far as one can judge from the illuminations of the twelfth century, the fashion . . . did not long maintain its ground. It was, however, afterwards revived' (*Dress and Habits*, 1.105–06). See also Henry, 3.586.

70.22 out-heroding outdoing; see *Hamlet*, 3.2.13.

71.8–10 well mounted . . . bearing upon his hand a falcon Strutt records of John that 'his partiality for *fine horses*, *hounds*, and *hawks*, is evident, from his frequently receiving such animals, by way of payment, instead of money' (*Sports and Pastimes*, 5).

71.28 rheno see *Dress and Habits*, 1.97–98: 'The RENO or RHENO was a garment made of the most pretious furs; and, consequently, it could not have been purchased but by persons of great wealth. Orderic Vitalis . . . places the *reno* among the royal habiliments, and clearly distinguishes it from the *chlamis*, or *long mantle*; an ancient author, cited by Du Cange, informs us, that the *reno* covered both the sides of the body and the shoulders; and another writer expressly says, that it descended as low as the navel: it must, therefore, have been a garment as much calculated for warmth as for ornament, and probably appropriated to the winter only.'

71.36 daughter of Zion frequently used in the Old Testament (e.g. Isaiah 1.8), often with symbolic meaning, but here it simply refers to Rebecca as a Jewess. Zion was a hill in the precincts of Jerusalem but later the name was given to Jerusalem itself, and figuratively, to the Jewish people.

71.41–43 a sort of Eastern dress . . . turban in fact medieval Jews dressed like Christians, apart from the distinctive badge or hat which they were later obliged to wear to identify themselves as Jews (see note to 47.31–33).

72.5 simarre term used vaguely for a light dress or robe for a woman, often in works with Middle Eastern or Persian settings.

72.18 bald scalp of Abraham while there is no biblical reference to Abraham's being bald, he did die at a very old age (see Genesis 25.7).

72.20 wisest king who ever lived Solomon; see 1 Kings 4.30–31.

72.22–23 Bride of the Canticles . . . lily of the valley to Solomon is traditionally attributed the biblical love poem, the Song of Songs, or Canticle of Canticles, in which the bride is described as 'the rose of Sharon, and the lily of the valleys' (2.1).

72.27 Mammon of unrighteousness Luke 16.9; *mammon* means 'riches'.

72.27–28 the Marquis of Marks, the Baron of Byzants the mark was a money of account equivalent at this time to two thirds of a pound sterling; the byzant was a Byzantine gold coin of varying value, used in England and elsewhere in Europe at this time and later.

72.29–30 not a single cross . . . dancing there proverbial: see *ODEP*, 180. A cross was often depicted on coins and, according to Thomas Hoccleve's *De Regimine Principum* (1411–12), 'The feend, men seyn, may hoppen in a pouche/ Whan that no croys there-inne may a-pere' (stanza 98).

72.43 high places of the synagogue the Hebrew term translated as 'high places' in the Old Testament refers to hills or elevated platforms used for sacrifice, but John perverts the phrase by using it of the best seats in the synagogue.

73.5–6 last Saxon monarchs of England Edward the Confessor (reigned 1042–66) and Harold II (d. 1066), each named elsewhere as an ancestor of Athelstane. The text implies that both Edward and Harold were of the 'ancient royal race' of the kings of Wessex which stretched back to the 5th century. This was true of Edward but not of Harold who, although married to Edward's sister, was the son of Earl Godwin (d. 1053) and his Danish wife Gytha. Harold had children but Edward was childless.

73.13 Unready since at least the 16th century the Anglo-Saxon king Ethelred II (reigned 978–1016) has been referred to as 'Ethelred the Unready', where *unready* (from *rede* 'advice') originally meant 'ill-advised'. This was a version of the earlier nickname *Unrade* meaning 'lack of counsel or wisdom'. However, *unready* was later misunderstood as the negative of *ready* and taken to mean 'unprepared, slow, hesitating'. Scott so uses it here.

73.26 vis inertiæ *Latin* force of inertia; here used metaphorically for sluggishness.

73.33 free companions Scott probably took the use of *companions* in this sense from Berners (Berners's Froissart, Vol. 1, Ch. 215).

73.33 Condottieri strictly leaders of troops of mercenary soldiers, but here used for the troops themselves just as Mrs Radcliffe appears to use the term in 1794 (*The Mysteries of Udolpho*, ed. Bonamy Dobree (London, 1966), 358).

74.18 Wat Tyrrell reputed to have shot the arrow which killed William II (William Rufus) in 1100 as he was hunting in the New Forest.

74.20 grandfather William Rufus had no children. John was descended from his brother, Henry I (reigned 1100–35).

74.24 St Grizzel Griselda, who suffered with exemplary patience her husband's testing of her obedience, and heroine of a story in Boccaccio's *Decameron* (1351–53), taken up in Chaucer's 'The Clerk's Tale' (via Petrarch's Latin translation) and in Thomas Dekker's *Patient Grissil* (1603). In none of these was she canonised. Although the story has ancient origins, Boccaccio first gave it the form associated with the name Griselda in which it became popular throughout Europe.

74.32 rulers of the land see Isaiah 16.1.

75.4 shield of brawn dish made by cooking, in a mould, meat placed inside the thick skin of a boar: see note to 57.7.

76 motto John Dryden, 'Palamon and Arcite' (1699), 3.580–86.

76.13 halidom holy thing, or relic, but the occasional use of spellings like *halidame* and *holidame* suggests that it was taken by folk etymology to refer to the 'holy dame', the Virgin Mary.

76.28 Waldemar Fitzurse fictional character, but at 299.16 he is said to be the son of Reginald Fitzurse, one of the murderers of Thomas a Becket in Canterbury Cathedral in 1170. The name *Fitzurse* means 'son of a bear'.

77.21–28 by touching his shield . . . actual battle detail borrowed from the Jousts of St Inglebert (see note to 67.18) where, however, each knight displayed two shields; one to be touched for arms of courtesy, the other for sharp weapons.

77.27 at outrance with maximum force or violence, a phrase used in English from the 15th to the early 17th centuries and also known to Scott in its French form 'a oultrance', in La Sale's 15th-century romance *Jehan de Saintré* (186, 228) of which he had a copy (Paris, 1724: *CLA*, 107) and which he had used in compiling his 'Essay on Chivalry'.

78.41 Wardour Manuscript see 12.33 and note.

79.1–4 contemporary poet . . . we trust S. T. Coleridge, 'The Knight's Tomb' (written 1817), lines 9–11. Although the poem was not published until 1834, James Gillman says that Coleridge quoted these lines to a friend who repeated them to Scott the following day, and that their appearance in *Ivanhoe* led Coleridge to identify Scott as the author of the Waverley Novels (*The Life of Samuel Taylor Coleridge*, 2 vols (London, 1838), 1.277).

79.7 place . . . no more see Psalm 103.16.

79.17 Barbaric normally 'uncivilized' or 'savage' but here used as an adjective for the noun *Barbary*, a name for the Mediterranean coast of Africa ruled by the Saracens or, more generally, the Saracen world. The same music is later called 'Saracenic' (81.39).

80.31 attaint as both noun and verb in this sense *attaint* had only a short life in English and it is probable that Scott revived the word from Berners's Froissart: e.g. 'The first course, they strake eche other on their helmes a great attaynt' (Vol. 2, Ch. 168).

82.6 Desdichado *Spanish* unhappy, or suffering misfortune. Scott may have confused it with *desheredado*, which means 'disinherited' or 'underprivileged'.

82.28–29 look your last . . . paradise see Luke 23.43. Hailes quotes from Fordun the defiant words of a 14th-century Scots warrior about to enter the lists against an English knight: 'Brother, . . . Prepare for death, and confess yourself, and then you shall sup in Paradise' (David Dalrymple, Lord Hailes, *Annals of Scotland*, 2 vols, (Edinburgh, 1776–79), 2.273).

83.5 device . . . one horse this device was used on the Seal of the Temple (see Laurent Dailliez, *Les Templiers et les Règles de l'Ordre du Temple* (Paris, 1972), 166). However, only the Grand Master was allowed to bear any device on his shield (see note to 25.13–14), and this device was not the one he bore.

83.8 their suppression see note to 307.13–19.

83.9 a raven . . . skull a raven was traditionally a harbinger of misfortune and death. More especially it was depicted as feasting on the bodies of the dead and picking skeletons clean, as the two ravens do in the Scottish ballad 'The Twa Corbies'.

83.10 Gare le Corbeau *French* beware of the raven.

84.37 Cave, Adsum *Latin* beware, I am here; the motto of the Jardine family of Jardine Hall, Dumfriesshire.

85 motto 'The Flower and the Leaf', a 15th-century poem once attributed to Chaucer, here quoted in Dryden's version, lines 175–77, 184–89.

85.28 agnus castus the name of a tree once held to be the protector of chastity.

86.37 Earl of Salisbury the Earl of Salisbury in 1194 was William Fitz-Patrick (d. 1196) but he does not appear to have accompanied Richard on the crusade. Scott probably refers to the more famous earl, William, known as Longespée or Longsword (d.1226), who married Fitz-Patrick's daughter and heir in 1198, and who, contrary to historical fact, is depicted in the romance *Richard Coeur de Lion* as a companion of Richard on the crusade (Ellis, 2.210, 249, 252, 260).

86.39 Sir Thomas de Multon, the knight of Gilsland see note to 51.1. However, the first Thomas de Multon who could legitimately be known as the 'knight of Gilsland' was a different person (fl. 1242–70). Through his marriage to Maud de Vaux, whose family had held the barony of Gilsland since 1158, he came to be known as Multon of Gilsland.

86.43 Over God's forbode *oath* God forbid! See 'Adam Bell, Clym of the Clough, and William of Cloudesly', Part 3, line 259: Percy, 1.159; Child, 116.

87.5 gigantic limbs the *Itinerarium* describes Richard as being tall with long arms and legs (Bk 2, Ch. 5; 1.144).

87.31–33 Laying one hand . . . the stirrup the same feat is described in 'The Book of Heroes', Henry Weber's version of *Das Heldenbuch* by Wolfram von Eschenbach, with the following footnote: 'This was reckoned one of the requisites of a knight; and in some countries no nobleman could succeed to certain lands possessed by his ancestors, without leaping upon his horse completely armed, and without touching the stirrups' (*Illustrations of Northern Antiquities from the Earlier Teutonic and Scandinavian Romances* (Edinburgh, 1814), 117). Lockhart claims that Scott's contribution to the volume was considerable, though only acknowledged with regard to the abstract of *Eyrbiggia Saga* (Lockhart, 3.114).

88.25 ducal crown the coronet to which Scott refers is that of a marquess, which has, 'on a jewelled circle of gold, four strawberry leaves and four pearls, alternately' (Bernard Burke, *A Genealogical and Heraldic Dictionary of the Peerage and Baronetage of the British Empire* (London, 1859), xiii).

89.36 Barbary see note to 79.17. Barbary horses, much prized for their speed, were not introduced into England until the early 17th century.

89.37 sequins Italian gold coins worth about nine shillings; also known as *zecchins*. The earliest English references to these coins date from the 16th century.

89.38 Joseph Pareira . . . Milan by the late 14th century the armourers of Milan were famous for their work but the name Pareira does not appear among them.

90.4 Philistine a warlike people who inhabited the coastal plains of Palestine and traditional enemies of the Israelites.

90.7–9 Ogg . . . sword of our fathers Og, King of Bashan, and Sihon, King of the Amorites, were Canaanite kings, killed in battle against the Israelites (see Numbers Ch. 21; Deuteronomy 3.1–7).

90.10–11 for a prey and for a spoil see Ezekiel 7.21: 'I will give it into the hands of the strangers for a prey, and to the wicked of the earth for a spoil'.

92.16 Needwood and Charnwood Needwood was a royal forest beside the River Trent in Staffordshire and Charnwood wooded upland country in NW Leicestershire.

93 motto Marlowe, *The Jew of Malta* (first performed *c.* 1592), 2.1.1–6.

93.20 presaging raven see note to 83.9.

93.36–37 Norman bonnet see Henry, 3.584: 'The caps or bonnets of the

Anglo-Normans were made of cloth, or furs'.

94.2 barbed steed horse wearing battle armour; see *Richard III*, 1.1.10.

94.3–5 long robe ... hood Strutt describes the Normans as wearing a 'long tunic' which was 'never worn by the lower order of the people', and also a gown which resembled the tunic but was looser, having long, large sleeves and a large hood 'which occasionally was drawn up over the head to defend it from the weather' (*Dress and Habits*, 1.93, 95).

94.33 zecchins see note to 89.37.

95.26 squire-at-arms apparently Scott coined this expression, basing it on the term *man-at-arms*, meaning a soldier, or fully-armed knight. Compare Keats's coinage *knight-at-arms* ('La Belle Dame Sans Merci', line 1).

96.30 estrada estrado, *Spanish* meaning a 'dais' or a 'room to receive guests'.

96.36 twelve Holy Fathers of our tribe the twelve sons of Jacob, the 'fathers' of the twelve tribes of Israel.

96.42 blotch of Egypt plague of boils (*blotch* means 'boil, eruption of the skin'), the third of the plagues inflicted by God on the Egyptians to induce them to allow the Israelites to leave Egypt: see Exodus 9.8–12.

96.43 Gulph of Lyons Gulf of Lions, where the Rhone flows into the Mediterranean.

97.2–3 robed the seething billows ... aloes see *The Merchant of Venice*, 1.1.33–34.

97.3 myrrh and aloes both are mentioned in the Old Testament, sometimes together, e.g. Psalm 45.8.

97.16 dispersed children of Zion the Jews living outside Palestine, sometimes known as the *diaspora*. While the phrase *daughter(s) of Zion* (see note to 71.36) is used in the Bible, *children of Zion* is not.

97.20 the herb which flourishes most ... trampled see *1 Henry IV*, 'the camomile, the more it is trodden on the faster it grows' (2.4.388–89); John Lyly, *Euphues, The Anatomy of Wyt* (1579), 'though the Camomill, the more it is trodden and pressed downe, the more it spreadeth' (*Complete Works*, ed. R. Warwick Bond, 3 vols (Oxford, 1902), 1.196).

97.27 Sabaoths Aramaic word meaning 'armies'; it occurs untranslated at Romans 9.29 and James 5.4 in the original Greek text, the Vulgate and the Authorised Version, and from the 14th to the 18th centuries was often mistakenly used in English as an alternative to *Sabbath*.

97.27–28 'tis a good youth see *As You Like It*, 3.5.112: 'It is a pretty youth'.

97.33 the new Temple the Temple in Jerusalem was destroyed in AD 70 and has never been rebuilt.

98.5 Nazarene Christians, so called because Nazareth was the home town of Jesus.

98.10–11 veil thyself Jewish women wore material covering the head and shoulders but were not normally required to cover their faces.

98.27 monies sums of money; often used instead of the singular form in Elizabethan English. Shylock uses the word frequently on his first appearance in *The Merchant of Venice* and, presumably from this, later writers like Scott identified it as a Jewish mannerism of speech.

99.23 wild bulls of Bashan see Psalm 22.12: 'Many bulls have compassed me: strong bulls of Bashan have beset me round'. *Bulls* here means figuratively 'enemies'; Bashan was the broad fertile region east of the Sea of Galilee and was celebrated for its cattle and sheep.

99.42–43 clipt within the ring pieces were often clipped from the edge of coins to obtain the metals of which they were made. Coins made by the hand-hammering method were always liable to suffer from clipping, particularly as they were seldom exactly circular, and a ring around the sovereign's head was early introduced to discourage a practice that was only stopped by the introduction of machine-made coins with graining or lettering on the edge in the 16th and 17th centuries.

100.24–25 gone somewhat beyond me outwitted me, got round me; a 17th-century expression: see *Henry VIII*, 3.2.408.

100.28 Goliath the Philistine . . . beam see 1 Samuel 17.4–7: Goliath was 'six cubits and a span' tall, that is, between three and four metres, and 'the staff of his spear was like a weaver's beam'.

100.37–38 fawns, forest fiends, white women it was the Romans who believed in fauns (minor gods associated with woodland) but the Germanic peoples had stories of similar wood-sprites (see Jacob Grimm, *Teutonic Mythology*, trans. James Steven Stallybrass, 4 vols (London, 1880–88), 2.478–87); Scott's forest-fiends apparently belong to the same class of beings. The Germanic peoples also had stories of white women, generally beneficent creatures associated by Grimm with Germanic goddesses (see Grimm, 1.272–81, 3.962–69).

100.42 necromancers and cabalists necromancers claimed to communicate with the dead and foretell the future; cabalists, or cabbalists, dealt in mysterious or magical arts: see note to 232.18–19. The charge of dealing in forbidden magic was frequently made against the Jews in the Middle Ages although the terms *necromancer* and *cabalist* do not appear until the 14th and 16th centuries respectively.

101.23 redeem thy bondage in the Anglo-Saxon period slaves were sometimes manumitted by their masters; they could also purchase their own freedom. Turner (4.134–35) cites a number of cases of such purchase.

101.24 brother as free of thy guild as the best free member of a guild, an association of tradesmen or merchants in a town.

101.25–26 freeman's sword and buckler see note to 274.10.

101 motto *The Two Gentlemen of Verona*, 4.1.3–10.

102.18 St Nicholas's clerks highwaymen, as in *1 Henry IV*, 2.1.59–60; so called either because St Nicholas came to be regarded as the patron saint of thieves or, as Scott believed (see his footnote to 357), with reference to 'Old Nick', the devil, jocularly referred to as a saint.

104.33–34 stream . . . fathers in the wilderness see Exodus 17.6.

105.13–14 dogs . . . dogs proverbial, recorded from the 16th century onwards: see *ODEP*, 194–95.

105.17 made good proved to be true.

105.24 Hebrew Jew *1 Henry IV*, 2.4.172.

105.26 Gandelyn from the ballad 'Robin Lyth' printed by Ritson (*Ancient Songs* (London, 1790), 48: Child, 115) but the Robin of the title is apparently not Robin Hood.

105.37 Miller 'Much the millers sone', a companion of Robin Hood in 'A Lytell Gest of Robyn Hode' (Ritson, 1.3, Fytte 1, line 14: Child, 117) and other tales of the outlaws.

106.2–3 after the fashion . . . moulinet in *Quentin Durward* (1.26.5–9) Scott describes this action as a 'significant flourish with [a] pole which is called *le moulinet*, because the artist, holding it in the middle, brandishes the two ends in every direction, like the sails of a windmill in motion'. *Moulinet* is the diminutive of *moulin*, 'mill'.

106.6–7 doubly a thief millers were traditionally considered to be dishonest in their weighing of the corn, as implied by the proverb 'an honest miller has a golden thumb' (*ODEP*, 532), referred to by Chaucer ('General Prologue' to *The Canterbury Tales*, 1 (A), 563), which suggests that there are no honest millers.

106.15 for want of a sacred poet see Horace, *Odes*, 4.9.28, 'Carent quia vate sacro', meaning 'because they lacked a sacred poet', where *sacred* means 'making sacred', that is, 'making famous'.

108 motto 'The Knight's Tale', *The Canterbury Tales*, 1 (A), 2599–610, modernised. Scott's description of the tournament has been influenced by the battle between Palamon and Arcite and their followers in 'The Knight's Tale' (*The Canterbury Tales*, 1 (A), 2483–662) including such elements as rules for limiting the extent of the fighting, the details of the actual fight and the role of the heralds.

110.38–39 throw down his leading-staff tournaments are similarly ended in *Jehan de Saintré* (128, 186, 267).

111.25 Laissez aller *French* let them go. Strutt quotes a medieval 'ordinance for the conducting of the justs and tournaments, according to the ancient establishment'. It sets out that the combatants shall continue fighting 'so long as the speakers shall give them permission, by repeating the sentence, LET THEM GO ON'. A footnote gives the original words as 'Laisseir les aler' (*Sports and Pastimes*, 105). These words are used for the same purpose in *Jehan de Saintré* (126).

112.6 Beau-seant , name of the silver and black gonfalon, or banner, of the Knights Templars. The term was actually *le gonfalon baussant*, with *baussant* used in its original sense meaning 'half one colour, half another'. The form *beau-seant* was a later corruption of the word. See Favine, 2.402: '*they were and shewed themselves wholly* White *and fayre towards Christians, but Blacke and Terrible to them that were Miscreants*'.

112.16–21 The splendid armour . . . terror or compassion compare Sir Philip Sidney, *Arcadia* (completed 1581): 'And now the often-changing fortune began also to change the hue of the battles. For at the first, though it were terrible, yet terror was decked so bravely with rich furniture, gilt swords, shining armours, pleasant pencels, that the eye with delight had scarce leisure to be afraid: but now all universally defiled with dust, blood, broken armours, mangled bodies, took away the mask, and set forth horror in his own horrible manner' (Bk 3, Ch. 8; *The Countess of Pembroke's Arcadia*, ed. Maurice Evans (Harmondsworth, 1977), 473; see *CLA*, 101). As there are no exact echoes, the passage may owe more to Froissart, whom Scott describes as delighting in the description of scenes of mixed glory and horror (see 'Essay on Chivalry', *Prose Works*, 6.79).

112 footnote see Favine, 2.402, and note to 112.6.

114.5 stood him in the more stead was the more service to him.

114.25–26 champion in black armour . . . horse according to the romance *Richard Coeur de Lion*, Richard appeared at the tournament at Salisbury (see note to 51.1) in several disguises. His first suit of armour was black, and he rode a horse of the same colour (Ellis, 2.186).

114.33 Le Noir Faineant variation on the well known phrase *roi faineant* (king who does nothing, or sluggard king) a term applied to the later Merovingian kings of France.

115.34 Gentle and Free . . . Ashby the words *gentle* and *free* are both used here in the sense of 'noble', and were often paired in this way in medieval texts, as in 'sire Thomas of Multone, gentil baroun ant fre' in 'The Execution of Sir Simon Fraser' (line 107; see *Historical Poems of the XIVth and XVth Centuries*, ed. Rossell Hope Robbins (New York, 1959), 14–21).

116.4–6 nowhere to be found . . . forest glades see *Richard Coeur de Lion*, where Richard, after defeating three knights, 'plunged into the forest, and disappeared' (Ellis, 2.187).

117.6–7 placed . . . the splendid chaplet see *Sports and Pastimes*, 108: 'as a peculiar mark of their esteem, the favourite champions [in tournaments]

received the rewards …
quality'.

117 motto William W…
attribution to the *Iliad* is und…
(specifically Pope's translations…

117.36–37 doctrine . . . antipa…
innate sympathy and antipathy to explai…
attracting iron (sympathy) and water exting…
Middle Ages these notions would have been we…
History (e.g. 20.1 and 24.1).

118.8–9 fiefs of the crown feudal estates granted …
on condition of service to the king.

118.22 communis mater *Latin* universal mother. See Gala…
'Jerusalem . . . is the mother of us all' although the Vulgate, the Latin B…
Aymer would have used (see note to 291.41–42), here reads 'mater no…
('our mother'): here, as elsewhere in the Waverley Novels, it seems Scott is n…
using the nominal source text but himself translating into Latin.

118.24–26 crusaders . . . Ascalon Richard spent some time at Ascalon, a coastal city 70 kms SW of Jerusalem which had been in biblical times one of the five principal cities of the Philistines, but he got closer to Jerusalem than this. In December 1191 Richard and his army reached Beit-Nuba, only 20 kms from Jerusalem, and within sight of the Holy City. Richard decided not to risk trying to take Jerusalem and instead signed a five-year treaty with Saladin which gave Christians freedom to visit the Holy Places. Richard of Devizes records that two men who had visited Jerusalem tried to persuade Richard to enter the city 'but the proud swelling of his great heart would not allow him to enjoy as a privilege from the pagans what he could not have as a gift from God' (*The Chronicle of Richard of Devizes of the Time of King Richard the First*, ed. John T. Appleby (London, 1963), 84).

119.7–8 rose of loveliness . . . camphire see The Song of Solomon 1.13–14.

119.10–11 minor . . . royal disposal in marriage a feudal superior had the right of guardianship over his vassal's heir where the heir was a minor and the right to give the heir in marriage; where the king was the feudal superior these rights belonged to the king. John's claim is untenable as he is neither king nor regent.

119.22 De Bigot Roger le Bigod, or Bigot (d. 1221), Earl of Norfolk, Hereditary Steward of the Household.

119.25 bones of Becket after Thomas a Becket (1118–70), Archbishop of Canterbury, was assassinated in his cathedral at the instigation of the king (see Scott's footnote to 299), he was canonised in 1173 and his shrine at Canterbury Cathedral became a favourite site for pilgrimage.

119.26 casting pearls before swine proverbial: Matthew 7.6; *ODEP*, 617.

119.37 fleurs-de-lis heraldic lilies; three fleurs-de-lis appear on the French royal coat of arms.

119.41 "Take heed . . . unchained" according to Hoveden, the French king, hearing of the agreement for Richard's release in 1193, at once sent word to John to take care of himself because the devil was now let loose (Hoveden, 3.216–17). Scott took the story, with the use of the word 'unchained', a free translation of the Latin *solutus*, from Henry, 3.154-55.

120.6 draw our party to a head this seems to combine two senses of *head* and means 'to bring our supporters to the crisis point' (*OED*, *head*, sb., 31) and 'to bring out our supporters as a force in rebellion' (*OED*, *head*, sb., 30). Compare also *Cymbeline*, 3.5.25.

…ssionary in the Ardennes in France. He …er being associated with a legend originally …ile hunting one Good Friday he found a stag with a

…arket town about 20 kms east of Cambridge, famous for its … and for the training of horses on its heath since the time of James VI … (1566–1625).

[1]21.8 merry-men followers of a knight or outlaw chief; traditionally, though not in this instance, applied to Robin Hood's band of outlaws.

121.20 Locksley according to Dobson and Taylor (*Rymes of Robyn Hood*, 286–87) the association of Robin Hood with the town of Locksley can be traced to an anonymous prose life in the Sloane Collection in the British Library. It was then incorporated into the later ballads. Robin Hood is addressed as 'Locksly' in the 17th-century ballad 'Robin Hood and Queen Katherine' (Ritson, 2.86, line 66: Child, 145), and in the 18th-century ballad 'Robin Hoods Birth, Breeding, Valour, and Marriage' we are told that Robin was born 'In Locksly town, in merry Nottinghamshire' (Ritson, 2.2, line 5: Child, 149).

121.23 nobles gold coins, first minted by Edward III (1327–77), valued at one third or one half of a pound.

121.39 shoot boldly round shoot boldly one after the other.

122.1 a shot at rovers a shot at a chosen mark, which could be at any distance from the archer.

122.15 devoted doomed; but as this meaning does not sit well in the context it was changed in the Magnum to 'bold'.

123.23 split to shivers this feat is attributed to Clym of the Clough in a ballad stanza quoted by Andrew Lang in his notes to *Ivanhoe* (Border Edition (London, 1891), 671), but the stanza does not appear in known versions of the ballad 'Adam Bell, Clym of the Clough, and William of Cloudesly' (Child, 116), and has not been traced.

123.30–34 a mark . . . willow bush this whole episode, including the use of a rod as a target and its cleaving in two, closely follows a story told of William of Cloudesly in the ballad 'Adam Bell, Clym of the Clough, and William of Cloudesly', Part 3, lines 193–212: Percy, 1.156–57; Child, 116.

124.2 sixty knights medieval writers differ on this, e.g. Layamon, the first to give a figure, says 1600 or more (*Brut*, ed. G. L. Brook and R. F. Leslie, 2 vols, Early English Text Society, OS 250, 277 (London, 1963, and Oxford, 1978), line 11434) but Malory gives the figure as 150 (*Morte D'Arthur*, 1.72: Bk 3, Ch. 1).

124.10 I give him the bucklers I own myself beaten by him: see *Much Ado About Nothing*, 5.2.15–16.

124.27 split the willow rod as well as being attributed to William of Cloudesly (see note to 123.30–34) this part of the story is also told of Robin Hood in 'Robin Hood and Guy of Gisborne' (Ritson, 1.121, lines 125–28: Child, 118).

124.33–34 never did . . . shaft in 'A Lytell Gest of Robyn Hode' Robin himself claims 'I was commytted the best archere,/ That was in mery Englonde' (Ritson, 1.77, Fytte 8, lines 75–76: Child, 117).

125 motto Thomas Warton, 'Ode for the New Year, 1787', lines 1–6.

125.23–26 Lord Hastings . . . historical fame William, Lord Hastings (1430?–83), executed by Richard III. See *Richard III*, 3.4.

125.26–28 castle and town of Ashby . . . Roger de Quincy . . . in the Holy Land Scott here confuses different generations of de Quincys. Robert de Quincy was a companion in arms of Richard I in Palestine. His nephew, Roger de Quincy (d. 1264), succeeded to the Earldom of Winchester in 1235. Roger's daughter married Alan la Zouch (d. 1270) of Ashby but in 1194 the lands of Ashby de la Zouch belonged to William de Belmeis (d. 1199).

125.34 swept the country cleared the surrounding area.

125.38–39 Danish families in the N and E of England there was extensive settlement by Danes after the Viking invasions. Ashby de la Zouch falls within this area.

126.10 memorable example . . . Ireland in 1185. According to Giraldus Cambrensis, Henry II sent his son John, then about 18, to govern Ireland. Received by the Archbishop of Dublin and other dignitaries at Waterford, John alienated them by treating them with disrespect and pulling their beards (*Opera*, ed. J. S. Brewer, James F. Dimock, and George F. Warner, 8 vols (London, 1861–91), 5.389).

126.12 buying golden opinions see *Macbeth*, 1.7.32–33.

126.37 waggoner's frock a frock was a loose-fitting garment reaching to the knees or lower, worn as an overall by various workmen including waggoners.

126.41 Charlemagne Charles the Great (742–814), king of the Franks, crowned as Roman Emperor in 800.

126.43–127.3 to what purpose . . . frost this story is told by the Monk of St Gall (*Early Lives of Charlemagne*, trans. A. J. Grant (New York, 1966), 104) and is quoted by Strutt (*Dress and Habits*, 1.40), Turner (4.82) and Henry (2.589). Scott has bowdlerised the passage which speaks of retiring to empty the bowels, while he refers to being seated.

127.4–6 short cloaks . . . princes of the house of Anjou see *Dress and Habits*, 1.97: 'the short mantle of Anjou, said to have been introduced by Henry the Second, who was from that circumstance surnamed *court* or *short mantle*'. The House of Anjou in England comprises Henry II and his sons Richard I and John; Henry's father was Count of Anjou, a possession lost by the English crown during the reign of John.

127.17 simnel-bread and wastle cakes simnel bread was made from fine flour, 'prepared by boiling, sometimes with subsequent baking' (*OED*, *simnel*). *Wastel*, an obsolete term revived by Scott, meant 'bread from the finest flour'. The Prioress in the 'General Prologue' to *The Canterbury Tales* pampered her dogs with 'milk and wastel-breed' (1 (A), 146–47). The term *wastle cake* is apparently Scott's own coinage.

127.20–24 though luxurious . . . inferior strain see Henry, 3.569–70: 'The English . . . were much addicted to excessive eating and drinking, in which they sometimes spent both day and night, without intermission. The Normans were very unlike them in this respect, being delicate in the choice of their meats and drinks, but seldom exceeding the bounds of temperance.' The comments derive from William of Malmesbury, 2.305–06.

127.27–28 his death . . . ale at King's Lynn, in 1216, John was struck down by dysentery and fever, apparently brought on by fatigue and over-indulgence in peaches and a new kind of beer. He died a week later.

127.39 dried his hands upon a towel Scott refers in his 'Essay on Chivalry' to a romance in which 'we read of the high birth and breeding of a page being ascertained, by his scrupulously declining to use a towel to wipe his hands, when washed before he began to carve, and contented himself with waving them in the air till they dried of themselves' (*Prose Works*, 6.52).

128.1 Karum-pie mentioned by Henry (3.590) as one of several dishes 'the composition of which, I imagine, is now unknown'.

128.5 beccaficoes from an Italian word meaning 'fig-pecker', a name given to small migratory birds of the genus *sylvia*. They were highly prized in the autumn when they were fattened by the fig and grape harvests.

129.17 hold me a Saxon see note to 16.24–29.

130.3 head and front of the offence see *Othello*, 1.3.80: 'the very head and front of my offending'.

130.5 nidering mistaken form of the Old English *nithing* ('villain') used in the 1596 printed text of William of Malmesbury from which Henry took the story of how William Rufus, rousing support for himself against the Norman uprising (see note to 17.21), 'called them his dear English, exhorted them to collect their countrymen, under the penalty, that every one who did not come, should be called a *Nidering*, a name which he knew none of them could endure' (Henry, 3.363; see William of Malmesbury, 2.362). In the footnote this is misremembered as a story about William the Conqueror. After Scott borrowed *nidering* from Henry it became through his influence popular in literary works, while historians revived the correct form, *nithing*.

130.42–43 Bartholinus . . . Danes see Henry, 2.539: 'To call a Dane a *Nithing*, was like setting fire to gun-powder, and instantly excited such a flame of rage, as nothing but his own blood, or the blood of the offender, could extinguish'. Henry cites Thomas Bartholin (1659–90), *Antiquitatum Danicarum de causis contemptae a Danis adhuc gentilibus mortis libri tres* (Copenhagen, 1689), 98: *CLA*, 99.

132.3 St Thomas St Thomas a Becket: see note to 119.25.

132.6 conclamatum est *Latin* it has been shouted; i.e. the celebrations are over.

132.6 poculatum est *Latin* it has been drunk. The Prior creates a new verb from the noun *poculum* 'a drinking cup, a drink'.

132.34 hand-writing on the wall see Daniel 5.5–31. A hand appeared and wrote on the wall a message which foretold the fall of King Belshazzar. See also note to 30.26–27.

132.34–36 they have marked . . . shake the wood referring to the return of Richard Coeur de Lion but also recalling a symbolic reference to a lion coming from the forest to punish the Jews in Jeremiah 5.6.

133 motto Joanna Baillie, *Count Basil: A Tragedy* (1798), 2.3.169–74.

134. 11 days of King Arthur . . . army Geoffrey of Monmouth records that in one battle Arthur killed four hundred and seventy Saxons (*Historia Regum Britannie*, ed. Neil Wright (Cambridge, 1985), 104; *CLA*, 27).

134.18–21 Duke Robert of Normandy . . . nation Robert (1054?–1134), eldest son of William I, became Duke of Normandy in 1087 on his father's death but his two brothers, William II (reigned 1087–1100), known as William Rufus (i.e. William the Red), and Henry I (reigned 1100–1135), were successively preferred as kings of England.

134.22–24 bold knight . . . Holy Sepulchre Robert displayed bravery and skill in combat but little judgement in his administration of Normandy. In 1096–99 he took part in the First Crusade which captured Jerusalem from the Muslims.

134.24–25 blind . . . Cardiffe Robert was imprisoned from 1106 until his death in Cardiff in 1134. The account of his release in 1107 or 1109, his plotting treason and being recaptured and blinded appears to be a later embellishment.

135.11 Christmas gambols and quaint maskings see *The Taming of the Shrew*, Induction, 2.135. Gambols were acrobatics, while maskings (or masques) were a form of court theatre where the performers were often courtiers. Neither term is found in the Middle Ages but the Christmas period was traditionally a time of revelling, including, by the later Middle Ages, feasting, dancing, tumbling, mummery and the wearing of disguises, costume, and masks.

135.38–136.5 He told how . . . brides' families based on Judges 19–21, but re-told in a medieval context with some elements of Livy's story of the rape of the Sabine women (*Ab Urbe Condita*, Bk 1, Ch. 9).

136.28 convent of Saint Wittol, or Withold the Benedictine abbey at

Burton, founded *c.* 1004, was not dedicated to Withold (see note to 20.14). De Bracy plays on the word *wittol* meaning 'cuckold' or 'fool'.

138 motto Thomas Parnell (1679–1718), *The Hermit*, lines 1–6.

140.14–16 zig-zag moulding . . . Saxon churches see Turner, 4.456: the 'universal diagonal ornament, or zig-zag moulding, which is a very distinguishing trait of the Saxon architecture'. This design is in fact Anglo-Norman, the earliest English example (*c.* 1104) being found in Durham cathedral.

140.25 Saint Julian according to tradition Julian the Hospitaller, having killed his own parents through a mistake of identity, went as a penance to live with his wife near a ford where they assisted travellers and sheltered the poor.

140.31 Pass on, whosoever thou art for the events in this chapter see the Middle English narrative poem, known to Scott as *The Kyng and the Hermite* (*Remains of the Early Popular Poetry of England*, ed. W. Carew Hazlitt, 4 vols (London, 1864–6), 1.12–34), which concerns an unidentified King Edward and an unnamed Hermit. For Scott, 'the identifying the irregular Eremite with the Friar Tuck of Robin Hood's story, was an obvious expedient' (Magnum, 16.xviii).

141.5–6 pater . . . aves . . . credo *Pater noster* ('our father'), the Lord's Prayer; *Ave Maria* ('hail Mary'), the words of the angel to Mary in Luke 1.28 used in devotions; *credo* ('I believe'), the creed.

141.19 told bead said his prayers using a rosary to keep count.

143.19–20 yellow hair . . . sparkling Henry tells us Richard had yellow hair and 'blue and sparkling' eyes (3.163); he cites the *Itinerarium* as his source but it does not mention Richard's eye-colour and describes his hair as between red and yellow (see Bk 2, Ch. 5; 1.144).

143.41–42 well of St Dunstan . . . Britons a well, known as 'Friar Tuck's Well', lies on the east of Fountain Dale in Nottinghamshire, an area associated since the early 19th century with the 'Fountaines dale' mentioned in the ballad of 'Robin Hood and the Curtall Fryer' (Ritson, 2.65, line 153: Child, 123; see also *Rymes of Robyn Hood*, 301–02). Possibly Scott was thinking of this well, but linking it with St Dunstan is his own invention. Stories of mass baptisms are told of various British saints, e.g. Paulinus, Alban, Augustine of Canterbury, and Germanus, but not of Dunstan.

144.6 win the ram Chaucer's Miller at 'wrastlynge . . . wolde have alwey the ram' ('General Prologue' to *The Canterbury Tales*, 1 (A), 548). According to Strutt, 'Anciently this animal was the prize most usually given upon such occasions' (*Sports and Pastimes*, 64).

144.6 win . . . the ring carry off the prize. Originally used of a sport in which riders tried to carry off a suspended ring on the point of their lances.

144.6–7 quarter-staff contest fought with a pole six to eight ft long held with one hand in the middle and one half-way between the middle and the end.

144.6–7 win . . . the bucklers come off winner: see 124.10 and note.

144.10–11 thoughts . . . are according to the flesh see John 8.15.

144.13–16 Shadrach, Meshech, and Abednego . . . Saracens see Daniel 1.5–20. The king in the biblical version is Nebuchadnezzar, King of Babylon but see note to 25.30.

144.25 Copmanhurst see note to 27.28.

145.37 no forks a drawing of a Saxon feast, referred to by both Strutt and Turner, shows the table set with 'a knife, a horn, a bowl, a dish, and some loaves' (Turner, 4.73). Forks did not become common in England until the late Renaissance (see Madeleine Cosman, *Fabulous Feasts* (New York, 1976), 16).

146.14–16 Waes hael . . . Drink hael see note to 45.11.

146.19–20 thews and sinews the phrase, giving *thews* the implied sense of 'muscles', was adopted by Scott, perhaps from 'The Marriage of Sir Gawaine', Part 1, line 30 (Percy, 3.12; Child, 31); it appears frequently in later writers with *thews* having the implied meaning 'muscles'. However, the word had meant, less specifically, 'bodily strength' or, as Shakespeare uses it, 'bodily proportions implying strength' (*Julius Caesar*, 1.3.81; *Hamlet*, 1.3.12).

147.15–16 scissars of Dalilah . . . Goliath Delilah cut off Samson's long hair in which his strength lay so that his enemies could capture him (see Judges Ch. 16); Jael killed the sleeping Sisera by hammering a tent-peg into his head (see Judges Ch. 4); David used the sword of Goliath (see note to 100.28) to cut off his head after he had felled him with a slingshot (see 1 Samuel 17.51).

147.16 tenpenny nail large nail, originally one sold for tenpence a hundred.

147.36 drink, sing, and be merry see 1 Esdras 9.54 in the Apocrypha.

147.37 lay in the 12th century a *lay* was a narrative poem sung or recited by minstrels but from the 16th to the 18th centuries the word was used to mean simply 'song'.

147.39 grey covering grey was worn by the Franciscan friars; the order, founded in 1209 and reaching England in 1224, was committed to personal and institutional poverty.

147.40 flagon usually a bottle or container for serving drink but here seemingly a drinking cup.

148 motto see Thomas Warton, 'Inscription in a Hermitage at Ansley Hall in Warwickshire' (1777), lines 25–30, 37–40.

148.21 wine and wassel *Macbeth*, 1.7.64; *wassel* is liquor in which healths are drunk or, more generally, revelling. See also note to 45.11.

148.21–22 Allan-a-Dale, the northern minstrel see the ballad 'Robin Hood and Allen a Dale', where Allen a Dale 'chanted a round-de-lay' (Ritson, 2.47, line 12: Child, 138). However, in the ballad it was Robin Hood himself who masqueraded as 'a bold harper . . . the best in the north country' (Ritson, 2.49, lines 63–64).

148.29–30 sirvente . . . vulgar English see Magnum, 16.262: 'The realm of France . . . was divided betwixt the Norman and Teutonic race, who spoke the language in which the word Yes is pronounced as *oui*, and the inhabitants of the southern regions, . . . [who] pronounced the same word *oc*. The poets of the former race were called *Minstrels*, and their poems *Lays*: those of the latter were termed *Troubadours*, and their compositions called *sirventes*, and other names. Richard, a professed admirer of the joyous science in all its branches, could imitate either the minstrel or troubadour. It is less likely that he should have been able to compose or sing an English ballad.'

148.34 scorned the parings of the devil's hoof there is a legend about Dunstan's encounter with the devil (see note to 152.1) but it does not concern the devil's hoof.

149.5 The Crusader's Return by Scott.

149.12 foughten field battle-field; a stock phrase in the 16th and 17th centuries.

149.23 Tekla or Tecla, a saint in early legends of very dubious historicity, supposedly born in Iconium (see note to149.37), a convert of St Paul and the first woman martyr of Christianity. The implication here is that Tekla is a western European woman to whom the crusader returns but, though she was known in the West, her cult was not particularly popular and her name does not seem to have been used as a Christian name in western Europe in the Middle Ages (*ODECN*, 276).

149.32 listed field at Ascalon a *listed field* is a place prepared for a tournament. During the crusade Richard's army was for some time at Ascalon, a coastal city SW of Jerusalem; the *Itinerarium* records a splendid celebration of Easter in 1192 (Bk 5, Ch. 17; 1.329) but makes no specific mention of a tournament.

149.37 Iconium the ancient and medieval name for the Turkish town of Konya, which the Rum Seljuk Turks made their capital in the 11th century. It fell to the Emperor Frederick Barbarossa's army in 1190 but the sultan was not killed.

149.47 Syria's in Scott's time the term *Syria* covered all the countries along the eastern coast of the Mediterranean including the Holy Land as in Ellis's version of *Richard Coeur de Lion* (Ellis, 2.219, 229). See also Milton's *Paradise Lost* (1.421).

150.29 derry-down meaningless words used, often together, in the choruses of popular songs from the 16th century onwards.

150.34 Byzantium the ancient name, sometimes used in the Middle Ages, for Constantinople (modern Istanbul), the capital of the eastern Roman Empire from 330.

150.42–43 chorus ... misseltoe there is no evidence for this assertion; Scott may have been influenced by Ritson who, in reprinting 'The Three Ravens' (which contains this chorus) from a book of 1611, claimed the ballad was much older than 1611 in origin (*Ancient Songs* (London, 1790), 155).

151.15 porridge of plumbs plum-porridge was made with prunes, raisins, currants etc., and eaten at Christmas.

151.33 scorn it with my heels proverbial: see *The Merchant of Venice*, 2.2.8; *ODEP*, 705.

151.34 Two masses daily, morning and evening see note to 35.36–37.

151.38 Exceptis excipiendis *Latin* except for what needs to be excepted.

151.42–43 goes about ... like a roaring lion see 1 Peter 5.8.

152.1 tongs of St Dunstan see note to 21.29. One night when Dunstan was working at metals, the devil came to tempt him. Dunstan seized his nose with his red hot tongs and the devil let out a roar which woke the whole neighbourhood.

152.2–4 Saint Dunstan ... Saint Thomas a Kent for St Dunstan see note to 21.29. St Dubricius (d. *c.* 550) was a monk and bishop who, according to some legends, became archbishop of Caerleon and crowned King Arthur. The English Winebald (d. 761) became the abbot of a German monastery. Winifred, another 7th-century saint, was the subject of various legends. St Swithbert (647–713) was a Northumbrian monk, a missionary to the Frisians. St Willick is possibly St Wilgis (fl. *c.* 700), the father of the missionary St Willibrord, or St Willigis (d. 1011), Archbishop of Mainz. St Thomas a Kent is Thomas a Becket (see note to 119.25).

152.5 cut and long tail *proverbial* horses or dogs with long tails or cut tails, hence, all kinds: *ODEP*, 134.

152.7 morning vespers vespers are prayers said towards evening. The morning prayers are matins, prime and terce.

152.8 fast and furious grew the mirth see Robert Burns, 'Tam o' Shanter' (1791), line 144.

152.13 Ariosto Lodovico Ariosto (1474–1535), best known for his romantic epic *Orlando furioso*. In his 'Essay on Romance' Scott remarks that 'although he torments the reader's attention by digressing from one adventure to another, [he] delights us ... by the extreme ingenuity with which he gathers up the broken ends of his narrative, and finally weaves them all handsomely together in the same piece' (*Prose Works*, 6.195).

152 motto not traced; probably by Scott.

152.25 Ettrick Forest the name for a large part of Selkirkshire although in Scott's day the ancient forest to which it originally applied had long since disappeared.

153.25 glaive word used at different times to refer to three different weapons: first, in the late 13th century, a lance or spear; by the 15th century, a halberd (see note to 303.41), often bracketed with a bill (see following note); later, a sword. Which of these Scott has in mind is unclear; the glaive was not an Anglo-Saxon weapon and the term derives from French.

153.25 brown-bill a *bill*, apparently a kind of broad-sword, is mentioned in Old English poetry, but the *brown-bill*, a kind of halberd painted brown, belonged to the 16th and 17th centuries.

154.18 Abbot Waltheoff apparently fictitious, but probably named after Waltheof, Earl of Northumberland (d. 1076), who led the northern resistance to William I.

154.34 ancestors . . . Scandinavia the Normans originated from the Vikings, or Norsemen, who invaded France in the early 10th century and were granted land around Rouen.

154.37–38 black dog . . . howled most piteously this combines two superstitions: black dogs (which are associated with the devil) and howling dogs are both traditionally omens of death or disaster.

155.3 pay the piper *proverbial* pay the price, i.e. suffer the consequences, from the notion, found from the 17th century, that 'those who dance must pay the piper': see *ODEP*, 615.

155.5 Burton . . . liquor ale was probably brewed at Burton Abbey from soon after its establishment in 1002 but the first recorded mention of it is in 1295 (*The English Counties*, ed. C. E. M. Joad (London, 1948), 363).

155.8 monk, a hare, or a howling dog see Jacob Grimm (*Teutonic Mythology*, trans. James Steven Stallybrass, 4 vols (London, 1880–88), 3.1119–28) on superstitions about various people or animals considered unlucky to meet when setting out. He cites (3.1120) John of Salisbury amongst others on the inauspiciousness of meeting a priest or other religious or a hare. Reginald Scot reports that hunters who encountered a friar or priest would abandon their hunt (*The Discovery of Witchcraft*, 3rd edn (London, 1665), 114: *CLA*, 123). Grimm (3.1128) suggests that domestic animals like dogs were rarely included in such superstitions, but see note to 154.37–38.

156.1 St Edmund b. 841, king of the East Angles, killed by Danish invaders in 870 for refusing to submit to them or deny his faith.

156.1–2 St Edward the Confessor see note to 73.5–6. Known as 'the Confessor' because of his reputation for religious devotion and good works, he came, after his death, to be regarded as a patron saint of England until overtaken in that role by St George (see note to 162.15).

156.17 hog dear to St Anthony St Antony (251–356), a hermit born near Memphis. One of his emblems in art came to be a pig and he was considered to be the patron saint of swineherds.

158.17–19 lament, like Hotspur . . . action see *1 Henry IV*, 2.3.29–30.

159 motto Joanna Baillie, *Orra: A Tragedy* (1812), 3.1.44–48.

160.3 smite them, hip and thigh destroy them utterly: Judges 15.8.

160.17 tables of our law the two stone tablets on which the Ten Commandments were inscribed; see Exodus 31.18.

160.18–19 our captivity the captivity of Judah in Babylon which began in 586 BC: see note to 250.17–18.

160.40 that revelation . . . believed the law as written in the Old Testament and as revealed by God to Moses.

162.15 white dragon according to the 12th-century Geoffrey of Monmouth's interpretation of events related by the 8th-century Nennius, this was the symbol of the Saxons (*Historia Regum Britannie*, ed. Neil Wright (Cambridge, 1985), 74).

162.15 Saint George although known to the Anglo-Saxons, St George was still not established as England's patron saint by this period. His gradual move towards this role was accelerated when in 1348 Edward III founded the

Order of the Garter under his patronage.

162.42 laid about him like a lion proverbial: see *ODEP*, 72.

164.18–19 give him leg bail run away from him.

165.7–8 draw a bow . . . cow-keeper see *King Lear*, 4.6.87–88. Shakespeare reads 'crow-keeper' (scarecrow); the reading 'cow-keeper' came from Nahum Tate's version of the play (1681), or the 2nd edition of Nicholas Rowe's Shakespeare (1714), or Alexander Pope's edition (1725).

165.11 Our heads are in the lion's mouth proverbial: see Psalm 22.21, 2 Timothy 4.17, and *ODEP*, 467.

165 motto untraced; probably by Scott.

165.24 St Clement d. at the end of the 1st century, third after Peter in the see of Rome, first of the Apostolic fathers, venerated as a martyr.

165.40 St Nicholas see note to 102.18. Ironically St Nicholas was also the patron saint of travellers.

166.1 Watling-street the English name for the Roman road running from near London to Wroxeter; also applied, as here, to other Roman roads: in 'A Lytell Gest of Robyn Hode' the Great North Road passing through Doncaster is called 'Watlynge strete' (Ritson, 1.38, Fytte 4, line 18: Child, 117).

166.25–26 The nearer the church . . . God proverbial, recorded from the 14th century onwards: *ODEP*, 557.

166.26 cockscomb cap resembling a cock's comb in shape and colour, part of the traditional garb of the fool: see note to 19.7.

166.27 black sanctus the sanctus is the angels' song, 'Holy! Holy! Holy!' (Isaiah 6.3) used in the Christian liturgy but the black sanctus is a burlesque or black magic version such as the 16th-century 'Black Sanctus, or monke's hymne to Saunt Satane' (see Thomas Evans, *Old Ballads, Historical and Narrative*, 4 vols (London, 1784), 3.242–44: *CLA*, 172).

166.32 trowl the brown bowl to me see 'Trowl the bowl, the nut-brown bowl', the chorus of 'The Second Three-mans Song' printed at the beginning of editions of Thomas Dekker's *The Shoemakers' Holiday* (1600).

166.33 Bully boy term of endearment, 'good friend'.

167.23 De profundis clamavi *Latin* out of the depths have I cried: Psalm 129.1 in the Vulgate (AV 130.1), included in the cycle of psalms said at the evening Office of Vespers.

167.27 devil's mattins unholy racket: Marlowe, *The Massacre of Paris* (written *c.* 1592), line 448, and Jonson, *The Sad Shepherd* (written *c.* 1635, printed 1641), 2.6.65. See also note to 166.27.

168.16 monk of the church militant play on words, alluding to the common phrase *the church militant* meaning 'the church here on earth warring with the powers of evil'.

168.22–23 as well as the beggar knows his dish i.e. his alms-dish: proverbial, recorded from the 16th century onwards (*ODEP*, 41).

168.37–38 truss my points see 169.5–7.

168.41 transmew transform, transmute. By Scott's time an archaism; used by Chaucer and Spenser, and by Thomson in his Spenserian imitation 'The Castle of Indolence' (1748), Canto 2, line 372.

169.2–3 broad-cloth penitent . . . confessor broadcloth was a fine, double-width black cloth used mainly for men's clothing. Sackcloth, a coarse, rough material, was more usually associated with penitence (e.g. see Matthew 11.21). Wamba is possibly playing on the word 'sack', which in another sense was applied to a loose upper garment hanging down from the shoulders, worn by the *fratres saccati* or 'sacked friars'.

169.3 motley the material used in a parti-coloured costume worn by jesters and fools; see note to 19.7.

169.31 daughter Rowena was Cedric's ward, not his daughter.

169.41 desire to continue unknown Richard did not keep his arrival secret. He landed at Sandwich and proceeded openly to London. Later in the year he did indeed visit Sherwood Forest but, once again, openly, not in secret (Hoveden, 3.240).

170.15 get behind me see Luke 4.8. Jesus rejects Satan's offer of power in the words 'Get thee behind me, Satan'.

170.17 partisan long-handled spear whose blade had lateral cutting projections; it was a weapon of the 16th and 17th centuries.

170.43 Clerk me no clerks compare *Richard II*, 2.3.87: 'Grace me no grace, nor uncle me no uncle'.

171.5 Jack Priest *The Merry Wives of Windsor*, 1.4.106, 2.3.28: the generic name *Jack* was often prefixed to a noun indicating a person's trade thus forming a nickname, often used contemptuously.

171 motto Joanna Baillie, *Orra: A Tragedy* (1812), 3.2.13–19.

171.28 were taking were being taken.

171.28 in behalf of in the interests of, for the benefit of.

172.12–13 the fiend laughs, they say, when one thief robs another proverbial: compare *ODEP*, 810.

172.40 dispensation even the Grand Master could not legitimately grant a dispensation from the vow of celibacy.

173.12–13 merit acquired . . . Saracens see note to 255.29.

173.31 Torquilstone fictitious place; the name is based on that of its former owner (see note to 175.16).

174.26–28 a large room . . . monasteries in his 'Essay on Border Antiquities' (1814) Scott describes the 'Saxon style of architecture' as 'massive round arches, solid and short pillars, much gloom and an absence of ornament', and cites the Chapter House at Jedburgh Abbey as a 'very perfect specimen' of this style (*Prose Works*, 7.39). Actually the earliest parts of the existing abbey at Jedburgh date from the 12th century and imitate features of Anglo-Norman architecture.

175.15 my father there is a gap of nearly one hundred and thirty years between these events and the time in which *Ivanhoe* is set.

175.16 Torquil Wolfganger the Danes introduced the name *Thorkell* into England and it was used there until the 13th century. *Thorkell* was adopted into Gaelic as *Torcail* and then anglicised as *Torquil* giving Scott the inappropriate form he uses here (see *ODECN*, 280–81). *Wolfganger* ('wolf-walker') is not a recognised Anglo-Saxon nickname but may possibly have been suggested to Scott by the name Ganger-Hrolf (see note to 220.30).

175.16–18 the valiant and unfortunate Harold . . . Tosti see note to 73.5–6. Harold became king of England in January 1066 and was soon faced with two nearly simultaneous invasions. The Norwegians landed near York and then joined Harold's brother Tostig, Earl of Northumbria, but were defeated at the Battle of Stamford Bridge 11 kms E of York in September 1066, where Tostig was killed. While Harold celebrated, William, Duke of Normandy, landed with an army at Pevensey. Harold marched south and confronted the Normans at Hastings on 14 October but his army was defeated and he himself killed.

175.35–43 What terms . . . twelve inches more see Turner, 3.371. The story is narrated by Snorri Sturluson in *Heimskringla* (*King Harald's Saga*, trans. Magnus Magnusson and Hermann Palsson (Harmondsworth, 1966), 150).

176.9 Stamford . . . Welland see note to 175.16–18. In a Magnum note (16.314) Scott writes: 'A great topographical blunder occurred here in former editions' and explains he confused Stamford Bridge 11 kms E of York with Stamford on the River Welland, now in Lincolnshire.

176.19 descended of Harold's blood see note to 73.5–6.

176.30–32 When that window . . . staining it compare Benedict Biscop who, having founded a monastery at Wearmouth in 674, brought glass-makers from France to glaze the windows of the church and monastery and to teach the art of making glass: see Bede's *Historia Abbatum* in his *Works*, ed. C. Plummer, 2 vols (Oxford, 1896), 1.368.
177.19 Hardicanute King of England (reigned 1040–42): at the age of about twenty-four, while drinking at a wedding feast, he fell to the floor in convulsions and died.
177.31–32 white rod of office long, slender rod, often made of white wood, carried as a sign of office by various kinds of officers.
178.31–35 It was repeated . . . vapour Ian Duncan in his edition of *Ivanhoe* suggests a parallel with Ariosto's *Orlando furioso* (Canto 22, stanzas 18–23) where Astolfo first blows his horn to clear an enchanted palace of its inhabitants and then lifts a slab at the threshold after which the palace dissolves in smoke and mist.
179 motto *The Merchant of Venice*, 2.8.15–17.
179.39–180.1 delivered . . . fowler see Psalms 91.3, 124.6–7.
180.9 wiry Scott envisages the scene as a picture and the application of this term to lines in pictures, particularly etchings, seems to be a technical usage of this period; the *OED* (*wiry*, 2b) cites examples by William Blake (1809) and James Smith (1815).
180.10 Rembrandt the Dutch painter (1606–69).
180.21 passions of the mind the subtitle of Joanna Baillie, *A Series of Plays: in which it is attempted to delineate the Stronger Passions of the Mind* (London, 1798).
181.26–27 after the just measure . . . Tower of London the English monetary pound was originally a pound weight of silver and the standard pound was kept in the Tower of London.
181.36 mark according to Henry's statement (3.543) that the value of gold to silver in the early 12th century was one to nine, Front-de-Bœuf's exchange rate offers Isaac no relief since a mark weighed two thirds of a tower pound (see previous note).
182.11 keys . . . loose see Matthew 16.19.
182.26–29 on that warm couch . . . lest the roast should burn in a Magnum note Scott quotes an account of similar torture, including the anointing with oil, from the time of Mary, Queen of Scots (Magnum, 16.329–35)
183.10 dross worthless matter; often used to express the 'true value' of gold and silver.
184.26 at a short day soon.
184.34 Fitzdotterel character in Ben Jonson, *The Devil is an Ass* (first performed 1616): *fitz* means 'son of' and *dotterel* 'fool'.
184.37 Talmud a body of Jewish law and commentary from the early centuries of the Christian era.
185.8–9 handmaiden . . . days of old a concubine was married to a man but with inferior rights to a regular wife; Abraham took his wife's handmaid for his concubine, as did Jacob (Genesis 16.3; 30.4).
186 motto see *The Two Gentlemen of Verona*, 5.4.55–58.
187.22–23 long luxuriant hair . . . tresses towards the end of the 12th century, 'the men curled their hair with *crisping-irons*' (*Dress and Habits*, 1.100–01).
187.29–30 turned up . . . ram see note to 70.22.
187.35–36 St Michael . . . Prince of Evil see Revelation 12.7.
188.41 knight's girdle *cingulum militare*, a wide hip-belt of metal plates elaborately ornamented or made of gold or silver, used from about 1360 to about 1450; before this a simple waist-belt was worn.

191.33 thrice-tempered steel is tempered (i.e. hardened) by being heated then immersed while still hot in cold water.

191.37–38 hoarse-winded blowing far and keen *Albania: a poem addressed to the Genius of Scotland* (London, 1737), line 258. The poem, by a 'Scots clergyman' who has never been identified, was republished in *Scotish Descriptive Poems*, ed. John Leyden (Edinburgh, 1803).

192.5 liberties of England it was widely assumed in the 18th and 19th centuries that the beginnings of Parliamentary government, freedom from imprisonment except by due process of law, and trial by jury were secured by Magna Carta, the declaration that the barons forced John to sign at Runnymede in 1215.

192.9 Henry see note to 8.16.

192.12 Saxon Chronicle the Anglo-Saxon Chronicle, a history of England in annal form, first compiled in the 9th century and progressively added to in Peterborough until 1154. The passage cited is from the 1137 entry and is quoted by Henry (3.576–7).

192.13 King Stephen reigned 1135–54.

192.25–26 cruel . . . description this sentence also forms part of the passage quoted from Henry.

192.28–33 Empress Matilda . . . Norman nobles this story is told of Matilda (1080–1118), daughter of Malcolm III of Scotland and wife of Henry I of England, but Scott applies it in part to her daughter, another Matilda (1102–67), whose first husband was the Holy Roman Emperor and who disputed the English throne with Stephen. Her son by her second husband, Geoffrey of Anjou, became king as Henry II.

193.8 recorded by Eadmer see Henry (3.577). Eadmer (*c.* 1055–*c.* 1124) wrote of contemporary events; for this story see his *Historia Novorum in Anglia*, ed. Martin Rule (London, 1884), 126–31.

193 motto John Home, *Douglas* (first performed 1756), 1.305.

193.32 Urfried the name was possibly suggested by Turfrida, wife of Hereward (see note to 30.6), mentioned by Turner (4.173).

193.32–33 stand not . . . up and away compare *Macbeth*, 3.4.119–20.

193.40 Zernebock Czarnobog, or Zcernoboch, the Slavonic black god of evil. Scott follows Turner who names 'Zernebogus, or the black malevolent, ill-omened deity' (4.23) as a god of the Saxons. In fact neither the continental Saxons nor the Anglo-Saxons worshipped him.

194.1–2 spun out the hemp on my distaff the distaff was a cleft stick about 3 feet long on which the flax was wound and which was held under the left arm with the fibres of the flax being drawn from it through the fingers of the left hand, and twisted by the right, with the aid of the spindle round which the thread was wound. The spindle was a hooked rod which was made to revolve and to draw the fibres into thread.

194.6 What devil's deed have they now in the wind? proverbial: 'to have one in the wind' (*ODEP*, 892), recorded from the 16th century onwards. There is also a suggestion of 'the devil is busy in a high wind' (*ODEP*, 181).

194.10 unguent normally means 'ointment', but 'black unguent' refers to ink.

194.16 Egyptian gypsy, a sense current from the 16th to the 18th centuries.

194.19–20 men know a fox by the train proverbial, recorded in the 16th and 17th centuries: see *ODEP*, 284.

194.40 gates of death Job 38.17, Psalms 9.13 and 107.18.

195.2 My thread is spun out it appears that Urfried has literally finished her spinning but is also referring to the classical Greek and Roman notion of the thread of a person's life being spun, measured out and cut by the Fates. See also note to 269.27 which suggests that Scott may have associated this notion with the Nordic Valkyries.

195.24 **Damocles** invited to a splendid feast after flattering Dionysius the Elder, tyrant of Syracuse (405–367 BC), by praising his greatness, Damocles looked up and saw a sword hanging over his head by a single hair. See Cicero (106–43 BC), *Tusculanae Disputationes*, Bk 5, Ch. 21, in *Works*, 28 vols (London, 1960), 12.486.

196.18 **called in ... Gentiles** see Romans 11.25.

196.43–197.1 **these pearls are orient** see *A Midsummer Night's Dream*, 4.1.51, and Marlowe, *The Jew of Malta* (first performed *c.* 1592), 1.1.87; the most esteemed pearls came from the Orient.

197.12 **bright lily of the vale of Bacca** combines 'the lily of the valleys' (Song of Solomon 2.1 and note to 72.22–23) and 'the valley of Baca' (Psalm 84.6).

197.26 **witch of Endor** the woman who called up the spirit of Samuel for Saul; see 1 Samuel 28.7–25.

197.27 **rose of Sharon** see note to 72.22–23.

197.32–33 **union ... synagogue** the doctrine that the marriage of Christians to Jews was prohibited, and that such marriages (when contracted without dispensation) were invalid, is found from early in the history of the Christian church and was universally accepted by the late twelfth century. Similarly, on the basis of Old Testament passages such as Deuteronomy 7.1–4 and Nehemiah 10.31, the marriage of Jews with non-Jews was considered to be prohibited and invalid.

197.35 **Despardieux** a corruption of the French phrase *de par dieu*, meaning 'in God's name' or 'by God'.

197.35 **queen of Sheba** the rich queen who visited Solomon: see 1 Kings Ch. 10.

197.36–37 **the most Christian king** title used by the kings of France after it was bestowed on Louis XI in 1468 by Pope Paul II.

197.37 **Languedoc** large area in southern France with its capital at Toulouse.

197.39 **par amours** *French* by way of (sexual) love; i.e. as a lover rather than as a husband.

198.7–8 **daughter of Sirach ... Ecclesiastica** an allusion to Ecclesiasticus, or The Wisdom of Jesus, Son of Sirach, one of the apocryphal books of the Bible, *Ecclesiastica* being a feminine form of *Ecclesiasticus*. Bois-Guilbert's jibe 'gravely and well preached' also suggests the canonical book Ecclesiastes, otherwise known as The Preacher.

198.12 **wisest of monarchs, ... his father** Solomon and his father David. Solomon 'loved many strange women' and had 'three hundred concubines' (1 Kings 11.1, 3), and David committed adultery with Bathsheba (2 Samuel Chs 11–12).

198.24 **subject to my will by the laws of all nations** the earlier custom of reducing captives of war to slavery, on which Bois-Guilbert's claim seems to rest, had generally been abandoned in Western Europe by the 12th century.

198.41 **degradation** this involved being deprived of his position as a Templar, losing the powers and privileges of the Order and being handed over to the secular courts for punishment.

199.39 **May my arms be reversed** it was a sign of dishonour for the coat of arms of a knight to be reversed, i.e. turned upside down.

200.31 **Landes of Bordeaux** area of sand dunes, marshes and lagoons to the south and west of Bordeaux.

200.37 **Castile** region of central Spain, and from 1037 a kingdom, which in combination with Leon and Aragon had by the 16th century developed into modern Spain.

200.37 Byzantium see note to 150.34.

200.39 Gascon native of Gascony, a former province of SW France; Gascons were reputed to be braggarts.

201.14–15 revenge is a feast for the gods . . . reserved it see Romans 12.19: 'Vengeance is mine; I will repay, saith the Lord', and Psalm 94.1: 'O Lord God, to whom vengeance belongeth'.

201.17–18 ambition . . . bliss of heaven itself refers to the legend that Satan (Lucifer) was an angel who had been thrown out of heaven for his ambitious pride.

201.32 baton of Grand Master see note to 305.4.

201.36 Messias the Messiah, a saviour who would arrive and liberate the Jews.

201.42–43 within our secret conclaves . . . derision among the accusations brought against the Templars in 1308 was that they 'while professing to be Christians, in fact, when they were received into the Order, denied Christ three times and spat three times on his image' (Malcolm Barber, *The Trial of the Templars* (Cambridge, 1978), 45).

202.15–16 Gold . . . touch-stone the quality of gold or silver can be tested by the colour of the mark made by rubbing it on basanite (touchstone), a smooth, black fine-grained quartz or jasper.

202.21 bold bad man Philip Massinger, *A New Way to Pay Old Debts* (first performed 1625 or 1626), 4.1.160.

202 motto Oliver Goldsmith, *She Stoops to Conquer* (1773), Act 4, in *Collected Works*, ed. Arthur Friedman, 5 vols (Oxford, 1966), 5.189.

203.12 St Niobe the mother of twelve children, Niobe was scornful of the goddess Leto, for having only two, Apollo and Artemis. In revenge, they killed all of Niobe's children. The gods, in pity, turned the grief-stricken Niobe into a block of marble which spouted water like tears.

203.15 Apollyon the name of 'the angel of the bottomless pit' in Revelation 9.11 and the Prince of Darkness whom Christian meets in the Valley of Humiliation in Bunyan's *The Pilgrim's Progress* (1678).

203.42 Pan to Moses . . . horn Alexander Pope, *The Dunciad* (1728), 3.110, on the christianisation of heathen temples and statues in Rome. Statues of the horned Greek god Pan were reinterpreted as representing Moses who was believed, because of the Vulgate's mistranslation of a word in Exodus 34.29, to have had horns on his head after talking with God on Mount Sinai.

204.4 our Lady of Bethlehem Mary, the mother of Jesus. In his 'Essay on Chivalry' (1818) Scott says, 'Each champion had his favourite saint, to whom he addressed himself upon special occasions of danger . . . but the Virgin Mary . . . was an especial object of the devotion of the followers of Chivalry' (*Prose Works*, 6.19–20).

204.21 by mastery *Scots* by force.

204.23 Hargottstandstede apparently fictitious; perhaps inspired by *Hergotestane* which appears in a list of Anglo-Saxon place-names in Turner (4.235). *Stede* means 'place' in Old English.

204.42 trysting oak an oak tree serving as an arranged meeting-place. A trysting tree is mentioned frequently in the Robin Hood ballads, and a number of ancient trees have been associated with Robin Hood, including the Major Oak in Sherwood.

204.43 Harthill-walk Harthill is a village about 13 kms S of Rotherham.

205.26 in the fact in the act.

205.40–41 shafts of a cloth-yard in length see 'The More Modern Ballad of Chevy Chace', line 179: Percy, 1.243; Child, 162B.

205.41–42 French crown French coin decorated with a crown; first issued in the 14th century.
206.16 machines military machines used in attacking fortified places, such as a siege-tower used to scale the walls or a mechanical catapult used to hurl stones and batter down the walls.
206.29 green-wood since at least the 16th century 'the green-wood' has traditionally been regarded as the home of outlaws and particularly of Robin Hood.
206.40 Engelred fictitious character.
208.5 the crook of St Dunstan shepherd's crook, or hooked staff, symbol of the episcopal office which Dunstan held as bishop of Worcester and London and archbishop of Canterbury.
208.12 cut a caper gave a little dance.
209.4–5 russet a coarse woollen cloth, grey, brown or dull red, worn by poor people and labourers; the context implies it is the dress of friars, as motley is of fools, but no such special identification of the term with friar's dress has been traced.
209.18 Time wears *The Merry Wives of Windsor*, 5.1.7.
209.25 Pax vobiscum *Latin* peace be with you.
209 motto untraced; probably by Scott.
209.40 St Francis St Francis of Assisi (*c.* 1181–1226), founder of the order of Friars Minor, or Franciscan Friars. See also note to 147.39.
210.11 grey-goose shaft arrow. See *Sports and Pastimes*, 47, where grey-goose wing feathers are 'preferable to any others for the pluming of an arrow'. In 'A True Tale of Robin Hood' by Martin Parker (*c.* 1600–*c.* 1656), Robin's band let fly with 'the gallant gray-goose wing' (Ritson, 1.138, line 233: Child, 154); and in 'The More Modern Ballad of Chevy Chace', the 'grey-goose wing' is on a 'shaft' (Percy, 1.243, lines 182–83: Child, 162B).
210.30 quidam . . . latrones *Latin* a certain traveller fell among thieves. See Luke 10.30. The wording is not that of the Vulgate.
210.35–36 nomen illis legio . . . legion see Mark 5.9: 'Legio mihi nomen est, quia multi sumus', translated in the AV as 'My name is Legion: for we are many'.
210.39 cor meum eructavit Psalm 44.1 in the Vulgate (AV Psalm 45.1). The opening words read 'Eructavit cor meum verbum bonum' which mean literally 'My heart has vomited a good word'. The first three words (often printed at the head of English versions of the psalm) have been taken alone and interpreted incorrectly as 'My heart has burst out', hence Wamba's gloss 'I was like to burst with fear'.
211.24–25 St Dunstan, St Dennis, St Duthoc for St Dunstan see note to 21.29; St Denis, patron saint of France, was the first bishop of Paris and died as a martyr in the 3rd century; St Duthac (d. 1065) was Bishop of Ross but little is known of his life beyond a few legends.
211.27 salvete et vos *Latin* and greetings to you.
212.2 better look long before ye leap in the dark combines 'look before you leap', found in this form from the 16th century and in other forms since the 14th century (*ODEP*, 482) and the phrase 'a leap in the dark' found from the late 17th century (*ODEP*, 450).
213.4 John-a-Duck's mare not identified.
213.7 stool-ball ball in the game of the same name; something like cricket, it was originally played by hitting the ball with the hand, probably with a stool as a wicket. References to it appear from the 15th century.
213.17–21 fool's cap . . . bauble . . . cockscomb the *fool's cap* is described by Scott at 19.20–28. A *bauble* was a court jester's mock symbol of office

consisting of a baton with a carved head with asses' ears at one end. For *cockscomb* see note to 166.26.

213.39–40 Watch and ward normally 'watching and guarding' but here used as 'watchman and guard'.

214.18–19 Et vobis . . . vestra *Latin* and with you—I beg you, most reverend sir, for your pity.

214.37 Ifrin probably Ifurin, the hell of the ancient Gauls, not of the Anglo-Saxons or Norsemen.

214.38 Odin and . . . Thor for Odin see note to 29.34. Thor, one of the most important of the Norse gods, was known to the Anglo-Saxons as Thunor but the Vikings had made the form Thor well-known in England.

215 motto see George Crabbe, 'The Hall of Justice' (1807), 1.5–8, 27–32.

216.15–16 render an account of his stewardship explain his actions to God: see Luke 16.2.

217.23 Ulrica a modern German (rather than Anglo-Saxon) female form of the male name found in Old English as Wulfric.

217.35 bodkin short, pointed weapon (the original meaning): see 'The Reeve's Tale', *The Canterbury Tales*, 1 (A), 3960, and *Hamlet*, 3.1.76.

218.15 mask of a spirit of light i.e. the appearance of an angel.

218.41–42 royal Confessor . . . ulcers of the body the disease *scrofula*, a tubercular infection of the lymphatic glands, was known as the *king's evil*, and it was widely believed that a touch from the royal hand would cure it. Edward the Confessor was the first monarch reported as 'touching for the king's evil'.

219.1 stern prophet of wrath compare Romans 13.4: 'the minister of God, a revenger to execute wrath'.

219.7 Woden, Hertha and Zernebock for Woden see note to 29.34, and for Zernebock see note to 193.40. *Hertha* is an alternative form of the Teutonic 'Nerthus', or Mother Earth, whose worship is described by the Roman author Tacitus (AD 55–120) in Chapter 40 of his *Germania*. Modern editions and translations generally use the form beginning with 'N' but in earlier editions the form with 'H' was common. Some scholars then took the name to be *Hertha* with the feminine Latin ending 'a' rather than the masculine 'us'.

219.7 Mista . . . Skogula two of the Valkyries, female spirits of Norse mythology, who attended the god of war and conducted slain warriors to Valhalla (see note to 269.27). Thomas Gray uses the form *Mista* in 'The Fatal Sisters: An Ode' (line 17); there is a list of Valkyries in Thomas Bartholinus, *Antiquitatum Danicarum de causis contemptae a Danis adhuc gentilibus mortis libri tres* (Copenhagen, 1689), 554: Bk 2, Ch. 12 (*CLA*, 99).

220.25–26 scallop-shell of Compostella see note to 40.39.

220.29 onslaught the context suggests that Scott saw this as an Anglo-Saxon term but it does not appear in English until the 17th century and may have been borrowed from Dutch or German.

220.30 their war-song of Rollo Rollo (Ganger-Hrolf) was the leader of the original Norse invaders of France, ancestors of the Normans (see note to 154.34). However, Cedric may here confuse the war-song of Rollo with the *Song of Roland* since Henry, citing William of Malmesbury and others as his source, had recorded how, at the Battle of Hastings, 'the Normans advanced, singing the famous song of Rolland' (Henry, 3.3; see William of Malmesbury, 2.302).

221.1 St Withold of Burton see note to 136.28.

221.13 proof *either* tested ability to resist penetration or, *figuratively*, armour of this quality.

221.23 canst read, Sir Priest? the problem of ill-educated clergy was a continuing one. In the 1260s the diocesan synod of Winchester directed that 'since many ignorant and illiterate persons . . . usurp the pastoral office, we enjoin both our Official and the archdeacons . . . that personally they make frequent and anxious inquiry whether any rectors or vicars are greatly deficient in learning' (*English Historical Documents, 1189–1327*, ed. Harry Rothwell (London, 1975), 703).

222.4–5 necessity . . . sharpens invention proverbial, recorded from the 16th century onwards: *ODEP*, 558.

222.10–11 he of St Ives . . . mass see 'Robin Hood and the Bishop': 'Then Robin Hood took the bishop by the hand,/ And bound him fast to a tree,/ And made him sing a mass, God wot,/ To him and his yeomandree' (Ritson, 2.23, lines 90–93: Child, 143). St Ives, 8 km E of Huntingdon, had a Benedictine priory cell dependent on Ramsey from the early eleventh century.

222.13 Gaultier of Middleton apparently a fictitious character.

222.14 chapel at St Bees village on the W coast of Cumberland. A small Benedictine priory cell, dependent on St Mary's York, was established there in the early 12th century.

222.39–40 Turning then back . . . to the donor see the story in William of Malmesbury (1.143), and retold in Henry (2.70) and Turner (3.27–28), of how Anlaff, disguised as a minstrel, visited the tent of King Athelstan, played before him and was rewarded with a coin. 'An absurd pride would not suffer Anlaff to carry off this money; but when he had got at some distance from the King's tent . . . he deposited it in the ground' (Henry, 2.70).

222.40–41 thy money perish with thee Acts 8.20 (the words of Peter when he rejects the money offered by Simon the sorcerer).

223.32 doit small Dutch coin worth half an English farthing, not found in England until the 15th century.

223.36 Saint Genevieve *c.* 420–*c.* 500. Having correctly foretold that Attila and his Huns would bypass Paris she came to be seen as the city's protectress and patroness.

224.8–9 immunities see note to 16.3.

224.32 red cap worn by cardinals, a privilege granted by Pope Innocent IV after the first Council of Lyons in 1245.

224.37 take heart of grace pluck up courage: proverbial: *ODEP*, 364.

225.1–6 Norman saw . . . all the four probably by Scott. The phrase 'the Norman yoke' was popular from the 17th century as a way of describing the Norman's substitution of feudalism for the supposedly freer or more democratic Anglo-Saxon system of government: see Christopher Hill, 'The Norman Yoke', in *Puritanism and Revolution* (London, 1958), 50–122.

225.25 man of mould mortal man: *Henry V*, 3.2.21. The phrase occurs from the 14th century onwards.

226.7 drawn by wild horses tying the limbs of a person to four horses and then using the horses to tear the body apart was formerly used as a method of execution. The expression is proverbial: see *ODEP*, 889.

226.13 seven kingdoms see note to 30.6.

226.14 House of Anjou see note to 127.4–6.

226. 14 confer . . . their wards a woman was able to inherit land but her feudal lord held the right to choose a husband for her. Rowena apparently holds her lands directly from the crown with the king as her feudal lord.

226.22–23 Wittenagemotes the Anglo-Saxon assemblies of the *witan* or wise men, called to advise the king.

226.23–24 whose bones . . . builded most of the Anglo-Saxon kings of Wessex and later of all England (Athelstane's supposed ancestors) were buried in the Old and New Minsters at Winchester. Edward the Confessor was buried in his newly consecrated monastery church at Westminster and Ethelred at Wimborne Minster.

226.37 St Bennet St Benedict of Nursia (*c.* 480–547) whose rule of life for his monks at Monte Cassino became the basis of monastic discipline in Western Christendom.

226.37 bull-beggars originally a bull-beggar was a spectre, an object of terror, a bugbear. It is sometimes used more loosely or figuratively, apparently with a pun on *beggar* and *bull*, either with reference to papal bulls or perhaps to the verb *bull* meaning 'fool' or 'cheat'.

227.8–10 honourable imprisonment . . . in treaty for ransom an elaborate system of ransoming those captured in battle developed in the Middle Ages. Noble captives could be ransomed for large sums and it was expected that they would be treated well during their captivity. By contrast common soldiers who could not command a high ransom were often much less well treated.

227.13 thou underliest it you have already been subjected to it.

227.14 There lies my glove to throw down one's glove, or gauntlet, was to issue a challenge to battle.

227.19–20 by the belt of Saint Christopher a number of stories attach to St Christopher, the patron saint of travellers, but none is concerned with a belt. According to tradition he was martyred in Asia Minor in the 3rd century.

227.25 Deus vobiscum *Latin* God be with you.

227.37–38 Saint Augustin . . . De Civitate Dei St Augustine of Hippo (354–430) wrote his influential *De Civitate Dei* ('The City of God') between 413 and 426.

227.42 Sancta Maria *Latin* St Mary.

228.2–3 Si quis . . . Diabolo *Latin* if anyone, at the tempting of the devil. A canon of the Second Lateran Council (1139) under Innocent II begins 'Item placuit ut si quis, suadente diabolo' (*Conciliorum Oecumenicorum Decreta*, 3rd edn (Basle, 1973), 176) and was popularised as 'Si quis suadente diabolo' in the *Decretum* of Gratian (C.17, Q.4, c.29) some twenty years later (see *Corpus Iuris Canonici*, 2nd Leipzig edn, 2 vols, ed. E. Friedberg (Graz, 1959), 1.822).

228.6 men of Belial term frequently used in the Bible to mean wicked and worthless people: e.g. see Judges 19.22; 2 Chronicles 13.7.

228.7–8 Touch not . . . nought of evil see 1 Chronicles 16.22.

228.12 helped of assisted by.

228.33 raise a bank build an artificial earthwork for military purposes: compare 2 Samuel 20.15.

228.38 Saint Dennis see note to 211.24–25.

229.42 make a shaft or bolt of it proverbial: *ODEP*, 718.

230.10 rascaille 14th and 15th-century spelling of the word *rascal* with the obsolete meaning 'rabble', revived by Scott as both a noun and an adjective.

230.14 Some hilding fellow *2 Henry IV*, 1.1.57; *hilding* means 'contemptible'.

230 motto untraced; probably by Scott.

231.12 Rabbi Jacob Ben Tudela the name is fictitious. However, Tudela is a city in Navarre, in Spain, associated with several notable Jews including the 12th-century traveller, Benjamin Ben Jonah of Tudela, sometimes given the title *Rabbi*.

231.17–18 Ishmael and . . . Edom for Ishmael see note to 59.19. Edom was the land between the Dead Sea and the Gulf of Aqaba; the Edomites were traditional enemies of the Jews.

231.22 Beard of Aaron see Psalm 133.2 which is referring to Exodus 30.25, 30.

231.31–32 Miriam . . . Byzantium Jews were known to use magic herbs and charms for healing, divination and other purposes, and even the highly respected rabbi and physician Elijah Mehahem ben Rabbi Moses of London (*c.* 1220–84) taught and used both medical and magical prescriptions (see Cecil

Roth, 'Elijah of London', *Transactions of the Jewish Historical Society of England*, 15 (1946), 52–53, and A. Marmorstein, 'Some Hitherto Unknown Jewish Scholars of Angevin England', *The Jewish Quarterly Review*, 19 (1928–29), 17–36). Miriam and Manasses appear to be fictitious characters. See also note to 311.28–31.

232.18–19 cabalistical art . . . sages of Israel the term *Cabbala* originally referred to oral traditions of the Jews not contained in the Hebrew Bible but later came to apply to a system of mystic biblical interpretation and magic contained in various 'cabbalistical' writings and practised by some Jews in the Middle Ages.

233.36 Idumea another name for Edom (see note to 231.17–18).

234.6 sons of Belial see note to 228.6.

234.17 all the heady tumult of a confused fight see *I Henry IV*, 2.3.52.

235.13 turban'd and caftan'd damsel see note to 71.41–43.

235.34 jessamine jasmine. The shrub may have been known to minstrels in Europe by the time of *Ivanhoe*, but is not mentioned in English writing until the 16th century.

239.8 horn . . . exalted the horn, in biblical language, symbolised power and might, and the horn lifted up, or exalted, signified victory and triumph; e.g. see 1 Samuel 2.10.

239.26 Juvenal's tenth satire Scott's reference to an 'enriched traveller' suggests he is thinking of Johnson's 'The Vanity of Human Wishes' (1749), lines 37–44, an imitation of Juvenal, rather than the original poem.

239.36–37 haste . . . more than good speed proverbial: 'No more haste than good speed' (*ODEP*, 356).

239.41–42 Reversing Shylock's position see *The Merchant of Venice*, 2.5.14–15.

240.31 middle course betwixt good and evil compare 'Virtue is found in the middle' (*ODEP*, 861) and *The Merchant of Venice*, 1.2.7.

241.3 lay leaguer before besiege. The phrase seems to be Scott's own; the normal wording is 'lie in leaguer before'.

241 motto see Friedrich von Schiller, *Die Jungfrau von Orleans* (1801), 5.11.11–12, probably translated by Scott.

243.13–14 quiver rattleth . . . shouting see Job 39.23, 25.

243.15 war-horse of that sublime passage see Job 39.19–25.

244.35–36 Something resembling . . . black shield in heraldry it is a solecism to place a colour (e.g. blue or black), not on a metal (gold or silver), but on another colour. Scott answered critics of his heraldry by arguing in a Magnum note that 'all the minutiæ of its fantastic science were the work of time, and introduced at a much later period' (17.99).

244.37 fetterlock and shacklebolt a fetterlock is a device like a padlock fixed to a horse's foot to prevent it running away; a shacklebolt is the bar used in a shackle, a fetter for humans or horses. Both were used as heraldic devices.

245.10 nakers this word appears in normal English use only in the 14th to early 16th centuries; see 'The Knight's Tale', *The Canterbury Tales*, 1 (A), 2511, and Berners's Froissart, Vol. 1, Ch. 147.

245.14 En avant *French* forward.

245.15 a la rescousse *French* to the rescue.

245.21 phrase of the time, so 'wholly together' a 16th-century phrase; see Berners's Froissart, Vol. 1, Chs 31, 81, and Richard Grafton's *Chronicle at Large, and Meere History of the Affayres of England* (1569), 2 vols (London, 1809), 2.269: *CLA*, 28.

245.30 armour of proof see note to 221.13.

246.15 blench from the helm lose courage and give up steering the ship.

246.41–43 Many of those valiant feats . . . places e.g. the skirmish at the barriers of Cambrai in Berners's Froissart, Vol. 1, Ch. 44.

247.21–22 Great God . . . brethren see Genesis 1.26: 'And God said, Let us make man in our image'.

247.28 Saint George strike for us an appropriate sentiment for a crusader. Various stories were told of St George coming to the aid of crusaders in battle, including one, related in the romance *Richard Coeur de Lion* (Ellis, 2.249), of his coming to aid Richard.

248.19 derring-do in *Troilus and Criseyde* Chaucer speaks of Troilus being outstanding 'In durryng don that longeth to a knyght' (5.837) i.e. 'in daring to do that which belongs to a knight'. In 1430 Lydgate repeated Chaucer's words in his *Chronicles of Troy* (2.16) but they were later misprinted as 'in derrynge do', and Spenser uses this form incorrectly as a noun phrase in *The Shepheardes Calendar* (Oct., 65) where the original glossary explains it as 'manhoode and chevalrie'. From him it was taken up by Scott and later writers.

248.29 assoilzie absolve. *Assoilzie* is a Scottish form in 1819 still in use as a legal term, but in English the old form of the verb, *assoil*, had been superseded by *absolve*.

249.8 breath of our nostrils see Genesis 2.7: 'And the Lord God formed man of the dust of the ground, and breathed into his nostrils the breath of life'. Scott uses the phrase as equivalent to *breath of life*, meaning 'all that makes life worthwhile'.

249.13–14 passing through the fire to Moloch see 2 Kings 23.10. Moloch, or Molech, was an Ammonite god whose worship involved sacrificing children as burnt offerings.

249.26 wandering bard in the Middle Ages minstrels often wandered from place to place seeking an opportunity to display their skills.

249.38 emprize see *Jehan de Saintré* (72, 94, 101, 181, 233, 239, 277) where La Dame des Belles Cousines regularly rejoices at Jehan's deeds of emprize.

250.7 Gideon successful leader of the Israelites against the Midianites (see Judges Chs 6–7).

250.7 Maccabæus Judas, son of Mattathias, a central figure in the struggle for Jewish independence in the 2nd century BC. The story of Judas and his brothers is told in the two Books of the Maccabees in the Apocrypha.

250.17–18 redeem the captivity of Judah Judah was the name of the fourth son of Jacob (see note to 53.23–24) and also of the tribe descended from him. After the destruction of the northern kingdom of Israel (see note to 286.11–12) Judah remained as the only Hebrew kingdom and came to represent the whole Jewish people, but it was conquered by the Babylonians in 597 BC and many prominent Judeans were sent into exile in Babylon, and in 587–86 BC Jerusalem was destroyed. See 2 Kings 24.1–25.6.

251 motto untraced; probably by Scott.

251.22–23 powerful limb lopped off . . . enterprize see *1 Henry IV*, 4.1.28–9, 43: 'This sickness doth infect/ The very life-blood of our enterprise . . . A perilous gash, a very limb lopp'd off'.

252.16–17 parish-butt on a holy-day even the later medieval kings made various efforts to encourage archery practice and Strutt records that an ordinance of Edward IV directed 'that butts should be made in every township, at which the inhabitants were to shoot at, up and down, upon all feast days' (*Sports and Pastimes*, 43).

252.19 make a virtue of necessity proverbial: *ODEP*, 861.

254.10–11 chief captain . . . great sum see Acts 22.28.

254.14 hard as a nether millstone proverbial: see Job 41.24 and compare *ODEP*, 352. The lower of the two millstones was firmly fixed and very hard.

254.24–25 unshod Carmelites the Order of Our Lady of Mount Carmel was founded in Palestine in about 1154 by St Berthold (d. *c.* 1195) but the first Carmelite community in England was established in the 1240s. The communities of Discalced ('Unshod') Carmelites, which arose from the reforms led by Teresa of Avila (1515–82), were required to go barefoot, except in cold lands.

254.32 unhouseled not having received the Eucharist: *Hamlet*, 1.5.77.

254.34–35 recks neither . . . hell does not care about either heaven or hell: see Milton, *Paradise Lost* (1667), 2.49–50.

255.4 night-raven see *Much Ado About Nothing*, 2.3.77, and note to 83.9.

255.6 evil angel compare *Julius Caesar*, 4.3.279.

255.14–15 war against his . . . father John rebelled against Henry II in 1188.

255.29 men canonized . . . Saracens *canonized* is perhaps used in the figurative sense, meaning 'honoured like a saint'. For most crusaders, rewards stopped short of canonisation, although in the time of Leo IX (Pope 1048–54) soldiers of the papal army who fell in the battle of Cività were recognised as Christian martyrs and reckoned as saints (Carl Erdmann, *The Origin of the Idea of Crusade*, trans. M. W. Baldwin and W. Goffart (Princeton, 1977), 123). Indulgences were promised by Gregory VII (Pope 1073–85) to those who died in battle for the cross, and, from the time of the Council of Clermont (1095), to anyone who 'journeys to Jerusalem to liberate the church of God' (Erdmann, 331). Manegold of Lautenbach (*c.* 1085) wrote, 'Whoever kills in the defense of the church, or otherwise oppresses the pagan who devastates it, is known to incur no guilt, but rather to deserve praise and honor' (see Erdmann, 236) and St Bernard wrote that 'to inflict death or to die for Christ is no sin, but rather, an abundant claim to glory' (*De Laude Novae Militiae*, Ch. 3, in *Works*, 8 vols (Kalamazoo, 1977), 7.134).

257.6 Hengist and Horsa see notes to 29.14 and 51.9.

257.26 Mista, Skogula, and Zernebock see notes to 219.7.

259 motto *Henry V*, 3.1.1–2, 25–8.

259.30 by the Saint Christopher . . . baldric see the Yeoman in the 'General Prologue' to *The Canterbury Tales*, 1 (A), 115, who had 'a Cristopher on his brest of silver sheene'. It was believed that a person who looked on the image of St Christopher would be protected from harm that day. See notes to 70.5 and 227.19–20.

263.1–2 Mountjoye Saint Dennis the war-cry used by the French in the Middle Ages. *Montjoie* was used as a name for the standard of the early French kings, the oriflamme, which they received at the hands of the Abbot of St Denis when setting out for war. The Abbey of St Denis is in N Paris and was the burial-place of the French monarchy. For St Denis see note to 211.24–25.

263.23 Thou art mad to say so see *Macbeth*, 1.5.28.

263.30 Saint Nicholas of Limoges amongst the various saints of this name there was no St Nicholas of Limoges. The best known St Nicholas, bishop of Myra (d. *c.* 350), was adopted as the patron saint of many places, including Lorraine in northern France, but not of Limoges.

263.40 Hand and glove i.e. I swear by my hand and glove. Swearing by one's hand was once a common form of asseveration.

264.26 dagger of mercy in his 'Essay on Chivalry' Scott writes: 'The knight had also a dagger which he used when at close quarters. It was called the dagger of mercy, probably because, when unsheathed, it behoved the antagonist to crave mercy or to die' (*Prose Works*, 6.75).

264.26–27 yield thee . . . but a dead man see Berners's Froissart: 'yelde you my prisonere: rescue or no rescue, or els ye are but deed' (Vol. 1, Ch. 342). (Duncan)

264.33–35 I yield me . . . submission Richard's return to England was not secret but the news did not immediately reach all areas. A fortnight after his

landing, the people in the castle of Tickhill sent two knights to see if the king had indeed returned (Hoveden, 3.238) before they were willing to surrender it to him.
265.32–35 the door . . . his casque see Madeleine de Scudéry, *Artamenes, or The Grand Cyrus* (London, 1653), 123 (*CLA*, 102): 'we saw the dore of our Chamber opened, and the King of Assyria enter: with his Arms all broken, and stain'd with blood in divers places: his scarfe all torn and bloody and his plume all ruffled, broken and bloody likewise'.
265.41 born of woman biblical phrase: e.g. see Job 14.1.
266.12 Hound of the Temple in the Bible dogs are considered unclean animals which were not allowed to enter holy places.
268.7–8 the hasty hand catches frog for fish derived from the proverb recorded from the 16th century onwards: 'to fish well and catch a frog' (*ODEP*, 263) meaning 'to achieve very little after a great effort'.
268.12–13 if wilful will to water . . . drench compare 'A wilful man must have his way' (*ODEP*, 890).
268.28 demi-courbette technically a *courbette* or *curvet* is a leap in which a horse raises his two front legs together, and raises his two hind legs with a spring before the forelegs touch the ground again; more generally it refers simply to a frisking or leaping movement.
269.9 hawks abroad compare 'ware hawk': *ODEP*, 867. A 'hawk' was an officer of the law.
269.12 redeemed word and glove fulfilled the pledge (see note to 263.40).
269.13 Preceptory of Templestowe a *preceptory* was a religious house of the Templars; see footnote to 302. Scott invented the name *Templestowe* but there were a number of Templar preceptories in Yorkshire, three of whose names began with 'Temple': Temple Hirst, Temple Newsam and Temple Cowton (Thomas W. Parker, *The Knights Templars in England* (Tucson, 1963), 35).
269.21 Furies the three Greek goddesses, the Erinyes or Eumenides, who punished the crimes of those who escaped or defied public justice.
269.23 scalds strictly speaking, *scalds* were, as Scott later explained, 'the minstrels of the ancient Scandinavians' (Magnum 17.148) but Scott applies the term here to Anglo-Saxons.
269.23–24 long dishevelled grey hair . . . head compare Thomas Gray, 'The Bard' (1757), lines 19–20.
269.27 Fatal Sisters see Thomas Gray, 'The Fatal Sisters' (1768). A translation from the Old Norse poem *Darraðar Ljóð*, it depicts the Valkyries (see note to 219.7) *weaving* 'the crimson web of war' (line 25) and singing 'We the reins to slaughter give,/ Ours to kill and ours to spare' (lines 33–34). However the reference to *spinning* suggests some influence from the classical notion of the Fates (see note to 195.2).
269.28–29 barbarous hymn in a Magnum note (17.148), Scott explains: 'these verses are intended to imitate the antique poetry of the Scalds—the minstrels of the old Scandinavians . . . The poetry of the Anglo-Saxons, after their civilisation and conversion, was of a different and softer character; but in the circumstances of Ulrica, she may be not unnaturally supposed to return to the wild strains which animated her forefathers during the time of Paganism.'
269.33 Sons of the White Dragon see note to 162.15.
269.35 Hengist see notes to 29.14 and 51.9.
269.41 Zernebock see note to 193.40.
270.6 Valhalla in Scandinavian mythology, the 'hall of the slain', a place of feasting and drinking for the souls of heroes killed in battle.
270.32 Horsa see notes to 29.14 and 51.9.

271 motto untraced; probably by Scott.

271.19 Adam . . . verdant apron see Genesis 3.7: after Adam and Eve had eaten the forbidden fruit, 'they knew that they were naked; and they sewed fig leaves together, and made themselves aprons'.

272.8–9 in these glades . . . kingdom see Ritson, 1.vi: 'These forests, in short, were his territories; those who accompanyed and adhered to him his subjects . . . and what better title king Richard could pretend to the territory and people of England than Robin Hood had to the dominion of Barnsdale or Sherwood is a question humbly submitted to the consideration of the political philosopher'.

272.12 curtal Friar a 'short-frocked' friar, a Franciscan, so called because of their short cloaks. See also note to 361.14.

272.14 Over God's forbode see note to 86.43.

273.30 theow and esne both words mean slave or serf. See Turner, 4.127: 'This unfortunate class of men . . . are frequently mentioned in our ancient laws and charters, and are exhibited in the servile condition of being another's property, without any political existence or social consideration'. For a discussion of the status of the *theow* see F. W. Maitland, *Domesday Book and Beyond* (Cambridge, 1897), 26–30.

273.31 folk-free and sacless common way of expressing the gift of freedom to a slave in Anglo-Saxon manumissions. See Turner, 4.134: 'Aluric, the canon of Exeter, redeemed Reinold and his children, and all their offspring . . . and Aluric called them free and sac-less, in town and from town'; on the next page Turner defines the rare word *folk-free* as 'free among the people'.

273.32 hyde measure of land, generally considered to be enough to support a freeman and his family; it varied in size throughout the country.

273.33 Walburghham an invented name, which Scott may have based on the woman's name *Walburge* included in Verstegan's list of Anglo-Saxon names (*A Restitution of Decayed Intelligence* (London, 1628), 271), or on the Sussex place name *Walberton* which derives from *Walburgetone*.

274.10 serf . . . the freeman must forth to the field see Henry, 2.412: 'slaves were excluded from . . . all military services, except in cases of the greatest national distress and danger. But when a slave was made free, a spear was put into his hand as one mark of his freedom, and he was thenceforward permitted to bear arms, and subjected to military services'.

274.11 Oldhelm of Malmesbury probably a reference to St Aldhelm (*c.* 640–709), Abbot of Malmesbury. His works include a collection of riddles in Latin but not proverbs.

274.11–12 Better a fool . . . fray compare 'Better come at the latter end of a feast than at the beginning of a fray' (*ODEP*, 52).

276.18 supping in Paradise see note to 82.28–29.

277.37–39 wind three mots . . . rescue see 'Robin Hood and the Shepherd' (Ritson, 2.55, lines 60–61: Child, 135), where Robin Hood summons his men to his assistance in this way.

277.38 Wa-sa-hoa see Scott's footnote and compare the 15th-century *Boke of St Albans* for shouted cries used while hunting hares: 'And thenne (so ho so ho) thryes and no moo./ And then say (Sa cy avaunt so how) i thou praye' (lines 1458–59): Lady Juliana Berners, *The Book Containing the Treatises of Hawking; Hunting; . . . known as the Boke of St. Albans* (London, 1810), 503: *CLA*, 208.

278.15 tenth part from Genesis on (e.g. see Genesis 28.22) a tenth part of the produce of the land was to be given to God as a sign of homage and gratitude. The payment of tithes was made law in England in 900.

279.11–12 Saint Hermangild in this context perhaps St Ermengild (d. *c.* 700), a queen of Mercia who became Abbess of Ely, rather than the Visigoth

Hermenegild (d. 585). Alternatively, as with 'Saint' Grizzel (see note to 74.24), Scott may have been thinking of the woman called Hermengyld in 'The Man of Law's Tale', *The Canterbury Tales*, 2 (B1), 533.

279.14 wet mass a play on the term *dry mass*, a service in which communion is not celebrated, and the phrase *a wet night* meaning 'a night of drinking'.

279.20 Sathanas Satan. This form of the name is used in the Wyclif version of the Bible and in *The Canterbury Tales* (e.g. in 'The Miller's Tale', 1 (A), 3750).

279.37 mulled see John Fletcher, *The Loyal Subject* (first performed 1618), 4.6.23–25: 'Do not fire the Cellar,/ There's excellent wine in't Captain, and though it be cold weather,/ I do not love it mul'd'.

280.1–2 rescue or no rescue see note to 264.26–27.

280.4–5 thunder-dint and levin-fire thunder-clap and lightning: see 'The Wife of Bath's Prologue', *The Canterbury Tales*, 3 (D), 276.

280.13 the seed has been sown in good soil see the parable of the sower, especially as told in Mark 4.3–32.

280.38 the Promise the promise of God to Abraham that his descendants would become a great nation; see Genesis 12.1–3, 17.19.

281.4 Saint Thomas of Kent see note to 119.25.

281.23–24 I will stand thy blow . . . mine in a Magnum note (17.170) Scott cites a parallel to this story in the romance *Richard Coeur de Lion*. The son of the king of Almain offered to exchange blows with Richard. 'The King stood forth like a true man, and received a blow which staggered him. In requital . . . he returned the box on the ear with such interest as to kill his antagonist on the spot.' See Ellis, 193–94.

281.26–27 Goliah of Gath in his brazen helmet Goliath, the giant from Gath defeated by David, wore 'an helmet of brass' (1 Samuel 17.5); his name quite often appears in English texts as 'Goliah'.

281.35–36 Genam meam dedi vapulatori . . . smiter see Isaiah 50.6; Lamentations 3.30. The wording is not that of the Vulgate.

282.2–3 the piper . . . nether chops proverbial: see *ODEP*, 627. *Nether chops* means 'lower jaw'.

282.6 leopard . . . spots proverbial: see Jeremiah 13.23; *ODEP*, 456.

282.10 all masters, and no men compare 'Where every man is master, the world goes to wrack': *ODEP*, 230.

282.22 hilding fellows see note to 230.14.

282.24 cardecu French silver coin, a quarter of a gold écu, first struck in 1580 when it was worth about two shillings.

282.27 pert as a pyet see 'The Reeve's Tale', *The Canterbury Tales*, 1 (A), 3950. A 'pyet' is a magpie.

282 motto *Coriolanus*, 1.6.32–36.

283.1 manus imponere in servos Domini *Latin* to lay hands on the Lord's servants. See Psalm 105.15: 'Touch not mine anointed'. Priests were anointed with oil when they were consecrated.

283.3 excommunicabo vos *Latin* I shall excommunicate you.

283.16 nebulo quidam *Latin* a certain good-for-nothing man.

283.19–20 gymmal rings rings made of two, or sometimes three or four rings, linked or intertwined.

283.21 pouncet-box small box with a perforated lid, used for perfumes. The word was coined by Shakespeare: see *I Henry IV*, 1.3.38.

283.25 gospel of Saint Nicodemus one of the apocryphal books of the New Testament, containing the acts of Pilate, and an account of Christ's descent into Hell. It was well-known in the Middle Ages but Nicodemus was not normally referred to as a saint.

283.37 your place will know you no more see Psalm 103.16.

284.4 Deus faciet salvum benignitatem vestrum *Latin* God save your reverence.
284.9 morris-dancer dancers in the morris dance, popular in England from the 15th century, usually represented various characters including Maid Marian and Friar Tuck.
284.11 Saint Andrew's day in Scotland in the Middle Ages St Andrew's Day (30 November) was a common date for settling debts and making payments. From the late 17th century it was replaced in this role by Martinmas (11 November).
284.14–16 facite vobis . . . iniquity see Luke 16.9.
284.19 I can well of woodcraft see the description of the Yeoman in the 'General Prologue' to *The Canterbury Tales*, 1 (A), 110: 'Of wodecraft wel koude he al the usage'. Here *can of* means 'know about'.
284.27–28 as the legend . . . free for a blast 'Free for a blast' was the family motto of the Clerks of Penicuik: see *Ivanhoe*, ed. F. A. Cavenagh (1921), 345.
284.35–36 hold a candle to the devil give assistance to wrong-doing, a proverbial expression recorded from the 15th century onwards (*ODEP*, 377).
285.5–6 live upon the fat . . . lees see Isaiah 25.6 ('a feast of fat things, a feast of wines on the lees') and Nehemiah 8.10 ('eat the fat, and drink the sweet').
285.18 propter necessitatem . . . depellendum *Latin* in case of necessity and to drive out the cold. The phrase seems to be Scott's own, but the idea of drinking to keep out the cold is familiar in Roman literature.
285.28 A sentence see *The Merchant of Venice*, 4.1.299.
286.11–12 ten tribes . . . Assyrian bondage in 722–21 BC the Assyrians conquered the kingdom of Israel (formed in the 10th century BC by the secession of the ten northernmost of the twelve tribes of Israel) and carried off a large part of the population to live in Assyria.
286.16 gnawing adders . . . state compare *1 Henry VI*, 3.1.72–73: 'Civil dissension is a viperous worm/ That gnaws the bowels of the commonwealth'.
286.18–27 Holy father . . . poor strangers see *The Merchant of Venice*, 1.3.101–24.
286.26 curse of Egypt see note to 96.42.
286.31 latro famosus celebrated or infamous robber. The phrase appears in the title of a document directed against infamous thieves ('contra famosos latrones') by the Bishop of Durham in the reign of Henry VII which Scott included as an appendix to the Introduction to *Minstrelsy of the Scottish Border* (ed. T. F. Henderson, 4 vols (Edinburgh, 1902), 1.200–06). Ritson quotes John Major as describing Robin Hood and Little John as 'famatissimi latrones' i.e. very notorious robbers (Ritson, 1.ix; see John Major, *Historia Majoris Britanniae*, ed. R. Freebairn (Edinburgh, 1740), 128).
287.21–22 Ichabod . . . house see 1 Samuel 4.21. *Ichabod* means 'no glory'.
288.5 buskins boots, or leather leggings. The word is common to several European languages, and according to the *OED* is used in English from the 16th century.
288.13 Saint Robert Aymer, a Cistercian, probably refers to St Robert of Molesme (*c.* 1027–1111), abbot of Cîteaux, or possibly to St Robert of Newminster (*c.* 1100–59), a Cistercian abbot in Northumberland.
288.18–19 spoilers arise against me see Jeremiah 6.26, 12.12, 48.8.
288.19–20 given as a prey . . . Egypt see 2 Kings 21.14, Jeremiah 49.32, and Ezekiel 7.21.
288.22–27 verbum Domini . . . treasures to others see Jeremiah 8.9–10. However, for *agros* (fields) the Prior has substituted *thesauros*

(treasures) and 'others' is a loose translation of *hæridibus alienis* which means 'alien heirs'.

289.3 Diccon Bend-the-Bow both common nicknames, *Diccon* being a diminutive of Richard and *Bend-the-Bow* a name for an archer. Compound nicknames like *Bend-the-Bow* were common after the Norman Conquest.

289.17 scatter us like dust see Psalm 18.42; Isaiah 41.2.

290.8 earth-worm Scott has revived the earlier use of this term 'as a disparaging designation for a human being' (*OED*, *earthworm*, 2a).

290.16 Saint Hubert see note to 120.31.

290.27 Holderness peninsula between the River Humber and the North Sea, an area still famous today as a habitat for estuarine birds, including geese.

290.35 Preceptory see note to 269.13 and footnote to 302.

290.38–39 naught for naught see note to 65.1–2.

291.25 inter res sacras *Latin* among sacred things.

291.41–42 lapides pro pane . . . Vulgate hath it see Matthew 7.9. The Vulgate reads: 'quis est ex vobis homo, quem si petierit filius suus panem, numquid lapidem porriget ei?'. The AV reads: 'what man is there of you, whom if his son ask bread, will he give him a stone?'.

292.3 lawful spoiling of the Egyptians see Exodus 3.21–22, 12.35–36. The Israelites, following the instructions of the Lord given to Moses, borrowed jewellery and clothing from the Egyptians and took it with them when they left Egypt; thus 'they spoiled the Egyptians'.

292.4–5 excommunicabo vos *Latin* I shall excommunicate you.

292.7 pouch up put up with. See *King John*, 3.1.200: 'Well ruffian, I must pocket up these wrongs'.

292.9–10 ossa ejus perfringam . . . bones the breaking of bones is a common biblical image, signifying conquest or severe punishment: e.g. see Numbers 24.8, 'he shall eat up the nations his enemies, and shall break their bones'.

292.19 hedge-priest contemptuous term for an illiterate or uneducated priest revived by Scott from Elizabethan English; see *Love's Labour's Lost*, 5.2.538.

292.30 Sheva the name of one of King David's scribes: see 2 Samuel 20.25.

293.12–13 Good fruit . . . sorry tree compare Matthew 7.17: 'every good tree bringeth forth good fruit; but a corrupt tree bringeth forth evil fruit'.

293.35 fellowship band of companions; the word is common in Malory who writes of a 'fair fellowship of knights' (*Morte D'Arthur*, 1.159: Bk 6, Ch. 6).

294 motto *King John*, 3.3.60–63.

294.40 Achitophel see 2 Samuel Chs 15–17 which record Absalom's conspiracy with Ahitophel against King David. Dryden used this story in his satire *Absolom and Achitophel* (1681) and Scott's spelling suggests Dryden's version was in mind.

295.4 holped up helped, here used ironically. See *The Comedy of Errors*, 4.1.22: 'A man is well holp up that trusts to you'.

295.43–296.1 bloody with spurring . . . speed see *Richard II*, 2.3.58.

296.3 from the crest to the spur see *Henry V*, 4.6.6.

296.13 I alone . . . tell you see Job 1.15.

296.25 Plantagenet the name given by modern writers to the kings of England from 1154 (Henry II, his sons Richard I and John, and on), descendants of Count Geoffrey of Anjou (see note to 127.4–6). Although based on the sprig of broom (Old French *plante geneste*) used as an emblem by Geoffrey, the name was apparently not in use before the 15th century.

296.35 Sir Guy, . . . Sir Bevis Guy of Warwick and Bevis of Hampton, heroes of early 14th-century romances which bear their names. Ellis, by claiming that these romances 'may possibly be founded on some Saxon tradition'

(Ellis, 2.4) and by categorising them as 'Saxon Romances', may have led Scott to believe them current in the 12th century.

297.5 take sanctuary take refuge. According to medieval law a felon convicted of anything but sacrilege or treason could take refuge in a church for up to 40 days, and during this time any person attempting to take him from the church incurred excommunication.

297.5–6 church of Saint Peter York Minster.

297.6 Archbishop Geoffrey (*c.* 1153–1212), illegitimate son of Henry II, elected Archbishop of York in 1189, and enthroned in 1191. See also note to 297.30.

297.16 by the light of Our Lady's brow perhaps a reference to the halo with which the Virgin Mary is traditionally depicted.

297.27 heads set on Clifford's Gate the heads of traitors were sometimes set on the gates of York but none is called Clifford's Gate. However, the keep of York Castle, on top of which traitors were apparently hanged, is known as Clifford's Tower. Although there is no written evidence of it bearing this name until the 16th century Scott may have known the claim that Clifford's Tower 'has long born that name, and if we may believe tradition, ever since it was built by the conqueror; one of that family being made the first governor of it' (Francis Drake, *Eboracum: or, the History and Antiquities of the City of York* (London, 1736), 289).

297.29 horns of the altar see note to 41.21.

297.30 peace with King Richard Richard was angry over the failure of Geoffrey (see note to 297.6) to respond to his summons to appear before him at his prison cell in Germany in 1193. Geoffrey had been, and still was, embroiled in an ecclesiastical power struggle at home.

297.31 Robert Estoteville William de Stuteville (d. 1203), son of Robert de Stuteville (d. 1186), remained in England during the Third Crusade. He was one of those 'for whom the King has sought absolution from their vow [to go on crusade], alleging their bodily infirmity and the need of their counsel for the preservation of his realm' (*The Chronicle of Jocelin of Brakelond*, trans. and ed. H. E. Butler (London, 1949), 135).

297.32 Earl of Essex see note to 393.2–3.

298.4–5 Our Uncle Robert . . . Cardiffe see notes to 134.18–21, 134.22–24, 134.24–25.

298.6 grandsire Henry i.e. John's great-grandfather, Henry I, brother of Robert, Duke of Normandy.

298.29 Lancelot de Lac and Sir Tristram although in France *Lancelot* by Chrétien de Troyes was written in the 1170s, Lancelot's central place in English Arthurian legend belongs to the 14th and later centuries rather than to the 12th. In Malory Lancelot is the greatest of all King Arthur's knights: 'in all tournaments and jousts and deeds of arms, both for life and death, he passed all other knights' (*Morte D'Arthur*, 1.152: Bk 6, Ch. 1). The tradition in which Tristram becomes one of the major Arthurian knights developed in the mid-13th century, and he also figures prominently in Malory.

298.30 encountering gigantic knights see *Sir Tristrem*, ed. Walter Scott, Fytte 3, stanzas 40–46, in *Poetical Works*, 5.279–82.

299.14 stained the steps of his own altar see note to 119.25.

299.16 Reginald Fitzurse hath left a son Waldemar is a fictional character.

299.28–29 Stephen Wetheral, Broad Thoresby . . . Hugh Bardan fictional characters but Wetheral, Thoresby and Bardon are all north country place-names which came later to be used as surnames. Moreover, there was a Hugh Bardulf who, although appointed by Richard as one of the justiciars of England (Hoveden, 3.28), refused to attack the castle of Tickhill which belonged to John because he was John's vassal (Hoveden, 3.206).

299.28 spears i.e. spearmen, a term current at the time in which *Ivanhoe* was set, and frequently used in Berners's Froissart (e.g. Vol. 2, Ch. 24), an early 16th-century text, but dropping out of use before the 17th century.

300.11 Chancellor secretary to the king, with important executive responsibilities.

300.22 High Marshal one of the chief officers of the kingdom with various responsibilities, but the context suggests that Scott is thinking of *marshal* in the sense of a military commander.

300.43 Hexhamshire area around Hexham in Northumberland.

300.43–301.1 Tynedale and Teviotdale the valleys of the North Tyne in Northumbria and of the Teviot in the Scottish Borders. Until the late 16th century both were considered to be beyond the rule of law.

301.3–4 knows each glade . . . high-wood see Milton, *Comus* (performed 1634; published 1637), 311–12.

301 motto untraced; probably by Scott.

301.22 tiger of Hyrcanian deserts Hyrcania was a district of Asia, SE of the Caspian (Hyrcanian) Sea. The phrase in one form or another is common in English literature: see *3 Henry VI*, 1.4.155 ('tigers of Hyrcania'), and *The Merchant of Venice*, 2.7.41 ('Hyrcanian deserts').

302.16 Children of the Promise the Jews; see note to 280.38.

302.16 a stumbling-block and an abomination terms frequently used in the AV; abominations were particular sins against God, and together they were referred to as 'stumbling blocks of iniquity', preventing the Jews from approaching God. See Ezekiel 14.1–11.

302.21–23 Lucas de Beaumanoir . . . Grand Master chief official of the Templars. Lucas de Beaumanoir is a fictitious character; the Grand Master Robert de Sablé having died in 1192 or 1193, there was a gap until he was succeeded in 1194 by Gilbert Erail. The name Beaumanoir (*French*, beautiful manor) was probably suggested by a chapter 'Which discourseth on Appeales' by Phillip de Beaumanoir, in Favine, 2.434.

302.28 strong and outstretched arm see Jeremiah 21.5 and Psalm 136.12.

302.28–29 correct . . . punish . . . countenance . . . kindled in anger common terms in the AV.

302.31 sons of Belial see note to 228.6.

302.34–35 destroyer biblical term which in addition to its normal meaning describes God's purpose for the wicked: see Psalm 37.38.

303.4 glove the overall meaning is clear but the precise significance attached to *glove* is not. Perhaps Scott had in mind a mailed fist, i.e. a fist enclosed in a glove of armour.

303.5 holy David over Edom David put garrisons in Edom: see 2 Samuel 8.14.

303.6 of . . . sweet savour i.e. pleasing to the Lord, as in the burnt offerings of the Israelites: Exodus 29.18.

303.10–11 his face . . . seven times heated see Daniel 3.6, 19.

303.14 rending his clothes e.g. see Joshua 7.6.

303.15 daughter of Zion see note to 71.36.

303.16 captivity of Israel see notes to 250.17–18 and 286.11–12.

303.23 Daniel . . . den of lions cast into a lions' den for worshipping God, Daniel was protected by an angel and escaped unharmed 'because he believed in his God' (see Daniel 6.10–23).

303.30 confounded and brought to shame see Psalms 35.4, 71.24.

303.41 halberdiers soldiers armed with a halberd, a weapon much used in the 15th century, with an axe-like blade balanced by a pick and topped by a spear-head on a handle from five to seven feet long (see also note to 153.25).

304.4–5 false brethren ... Order see Rule in English, Ch. 21 (de Curzon, 67): '*certaine false brethren in the parts beyond the Mountaines*'. For 'false brethren' see 2 Corinthians 11.26 and Galatians 2.4. Scott interpreted the location as 'in the mountains of Palestine', but it may have referred to the brotherhood in Armenia (see Laurent Dailliez, *Les Templiers et les Règles de l'Ordre du Temple* (Paris, 1972), 61, note 58).

304.9–10 In many words ... sin see Proverbs 10.19; Rule in English, Ch. 17 (de Curzon, 40).

304.10–11 Life and death ... tongue see Proverbs 18.21; Rule in English, Ch. 17 (de Curzon, 40).

304.36 high-born knights when a knight was admitted to the Templar Order, he was asked if he was a knight and the son of a knight, or whether he was descended from the knighthood through his father so that he should and could be a knight, and whether he was born of a legal marriage. See the supplementary rules, Chs 337, 431 (de Curzon, 194, 234).

304.39 the rule of Saint Bernard the Templar Rule owed much to the Benedictine Rule as interpreted by the Cistercians. How far St Bernard (1090–1153), founder and Abbot of the Cistercian house at Clairvaux, and secretary to the Council of Troyes, was responsible for it is a matter of debate, but Scott read in Favine: 'The Fathers in this Holy Councill at *Troyes*, gave command to the Reverend Abbot Saint *Bernard*, to have the perusing of those Rules and Vowes .... Saint *Bernard* did set downe the Rules of this Order in Latine' (Favine, 2.401; de Curzon, 16).

304.40 Burrel cloth coarse woollen cloth, probably of a brown or red-grey colour, of a kind peasants would wear. See Rule in English, Ch. 20 (de Curzon, 28): '*We command that the garments bee ever but of one colour, for example, White or Blacke*, or as it may be Burrell'.

304.40–41 justly fitted to the size of the wearer see Rule in English, Ch. 20 (de Curzon, 27–28), which requires that a Templar's garment should be '*a meete measure with him that uses it, acording to every mans severall size*'.

304.41 octangular see note to 40.25.

305.1–2 softest lambskin see Rule, Ch. 23 (de Curzon, 29), which allowed the use only of lambskin or ramskin in winter clothing.

305.4 abacus a mistake for *baculum*, a Latin word for a staff. The Rule (Ch. 68) refers to the Master holding 'Baculum, & Virgam', a staff and rod, 'the staffe to support the infirmities of the weake, and the rod to correct the defaults of delinquents' (Rule in English, Ch. 68; de Curzon, 50).

305.6–7 the cross of the Order ... orle see note to 40.25.

305.10 Preceptor the head of a Preceptory (see note to 269.13 and footnote to 302) responsible for the training and discipline of the knights.

305.17 to be dissolved and to be with the just compare the Vulgate's *dissolvi, et esse cum Christo*, 'to be dissolved and be with Christ' (Philippians 1.23) where the corresponding AV passage reads 'to depart, and to be with Christ'. St Bernard in his *De Laude Novae Militiae* (see note to 304.39) adapts the Vulgate passage. Either St Bernard or the Vulgate itself could be Scott's source.

305.20 Temple Church the round church of the Templars in London, consecrated in 1185 and still standing.

305.20 Robert de Ros Scott is thinking of a sepulchral effigy bearing the coat of arms of the de Ros family in the Temple Church but it belongs to a slightly later date. It has been identified by various writers as that of Robert de Ros (d. 1227), a benefactor of the Templars, or of a later member of the family.

305.22–23 William de Mareschal *c.* 1147–1219, 1st Earl of Pembroke, another benefactor of the Templars, likewise not dead in 1194. He was buried in the Temple Church and one of the still existing effigies there has been uncertainly identified as his.

305.26 **Conrade Mountfitchet** Scott possibly took the surname from Gilbert de Montfichet, a benefactor of the Knights Hospitallers mentioned by William Dugdale, *Monasticon Anglicanum* (London, 1693), 204.

305.32–33 **the roaring lion . . . whom he may devour** see 1 Peter 5.8.

305.36 **Ut Leo semper feriatur** *Latin* that the lion [i.e. the devil] should always be struck down: Rule, Ch. 48 (de Curzon, 58), and see 1 Peter 5.8.

305.43 **no gold upon stirrup or bridle-bit** see Rule, Ch. 37 (de Curzon, 54).

306.2–3 **They are forbidden . . . another** see Rule in English, Ch. 46 (de Curzon, 56): 'That none catch one Bird with another'.

306.3–4 **shoot beasts . . . game** see Rule in English, Ch. 47 (de Curzon, 57).

306.6–8 **forbidden to read . . . hours of refection** Templars were not allowed to send or receive letters without permission or read them except in the Master's presence (Rule, Ch. 41; de Curzon 47–48) and were to listen to '*sacred reading*' during meals (Rule in English, Ch. 9; de Curzon, 34).

306.8–9 **commanded to extirpate magic and heresy** the Templars were not specifically directed to wipe out magic and heresy in their Rule; Scott anticipates the charges of heresy and black magic brought against them when the order was suppressed.

306.12 **eating flesh but thrice a-week** see Rule in English, Ch. 10 (de Curzon, 35).

306.12–13 **the accustomed . . . body** see Rule in English, Ch. 10 (de Curzon, 35): '*the accustomary feeding of the flesh, is the necessary corruption of the body*'; Scott correctly interprets the Latin as 'feeding on flesh'.

306.14 **water** see Rule in English, Ch. 16 (de Curzon, 38); whether knights had only water or '*a competent mixture of wine with . . . water*' was left to the Master.

306.20–24 **we were forbidden . . . paradise** see Rule in English, Ch. 56 (de Curzon, 69): '*It is a dangerous thing to assemble or joyne together Sisters, because the auncient enemy hath drawne many from the right path of Paradise by the company of women*'. The 'Ancient Enemy' is the devil.

306.27–28 **ut omnium mulierum fugiantur oscula** *Latin* that the kisses of all women should be avoided: Rule, Ch. 72 (de Curzon, 69).

306.30–31 **Hugh de Payen . . . blessed Seven** the founders of the Order, Hugh de Payen and Godfrey de Saint-Omer, were joined in 1118 by seven others: André de Montbard, Gondemarc, Godefroy, Roral (Rossal), Payen de Montdésir, Geoffroy Bisol and Archambaud de Saint-Agnan (Saint-Anian).

306.38 **streaks of leprosy . . . houses of old** Leviticus 14.37.

306.41 **basilisk** fabulous serpent supposed to have been hatched by a serpent from the egg of a cock. Its look was fatal.

307.1–2 **Slay the sinners . . . brand of Phineas** see Numbers Ch. 25.

307.5 **purify the fabric of the Temple** compare the cleansing of the temple: Mark 11.15–17.

307.6–7 **unclean stones . . . out of the building** see Leviticus 14.40.

307.13–19 **our presumption . . . demolished** Beaumanoir foresees events of the 14th century when, beginning with arrests in France in 1307, the Templars were charged with heresy and immorality (see Malcolm Barber, *The Trial of the Templars* (Cambridge, 1978), 248–52) and finally suppressed by the papal bull *Vox in excelso* of 22 March 1312.

307.19–20 **Temple . . . place thereof . . . nations** compare Lamentations Chs 1 and 2, and John 11.48.

307.24–25 **wickedness of this generation** see Matthew 12.45.

307.34–35 aspirants . . . knights see Rule, Ch. 24 (de Curzon, 30).
307.36 awaiting his permission permission had to be granted for the simplest actions, even, for example, for a brother to shorten his horse's stirrups or other straps (see supplementary rules, Ch. 144; de Curzon, 113–14).
307.39 Damian the name of the squire in 'The Merchant's Tale'; in the same context of the tale January is said to sing 'ful murier than the papejay' (*The Canterbury Tales*, 4 (E), 2322).
307.41–42 jangling as pert and as proud as any popingay proverbial: see 'Als prowd as ony papingo', *The Frieris of Berwik* (*c.* 1500), line 142. Scott also conflates two lines from Chaucer: 'proud, and peert as is a pye' ('The Reeve's Tale', *The Canterbury Tales*, 1 (A), 3950) where *pye* means 'magpie', and 'thou janglest as a jay' ('The Man of Law's Tale', *The Canterbury Tales*, 2 (B1), 774).
308.3 Preceptor see note to 305.10, but the title was also given to other Templars in positions of authority and thus to Bois-Guilbert.
308.4–5 who may not walk . . . Master see Rule in English, Ch. 33 (de Curzon, 44–45): 'That none is to walke according to his owne will'.
308.5–6 In the hearing . . . obeyed me Rule in English, Ch. 33 (de Curzon, 45): a translation of the Vulgate's 'in auditu auris obedivit mihi' (Psalm 17.45; AV Psalm 18.44).
308.17–19 the staff and the rod . . . delinquents Rule in English, Ch. 68 (de Curzon, 50). For 'staff and the rod' see Psalm 23.4, and note to 305.4.
308.39 misbelieving jaws compare *The Merchant of Venice*, 1.3.106.
309.16 Armenian cap probably a high pointed hat. Jews were required by the Council of Vienna in 1267 to wear a high pointed hat, the *pileum cornutum* (Cecil Roth, *A History of the Jews in England*, 3rd edn, (Oxford, 1964), 95), and people are shown wearing high pointed hats in illustrations to the 13th-century Armenian *Gospel of Haghbat* (Sirarpie Der Nersessian, *The Armenians* (London, 1969), 147).
309.28 De Lectione Literarum *Latin* concerning the reading of letters: Rule, Ch. 41 (de Curzon, 47). The translation reads: '*It is in no wayes lawfull to any Brother, eyther to receive himselfe Letters from his parents, or from any other, nor to send him Letters,* without the command of the Master, or Steward. After that the Brother have leave, if they please they may bee read in the Masters presence.'
309.37 fanners to purge the threshing-floor see Matthew 3.12.
310.2–3 Bacchus . . . Venus respectively Roman god of wine, and goddess of love and beauty. Pagan goddesses are often addressed as 'Lady' in medieval texts.
310.10 Witch of Endor see notes to 197.26 and 100.42.
310.15 Invenientur vigilantes *Latin* they will be found watchful: see Luke 12.37. The Vulgate reads 'invenerit vigilantes'.
310.21 Vinum laetificat cor hominis *Latin* wine makes glad the heart of man: Vulgate Psalm 103.15; AV Psalm 104.15.
310.21–22 Rex delectabitur pulchritudine tua *Latin* the king will take delight in your beauty: see Vulgate Psalm 44.12; AV Psalm 45.11. The Vulgate reads: 'Et concupiscet rex decorem tuum'.
310.24 den of thieves Matthew 21.13.
310.25 Pr. S. M. Jorvolciencis abbreviation of the Latin *Prior Sanctae Mariae Jorvolciencis*, 'Prior of St Mary's of Jorvaulx'.
310.33 the hand of God is upon us that is, in anger; see 1 Samuel 5.11.
311.15–18 devouring enemy . . . the lion the devil; see 1 Peter 5.8.
311.18 semper percutiatur leo vorans *Latin* may the devouring lion always be struck down. See note to 305.36 and 1 Peter 5.8.
311.19 abacus see note to 305.4.

311.28–31 Miriam . . . burned at a stake see note to 231.31–32. Jews were held by many to use supernatural powers for healing, and to practise witchcraft and sorcery. Laws specifically against witchcraft were not passed in England until the 16th century, but witchcraft was frequently associated with heresy, for which the punishment (common law at first, in 1401 confirmed by the statute *De Heretico Comburendo*) was burning at the stake.

312 motto untraced; probably by Scott.

312.11 President term applied from the 14th to the 16th centuries to the head of a religious house.

313.10–12 De commilitonibus . . . carnis *Latin* concerning the brethren in arms of the Temple in the Holy City, who frequent the company of worthless women for the gratification of the flesh. Scott invented this chapter although it conforms to the general spirit of the Rule.

313.26 rolled away . . . understanding see Joshua 5.9 ('This day have I rolled away the reproach of Egypt from off you') and Ephesians 4.18 ('Having the understanding darkened').

313.35 Saint Magdalene . . . virgins Mary Magdalene was one of the followers of Jesus and the first person to see him after his resurrection (Mark 16.9). The preceptor confuses with hers the story of St Ursula and the eleven thousand virgins who according to a much-elaborated legend were slain by the Huns at Cologne on account of their Christian faith.

314.6 chastisement . . . stripes see Isaiah 53.5.

314.6–7 staff . . . rod see note to 308.17–19.

314.14 sweet and acceptable offering see Jeremiah 6.20: 'your burnt offerings are not acceptable, nor your sacrifices sweet unto me'.

314.17–19 burst the bands . . . heaps upon heaps see Judges 15.13–16.

314.21 die the death be put to death. Originally from Mark 7.10, and used by Shakespeare. Samuel Johnson in his edition of Shakespeare, commenting on *Measure for Measure*, 2.4.165, notes that it 'seems to be a solemn phrase for death inflicted by law'.

314.22–29 the laws of England . . . domain baronial courts dealt with disputes between lord and vassal and between vassals, and had powers of jurisdiction over such matters as land, inheritance, feudal service, wardship, marriage etc. Little is known about their involvement in such matters as witchcraft and sorcery (Richard Kieckhefer, *Magic in the Middle Ages* (Cambridge, 1990), 188). Moreover the powers of baronial courts had already been considerably reduced in the reign of Henry II (reigned 1154–89) and they did not have the absolute powers which Beaumanoir claims for them. For the judicial powers of the Templars see note to 393.15.

315.10–11 le don d'amoureuse merci *French* translated by Scott in his 'Essay on Chivalry' as 'the boon of amorous mercy' (*Prose Works*, 6.31) and meaning 'the granting of sexual favours'. The phrase comes from La Fontaine (1621–95), 'L'Oraison de Saint Julian', line 312.

315.26 sin-offering special sacrifice offered by the Israelites to atone for sin and defilement: see Leviticus 4.1–35, 6.24–30.

316.1 painted piece of Jewish flesh and blood *painted* was formerly used of colouring the face with make-up; its biblical associations are with the evil Baal-worshipper Jezebel (2 Kings 9.30) and with whoredom and the profanation of the Lord's sanctuary (Ezekiel 23.40).

316.2 wild-goose chase *proverbial* hopeless quest: see *ODEP*, 889.

316.26 in flagrant delict translation of the Latin *in flagrante delicto*, meaning 'in the very act of committing the offence', used particularly of adultery.

316.29–30 petty quarrels . . . Burgundy this was not a time of particular conflict between Flanders and Burgundy. Scott is probably thinking of conflicts in the 15th century between the Flemish and their rulers (some of which are reflected in *Quentin Durward*) after Flanders came under Burgundian control in 1384.

316.38 Perish a thousand . . . baubles see Oliver Goldsmith, *She Stoops to Conquer* (1773), 2.1: 'Perish the baubles! Your person is all I desire.' (*Collected Works*, ed. Arthur Friedman, 5 vols (Oxford, 1966), 5.114).

317.39 Maison-Dieu the Templars had a preceptory at Ewell, in Kent, but there were no Templar houses called Maison-Dieu. The term *maison-dieu* (literally 'house of God') was used for hospitals or poorhouses; the hospital of St Mary in Dover which later came to be called *Maison-Dieu* did not belong to the Templars and was not founded until the early 13th century.

319 motto untraced; probably by Scott.

319.31 Preceptors see notes to 305.10 and 308.3.

320.11–12 Venite exultemus Domino *Latin* come let us sing to the Lord (Vulgate, Psalm 94.1; AV Psalm 95.1), used daily in the office of Matins, and mentioned in Rule, Ch. 7 (de Curzon, 26).

320.18 the rushing of mighty waters Isaiah 17.12.

320.23 Knights Companions there was no such named rank in the order of the Temple but Scott uses it here and at 321.22 as a term for the ordinary rank of knights. However at 320.40 he seems to suggest, inaccurately, that there were both knights and companions in the order as there are in some modern chivalric orders.

320.31 Prince of the powers of this world the devil: see John 12.31, 14.30, and 16.11 ('the prince of this world') and Ephesians 2.2 ('the prince of the power of the air').

320.35–36 Semper Leo percutiatur see note to 305.36.

321.6 fifty-ninth capital de Curzon, 42.

321.27 holy places purified . . . by the blood compare Leviticus 8.14–15.

321 footnote Rules . . . St Bernard see note to 304.39. Most editions of St Bernard's works only include the *De Laude Novae Militiae*, a treatise he wrote in the early 1130s to encourage the Templars. Scott may have known an edition which also contained the Rule but there is no such edition in the Abbotsford Library or the Advocate's Library (now the National Library of Scotland). The phrase 'the Rules of the Poor Military Brotherhood of the Temple' translates the title of the Templar Rule: *Regulae Pauperum Commilitonum Templi*.

322.3 Auferte malum ex vobis *Latin* remove the evil thing from amongst you: Rule, Ch. 68 (de Curzon, 50), and see 1 Corinthians 5.13.

322.6–7 Quod nullus juxta . . . incedat *Latin* that none is to walk according to his own will: Rule, Ch. 33 (de Curzon, 44–45).

322.8 Ut fratres . . . excommunicatis *Latin* that brothers should not share with excommunicated persons: Rule, Ch. 57 (de Curzon, 24).

322.9 Anathema Maranatha that is, excommunication, as threatened by the Templar Rule: Rule, Ch. 57 (de Curzon, 24); and 1 Corinthians 16.22. *Anathema* means 'cursed with God's disfavour'; the exact meaning of *maranatha* is unclear but is interpreted as part of a formula of solemn cursing.

322.10–11 Ut fratres . . . mulieribus *Latin* that brothers should not spend their time amongst foreign women. This would appear to have been invented by Scott; the Rule forbids relations with *all* women (Rule, Ch. 72; de Curzon, 69).

322.13 Ut Fugiantur oscula *Latin* that kisses should be avoided: Rule, Ch. 72 (de Curzon, 69).

322.15–16 cut off . . . from our congregation see Exodus 12.19; Numbers 19.20.

322.16 right hand . . . thereof see Matthew 5.29–30.

322.18–19 De osculis fugiendis *Latin* on avoiding kissing. This refers to the same rule as in 322.13 but the words are Scott's.

323.26–27 Thirteen pater-nosters . . . vespers see Rule in English, Ch. 2 (de Curzon, 22).

323.28 Thrice a-week . . . flesh see Rule in English, Ch. 10 (de Curzon, 35).

323.43 Moslemah used erroneously as the plural for *Moslem*.

324.12 possessed . . . dumb devil that is, he is possessed by a devil which will not allow him to speak. For the story of a similar spirit cast out by Christ see Mark 9.17–27.

324.13 Avoid thee, Sathanas banish yourself, Satan; a relatively rare reflexive usage. Compare 'Auoyde fro me Sathan' in Coverdale's version of Matthew 16.23.

324.31 mystery of iniquity 2 Thessalonians 2.7.

325.23 The lion of the tribe of Judah hath conquered see Revelation 5.5, a Christian text referring to Jesus, and therefore unlikely to be written on a Jew's box. However, the image of Judah as a lion originated from the Old Testament: see Genesis 49.9–10.

325.41 Higg, the son of Snell see Turner's chapter on 'Classes and Conditions of Society' where Snel and Hig are listed as Anglo-Saxon slaves who were given their freedom (4.133, 134).

326.1 arise and walk see Matthew 9.5.

326.17–19 It was not the wont . . . strangers see note to 98.10–11.

326.29 it suits not a maiden . . . such rude grooms Rebecca's words echo those of Mary, Queen of Scots as she prepared herself for execution: 'The executioners offered their assistance, but she modestly refused it, saying, she had neither been accustomed to undress before so many spectators, nor to be served by such grooms of the chamber' (*Tales of a Grandfather*, in *Prose Works*, 23.185).

326.32 elders among your people common biblical phrase: e.g. see Exodus 19.7.

327.29 women of good women of good standing, Scott's variation on the obsolete phrase 'man of good'.

328.14 milk-white swan an accusation based on folklore rather than witchcraft. There are various stories of swan-maidens who could change at will between human and swan form, and although the known versions come from Germany and Scandinavia it is probable that such stories also circulated in England: see Jacob Grimm, *Teutonic Mythology*, trans. James Steven Stallybrass, 4 vols (London, 1880–88), 1.426–30.

329.42 challenge obsolete sense of the word, meaning to demand as one's right. See 'The Franklin's Tale', *The Canterbury Tales*, 5 (F), 1324–25: 'Nat that I chalange any thyng of right/ Of yow, my sovereyn lady, but youre grace'.

329.43 trial by combat form of 'trial' introduced to England by the Normans, which, 'like other ordeals, was an appeal to the judgement of God for the discovery of the truth or falsehood of an accusation that was denied . . . founded on this supposition,—*That Heaven would always interpose, and give the victory to the champions of truth and innocence*' (Henry, 3.355). Those considered legally unable to defend their own cause could have champions to fight on their behalf.

330 motto see *Richard II*, 4.1.46–48, which reads, 'to the extremest point/ Of mortal breathing.'

330.32–34 delivered in thunders . . . fire see Exodus 19.16–18 (the delivery of the Ten Commandments to Moses).

330.34 recalled see Matthew 5.17: 'Think not that I am come to destroy the law, or the prophets: I am not come to destroy, but to fulfil.'

332.5–6 field . . . foughten see note to 149.12.

332.11 well know we . . . angel of light see 2 Corinthians 11.14: 'Satan himself is transformed into an angel of light'.

334.3 **disposer of all** see Proverbs 16.33.

334.3–4 **turn back the captivity of Judah** see Jeremiah 29.14, 22; Zephaniah 3.20; and note to 250.17–18.

334.16 **Buthan** perhaps suggested by the street name Bootham in York.

334.26 **my soul is disquieted** see Psalm 42.5.

334.29 **Be of good comfort, brother** see Matthew 9.22; 2 Corinthians 13.11.

334.30–31 **mammon of unrighteousness** Luke 16.9; *mammon* means 'riches'.

334.32–33 **signet . . . the evil genii** in the Koran it is recorded that God gave Solomon power over the wind and over genii, or *djinn* (Koran, 34.12–13). Tradition has it that he exerted this power by means of his signet, inscribed with the name of God: see H. A. R. Gibb and J. H. Kramers, *Shorter Encyclopaedia of Islam* (Leiden and London, 1953), 550.

335.4 **cupping apparatus** glass or horn cup sometimes used in blood-letting (see next note). It was alternately pressed on the skin and pulled away, thus sucking out the blood.

335.5 **phlebotomy** blood-letting, opening a vein to let blood flow; a common practice based on the belief that certain illnesses were caused by too much blood in the body.

335.7 **throw dust on his grey hairs** sign of mourning found in the Bible: see Joshua 7.6; Job 2.12; Lamentations 2.10.

335.12 **Benoni** *Hebrew* son of my sorrow; the name given by Rachel to her last son, in giving birth to whom she died (Genesis 35.18); his father renamed him Benjamin.

335.12–13 **bring down my grey hairs to the grave** Genesis 42.38: words spoken by Jacob in his fear of losing his son Benjamin.

335.13 **the bitterness of my heart** see Job 7.11.

335.13–14 **curse God and die** Job 2.9.

335.15–16 **art thou a father . . . like unto these?** 'father' meaning a senior and respected person as in Acts 7.2. See John 3.10: 'Art thou a master of Israel, and knowest not these things?'.

335.18–19 **Daniel . . . lions** Belteshazzar was the name given to Daniel in the palace of Nebuchadnezzar (Daniel 1.7). See also note to 303.23.

335.18 **Daniel, which** an AV usage: see Matthew 5.10; 1 Corinthians 15.57.

335.22–23 **wither . . . gourd of Jonah** see Jonah 4.6–7: God prepared a 'gourd' (a tree bearing gourds or large, fleshy fruits) to give Jonah shade but the next day he prepared a worm which attacked the gourd so that it withered.

335.23 **child of my old age** compare 'son of his old age', Genesis 21.2; 37.3.

335.24–25 **the darkness of the shadow of death** see Job 3.5; Psalm 107.10, 14. The 'shadow of death' is used 19 times in the AV: e.g. see Psalm 23.4.

335.28–29 **mine eyes . . . fountains of water** see Jeremiah 9.1: 'Oh that my head were waters, and mine eyes a fountain of tears'.

335.32 **Adonikam** name of an Israelite family, meaning 'my Lord has arisen': see Ezra 2.13; Nehemiah 7.18.

335.33 **the Promise** see note to 280.38.

335.35–36 **strong man** see 1 Samuel 14.52; Psalm 19.5; Proverbs 7.26 etc.

335.40 **her who hath none to help her** see Isaiah 63.5: 'there was none to help'.

336.6 **the house of bondage** used 9 times in the AV: e.g. see Exodus 13.3.

336.7 say unto him . . . even unto Wilfred prefixing of *even* to a repetition or explanation is typical AV style: e.g. see Proverbs 22.19, 'I have made known to thee this day, even to thee'.

336.12 Cordova major city of Moorish Spain and, in the 10th and 11th centuries, a significant Arab and Jewish cultural centre where Jews were generally treated with tolerance and held positions of influence. However, by the 1190s the Almohads had conquered southern Spain and had forbidden the practice of the Jewish religion.

336.13 Boabdil the Spanish name for Abu 'Abdu'lla Mohammed (Mohammed XI), last Muslim sultan of Granada (1482–92). During his reign Jews enjoyed the same rights and freedoms as other subjects.

336.19–20 flesh of my flesh . . . bone see Genesis 2.23.

336.22 Girth up thy loins see note to 59.33.

336.26–27 men of blood see the alternative, marginal version of 2 Samuel 16.7.

336.29–30 hath compassion common biblical phrase: e.g. see 2 Kings 13.23, 'the Lord was gracious unto them, and had compassion on them'.

336.34 Be of good courage common biblical phrase: e.g. Psalm 27.14.

337.6–7 as thy heart desires common biblical phrase: e.g. see Psalm 21.2.

337.10–11 free guild-brother member of a guild: see note to 101.24.

337.12 mancus rather than being a coin of the Anglo-Saxon period, a mancus was a unit of money used in accounts, one mancus being the equivalent of thirty pence. However, Henry believed 'that the *mancus* was a real gold coin' (2.498).

337.18 flying post mailcoach using relays of horses, an express.

337 motto see Anna Seward (1747–1809), 'From thy waves, stormy Lannow, I fly': *The Poetical Works of Anna Seward*, ed. Walter Scott, 3 vols (Edinburgh, 1810), 1.158.

337.33–338.22 When Israel . . . sacrifice Rebecca's hymn tells the story of the wanderings of the people of Israel (see Exodus 12.28–19.2) in a manner reminiscent of e.g. Psalm 107. It draws heavily on language, imagery and quotations from the Bible (see below).

337.33 Israel, of the Lord beloved see Psalm 60.5, where the psalmist speaks of Israel as God's beloved.

337.34 the land of bondage see Deuteronomy 5.6.

337.36 guide in smoke and flame see Exodus 13.21.

337.41 the choral hymn of praise e.g. see Exodus 15.1: 'Then sang Moses and the children of Israel this song'.

337.42 trump and timbrel see Psalm 150.3–4.

338.1 Zion's daughters see note to 71.36.

338.3 portents the 'signs and wonders' that God sent in the land of Egypt: see Exodus 7.3–12.51.

338.5 Our fathers would not know Thy ways see Psalm 95.10: 'It is a people that do err in their heart, and they have not known my ways.'

338.13 long-suffering characteristic frequently attributed to God, e.g. in Psalm 86.15.

338.13 slow to wrath see Nehemiah 9.17 and Proverbs 14.29.

338.14 A burning and a shining light John 5.35.

338.15 Our harps . . . streams see Psalm 137.1–2.

338.17 censer round our altar beams see Leviticus 16.12.

338.19–20 The blood of goat . . . prize see Micah 6.6–8; Isaiah 1.11.

338.21 A contrite heart Psalm 51.17.

339.16–17 a parting . . . not bread see Isaiah 55.2.

339.19 the Rock of Ages from the AV's marginal note to Isaiah 26.4; the

AV text itself reads 'everlasting strength'. The phrase is best known from the hymn 'Rock of Ages, cleft for me' by A. M. Toplady (1740–78).

339.31 bucklered defended; a rare verb found in Elizabethan drama, e.g. 'buckler falsehood with a pedigree' (*3 Henry VI*, 3.3.99).

340.22 trim their bark balance their boat, distribute its load to keep it on an even keel.

341.30 breath of my nostrils see note to 249.8.

342.21 a hissing and a reproach see Jeremiah 29.18.

342.23–24 mountains . . . nearly scaled in classical mythology the giants piled mountains on mountains in an attempt to reach the heavenly home of the gods; see Ovid (43 BC–AD 18), *Metamorphoses*, 1.151–53.

342.30 the Regent there was no regent during Richard's absence and he retained ultimate authority himself. However he entrusted wide powers to various individuals, at first mainly to William de Longchamp, Chancellor and Bishop of Ely from 1189, but, after he was removed in 1191 by John's supporters for his tyrannical behaviour, the principal conduct of government lay with Walter de Coutances, Archbishop of Rouen.

343.7 Conrade, Marquis of Montserrat member of an Italian crusading family, Conrad of Montferrat was chosen as King of Jerusalem in 1192 but was assassinated twelve days later. Montserrat seems to be Scott's normal spelling although the correct name was Montferrat; Scott's usage arises from misreading an 'f' as a long 's' and is not unique in the period (e.g. see David Hume, *The History of England*, 8 vols (Edinburgh, 1810), 2.14, although earlier editions spell the name correctly).

343.18 Mount Carmel see note to 51.34.

343.19–20 exchange . . . sceptre become a king rather than Grand Master of the Templars.

344.1 elements medieval philosophers believed that all matter, including the human body, was compounded from the four 'elements', earth, air, water and fire.

344.14 daughter of Jacob i.e. a Jewish woman. See note to 53.23–24.

344.15 Comforter when used as a proper noun 'the Comforter' is a New Testament term normally applied to the Holy Spirit (e.g. John 14.26) whose existence is not part of Jewish belief; it occurs, however, as a common noun in Lamentations 1.16, 'the comforter that should relieve my soul'.

344.15–16 hide his face from his people common Old Testament phrase: e.g. see Isaiah 8.17, 'the Lord, that hideth his face from the house of Jacob'.

344.17 in sincerity and in truth Joshua 24.14.

344.34–35 the gourd . . . the cedar a gourd (see note to 335.22–23) is not a large tree; the cedar tree is tall and is frequently mentioned in the Bible, e.g. 2 Kings 19.23; Ezekiel 17.3.

344.36–40 Divine Presence . . . Jacob in Exodus 25.17–22 the mercy-seat which covered the sacred Ark of the Lord is described as having two golden cherubim, one at either end. Numbers 7.89 tells how Moses 'heard the voice of one speaking unto him from off the mercy seat that was upon the ark of testimony, from between the two cherubims'. Its message was that the Levites (the descendants of Levi, the third son of Jacob) were to serve in the tabernacle on behalf of the other members of the congregation.

344.43–345.1 trampled down . . . mire of the ways see Isaiah 10.6; Micah 7.10.

345.3 Adonikam see note to 335.32.

345.24–25 garden of the sluggard . . . blossom see Proverbs 24.30–31, 'I went by the field of the slothful . . . and, lo, it was all grown over with thorns, and nettles had covered the face thereof'. The wording is probably influenced by Isaac Watts's hymn, 'The Sluggard', itself based on Proverbs, and Christ's parable of the sower in Luke 8.7: 'And some fell among thorns; and the thorns sprang up with it, and choked it'.

345.33 **forgave her executioner** compare *As You Like It*, 3.5.3–6: 'The common executioner,/ Whose heart th'accustom'd sight of death makes hard,/ Falls not the axe upon the humbled neck/ But first begs pardon'.

346.1 **lay down life . . . garment** compare *Measure for Measure*, 3.1.105–07.

347.14–15 **armed image of Saint George. . .procession** St George is one of the Nine Worthies who according to Strutt 'appear to have been favourite characters, and were often exhibited in [16th century] pageants', the effigies in some cases being 'probably nothing more than images of wood or pasteboard' (*Sports and Pastimes*, xxvii).

348 **motto** see Colley Cibber, *The Tragical History of King Richard III* (1700), 5.4.121; this is a revision of Shakespeare's play.

348.7 **Saint Botolph** Botulf (d. *c.* 680) was a very popular saint in medieval England but details of his life are sketchy. He established a monastery, perhaps at Boston ('Botulf's Stone') in Lincolnshire.

348.38 **take the lee-gage** keep to the lee-ward, i.e. keep away from the wind.

348.39 **makes all split** makes everything go to pieces, makes everything give way: see *A Midsummer Night's Dream*, 1.2.24.

349.8 **faithful as steel** proverbial: compare 'as true as steel' (*ODEP*, 840).

350.17 **Malkin** diminutive of *Mald* (i.e. Matilda, Maud); a familiar name in the Middle Ages, occuring e.g. in 'The Nun's Priest's Tale', *The Canterbury Tales*, 7, 3384 (B2 4574).

350.18–19 **the juggler's steed . . . amongst the eggs** as Duncan points out Scott combines the idea of an 'egg-dance' where a human dancer danced a hornpipe amongst eggs without breaking them (see *Sports and Pastimes*, 173), with an account of 13th-century dancing horses (see *Sports and Pastimes*, 184).

350.29 **Fructus Temporum** *Latin* the fruit of the times. The first part of the *Croniclis of Englonde with the Frute of Timis* (published in St Albans in 1483) begins with the words 'Hic incipit fructus temporum', that is 'Here begins the fruit of the times' (A4r).

350.39 **rowels** small wheels with sharp points on the end of spurs. However, according to Strutt, the 'rowel does not appear in any delineation till the latter end of the 13th century' (*Horda*, 1.48).

351.1 **Grange** outlying farmhouse and barns belonging to a monastery where tithes of grain and other produce could be stored.

351.24 **cold rheum** rheumatism.

351.29 **pacing nag** horse trained to move with a smooth and even motion by lifting the legs on the same side together

352.2 **Diggory** the name goes back to the medieval romance *Sir Degore* (*ODECN*, 84). It came to have comic associations after being used by Goldsmith as the name of a character in *She Stoops to Conquer* (1773).

352.25 **good cutting falchion** originally a curved sword but later a term for any sword; see *King Lear*, 5.3.276, 'my good biting falchion'.

352.36 **mopping, mowing** see *King Lear*, 4.1.62–63.

352.42 **virelai** form of lyric with stanzas linked by common rhymes, a pattern which Scott does not follow. It was popular in France and in England in the 14th century but unknown in the 12th century. See 'The Franklin's Tale', *The Canterbury Tales*, 5 (F), 948; Spenser, *The Shepheardes Calendar*, November, 21; and Dryden, *The Flower and the Leaf*, 365.

352.43 **stiff and mellow burthen** see the 'General Prologue' to *The*

Canterbury Tales, 1 (A), 673–74: 'This Somonour bar to hym a stif burdoun'. The burthen or burden is the bass part.

353.3–19 Anna-Marie . . . Tybalt, my love by Scott.

353.23 came by the cudgel were beaten.

353.31–354.15 There came three merry men . . . say him nay by Scott.

354.1 Hur's a gentleman . . . of Wales it was a literary convention to represent Welsh (and Gaelic) speakers as using *her* in place of 'he' or 'him' (see *OED*, *her*, personal pronoun, 2b).

354.25 Heaven forefend may Heaven prevent it: see *1 Henry VI*, 5.4.65.

354.29–30 trees have ears as well as stone walls see the proverb 'walls have ears': *ODEP*, 864.

354.41–42 that which is the root of evil i.e. money: see 1 Timothy 6.10, 'the love of money is the root of all evil'.

355.1 good fellows see note to 360.18.

355.6 Abbot of Saint Bees see note to 222.14; compare 222.10–11, where a similar story is told of the abbot of St Ives.

355.9 yeomanly service see *Hamlet*, 5.2.36.

355.18–19 seven-fold usury . . . loans see Luke 6.35 ('But love ye your enemies, and do good, and lend, hoping for nothing again; and your reward shall be great') and compare Proverbs 6.30–31 where a thief who is found 'shall restore sevenfold'. In the Bible 'seven' is a potent figure but is sometimes used just to indicate a large number.

356.5 you have neither lions nor wolves see Zephaniah 3.3: 'Her princes within her are roaring lions; her judges are evening wolves'.

356.27 know my gamut the gamut was the scale of all the known notes in medieval music, hence 'know my notes'.

357.7 king of the nine-pins the tallest pin, or king-pin, placed centrally in a game of skittles.

357.12 morrion an infantry helmet of a type used in the 16th and 17th centuries.

357.14–15 Clerks to Saint Nicholas see note to 102.18.

357.33–34 Ha! Saint Edward! Ha! Saint George! . . . every invocation in his 'Essay on Chivalry' Scott relates how 'Edward III., fighting valiantly . . . before the gates of Calais, was heard to accompany each blow he struck with the invocation of his tutelar saints, Ha! Saint Edward! ha! St George!' (*Prose Works*, 6.20). For Edward the Confessor see note to 156.1–2; for St George see note to 162.15; see also note to 247.28.

359.18 thy disobedience to thy father Richard rebelled against Henry II in 1173–74 and 1188.

360.18 Prince of good fellows *good fellows* could mean 'thieves' (see footnote to 357), but see also Henry V's description of himself as 'the best king of good fellows' in *Henry V*, 5.2.240.

360.25–26 When the cat . . . mice will proverbial: recorded since the 16th century in this form and earlier in other forms (*ODEP*, 109–10).

360.38 Confiteor *Latin* I confess. However meagre his scholarship, the friar would have been familiar with this term from the confession at the beginning of the Mass.

361.3–4 mouth drawn down . . . tassels at the mouth of a purse see Ben Jonson, *Everyman out of his Humour* (first performed 1599), 5.6.35.

361.14 Friar Tuck Friar Tuck does not play a significant part in the original Robin Hood ballads. Dobson and Taylor see him as a fusion of two different friars, a 15th-century outlaw, Robert Stafford, who called himself 'Frere Tuk', and the jovial friar of the morris dances (*Rymes of Robyn Hood*, 41). The first record of his being associated with Robin Hood is in a dramatic fragment of the late 15th century (see *Rymes of Robyn Hood*, 203–07) and about

1560 he appeared in 'The Playe of Robyn Hood' (see Ritson, 2.192–203) as 'a jolly fryer', and subsequently in chapbooks as Scott's reference to 'penny-histories' makes clear (see note to 6.24). Scott developed this image in *Ivanhoe* and thus ensured him a central role in subsequent tellings of the Robin Hood story. He also identified him with the friar of 'Robin Hood and the Curtall Fryer' but was not the first to do so: the 17th-century Percy Folio calls this ballad 'Robine Hood and ffryer Tucke' (*Bishop Percy's Folio Manuscript*, ed. John W. Hales and Frederick J. Furnivall, 3 vols (London, 1868), 1.26). This version had not been published in Scott's time, but Scott knew the contents of Percy's Folio Manuscript, and Ritson had speculated that Friar Tuck might be the curtal friar (Ritson, 1.xxvi).

361.16 Lord's anointed the king, who was anointed with oil at his coronation; see also note to 283.1.

361.17 sits the wind there compare 'Sits the wind in that corner' (*Much Ado About Nothing*, 2.3.91).

362.12 vert and venison green vegetation (vert) in a forest serving as a cover for deer and the deer (venison) that are in it; a standard phrase.

362.21 hogsheads large casks. A hogshead of ale contained 48 gallons (218 litres) or 51 gallons (232 litres) outside London.

362.21–22 of the first strike of the highest strength. This usage is without parallel in other authors and may be a mistake.

362.26–27 turn our game into earnest compare 'The Miller's Prologue', *The Canterbury Tales*, 1 (A), 3186.

363 motto see Act 2, Air 11 of *Love and Loyalty* (1788), an opera by Andrew MacDonald.

363.37–38 lonely journies see the *Itinerarium*, Bk 4, Ch. 28; 1.286–88: after Richard had set out with a very small company and been attacked by the Saracens, his followers urged him not to ride out in this lonely way any more since on his safety depended the safety of all but Richard took little notice of the advice.

364.21–22 Estoteville and Bohun see notes to 297.31 and 393.2–3.

364.23 Salisbury see note to 86.37.

364.24 Beauchamp, in Warwickshire the Beauchamps were not associated with Warwickshire until the time of William de Beauchamp (d. 1298) who inherited the earldom of Warwick from his mother.

364.24 Multon see notes to 51.1 and 86.39.

364.24 Percy the family of Percy was descended from Sir William de Percy who accompanied William the Conqueror to England, and who received grants of land in Yorkshire. By 1194 the Percy inheritance was in the hands of Maude and Agnes, daughters of William de Percy (d. 1175). 'Percy' at this time may have been Henry (d. 1198), eldest son of Agnes, who took his mother's name. Scott's 'in the north' suggests he was thinking of Percy coming from Northumberland with which the family later became strongly associated but they did not hold land there until the 14th century.

364.25 Chancellor William de Longchamp (d. 1197) was Richard's chancellor and had the principal charge of the kingdom in the early part of Richard's absence on the crusade. After being deprived of power (see note to 342.30) he left England and later joined Richard in Germany. When Richard was released from captivity Longchamp returned to England as chancellor.

365.19–22 brilliant and rapid meteor . . . universal darkness see Alexander Pope, *The Dunciad*, Book 4 (1743), 634, 656: 'The meteor drops, and in a flash expires/ . . . And universal darkness buries all'.

365.33 with advantage with improvements. See *Henry V*, 4.3.50–51: 'he'll remember, with advantages,/ What feats he did that day'.

366.2–4 they who jest . . . claws Roger of Hoveden tells how, outside the walls of Messina in 1191, a playful battle with canes between Richard I and William des Barres led to the king's becoming enraged with his opponent, banning him from his presence and declaring everlasting enmity between them. It took the combined entreaties of the King of France and other leaders to persuade Richard to revoke his words (3.93–94).

366.3 **toying with the lion's whelp** see *Antony and Cleopatra*, 3.13.94.

366.13 **Saint Christopher** see note to 259.30.

366.15 **Scathlock** Will Scathlock, Scadlock or Scarlett, a follower of Robin Hood. In 'A Lytell Gest of Robyn Hode' he is one of the two men who remain with Robin Hood at the king's court for a full year (Ritson, 1.77, Fytte 8, lines 69–72: Child, 117).

366.16 **Norman blast** compare 284.28–32.

366.16–17 **on peril of your life** at the risk of your life (if you do not obey me).

368.4 **King's untimely death** Richard died in April 1199 from gangrene arising from a cross-bow bolt wound which he received while besieging the Castle of Chaluz in France. He was forty two and had been king for only ten years.

368.4–5 **Charter of the Forest** this was granted later than the reign of John; see note to 42.37–38.

368.7 **treacherous death** at the hands of his cousin, the prioress at Kirklees, to whom he went to be 'bled', as recounted in the ballad 'Robin Hoods Death and Burial' (Ritson, 2.183–87: Child, 120).

368.8 **black-letter garlands** collections of ballads in the 'black-letter' (or Gothic) type in which these early anthologies were printed.

368.10 **Now cheaply . . . weight in gold** see John Ferriar, *The Bibliomania* (London, 1809), line 65: 'Now cheaply bought for thrice their weight in gold'.

368.16 **this ancient Saxon fortress** Scott was not alone in believing that the central keep of Conisbrough Castle was of Anglo-Saxon origin. In his notes to the Magnum (17.338–39) he quotes the opinions of Richard Gough that the name 'Coningsburgh' would 'lead one to suppose it the residence of the Saxon kings' (Camden's *Britannia*, ed. Richard Gough, 2nd edn, 4 vols (London, 1806), 3.267). Later research has shown that the earliest parts of the existing castle date from the late 12th century. Scott's direct knowledge was limited: in 1811 he wrote to J. B. S. Morritt, 'I once flew past it in a mail-coach when its round tower and flying buttresses had a most romantic effect in the morning dawn' (*Letters*, 3.41) and in 1829 when writing his note for the Magnum he regretted that he had had no more than 'a transient view' (Magnum, 17.335) as he passed it on his return from Paris in 1815 (see Donald Sultana, *From Abbotsford to Paris and Back: Sir Walter Scott's Journey of 1815* (Far Thrupp and Dover, New Hampshire, 1993), 144).

368.20–21 **as its Saxon name implies . . . kings of England** see quotation from Richard Gough in note above. The name *Conisbrough* is derived from the Old English *Cyningesburh*, 'the king's fortified place', the name being recorded as early as a document of 1000–04 (see Stephen Johnson, *Conisbrough Castle*, 2nd edn (London, 1989), 18). At the time of the Conquest the manor of Conisbrough was held by King Harold.

368.33 **Heptarchy** see note to 30.6.

368.34 **barrow** mound of earth or stones erected over a grave, a common procedure in the early Anglo-Saxon period. There was a mound known as the 'Grave of Hengist' on the west side of Conisbrough Castle but it may simply have been a bank on the outer slope of the ditch: see *The Victoria History of the Counties of England: Yorkshire*, 3 vols (London, 1912), 2.30.

368.35 **various monuments** see Camden's *Britannia*, ed. Richard Gough, 2nd edn, 4 vols (London, 1806), 3.267, and Magnum, 17.338: 'On the south side of the church-yard lies an ancient stone, ridged like a coffin, on which is carved a man on horseback; and another man with a shield encountering a vast winged serpent, and a man bearing a shield behind him. It was probably one of the rude crosses not uncommon in churchyards in this county'.

369.3–4 **armorial bearings... unknown to the Saxons** while the Saxon kings had personal insignia, a formalised system of hereditary devices only began to develop in England after the Norman Conquest, and was still not fully established in the later 12th century. Tournaments helped popularise it among the nobility.

369.5–6 **white horse** Scott here follows Verstegan who claimed that Hengist 'was doubtlesse a Prince of the cheifest blood, and Nobillity of Saxony... his wepen or armes being a leaping white horse or *Hengst*, in a read field;... which was the ancient armes of Saxony' (*A Restitution of Decayed Intelligence* (London, 1628), 120).

369.36 **Welch bards** the ancient Celtic bards recorded traditional history, laws and genealogies etc. in verses, usually sung to the harp. Later, in Scots, the term was applied more loosely to a wandering minstrel, as in *The Lay of the Last Minstrel* (Introduction, line 7; *Poetical Works*, 6.43).

369.38 **rotes** plucked or bowed instrument, descended from the ancient lyre. Scott's inaccurate footnote may have come from Charles Burney's *General History of Music* (1776–89) which claims 'the instrument called a *rote*... had first its name from *rota*, the *wheel* with which its tones are produced' (ed. Frank Mercer (London, 1935), 594n). It was in fact a plucked or bowed instrument, descended from the ancient lyre, and closely related to the crowd.

369.39 **Saxon genealogical poem** amongst the surviving Anglo-Saxon poetry there is no purely genealogical poem although poems such as *Beowulf* show an interest in genealogy, and the *Anglo-Saxon Chronicle* includes genealogical accounts of the ancestry of the Anglo-Saxon kings.

370.20–21 **white wand of office** see note to 177.31–32.

370 **motto** John Webster, *The White Devil* (published 1612), 5.4.54–58.

371.22 **Woden** see note to 29.34.

371.28 **Waes hael** see note to 45.11.

371.36–37 **rude chapel... buttresses** on the second floor of the tower of Conisbrough Castle there is such a chapel built inside the thickness of the walls and a projecting buttress.

372.11 **Zernebock** see note to 193.40.

372.11 **Apollyon** see 203.15.

372.14 **Saint Edmund** see 156.1.

372.24 **untimely bier** *Richard II*, 5.6.52.

372.30 **oratory** small chapel or room for private worship. For the description see Gough (see note to 368.16) as quoted in the Magnum (17.339).

372.36 **wimple** head-covering of material folded to cover the hair, chin, sides of the face and neck, now only used by some nuns but then more widely worn. Edith's wimple, however, leaves her hair visible.

372.37 **black cypress** light, transparent material, used in mourning clothes. The term does not appear in English until the later Middle Ages.

373.4 **in especial** especially; Scott's revival of an expression which apparently went out of use before 1600.

373.9 **Adeling** modern form (with *atheling*) of an Old English word meaning 'a member of a noble family, a prince', which by later writers is often restricted to the sense of 'a prince of the royal family'. It was not normally used as a Christian name.

373 **hymn** by Scott. It is not in the manuscript.

373.23–24 **Dust... all must** see the funeral service in the Book of Common Prayer, 'earth to earth, ashes to ashes, dust to dust'; Genesis 3.19, 'dust

thou art, and unto dust shalt thou return'; and Ecclesiastes 3.20, 'all are of the dust, and all turn to dust again'. The rhyme echoes a song in *Cymbeline*: 'Golden lads and girls all must,/ As chimney-sweepers, come to dust' (4.2.263–64).
375.4 Richard of Anjou see note to 127.4–6.
375.15–17 Matilda . . . Edgar Atheling . . . heir to the monarchy after the death of his great-uncle Edward the Confessor in 1066, Edgar Atheling (d. 1125) was the next in the line of descent from the Anglo-Saxon kings. His sister Margaret married Malcolm III of Scotland, and their daughter Edith (also known as Matilda) married Henry I, great-grandfather of Richard.
376.12 burst his bloody cerements see *Hamlet*, 1.4.48.
376.25 Mort de ma vie *French* death of my life. This expression is found in editions of *Henry V* (3.5.11 and 4.5.3) although the original quarto edition reads 'Mordeu ma vie' and 'Mor du ma vie', on which the readings in modern editions, 'Mort Dieu, ma vie!' meaning 'God's death, my life', are based.
376.31–32 departed spirit . . . revisit compare *Hamlet*, 1.4.45–51.
376.33–34 do aught . . . speak to Cedric compare *Hamlet*, 1.1.130–32.
377.20 oubliette secret dungeon, with access only through an overhead trap-door. Scott took the term from the French.
377.26 Jeremy normally an anglicisation of *Jeremias*. However it is possible that Athelstan, with his mind on food, was here thinking of St Jerome (*c.* 342–420), who lived a life of extreme asceticism.
377.28 Twelfth-night the eve of Twelfth-day, or Epiphany, which occurs twelve days after Christmas; formerly kept as a day of merry-making.
377.32 rood of Bromeholm see note to 52.33.
378.3–4 Do rocks melt with the sun? see Robert Burns, 'A Red Red Rose', line 10.
378.17 beside the staple i.e. outside the staple, or hoop into which the bolt fitted.
379.1 devil's mass see notes to 166.27 and 167.27.
379.9 for a count's ransom compare *king's ransom*, i.e. Richard is prepared to bet a large sum of money on the 'pot-companion' being Friar Tuck.
379.11 be the devil, an he will *Twelfth Night*, 1.5.120.
379.25 corpse-hood the hood of the grave-clothes. The term seems to have been invented by Scott.
380.13–14 male descendant of the Holy Confessor Cedric refers generally to the Saxon royal line as Edward the Confessor had no children: see note to 73.5–6.
380.29 Wolfram this name is presumably intended to suggest that the abbot is of Anglo-Saxon ancestry, but is German, rather than Old English, in origin.
381.4 renounce and abjure terms associated with the oaths of allegiance to the reigning Hanoverian monarch and renunciation of James VII and II and his descendants required of holders of public office in the 18th and 19th centuries.
381.20 to boot in addition.
382 motto *Richard II*, 1.2.50–53.
382.15 execution executions were public spectacles until 1866, and often attracted huge crowds; e.g. in 1807 the public execution of John Holloway and Owen Haggerty drew 45,000 spectators and in 1824 that of Henry Fauntleroy 100,000 (David D. Cooper, *The Lesson of the Scaffold* (London, 1974), 7–8).
382.16–17 meeting of radical reformers 1819 was a year of turbulent political agitation in Britain with speakers calling for radical reforms drawing large crowds. Scott was deeply worried by these events and strongly opposed to the reformers' demands.
382.19–20 in the heroic language . . . dunghills terms used in the early

18th-century disputes between journeymen tailors and their masters over better wages and working conditions. Those who refused to comply with the masters' terms were known as 'flints', and those who complied as 'dungs' or 'dunghills'.

382.34 **Beau-seant** see note to 112.6.

383.10 **familiar spirits** evil spirits or demons attending a witch.

383.37 **translated** taken to heaven without dying, as was said of Enoch (see Genesis 5.24 and Hebrews 11.5).

383.39 **death-meal** that is, funeral feast. Scott seems to have invented the term.

384.19 **sacring-bell** sanctus bell, a small bell rung at the time of the elevation of the bread and wine in the communion service. However, it is possible that Dennet is using the word as it was sometimes used in post-Reformation times to mean a small bell rung as a summons to worship.

384.22 **Cheshire round** kind of rough dance, first noted in the *OED* in the 18th century. Compare Farquhar's 'he shall box, wrestle or dance the Cheshire Round with any man in the country' (*The Recruiting Officer* (1706), 5.5).

384.26 **bell and ram** for *ram* see note to 144.6. A small gold or silver bell was sometimes awarded as the prize for victory at races and other contests, hence the expression *to bear the bell* meaning 'to carry off the prize'.

385.9 **Saint Hubert** see note to 120.31.

385.34 **basnet-cap** a basnet or basinet was originally a hemispherical helmet without a visor, worn under the fighting helmet (or helm), as in *Guy of Warwick*: 'An helm he had on his heved set,/ And ther-under a thick basinet' (Ellis, 2.76). Ellis glosses it as 'scull-cap' and Scott also recognised it as a cap since in *The Betrothed* (1825) we read 'The bacinet, or steel cap, had no visor' (1.40.2–3). Hence the creation of the nonce-word *basnet-cap* would have been a natural step for Scott. The first and subsequent editions read 'barret-cap' here but the manuscript could be interpreted either way and 'basnet-cap' makes stronger sense. Bois-Guilbert wears the basnet while his esquire carries the fighting helm.

385.43 **godfathers** used here to denote the 'seconds' attending a knight involved in single combat; this is not a normal English meaning but a rendering of the French word *parrain* which, like *godfather*, originally meant a male sponsor at baptism but later developed this extended meaning.

386.16–17 **vessel of wrath** Romans 9.22: 'the vessels of wrath fitted to destruction'.

387.11 **Te igitur** *Latin* thee therefore; the opening words of the Canon of the Mass, and, by association, the book containing them.

388.12 **raise me up a deliverer** see Judges 3.9, 3.15.

388.28 **I have no portion in thee** I have nothing to do with you. See 1 Kings 12.16 and 2 Chronicles 10.16: 'What portion have we in David?' which in context means 'What have we to do with David?'

388.41 **Sadducees** members of a Jewish sect at the time of Christ who believed the soul died with the body: see Matthew 22.23; Acts 23.8; and Flavius Josephus, *The Antiquities of the Jews*, Bk 18, Ch. 1, Part 4.

389.2–3 **Soldan of Trebizond** a soldan (or sultan) is a ruler of a Muslim state but in the 1190s Trebizond (modern Trabzon in Turkey) was part of the Byzantine Empire and it remained a Christian city until 1461.

389.7–8 **blot . . . scutcheon** stain on my reputation.

389.9 **Tempter . . . begone!** compare the words of Christ when tempted by the devil: 'Get thee hence, Satan' (Matthew 4.10).

389.12 **avoid thee, in the name of God!** see note to 324.13.

389.28 **Greek fire** combustible matter frequently used in 12th-century warfare, so named because it was first used by the Greeks of Constantinople. 'It is said to have been a composition of sulphur, bitumen, and naphtha. It . . . burnt with a livid flame; and so intense a heat, that it consumed not only all soft combustible substances, but even stones and metals. . . . One of its most singular properties was, that it burnt in water, which did not in the least abate its violence' (Henry, 3.477–78).

389.37 ring noon from the custom of ringing the time of day with bells. Used figuratively, as here, by Jonson: 'till this Ash-plant/ Had rung noone o' your pate'. See *A Tale of a Tub* (licensed 1633), 2.2.23–24.

390.16 Monseigneur *French* my lord. In the Middle Ages such titles as *monsieur*, *monseigneur*, and *lord* were commonly prefixed to the names of saints and in *Jehan de Saintré* we find more than one reference to 'monseigneur Saint George' (102, 107, 120, 130).

391.4 to his keeping I commit myself see 1 Peter 4.19: 'let them that suffer . . . commit the keeping of their souls to him'.

391.18 Faites vos devoirs, preux chevaliers *French* do your duty, gallant knights. *Faites vos devoirs* is a regular phrase used in directing knights to begin a tournament in *Jehan de Saintré* (110, 117, 266).

391.23–24 Laissez aller see note to 111.25.

392.2–3 died . . . own contending passions for events which may have suggested the idea of Bois-Guilbert's sudden death to Scott see *Letters*, 5.499, 501.

392.4 judgment of God alluding to the belief that trial by combat allowed God to judge the issue.

392.5 Fiat voluntas tua *Latin* may your will be done: Matthew 6.10.

392 motto John Webster, *The White Devil* (published 1612), 4.1.116.

392.32 Bohun see note below.

393.2–3 Bohun . . . England Henry de Bohun (d. 1220), hereditary Constable of England. He was created Earl of Hereford early in the reign of John but was never Earl of Essex. His son Humphrey (d. 1275) succeeded him as Earl of Hereford and some time later inherited the earldom of Essex from his mother. In the MS Scott here wrote 'Humphrey de Bohun Earl of Hereford and Essex' and it would appear that an attempt was made later to identify the correct Bohun but without getting the details correct.

393.13 hand is in the lion's mouth proverbial: see *ODEP*, 346.

393.15 immunities . . . our Order the Templars enjoyed extensive religious privileges granted by the Pope and secular privileges and immunities granted by the monarchy and by the powerful lords of the country. They had the power to hold their own courts and had jurisdiction not only over their own tenants and slaves, but also over any wrongdoers found on their estates. Richard I's *Carta fratrum milicie Templi. De libertate* of 1189 (*The Records of the Templars in England in the Twelfth Century: The Inquest of 1185*, ed. Beatrice A. Lees (London, 1935), 139–40) lists their privileges and immunities, adding 'excepta sola Justicia mortis et membrorum', i.e. 'with the sole exception of sentences of death or in respect of limbs'. A Templar could only be brought to court by the king himself or his chief justice (Thomas W. Parker, *The Knights Templars in England* (Tucson, 1963), 27).

393.23–24 Quare fremuerunt Gentes *Latin* why have the nations complained? (Psalm 2.1).

394.2–3 your ladies . . . broken lance see *Troilus and Cressida*, 1.3.281–83: 'he'll say in Troy, when he retires,/ The Grecian dames are sunburnt and not worth/ The splinter of a lance'. Richard's implication is that the Templars' ladies are not true ladies but peasant women, sun-burned from working in the fields.

394.12 scandal and offence the two words often occur together, probably as an allusion to the Vulgate text of Romans 9.33, 'Ecce pono in Sion lapidem offensionis, et petram scandali', corresponding to the AV's 'Behold, I lay in Sion a stumblingstone and rock of offence'. As used here by Scott, both words seem to have more or less the meaning *offence* has today.

394.21 splendour of Our Lady's brow see note to 297.16.

394.38 strong man see note to 335.35–36.

395.28–29 maugre his consent variation on the more normal Middle English phrase *maugre his will* meaning 'against his will'.

395.37–41 he received him . . . pacified as Henry relates (3.157), John, who had fled to Normandy before Richard's return, came and begged forgiveness when Richard himself crossed to France shortly afterwards. Richard forgave him. Henry cites as a source Matthew Paris (see *Chronica Majora*, ed. Henry Richards Luard, 7 vols (London, 1872–83), 2.404–05: see *CLA*, 252).

396.7–9 punishing . . . their principal the subordinates mentioned in the novel are fictitious but a 13th-century poem (in 1819 not yet in print) records that Richard, while pardoning John, planned to punish some of his associates: see *L'Histoire de Guillaume le Maréchal*, ed. Paul Meyer, 3 vols (Paris, 1891–1901), lines 10409–13.

397.23–24 cock which would not fight proverbial, recorded from the 19th century onwards: see *ODEP*, 131.

397.42 noble Minster of York the building standing in 1194 was begun in 1070 by Thomas of Bayeux with its choir rebuilt by Archbishop Roger of Pont-Leveque (1154–81). Construction of the present minster started in the 1220s.

398.5 She of Rome the Catholic Church.

398.21–24 Edward the Third . . . disappeared see Historical Note, 403.

399.8 fearful odds *Henry V*, 4.3.5.

399.19 Mohammed Boabdil, King of Grenada see note to 336.13.

399.28–29 Ephraim . . . dove see Hosea 7.11: 'Ephraim also is like a silly dove without heart'. Scott changes 'without heart' to 'heartless' which in the context is probably to be understood as meaning 'disheartened' but the original Hebrew phrase means 'without understanding, witless'.

399.29 Issachar . . . drudge see Genesis 49.14. The manuscript reads 'Issachar an ass', which is closer to the biblical text.

399.38 there is a gulph betwixt us see Luke 16.26: 'between us and you there is a great gulf fixed'.

401.14 under weigh common but mistaken variant of 'under way', from an association of ideas with 'weighing anchor'.

401.21 too curiously *Hamlet*, 5.1.200.

401.32 Charles of Sweden Charles XII, king of Sweden (1697–1718), achieved great military success but was finally killed at the siege of the fortress Fredriksten in Norway.

401.33–36 His fate . . . Tale see Samuel Johnson, 'The Vanity of Human Wishes' (1749), lines 219–22. Johnson's 'barren' was replaced by 'foreign' because the scene of Richard's death could not properly be described as barren; however, in view of Richard's strong identification with his French domains, the word 'foreign' is not appropriate. Similarly Johnson's 'dubious' was replaced by 'humble' because, while there was some argument about who killed Charles, the identity of Richard's killer was known.

GLOSSARY

This selective glossary defines single words; phrases are treated in the Explanatory Notes. It covers archaic and technical terms and occurrences of familiar words in senses that are likely to be strange to the modern reader. For each word (or clearly distinguishable sense) glossed, up to four occurrences are normally noted; when a word (or sense) occurs more than four times in the novel, only the first instance is given, followed by 'etc.' Orthographical variants of single words are listed together. Often the most economical and effective way of defining a word is to refer the reader to the appropriate explanatory note.

abbey-stede monastery and its estate 285.5
abidden remained 272.15, 310.26
abroach broached, opened 369.20
accoutred equipped, dressed 87.29, 25.4, 18.29, 277.27
adamantine invincible, unbreakable 345.20
affirmance assertion 328.41
agraffe clasp 72.15
alchemist someone skilled in the supposed science of converting baser metals into gold 197.13
alderman see note to 21.22
alembic distilling apparatus used by alchemist 197.15
aloes fragrant resin or wood of the agollach 97.3
ambuscade ambush 61.32, 367.34
amice hood or hooded cape of grey fur worn by members of religious orders 148.10
an, an' if 20.33 etc.; and 262.21
anchoret, anchorite hermit 27.28 etc.
apaid rewarded 351.31
appellant someone appealing against a conviction by demanding trial by combat 333.5, 333.8, 333.11, 387.33
approve prove 109.41
arbor see note to 49.8
arrest sentence, decree 30.13 (see note)
asper small Turkish silver coin 334.37
assoilzie absolve 248.29
attainted convicted 332.34
avaunt go away 219.27, 258.21, 348.2
aves see note to 141.5–6
avised made aware 279.40; gave information of 302.25
avouch affirm 325.29, 383.33; to vouch for the truth of 332.40; prove 341.14; confess 380.40
awful awe-inspiring 87.24, 337.36, 344.38
azure blue 244.37
baldric, baldrick belt worn diagonally across chest for sword or bugle 25.26 etc.
ballat ballad 148.30
ban curse 213.36
bandeau narrow head-band 19.24
banderole ribbon-like flag with a crest or inscription 25.10
banditti outlaws, bandits 37.6 etc.
Barbary see note to 79.17
barbed (of a horse) wearing battle armour 94.2
barbican fortified gateway 173.40 etc.
barely simply, only 383.28
barrow grave-mound 368.34 (see note)
bartisan, bartizan small projecting battlemented area 196.9, 199.13, 228.37, 243.2
basnet-cap steel cap 385.34 (see note)
basta enough! no more! 213.6
battlement indented parapet 97.33 etc.; battlemented area 196.9 etc.
bauble see note to 213.17–21
bead rosary bead 141.19, 167.5, 229.28, 371.43

beams *verb* shines brightly 338.17
bearded confronted, opposed 132.23
beccafico kind of small bird 128.5
beech-mast fruit of beech-tree 20.18
behoof benefit 396.16
Benedicite *Latin* bless us! 251.31
benison blessing 54.26
beseem be right, be fitting 52.16
beshrew curse 53.26 etc.
besom broom 13.33
bestad, bestead beset (by enemies) 114.35, 252.34, 277.37
bewray divulge, betray 298.12, 298.14
bezant, byzant Byzantine gold coin 72.28 etc.
biggin child's cap 223.33
billet note 119.28, 119.36, 119.38, 120.3
black-letter Gothic typeface 368.8
blench turn away 182.39, 246.15, 255.9
blotch boil 96.42
bodkin short, pointed weapon 217.35 (see note); hair or hat-pin 363.36
bonnet brimless head-gear, cap 71.10
boon *noun* gift 56.35; favour, request 237.3 etc.
boon *adjective* jolly, convivial 168.13, 306.15, 357.4
boss raised ornament 372.43
brake thicket, patch of dense bushes or low trees 357.9, 277.21
brawl scold 365.2
brawling wrangling 281.20-21, 281.22
breviary book containing the psalms, hymns, collects and readings for each day which those in religious orders had to recite 221.24, 350.31, 384.20
brilliants diamonds of the finest cut 72.15
broach spit, spiked rod for holding meat while it is being roasted 43.10
brook endure 236.36, 339.39, 360.33
brown-bill see note to 153.25
bruising boxing 382.15
bruit rumour 251.34
buckler *noun* shield 65.20, 101.25-26, 147.31, 170.17
buckler *verb* shield, defend 331.31, 394.9
buckram coarse, stiffened linen 61.5, 168.36
budget pouch or bag 228.18
bull-beggar see note to 226.37
bull-feast bull-fight 66.35
burgher citizen 69.13
burthen burden 61.10 etc.; chorus 166.31; bass part 352.43
buskins boots or leather leggings 288.5
butt[1] large wine or ale cask of varying capacity 30.28 etc.
butt[2] target 314.41
buxom jolly, lively 283.41, 365.8
byzant see **bezant**
cabalist see note to 100.42
cabalistic see note to 232.18–19
cabalistical see note to 232.18–19
caitiff *noun* wretch 228.1, 250.33, 286.32
caitiff *adjective* captive 241.15, wretched 382.5
can know 284.19
canary light, sweet wine from the Canary Islands 146.3
cankers cancers 66.20
cap-a-pee from head to foot 78.28, 385.31
capul horse 334.16
caracole *noun* capering about 71.32
caracole *verb* caper about 71.32
carcanet necklace 400.21
cardecu old French silver coin 282.24 (see note)
career course 75.33, 88.4, 323.23; charge 83.42 etc.; speed 357.26, 391.26
carol *noun* song 353.20, 253.28
carol *verb* sing 353.16
cartel written challenge 204.5, 205.20
casque helmet 84.42, 116.38, 116.41
cassock long loose coat or gown 163.25 etc.
castellated with battlements, like a castle 32.33
censer container for burning incense 338.17
centrical central 120.7
cerements grave-clothes 376.12
certes truly 61.20, 188.31, 354.41
chaffer deal, haggle 100.30
challenge *noun* act of demanding as a right 331.10
challenge *verb* demand as a right 329.35, 329.42, 331.25
chamfrom brow armour for horse 25.4
chaplet wreath worn on head 116.20, 116.34, 117.7, 117.9

chapter assembly of members of a religious order 137.15 etc.
chivalry see note to 17.4-5
choleric inclined to anger, fiery 34.25
cholic pains in the stomach 65.4
chops jaw 282.2-3
churl serf, peasant 30.16 (see note) etc.; rude and ill-bred person 72.41 etc.
cimelia treasures 291.11
circumvallation outer ring of defences 368.41
clerk cleric 144.20 etc.
cliff cleft 139.34
clip cut off a piece at the edge of a coin 99.42
clout mark shot at in archery 123.17
cockscomb see note to 166.26
collop slice 285.37
commons the common people, not nobles 400.31
companion member of an order of knights 320.23, 320.40
conditioning on the condition that 360.31
condottieri mercenary soldiers 73.32
conformable compliant 236.38, 279.30, 284.34, 350.37; conforming 364.14
confrere fellow member of an order 308.3
congee low bow of obeisance 72.35
conjuring beseeching 74.4
consuetude custom, habit 307.9
convent monastery 23.32 etc.
cope long cloak worn by monk or friar 40.13 etc.
cope-stone top stone of building 306.24
coping sloping (stones) on top of wall 262.20
cord rope worn as girdle by monk or friar 151.24 etc.; hangman's rope 182.42
corpse-hood hood of grave clothes 379.25 (see note)
corslet defensive armour covering trunk of body 143.18 etc.
costume see note to 12.5
couch *noun* bed 21.33 etc.
couch *verb* lower (a lance) ready to charge 206.4; express in words 332.32
counter-buff return blow 361.22, 377.7
counterpoize weight used to counterbalance the drawbridge 262.5
course encounter, charge (in a tournament) 50.19 etc.
courser heavy horse for armed knight 65.21, 382.3; light, swift horse 25.39
cow-keeper cowherd 165.8
craven *noun* coward 121.32, 246.15, 297.13
craven *adjective* cowardly 199.8, 206.6, 248.35
credo the creed 141.6
crisping-tongs instruments for curling hair 283.21 (see also note to 187.22-23)
crook see note to 208.5
crosier bishop's staff 361.14
crouch bow down in submission 340.27
crow crow-bar 262.39
crowd plucked or bowed lyre, fiddle 369.37
crowder player on a crowd 188.32
cubit length of forearm 28.43 (see note)
curée see note to 49.8
curfew enforcement of covering fires at set time in the evening 36.33
curtal see note to 272.12
cypher number 355.21
cyphering numerical calculations 355.15
cypress light, transparent material 372.37
danger see note to 63.33
death-meal funeral feast 383.39 (see note)
degradation demotion 315.43
demi-courbette see note to 268.28
demivolte half-turn made with the horse's forelegs raised 28.14
depredator plunderer, robber 66.16
derive transmit 311.26
despoil plunder, rob 62.17 etc.; strip 392.15
devices heraldic emblems, coats of arms 78.42 etc.
devoir one's best endeavour, one's duty 332.40, 387.4, 387.23
dingle hollow 152.17, 162.5, 301.3
diocesan bishop of a diocese 291.35, 361.9
disclaimed refused 71.21
discover reveal 95.28, 159.12; catch

sight of 113.2; discern 119.1; betray 95.28
disport sport 146.25
dissolution death 256.22; breaking apart 364.6
doff take off 98.15 etc.
doit Dutch coin of small value 223.32 (see note)
dole food and money given as charity 383.39
donative donation 90.27
donjon central tower of castle 173.33, 220.19
draff swill, dregs 98.41
drench drown 222.30, 268.13
dross worthless matter 183.10
drudge someone who does heavy and disagreeable work 36.30, 399.29
dunghills see note to 382.19–20
edge-tool implement with sharp edge for cutting, e.g. a knife 19.36
embattled battlemented 196.6
embrasure indentations in battlemented parapet 196.10, 200.1, 245.26
emir Muslim ruler, chieftain or governor 306.17
emprize chivalric adventure 248.36, 249.38
encomium high praise, eulogy 144.1
endearment love 217.33
engine military machine or weapon 270.29; plot, device 317.35
enlarge speak at length 316.25
enlargement release 185.13
enow enough 272.22, 290.29
epopeia epic 5.33
errant wandering in search of adventure 102.13 etc.
escutcheon shield bearing coat of arms 79.5
esplanade open level space 67.41
esquire knight's attendant 391.12, 398.7
essay attempt 346.32
essoine, essoyne excuse for not appearing 332.38, 387.28
event outcome 16.30 etc.
extremities extremes 186.19
falchion sword 352.25
falcon-ways like a falcon 136.30
fellowship band of companions, company 258.14, 293.35 (see note)
felon foul, wicked, cowardly 358.1, 358.13
fence shield. protect 251.21
feof, fief estate held by feudal tenure 240.27; 117.40, 118.8, 129.11, 129.15
field battle 332.5
fit bout 13.7, 13.17
flagon see note to 147.40
flatlings with the flat side 377.6
flints see note to 382.19–20
flitch side (of bacon) 260.7, 384.20
flox-silk floss-silk, fine filaments of silk 119.36
folk-free see note to 273.31
foot-passenger pedestrian 109.6
forbode prohibition 86.43, 272.14
forefend avert, prevent 272.21
forfeit penalty for not observing rules 103.7, 103.9
fortalice fortress 221.21
fortuned happened 334.18
fosse moat 32.38, 32.42
foughten see note to 149.12
franklin see note to 16.3
free open 222.37
frock monk or friar's habit 208.37 etc.; see also note to 126.37
furniture harness etc. worn by a horse or mule 23.30, 385.30
gaberdine see note to 53.24-25
gage *noun* pledge to do battle 329.43 etc.
gage *verb* pledge, expose to risk 52.17, 76.34, 276.6; wager 77.5, 146.1, 230.6
gambols see note to 135.11
gammon haunch of bacon 47.12, 60.5, 260.25
garland anthology 368.8
Gascogne from Gascony 272.19
gaud toy, showy ornament 53.18, 291.23
gentile non-Jew 59.18 etc.
ghostly spiritual, religious 209.9 etc.
girth surround 86.16; gird 336.22
glaive see note to 153.25
glance *noun* gleam 357.12
glance *verb* gleam 64.15, 142.2, 244.41, 270.49
glee-man minstrel 148.37
goodly good, fine 51.30 etc.
good-man male head of household 151.21
good-wife female head of household 151.21

gorget collar 18.43; throat armour 18.43, 116.41, 357.21
grace-cup last drink at end of meal 53.9
gramercy thanks 65.12 etc.
grange farmhouse with attached farm buildings 189.11, 189.15; monastery's outlying farm and store-house 351.1 (see note)
grist corn to be ground in mill 143.15
guerdon reward, recompense 50.36, 237.9, 351.28
guild association of merchants or tradesmen in town 101.24, 260.5
guild-brother member of a guild 337.10-11, 369.24-25
guilder Dutch silver coin 99.16
gull take in, cheat 53.18
gust relish, enjoyment 369.25
gymmal see note to 283.19–20
gyves shackles 63.32, 154.9, 288.41
hackney middle-sized horse used for everyday riding 25.2
hacqueton padded jacket worn under mail armour 231.4
halberdier soldier armed with a halbert 303.41 (see note), 318.40
halbert for 260.10 etc. see note to 303.41
halfling see note to 53.20
halidom(e), haly-dome for 76.13 etc. see note to 76.13
hap *noun* fortune, chance 325.10
hap *verb* chance 332.13
harbourage shelter, lodging 27.2, 140.26, 236.26
harness armour 164.27, 392.32
harrying plundering 221.6
hatch half door 145.11, 146.8, 147.19
hatchment coat of arms displayed on tomb 249.21
hauberk coat of mail 18.23, 261.29
hedge-priest see note to 292.19
helm[1] helmet 65.19, 108.17
helm[2] wheel or handle for steering ship 246.15
helmed helmeted 270.11
hership raiding, plundering 37.38
hest command 193.32
hilding contemptible 230.14 (see note), 282.22
hind see note to 7.43
hollo *noun* shout of encouragement 74.12
hollo *verb* call to hounds 284.20
holy-rood holy cross 375.25
houghed disabled by cutting the hamstring 360.32
houris beautiful maidens of the Muslim paradise 30.24
howlet owl 221.5
humming strong (of liquor) 280.3
hurley burley strife, commotion 65.9
hutch wooden box frame 57.16
hyde see note to 273.32
imp demon 152.2
impeach call in question, discredit 38.6 (see note), 49.41, 324.19; accuse 388.16
incomings income 285.7
infidel unbeliever 28.23 etc.
ingrossed written out in due legal form 332.28
inheritance birthright 46.39, 103.37
invested covered, adorned 40.27
jangle argue, carry on 285.16, 356.40; chatter 307.41
jangling clanging 27.32
jealous suspicious, fearful 31.2, 121.38, 207.39; vigilant in guarding 316.6
jelly-bag bag used in straining jelly 19.27
jennet small Spanish horse 23.38 etc.
jeopard endanger, risk 260.1
jessamine jasmine 235.34 (see note)
keeping see note to 12.5
kirtle woman's gown 36.20 (see note), 44.11; man's tunic 135.2
laical non-clerical, lay 291.27
largesse gift, alms 26.31; generosity, generous giving 78.17-18, 90.26
leach, leech *noun* doctor 183.5 etc.
leaguer besieging force 241.3
leech *verb* heal 153.22
lee-gage see note to 348.38
leman lover, mistress 282.25
levin-fire lightning 280.5
liard small French coin 273.3
linked made of interlocking rings 24.35, 24.39
list choose, please 160.24 etc.
listed set up with lists for a tournament 149.32
lists see note to 30.34
loadstar object of one's attention or hopes 188.10
loop-hole narrow vertical window 179.12, 371.38, 372.32
lurcher cross-bred dog, usually from a

sheepdog or collie and a greyhound 20.25
mace heavy club with a metal head 110.26, 268.16
machicolles projecting parapet with opening for dropping stones or molten lead on attackers below 200.1
mail[1] armour made of linked rings 24.35 etc.
mail[2] travelling bag 222.12, 228.17, 283.1, 283.5
mail-coat coat made of mail 221.7
major-domo head servant or steward 38.11
malapert impudent, presumptuous 252.2, 295.32
malison curse, or malediction 273.34
malvoisie malmsey, a sweet wine 222.30
mammocks shreds, broken pieces 208.28
manciple servant in charge of buying provisions for a monastery 350.42, 351.1
mancus for 337.12 see note
mangonel military machine for hurling stones 220.21, 327.43
manhood courage, valour 226.26
mantelet moveable defences under whose cover assailants could advance to attack a fortified place 228.39
maravedi small Spanish coin; worth about one sixth or eighth of an English penny 290.11
mark equivalent to two thirds of a pound sterling 72.27 etc.
maroquin made of Morocco leather 71.29
marry exclamation or mild oath expressing some surprise 29.25 etc.
maskings see note to 135.11
mastiff large dog with big head and drooping ears 20.25, 142.1
matins, mattins prayers said at daybreak 57.24, 310.24, 351.34, 323.27; see also note to 167.27
mattin morning 52.35
mattin-song matins 349.18
maugre despite 281.5; see also note to 395.28–29
mechanic artisan, tradesman 369.35
meed reward 117.9 etc.
mell concern oneself 281.5
mellay battle, close combat 249.7, 256.41, 266.37-38
mendicant beggar 183.34, 369.32
merk see **mark**
merry-men see note to 121.8
mess cooked food 48.20, 48.31
minever see note to 34.40
minion favourite (used abusively) 117.38, 189.22, 342.7, 347.4; hussy 194.25, 214.42
minstrel see note to 12.27
misbeliever a non-Christian 309.20, 361.31
missal mass-book 142.12
monies sums of money 99.20 etc.
mopping grimacing 352.36
morat see note to 39.1
morrion helmet 357.12 (see note)
morris-dancer see note to 284.9
morte horn note blown at death of deer 49.6
mortier cap once worn by high French officials 24.11
mot note on a horn 277.37, 277.42, 278.7, 354.22
motley see note to 169.3
mowing grimacing 352.36
mummery play-acting 120.8 etc.
murrain plague, pestilence 22.17
muscadine muscatel, sweet wine made from muscat grapes 89.29
Musselman Muslim 58.16
myrrh perfumed gum 97.3, 119.8, 325.30
mysteries religious doctrines 202.12, 311.22, 279.23, 280.14
natheless nevertheless 233.43, 287.24
Nazarene Christian 98.5 etc.
necromancer see note to 100.42
neophyte, neophite beginner 10.16; novice in religious order 386.24
nether lower 254.14, 282.2
night-mare see note to 20.14
nigromancy necromancy: see note to 100.42
nine-pins skittles 357.7
noble gold coin equal to one third or one half of a pound 121.23, 124.15, 124.30
nombles see note to 49.8
nook piece 147.37, 378.14, 379.16
Norman-French form of French used in Normandy and Norman England 9.7 etc.
object attribute as a fault 127.23;

bring forward as objection 134.17
obsequies funeral rites 369.1, 374.23, 381.37, 392.18
onward *adjective* straightforward 50.29
oriel upper-storey projecting window 299.39
orisons prayers 168.15, 361.40
orle see note to 305.6–7
oubliette secret dungeon 377.20 (see note)
out-herod out-do 70.22
outlandish foreign 194.14
outrecuidance presumption 223.25,43
pacing trained to move smoothly, lifting the legs on the same side together 351.29
palfrey horse for ordinary riding (not a war-horse) 23.41 etc.
pallet straw bed 60.2-3
palmer pilgrim from the Holy Land 32.15 etc.
panier basket 180.35
parapet protective wall on rampart or turret 196.10 etc.
parched dried, roasted 142.37
partisan, partizan for 170.17 etc. see note to 170.17
passenger traveller 140.23; passer-by 369.11
passing very 173.11
paste vitreous compound used in artificial gems 12.28
patch jester, fool 224.34
pater the Lord's Prayer in Latin 141.5
pater-noster the Lord's Prayer in Latin 323.26
patriarchal see note to 6.6–7
patrimony the church's endowment with land and property 5.14, 291.25; property inherited from ancestors 38.28, 184.36
patter recite (mechanically) 146.35, 229.18
pavisse large shield covering whole body 228.40
Paynim *noun*, *adjective* pagan, non-Christian, especially Muslim 149.41, 306.10, 361.31
pea-cod pea-pod 164.8
pennon long, narrow flag 55.13, 230.5, 244.29
pent-house small sloping roof projecting from front of building 23.16
peradventure perhaps 223.34-35 etc.
periapt charm, amulet 311.22
physiognomist someone who reads people's characters by observing their faces 190.41
pigment wine with honey and spices 39.1-2
pinfold pen or pound, fold for sheep or cattle 143.28
plat patch 139.30
plate armour made of sheets of metal 25.38 etc.
plate-coat coat made of plate 252.7
plenty abundant provisions 146.25
points see note to 168.37–38
poniard short knife, dagger 145.15 etc.
popingay parrot 307.42
postern side or back entrance 26.34 etc.
pot-companion drinking companion 379.7
pottage thick soup or porridge 48.21 etc.
pouncet-box perfume box with perforated lid 283.21 (see note)
pranked brightly or showily dressed, adorned 306.1
prating chattering 352.7
preceptor head of a preceptory 302.41 etc. See also note to 308.3
preceptory religious house of the Templars 198.11 etc.
pregnant weighty, significant 331.24
presence royal presence 135.36
presently immediately 119.19 etc.
prick spur a horse, ride 150.37
prior see note to 25.43
professor professional boxer 382.16
proof *noun* see note to 221.13
proof *adjective* impenetrable 210.11, 262.43
provost supervisor 121.30, 122.4, 122.17
puissant powerful 333.6
pummel knob on hilt of sword 69.1; saddle-bow 87.31
punctilio trifling rule of conduct 151.40
pursuivant attendants to the herald 67.15, 94.38
pursy fat 351.37; short-winded 377.25
pyet magpie 282.27
pyx container for reserving

communion bread consecrated at mass 285.32
quaint elegant, beautiful 65.18, 187.23; ingeniously contrived 135.11
quarter-staff see note to 144.6-7
quean disreputable woman, harlot 313.40
quiddities quibbles 260.6
quittance receipt 100.20, 286.1, 290.41
quondam former 281.12
rabbin rabbi 232.17,20
rack frame for stretching people as a means of torture 58.34
rascaille *noun* rabble 356.21
rascaille, rascal *adjective* belonging to the rabble 230.10 (see note), 229.33, 230.10, 251.26
recall revoke 330.34
recheate series of notes sounded on a horn in hunting 49.6
reck care 254.34, 266.3, 272.10, 275.34; matter 280.26
recreant *noun* someone confessing defeat 382.5
recreant *adjective* confessing defeat 333.14; false, unfaithful to duty, cowardly 257.42, 346.20, 346.39
regaling feasting themselves 379.20
regularly in accordance with the rules of a monastic order 305.3
reliquary container for religious relic 44.9 etc.
reprehension reprimand 283.11, 327.7
retort throw back 132.26, 186.3, 245.11
retrograde go back 230.32
rheum see note to 351.24
ring see note to 99.42–43
rood[1] cross 52.33 etc.
rood[2] land measurement, approx. 1012 square metres 254.26
rote see note to 369.38
rout disorganised band of soldiers 229.33
rowel sharp-pointed wheel on spurs 350.39 (see note), 393.40
runlet small barrel or cask 146.3, 279.38, 280.21, 362.21
rusted rancid 223.9
ruth pity, compassion 280.10, 280.40
sable black 72.3 etc.
sack kind of white wine 168.38 etc.
sacless see note to 273.31
sacring-bell see note to 384.19
sacristan official in charge of sacred vessels and vestments in religious house 372.4 etc.
sally-port opening in fortifications for making a sally on an enemy 222.25 etc.
Saracen *noun* see note to 25.30
Saracen *adjective* of the Saracens 58.16 etc.
satellite attendant 181.12, 240.4
scald see note to 269.23
scandalize slander 309.2
scatheless unharmed 105.28
scion offshoot, descendant 157.22, 267.3, 375.23
Sclaveyn pilgrim's mantle 40.38
scout someone sent out to reconnoitre 299.29
scout-master chief of the scouts 299.29, 300.33,35
scrip small bag or wallet 18.29, 19.34, 53.19
scrivener professional scribe or penman 12.41
scutcheon shield on which coat of arms is depicted 389.8
sea-coal coal (not charcoal) 353.41
seethed boiled, stewed 48.21
seething boiling 229.20
selcouth strange, unusual 244.28
sendal fine silk material 263.13
seneschal steward, overseer of domestic affairs in noble household 27.19
sepulture burial 377.22
sequin zecchin 89.37 (see note)
serf see note to 19.41
sewer servant in charge of serving food at table 177.31 etc.
sexton grave-digger 298.8; sacristan 379.14
shambles meat-market 222.28
shaveling *contemptuous* monk, friar or priest 171.1, 203.37, 211.8, 226.43
shekel coin of the ancient Hebrews 53.19 etc.
shift available way of achieving one's purpose 223.3
shivers splinter 83.19, 83.41, 123.23
shrift confession 220.36
shrive hear the religious confession of (someone) 132.8
sigil occult sign or device 311.21

simarre loose, light robe 72.5 (see note)
sin-offering see note to 315.26
sirrah form of address used to an inferior 42.2, 46.3, 124.16
sith since 122.18
skill help, avail 381.35
slinger soldier armed with a sling 33.4
slot track or trail of an animal 301.1
slot-hound sleuth-hound 239.3
slough bog, swamp 20.39
slow-hound sleuth-hound, kind of blood-hound 35.21
soldan sultan 149.37, 389.2
solere upper room, room exposed to sun 54.21
sooth truth 233.28, 356.39
sorry worthless, bad 293.13
sortilege divination by casting lots 321.19
soubriquet nickname 73.10-11
soul-scat gift to church on someone's death 276.28, 372.2
spears spearmen 299.28
sped see **speed** *verb*
speed *noun* helper, guardian 53.24
speed *verb* assist 140.42, 152.5, 276.23, 364.3; kill 190.31, 252.8; fare 303.32
springal youth 114.21
squire well-born young man attendant on knight 25.3 etc.
squire-at-arms see note to 95.26
stead place 212.11, 212.12, 237.3; estate 273.33
stiff-necked stubborn 46.42
stock-fish dried fish, usually cod 351.36, 351.41
stole narrow strip of silk or linen worn over shoulders by priests 362.28, 379.39
stool-ball see note to 213.7
stoup large jar or bottle or small cask 146.3 etc.
straight lay out a corpse for funeral 255.42
straitness narrowness 61.2
stripes blows, strokes 314.6
strophe stanza 269.28
sultana see note to 43.34
sumpter carrying packs and baggage 24.1, 159.5, 161.13
sward grass, turf 17.31, 106.36, 152.20
swart dark, swarthy 40.28
sybil witch 193.18, 194.25
talent largest Jewish monetary unit 99.30, 233.31
targe shield 352.26
tell count 99.32 etc.
tenpenny see note to 147.16
thews see note to 146.19–20
thrall serf or slave 19.2, 19.16
thunder-dint thunder-clap 280.4-5
tilt-yard area set aside for tilting or tournaments 160.23 etc.
tine pointed branch of an antler 227.17
tippet cape, short cloak 71.28
toll-dish dish for measuring toll of grain due to miller 105.43
totterish unsteady, tottery 282.11
totty unsteady, tottery 378.16
tournament for 38.1 etc. see note
tournay, tourney tournament 56.13 etc.
traffic trade, commerce, business 98.7 etc.
train animal's tail 194.20
tra-li-ra musical embellishment 284.29
translate transform 153.2; take to Heaven without dying 383.37
transmew transform, transmute 168.41 (see note)
traverse contradict, prove wrong 9.1
treat negotiate, deal 223.4 etc.
tregetour juggler 379.30
trenched encroached 367.4
trencher plate or platter, flat piece of wood for serving or carving meat 35.27, 45.27, 127.26, 143.9
trencher-man eater 146.21
trivet *noun* three-legged table 142.21
trivet *adjective* three-legged 40.8
troubadour medieval love poet 30.12 (see note), 49.17, 188.5, 352.6
trow think, believe to be true 60.35 etc.
trowl pass around 166.32, 166.34, 166.36
trumpet trumpeter 67.14 etc.
truncheon short staff carried as a symbol of office or authority 83.34 etc.
truss see note to 168.37–38
tush exclamation expressing impatience and contempt 28.6
twain two 150.33, 384.24
tythes payments to support the

church, one tenth of the produce of the land 284.12
uncanonical against the rules (canons) of the Church 151.31-32
unguent ointment 194.10 (see note), 325.6, 325.17, 325.27
unhouseled not having received the eucharist 254.32
unshriven not having made confession to a priest 254.32, 391.38
urus aurochs, extinct species of wild ox 146.11
usage interest (on money lent) 65.6, 355.21; treatment 194.26, 283.10, 283.12, 283.13
usurer one who practises usury 232.24, 288.43, 313.22
usurious exorbitant 66.19; demanding exorbitant interest 184.35
usury lending money at interest 53.18, 181.43, 183.3
vagabond wandering 249.28; good-for-nothing 252.25
vail take off (headgear) as sign of respect 51.37
vair see note to 34.40
van forefront 261.27
vantage advantage 281.25, 281.33, 342.6; benefit 289.41
varlet rogue 96.13
venerie hunting, the chase 284.32
vesper-bell bell for vespers 42.22
vespers prayers said towards evening 52.30, 151.34, 323.27, 355.31; see also note to 152.7
vizard mask 164.15, 187.21
voice approval, support 42.29
voluntaries volunteers 260.40
warden ranger of a forest 42.34
warder baton used to signal beginning and end of tournament 114.18, 115.16
wassel see note to 148.21
waver swing, wave in the air 22.4
weal welfare, prosperity 153.42 etc.
weasand gullet 376.39
weeds clothes 40.35
ween expect, believe 37.38, 244.38
whereabout whereabouts 166.17
white white target in archery 74.14
whittle large knife 18.34, 124.13
whole whole quantity 100.38
wicket small gate for pedestrians 61.2, 101.18, 180.14
wight person 151.14
wind wrap in grave-clothes 370.27
witcheries deeds of witchcraft 318.3, 321.19, 329.18
withal, withall with 30.4 etc.; in addition to 325.7
without outside 220.17
woodcraft skill in hunting and other forest pursuits 278.6, 284.19, 284.34, 285.37
woodman wood-cutter 247.9
woodsman huntsman 29.11 etc.
wot know 86.12 etc.
yeoman footsoldier 65.26; servant in royal or noble household 68.26, 93.35; freeholder, well-off, respectable commoner, 69.13 etc.; member of king's bodyguard 124.32, 135.6, 361.35
yeomanlike yeomanly 122.9
yeomanly *adjective* befitting a yeoman, worthy, good 355.9
yeomanly *adverb* in a way befitting a yeoman, generously, courageously 106.37, 247.30
yeomanry yeomen collectively 68.11, 122.7, 147.20-21, 230.18
zecchin Venetian or Turkish gold coin 94.33 etc. and see note 89.37